Copyright © 2022 Lauren Koetting

Published by Wild Lark Books

Wild Lark Books
513 Broadway Street
Lubbock, Texas 79401
wildlarkbooks.com

First Printing, 2022

eBook Available
Fiction | Magical Realism | Christian Fantasy

All rights reserved. No part of this book may be reproduced in any manner whatsoever without written permission except in the case of brief quotations embodied in critical articles and reviews.

To request permission, please use the following contact information:
info@wildlarkbooks.com

This is a work of fiction. Unless otherwise indicated, all the names, characters, businesses, places, events and incidents in this book are either the product of the author's imagination or used in a fictitious manner. Any resemblance to actual persons, living or dead, or actual events is purely coincidental.

A Note From the Publisher

When we first met Lauren to discuss her vision for GRACE OF DEMONS: THE DEVIL'S EVE, it was clear she wanted to present her work to readers just as she had written it, preserving every facet of its original conception.

At Wild Lark Books, we believe in honoring authors as artists and serving them in all capacities in their endeavors. Lauren's passion for the story she has written is inspiring, and we are honored to be able to support her.

Thank you for being a part of that journey.

#SupportArtReadBooks
Wild Lark Books

GRACE OF DEMONS

Support Authors

WILL YOU HELP SUPPORT AN ARTIST?

Wild Lark Books is an independent publisher that supports authors as artists. As with all works of art, reviews help build audiences and spread the word.

Please support this author's artistry by submitting reviews. It would mean the world to us!

shop.wildlarkbooks.com
librarything.com
bookshop.org
goodreads.com

Support Art. Read Books.
Wild Lark Books

GRACE OF DEMONS

The Devil's Eve

LAUREN KOETTING

Wild Lark Books

To the good among evil,
and to the One who knows them all.

Contents

Support Authors iv
Dedication vii

1	1
2	7
3	17
4	18
5	25
6	70
7	83
8	92
9	132
10	152
11	174
12	186
13	197
14	205

15	259
16	264
17	282
18	307
19	329
20	357
21	360
22	380
23	390
24	395
25	410
26	439
27	464
28	476
29	492
30	517
31	541
32	550
33	578
34	599
35	638
36	714

About The Author 734

I

Detective Benson Crane was in no mood for small talk as the rookie cop lifted the yellow crime scene tape for him. It was past midnight and cold and rainy, and here he was, having been once again rudely awakened from his sleep to respond to a call, now ducking under crime scene tape and being far too jovially addressed by some fresh-faced newbie who was apparently unaffected by both the lateness of the hour and the fact that someone had just died.

"Doin' all right, there, Detective?" asked the rookie as Crane grunted under the tape. "Heck of a shower we're getting."

Crane, though well known to the entire police force to be a bit of an asshole at times (and not one bit ashamed of it), made a monumental effort to respond with a halfway-friendly "Sure is" before turning away from the kid and rolling his eyes. These guys kept getting younger and younger. He had suspected for some time he was getting too old for this, but damn...did he have to get slapped in the face with that fact this late at night?

He proceeded up the few concrete steps to the museum's front entrance, where his partner of six years, Detective Myron Banks, was awaiting his arrival. Banks was more than a decade younger than Crane but a good cop and a hard worker, and Crane had nothing but respect for the man. He wasn't annoying, either, which was a rare and exceedingly pleasant bonus.

"What do we got, Banks?" Crane asked as Banks opened the front door and let him in to the museum lobby.

"I only know what the patrol guys were able to tell me before you got here," Banks replied. "We have a dead body—one of the night guards, male, early thirties. And then we have the other guard who found him. He's about sixty and extremely upset. Looks like he saw a damn ghost. Paramedics are up there with him now in the security office." Banks nodded his head toward a set of stairs off to the right of the reception desk. "The deceased is Joshua Ellis. No apparent signs of a struggle or a break-in or anything. The body's in the east wing over there. Heart attack, maybe, from the sound of it."

"Early thirties? Awful young for a heart attack," Crane mused as he removed his coat and shook the rain from it before draping it over a wooden bench beside him. "Is that what the ME decided?"

"She wasn't finished yet," Banks answered. "We can go see how her assessment is coming along. I haven't actually seen the body yet."

"Any idea what scared the other guard so bad?" Crane asked as he followed Banks to the east wing entrance.

"No, we'll have to talk with him later," Banks explained. "I saw him when I first got here; he's in no shape to answer questions right now. But he told the uniforms there was someone else in there. He was sure he had seen another figure when he found Ellis. More questions than answers right now, I guess."

"Yup," Crane agreed. They'd put the pieces together eventually, though; they always did. He decided to save further questions until after he saw the body. He had been glancing around the lobby as they walked, and he now found himself reminiscing on the few times he and his wife had brought the kids here, back when they were young. The place hadn't changed much, at least not in the lobby. There was still the same reception desk where cheery old ladies would greet visitors and prompt them to sign the guest book, and beyond that was still the same copper statue of Atlas holding the world. Visitors would walk past him to get to the main exhibit hall, which branched off to the smaller permanent exhibit rooms. He wondered if they still had the dinosaurs in there. Those were always his favorite, and the kids' favorite, too. This wasn't a huge museum; it was run by the university and requested only donations as an entrance fee, but it enjoyed the benefit of several wealthy patrons and had brought in lots of interesting traveling exhibits over the years. It was really a nice little place to visit, in Crane's opinion. He wasn't an art fan, but the history stuff was kind of entertaining sometimes. His anniversary was coming up in a couple months...maybe he'd bring the missus here for an afternoon. That'd be nice.

The doors to the east wing had been propped open. Crane and Banks proceeded through them to a small foyer, set up with some introductory placards and large, eye-grabbing posters explaining the exhibit visitors were about to see. Crane wasn't about to read all of it, but he gathered the main idea was to entice visitors to set foot on a "fantastic journey through the history of weaponry." He had been only marginally interested in the exhibit itself, but the weaponry thing could possibly be motivation for a theft. Possibly. But Banks had said there were no signs of a break-in...he had to rein in his thoughts for now. No sense considering all the possibilities just yet.

The detectives continued to the exhibit's interior doors, which were likewise propped open. The lights had been turned on in here, though the overheads were fairly dim. In this first room, lighted glass cases on one wall held spears, arrowheads, stones—the early days of humanity's arms. A hunting scene of wax figures was set up along the opposite wall. The display included special flickering lighting, ample artificial foliage, and small hidden fans, bringing life to the torches held by the hunters and giving the whole gruesome scene, including the hunters' terrified prey, a dynamic realism that would certainly inspire awe in its viewers. During the day, it would be a great visual entertainment, but in the middle of the night, casting eerie shadows and backed by timely rumblings of thunder outside, it was altogether unnerving.

This room filtered into a short hallway leading to the next room, which was much larger. It had been set up with wide aisles and cordoned off to filter visitors through the exhibit chronologically. There were more glass cases and more wax figure displays throughout, each showing some different milestone in the evolution of weaponry and each as vicious and macabre as the last. Crane was following Banks through the exhibit, trying to take in any potentially pertinent details, but he found himself simply creeped out by these damn displays. *Thank God they're not animatronic*, he thought to himself as they finally arrived at the body, covered by a sheet. It was conveniently located in the center of the walkway, lying on the floor between displays of blue-uniformed Yankees and gray-coated Rebels, each with a rifled musket or a bayonet pointed at his American brothers on the other side of the aisle. *No shortage of carnage here*, Crane thought as he looked at the gaping hole opened in the chest of a young Rebel soldier, *but that's not even the real murder scene.* He was surprised to note, once he could pull his gaze away from the violent wax-figure display, there was, in fact, no clear evidence of any crime here. The whole exhibit looked completely untouched, and there was no blood or debris on the floor in the area of the body. Maybe this was just a heart attack after all.

Dr. Patricia Reyes was standing nearby, writing notes on a clipboard. The angle from Crane's perspective made her head appear dangerously close to the muzzle of a prop rifle, and he had to restrain himself from instinctively reaching out to push the fake firearm away.

Dr. Reyes had been the medical examiner for about ten years

now, and Crane had worked with her on several occasions. She, like Banks, was easy to deal with. Having come from a much larger county, she had developed a great distaste for politics and other such bullshit, and Crane appreciated that. She looked up and nodded to acknowledge the detectives' presence. Her face appeared drawn and pale, but perhaps that was on account of the dim lighting or the shadow from the ball cap she was wearing.

"I'm afraid I can't tell you much just yet," she said, sounding very tired. "There's no evidence of any defensive wounds...or any wounds whatsoever, for that matter. Could be a heart attack or stroke or something similar, but there's really no evidence of any of those things, either. He appears to have been a healthy young man." She turned and stared down at the sheet as she continued. "It's strange. I'll have to do a full autopsy and check medical history, of course, but...I can't explain it. I understand the other guard heard a scream and immediately investigated, finding his partner here, and that's when he called the police." She paused as if awaiting confirmation.

"That's what I understand so far," Banks affirmed. "He swore he saw someone else, too, which is why they called us in for a potential homicide investigation. Does his story not track with what you've seen?"

"Well..." Patricia hesitated again, seemingly reticent about sharing her thoughts on the matter. A long second later, however, she stated, "The body is too cold. *Way* too cold. The bodies in the morgue aren't this cold."

"That's impossible," Crane blurted out. He immediately regretted it, because he prided himself on being open-minded when it came to investigations. He knew he didn't know everything, and he had learned long ago that practically nothing was impossible. "I mean," he corrected himself, "how is that possible? He can't have been dead for more than an hour, maybe even less than that."

"Maybe an autopsy will shed more light on it," Patricia replied.

"I shouldn't conjecture at this point. But...there is something else." She looked from Crane to Banks and then back to Crane. He didn't know her too well personally, but he knew her at a professional level, and he could tell something had thrown her. She didn't have the matter-of-fact air or the confidence he was used to seeing in her. Maybe it was stress or tiredness, but Crane wondered if it might be more from empathy. Dr. Reyes was used to death, but she was still human, and even the most hardened individuals sometimes found themselves shaken by a murder investigation. But this wasn't a bloody or particularly disturbing scene (aside from the wax figures, anyway), and, hell, they weren't even sure this was a murder. Maybe the deceased reminded her of someone she knew.

After what seemed like a long moment, Patricia dropped to a knee and reached for the sheet. The detectives joined her nearer the floor, Banks having a far easier time than Crane as they crouched by the body. Before pulling the sheet away, Patricia sighed and looked at each of them again, her brows furrowed into a visage of either confusion or anxiety; Crane wasn't sure which.

"The eyes aren't right," she said. "They're just not right."

And with that brief statement, delivered in a voice colored with exhaustion, unknowingness, and a hint of sadness, Patricia pulled the sheet away from the body, exposing the face. Crane instantly lifted a fist to his mouth and bit into his knuckles to prevent any audible reaction from himself. He was only vaguely aware of his partner's immediately standing to turn away from the sight. He tried to force himself to look into the eyes, but not for long. He felt sick. These eyes were completely black, devoid of all light...no color, no reflections...like holes ripped open in the fabric of time and space...but not holes...just shineless, lifeless black orbs...dead. Dead, and without any trace of having once been alive. No...these eyes were definitely not right.

2

Iris Wakefield sighed audibly as she trudged grudgingly up the dimly lit stairs to her employer's second-floor office, purse in one hand and a venti Starbucks coffee in the other, just as she had done practically every workday for the last eight years. And, just as she had done practically every workday for the last eight years, she wondered whether it was a series of bad decisions that had brought her here, or whether it was simply a symptom of the human condition to live in mediocrity. She had attended college on a full academic scholarship after having graduated high school at sixteen, and with credits earned for advanced courses, she had effectively skipped her freshman and sophomore years at the university. Schoolwork had always come easy to her, as had the shunning of frivolous social engagements, so it was no particular difficulty for her to earn a PhD in behavioral psychology, graduating *summa cum laude* with a stellar academic record that had also included Phi Beta Kappa membership and a master's in theology. Yet here she was, once again ascending a creaky, cheaply carpeted stairway that already reeked of someone's poached-egg breakfast overlying a hint of bleach left by last night's cleaning crew. *God, this place is gross,* she thought to herself.

She reached the second floor and turned the corner, arriving at the glass door proudly bearing a cheap vinyl cling of the company's name and logo: Eden Compliance & Engineering. It was certainly not Eden, and "engineering" was a stretch of their actual services, in Iris's opinion, but somehow the owners got away with the name. The logo was, uncreatively, a large tree, with roots shooting from the Eden name. Iris sighed before opening the door, but she was pleasantly surprised to find the morning receptionist was not at the front desk. The requisite "Fine, thanks, and you?" in response to the inevitable daily greeting and well-being inquiry had always been trite but had, over time, grown increasingly obnoxious, so any morning without it was a small blessing.

With eyes downcast, Iris proceeded down the hallway to her tiny office. It was a shithole, but she was lucky to have it. Some people who had been with the company just as long were still stuck in cubicles, with nothing but partitions to shield them from their annoying coworkers. Sometimes Iris wondered if these people found their colleagues, herself included, as irritating as she found them. Perhaps they didn't...but she would never be able to answer how that was so.

She set her bag and coffee on the cheap laminate desk and sat down. As she waited for her computer to boot up, she looked with loving sadness at the single photograph displayed on the wall. It showed her sixteen-year-old self with her parents and maternal grandmother, posing with smiles and souvenirs near the giant *Jaws* display at Universal Studios in Orlando. It was Iris's favorite memory, that last family vacation they had taken. They weren't her biological family, but they were the only family she had ever known, and they had somehow loved her unconditionally—a phenomenon which Iris still couldn't truly understand, even after all her psychology courses. The Wakefields had adopted her as a baby, and they had given her every thought and every care they would have given their own child, had they been able to conceive. They were hard-working, middle-class people who owned a small print shop and never had a great surplus of finances, but all the bills were always paid on time, and each summer they'd take a little family vacation somewhere. Iris's mother, in particular, had always ensured that birthdays and holidays were celebrated, too. They raised Iris in the Catholic Church and had never relented in the daily practice of their faith. The Wakefields were genuinely good people, a rare and beautiful example of what humanity was capable of being, and yet the world had given them little to show for it. They had led quiet, unimportant lives by worldly standards, and yet theirs had been the only lives of importance in Iris's world. The only consolation Iris had since the awful night six months after that photo had been taken was the fact that the drunk who killed her parents had been thrown through his own windshield and violently splattered against a concrete retaining wall. She knew it wasn't healthy or properly Catholic of her, but to this day she still hoped that sorry excuse for a human being was suffering in eternal fire and brimstone amid incessant wailing and grinding of teeth. Sadness was a difficult emotion, and she found anger much more palatable.

The death of her parents had changed her, and not for the better. She became increasingly jaded and cynical, and after her grandmother passed away after a brief illness two years later, she had no desire to pursue much in life. She had finished her PhD and hoped somehow that was some small consolation to her family, who she hoped was watching her and praying for her from Heaven. She wasn't really sure in what she believed anymore, but she still hoped in the eternity of beautiful souls like those of her small family, and it pained her greatly each time she worried she was a disappointment to their memory.

A gruff rap on the doorframe brought her out of today's reverie. "Hey, girl, how was your weekend?"

Iris didn't have to look at the coworker now standing in her office, uninvited, to know it was Matilda Gordon, quite possibly the most insufferable and unintelligent person she had ever met. With her inbred, backwoods drawl, the girl had somehow turned the word "weekend" into three syllables, and now she eagerly awaited not Iris's actual response, but rather the tacit invitation that Iris's response would necessarily extend for her to speak about her own weekend.

"Oh, it was fine, thanks," Iris replied in a deadpan tone, hoping the terseness and clear disinterest might somehow encourage this cow to leave her office, yet knowing it wouldn't be so.

Per usual, Matilda heard the reply and promptly sat her wide rear-end in the guest chair facing Iris's desk, already babbling off some far-fetched story about her weekend adventures and subsequent misfortunes, which, if any of her inane stories were to be believed, poor Matilda had more than her fair share of. This time, the story had something to do with a goat, an ill-timed gust of wind, and a busted transmission on her new husband's pickup (how anyone could stand to be married to such a loud-mouthed simpleton was beyond Iris's understanding). Iris might have tried to be nice and actually listen, except that her focus had been unfortunately drawn to the shortness of Matilda's dress and the thick, lumpy white legs that protruded from it. Clunky wedges completed the outfit and compounded the overall weight of her presence. A grease stain on her chest and an asymmetrical, butt-shaped face framed in stringy brown hair were the finishing, signature touches on the Matilda Gordon package. Considering the chubbiness of her cheeks and her pug-like, mashed-in visage, it was truly amazing she could even see out of her squinty eyes. Iris noted with some amusement that Matilda's heavy eyeliner and mascara had gone rogue on her right eye and were now speckling the puffy cheek below.

"So, yeah, I was like, 'Uh, no, you can make your own dinner,'" Matilda finished with a tiny, scoffing giggle, after what felt like an eternity. Iris tightened her lips into something she hoped resembled a smile, because no matter how much she hated her coworkers, she still didn't want to be mean to them—at least not to their faces. Apparently, the "smile" passed Matilda's test, because she then continued, "Anyway, we ended up going to Kay-han's for dinner after all."

Before she could resist the impulse to engage in this trivial conversation, Iris asked, "Kay-han's? What is that? I've never heard of it."

Matilda, clearly excited to know something Iris didn't, puffed her chest out a little and tilted her head slightly to the side, replying, "You haven't heard of it? It's SO good! It's, like, Mongolian food. I got sesame beef with spinach."

The word "spinach" had actually come out with a "j" sound at the end, but even more appalling to Iris was the realization that the restaurant to which Matilda had been referring was, in fact, Khan's Mongolian Grill. Perhaps the poor girl had never taken a history course. *K-han's, ha,* Iris thought to herself. *How can anyone be this dumb?* She managed to avoid the temptation to correct Matilda's embarrassing ignorance, allowing the girl to segue into another of her favorite conversation topics—the fact she had recently taken and somehow passed some exam that allowed her to string some letters after her name in her email signature. Annoying as she had been before, Matilda had been even more obnoxious ever since, acting as though she were the most important and educated person in the office (never mind there were three registered professional engineers who worked there, and Iris herself held a PhD), and beaming at every opportunity she had to remind others of her new "certification." Funny enough, she could still be found multiple times per day in the cubicles of other employees, asking dumb questions to which an "expert" such as she should already know the answers.

"So, are you busy? I'm SO swamped. It's like, ever since I passed my test, I have so much to do," Matilda said. She scrunched up her face and rolled her eyes in mock frustration. Iris forced a half-smile again, though her patience was now completely gone, and swallowed the incredible desire to get up and punch this fat, incompetent, "certified" idiot in her rubbery face. She was spared having to reply, thanks to a sudden ring of her telephone. *Thank God*, she thought as she lifted the phone. Matilda dutifully arose from the chair and took her leave after mouthing something from her lipstick-encrusted pie hole, to which Iris nodded as she held the phone to her ear.

"This is Iris," Iris said into the phone, wondering what dumbass client needed what stupid piece of information now.

"Dr. Wakefield?" The masculine voice on the other end of the line was smooth and rich, like a polished piece of mahogany. "My name is Loomis Drake. I've taken a great interest in the article you published on behavioral modification in patients with dissociative identity disorder. I'm looking to start up a subsidiary company that would specialize in this type of research, and I would very much like you to be involved from the onset."

Iris had only halfway registered the words following "Loomis Drake." He was known worldwide as a multibillionaire who owned numerous companies involved with various research and development in fields like technology, pharmaceuticals, engineering, manufacturing...you name it. He had also received rampant recognition and acclaim for his companies' countless service projects in impoverished neighborhoods and third-world countries across the globe. He had done a great deal of good in the world, and it seemed he was tirelessly committed to continuing it. And to top it off, he had thrice been named *People* magazine's "Sexiest Man Alive." Iris would have dismissed this as a prank phone call, except she didn't really know anyone outside this office, and no one in this office would have the cunning or cleverness to undertake such a scheme. And, of course, she wanted to believe it was real.

Sensing her dumbfound state over the phone, Drake continued, "It is quite common for me to encounter silence when I place a call like this. I suppose that is one cost associated with the publicity I've received." He paused and chuckled demurely before proceeding. "But, I assure you, I am indeed who I claim to be. I do my homework very carefully, and I know what value you can add to my new endeavor. That is why I wanted to make this phone call personally. Iris, would you be interested in visiting my office and discussing this in person?"

Still awestruck, Iris managed to clear her throat and reply, "I would be very interested, thank you. It sounds like a great opportunity." She winced inwardly after she spoke the words, realizing Loomis Drake must of course know this was a great opportunity, making it quite stupid of her to say so.

If he had rolled his eyes on his end of the line, he made no vocal indication of it. He simply answered in his good-natured and charming timbre, "Excellent. I will have my secretary contact you to make some travel arrangements. You'll of course be taking a private jet. I assure you every comfort I myself would expect on the flight. I'll let you get back to your work now, but I very much look forward to meeting you soon."

"Likewise," Iris replied. "Thank you, Mr. Drake." Why she felt so instantly subservient to this man, she could not explain.

With another charismatic chuckle, Drake said, "It is I who should thank you, and please, call me Loomis. Goodbye for now, Dr. Wakefield." And with that, the call went silent.

Iris very slowly set the phone back down on its cradle, staring unseeingly at her computer screen, dumbstruck, nervous, excited, and wondering what the hell had just happened.

***

Loomis Drake ended the phone call and casually leaned back in his leather chair, smiling to himself as he reflected on the plans he had already set in motion and on all that was to come. Very soon he would have what he needed, and then no one—and nothing—could stop him. Satisfied with himself, he took a moment to soak in all the titillating opulence around him. It seemed most multibillionaires these days opted for modern, minimalistic decor, but he had always much preferred rich, heavy, dark Victorian and Renaissance styles and all the wealth and class they so beautifully and clearly affirmed. He relished the oversized leather chairs and sofa; the thick, intricately carved and well-polished wooden tables and desk; the dark, heavy drapes in the windows; the gilded frames housing the works of Rembrandt, Renoir, Botticelli, Goya, and others—originals, of course, whenever originals were available and could be framed and displayed. This was a room that pulsed with royalty, a superiority and a divine sovereignty he deserved and would soon claim for himself.

He rose and strode nonchalantly to his bar, where he poured himself a generous couple of shots of twenty-year-old scotch in a crystal glass. It was seven in the morning, but who would judge him? He practically owned this world, and what he didn't own, he could buy. Or take.

He returned with his drink to his desk, where he once again reviewed the open file on his computer, a photograph of the Dr. Iris Halcyon Wakefield to whom he had just spoken. He felt some mild amusement as he looked at her, thinking how very easy it would be to take what he needed from her. She was thirty-three now and had apparently never questioned her own origins, according to what information he had gathered on her. She was ignorant of where she had come from and what she had, and that would make his endeavor a simple one. She was not as strikingly attractive as the women with whom he usually preferred to associate, but neither was she bad-looking. She appeared to be on the fit side of average, and she had rather pleasing auburn hair and truly mesmerizing green eyes. Well, mesmerizing if one cared much about eyes, which Loomis himself did not. She would be easy. They were all easy.

He finished the scotch, then stood and removed his suit jacket and draped it on the back of his chair. He unfastened his cufflinks and carefully rolled up the sleeves of his shirt, then reached over to the intercom and buzzed the secretary out front. "Yvette? Please come here. I would like your assistance."

***

"Yes, sir, Mr. Drake," Yvette immediately replied through the intercom, hoping her voice didn't sound too anxious or excited. She grabbed her cell phone and used its camera to check her makeup, then she tousled her dark hair and leaned down to put her uncomfortable, strappy, spike-heeled shoes back on. She stood from her chair, undid one extra button on her blouse, smoothed the front of her short, form-fitting skirt, tousled her hair again, and then took a deep breath as she walked back to her boss's office, ready and very willing to provide whatever assistance he requested.

***

After a brief moment, during which Loomis had no doubt Yvette had been primping in preparation for entry into his presence, the door to his office opened, and Loomis smiled broadly at the twenty-something-year-old girl who had just entered, noting her brown eyes were already wide and dilated with lustful desire. She was small and tight, yet generously endowed in the right places, and young but far from innocent, as he well knew. Just as he had so many before her, he had seduced her without even trying. It was natural and routine for a man with his looks—smooth, olive-toned skin and deep brown eyes; chiseled features; thick, dark hair; tall stature; a slenderly muscular build. The billions of dollars in his bank accounts made it even simpler. Most women were complete and utter trash, just like Yvette, all too eager to give themselves up to any man who showed them some positive attention, especially when the man was attractive and wealthy and charming, which Loomis Drake certainly was. He found pleasure not in the actual activities he undertook with these women, but solely in the knowledge he could so easily debase them, over and over and over. He in fact had no actual feelings for Yvette or anyone else, and his enjoyment of them was an ecstasy of vice rather than a physical entertainment. They were all such trash, and he enjoyed making that evident, even if they were too dumb to recognize it.

Still smiling at her with his perfect, white teeth, Loomis approached Yvette and placed his hands on her hips. "I see you're wearing my favorite outfit of yours," he said in his resonant, sultry voice.

She blushed slightly and replied, "Yes, Mr. Drake," with a small smile. Her eyes practically screamed for him. *So easy*, he thought.

Loomis turned her body and gently walked her to the sofa, then pressed a hand lightly but authoritatively against her back, bending her over the back of the couch. He smirked with malice as he continued to press on her with one hand, unzipping his trousers with the other. He then lifted her skirt from behind her and was pleased to see she was wearing no panties—the tawdry, worthless slut—and she had very clearly been aroused simply by the *thoughts* of what he was about to do to her.

So easy.

3

On the holy mountain, far from the reaches of Earth's human hands and guarded by a mystical presence, the sounds of flame and a metallic hammering echoed with rhythmic regularity, like a heartbeat from the mountain's granite depths. Within a cavernous space, cloaked in shadow but for the dancing light from a burning furnace, there stood a solitary figure before an iron anvil, a strong right arm pounding into form a metal shield. His expression was hard-set in a grave sense of duty as he hammered the still-glowing bronze, eyes focused and unblinking, unfazed by the sparks and embers that arose from every beat of this mountain's metallic heart. An hour before, during his evening meditation, he had felt the sure and grim realization of a dark prophecy now being fulfilled. Centuries had passed without incident, but now was the time; of this he was certain. War would be unleashed, suffering would feast upon the human race, and faith would be tested. Souls would be lost. But his sacred vocation remained, and he would take action. The master of the house would not find this servant sleeping.

4

The rain had subsided into a cold mist by the time the detectives left the museum. Feeling tired and heavy, more in an emotional sense than in the physical one, Crane followed the final directions from his GPS and pulled his sedan along the curb in front of a small, nondescript residence. In his rearview mirror, he saw the headlights of Banks's car cutting the darkness as he turned the corner and parked behind him. Shaking his head sadly, Crane took a deep breath and grunted his way out of his vehicle, meeting Banks at the edge of the driveway. The yellow glare of a nearby streetlamp, illuminating the damp, eerily quiet night air, cast deep shadows across his partner's solemn face as he stood beneath it, making the dread hanging over both of them even more apparent. This was one of the parts of his job that Crane absolutely hated, and it never got any easier.

"You want me to do the talking this time?" Banks asked quietly, staring at Crane with a concerned expression.

"No," Crane sighed, steeling himself. "I'll handle it." His voice sounded surer than he felt. How the hell was he supposed to explain the young man's death when they didn't even have a clue what had happened?

They followed a short, cracked concrete walkway to the porch, and Crane pulled out his credentials as he pressed the doorbell.

He heard the buzz shatter the silence of the home's interior, and a small-sounding dog began barking in response. A light turned on inside one of the windows, and Crane took one last calming breath as the porch lamp was similarly lit. A second later, a tall, thin man of about sixty or so opened the door, squinting through the glass of the still-shut storm door.

"Stephen Ellis?" Crane asked. The man's face creased with anxiety as he gave a curt nod. "I'm Detective Benson Crane," he continued, holding up his identification, "and this is Detective Myron Banks. May we come in?" Banks similarly displayed his ID, but Crane knew the man standing in front of them in his sleeping clothes and bathrobe wasn't really looking at their badges. Anyone on the receiving end of this kind of visit at two in the morning would know only bad news was coming; they didn't tend to question credentials.

Stephen didn't hesitate to open the door to them, and he led the detectives through a small entryway and into a modest den, simply furnished and minimally decorated but for a series of family photos hung in frames along one wall. *Damn*, Crane thought, *why did there have to be photos?* He supposed it wouldn't be any easier to deliver terrible news even in a sterile environment. The absence of evidence of happy memories with the deceased was hardly evidence of an absence of happy memories, but...well, having to see the photos always made this process that much more painful.

Stephen covered his mouth with one hand as he motioned an invitation for the detectives to sit. He seated himself on the edge of a worn recliner, and Crane and Banks sat on the couch across from it. Oppressive sadness seemed to hang over the room already, nearly smothering the dim light from the table lamp at Stephen's opposite side. A spindly white-and-brown terrier bounded into the room and suddenly went still, as if sensing there was something horribly amiss.

"Is it...?" Stephen choked, his gray eyes tearing up.

"Mr. Ellis," Crane replied dutifully, meeting the man's worried gaze, "I'm afraid we do have some bad news." The man swallowed audibly, and he appeared to be holding his breath. *God, I hate this*, Crane thought, feeling his own heart aching for this stranger. After a pause and a deep inhalation, he made the announcement. "Your son, Joshua, died tonight while on duty at the museum."

Stephen closed his eyes tightly and covered his face with one hand, shaking his head as noiseless sobs racked his body. After a moment, the man nodded, rubbed his eyes, then addressed Crane with a trembling voice and a quivering lip.

"What?" he asked weakly, shaking his head again in a subconscious denial. "No...no, there must be some mistake. How can that be? What...what happened to him?"

"Actually, sir," Crane answered, "we aren't sure yet what happened. He was performing a standard security patrol and was discovered by a fellow guard shortly after. We're investigating to determine the cause of his death."

"He was healthy," Stephen said, disbelief clouding his tone, although he was clearly trying to accept the reality being delivered to him. "How...how can he be...*dead*?"

"We don't know yet, but, with your permission, we would like to perform an autopsy," Crane replied. "There is no obvious explanation right now, but we want to find out for you." Cautiously, he added, "We haven't yet been able to rule out foul play."

Stephen's eyes widened. "Foul play?" he repeated incredulously. "Who would want my son dead?"

"We have no evidence of anything yet," Banks answered calmly, giving Crane a break. "Can you tell us a little more about Joshua? Anything you can share may prove helpful."

The man ran his fingers along his stubbled jawline, his eyes distant. He sighed and made a visible effort to compose himself, then spoke. "Josh was always a good kid," he said. "He was smart and hard-working, and he loved helping people. He went to college on a full scholarship and graduated with a degree in criminology. He wanted to go into law enforcement. He planned to put in some time with the local police force, then work his way to the FBI." He paused, took a labored breath, then continued, "But his mother, my wife, died after a long battle with cancer not long after he graduated. He didn't want to...he didn't want to leave me alone, so..." He slumped over his knees, resting his face in his hands as his thin frame shook with grief.

"We understand how difficult this is for you," Banks offered compassionately. "If you would like us to come back later—"

"No, no," Stephen interrupted, sitting up again and collecting himself. "It's all right. It isn't going to be any easier for me to talk later than it is now. Josh worried about my being alone here. I'm a Navy veteran, and I was injured years ago while overseas. Never been able to work consistently since then. So when my wife died, Josh gave up all his dreams so he could stay here with me. I begged him not to. I didn't want him trapped here. But he was every bit as stubborn as I've always been. He stayed here with me and took the security job at the museum, and it's been just the two of us for all these years now. He *sacrificed* for me. He missed out on so much because of me—his career, his friends, his *life*. He helped me with the bills, the house, my doctors, everything...I...God, I pray he doesn't resent me now." Breaking down once more, he allowed the welling tears to drain down his weathered cheeks as he laid his face in his palms.

"Sounds like family was everything to him," Crane replied, struggling to keep his own voice steady. "I'm sure he never resented you."

After a minute, Stephen managed a small, grateful smile through his sorrow. "Hope you're right, Detective." He fell quiet for a second, in reflection, then cleared his throat and said, "I don't know if that was the kind of information you needed..."

"It's very helpful, thank you," Banks assured him, his baritone voice proving it could be just as comforting as it could be intimidating. "Can you tell us if Josh had any health issues? Anything you were aware of?"

Stephen roughly brushed the tears from his face and shook his head. "Not at all," he answered solidly. "Besides my war injury and my wife's cancer, we've always been really healthy people. I think Josh might have taken three sick days in all his years at the museum."

Banks nodded thoughtfully, then glanced sideways at Crane, his eyes asking if there were any further questions. Crane gave a nearly imperceptible shake of his head, then swallowed and addressed Stephen again. "Mr. Ellis," he said, fishing a few different business cards from his wallet, "we are truly sorry for your loss. This is never easy, but we do want you to know there is support available if you need it." He placed the cards in Stephen's gently shaking hand and continued, "Detective Banks and I will update you when we know more, but please, don't hesitate to contact us before then if you need anything. You have my number there, along with some contact information for various support services. And we'll arrange to have Josh's personal effects gathered for you."

Stephen looked vacantly at the cards as he asked, "Can I see him? Can I see my boy?"

God, help me, Crane prayed. He could feel Banks go as cold as stone next to him even as his own heart fell into his stomach. That was the one question they had both been dreading more than anything. He couldn't lie to this man, nor could he prevent him from seeing the dead body of his son, but...how could he prepare anyone to see those *eyes*?

Crane cleared his throat and answered falteringly, "We can

arrange that if you choose to...but, Mr. Ellis...I...I suggest you might not want to remember Joshua in that way."

Stephen looked at Crane with directionless eyes that were full of pain, not responding for several seconds. The little dog trepidatiously approached its grieving owner and lay down at his feet, placing its chin on his slipper. At length, Stephen sighed shakily and turned his eyes toward the ceiling, staring distantly as though hoping to see God Himself up there. He eventually returned his gaze to Crane and nodded. "Maybe you're right," he said. "Maybe you're right."

Crane silently thanked God that the man was not pursuing the viewing of Joshua's body, at least for now. He hadn't yet recovered from seeing those death-black eyes himself, and he couldn't imagine trying to console the young man's father if he saw those soulless holes where once he had seen the eyes of his son. Rising slowly from the couch, with Banks following his lead, he asked, "Is there anyone we can call for you? A relative or a friend or neighbor, maybe? Someone who could stay with you or at least check in on you?"

Running a hand through his thin, gray hair, Stephen stood from his recliner, obliging the dog to move away, and sighed. "That isn't necessary," he said, forcing a wan smile. "I'll talk with my neighbor tomorrow; he's been a big help to Josh and me over the years. But I'll be fine on my own for tonight. I've still got Sadie here with me, after all." He nodded as cheerfully as he could toward the wiry terrier below him, but there was little actual mirth in the gesture.

"Okay," Crane replied, "if you're sure."

"I'm sure," Stephen confirmed, his voice stronger than before, but still darkened by hurt and exhaustion.

Crane nodded at him, recognizing a deep strength and fortitude in the man, despite the grief he was feeling right now. "We'll drop back by later to see how you're doing," he said, "but, like I said, you call us if you have questions or need anything from us."

"I will," Stephen answered. "Thank you, Detectives." He looked at each of them and then started numbly toward the front door, ushering them out.

Minutes later, Crane was standing again in the cold mist, staring up at the hazy night sky and wishing he had retired last year. He was dog-tired and completely sickened by this whole strange incident. Whatever had happened at the museum, it had cost much more than the single life of a good young man.

"Go home and get a few hours of sleep," Banks suggested, clapping Crane on the shoulder and startling him out of his brief reflection. "This is going to be a rough one, but...we'll figure it out."

Crane smiled grimly at his partner, who returned the same weakly comforting expression. "Sure," he agreed anemically, his tone disclosing his uncertainty. "See you at the office," he concluded solemnly.

Both detectives got into their cars and drove away, but the images of Joshua Ellis's deceased body and his grieving father remained vividly etched in Crane's mind, and he wondered if he would ever sleep again.

5

Iris couldn't remember the last time she had felt this excited. She was a bit anxious, too, but the tinge of nervousness didn't compare to the elation she was feeling as she packed her overnight bag. Loomis Drake's office had indeed contacted her shortly after that brief but magical phone call from the man himself. The arrangements had been made quickly and easily, with practically no inconvenience to her, and now she was unashamedly looking forward to the luxury she had been promised. A limousine would pick her up at home to take her to the airport, where a private corporate jet would be awaiting her arrival. She would be flown to Portland in style and comfort, with no screaming babies or yammering businessmen or oversized passengers to turn her flight into the floating microcosm of hell that most commercial flights tended to be. She would then be driven to the hotel, a five-star beauty owned by her hopefully soon-to-be employer. She could spend the afternoon and evening as she pleased, and Loomis's office had already overnighted to her a credit card for meals and other expenses. Her interview would be the following morning, and considering her ecstasy for this opportunity, there was no room for any doubt about her success there. She had complete confidence that tomorrow would be the beginning of a new chapter in her life, and although time and cynicism had made her averse to change, she was now ready for it. After yesterday's unsolicited forty-five-minute random commentary from Matilda (which Iris had hoped but unfortunately failed to tune out, instead falling victim to the unwanted imagery of Matilda in a swimsuit as she had detailed for Iris all the fad dieting and two-a-day workouts she intended to start "soon" in preparation for next summer), Iris was finally ready to get the hell out of Eden and make a change. The lengths to which Loomis had already gone to make her travel and interview more a pleasure than an onus boded well. If he would treat a potential employee this way, surely he must treat his employees even better. This would be the chance of a lifetime for her to start using her education for something meaningful and to make the kind of money she had previously imagined only in daydreams. So, as she tossed some travel items into her bag and enthusiastically sang along with the old classic rock track playing on her stereo, she was the embodiment of self-assurance and satisfaction.

It was early evening, but autumn's premature dusk had already set in, and Iris was fully prepared for a prompt bedtime. She wanted not only to be well rested for the trip, but also to look her best. She knew appearance wasn't everything—in fact, it shouldn't mean anything—but she was admittedly prone to a touch of vanity, and getting some extra sleep in hopes of waking to a fresher-faced reflection was a palatable idea, especially in consideration of the party she'd be meeting. It wasn't every day a girl would have the opportunity to chat with a good-looking billionaire, and while her deep and naturally pessimistic belief was that a man like Loomis Drake would have no romantic interest in someone like her, she still felt a seed of desire for things to happen as they always did in the love stories of books and movies she claimed to hate. It irritated her to have such a thought, but her attempts to remove it from her mind were unsuccessful.

She finished packing what she could before morning, then

turned off her music and moved to the bathroom, removed the hair tie from her signature messy bun, brushed through her long hair, and undressed. She stepped into the shower and turned on the water, hotter than usual, and found her thoughts slipping right back to Loomis Drake as she shampooed. The warmth and steam were relaxing, and she allowed herself to fantasize for a moment about the man she had seen so often in the media and would soon meet face to face. How might she want things to happen? Maybe some little-known common interest they might share, leading to some unexpectedly meaningful conversation they would choose to continue after the interview...over coffee or drinks or dinner. Loomis would be mystified by her rare and enticing blend of classic elegance and modern, down-to-earth realism—a concoction he would find exotic in comparison to whatever vanity-gluttoned, airheaded bimbos he must usually engage with. Iris would be a breath of fresh air, perhaps less glamorous than what he could have, but far more appealing in brains and substance. He would be immediately smitten with her. In Iris's fantasy, the two of them would find they shared a similar distaste for humanity's general hypocrisy, and Loomis would admit that all his herculean efforts in charity were motivated more by a desire to change people's behavior than by heartfelt pity or sympathy. They would find they had compatible ideals and instant chemistry, and the time they spent together would be romantic and magical.

As she lathered soap on herself, enjoying the stream of hot water on her back, she imagined what wonderful sensations she might feel when Loomis would touch her. She would be shy at first, nervously accepting a light stroke across her hand but secretly desiring more, just as he would be. Perhaps he would guide her toward a seat, with a steady, masculine hand placed low on her back in just the right combination of gentility and authoritativeness. As the fantasy played out, he would have a strong arm around her hips, pulling her close to him so she could feel a muscular chest pressed against the softness of hers. He would reach with his other hand to gently guide her head toward his as he would lean in for a kiss...

Iris shook her head there and lowered the water temperature, rudely interrupting the dreamy, broken scenes of her own fantasy. That down-to-earth realism had reared its sometimes-ugly head. She was only kidding herself; sexy billionaires like Loomis Drake knocked elbows with glitzy, beautiful women like models and actresses and pop stars. What the hell would he ever see in an introverted homebody who preferred watching football or lifting weights to getting mani's and pedi's with "the girls" after drinking mimosas at some ritzy brunch locale? Those primped social butterflies were the women who hung on the arms of billionaires at elite social engagements. Iris could consider herself to pass as "pretty," but that was a far lower echelon than "glamorous," and besides that, she had been told she was intimidating—and that was probably just the euphemism people used when speaking to her face. She imagined the flies on the wall would have heard the terms "bitchy" and "stuck-up" used in reference to her more than once, assuming anyone was talking about her, anyway. Whatever. She was, if nothing else, true to what she was. She wouldn't pretend to be anything she wasn't or to enjoy anything she didn't like. If people wrongly perceived her genuineness as elitism and bitchiness, so be it. But in such a reality, it was foolish of her to entertain fantasies like this one about Loomis Drake. Ultimately, it would only cause her pain. So she dashed the idea as best she could and emerged from the shower vowing to approach her interview with nothing but business on her mind.

Partially deflated by the pessimistic shattering of her little daydream, Iris finished her nightly hair- and skin-care routine and climbed into bed. She looked up at the ceiling for a moment, more nervous now. She hadn't really prepared for her interview, and although that wouldn't normally cause her any consternation, she had allowed a river of her own thoughts to erode her sense of self-worth. She already felt grossly inferior to Loomis Drake, for no real reason at all. She had been out of the habit of praying for some time, but now she closed her eyes and asked very simply, *Lord, please help me to do well in my interview.* At a loss for anything further to say to God, she opened her eyes, rolled over, turned out the bedside light, and shoved her face into her pillow, hoping sleep would not delay. As it finally began its descent upon her, her thoughts became wispy and distant, floating right back to the arms of Loomis Drake...

***

"Good morning, ma'am," the driver said as he took Iris's bag from her and loaded it into the trunk. He was a short black man of about sixty, with eyes that sparkled with kindness and warmth. His face was open and jovial, with round cheeks and a small, white beard, reminiscent of jolly old Saint Nick. Iris couldn't help but smile at him, and she felt instantly at ease.

"Good morning," she replied. "Thank you for picking me up."

"Aw, don't mention it! I'm gettin' paid for it," he said in a laughing voice. He allowed no time for Iris to respond before he continued, "Well, now, of course I'm joking. I *am* getting paid for it, but I'd just as gladly do it for free! When Mr. Drake asks me to help get someone to him, I know it's important! He doesn't meet with just anyone, you know."

Iris chuckled at the man's good-natured humor. "I admit, I was surprised when he called me," she said. "I don't know what help I can be to someone like him."

The driver had closed the trunk and opened the rear door of the limousine, graciously waving an invitation for Iris to enter. "Well, now," he remarked easily, "I once felt that very same way, but Mr.

Drake sees value in everyone. He's a real great man. Real great man. I wouldn't work for anyone else!"

Iris smiled as she took a seat in the plush leather interior, surprised to learn this man actually worked for Loomis. Wouldn't it have made more sense to coordinate a local driver for her twenty-minute ride to the airport? To her knowledge, the nearest office of any Drake company was at least a two-hour drive away. Not that she didn't appreciate the extravagance of the arrangements as they were, though. And the man's loyalty to Drake was a good sign. If even a driver was so happy in his position, surely she would find a comfy place in Loomis's employ, too. She had always believed work would be hell no matter where or among whom it was, for why else would it be called "work," if not to be made synonymous with toil, drudgery, and all the vanity lamented in the book of Ecclesiastes? Perhaps Loomis, however, would finally prove her wrong.

The man had entered the driver's seat and turned to face Iris through the open screen separating the front from the rear. "What music you want me to put on for you, Miss?" he asked. "I can get just about anything in here! Or maybe you want me to keep it quiet?" He paused and laughed at himself. "Oh, and hey," he soon continued, "there's drinks back there, too, in that little fridge there. Water, sodas...you just help yourself!"

On any normal day, Iris would find the man's verbosity an annoyance, but today, maybe the start of a new era for her, she could only grin at his cheerful deluge of helpfulness and servitude. "I don't need anything, but thank you," she replied. "And as for the music, I don't really have any preference." It was a lie, but she felt compelled by graciousness to say it. "Why don't you just play whatever you'd like to listen to?" She hoped to God it wasn't country.

"Well, all right now," he answered, "but you just let me know if you don't like it!" He poked around on some touchscreen buttons up front, and to Iris's surprise, the vehicle was soon filled with

orchestral music. She recognized the piece as one of Vivaldi's *Seasons*, and it pulled her memory back to her days in the high school orchestra, where she always sat second chair because of an Asian kid who devoted more time to practice than she had ever been willing to spend. She smiled to herself as she recalled one audition that had gone so well for her that the guy had actually started to sweat his first-chair position upon seeing the close margin in the results their conductor had posted. He had sworn then to practice even more, and, to Iris's amusement, he probably had done just that. The brief reminiscing bolstered her confidence as the driver took her to the airport. She had never been concertmistress in high school, but soon she would be working for Mr. Loomis Drake, famed billionaire and three-time "Sexiest Man Alive"!

She sat comfortably in the limousine and watched the scenery pass by outside the tinted windows, seeing the city's commercial and residential areas giving way to industrial and agricultural lots as they neared the airport. The driver took her to a private hangar some distance from the main terminal. She had seen this other runway and building before and had often wondered what they were used for. Now, there sat on the tarmac a small, sleek twin-engine jet, a pearlescent sapphire blue exterior glittering under the morning sun. There was no gauche logo or company name to mar its aesthetic appeal, only a simple white identification number on the fuselage near the cockpit. The driver pulled the car around to a gravel area just beyond where the plane sat, then turned off the engine and exited, moving to open the door for Iris. While she waited for him, she looked back through the rear window and saw the door of the plane had opened, and steps had been lowered. A woman and two men had descended to the tarmac and now stood with perfect posture and polite smiles as they awaited their special passenger.

"Here we are, Miss," the driver said as he opened the door and extended an arm to help her out of the car. "I'll grab your bag for you, and we'll go over there and meet your crew!" He chuckled and added, "They'll be the best you'll find anywhere; I guarantee it! And there's not a better plane that money can buy! I'm just assumin' that, anyway. Haven't actually flown in one of those beauties myself, but Mr. Drake don't tend to cut corners! You'll have a blast!"

They reached the group at the plane, and the driver set down Iris's bag and greeted each of them warmly, receiving a kiss on the cheek from the woman, a firm handshake and slap on the back from each of the men, and a chorus of how-are-you's and good-to-see-you's. Iris stood at a slight distance, feeling suddenly awkward, as she often did among groups of more than two people.

Eventually, the driver turned and invited Iris closer, introducing her to the crew. "This here is Miss Iris," he said. "Well, I suppose that's Dr. Iris. Er, Dr. Wakefield. They tell me she's headed up to interview with Mr. Drake personally, and I've been tellin' her how great he is. I told her she's going to have a great time, so you all better see to it!"

"Welcome, Dr. Wakefield," the woman said with a warm smile as she offered a hand in greeting. She was probably a little younger than Iris and quite breathtaking—exactly what one might expect of a flight attendant if one's experience came only from movies. She wore a long, tailored beige coat over her uniform, but the lengthy brunette hair under the blue pillbox hat and the hose-clad legs standing in patent leather pumps were evidence enough she was dressed the part. It was as though she had just stepped off of the silver screen. "I'm Lorelei, your flight attendant," she continued, her voice tinged with just enough of a British accent to be charming without causing irritation. "Anything you need, love, you just let me know! I'll take good care of you." Being referred to as "love" by a stranger would have annoyed Iris on any other day, but for some reason, today she found it rather pleasant.

One of the men now likewise extended his hand to Iris,

introducing himself. "I'm your pilot, James, at your service, Doctor!" Iris concealed an internal swoon as he firmly shook her hand. *Oh, Jesus, he's Australian*, she thought upon hearing his voice. He had tan skin and a delightfully rugged appearance, his face nicely stubbled with the same sandy brown hair that adorned his head, contrasting most beautifully with a pair of piercing blue eyes and a model-quality white smile. *Hot damn, if I can't have Loomis Drake, I would definitely settle for this hunk*...Iris swallowed hard and tried to refocus her thoughts. It wasn't often she found herself salivating over a guy like some ditzy teenaged schoolgirl; she liked to consider herself above that kind of behavior. But...a little occasional objectification never hurt anyone.

James had been speaking as Iris lost herself in his masculine beauty and tantalizing accent, but she had only partially registered his words. He had introduced the other man, the co-pilot, who had, in turn, cordially shaken her hand. *Crap, what was this guy's name?* Iris hoped it wouldn't come up at all during the flight. That would be a dead giveaway that she had the hots for James, a scenario so embarrassing that she would have no choice but to jump from the plane.

"Yeah," James was saying when Iris finally tuned back into the conversation, "ol' Ken here's just cruising along waiting for retirement; lets me do all the real work. Ain't that right, mate?" He gave the co-pilot a good-natured backhand to the gut, at which the co-pilot, whom Iris could now thankfully identify as Ken, chuckled in agreement. She was amused by the group's playful banter. They all seemed genuinely happy in their work and fond of one another—exactly the experience she had always believed to be impossible in any real-life job.

"Gentlemen, let's not keep the good doctor waiting," Lorelei interjected after having added a tiny musical laugh to the ribbing. She turned to Iris and continued, "These two are a right mess, love, but I'll see to it they behave! We'll get ready and head out so you can enjoy your afternoon. Our flight's a touch over three hours, but Portland is two hours behind us here, so you'll have plenty of time to relax and enjoy yourself. You'll absolutely adore it there!"

The driver wished Iris good luck, said his goodbyes to the crew, and then returned to the car and departed. James and Ken boarded the plane, Ken taking Iris's small suitcase up for her, and they began their preparations as Lorelei ushered Iris up the steps in front of her. The plane's interior was a roomy and luxurious abundance of pristine white leather. Iris had walked through the glorified cattle cars they called "business class" on the plebeian flights her office would stick her on, and at the time, even those had seemed nice in comparison to the miserable "economy class" sardine cans she always had to sit in. But this…this was something completely new to her experience, something well beyond the average man's wildest dreams of affluence. This was real money announcing its presence in stylish fashion. Lorelei directed Iris to her choice of several oversized seats, laid out in a spacious semi-circle around a white table, each with its own side table. There was a flatscreen monitor mounted from the ceiling near the front of the seating area, completing what was essentially a flying conference room. Iris wished her family were still alive to hear her tell of this; they would have been so excited for her to have this experience. She felt the faint onset of sadness as she reflected on them and how they were gone—how she had no one left in this world to really talk to. There were her coworkers, but frankly she couldn't stand any of them for more than a brief and superficial "How're you doing? Good? Good." She had a couple of high school friends who sort of kept in touch, but they had moved away and gotten married and had kids, and she spoke to them only via text message maybe once a year when they'd wish her a happy birthday. The excitement of this experience was replaced by a sudden and profound loneliness she would have had difficulty shaking if not for

Lorelei's sweet, tuneful English voice asking her what she would like to drink.

"I can get you just about anything you like, love," she said. "Well, after takeoff, of course. Coffee, tea, water, juice…" She paused, smiled, and then conspiratorially inclined her head toward Iris. "Or something stronger, if you like! It's a bit early for most, but we won't tell anyone," she finished with a wink.

Iris smiled, with true mirth and not the forced toleration with which she usually smiled at people, and asked for coffee and water.

"It'll be here as soon as we're at our cruising altitude," Lorelei replied. "Now, we don't anticipate needing any of this, but you understand I have to go through the safety speech, love. Just standard operating procedure." She explained the safety features of the aircraft and how to use an oxygen mask and what to do in case of a water evacuation, and she pointed out the restroom behind a navy curtain in the back. Iris listened respectfully and hoped she would need neither the safety features nor the restroom during this flight.

James's voice came out over an intercom, whimsically identifying himself as "your Captain speaking" and telling "all passengers" to take their seats for departure. "We're expecting three hours, twenty minutes' flight time, clear skies here…maybe a bit of light rain as we near Portland. That lovely lady back there is Lorelei, your flight attendant, and she'll take good care of you. Your co-pilot up here with me today is Ken; he'll be doing crossword puzzles and eating donuts while I get you safely to your destination! So, Dr. Wakefield, sit back and relax. You're in good hands!"

The plane's engines had started, and Iris was amazed at how quiet and smooth they were. *Billionaires can afford better technology than the rest of us*, she mused. As it always did, the takeoff amazed her. She stared out the window as the craft sped along and then rose into the air, thinking to herself, *Look what mankind can do!* It was the same thought she had each time she flew, and she knew it was a sheltered thought. Mankind had gone to the moon and sent craft to Mars and well beyond; mankind had cloned DNA and built everything from gigantic skyscrapers to microcomputers. Getting a plane in the air was hardly an achievement at this point, but Iris still found in herself a childlike wonder at it.

Shortly after takeoff, Lorelei disappeared behind a navy curtain near the front and returned with a silver tray holding a large cup of hot coffee, a bottle of spring water, and a handful of Biscoff cookies on a napkin. "Any refills or anything you need, just press this button here, love," she told Iris. "There's Wi-Fi and streaming television," she added, nodding at the monitor. "You just make yourself at home." With another smile, she disappeared once more behind the curtain, and Iris was left in quiet solitude to enjoy her refreshments and once again consider how wonderful it was going to be to meet Loomis Drake and maybe grab a piece of this lifestyle for herself.

About two hours had passed when she looked up from the book she had brought and glanced again out the window, noting the sky was now flecked with gray clouds. She had finished a second cup of coffee and started a second bottle of water. She had been too self-conscious to ask for more cookies, but Lorelei had brought her two more packages, anyway, and Iris was very happy about that. She set the book on the table, took a small bite of her fifth or sixth cookie, and then stretched her arms overhead and yawned. It was a fantastic way to fly, but she was growing bored. Suddenly, a tiny jolt startled her, causing her heart to race and her attention to go immediately to the window. It was darker, certainly, but...pilots could fly in rain, couldn't they?

There was a sound of static and then the click of the speaker as James announced from the cockpit, "Ladies, please take your seats and buckle up. We've hit a bit of turbulence here. Nothing too major, but...things might be rough for a while." He spoke slowly and calmly, but Iris was sure she had heard some layer of anxiety in his voice. She dismissed the thought, though, knowing she tended to overreact to any non-routine movements or noises on a plane. She inhaled deeply and tried to calm her nerves. *God, please get us there safely,* she prayed. It didn't make her feel any more at ease.

After a brief respite, the plane shook more violently, then dropped suddenly for an instant before regaining its altitude. It had been enough to give Iris that weightless, chilled sensation in her spine that she experienced during the big drops on roller coasters. There, it was fun; here, it was terrifying. She wanted to look out the window again, but she was suddenly very afraid. *God, help us...*

Lorelei came back from behind the curtain, grabbing the nearest seat to steady herself as soon as she could, and asked Iris if she was all right. Another, more pronounced lurch almost caused her to fall into Iris's lap.

"I'm fine," Iris lied. "You should sit down, Lorelei. This is some bad turbulence."

"Oh, no, love," Lorelei replied in a breathy voice as she sat in the chair beside Iris and fastened the seat belt. "I've been through worse." There was no sincerity in her tone, and Iris could tell the girl was panicked. The lights suddenly went out as one wing dipped to an alarming degree, sending the beverage tray and book flying from the table. Against her better judgment, Iris looked outside to see purple jags of lightning veining the sky. James was clearly fighting to right the plane in the storm, and there was a sickening oscillation as he tried to reorient the aircraft.

The speaker again came on, and James, probably unaware anyone outside the cockpit was hearing him and now completely omitting any calm and reassuring veneer for his voice, cursed sharply, "Fuck! I'm losing her," as the plane tilted sideways once more. *No way this is happening...no way,* Iris thought. *God, Jesus, please, help!* She glanced at Lorelei, now pale and teary-eyed, then she heard a thunderous explosion from one of the engines. Lorelei screamed as the nose fell and oxygen masks descended from above them amid a wailing of alarms and a crimson pallor of flashing emergency lights. The aircraft was spinning and falling uncontrollably, and Iris only vaguely noted the flames and smoke illuminated outside the window. Fear had full grasp of her mind and body now, and she couldn't think or move. A second explosion thundered and ripped a hole in one side of the plane, sucking everything toward its yawning maw with a deafening hiss. There was a distant-sounding grind of metal and a hot, sulfuric smell as Iris closed her eyes to the reality being torn asunder all around her. She drifted into a subconscious limbo to await her impending demise.

***

Iris awoke with a cough, neither knowing where she was nor fully comprehending what had happened. She tasted grass and blood in her mouth, and she felt a dizzying, head-splitting pain when she tried to push herself up from the ground. Opening her eyes and finding them unable to focus, she blinked hard and attempted a deep, calming breath. The air, however, was filled with smoke that instantly made her cough again, doubling the pain in her head. She had to move, had to get away from wherever she was. Not trusting herself to stand just yet, she brought herself to her knees and hands and crawled toward the brighter area in her foggy vision. She wasn't seeing clearly, but the smoke was less dense here, with a soft breeze bringing fresh air with it. Slowly and distinctly, like systems rebooting in sequence, her senses finally started to operate again. There was a cold, light rain falling on her. Her ears were ringing in her head, but she could feel an echoing expanse of natural land around her. She guessed she was nowhere near a city. Her eyesight was blurry but had started to return to normal, and she could see black smoke billowing from golden-orange flames down below the higher area to which she had crawled. At the origin of the fire was part of what was left of the jet, and she realized the nightmare had been real. The plane had crashed, and somehow, inexplicably, she had lived to tell about it, though she couldn't imagine wanting to recount the horror for anyone. Other smaller fires burned apart from the largest one, dotting a lengthy distance with their illuminated areas of wreckage and debris.

I have to check for them, she thought, remembering the group that had been up there with her. If she had lived...it didn't look promising, but maybe they had, too. Having recovered enough to determine she was not terribly injured—aside from an awful headache, nausea, and a slight limp—she carefully made her way back toward the area from which she had come. It was downwind of the largest fire, but the wind seemed to have picked up so that the smoke was dissipating more quickly now. Covering her mouth and nose with her hand and trying to inhale as little smoke as possible, Iris surveyed the ground and all its debris. She found the seat she had been sitting in, now dirty, torn, and charred in places. It appeared the seat belt had ripped at some point, which must explain why she had been lying prone in the grass away from it when she had regained consciousness. She found another of the seats several yards away, this one turned on its side with its back facing where she stood. As she approached, she noticed a bit of brunette hair on the ground, extending from above the seatback. *Oh, God,* she prayed silently. *Oh, God, please let her be alive...*

"Lorelei?" she asked, hoping for a reply but expecting none. She moved to the front of the seat and found the girl still buckled in, giving her the appearance of hovering a few inches above the ground. Her body was limp, her limbs and head all lolled to the side, and her hosiery and dress were torn and stained. Iris swallowed and forced herself to get closer. She reached out to move the hair out of Lorelei's face, but before her hand arrived there, she noticed a large piece of twisted metal protruding from between the girl's arms. Feeling sick, but dutifully inspecting anyway, she carefully moved Lorelei's top arm and saw the wreckage stuck deep in her abdomen, just under the rib cage, a vast, scarlet flower of blood coloring her dress all around it. The sight brought involuntary tears to Iris's eyes. She had seen carnage and death in movies and video games, and she had always believed herself to be the kind of woman who would handle a crisis well, but her current reality was proving much harsher and more difficult to cope with than she could have imagined. Blinking away her tears, she brushed Lorelei's hair to the side. The girl's eyes were closed, and her lips and chin were bloodied. The logical part of Iris's brain told her Lorelei was dead, but the more sentimental part was still tragically hoping for some miracle, like a child believing an endless stream of prayers might resurrect a deceased pet. She felt at Lorelei's neck for any pulse, but of course there was none.

Iris shook her head sadly and took a shuddering breath, ignoring the smoke still in the air. The rain and wind had dispersed it enough by now that she could breathe without choking. She left Lorelei and headed for the larger part of the wreckage, stepping carefully over broken pieces of airplane and avoiding the patches of fire still burning as she approached what was left of the fuselage. One side had been torn out, and the opposite side had apparently been badly damaged by trees and rock as the plane had come down. Electrical wires were exposed in places, and she was careful to avoid them, particularly after noticing sparks from one of the bundles. As she examined the ruined remnants of what had been such a sleek, elegant jet, she found it increasingly astounding that she was even alive.

Eventually, she reached what had been the cockpit. The nose of the plane was buried in the ground, and with the plane tilted as it was toward one side, there was no way for her to see in through the outside windows to where James and Ken had been seated. *I should leave*, she thought. *They can't have survived this. I should just get away, try to find help.* But even as she thought it, she knew she couldn't do it. First, she *had* to know for sure whether anyone else had survived; and, second, she had no idea where she would go for help, anyway. So she climbed through a part of the fuselage to the cockpit door. It was broken on its hinges, and the frame around it had been bent, jamming it too tightly to pull open. She couldn't see well in the dimness of the wrecked plane, so she left where she was and looked around for anything she might use as a crowbar. She wasn't sure she'd even have the strength to pry the door open, but she was certainly going to try.

As she searched for something suitable, Iris found a tiny package of Biscoff cookies lying on the ground, seemingly unharmed and very incongruous with the destruction and tragedy surrounding it. It instantly reminded her of Lorelei, who had been so kind and sweet to her and was now hanging dead in a white leather chair in the middle of nowhere, mercilessly impaled by a wayward cut of metal. *Why couldn't that poor girl have been as fortunate as this stupid package of cookies?* She had to wipe tears from her eyes at the thought.

She finally found a long, thick piece of metal that might prove helpful and carried it back to the cockpit entrance, shifting her position until she felt stable footing and could insert the bar into the gap between the door and the frame. After a few failed attempts, she was able to move the door enough so that it swung open into the cockpit area. Its weight on the broken hinges was too great, and the door fell from its place and plummeted downward, striking the side of the plane that had settled into the grass and foliage below. Careful to maintain her footing, Iris climbed into the cockpit, noting the pilot's and co-pilot's chairs in front of her. It was black and sooty in here, with a disgusting stench of burnt meat. She winced at the grotesqueness of the place and fanned the heavy, stale air out of her face as she entered with a cough. Though the plane's windows had shattered in the crash and were now upturned toward the sky, the overhanging evergreens had prevented much rain from falling in here and clearing the space. Iris knew what she would find, and she didn't want to find it, but to leave now and live the remainder of her life not being sure seemed a worse scenario than braving the horror for a moment.

She coughed again and then quietly implored the air, "James? Ken?" Unsurprisingly, she was answered by silence.

She reached out one hand and grabbed the back of Ken's seat, attempting to use it for balance. A blackened crust sloughed off at her touch, and the seat shifted on loosened, broken bolts in the floor. She saw Ken's head droop sideways, recognizing the slightly bald spot in his brown hair. Moving slowly closer, she was able to get a clearer view of the two men, balancing herself on equipment boxes built into the plane's floor. She swallowed her scream but couldn't prevent herself from crying. Both were practically unrecognizable, the flesh of their faces badly burned and even missing in places, either from the fire or from glass or metal that had broken apart and stripped it away. What remained were ruined, skeletal shadows of what these men had been in life. Iris tried not to focus on the grisly scene in front of her, but even as she tried to pull her attention away, she felt the hideous images being imprinted on her memory —of James's white teeth, bloodied and blackened and horrifically exposed from a now-missing cheek, and of Ken's one wide-open eye, left blind in death but still visible for the living, laid open by a patch of burned-away skin. Suddenly very nauseated, Iris turned and quickly stumbled out of the cockpit and out of the fuselage to the open, rainy air, where she fell to her knees and vomited.

Long minutes passed while she sat on her knees, resting on her heels, holding her face in her hands and weeping until finally she had cried out all the overpowering emotions she had experienced in such a short time. The rain had subsided, but the sky remained overcast and dreary, and the haunting remnants of the crash still lay about her in desolate, quiet remembrance of the three lives she had just seen extinguished by a devastating tragedy. Logic eventually began speaking to her mind again, and she realized there was nothing she could do here. She debated whether she should stay, hoping for help to arrive, or whether she should leave, trying to make her way to wherever civilization might be. *What do I do now, Lord?*

There was, of course, no booming voice from the sky to answer her, no bright lights or stars to guide her. But she hated the feeling of this place, this crash site and its ambience of death. So she rose to her feet and began walking, neither knowing nor truly caring where she might be going. In numb, mindless indifference, she moved away from the wreckage until her toe struck a light but solid object on the ground. Looking down, she saw her purse, as pristine as that package of cookies she had found. She scoffed at the irony of it, then bent down and picked up the bag, slinging its strap across her torso as she proceeded forward into the mountain wilderness.

***

Iris hiked along the tree line for some time and started to wonder if sojourning alone into unknown territory without provisions had been the best idea. The shock of the crash and its aftermath and the disbelief in its nightmarish reality had finally begun to fade into an acceptance of her current circumstances, and she found herself thirsty, hungry, and cold. She continued onward nonetheless, not really certain why she was doing so. Perhaps she was being steered by some supernatural guiding hand, or, more likely, she was subconsciously attempting to deny the plane crash by removing herself from the evidence of it.

Eventually, she heard what sounded like running water, and she followed the sound until she reached its source, a flowing stream that held the clearest water she had ever seen. It had cut its course down the mountain in a rocky but shallow draw, and the trees had given it its space. Elated, Iris moved quickly but carefully toward the water, kneeling on a stone near its edge. The drizzle had stopped at some point, and pleasantly warm sunlight had broken through the clouds, clothing the scene with vibrant hues. The beauty of this place momentarily astounded her, and she forgot her thirst for a moment as she surveyed her surroundings. They were flawless. The trees and foliage all around were deep green; the water was clearer than perfect glass; the stones on the ground and in the riverbed were a smooth slate gray; and...there was a *feeling* to the place—a comforting, unhurried, peaceful solitude, as though it had been left completely untouched by mankind.

She had no qualms about drinking the water here, though anywhere else, she would have been more likely to die of thirst than to drink from an untreated source, considering the videos she had seen about waterborne intestinal parasites and other undesirable things. Here, however, she felt safe, and she was grateful for the refreshment this brook offered.

A sudden rustling downstream caught her attention and immediately sent a current of adrenaline through her veins. She had been stupid and unthinking enough to leave the crash site without any weapon, and she had no idea what wildlife might be out here. Eyes wide, she sat unmoving as she felt the sound draw nearer and then cease. She slowly turned her head and then found herself paralyzed with fear at what she saw, then heard.

***

Farther up the mountainside, a motionless figure stood poised on the stones out in the river, fishing spear at the ready. Having studied his current target, darting its glittery patterns just under the crystal surface, he had slowed his breath and timed his heartbeats, preparing to strike. In the split second before his movement, a distinctive cry turned his head sharply downstream, and fishing instantly became a distant memory. It was a sound he hadn't heard in years, but that piercing howl was as unmistakable now as it had been when last he had heard it. He had hoped then never to hear it again. It could mean only trouble, the approaching of some new and terrible threat like the one years ago that had left him alone to face whatever was now drawing near. Dropping the spear and reaching instinctively for the short, heavy blade strapped at his thigh, he withdrew to the river's edge and, impelled by the courage born of his noble duty, proceeded with haste through the pines toward the source of that heartrending sound.

***

Iris's mind had been thrown into a bewildered panic, but her senses were still intact, and she both heard and felt the sound. It was something between a wolf's howl and a banshee's wail, piercing and terrifying and threatening, and it emanated at a painfully loud volume from somewhere deep within the great beast that now loomed before her. This was unlike any animal she had ever seen in reality or nightmare. It was, in appearance, an exotic amalgam of a giant wolf and a lion, but it had a presence, an air, far more powerful than any normal creature's. Its fur was a shining, heavy coat of an almost luminous white, with radiant flecks of silver and an inexplicable cleanliness, a complete lack of any evidence that this was a wild animal dwelling in a mountain forest. As it howled, it bared a set of large and perfect teeth, pearly and somehow beautiful in spite of the danger they clearly held. Most striking of all, if there could be any outstanding feature on a being so wholly astounding, were the eyes, which had not left Iris's since the moment the beast had first appeared. They were a rich golden hue, blazing like fire as they held Iris's gaze. These eyes were not wild; they were not the eyes of a beast. There shone from within them a light of intelligence and of feeling—the brilliant markings of a soul that made them seem almost human. Even had she been able, Iris might not have wanted to pull her eyes away from those of this unquestionably magnificent creature. It was obviously powerful and obviously dangerous, but also undeniably beautiful.

Though Iris had beheld the animal for only a brief moment, awe and fear had created a sense of surreal eternity for her. Sometime within the pause, two more of the beasts had flanked her on either side, and she now became vaguely aware of their presence. These two, though somewhat smaller in stature, were equally magnificent and intimidating, and she realized with a faint numbness that her life was about to end. These creatures, whatever they were, had clearly perceived her as a threat, and they had left her no hope of escape. Neither the river nor the trees would offer any refuge. Still, instinct drew her away from them, and she rose slowly from her knees to her feet to take a few timid steps backward, neither lowering her eyes nor turning her head. The wolves, or lions, or whatever they were, followed with calculated and oddly graceful movements as they gradually and methodically closed the trap they had set. Iris had nowhere left to go. A long, breathless second passed, and the world faded away from her perception as a swift and seemingly weightless leap brought the first great wolf hurtling toward her. She lunged away from the muscular frame of her beastly assailant, only to slip on the damp granite beneath her and fall to the sodden ground of the riverbank. Her head struck one of the stones there, leaving her dazed and helpless as warm blood trickled down into her ear from the gash. In her mind's ensuing confusion, she noted with a sort of drunken approval how beautiful the sky was above her, then she lost all consciousness.

***

Having reached the source of the gut-wrenching howl, the man paused to assess the situation, standing at the edge of the pines and staring downstream at the unbelievable scene playing out before him. It was not one, but three Empyreal Hounds, the largest in the middle clearly an Alpha. They had entrapped a young woman who looked anything but threatening, but he knew all too well that appearances were deceiving, and for three Empyreal Hounds to descend upon a visitor to the mountain, this woman must be a very serious threat. As the girl remained motionless among the Hounds, seemingly yet unaware of the two flanking her, the man ventured closer, taking quiet, careful steps so he would not alert her to his presence. As he approached from behind, surreal auras of light subdued his physical vision, clearing his mind and allowing him to see as most mortal beings could not—to see with the heart, with the soul; to behold the spirit, the true nature, of another. What he saw now frightened him, but he would bravely press forward and do what had to be done, for his failure now could usher in the total annihilation of the human race.

The wicked being was securely trapped on three sides by the holy Empyreal Hounds, and their command of her attention would allow a simple surprise attack. The man's hand was still wrapped around the handle of the blade at his hip, and he now withdrew it with a stoic and deliberate rush from its leather sheath as he took quick, long strides toward his target, raising the knife as he neared. Suddenly, the Alpha Hound lunged toward the girl, who instinctively sidestepped in an attempt to avoid the assault. She fell, hitting her head against the rocks along the river. The man paused at the sudden movement from the Hound, but now was the time to strike. To his amazement, however, the Hound moved in front of him, standing its massive frame over the girl's dazed or unconscious body in a posture that appeared almost protective. Though besotted by the strange turn of events, the man dutifully ceased his offensive and sheathed his blade. The Hound stared into his eyes, and he stared back, letting the noble beast speak to him, not in audible sounds or words, but in the quintessential reshaping of a mortal mind and a mortal will by an invisible, omnipotent hand. Though instinct guided him otherwise—to kill this evil intruder—the man obediently nodded his understanding to the Hound. He moved toward the girl, lying limp at the river's edge, the Hound moving silently aside as he approached. He picked her up and turned upstream, carrying her to his dwelling, where none such as she should be allowed.

***

Iris opened her eyes slowly and squinted in the light that filled this room. As her vision adjusted, she looked around groggily, unsure of what had happened and where she was. She was lying on a small couch inside a rustic-looking den that was sparsely furnished, but clean and somehow elegant. The wooden furniture was solid and well maintained, with intricately carved accent designs that spoke of an antique origin. Immediately before her was a coffee table; beyond that was a large stone fireplace containing the remnants of a fire from perhaps the night before. It felt like a cozy, comfortable place, and although Iris had no recollection of arriving here, she was glad she had.

She sat up and pressed her fingers against the pain in her temple, finding a cloth bandage and some kind of poultice there. She looked around, wondering who had brought her here and cared for her, and she was startled to see a man sitting silently in a chair beside the table. He was intimidating in both physique and presence. He was very muscular, with a broad chest and broad shoulders. His face was strong and noble, with an aquiline nose; a heavy brow; high, defined cheekbones; and a square jaw. His eyes were a brilliant sky blue, full of wisdom and kindness and preternatural keenness. His eyebrows and his hair, which appeared to be pulled back in a ponytail, were a silvery white, contrasting sharply but beautifully with his deeply tanned skin. There were a few small scars that looked like burns spattered across his face, but these didn't detract from his appearance; in fact, they enhanced it, adding a rugged, virile facet to his aristocratic, refined persona. The man was perhaps fifty or sixty, given the lines in his face and the experience evident in his eyes, although it was very difficult to tell. Whatever his age, he was obviously fit and highly disciplined with regard to physical maintenance.

He focused on Iris as she stared at him in confusion, saying nothing. His gaze was not threatening, but it was certainly sharp. It felt as though he were sifting through all her secrets, like he could read her past thoughts and memories like an open book. Iris felt like a child who had just been caught with her hand in the cookie jar...by a priest. She knew she had no reason to feel that way, but the man's stare was unnerving nonetheless. Finally, she broke the silence, which she found awkward, though her unspeaking host seemed completely unfazed by it.

"You brought me here?" she asked, her voice gravelly from a period of disuse. She cleared her throat and continued, pointing to her bandaged head, "You did this?"

"I did," the man replied, in a voice that was deep and dignified—not loud, but intrinsically authoritative. It was a voice that resonated with both patrician gentility and exacting incisiveness, very accurately reflecting what Iris had already sensed in him. His presence felt rigid and piercing but also mysterious and beautiful, like an ornately engraved antique sword wielded by a king.

Iris waited for further comment from her rescuer, but none came. "Thank you," she said quietly, truly grateful for the help this man had given her and intrigued by him, though a bit deflated by his somber quietude. She wasn't a fan of conversation with strangers, but this seemed an appropriate time for the man to make an effort to welcome her and show some concern for her. His elite stare-down and monk-like silence were going to make this a tedious stay. She was too exhausted at this point to be the one making conversation, however, so she said nothing more.

After a minute, the man's voice cut distinctly, though somehow serenely, through the quiet of the room. "Would you like some tea?" he asked simply.

Roused by the offer, Iris perked up where she sat and graciously replied, "Yes, please; that would be nice." Perhaps, after all, he was just a shy man unused to visitors. Perhaps this was his effort to be hospitable and caring. She knew she should be understanding of him and his situation. It seemed he was up here in the mountains alone, and he probably liked it that way. Her appearance had shaken his routine and perhaps even unsettled him more than his expression might let on.

The man stood gracefully from his seat and left the room, headed toward a kitchen that Iris could only halfway see from where she sat. He was very tall, easily clearing six feet, and for a man so large and imposing, he had a smooth and agile gait. There were no stomping footsteps nor creaking floorboards beneath him. As he walked away, Iris realized how strangely he was dressed. He had heavy, knee-high leather boots laced up over brown tights that made no secret of the statuesquely muscular legs they were enveloping. A loose-fitting, crimson-colored linen shirt covered his torso all the way to the upper portion of his thighs, but even the extra fabric in the sleeves couldn't conceal the substantial muscles in his arms. A leather vest and a corded leather belt completed his attire. From behind, Iris saw the man's hair was in fact held back in a silvery-white ponytail, extending almost midway down his back in smooth waves. It would have been an appropriate ensemble for a Renaissance fair, perhaps, but for everyday wear, it was…exotic.

He returned shortly, carrying a teacup on a matching saucer, which looked humorously small in his large hand. He set it carefully in front of Iris on the table, then swiftly and easily sat back in his chair, his movements dexterous and muted. Iris thanked him, receiving a silent nod in reply, then turned her attention to the cup in front of her, bringing herself to the edge of the couch so she could reach the tea while resting her elbows on her knees. She carefully raised the saucer and cup toward her lips, aware of the man's gaze on her. The tea had an herbal aroma that was somewhat unfamiliar but not altogether unpleasant. She blew softly across the top of the cup for a moment, hoping to avoid burning her mouth as she took a hesitant sip. It was a wonderful tea, with the distinct flavor of licorice and an unknown medley of something citrusy but sweet. She relaxed slightly and savored the beverage, momentarily forgetting why she had found the silence here so awkward. This was, in fact, a very pleasant place, and the quiet and solitude were a welcome respite from the vicious events of this day.

After Iris had finished the cup and replaced both it and the saucer back on the table, the man asked, "Did you like it?" Once again, his tone was pointed, almost like an accusation, but not overtly threatening.

"I did like it," Iris replied truthfully. "It was very good." She hesitated a second, debating internally, then continued, "What's in it?"

"It is primarily licorice and lemongrass, with saffron and dandelion and spearmint, and a few other things," he said. "I blend it myself," he added before falling silent once more.

"It's wonderful," Iris said.

"I am surprised you enjoyed it," the man stated. "Truthfully, I expected a different reaction."

Iris furrowed her eyebrows quizzically, then asked, "Really? It's different, but it's good. I think it's wonderful. I'm used to store-bought tea in pre-packaged bags. This is much better." She found it rather sad the man had expected his tea to meet with a negative reaction from what must be his first visitor in a very long time, and she was glad she could genuinely compliment it for him.

Without replying, the man stood from his chair, took the cup and saucer from the table, withdrew to the kitchen once more, then returned with another full cup of hot tea. Iris smiled at him as he set the saucer carefully in front of her, but he wasn't looking at her. With slight disappointment, she cast her eyes down to the tea as the man moved back toward his chair. She was suddenly startled by the icy whisper of a blade being withdrawn from its sheath. Eyes widening with concern, she turned slowly to face the man next to her. He had pulled a large, heavy knife from the leather sheath near his hip and had set it within close reach on the corner of the table nearest him. Though he was seated, his posture was anything but relaxed. His blue eyes were like daggers as he stared at her, and there was a cold, stony gravity emanating from him. He looked like a marble statue of a Roman god or a Greek warrior that had been carved by man but then imbued with life by a supernatural force, awoken from stone to vanquish a powerful enemy, and although Iris had no idea what threat she posed, she knew for certain she had been labeled the enemy.

Watching her eyes dart toward the blade on the table near him, the man said, "No harm will come to you here, if your intentions are pure." Iris could feel the confusion make itself evident on her face. "Should I find your intentions are evil, however, you will meet your demise," the man continued, his voice slashing the tense air with quiet but lethal authority.

Iris could not allow herself to panic. She knew nothing of this man but what she had sensed from his demeanor and behavior, but that was enough to make her sure he would kill her if he believed it necessary. And that was her conundrum now—what would cause this man to believe her death was necessary? What was this talk of pure or evil intentions? Had she inadvertently stumbled into the arms of some religious zealot? A sociopath? A psychopath? There was precious little in this room to give her any idea how she might successfully reason with this man, and she knew she might have only seconds to formulate responses that would either subdue his animosity or trigger a deadly rage.

The man interrupted the confused meanderings of her thoughts with the sharp question, "Why are you here?"

Iris stared at the man, dumbfounded. In the pause before she replied, the man continued, "Answer me in full truth. That is all that is required. Do not trouble yourself to find the responses you believe I desire; I will recognize deceit immediately." Iris didn't doubt his final statement at all. This was no ideal situation, but definitely her best option now would be to comply with his interrogation. As if sensing her internal decision to answer his questions, the man asked her again, "Why are you here?"

Iris swallowed and then replied, slowly, "I'm not here intentionally. I was on a plane, going to Portland. It crashed in the mountains. I survived; I don't know how. Everyone else is dead. I didn't know what to do, and I...I couldn't stay there, so I just started walking. I found the creek, and then there were these wolf things...I don't know what happened there. I guess that's where you found me. I guess...did you save me from them?" She stopped, but the man said nothing for what felt like a long time.

"They are not wolves," he finally stated. "They are Empyreal Hounds, and they saved *you* from *me*. I would have killed you there, for I see exactly what you are, but the Hounds made it clear I must spare you, at least for now."

Great, Iris thought. *I survive a plane crash only to wander into some crazy man's mountain hideaway. He's ready to kill me for whatever reason...I should have just died in the crash.* She looked briefly at the knife on the table. Maybe if she could make a surprise movement, she could knock the table over and grab the weapon from the floor before the man could react. He was too strong for her to fight, but if she had the knife, she might have a better chance at convincing him to let her go. She couldn't bring herself to try it, though. Not just yet.

"Tell me about your parents," the man said, his expression still focused and full of warning.

"What?" Iris asked in shocked reply, so stunned by the strangeness of the question that she couldn't withhold her verbal bewilderment. "What do my parents have to do with anything?"

As soon as the words were out, Iris regretted the outburst. If the man killed her right now, it would serve her right. She wasn't maintaining the appropriate composure. She hazarded a cautious glance at her captor, halfway expecting to find him angered and ready to kill, but he was still sitting like a statue. He said nothing, and Iris was grateful for a second opportunity to answer his question.

"I was adopted as a baby," she told him. "They were the best parents anyone could ask for. They and my mother's parents were the only family I ever had. They're all dead now. As for my biological parents...well, I know nothing about them. My parents offered once to help me find them if I wanted. I had no interest in it. They hadn't wanted me; I didn't see any reason I should want them. I don't even know their names, and I don't care."

The man's eyes narrowed, and his broad forehead wrinkled slightly, then his visage returned to its unmoving, stony mask. He waited several seconds before speaking again. "And why were you going to Portland?" he asked.

"A job interview," Iris answered. "Loomis Drake had contacted me about a week ago—"

"Loomis Drake?" the man interjected sharply, his eyes suddenly full of heightened concern.

Iris, taken aback by the man's startled interruption, responded hesitantly, "Yes...Loomis Drake. He called me personally and said he's starting a new company that will focus on the same research I did in college for my doctorate. He had come across a paper I had published and thought I might be an asset to his company."

"Indeed you would be an asset to him," the man stated with a note of derision.

What the hell is going on? Iris wondered. She was surprised this man would even know of Loomis Drake, and what the hell did he mean when he said she would "indeed be an asset" to him? The man's gaze left her momentarily as he stared forward at seemingly nothing, apparently deep in thought. Iris took another sidelong glance at the knife still on the table. This might be her chance to catch him off guard, to grab the weapon and get out of this insanity...but part of her was inexplicably intrigued by the man and his strange behavior. Despite her anxiousness and her hope to remove herself from a potentially dangerous situation, she was curious. It made her want to stay, and it caused enough hesitation that the man had roused himself from his faraway thoughts before she had acted on anything.

"What is your name?" he asked, his voice slightly gentler than it had been.

"Iris," she replied. "Iris Wakefield."

The man nodded slowly, as if in answer to some tacit question he had asked himself. He then drove his icy stare back into Iris's eyes before saying, "You truly have no idea what you are, do you?"

Iris found herself at a loss for words to offer in reply. How should a person be expected to answer such a question? Her response to the man was a quizzical and concerned expression.

The man took a deep breath and stood from his chair. Iris watched him as he picked up the tea she had left untouched on the table. "Your tea has gone cold," he said. He went back to the kitchen and returned quickly with a fresh, hot cup, which this time he held in front of Iris until she reached up and took the cup and saucer from him. *Damn me*, she thought. *I'm going to run out of chances to get away from here. He left the room, and I should have grabbed the knife and run...but I'm still sitting here because, why? Because I want to hear what this man's going to say? He's probably just crazy.* But even as she thought it, she sensed it wasn't true. The man may be unusual, and maybe even dangerous, but he didn't act insane. If anything, she felt he somehow had a stronger grasp on reality than most people did.

She balanced the cup and saucer on her lap, and the man returned to his chair. "Iris," he said softly, "drink the tea. I have things to tell you—things you will find difficult to believe. Things you may wish you had never known." Iris felt her heart beating faster as the man spoke in his sonorous, scythe-like voice. She was nervous, perhaps afraid, but she wanted to hear him out.

The man continued, "I am sorry for my behavior if it should have caused you any distress. You will understand my actions and my thoughts, perhaps, in time." He paused briefly, then said, "You will not want to hear what I tell you now, but I am obliged to tell you. And I hope, for your sake, you do what is right with the knowledge I impart to you." Iris looked into his eyes, staring directly back into hers, and she felt like he was somehow inside her head. She swallowed hard in the tense silence that now hung in the air, then she lifted the teacup toward her lips with a shaky hand. She pulled her eyes away from the man and looked down at the tea as she sipped it, waiting for him to continue.

"There is a reason you do not know your true parents," he stated. "It is good you never sought to know them, for you are correct they did not want you. But there are those who do want you now, because of what you are. He who seeks you now has ill intentions, and he is undoubtedly hoping and expecting you remain ignorant of your origins. It is imperative we disappoint him."

Iris set her tea on the table and breathed deeply, trying to calm her nerves. This was ridiculous. This man couldn't possibly know her or her parents. Whatever he was talking about was a delusional fantasy. She couldn't allow herself to be shaken by his fanciful posturing. She would listen awhile for now, but at the next opening, she would go for the knife. She didn't want to stay here any longer. It felt like a bad dream.

"I was truly stunned when you enjoyed the tea," the man said, the statement oddly out of place in relation to the strange, looming story he had seemed to be introducing.

With sudden impatience at being left treading the waters of confusion, Iris asked in exasperation, "Why? Why do you care if I enjoy this tea or I don't? Just get on with it."

The man, unaffected by her irritation, stared at her for a long moment, then answered her quietly, "There is holy water in the tea...and you are a demon."

Iris hadn't known what to expect the man to say, but had she made a dozen wild guesses, the you're-a-demon statement would not have been among them. She had obviously misjudged the man's sanity. Perhaps she had been away from psychology for too long. The guy was clearly a religious nut, and those were sometimes, ironically and unfortunately, the most dangerous kind.

"You do not believe me," he continued, "and I can understand why. But you will recognize the truth in time. You must, because your inability or unwillingness to accept what you are will result in the deaths of many innocent people. And I mean not only their mortal deaths, but the destruction of their souls."

Iris would have to work very carefully now. The last thing she wanted was to offend this man if he believed she was some evil presence, but the next-to-last thing she wanted was to hang around with him.

"I'm sure you mean well," she said cautiously, "but I assure you, I am no demon. I'm really a decent person. I'm sorry I disturbed you." She stood slowly from the couch and concluded, with as much confidence as she could muster, "Thank you for helping me, and thank you for the tea. I'll leave you now, and I won't bother you again." As she spoke, she moved around the table and began backing away from the man's chair toward what she hoped was an exit door.

To her dismay, the man arose immediately and said bitingly, in the loudest voice she had heard from him yet, "You may not leave yet, Iris—not until you have heard the full truth." The admonishing tone in his voice made her stop in her tracks. The man took a couple of long steps toward her, stopping directly in front of her. She looked up at him, towering above her, his muscular form making her feel very small and weak. "Please," he entreated, in a gentler tone. "Sit back down and listen to me. You must understand, I cannot allow you to leave like this."

Iris stood unmoving for a few seconds, unsure how to proceed. She wouldn't be able to escape. The knife was too far away, and the man was blocking her path to it, anyway. So she moved slowly back toward where she had been sitting on the couch. As she did so, she was pleased to see the man likewise returning to his chair. Now might be her last chance.

Shoving the whole table forward, knocking the cup and saucer and the knife to the floor, Iris pushed herself quickly over the tabletop to where the blade had fallen. She grabbed for the handle and panicked when she couldn't lift it. It felt as though it had become a part of the floor, as though she were trying to uproot a tree with a single hand. The man was already standing over her, watching her struggle in vain to pick up the weapon.

Iris felt tears forming in her eyes. He would definitely kill her now. It had been stupid for her to try this. *What the hell is wrong with this knife?* her mind screamed at her. *It can't be that heavy...*

A strong hand reached out and grabbed her upper arm, lifting her to her feet sternly, though not maliciously. "Sit," the man commanded, pointing to the chair he had been using. Iris, her face flushed with adrenaline and embarrassment, acquiesced.

He bent down gracefully, picked up the blade and sheathed it at his hip, then righted the table and set the cup and saucer back on it. Standing next to where Iris now sat, he told her, "This blade is enchanted with a magical spell. I am the only one who can wield it. I have told you, no harm will come to you here. I believe you have lived your life not knowing who or what you really are. I now believe you have been brought here by God for your protection and for the protection of mankind. I will not hurt you, but you must listen. You must hear the truth I can share with you. What you then do with that truth will be your own virtue or sin."

He looked down at Iris, sitting silently in the chair, still breathing quickly and obviously upset, clearly defeated by her own failed attempt at escape. He must have been convinced she would not try running again, because he moved away from her and sat quietly on the couch. Iris was still suspended in a mental state of disbelief, but the physical effort of tossing the table and trying to pick up the man's knife had somehow exhausted her body and mind to a point where she was ready to listen to him. She would listen without trying to formulate some plan of action as he spoke...because it really didn't matter. Whether she believed him or she didn't, whether she lived or died, what did it really matter? She should have died in the crash. That she hadn't seemed miraculous. Maybe God really had brought her to this man for a reason.

"Perhaps I have approached this in the wrong manner," the man said. "This is foreign to my experience, I will admit. I do not mean to alarm you, Iris, but I believe the truth, as it is, will unfortunately do just that. You must have many questions already. Ask them now, and I will answer you, so that you might learn the truth in a manner that suits you." He fell quiet, looking at Iris with an expression less severe and cold than what it had been. There was warmth in his eyes, and though Iris had thought him psychotic not long ago, she now believed she had been mistaken in thinking so. Yes, his words so far had been alarming and unbelievable, but there was still an unmistakable presence of confidence and truth in him. His was an almost holy presence.

She did indeed have many questions for the man, and the tension she had felt previously was now gone, as the man had relaxed slightly in his austerity. So she cleared her throat and asked, "Who are you?"

"My name is Auraltiferys," he replied. "I am the last remnant of a holy order known as the Knights of Heaven's Forge. We are, or we were, blacksmiths and priests, tasked with the creation and protection of weapons and relics in service to God."

Iris blinked several times. Today had been a whirlwind of impossibility already; why should she be surprised by the man's response? For that matter, why should she doubt it? "So," she proceeded hesitantly, "you're a blacksmith? Or a priest?"

"I am both," Auraltiferys answered.

Iris nodded slowly, still uncertain whether her brain was actually believing any of this. "So, the knife," she said questioningly. "That knife...you made it?"

"I did," he confirmed. "Its blade is inscribed with the runes of magic spells. Only my hands may lift it, and it cannot be used against me."

Of course, Iris thought. *Runes and magic spells...why not? Makes perfect sense.* "But you're also a priest? Like a Catholic priest? I thought magic was, you know, taboo," she retorted. The man, to her surprise, smiled a little. Even the slight change lit up his face in a way that radiated genuineness and goodness. He really was a beautiful man.

"The Roman Catholic Church knew of our Order once," he explained, "though our Order existed long before the Church was established. We worked together in harmony as part of the same Body of Christ after the Church was founded. Eventually, however, corruption and dissent within the Church made that collaboration a dangerous liability. We withdrew from the institution and hid our existence from future generations. Any who knew of us have long since died. My priesthood would not be recognized by the Catholic Church of your existence, but I am a Catholic priest. I can administer the sacraments and celebrate the Mass." He paused, then continued, "As for the magic, it is, like all things, given to us by God. It is, in itself, neither good nor evil, but as you know, humans have free will. Those with the knowledge of magic may use it as they choose, and, sadly, many have chosen darkness over light. It became evident long ago that magic could not be freely given to the world, for it would result in chaos and destruction. We have protected the knowledge as best we can from humankind, but angels and demons are fully aware of it, and the evil ones still use it as they can. As humanity has drifted farther from God, however, the demons have found it increasingly difficult to reveal magic to them. Humans are losing the ability to wield magic at all because they are losing belief in everything—good and evil alike. This, of course, is helpful to me in the protection of the knowledge of magic, but the sad truth it speaks of the state of the human race is most unfortunate."

Iris was fascinated by his explanation, but it left her with so many other questions...she couldn't possibly ask them all now, and besides, there were other more personal topics they needed to discuss, though she found it rather uncomfortable to return to them. After hesitating momentarily, she forced herself to address the elephant in the room. "You said I'm, um...a demon," she said tentatively, her tone inflecting a question mark at the end of her statement. "What...what did you mean by that?"

The blacksmith-priest's expression was serious as he answered her. "I have been given spiritual gifts that allow me to see as few men see," he said. "I can, when it is the will of God, read the hearts and minds of men. I can see through artificiality to the true natures of beings. You are a being with two natures. You are human, but you are also a demon, an angel of Hell."

"I don't understand," Iris blurted out. "I can't be a demon! That's not even possible! I can't be human *and* an angel. It doesn't make sense. Besides, I was raised Catholic. I'm still Catholic. I still go to Mass every weekend. I'm not perfect, but I'm not evil!" She had unintentionally allowed her words to come out in a rush of emotion and confusion.

Auraltiferys allowed her the outburst, then responded quietly, "I cannot explain how or why you exist as you do, but I can tell you with full certainty, you have both a human body and soul and a demonic nature."

"You think I'm possessed," Iris suggested.

"No, not possessed," Auraltiferys replied rather sternly. "You are both human and demon." He paused before adding quietly, "And...you're not just any demon."

Oh, God, Iris thought. *What the hell is it now?* She simply stared at the blacksmith, waiting for whatever hammer he was about to drop.

"Iris," he said haltingly, "you are...the begotten of Satan himself."

Iris shook her head forcefully for a second or two before the pain reminded her of the wound she had suffered. She clenched her teeth and pressed a hand to her forehead, took a deep breath, then laughed mirthlessly before speaking again. "You're telling me I'm Satan's daughter; is that what you're telling me? Do you realize how ridiculous you sound?" Her voice was louder and higher pitched now in her agitation. "I still go to Mass! I take Communion! How the hell do you explain that? Shouldn't it hurt me or kill me or something? *How do you explain that?*"

"I cannot explain it," Auraltiferys replied, his tone once again rife with authority and warning, though not unsympathetic. He sounded truly sorry he could not offer an explanation. "Angels do not proliferate as humans and animals do," he finally continued. "They are purely spiritual beings. However, there was once a little-known and much-unheeded prophecy of Satan's progeny. It was said he would, through the use of magic and relics, be able to give part of himself in spirit to a human form. If the prophecy came to pass, Satan's creation would be a perverted reflection of Jesus Christ. As Christ is consubstantial with the Father, so would this offspring be consubstantial with Satan, housed in a permanent human body."

Iris sat numbly, hearing but only halfway understanding, saying nothing. Auraltiferys continued in his low voice, "Perhaps you are the one whom that prophecy foretold. But never was it suspected you would have a human soul. I believe, though it is my opinion only, God must have ruined Satan's plan for you. He granted you a human soul, a body with His breath in it. Satan wanted an empty human shell animated solely by his evil spirit. Imagine his disappointment when God gave you humanity and, by necessary extension, a free will."

Iris swallowed. Could this really be possible? It was all so unbelievable. She didn't *feel* like a demon...then again, hadn't there been dozens of times in her life when she had felt like an outsider among the human race?

Auraltiferys studied her with an inquisitive gaze, as if hearing her thoughts as she had them. After a long silence, he spoke again. "Iris, you are very powerful. The Earth is the Devil's playground, and you walk it freely. His spirit is within you. The powers he possesses are yours, and you can exercise them even more readily than he, for you dwell in person among the human race. But you have been given a choice." He stopped and thought briefly before continuing. "The Empyreal Hounds would have had me destroy you, were you not meant to be here," he said. "Instead, they preserved you. They revealed to me your power and the potential it has for good. There are distressing events being played out as we speak. There is one who seeks to overthrow Satan as ruler of Hell, and he will destroy human souls as he goes. He will need your aid, for in the ranks of Hell, you are greater than he, but you can stop him. You can choose to fight for Heaven, for God, to save mankind."

Iris suddenly felt light-headed and weak. She didn't want to hear these fantastic stories anymore. This must all be a crazy dream. Maybe the plane crash was a dream, too. Surely she would wake at any moment. She found a timid voice in her throat and said tightly, "I'm going now. Thank you for everything, but I need to leave now." She stood from the chair and immediately felt the room spin around her. She attempted one wobbly step forward as dark rings closed in on her vision, and then she felt her body falling. *Wake up*, she thought. *Wake up.*

***

Iris opened her eyes and rolled over in the bed, reaching toward the small clock on her bedside table so she could check the time. The room was shaded in the blue-gray glow of the full moon's light seeping in through the blinds. *What a strange dream that was*, she thought. *And so vivid, so real.*

She tried to turn the little clock so she could see its face, but it seemed to be caught on something. Propping herself up on her elbow, she reached farther for the switch on her nightstand lamp. She pressed it, but the bulb remained dark. *That's strange...*

She suddenly felt a cold hand on top of hers, and with a startled cry, she shoved it away, jumping out to the other side of the bed. She hit the light switch on the wall next to her, to no avail; the room remained dark but for eerie moonlight. Across the bed from her stood a figure, shadowy and tall. A pair of gleaming, sinister yellow eyes shone from its face, like cats' eyes in a black window. Iris backed through the open door, then turned and ran through the darkness, trying to find her way out of the house. Nothing was as she remembered; once she left her bedroom, everything became a maze of hallways and doorways, each one masked in the dim, bluish hue of a moonlit midnight, each one leading nowhere. She finally stopped in her tracks, lost and confused, hoping the shadowy figure had disappeared. A slow, deep rasp of laughter came suddenly from behind her, so close she could feel the icy rush of air along the back of her neck. She screamed and ran forward, thankfully finding a door at the end of the dark, expansive room in front of her. This must be the one; this one looked different from all the others.

She threw open the door and stumbled outside, knowing the evil presence was still close behind her. She halted herself just before falling headlong into a great pit. What should have been a front yard or a street was instead a gaping hole in the ground, opened like a beast's mouth to swallow her, with tongues of flame flicking around as if to taste the air, to taste *her*. Smoke and sulfur billowed out of the pit, and with the suffocating stench came a terrible cacophony of pain-soaked voices and ghastly wails. She had run out of ground to cover. She turned and saw the shadow standing behind her, now an opaque and monstrous beast, taunting her for having run herself into a trap. It laughed its terrifying cackle, then extended two long, jagged arms toward her. She closed her eyes tightly and screamed, for there was nothing else she could do.

Suddenly, a metallic swish cut the air, and Iris opened her eyes to see Auraltiferys before her, his blade gouged into the chest of the evil shadow that had chased her. The entity disappeared, and Iris sensed the pit behind her closing itself as calmness descended into the place where she was. The last thing she saw was moonlight striking the silver-white hair and the noble features of the blacksmith, illuminating him with a beautiful, aural glow. The scene faded from her vision, and her eyes fluttered open, her body now awake on the same couch where she had sat before, this time warmed by a fire in the fireplace before her. By the flickering light of the flames, she could see Auraltiferys sitting in the chair nearby, his large arms resting gracefully on the armrests, and her heart was gladdened to feel his comforting presence there.

"Bad dream?" he asked, not looking away from the fire, his dignified countenance gilded by the light of the flames. His tone suggested the words were more a statement than a question.

Iris lay on the couch silently for a moment, her thoughts moving back to the dark hallways of the dream she had just had, and to the terrible presence that had pursued her there, and to the awe-inspiring savior who now sat so calmly by her side. Perhaps it had been just a dream, the wild meanderings of a mind that had been subjected to a multitude of strange physical and mental traumas in a short period of time—but she couldn't convince herself of that. There had to have been some meaning to the dream, or the *vision*, she had just experienced. In fact, she found herself hoping there was meaning to it. Whether it was dream or prophecy, she felt deeply indebted to the noble blacksmith who had appeared with stoic bravery to rescue her from a terrifying evil. And if logic was necessary, there was still the fact that he had taken her in and cared for her when she was hurt and in need. Whether she thought with her heart or with her head, Iris had decided she owed it to Auraltiferys to *try* to believe him. He had promised no harm to her, and she inherently trusted his word. If he were wrong, what trouble would it be? And if he were right...well, as unbelievable as that seemed, Iris had to admit it would be one hell of an adventure. How else could someone wind up here, in such an impossible set of circumstances, if not by the will of God? It was either that or coincidence, and she had finally decided which option she found less likely.

She sat up slowly and finally addressed the blacksmith, saying simply, "All right." He turned and met her eyes with his, one eyebrow raised slightly in an invitation for her to continue. "I want you to tell me everything, and..." She paused and swallowed. "And I'll try to believe you."

Auraltiferys blinked slowly and nodded once in acknowledgment. "I am pleased to hear it," he said, his strong but gentle antique voice carrying a note of approval that made Iris feel suddenly proud, like a child who had just been patted on the back by her father. She found herself smiling unintentionally before Auraltiferys continued. "It is growing late," he said, "and you have had enough stress for one day. I'll show you to a spare room so you can rest. There is much for you to learn. Make yourself ready, both physically and spiritually, for your former way of life ends tonight."

The gravitas in his final statement made Iris unequivocally nervous. She had been flying to Portland thinking she was ready for a change; now she was lost somewhere else and being told by some strange and magnificent man that her old life was passing away, and she no longer welcomed the change.

As if in reply to her racing heart and the fluttering in her stomach, Auraltiferys stood from his chair and extended his hand to her with an easy and gentle smile. "Do not be afraid," he said as she took his hand and rose from the couch. "All knowledge and strength you need are already within you, and you are not alone." Iris looked up at his eyes for an instant before dropping her gaze back to her feet, already fearing she might disappoint him.

Auraltiferys was quiet for a few seconds, then said, "You are welcome to join me for my evening prayers if you like."

Iris, quickly reflecting on her nightmare and feeling most unprepared to leave the blacksmith's side, graciously accepted the invitation. Perhaps an hour later, after a prayer session that made her ashamed of the emptiness and insipidness of every so-called "prayer" she had ever uttered, Auraltiferys led her to a bedroom that was quite monastic but had everything she would need—a bed with clean sheets and blankets and pillow, and a bathroom which, to Iris's surprise, included a functioning toilet, shower, and sink. He left her there alone for a short while, long enough for Iris to discover fresh handmade soap in the bathroom, then returned with some fresh clothes, handing them to her. "I haven't any clothing that would suit you," he stated apologetically, "but you may use these if you like. Is there anything else you may need?"

"No, thank you," Iris replied.

"Then, good night, Iris," he said. "Rest well. I will see you in the morning." With that, he turned and walked gracefully away, gently closing the door as he did so.

Iris showered, enjoying the soft feel and herbal fragrance of the soap she knew Auraltiferys must have made. She put on the shirt he had brought to her, over her undergarments. She might have been more comfortable without her bra, but she couldn't stand the thought of allowing a priest's shirt to touch her without it on. *That's stupid*, she thought. *It's just a shirt.* But the bra was staying on nonetheless.

She climbed into the small bed and closed her eyes, hoping sleep would not transport her back to that nightmare place with its evil shadow and pit of fire. As she drifted off, she enjoyed a slight scent of something like incense from either the sheets or the blacksmith's shirt; she wasn't sure which. Her last conscious thought was a muddled wondering whether Auraltiferys might be an angel.

6

Iris awoke to a faint, rhythmic rumble that she felt more than she heard. The shaded window above her bed was still quite dark, indicating an early hour. She listened intently from atop her pillow, trying to determine what the sound was, if it was sound at all. It wasn't loud, but it carried the feeling of thunder, and it seemed at once both distant and very near, as though she were listening to her own heartbeat from far away. Whatever it was, it probably meant Auraltiferys was already awake, and she should be, too. After all, she apparently had much to learn.

She yawned and shrugged off the blankets, then stood from the bed to get ready for this strange, new day. There was a lamp of some sort on the nightstand beside her, but she couldn't find any switch or dial that would turn it on. *Crap,* she worried, *does this place even have electricity?* She felt a momentary frustration at the antiquity of her current abode. One could call it "rustic charm" during daylight hours, but when the sun was down, it was nothing but archaic, third-world misery. Hadn't the lamp been on last night? It had to have been on—the sun had set before Auraltiferys had brought her to this room, and she hadn't prepared for bed in darkness. Even so, she couldn't remember either herself or the blacksmith turning it off. She ran her hands over its metallic dome and short stand, determined to find the trick to it, but her efforts were useless. The thing didn't even contain a glass bulb that she could find, and she started to wonder whether the object was even a lamp at all. Though only seconds had passed, her frustration was already beginning to border on anger when, as if in obstinate reply to her mental bashing of its apparent uselessness, the dome suddenly brightened and filled the room with soft, white light. Iris decided not to question what had caused it to work, settling instead for simple gratitude that the room was no longer dark.

She donned the same jeans and knee-high boots she had been wearing the day before, then debated whether she should remain in the shirt Auraltiferys had given her or change back into hers. She finally opted for her own clothing—a gray tank top partially covered by a fitted plaid button-up—then moved into the restroom. Looking at herself in the mirror, she realized with sudden horror she had washed off all of her makeup the night before and was now helplessly without it. She hadn't gone out in public, not even to the gym, without makeup since she was in junior high, and she didn't relish the thought of being around a man without it on, even if that man was a priest. *Oh, well,* she finally thought with dismal humor, *first day as a demon; might as well look the part.* She tied her reddish hair up into its usual messy knot high on her head and sighed one last time at the naked face staring back at her from the mirror. *Could be worse, I guess.*

After leaving the bedroom without even attempting to turn off the light, Iris moved down the short hallway and around the corner, back to the living area where she had been the previous day. Lights were already on in this room, casting a warm glow onto the furniture and the bookshelves beside the fireplace. There was no sign of Auraltiferys, and Iris didn't feel comfortable exploring the house to search for him, so she walked to the shelves and inspected the ornate spines of the large tomes they held. Few, if any, had titles stamped on them; most bore only scrollwork or other patterns, while some were labeled with runes or other symbols that were entirely foreign to her. She carefully pulled one off the shelf—a thick book with a cover of dark red leather—and placed it on her lap after seating herself on the couch in front of the fireplace. She probably wouldn't be able to read anything in it, but she needed to pass the time somehow until Auraltiferys showed up. Maybe there would be illustrations.

As she pulled on the cover, the book met her with a stubborn refusal to open. She pried from various places within the gilt-edged pages, all to no avail. She gave up after several seconds, then dropped the book with irritation on the table and tried a half-dozen others. None of them would open, and Iris had soon convinced herself she would prove an epic disappointment to the blacksmith, who believed she had great powers and might play some part in a dire battle against evil. She hadn't yet brought herself to believe fully in the magic Auraltiferys had spoken of, but he was certainly convinced of it, and his clear conviction and intense nature led Iris to want to believe him. There was certainly something strange about this place, something that simply *felt* different from the reality she was used to. There were those extraordinary wolves, and these books that wouldn't open…maybe science could explain it all away somehow, but she felt a gnawing little hope that the blacksmith was right about her, that he could teach her something about herself she had never known before. She couldn't help but think of her favorite singer, a musician whose lyrics had always been full of magic, telling tales of witches and wizards, dragons and rainbows, angels and demons. Maybe her musical idol had held some arcane knowledge, something substantial and real. Maybe his songs had been born from something more than a penchant for the fanciful and a voice for metal.

After a moment of curious reflection, Iris heard the door open behind her. Auraltiferys entered and gently closed the door behind him, greeting her with a quiet "Good morning." He had his sleeves rolled up to just above his elbows, muscular forearms exposed in sooty majesty. His face, too, was covered with dusty black, except for the areas just around his bright, cool eyes. When he spied the books dumped on the table in front of Iris, his expression took on a hint of amusement. "Having any luck with your studies?" he asked.

"I think you know I'm not," Iris replied.

His visage eased into a tiny smile, blue eyes shining like diamonds from the coal-black dust on his face. He moved closer and stood beside the table. "Choose one," he instructed, indicating the mess of books lying there. Iris leaned forward and picked up the red-leather volume once more. She held it out to the blacksmith, expecting him to take it from her. Instead, he passed his hand breezily over the cover, then said, "What I've just done, you can also do, but you limit yourself. Read what you can now, and I will return after I've cleaned up." He walked out of the room and left Iris holding the book, wondering what he had just done. Dubiously, she tugged at the cover once more...and it opened just as one would expect.

The thick, antique pages were a yellowy brown, but they were clean, fully intact, and completely legible—if Iris had known the language in which they were written. It looked like Arabic or something similar. *Well, this is useless*, Iris thought to herself, with no small amount of frustration. She shook her head and continued turning pages, hoping though not expecting to find an English translation somewhere inside. As she finally shut the cover and tossed the book back onto the table, Auraltiferys returned, his face freshly washed and cleanly shaven.

"Finished so soon?" he asked, quietly taking a seat in his chair.

"I can't read this," Iris answered, with an unintentional hint of anger. "If you have any in English, I'll be happy to take a look. I might even be able to muddle through something in German, but I don't even know what alphabet this is!"

Auraltiferys sighed softly. "Iris," he said, "you have within you a nature that is ancient, a nature that once existed in glory very near God Himself. You are an angel, with knowledge and power that surpass the understanding of humankind. Yet even as I tell you this now, your humanity precludes you from accepting the truth. You allow the limitations of human logic to obscure the radiance of your spiritual being. You must let go of your doubts and your fears and allow God's power to work through you."

Perfect, Iris thought sarcastically. *Here we go again…another "Give it up to God" sermon, complete with sides of "He has great plans for you" and "He will make you strong." Ugh.* She had never seen any evidence of God's supposed "great plans" for her. She remembered praying consistently and for a very long time that her life would take whatever direction God intended. Apparently, God's grand scheme for her had been that she should end up with a practically unused PhD and a mediocre job at a shithole company, with no friends or family except the full-of-bullshit people she worked with and couldn't stand. And now, as a sickly humorous epilogue to her story, God had planned that she should survive a plane crash, meet a crazy man on a mountain, be filled with a stupid hope that magic was real and that she could wield it, and then once more be forced to face what a disappointment she was. As her thoughts derailed into angry disillusionment, Iris's expression went unintentionally dark. The blacksmith, who had remained silent for a few seconds after his last statement, now spoke once more. This time, his voice had an even more distinctly cutting edge to it.

"Disappointment belongs to you, Iris, not to God," he announced. "He took an active role in your creation, although Satan had tried almost limitless means to prevent Him. Do you really believe He would have done so for no reason?"

Was Auraltiferys reading her thoughts? Iris would have to be less transparent if she didn't want the blacksmith-priest inside her head. She swallowed before replying to him. "Maybe God's reason was just to stick it to the Devil," she suggested drably. "And if that was the purpose, then I guess I've already fulfilled it, if what you say about me is true."

Auraltiferys's eyes narrowed. "You have too little faith," he said. Iris rolled her eyes in response, but the blacksmith continued, "Perhaps it has been for the best. Perhaps you would be too dangerous if you knew your own powers. As it is, it seems you will never know. You don't truly *want* to know, for if you did, you would believe what you have already seen. How much clearer must God make this for you? Even Thomas believed when he saw Jesus risen. You have seen magic at work, and still you disbelieve."

Maybe it was solely on account of Auraltiferys's priesthood that his statements made Iris feel like crap. She didn't want to doubt God or to lack faith. Back when her family had still been with her, she had been much more spiritual. She had even wondered for a brief time about becoming a nun. What the hell had happened to her? She felt some tears trying to well up in her eyes, and she stubbornly blinked them away.

"Okay," she said with a sigh. "It's not that I don't believe. I've seen some strange and inexplicable things here. And it's clear you're a man of great faith, and I respect that. I'm just not sure you're right about me. Maybe I'm just human, and maybe I just can't do this."

"I'm 'just' human, as you say," Auraltiferys responded.

"*Are* you?" Iris retorted suspiciously.

"Yes," the blacksmith replied with unquestionable finality, "and even in my simple human capacity, which is far more limited than your angelic nature would be, I can use magic for good. I have created thousands of weapons and shields and rings and scepters and crowns, all cast with magic that has protected God's people and has fought the forces of evil throughout the ages. I can read and interpret all of the books you see here, written in hundreds of languages, many of which are no longer known by anyone else on Earth. I can manipulate time; I can control nature's elements; I can heal the sick; I can exorcise demons. It is all by the grace of God and the power He has allowed me to use. Everything I can do, Iris, you can do—far more easily and with greater strength. The key, as ridiculous as it must sound to one as academically educated as you, is simply to believe that you can do it."

Iris sat in silence as Auraltiferys spoke, his dignified voice so full of conviction that she felt suddenly ashamed to be in his presence, like a child having just been rightly berated by her father. After a moment, she hesitantly reached for the book once more. She opened it and stared blankly at its cryptic pages, trying to concentrate on the simple belief that she could read the words. She felt the blacksmith's gaze on her, and it made her nervous. She could make no sense of the writing, and she knew Auraltiferys knew it.

"Maybe God doesn't want me using His power," she finally said, defeated. She was smart and a fast learner, and although this seemed a ludicrous expectation for anyone, she was still disappointed in finding herself unable to do as Auraltiferys had asked. "Look, if you can teach me, I can learn it; I don't doubt that at all," she offered.

"It isn't just a matter of learning," Auraltiferys replied. "It requires an ability and a willingness to let go of your limited nature and accept the limitless power of God within you."

"Yeah, I don't get how to do that," Iris rejoined with exasperation, "and maybe there's a reason for it. Maybe, if I really am Satan incarnate, then maybe God just refuses to 'work within me,' as you say."

Auraltiferys startled her with a disdainful scoff. "God does not withhold His power even from Satan," he stated coldly. "That is precisely why Satan has power at all. An infinite, all-loving God gives all of Himself to all His creation, and that includes you. Those in Hell have refused His love, but they haven't refused His power, and He will not take it from them." He sighed and leaned back slightly in his chair. "I would teach you," he continued, "and perhaps you could learn, but we simply haven't the time. I have seen a dark prophecy coming to fruition, and there are precious few powerful enough to prevail over it. The battle has already begun, and if you cannot realize your powers now, I fear you will succumb too easily to the temptations you will soon face. Good will almost certainly fall to evil, in calamitous and irreversible destruction."

The icy gravity of his statement filled Iris with profound uneasiness. Whatever Auraltiferys spoke of, he certainly believed, and it sounded terrifying. In the ensuing silence, she wondered if she really could help in this "battle," as the noble blacksmith seemed to believe. She wanted to keep trying, but she also feared failure. She was prepared to ask for another chance when Auraltiferys asked, "Are you hungry?"

Surprised and confused by the sudden and seemingly out-of-place question, Iris stammered, "Um...well, yes, I guess I am."

Offering no explanation, Auraltiferys simply stood and said, "Come with me."

Iris followed him through the kitchen and outside, along a worn path that led through tall evergreens down toward a clearing sided by rocky outcroppings of the mountain. The sun had begun to rise, illuminating the sky in a most fantastic and colorful way.

"Where are we going?" she finally asked as she struggled to keep up with the blacksmith's long, purposeful strides.

He didn't answer immediately. The two proceeded through the clearing and approached what appeared to be an entrance to a cave carved into the mountain's side. Here, Auraltiferys stopped and turned to face Iris. She looked at him expectantly, hoping whatever he had planned would somehow remove whatever mental block was preventing her from "realizing her powers," as he had phrased it. She also hoped there might be food involved, because, since he had mentioned it, she realized she was quite famished. Thirsty, too.

Auraltiferys looked down at her and shook his head sadly, although his expression was firm. "If I could allow you two thousand years, as I have been allowed," he stated, "I could help you learn what you already know."

Two thousand years? Iris thought in amazement. *What the hell is he talking about?*

"As it is, however," the blacksmith continued, "we have no time, and what you are makes you a treacherous vulnerability." Iris's eyes widened as he spoke, her stomach sinking with a sickening fear. In the same split second in which she decided to turn and run, Auraltiferys reached out and grabbed her, swiftly and easily draping her over his broad shoulder, pinning her legs uselessly against his chest. Iris screamed and tried hitting him, but the angle of her body made her punches pitifully feeble against the blacksmith's muscular back. She kept screaming and hitting, in complete futility, as he carried her toward the cave's entrance.

Amid her pleading cries, Auraltiferys quickly repositioned her and then threw her, flailing and screaming, into the black mouth of the cave. Iris was weightless for an instant and then felt her body slam into a cold, hard floor before she rolled downward for what seemed an eternity. She came to rest in a damp, pitch-black expanse, sore and doubtlessly cut and bruised from the fall. Looking upward, she could make out a tiny pinprick of light up at the cave's mouth until a distant-sounding rumble swallowed it and indicated that the good blacksmith had sealed the entrance.

"No!" she yelled. "Please, no! Let me out!" Even as she screamed, she knew no one heard her. She couldn't believe the betrayal she had just experienced. She couldn't believe she was trapped here, essentially buried alive, at the hands of a man so obviously holy. She hardly knew him, and yet she had liked him, in surprising contrast to the attitude she had toward most people. She had wanted to help his cause. She had wanted to be what he said she was. Was patience not a virtue? Could he not have given her another chance?

Iris sat unmoving but for convulsive sobbing that overtook her. Her nose dripped and her eyes burned. *Why, God? Why would you allow this? What the hell am I supposed to do?*

Eventually, the tears subsided, and Iris wiped her eyes and nose roughly with her hand, sniffling a few final times before attempting to collect herself. Should she try to escape? Maybe look for another way out? That was a terrifying thought—who knew what kind of precipices or vermin might lie in her path if she went exploring? There was no light down here.

She turned and felt for the wall down which she had rolled. She tried climbing, but the surface was slick and steep, and she couldn't find any footing in the dark. Giving up, she sat down with her back against the stone wall, listening to the cavernous silence around her and essentially resigning herself to death, closing her eyes and resting her head on the rock behind her.

***

Maybe she had fallen asleep, but she couldn't be sure. Iris opened her eyes to the darkness that still engulfed her. She leaned forward slightly, straining to hear something she thought she had heard. Was it a voice? No...it couldn't have been. It was probably a dream, or an echo of dripping water, or ringing in her ears. She pushed the thought aside and sat in silent stillness until, eventually, her mind wandered into reflection on what Auraltiferys had told her. What was it he had said? *God does not withhold His power even from Satan.* At a human level, that seemed stupid. If Iris were God, she would have revoked the Devil's magic license as soon as he had given her any lip, and she would have properly smitten him, too. But, in a spiritual light, Auraltiferys's simple statement made some sense. God had never pulled Himself away from any of His creation; He had simply given them His gifts and then allowed them their free will. If God allowed even Satan to continue using the power He had given him, why shouldn't Iris, whether she was a demon or a human or both, be able to wield that same power? She would use it only for good, of course. She would fight against evil. So wouldn't God want her to use this power? Wouldn't He want her to learn, and to be able to help Auraltiferys against the terrible forces that were apparently threatening, or soon to be threatening, her world?

She closed her eyes again and recalled the previous night, when she had joined the blacksmith for his evening prayers. She wanted to be angry at him for how he had tossed her down here, and for how he had told her such astounding things about her and her possibilities, only to let her be disappointed, but she could find no room for anger in her heart when she thought of him. The beauty and the genuineness of his prayers had amazed her, and she had marveled at how a man so tall and muscular and powerful could make himself seem so small and inconsequential before God. Maybe *that* was the simple key to all this: humility. It wasn't the first trait Iris had noticed about the man, but she realized now it was the trait from which all the blacksmith's nobility and dignity and wisdom and strength emanated. She had sometimes thought herself humble, but she knew it would be a full lifetime before she could be anything like the servant of God that Auraltiferys was. Unfortunately, she didn't have a lifetime left to learn true humility, because the blacksmith had just thrown her into a crash course on it. In true humility, either she was going to let God's power save her from this place, or she was going to face His judgment at her death.

Eyes still closed, Iris leaned forward onto her knees and exhaled slowly, praying in the silence of her mind. *Lord, I would ask you to tell me what to do, but I've never been able to hear you. Auraltiferys hears you, and he listens. He is your humble servant, and the most just and righteous man I've ever met. He speaks of a terrible battle happening, of powerful evil threatening humankind, and he says I can help. Lord, I want to help him. Please let me help. If you will that your power should work through me, so be it.*

Iris realized tears were leaking from her closed eyes. She opened them suddenly, blinking the droplets away, finding herself still enveloped in damp blackness. Had she expected to hear a little whisper from God? There hadn't been one. Or, if there had been, she was still too dense to hear or understand it. She stood and shook her head. Tears wouldn't get her anywhere. Crying didn't make her humble, and it didn't seem like a brief, even though fervent, prayer would get her out of this cave. She was once again frustrated with herself and her inability to do...well, anything useful. *Whatever*, she thought with apathy. *If God wants me to see, He'll let me see.*

She began walking forward, neither knowing nor caring where there might be rocky walls to stop her or falling stalactites to strike her or cavernous holes underfoot to swallow her. Three steps in, she felt a strange heat inside her, behind her eyes. It was not the heat of fever or tears, but it was a palpable and unmistakable sensation. She stretched her hand out in front of her, feeling for whatever might be there, and she was shocked by what she saw. Where her hand passed, light followed—inexplicable, visible light. She swept her hands around the room, and the cavern was illuminated by a pale, silvery luminescence. She stood in a huge, open space, with dark walls that glittered with dampness and stalactites and stalagmites that jutted like teeth from a high ceiling and an uneven floor beneath her. Water dripped slowly from some of the outcroppings overhead, and not far in front of her was a steep drop-off into a pool of water far below. Even in the dimness of the light that had appeared, Iris could see colorful crystals glimmering along the folds of stone that cascaded farther into the mountain. She stood still for a long moment, awestruck by the beauty of the cave and completely dumbfounded by the light that seemed to have come from within her own eyes. It felt as though she had willed the light into being, but she knew better. She didn't have that kind of power, but God did, and He had just let her borrow some of it.

She stared a minute longer at the scene around her, hoping to imprint it on her memory, and she realized a broad smile had appeared on her face. *Thank you, God*, she thought, finally understanding, at least in some small way, what it meant to feel God's presence. Then, eager to return to Auraltiferys and having no doubt she could do it, Iris returned to where she had first fallen. She pressed her hands against the worn stone wall and simply climbed as though an invisible ladder had been built there, leaving no need of handholds or footholds. She soon reached the top, where Auraltiferys had rolled a huge boulder across the cave's mouth. In a purely physical realm governed by science alone, a dozen men wouldn't have been able to move a stone of this size without mechanical assistance, yet Auraltiferys had moved it himself—or, more precisely, God had moved it for him, and so would He do for Iris. She laid her hand on the stone and moved it sideways, the massive rock rolling away as easily as a pebble. Warm, welcoming sunlight struck her face, and she could see Auraltiferys waiting on another stone not far from her, his posture erect and his strong arms crossed over his chest. Upon seeing her emerge from the cave, he stood and released his arms, and he grinned.

7

Detective Crane leaned back in his chair and heaved an exasperated sigh. The museum murder, if it was, in fact, a murder, had just happened last night, and already he had been forced to field calls from a disgruntled local museum curator, an even more disgruntled representative from whatever museum owned the weapons exhibit, two jackass insurance agents, a handful of obnoxious local reporters trying to nail a scoop, and a quaint but panicked English woman who claimed to have once owned the single item in the museum exhibit that had turned up missing. Apparently, word traveled fast in the museum business. Crane glanced down at an inventory photo that had been emailed to him by Dr. Marvin Whitakker, the curator of the university museum. It showed what appeared to be a copper spearhead, with some faint scuffs and a slightly worn carving of some emblems. It looked old, sure, but it didn't look particularly valuable to Crane's eye. Certainly not something to lose one's shit over, although the nasal, high-pitched voice of Marvin Whitakker over the phone seemed to indicate that he had lost his shit over it a few times already. Crane looked forward to meeting with the man about it later. Nothing like an agitated, squirrelly little academic to lift the work mood.

"Figured you'd have a rough morning," Detective Banks announced as he set a large cup of coffee on Crane's desk. "You look like hell already, brother."

Crane blew slowly through his teeth as he reached for the coffee cup, nodding in thanks to his partner. He would have been grateful for a cheap cup of gas station crap, but Myron had shot for the good stuff today. God bless him.

"Too old for this shit, Banks," Crane said, shaking his head and sipping the coffee as Banks sat down at his own desk, which faced Crane's.

"So what have I missed? I was feeling bad about leaving you here while I dropped the kids off, but now I'm thinking I'm okay with it," Banks said with a chuckle. He sounded jovial and upbeat, but Crane knew better. He could see Banks was forcing the levity. The body they had seen last night had shaken them both, and neither of them was looking forward to meeting with Dr. Reyes in the morgue for her findings.

"Well," Crane began, "it turns out there's an item missing from that weapons exhibit." He tossed the printed photo of the spearhead over to Banks. "The curator wants us to get with him at the museum later to discuss it. He insists on meeting about it in person. Sounds like a real prick. He's already called the museum that loaned the exhibit and their asshole insurance agents."

Banks studied the photo for a brief moment, pursed his lips, and then scratched his shaved head. "Great," he replied flatly.

"Yeah," Crane agreed. "We'll have to go back there anyway, I guess, because I damn sure didn't see how anything could have been taken."

"Maybe the guard took it?" Banks suggested. "Would he have had a key for the display cases?"

"Don't know," Crane responded. "We'll ask Dr. Marvin about it when we talk with him." He went silent for a minute, sipping coffee and making some mental notes.

"Any word on COD?" Banks asked, his voice suddenly clouded with some hesitancy. He didn't really want to discuss that body, and Crane felt the same way. This sure was a crappy job sometimes.

"Not yet," Crane said. As if in response to his reply, his desk phone suddenly rang. With a pointed glance at Banks, he lifted the receiver. After several seconds, he set the phone back down. "There it is," he addressed his partner. "Dr. Reyes is ready for us."

Banks sighed a little and ran his hand over his scalp. He stood up slowly, took a long, slow final sip of his coffee, and looked back at Crane. "You ready for this?" he asked.

Crane stood up, chugged the remainder of his coffee, and shrugged in reply.

***

Crane still hated the smell of the morgue, or the mortuary, or whatever this vile room was called. The sewers might have a worse scent, but here there was a disinfectant-and-formaldehyde bouquet pervaded by death that burned the nostrils and bludgeoned the spirit. The bit of menthol he had rubbed under his nose didn't sway it. As he and Banks entered Dr. Reyes's office, Crane glanced at his partner. Myron was an imposing fellow, tall and athletically muscular, a former pro football player who still looked fit enough to outplay any other tight end on the field. His stature, his unabashed confidence, and his usually serious expression tended to command respect from anyone, and yet at this moment, there was an air of uneasiness seeping through his dark skin. *At least it isn't just me*, Crane thought to himself.

The detectives found Dr. Reyes sitting at her desk with her face in her hands. Crane quietly cleared his throat to announce their presence to her. She immediately brushed some bangs away from her forehead and arose with a sigh.

"Sorry," she said, her voice exhausted and sad, completely devoid of the precise, businesslike tone Crane was used to hearing from her. "Come on in," she continued as she moved toward the examination room. She started donning her laboratory garb and pointed toward the clean lab coats hanging on a rack to the side to indicate that Crane and Banks should do the same. Once they had all suited up and put on surgical gloves and masks, they proceeded into the exam room, where the body of young Joshua Ellis lay on a cold metal table, covered by a sheet.

There passed what seemed an awkwardly long minute as the three stood there, staring silently at the veiled body lying before them. They had all seen the body before—and Patricia had probably seen more than enough of it for all of them—but none of them was looking forward to inspecting it again. Crane thought back on the night before: how he couldn't bring himself to focus on the eyes, how he hadn't even wanted to try to sleep afterward, how he probably wouldn't be sleeping for some time. He was afraid the cold, dark blackness of those dead eyes would appear before him the moment he drifted off. *I'm losing it*, he thought. *Should have retired last year.*

Patricia finally broke the silence, stating tiredly, "I'm afraid I can't offer you much on this one, gentlemen. This is...this is something else." She carefully pulled the sheet away from the head and torso, folding it atop the pelvis, leaving the hips and legs covered but exposing the majority of the body. Thankfully, she had graciously covered the face with a separate towel underlying the sheet, so those hellish eyes were still hidden from view. A grotesque Y-incision marred what was an otherwise fit and healthy-looking chest and abdomen, except, of course, for the terribly pale hue of the skin.

"Well," Crane began awkwardly, "uh...well, what can you tell us, Patty?"

"Anything is better than nothing," Banks added, clearly trying to bring some cheer to the bleak room.

The medical examiner inhaled deeply, seemingly immune to the stench of her surroundings, then exhaled slowly before speaking. "I'll just tell you the facts I know," she answered. "First, as I mentioned at the scene, this body was way too cold when we found it. When I first checked the temperature, it registered right around ten degrees Fahrenheit. That's ludicrous. I thought I must have made a mistake, but I checked again when the body arrived here, and then again after I completed the examination. I recorded readings of..." Her voice trailed off as she turned to grab a clipboard with her notes. "Readings of fourteen degrees and sixteen degrees," she concluded.

"It's getting *warmer*? How the hell?" Crane interjected. He could feel his eyebrows scrunched together in frustrated confusion, and he tried to relax them. His wife had told him he was only adding to his wrinkles every time he scowled like that.

"It is getting warmer," Patricia confirmed, "but that's probably because the surrounding air is warmer. Like I said, we don't even keep bodies that cold here. He was probably even colder before I got to the scene. It's impossible."

"Would dry ice cause something like that? Just thinking out loud," Banks suggested.

"No, I don't think so," Patricia replied. "Besides, there would be other evidence of that, like burns on the skin."

Crane scratched his head, more out of mental discomfort than from an itch. "Okay, so we've got a body that's inexplicably cold. What else?"

Patricia shook her head slightly, a defeated expression on her face, and answered, "There's no evidence of a cardiac incident or a stroke, or an aneurism, or anything else that could reasonably cause an otherwise healthy thirty-two-year-old to die suddenly. I found no evidence of poison or drug use, and there was no alcohol in the system. Which brings me to another...well, impossibility."

Great, Crane thought. *Should have retired.* He turned to glance at

Banks, who glanced back at him with a lifted eyebrow and an anxious look in his eyes. Patricia had paused to let the two detectives mentally prepare themselves for her next finding. After a moment, she stated, "There was no blood in the body."

Crane stared blankly at Dr. Reyes, blinking. He imagined Banks next to him was doing the same. What question could one ask after being told such a thing? They all knew there had been no blood at the scene. And so another long, quiet minute passed, three living, intelligent people standing there wondering what the hell the dead man might be telling them.

Finally, Banks propelled the conversation forward by asking hesitantly, "So...um...what else?" *Yup*, Crane thought. *That's about all that's left to ask, isn't it? Damn, we're screwed here.*

Patricia closed her eyes tightly and pinched the bridge of her nose with a gloved hand before composing herself again and answering. "Lungs are completely collapsed, and..." She paused to turn and pick up a metal tray that held a small object that looked like an irregular pebble. Holding the tray out so that Banks and Crane could have a closer look, she continued, "That's part of the heart."

Crane saw the look on Myron's face and might have liked to laugh at it, if the reality of this situation hadn't been so damned awful. He looked like a curious child trying to explain a magic trick to himself. He extended a gloved finger and poked the supposed heart piece, which made a hard scratching sound against the steel tray. Obviously, it was solid; nothing like muscle or tissue. More like stone.

"I've sent a sample to the lab," Patricia told them, "but I couldn't tell you what to expect. To my eyes, it looks quite literally like a heart that turned to stone." She again shook her head as she fingered absentmindedly at the gold cross necklace at her chest. "Then, of course," she added quietly, "there are the eyes."

Crane pressed his eyelids shut and lifted a hand to massage his forehead and temple. He really didn't want to look at the face again, and he knew that was the real reason his body was now trying to tell him he felt sick. Physically, he was fine, but mentally, he had a serious case of the I-don't-want-to's. He sighed, then lowered his hand and opened his eyes. "Let me guess," he said forlornly, "nothing there but more questions."

"Frankly," Patricia suddenly snapped, eyes blazing, "I don't want to look at them anymore." Her tone was strained and unprofessionally edgy. "No, there's nothing there but questions."

Crane's normal reaction to such an impetuous outburst by someone in the workplace would generally be to respond in kind, usually escalating the conversation to an even greater degree of anger. But he restrained himself here, knowing that those damn eyes had messed him up, too, and he had looked at them only for a couple of seconds. Poor Patricia had been trapped in the same room with them for hours, and only God knew how those black little orbs of darkness might have affected her. Thankfully, Banks had remained quiet, deferring to the senior detective to address the snippy remark from Dr. Reyes.

Crane cleared his throat softly, then said, in an empathetic voice, "Patty, listen, we all know the eyes are wrong. Hell, Banks and I could hardly stand to look at them at the scene." He saw Banks nod understandingly beside him. "If you've done your examination, and you say there's no medical explanation for this, then I don't see any reason you should have to look at the eyes again. We trust your judgment. But..." Crane considered stopping his mouth there, but words kept coming out before he could act on the consideration. "I do think Banks and I need to see them again in person before we start relying on the photographs only." *Shit*, he thought immediately. *Pictures would be just fine; why the hell did I say we need to see the eyes again? Fuck me.*

Patricia took a deep breath and relaxed considerably. "Thank you, Benson," she said, seeming suddenly much more like herself, though almost close to tears, which was most unusual. "Thank you," she repeated. "And I'm very sorry I snapped like that. I...I admit this one has really gotten to me." She walked around the table to the exam room door, pausing before she opened it to leave. "Take all the time you need, but...God be with you. This isn't in the record, and this is just my opinion, but honestly..." After falling silent for a few seconds, she took a shuddering breath and concluded, "Honestly, I think this was the work of something evil. Something *supernaturally* evil." Her gaze fell to the floor momentarily, then she looked back up at Crane intently. "That's not scientific," she said sharply, "and it's not professional, but, God damn me, that's what I believe." With that, she pushed through the door and exited the room, leaving the detectives standing together in stunned silence.

Banks continued staring at the closed door for several seconds after Patricia left, likely feeling much like Crane did: shocked and anxious. They knew the kind of professional that Reyes was, and for her to state such a far-fetched opinion was unheard of. If she thought this was something evil...well, scientific or not, Crane tended to think she was probably right.

Banks turned to Crane and shook his head. "You really wanna look at those eyes again?" he asked. "After all that? Shit, man. Shit."

"We have to," Crane said gruffly. "One last time, then we'll rely on photos. If we're gonna go out there and start telling people this guy was murdered and our primary fucking suspect is Dracula, then we better have crossed all our T's." *And dotted all our "eyes,"* his brain concluded in grim humor. He roused himself to move toward the head of the body on the table, then glanced at his partner briefly before removing the towel that covered the face.

Crane forced his gaze onto the black orbs resting in the pale, dead visage of poor Joshua Ellis. They seemed sunken and deflated, yet they were protruding in such a way that the eyelids would not cover them. There was no shine or color to them, only the absence of...anything. As Crane stood there looking at them, he felt his heart start to race, and sudden nausea overwhelmed him. He looked away instantly, swallowing hard to shove his stomach down out of his throat. A few seconds of staring into those messed-up eyes, and he had practically felt his own insides being pulled out of him. He turned and caught sight of Myron, who had already averted his gaze and was hunched over with his hands on his thighs and his head near his knees. When he stood up and looked back at Crane, he rubbed a hand brusquely across his face to remove the few tears that had trailed down his dark cheek. Crane hadn't realized until then that he was crying, too. He wiped his face with his gloved hand and quickly threw the towel back over Ellis's face, being careful to catch no glimpse of the dead eyes as he did so.

The detectives left the exam room in silence. When they arrived back at their desks, Crane sat down heavily in his chair and stared for a long time at his computer screen, seeing shapes and colors but registering nothing. He finally had the odd thought that he had forgotten how to blink.

8

After Iris's success in the cave, Auraltiferys had led her to an expansive library that stood some distance behind his residence, which was itself much larger than she had first noticed—there were probably a dozen large rooms on each of the home's two floors. The library was actually an additional wing of a big, Gothic-style church, ornately constructed with columns and spires and flying buttresses and adorned with a plenitude of stained glass. It was a breathtaking building, and Auraltiferys had been good enough to let Iris marvel at it for a moment, despite the apparent urgency of her training. It was more beautiful than any cathedral she had ever seen, even in photographs.

They entered through a side door that opened directly into the library, a huge, rectangular room that appeared to span the length of a football field, with violet-carpeted walkways lining a gleaming marble floor. Arranged in rows near the center, on plush rugs of the same violet carpet, were heavy, carved mahogany tables with built-in benches. Circular fire pits, encased in marble, were situated on the floor among the tables at comfortable distances. Faint aromas of leather and wood lingered in the cool air.

Along the visible portion of the library's periphery were intricately designed stone columns punctuating vast wooden shelves full of books and equipped with the rolling ladders Iris had thought existed only in movies. As she gawked at the height of the shelves, her eyes finally reached the vaulted ceiling, which was spectacularly decorated with glittering mosaic art depicting the crucifixion of Jesus, with two men hammering nails into his hands on the cross. Instead of Roman soldiers, the men shown in this piece appeared to be blacksmiths, as Iris inferred from the similar figure depicted below the scene in much the same pose, though working at an anvil instead of a cross. Above the crucifix was the Virgin Mary, wearing a crown of twelve stars, shown against a blue background that contrasted with the reds of blood and fire below her feet.

"That was a monumental task," Auraltiferys stated, looking up with Iris at the amazing work. "It was undertaken, obviously, after the crucifixion and resurrection of Jesus," he explained. "The Knights are part of the human family, too, although we live here separately from them. You might think we were preserved from sin, but we inherited it just as you did. This work was meant to remind us all, throughout the ages, that our hands, too, helped nail Christ to the cross, and to remind us that we, too, have an adoptive mother in Mary."

"It's beautiful," Iris replied. It truly was—the image was somehow perfect from every angle, and the bright, warm light radiating from sconces on the stone pillars below put highlights and shadows in just the right places to make the mosaic seem almost alive.

Auraltiferys gave her several seconds to appreciate the ceiling, then he gently cleared his throat, prompting Iris to follow him as he led her to one of the tables. He indicated with a graceful hand gesture that she should sit, which she did. The blacksmith sat across from her, contemplating her with his silvery-blue eyes. Iris adjusted her own posture to try to match his; she had a more dignified carriage than much of the general public and probably all of the hillbillies at her office, but she felt like a total slouch next to Auraltiferys.

"Had I any significant length of time in which to train you," the blacksmith said, "I would do things differently. It would not have been my first choice to subject you to a trial by fire."

"Right," Iris carelessly interjected. "Your *first* choice would have been to kill me." She wanted to kick herself as soon as the thoughtless words had left her mouth. With sudden nervousness, she tried to read Auraltiferys's expression. It was as sharp and cold as a blade, but not completely devoid of kindness—a blade wielded by an ally and not an enemy.

After a long pause, Auraltiferys responded, "Were you to see a demon before you, I should hope you would act defensively yourself."

Iris let her eyes fall to the table, heavy with guilt. She knew Auraltiferys was truthful in all he said, and although she didn't feel like Satan or like any demon, she trusted the blacksmith's assessment of her. Already, so much of what he had explained had been made evident right before her eyes, and she had, in fact, *felt* magical power from God working within her. She had experienced all this newness in her human mindset, which was the only one she really knew for now, but Auraltiferys's chilling reminder of her true nature forced a startling realization: If she couldn't acknowledge her own demonic nature, it might very well take her over before she even understood what was happening. *This isn't a matter of mortal life and death*, she reflected. *This is eternity—salvation or damnation.* She had better choose wisely.

The blacksmith's authoritative yet elegant voice brought Iris out of her momentary contemplation. "Iris," he said coolly, "you are not identical to Satan, and you do not belong to him, but neither are you completely *unlike* him. I hope you will not leave here believing yourself immune to evil. Undoubtedly, your human upbringing in

Christian spirituality and Catholic teaching has prevented you from realizing your own demonic nature, but it is right there within you, in fullness—the very same spirit that shunned God in arrogance and chose Hell as his eternity. You will have to direct your actions rightly, because the practice of magic may well awaken that spirit within you, and it will be stronger than you anticipate."

Iris swallowed, took a deep, shuddering breath, and looked back up at her tutor. "I understand," she replied weakly. "I mean," she added, "I don't feel like the Devil, but...I believe what you say, and I understand I'll have to be careful."

Auraltiferys's stare felt like a scalpel, cutting her right open. Iris was certain he could see all the not-yet-confessed sins she carried with her: every mean-spirited thought she had about her coworkers at the office, every impatient outburst she allowed within the confines of her car while driving in traffic, every suggestive fantasy she let her mind play out in daydreams. Under the blacksmith-priest's deep and profoundly uncomfortable scrutiny, she realized her "understanding" the need to be careful would not be good enough.

"Please," Auraltiferys said, "recognize how difficult a position this is for me. I see you are inclined toward goodness and righteousness, but I also see in you wickedness that far exceeds what a human alone is capable of. Whatever I help you to learn can be directed toward light or toward dark, and should you choose to use your abilities for evil, I will feel personally responsible for the ensuing damage. Yet I haven't any other option but to teach you, for that is how I have been directed by the Spirit, and I do see in you the possibility for real victory in the coming battle."

Iris silently nodded her understanding, though she still wondered what exactly the "coming battle" would prove to be.

"Create a fire for us, please," the blacksmith suddenly instructed, indicating with an easy motion of his hand the fire pit next to their table, his sharp eyes still trained on Iris.

Iris looked at the pit and closed her eyes, trying to recall the feeling she had experienced in the cave. It wasn't exactly emptiness, but it was something like it, though with a distinctly positive character, like the languid undulation of floating in a lazy river, embraced by a silent peace. She focused her mind on fire, and when she opened her eyes, the warm and pleasant flickering of a small group of flames greeted her. She sighed with relief, glad she had succeeded on the first try. Her series of failures before Auraltiferys's do-or-die lesson had been enough embarrassment for a lifetime.

Auraltiferys grinned slightly. "Do you know how you did it?" he asked.

Iris stopped herself from replying with something foolish, like "Magic, of course." She knew that wasn't what Auraltiferys meant in asking the question. So, after a brief pause for thought, she simply answered, "No, I don't." It was the truth.

Auraltiferys extended his hand out beside him and caught a large book, which he had apparently summoned from one of the shelves. *I'll never get used to this*, Iris thought to herself as the airborne tome landed in the blacksmith's strong hand with a dull thud.

Sliding the book in front of her, Auraltiferys replied, "It was a trick question. If you learn nothing else from me, learn this: *You* do nothing on your own. With practice, the magic will feel natural and immediate, as though *you* are the source of the power. Remember—always remember—you are not. You are but a wielder of power borrowed from God, and you will never fully understand how or why it works, because He is so far beyond your comprehension."

As Iris nodded, the blacksmith opened the book in front of her to one of its early pages. It appeared to be written in Latin, in verses like poetry. Auraltiferys indicated one of the verses with his finger and instructed Iris to read it aloud. She recognized only a few of the words from her grade school Latin classes; it was something about

God and fire. She expected she may have butchered some of the appropriate pronunciations, but Auraltiferys didn't correct her.

"So what does it mean?" she finally asked, after her brief recitation was met with silence.

Shaking his head, Auraltiferys answered, "Read again, with the same mindset you had when using magic. Your demonic spirit is ancient; Latin is, to you, neither a dead nor a foreign language."

Iris refocused, dropped her eyes from the blacksmith back to the page in front of her, and was amazed at the difference. The words were the same on the page, but they were no longer just groupings of letters to be sounded out; she actually understood them.

"It's a prayer for fire," she stated, mildly surprised.

"It is a *spell* for fire," Auraltiferys corrected. "One of many spells you might have used when I instructed you to create this fire," he continued, nodding toward the pit beside him. "Yet you achieved the same result without the words. That is because magic is, in essence, the instant granting of a prayerful request. There are as many magical methods as there are manners of prayer. Spells are structured prayers meant to focus the mind and will on specific requests. You can memorize them and use them, but to rely on them alone would severely limit you. I call them a basic practice, though I must specify they are in no way weak or ineffectual. Some spells, in fact, are long and complex, and few with the ability to use magic even know them."

Iris listened to the blacksmith as he spoke, then directed her attention back to the book, casually flipping through the pages and scanning the spells. These seemed simple enough. They were appeals for the physical command of natural elements, things like creating fire or drawing water from the ground or cutting wood or moving stone. As she glanced through the pages, she challenged Auraltiferys, "You told me before that very few human beings have the ability to practice magic anymore, but if magic is no different from prayer, then any child can do it. And, aside from the fact these are written in Latin, it seems as though anyone with the ability to read could use these spells. It would be the same as teaching someone to pray the Our Father or the Hail Mary."

"It would not be the same," Auraltiferys replied, his tone serious but not unfriendly. "You are correct in that anyone can read a spell," he continued, "but it takes a very particular state of heart and mind to allow God's power to effect an instant result, and that is, in your world, becoming increasingly difficult to achieve. Surely, Iris, you have noticed all the distractions that occur during prayer. You have noticed how thoughts wander, or how the mind questions whether anyone is listening, or how recited words become a careless chant of habit. Even the devout have trouble praying as they ought, however righteous and loving their intentions may be. Moreover, there is a tendency toward one-sided conversation, the propensity to let a stress-laden heart shout at God its deluge of fervent supplications without troubling oneself to listen for a response or to resign oneself to His will. Without proper belief and the requisite emptiness of self, a spell, as a prayer, is nothing but words."

"If that's the case," Iris asked, "then why bother hiding magic from humanity as you have?"

Auraltiferys narrowed his eyes slightly as he looked at her. Iris sensed he was mildly displeased with her argumentativeness, though she wasn't intending to be disrespectful; she was truly curious. There was a touch of suspicion in the blacksmith's gaze, too, and suddenly she understood his hesitation. To a man who had identified her as Satan, every word of hers must come with an inherent potential for ulterior motivation.

"Humankind is safer in ignorance of magic," he answered slowly and deliberately. "As difficult as it may be to practice magic well, it is even more difficult to maintain one's proper direction while practicing it. I fear you will learn this from your own experiences, likely sooner than later. As I have warned you, in magical practice, it is easy to stray into the erroneous belief that you direct your own power. That draws you closer to self, not to God, and that is dangerous. Think how self-centered you already believe the human race to be, Iris." He paused, piercing her with the icy daggers of his eyes as if to let her know he had entered her mind and found her true opinion of humanity sitting there. She did, in fact, find the human race to be horribly vain and self-serving, her own self not necessarily excepted.

"Can you then imagine how far from God they might end up?" he continued at length. "Our Order did not arrive at the decision without deep and prayerful consideration. We had visions of the turmoil magic could cause on the Earth. We were shown how easily Satan and his angels would turn mankind away from God to follow their own wills, straight to the damnation of their souls. Without knowledge of magic, humanity has one less temptation in their world, one less obstacle upon their spiritual journey."

Iris lowered her eyes as the blacksmith offered his gracious explanation. Of course he was right. The world was a hellhole already, with people incessantly at one another's throats, individually and collectively, metaphorically and sometimes literally, and she couldn't envision what the evening news would look like if even a quarter of those people had magical abilities they could use on demand. It would be a bloodbath, and prayer or not, one could be sure *that* magic wouldn't be drawing them any closer to God.

"Yeah, I see the problem," she agreed. She glanced through one last spell in the book, then looked back up at Auraltiferys. "So do you want me to memorize these?"

"It isn't necessary," he answered, standing up from the table, his impressive height making Iris feel very small as she remained seated. "Under other circumstances," he continued, "I would have had you study the simplest of these spells first, and then you would have practiced them through meditation under my guidance. As things are, however, you have already learned how to perform the magic yourself, in contemplative will, and that is the most advanced method. You have experienced the focus necessary for magic; you have felt God work His power through you. You will not have to rely on spells, though I recommend you study them on your own as opportunity allows. They can prove extremely beneficial for certain things. I imagine you will create many of your own as well. Spells are, of course, not limited to the words in the pages of these books."

Iris quietly closed the spell book and stood to join Auraltiferys. He put out the fire with unspoken magic and asked her to follow him. As they walked down the long, wide central aisle of the library, past several groupings of tables and hearths, he explained, "I am teaching you but a few things in a single breath of time. It will be only enough to help you guard yourself against the evils you will soon face. You have heard such words before; you have been taught to recognize the Devil at work on the Earth and to fight his temptations, but you are about to experience the powers of Hell in ways you have never considered. What I teach you here, you must compound exponentially with your own learning, and urgently so. You have little time, and not only because an evil scheme is nearly complete." Pausing next to a final set of shelves that abutted a broad marble stairway leading down into a separate area and pressing his eyes into Iris's with glittering, metallic gravity, Auraltiferys finished, "I assume you have a life you wish to return to."

Startled by the final statement, Iris realized she hadn't even thought about going home. With a timid shrug, she answered honestly, "I hadn't really thought about it. I guess after the plane crash, I just...I don't know; I haven't thought about getting home. I had scheduled a few days off from work to go to Portland for my interview, but...I guess the office will miss me if I don't show up on Monday." She sighed as the unpleasant thought of returning to Eden engulfed her like a thick, suffocating, black cloud.

Auraltiferys smiled sympathetically. "The life you return to will not be the same as it was," he conceded, "but you will adapt. You cannot remain here indefinitely. So, let us continue your brief lesson."

Iris followed him down the carpeted steps into a grotto, small only in comparison to the vast library from which they had just descended. A dozen thick, carved marble pillars, arranged in a wide circle, stretched from the floor of this area to a plane even with the floor of the library above. The decorative mosaic of the library ceiling had ended just before the stairs; here in the grotto area, skylights far overhead allowed sunlight to filter in and glisten on the polished surfaces of the massive columns, which Iris now noticed had multiple cubbies carved into them, displaying various bric-a-brac, much like a shop or a museum.

Auraltiferys approached a particular column and removed from one of its niches a golden scepter, engraved with runes and topped with an intricate finial set around a sizable iridescent gemstone. It appeared rather undersized next to the blacksmith's imposing figure, but Iris soon realized its heft when he handed it to her. Its weight was almost uncomfortable for her one arm, but the shameful thought of being unable to hold it prevented her from using two hands. She had always had substantial upper-body strength for a woman—a fact that had rarely gone unnoticed by others whenever opportunity for such observation existed—and she had taken perhaps an undue amount of pride in that. She didn't want a two-foot stick to appear too heavy for her. So she stubbornly held it with only one hand, trying to inspect it briefly before glancing quizzically at Auraltiferys, whose expression was one of either mildly surprised approval or subtle amusement; she wasn't sure which. She hoped he would get on with this lesson soon; she wouldn't be able to hold the weighty scepter for too long.

"Are you using magic right now?" he asked simply.

"What?" Iris replied, confused and slightly panicked by the question. "I don't think so. Why?"

With a brief and quiet snicker, the blacksmith answered, "You cannot use magic by accident. Are you or are you not using any magic?" His eyes were sparkling with mirth, although he continued to radiate a cool stoicism and seriousness.

"No, then," Iris responded, more sharply than she had intended. She knew the unintentional tone had stemmed from an internalized concern she might be doing something wrong without even realizing it. She felt her forehead pressed into a scowl and made a conscious effort to relax it.

"Well, then," Auraltiferys said, rather cheerfully, "I'm impressed you have held the scepter this long. You are stronger than you look."

"Damn right, I am," Iris answered. It was a good-natured response, but there was some true pride in there, too.

Auraltiferys replied with a raised eyebrow and a stern but not unkind expression, in tacit, forgiving admonishment. For a moment, Iris had forgotten she was being tutored by a priest, and she regretted her somewhat profane reply.

"Regardless," the blacksmith continued after a short pause, "it is easier to hold if you let magic bear the weight."

Iris couldn't believe how dense she was being. Everything Auraltiferys was doing with her today was meant to help her realize her magical abilities, and instead of focusing her thoughts and actions in that same vein, she was having to be prompted for everything. Angry at herself, she pressed her eyes closed, recentered herself, and then opened her eyes to the weightless, peaceful feeling of immersion in God's power. The once-heavy scepter now felt like nothing more than a pencil.

"This will take time," Auraltiferys said, recognizing Iris's displeasure with herself. "You have spent your life in a physical world governed by scientific laws and immutable impossibilities you've never questioned, so magic is not instinctive to you. That might frustrate you now, as I am training you, but in the long term, it will be more a benefit than a hindrance. Demons rely on magic instinctively because they must. They do not have physical, earthly forms. You, though a demon, are also human, and humans should never depend solely on magic. We are to labor as we can and reap the fruits of those labors, giving thanks always to God, using magic as a supplement only, to strengthen us in our battles against evil; to increase our knowledge and faith; to heal our wounds; to elevate the glory we give to God; and always in the appropriate spirit of humility, with prudential wisdom. Magic is not a substitute for work; it is an enhancement of one's work."

Iris sighed in reply, letting the scepter rest easily in her hand down at her side. "I don't know about all this," she said, notes of frustration and weariness in her voice. "You're telling me how urgently I need to learn magic, but then you warn me not to use it too much. How am I to know what's right? How do I trust myself with that? By the time I get home, you're going to have me too afraid to practice any magic at all."

"Good," Auraltiferys answered sharply, much to her surprise. She realized she had been hoping for some words of encouragement, and instead she had received the blacksmith's blunt approval of her doubts of herself, and that carried with it a painful sting. She remained silent, meeting her tutor's icy stare with eyes that pleadingly awaited some follow-up wisdom and perhaps a comforting thought. She had experienced more new things in the past day than she had experienced in probably the last five years, and she had never been particularly fond of the unfamiliar. She already knew she would be afraid once she left the blacksmith's side, and this suggestion that her fears were justified only exacerbated that anxiety. *I'll be better off leaving it all alone,* she thought. *Let this supposed battle happen without me; let the world burn or whatever else is going to happen. It won't be my fault.*

The blacksmith crossed his muscular arms in front of his chest, looking down at Iris from his lofty height, his eyes alight with the characteristic keenness that made him appear at once so intimidating and so holy. After searching her for a short moment, he said, more softly, "My words are harsh sometimes, Iris. I mean no offense with my abrasiveness. You are, however, a demonic entity, whether you sense it in yourself or you don't. I cannot coddle you, not only because such behavior is against my nature, but because to do so could instill in you a false sense of comfort and security. If you wonder how you will know what is right, if you doubt your own judgment, if you are afraid, then you are in a good place, because you will then necessarily seek God's guidance."

Iris brushed a tear away from her cheek with the back of her hand. "You do understand God doesn't really talk to me, right?" she asked shakily.

"When did you last ask Him to?" retorted the blacksmith in a quiet voice.

Iris rolled her eyes and sniffled, then extended her arm to return the scepter to Auraltiferys. "This is pointless," she said with exasperation. "I can't do this. I've prayed for purpose and guidance before, and I've ended up with practically beans to show for it. I work at a shitty company for a shitty boss with other shitty people; I have no family and no real friends; practically everyone who meets me thinks I'm a stuck-up bitch, and I'm either too afraid or too lazy to do anything to change any of it. You wanted me to help in some fight against evil, and I thought I wanted to do it. But if you're right about me, then I shouldn't be trusted with this."

"You've already been trusted with it," Auraltiferys answered stonily, not uncrossing his arms nor making any move to accept the scepter back from her. "You exist as you do because God has willed it, and you have arrived where you are because of His providence, whether you realize it or not. I would not be helping you discover your abilities for magic had I not been led by God to do it. So, you see, you have already been chosen for this. But I cannot tell you no danger exists on the road in front of you; that would be a lie. You will face lurid temptations, and you may very well stumble. Such danger would exist for you without magic, too. Nothing has changed here, Iris, except the scope of your perception. But your will is your own, and if you wish to turn away from this now, I'll not try to stop you."

The handsome, scarred face and the sparkling silver-blue eyes of the blacksmith were a breathtaking image of spiritual profundity as he spoke his words with elegant gravity. In the sunlight from overhead, amid the glittering marble and metallic relics of the columns, Auraltiferys looked like a saintly apparition. It might have been emotion coloring her vision, but in this particular moment, Iris believed it was something more than that, something that was opening her eyes in a different way. She could walk away. She could leave and never think of magic again; Auraltiferys would let her go. She knew she had freedom to choose. One path was illuminated by truth; the other was a road obscured by the shadow of avoidance. Either road could lead to Heaven or to Hell; that would be her choice, too.

With a short nod and a pointed look into the blacksmith's eyes, Iris slowly lowered the scepter. "Let's continue, then," she said quietly.

Auraltiferys inclined his head in genteel acknowledgment, then uncrossed his arms and placed his hands on his hips. "The items you see in this room are examples of the works of the Knights," he stated, segueing directly into her next lesson rather than continuing on the emotional detour Iris had presented. "These are relics, imbued with powers for specific purposes—physical manifestations of God's magic. Similar to the tangible religious articles you are used to, like statues, icons, crosses, crucifixes, or rosaries, relics are meant to focus the user's magical contemplation on exact purposes. The important difference is that relics hold within themselves actual power, which can be unlocked by anyone with any magical ability. In the hands of someone with no knowledge of magic and no ready capacity for it, relics are nothing more than the objects they resemble, but when used by a wielder of magic, relics are invaluable tools."

Iris lifted the scepter and inspected it again, more closely this time. Letting the magic work within her, she recognized the runic inscriptions, which indicated, simply, strength and prosperity. She wondered if she should know precisely what the scepter could do just by looking at it. She didn't know, and she hoped that was not a failure on her part.

"I recognize these runes," she offered, slowly rolling the scepter as she balanced it with her other palm. "Strength and prosperity. But what does it *do*?"

"Our relics are intentionally mysterious," Auraltiferys answered, as though he had heard her internal discourse. "One cannot know by looking at a relic what its powers are, but the runes will give you some general indication. The mystery has protected our works from being carelessly used by unqualified individuals. Only the more knowledgeable practitioners of magic can take a relic not intended for them and determine the item's powers, and the more capable the user, the simpler it is to unlock a relic. You, for example, in your magical capacity, should find it quite easy to hold a relic and *feel* what it can do."

"You mean, in my magical capacity as a demon," Iris interrupted, her tone suggesting her own distrust of herself.

Auraltiferys crossed his arms again and sighed. "I understand the identity crisis you have been propelled into," he answered, "but you will have to cope with it. Yes, your demonic nature has the greater strength when practicing magic, but your human nature puts you in a particularly advantageous position, because you have both a physical form on the Earth and the potential for a relationship with God that no angel nor demon can duplicate. You are unique, and for that reason, there is only so much guidance I can give you. You exceed even my own comprehension. But I do trust you are meant to learn of these things. I trust you are meant to realize your own abilities."

"And what if I turn evil because of it?" Iris asked.

After a long pause and another discerning stare, Auraltiferys replied, "Nothing can 'turn' you evil. Evil is a choice one makes."

"But if I'm the Devil—" Iris interjected.

"You're not the Devil," the blacksmith rejoined, his voice slicing the air like a knife. "You are his same spirit, but you are still a separate being. Let us not endeavor to contemplate what we cannot understand. I am trusting in the spiritual direction I have received to train you. So must you trust—if not in me or in my spiritual capacities as a priest, then in the goodness of your own soul. You would not argue to me that you are a bad person, would you?"

"No," Iris answered. She had never thought of herself as a bad person; not really. "But I'm not exactly a saint, either," she added after some hesitation.

"Will we continue upon this same endless cycle of argument?" Auraltiferys asked. "There is no comfort I can give you, Iris. I cannot tell you to shun your demonic nature; neither should you expect you will lose your human nature or your free will. You will have to learn to exist as what you are and direct yourself toward the end you choose." He fell silent and probed her for a moment with those silver-blue eyes. "God brought you here in full knowledge of what you are," he added quietly, with a hint of a smile in his tone. "Have a little faith."

Iris pressed her lips together in a thin line, took a deep breath, and nodded. She wished she could be unafraid, but the anxiety was inescapable. How could she ever fully trust herself if Satan's spirit was there inside her? How could she ever return to any sort of normal life now? And how could she ever hope to be welcomed into Heaven after her death? *Let it go*, she told herself. *No point worrying about that now.*

"Okay," she finally answered. "I'll try to...have more faith." She meant it, but she couldn't identify how she would do it, even in her own head.

The blacksmith smiled for an instant, more in his eyes than on his lips, and then he picked up where he had left off before his pupil's latest interruption. "As I was saying," he continued, "you are, by nature, a very capable wielder of magic, and you should be able to identify this relic's powers, simply by feeling and interpreting the power emanating from it. Try."

Iris sensed no need for waving the scepter around in grand fashion. Whatever power was in the relic would be there whether she flicked it around like a wand or held it still. So she pulled it closer to her chest, closed her eyes, then opened them to see a completely separate place before her. She stood at the edge of a cliff, overlooking a vast expanse of land. Two opposing armies approached, and in the almost boundless vision she now had, she could see with immediacy after every step of every warrior the series of consequences that would befall each side. She could see how one should move in order to protect another or to entrap another; she could see how strengths could prey on weaknesses and how each side could be led to sure victory. It was both remarkable and terrifying. Upon sharper focus, she discovered she had the ability to command the figures below her, to direct them by mere thought.

She removed herself from the vision after a minute, finding herself still in the cool grotto below the library, with Auraltiferys standing before her, carefully watching. Blinking the strange experience away from her eyes, she remarked, "That...that was really something."

"Indeed," Auraltiferys agreed.

"Perfect strategic vision," she mused, reviewing the spectacular craftsmanship of the scepter with a deeper appreciation. "The ability to direct entire armies...this would inevitably bring strength and prosperity."

With a gentle nod, Auraltiferys replied, "You can probably guess to whom the scepter was given, if you know your history." He paused to allow himself a small smile at Iris's thoughtful and then bewildered expression as she considered the possibilities, then he continued, "Of course, the power of the relic is undoubtedly more pronounced in your possession. Its original owner was less magically capable than you, and while the scepter was a great help to him, he never unlocked its perfect power. Relics can enhance the magical abilities of any user, but a user's limitations will likewise limit the relic's powers."

Iris had lost a certain amount of attention as she tried to pick out what historical figure must have held this scepter and used its power. She wanted to ask, but she gleaned from the blacksmith's mysterious smile that he would never answer her directly. He held out his hand to retrieve the relic, and Iris returned it to him with an expression she knew screamed of curiosity. As he placed the scepter carefully back into its marble niche, she asked, "If that belonged to whom I think it might have belonged..." She trailed off, suddenly afraid a dumb question was preparing its escape from her mouth.

"Yes?" Auraltiferys prompted, turning back to face her. His voice carried a welcoming invitation that assured Iris he would not deem any question a dumb one.

"Then why did he have it?" she asked skeptically. "How did he get it? I mean, if magic is a religious thing and these relics are religious things...he wasn't even Christian!"

Auraltiferys actually laughed, much to Iris's surprise. It lasted only a fleeting moment, but it was an elegant, dignified, beautifully joyful sound that brought an instant smile to her lips and a great comfort to her heart, though it also made immediately evident to her how narrow-minded her thinking had been. She knew how the blacksmith would answer even before he spoke. "God is Creator of all," he said, his tone full of reverence, "and He aids even those who do not know or believe the truth. Most relics, in fact, were fashioned long before Christianity came to be, and many holders of relics were not even monotheists. They may not have understood the true source of their abilities, but God would not have directed relics to them without purpose. Everything that happens, He either wills or allows, and He has His reasons."

"Right," Iris replied, with a touch of chagrin.

"Yours is a curious and questioning mind, Iris," Auraltiferys said cheerfully, motioning with his hand for her to start moving back up to the library. Walking beside her as they ascended the stairs, he added, "You must realize you cannot understand everything."

Iris sighed. "I know," she responded, "but that's how my brain is wired. I want to understand how things work and why things happen."

"It is not a bad thing," the blacksmith replied encouragingly. "But you've just discovered a facet of existence previously unknown to you, and the more you explore it, the more you will realize just how little you truly comprehend. Can you accept that?"

They reached the top of the stairs and paused in the library as Iris admired the ceiling mosaic once more. "I'll try to," she answered.

"That is enough," Auraltiferys stated confidently. He waited for Iris to turn her gaze from the ceiling back to him before he began leading her back through the library.

Walking quickly to match his pace, Iris commented, "This library is huge, and it was clearly set up to accommodate lots of people. Are you really the only one here?"

The blacksmith slowed his gait slightly, noticing Iris's difficulty in keeping up. "I am the only one here now," he said, "but it was not always this way." His voice was steady, but there was sadness in it, and Iris regretted having asked. "One day," he added, stoically, "I might tell you what happened here. For now, it is unimportant. Let it suffice to say, no place outside of Heaven is immune to evil."

Iris felt a cold nervousness suddenly in her stomach. She wondered what the backstory must be, but she wasn't about to press the issue. He had told her *something*, anyway—this mountain was not Heaven, and evil had once found its way here. She understood better now why Auraltiferys had first reacted to her demonic nature as he had.

They exited the library into the warm, sunlit peacefulness of the mountain's day, and Auraltiferys asked whether she felt like taking a walk. Her body felt thirsty and completely famished, but somehow the idea of a pleasant walk alongside the blacksmith seemed more appealing than food or anything else, so she agreed. They proceeded down a worn path that led away from the library and the church, eventually curving its way through a field of wildflowers unlike anything an earthly artist could have imagined. Vibrant color was everywhere around them, from the tiny white blossoms lining the golden sand of the footpath, to the reds and oranges and blues and violets of the taller flowers beyond, to the vivid, deep green of the trees just barely visible at the farthest edges of the meadow. As she and Auraltiferys walked in silence for a few minutes, Iris found her thoughts directed in fond memory to her mother and grandmother. They had both loved flowers, and though Iris had never shared their same enthusiasm for nature's beauty, she wished they could see this. Of course, if they were in Heaven, as she fervently hoped they were, then perhaps they had already seen things far more spectacular.

Pausing on the footpath as a gentle breeze swept like a brushstroke over the canvas of the field, moving its colors in tranquil waves, Iris called out to her tutor. "Hey," she said, prompting him to stop and turn his amiable sapphire gaze back toward her. "What is this place, really?"

After a momentary pause and a subtle smile, Auraltiferys returned a few steps closer to her and answered, "This is a holy place, and physically the nearest a living being can be to Heaven. Farther from Heaven than Eden was, but nearer Heaven than your Earth." He followed Iris's vision to the breathtaking scene around them and fell quiet. Iris sensed he found wonder in it still, even after having lived here for two thousand years or more. She could fathom neither his age nor his righteousness, but she hoped one day she might be something like him.

They eventually continued down the path, and Auraltiferys spoke again. "We must speak of what has brought you here," he said, "although nothing I say can prepare you for what lies ahead. As I have told you, a dark plot has been realized and is nearly complete, and if its creator succeeds, humanity will be lost to Hell."

"You're referring to the one who wants to overthrow Satan," Iris recalled.

"Yes," the blacksmith replied, leading her down a shaded fork of the footpath, through a wooded area. "And to overthrow Satan, he must either have you on his side or destroy you, because you necessarily hold as the begotten of Satan the same power that keeps him on his dark throne."

"I don't want Satan's throne," Iris stated. "Why do I have to be involved at all?"

"I suppose your involvement is not necessary," Auraltiferys answered, "but if you were to renounce your own claim to Hell as Satan's begotten, then there would be no one left to stop him but Satan himself, and the Devil is not as strong as he thinks he is. If the throne is taken from Satan, the one then upon it will be able to destroy the Earth. If you do choose to embroil yourself in this battle, it is the usurpation of humanity you will be fighting."

Iris swallowed, another bolt of anxiety striking her. *What am I getting myself into?* Even as she asked it of herself, she knew it didn't matter. Whether she wanted to be involved in some hellish game or not, she couldn't let humanity be destroyed if she had the power to intervene.

"I guess I understand," she said weakly. "So, what is this horrible plot, and how do I stop it?"

Auraltiferys left the path and stepped up a few solid footholds in a large, craggy outcropping of granite situated amid the cool shade of the evergreens, seating himself on a low, flat portion in the rock. He invited Iris to join him, which she did with cautious steps on the stone, and he answered, "The plot involves creation of a shadow entity capable of stealing human souls from their bodies, regardless of their will. It is a sick and twisted desecration of what God has created. To stop it, you must undo the black magic Loomis Drake has initiated."

Iris turned sharply toward Auraltiferys at the mention of Loomis, startled by the implication. She had forgotten the blacksmith's odd reaction when she had told him of her upcoming job interview with the handsome billionaire, and now she wasn't sure she wanted to hear what must be the truth.

"No way," she exclaimed, in a voice breathy with disbelief. "Are you saying *Loomis Drake* is trying to take Satan's place in Hell?" Nervousness was evident among the skepticism in her tone—as inconceivable as the notion was, she didn't think the blacksmith would lie to her.

"Indeed, he is," Auraltiferys answered, "and he has been for many ages. His amalgamation of dark magic has required extreme amounts of time and energy, and he must be quite frustrated to now find you in his way."

Wide-eyed, Iris repeated sharply, "*Many ages?* What do you mean? Loomis Drake is, like, forty years old."

Auraltiferys's expression was grave and serious, his eyes gleaming with what Iris interpreted as dire warning. "That body of his appears to be about forty years old," he said somberly, "but Drake himself is ancient, far older than even I am. He is a demon."

Iris felt suddenly cold, though she was unable to explain why. She didn't know Loomis Drake, but practically the whole world spoke highly of him. He was known to be charming and charitable and charismatic; that he was a demon seemed a complete impossibility.

Shaking her head and feeling her forehead scrunch in consternation, Iris argued, "That's impossible. He does so much good for so many people. He's known worldwide as a philanthropist—"

"Does a wolf not fare better wearing sheep's clothing?" Auraltiferys interjected. "Iris, don't be deluded. Loomis Drake is a demon, consummately evil and, in my opinion, possibly stronger than Satan himself. He *created* his own human vessel so he could inhabit the physical world, and he alone among the angels of Hell has proven capable of such insidious magic. If Satan knew how Drake had done it, I imagine you would have turned out far differently."

Iris sat quietly, her mind struggling to accept as truth the blacksmith's statements even as she began considering the ramifications of this alarming news. It was a stomach-turning thought, believing

Loomis Drake had known her true identity all along and had intended her as only a pawn in his perverse scheme to gain control of Hell. She recalled how she had, only a brief time ago, fantasized about romantic opportunities with the wealthy bachelor, and she now felt shockingly dirty for it. *Oh, dear God, please tell me Loomis Drake couldn't hear those thoughts*, she pleaded silently. She knew, or thought she knew, demons couldn't read minds, but that knowledge was no comfort. She felt unmistakably violated, regardless.

After a long, contemplative minute, during which Auraltiferys remained silent, Iris pulled her feet up to rest on the same portion of rock where she was sitting and wrapped her arms around her legs, hugging her knees close to her. "So he isn't even a possessed soul?" she inquired. "He's a full demon in a human body, allowed to walk the Earth as he pleases?"

"Yes," Auraltiferys replied, "and I need not describe to you how exceptionally dangerous that makes him."

"No," Iris sighed, "no...I get it." She flipped her long bangs away from in front of her face and began mindlessly twirling them with the fingers of one hand as she wondered how she could ever stand up to Loomis Drake now. She was already petrified of him.

"There is need for caution, Iris, but not fear," Auraltiferys said, his voice stern and authoritative but also carrying a breath of quiet reassurance. "I believe you are stronger than he is, or, more precisely, I believe you will become stronger than he is. Your only disadvantage is your newness to all this."

"Yeah...that, and being a weak-ass human," Iris blurted out dejectedly. She regretted the words as soon as she had spoken them, and not only because of the low-class descriptor she had chosen to use while speaking to a priest. Auraltiferys was, after all, a human being, too, and though he was unequivocally saintly, he was anything but weak, and Iris's immature little outburst was an insult to a man such as him. He was a paragon of what humanity had been created to be, and to generalize humanity as weak was to ignore the near-perfection in him. Iris expected a well-deserved lecture for the ill-advised statement, but a cautious glance toward her tutor revealed instead an austere expression that spoke volumes more than a lecture would have.

"Sorry," she apologized. She wanted to say more, but she didn't know where to begin.

"Drake will consider your humanity a weakness," Auraltiferys finally answered. "You will choose whether you prove him right or wrong."

With that profound statement, Auraltiferys stood and jumped down from the stone to the ground below, extraordinarily gracefully for a man of his supposed age—or for any man, for that matter. He looked toward Iris and waved her down. "Come," he called to her. "We will discuss more on the way home. I'm sure you must be quite hungry by now. I'll prepare something for you when we get back."

Iris hopped down to join him, energized by the promise of food. Auraltiferys pulled a canteen from a pouch on his belt and handed it to her before turning and embarking once more on the path. Iris took a few generous, refreshing sips of water then returned the canteen as they walked. "So how is it that Loomis Drake has been able to set such a terrible plan in motion?" she asked.

"Drake is a singular combination of exceptional qualities that distinguish him from all the rest of Hell," Auraltiferys replied, his expression darkening. "He is extremely intelligent, highly motivated, tirelessly driven, and very creative. Consider him the Leonardo da Vinci of the underworld. He has spent millennia studying the *science* of magic, and he has amassed a wealth of knowledge unparalleled by that of any other being, only God excepted. Through scientific study and trial using magic and relics, he eventually created a false human body for himself, and that has allowed him to live the past few hundred years of his eternal damnation on Earth, existing in whatever identities and circumstances have suited his purposes, and it has only made him stronger. He has direct access to records and relics that other demons could not hope to touch, even if they had the wherewithal to locate them. He has been able to identify and collect a number of magical relics with the particular powers he desired, and he has oriented them to create a collective magic, a compounding of spells upon spells that feed into one another, increasing their powers beyond what the relics were created to hold. His design has brought forth an *actual* being—this time not an artificial, empty body, but a demonic entity that exists as a substantial shadow. This 'shadow-demon,' like Drake, has access to Earth, and I believe it has already stolen at least one human soul."

"Seems like a ridiculous amount of work just to take souls," Iris suggested, her own voice weary from just the thought of all the effort Loomis must have put into this elaborate plan. "Could he not just tempt them the good old-fashioned way?" She meant the question to be humorous, but she then considered her own demonic nature and realized she should probably tone down her sometimes-off-color drollery.

"He can, and he still does," Auraltiferys answered, unperturbed by Iris's comment. "He has a more extensive grand vision for the shadow-demon," he added, "but I don't know what that is. I do know it will threaten the continued existence of humankind—that much I have sensed in dreams and trances. I fear there may be more at stake than the loss of souls."

"What more is there to stake?" Iris asked darkly.

"At one time," Auraltiferys replied, "I would have thought nothing. Whatever Drake's plan is now, though, it is darkness unlike any the world has seen. I pray you are able to stop it."

They neared the edge of the woods and continued along the path as it followed the boundary of a huge garden, surrounded by a low wooden fence. Fruit trees lined one half of the area, while various vegetables and herbs grew in neat rows on the side nearer them. Iris couldn't imagine how it was possible, but it seemed Auraltiferys alone was responsible for the garden's upkeep, and he seemed to be doing an amazing job at it. A dozen people could find ample work in such a wide acreage.

"May I ask something, um, potentially offensive?" Iris inquired gently, after a protracted silence.

"You may," Auraltiferys answered, opening his canteen and drinking as he walked.

"Why don't *you* stop him?" she asked. "I'd love to help, but, honestly, you seem much better equipped for the job."

The blacksmith returned his canteen to his belt and sighed. "I would gladly face Drake myself, but it would do no one any good," he said, his deep and elegant voice heavy with disappointment that seemed to be directed inward. "I would not be strong enough."

"It's all God's power, though, isn't it?" Iris countered. "God is strong enough to stop him."

"Of course God could stop him," Auraltiferys rejoined. "And Jesus could have saved Himself from the cross." He paused briefly to glance over at Iris, making deliberate eye contact. Once he had satisfied himself that she understood his reply, he turned his gaze back to the path ahead of them and continued, "I might be able to send Drake back to Hell, but it would be the end of the world before he would be locked there, and if he overtook the dark throne before then, my 'defeat' of him would be rendered inconsequential. You, however, can keep him from ruling Hell, from gaining the uninhibited evil freedom he cannot know under Satan's command. So, you see, Iris, this is a job for *you*, not for me. Besides, my place is here on the mountain. It is safe neither for me nor for this holy place for me to leave it unattended. The battlefields are on Earth and in Hell. Those are places for you, at least for the time being.

But, for as long as God wills it, I will be here if you should need me. I will provide you with whatever I can to aid you."

Iris nodded silently, mostly to her own thoughts, as they rounded the corner of the garden. She could see the blacksmith's home off at a distance. To her other side was another granite face of the mountain. An entrance had been carved into it, covered by wrought iron bars. Iron sconces were affixed to the stone on either side of the doorway, bright amber flames dancing within each one.

Noting her curious glance at the mysterious entrance, Auraltiferys paused to offer an explanation. "That is my forge," he said. "There are eleven others on the mountain, each one throughout human history assigned to only one blacksmith at a time. Now, mine alone still retains its holy fire." The graceful edge of his voice was again tinged with sadness, or perhaps loneliness. It awoke in Iris a sudden urge to hug him, which was, for her, quite atypical. She had never been particularly inclined toward physical signs of affection, and she sensed Auraltiferys was much the same in that regard.

Hoping instead her interest in the forge might lift his spirits, she asked, "Can I see inside?"

Auraltiferys stared back at her with a somber expression and piercing gaze. "You may not," he answered simply before turning away and continuing along the path toward the house.

Iris was taken aback by the rejection, and perhaps in a different setting, in different company, she might have retorted with something snarky, but she couldn't even bring her own mind to think anything negative of her tutor. There may be some icy contours to his persona, but she had no doubts about his true warmth and goodness, and if he didn't want her inside the forge, he must have good reason for it. So she brushed off the apparent rebuff and followed Auraltiferys in silence.

When they reached the house several minutes later, Auraltiferys motioned Iris through the den and into the kitchen, which was far larger and more modernly equipped than she would have guessed from the tiny portion she had seen from the couch the day before. The blacksmith pulled out a chair for her at the dining table, and Iris seated herself there as he proceeded around the counter. She watched him open what was apparently a refrigerator and remove a small pot, which he then placed on the stove. As it heated, he filled two tall glasses with cool water from the faucet and brought them to the table, handing one to Iris and drinking from the other as he stood beside her. After they had both finished that first round, which didn't take long, he refilled both glasses and returned, seating himself gracefully. Iris kept her gaze trained aimlessly on the beverage for half a minute, still feeling rather deflated by her new mentor's last comment. Eventually, though, she hazarded a glance up at Auraltiferys and was startled to find him watching her with trenchant interest.

Seeing her reaction, Auraltiferys blinked and softened his expression. "I see you accept my decisions as having good reason," he said, "but you are yet disappointed."

Once again surprised to hear the blacksmith practically narrate her own thoughts, Iris considered for an instant whether she should try to lie, to claim she had thought nothing of the sharp dismissal of her interest in the forge, but she knew it would be fruitless. One might as well try to deceive God.

With a small shrug, she replied, "I'm sure you have good reasons for all you do, but I admit, I *am* a little disappointed you don't trust me. Not that I blame you." *Satan isn't particularly trustworthy, after all*, she thought to herself.

"Trust has little to do with this particular decision," Auraltiferys answered decisively. "The forge is a holy place, and I go to great lengths to ensure its magic remains pure. That is what gives my works such great power. Any sin that enters will taint the magic of the relics created there; it will erode a relic's power just as it erodes a human soul."

Iris, fascinated by the brief explanation, realized she no longer had any desire to enter the forge. Her imagination painted a picture of fire consuming her as soon as she should set foot inside. It was odd, however, to think of Auraltiferys having to go to any "great lengths" to prevent sin from entering. There was no one here but him, and he was a saint.

"I see why you must keep me out, then," she finally responded.

Auraltiferys stood and walked to the stove, stirring the contents of the pot with a wooden spoon. Whatever it was, it was starting to smell quite tasty. After a minute, he removed a bowl from a cupboard, filled it with the food, placed a small spoon in it, and set it before Iris. He recited a blessing over the meal and then graciously motioned for her to eat.

"Aren't you having any?" she asked, surprised. Auraltiferys was a big, muscular man, and he must be even hungrier than she was.

"No," he answered. "I'm fasting." The reply reached Iris's ears just as she was swallowing a huge, wonderfully flavorful bite of the stew he had heated for her, and she felt a pang of guilt.

"Why?" she questioned, with some disbelief. She didn't even appreciate the obligatory fasting on Ash Wednesday or Good Friday; that anyone would voluntarily fast otherwise was difficult for her to comprehend. Even more difficult to comprehend was that someone already so obviously holy would engage in such unnecessary self-denial.

Auraltiferys appeared rather amused by her reaction. "I do it often," he replied easily, "to atone for my sins. I have no other priest here who can hear my confessions or give me absolution. So I fast, and I pray, and I live ascetically, striving to avoid all near occasions of sin and never allowing myself to become complacent." He relaxed slightly and leaned back into his chair, casually draping one beefy arm over the chair back and holding his water glass with the other. Seeing that Iris had not taken additional bites of food, he nodded toward the bowl and asked, "Do you not like it?"

"Of course I like it!" Iris exclaimed. "It's excellent! I just feel guilty eating in front of you now."

"You shouldn't," he responded. "To quote Saint Paul, 'Whether you eat or drink, or whatever you do, do everything for the glory of God.'"

Iris nodded and took another guilty bite of stew, trying to accept the blacksmith's reassurance. After swallowing, she said, "I don't see how someone like you could have any reason to atone for sins. You're so...saintly."

With a slight grin and an easy shaking of his head, Auraltiferys answered, "It may be easier for me to avoid sin, being here by myself in this place set apart from the completely fallen world, than it is for you and the rest of humanity to avoid it. But this is not Heaven, and there is no perfection here. I see your world, and I see the lack of faith and the hypocrisy and the sinfulness in it. The same once intruded upon this mountain, too, and as often as I have witnessed these things, whether in physical or metaphysical sight, I have had judgmental thoughts. I hold frustration and anger, too, Iris, much like you do. But the forge is no place for harboring those sentiments, and so I must do all I can to ask God's forgiveness. I do it not only for myself and for the sake of the works of Heaven's Forge, but also for all the human race."

He rose and went to the sink, filling a kettle with water and placing it on the stove to heat. He added a measure of a dry tea mix from a glass jar, replaced the lid, removed two teacups from the cabinet, and then waited patiently by the stove.

Iris finished her stew and watched Auraltiferys for a short moment, curious again about the mountain's encounter with sin, but afraid to bring it up. Finally, she emboldened herself enough to ask, quietly, "Will you tell me what happened here on the mountain?"

He looked over at her with an astute gaze, then nodded silently. He waited for the water to boil, then sieved the tea into the two cups and returned with them to the table. Iris pulled her cup toward her and lifted her eyes to meet the blacksmith's, eagerly awaiting his story.

Auraltiferys sighed heavily before he began. "I have not spoken of those days since they passed," he said. "I was all that was left." His eyes drifted far away, as if their steel-blue gaze was literally looking into the past. However long ago the mysterious event had been, Iris could see that time had not fully healed the wounds it had inflicted on her gracious host and tutor. She sat silently, realizing she had asked for something difficult for him to give.

"Back then," he finally continued, "our Order was more directly involved in earthly affairs. Certain Knights would travel between here and Earth, distributing or collecting relics and magical arcana. It tied us to the rest of humanity, but it also exposed us to greater temptations, and not all Knights throughout history have shared my fastidiousness in avoiding sin. One of our Order was targeted and tempted away, by none other than Loomis Drake. In exchange for I don't know what, he secretly cast a magical key to the mountain and gave it to Drake, allowing him simple access to this place, which otherwise would have been off-limits to him, as it takes acute knowledge and extremely powerful dark magic for a demon to enter here. Even had Drake been able to bring himself here, the act should have made him so weak that the whole effort would have been futile, but with the magic from a Knight's key, he could enter as he pleased, and so he did, bringing with him a particularly strong set of spells he should never have known." He paused, his eyes staring out into the afternoon sunlight through the window behind Iris.

"What did he do?" she asked quietly.

"He destroyed what could be destroyed," the blacksmith answered simply.

Iris was glad she had already finished the stew he had given her. The thought of her new demonic adversary having such evil power made her anxious, and there was no way she could have continued eating now even if she had wanted to.

"Why would he do that?" she questioned.

Auraltiferys roused himself and refocused his eyes on her, shrugging as he replied, "For five hundred years, I've asked the same question, and still I have no sure answer. All the knowledge and every relic he stole from us, he could have obtained by less violent means, and although he may have tempted some to Hell, I am certain he likewise sent good souls to Heaven that day. So his motivations elude me. Perhaps it was just a twisted message to us, an evil endeavor to show us even the holy is within his grasp. Perhaps he simply wanted to test his power; perhaps Earth had become an unfulfilling and mindless playground for him. Whatever his reasons, he proved both his strength and his depravity, and what he took away from here only made him stronger."

Iris dropped her eyes and shook her head, astounded by the blacksmith's tale. It hadn't been a particularly detailed recounting of Loomis's attack, but it had told her enough. She didn't need or even want the details. She took a timid sip of her tea and then set the cup back down and looked at Auraltiferys. "Do you fear him?" she asked softly.

With a stern expression and undeniable strength flashing in the ice of his eyes, he answered, "There is nothing he can take from me but a mortal body that was always temporary. I do not fear him. But I know what grave and irreparable damage he can inflict on humanity, and I believe he must be stopped before he succeeds in this plot he has begun."

Iris nodded slowly in agreement, wishing Auraltiferys could go into this battle instead. He was far more capable, and he was truly and utterly fearless. She, on the other hand, was already terrified of the beast that had already baited her and now awaited her submission, lurking in the beautiful and charismatic form of the sexiest man alive. After a long, quiet moment lost in her imagination's dreadful thoughts, she finished her tea and then leaned back in her chair with a sigh, staring at the ceiling. "I wish I were even half as intrepid as you," she murmured wistfully.

"I believe you are," the blacksmith answered her, his dignified voice a luxurious comfort. "You will find all the strength and courage you need," he continued. "And forget not that you have the advantage over him. He needs something from you, and he cannot take what you do not give."

Iris sat up straight once more and met her tutor's gaze. "That may be," she acknowledged, "but it sounds to me as though Loomis Drake has a knack for getting what he wants."

Auraltiferys studied her with his uncomfortable perceptiveness for several seconds before he stated, simply, "Demons *are* most adroit at manipulation."

He continued to stare at her, and Iris could hear in her head the unspoken message hidden in his cryptic response: The demon Loomis Drake had no capabilities she herself did not possess. It would be an even fight, assuming she could keep her wits about her and have a little faith.

The blacksmith remained quiet until he was satisfied Iris understood his meaning, then he added, "The gate to Hell is no wider open to you than is the gate to Heaven. You will choose where to enter when the time comes. Not even Drake can force your decision; remember that. You already know to be wary of him; you believe he holds great power, and that knowledge will make you cautious. Remain vigilant, and you will not be duped."

He finished his tea and then collected the dishes, walked them to the sink, and began washing them. Iris offered to help, but he graciously declined her assistance and had the dishes cleaned, dried, and put away in only a few minutes, after which he led her outside to practice various magical spells. Iris found, to her surprise, that the *feeling* in the magic was already becoming more natural to her, and she had little trouble completing the tasks Auraltiferys set for her. After perhaps an hour of practice, he challenged her to spar with him, and she quickly lost the confidence she had developed. She was afraid of both her tutor's substantial strength and her own unexplored demonic power, and she tried, unsuccessfully, to argue her way out of the exercise. If she could not defend herself against the magic of a human, Auraltiferys had told her, she could not hope to defend herself against Loomis Drake's demonic spells. So the blacksmith had thrown various attacks at her, quickly increasing the rapidity and the complexity of his blows until Iris, finally fed up with the multitude of strikes he had landed on her, focused an impressive and terrifying spell against him, summoning it somehow from recesses of her mind she hadn't even known were there. Auraltiferys had shielded himself, but Iris's counterattack had still packed enough of a punch to knock him to the ground, and she felt awful for it. Auraltiferys, however, completely unharmed, had arisen gracefully with a small chuckle and a nod of approval. He was pleased with her quick learning, and his belief in her abilities nerved her.

As the sun began its descent, Iris again joined the blacksmith-priest for his evening prayers, then she spent some time alone in the den, reading from a few of the magic books that had seemed so foreign to her just that morning. Auraltiferys returned a while later, carrying something in his hand.

"I am sending this with you," he said, handing to her a small, bronze amulet on a thin metal chain. The medallion had an appearance similar to that of a knight's shield, round but for a semi-circular cut-out on either side, with precise engravings of runes set around a deep red stone affixed in the center. "It was once an unbreakable shield given to the Knights Templar, repossessed by our Order after the Crusades. Its image was recently shown to me during meditation, and I was inspired to recast it and repurpose it, not knowing to what end exactly. I realize now, this piece is meant for you."

Iris turned the medallion over in her hands, again amazed by the blacksmith's artistry. "How do I use it?" she asked as she fastened the chain's clasp behind her neck.

"It is yet a shield," Auraltiferys answered, "though now in this form more useful in spiritual warfare than in militaristic endeavors. It is meant to focus your mind and heart on God, and I hope you will not fight it. But remember, its magic is only as strong as you allow it to be. It can help you direct your steps toward righteousness only if that is the path you seek. It cannot force you to shun evil, but it may help you avoid temptation, if you wish to avoid it."

The amulet's weight around her neck was considerable but not uncomfortable, and the explanation of its magic made its presence even more reassuring, even though it would not lessen her own responsibility to stay on the right course. A knight's shield had never guaranteed safety in battle, but it was an advantage to have it, nonetheless.

Iris reclined back into the sofa cushions with a sigh as Auraltiferys seated himself in his chair. "What happens after I leave here?" she asked him, tension in her voice. Her mind had drifted to those thoughts when the blacksmith had left her in the den, and she had dreaded having to ask, but her time on the mountain would soon run out, and she was going to be flung headlong into a dark and frightening reality. Shielded or not, she was not looking forward to the unavoidable future. Before she had inadvertently stumbled upon Auraltiferys's monastic and magical abode (or, more accurately, before God had led her to it), she had been the sole survivor of the crash of a plane taking her right into the lion's den. That wasn't something she could have planned for; it wasn't anything she was prepared to deal with. She wouldn't know what to do when she returned to the crash site (hell, she wouldn't even know how to get back to the crash site), and she wouldn't know how to handle Loomis Drake after that. Reality now seemed like an unbearable burden, a cross too heavy to carry.

"I will help you to return to Earth this time," Auraltiferys replied, his tone soft yet purposeful, like burnished steel. Iris wondered if he had somehow read the thoughts in her mind, again.

"Back to the plane crash?" she cut in, already trying to plan how she would find her way back to civilization from there.

"Wherever you want to be," Auraltiferys answered, prompting Iris to discontinue her survival planning. She sat up and looked at him quizzically. He sat straight and dignified in his chair, forearms lying easily atop the armrests, his noble visage and sharp, bright eyes giving him the appearance of a king. For an instant, as she looked at him, Iris completely forgot all the concerns she had held the moment before. She couldn't even recall what she had asked him.

"Anywhere on Earth is accessible from here, and this mountain is likewise accessible from anywhere on Earth," he explained. "I will recommend, however, that you go home. Drake will already know you did not perish in the crash, and he will seek you out again. It is best you stay away from him as long as he allows, so that you can increase your knowledge and practice what you have learned."

Iris felt some comfort at the thought of returning home, but it was fleeting. As usual, her brain dove straight into a sea of doubt as she considered the things that might happen, the possibilities that might lie at the frayed ends of the thread of reality upon which she had now embarked.

"Won't he wonder how I made it home?" she asked dubiously. "He'll know you must have helped me, and if he knows you helped me, he'll know I know what I am," she rambled, her words taking on an increasingly nervous edge. "I won't even have the advantage of surprise!" She might have continued with a litany of increasingly dreadful hypotheticals, but a look from Auraltiferys silenced her. It wasn't an expression of criticism exactly, but it prompted her to consider the possibility she might be sounding quite foolish.

"It matters not what suspicions Drake may have," the blacksmith stated plainly. "You have already obtained the ultimate advantage by learning your true nature. Drake would have had a simpler task ahead of him if you had not been led here to me, but the truth has not changed. You have always been what you are, and Drake must have at least considered the possibility that his dealings with you might open your eyes to your demonic self. That is not his intention, but he has never been one to leave evil to chance. I assure you, he has contingencies in place, and if he realizes you've become aware of your power, you will only prove a greater, and therefore more desirable, challenge for him."

Iris felt her stomach turn at her tutor's words. That she was merely an object of conquest was a disturbing realization; that the man hoping to conquer her was actually a demon made it even more appalling.

Auraltiferys watched her as she lost herself in thought, then he spoke again after a long moment. "Iris," he said firmly, rousing her, "you will never have all the answers. You have never had all the answers, and yet you have ended up exactly where you are meant to be. Question what you will, and seek knowledge and wisdom, for there is great virtue in them, but do not expect to see every possibility. You've grown exponentially in learning in a very short time, and you have only scratched the surface of your true capabilities, but the unknown will always exist for you, just as it exists for all but God alone."

Iris sighed and covered her face with her hands as she relaxed again into the sofa back. She let her hands drop to her sides and then looked over at Auraltiferys. "I don't like the unknown," she returned simply.

With a small grin, he replied, "Then that is how God will teach you to have faith. It is a fallen world, Iris. Life is not always comfortable."

Iris pursed her lips, feeling properly admonished, but then she smiled. She couldn't help but be enchanted by the blacksmith's simple wisdom.

Auraltiferys stood and stretched his back. "It has grown late," he announced.

Iris rose hesitantly from the couch, suddenly petrified the blacksmith might send her away immediately, and she didn't feel ready for that. She might never feel ready. "Can I stay here tonight?" she asked sheepishly.

"You may stay," Auraltiferys answered. "We will practice more tomorrow, and we will see that you are as prepared for what lies ahead as you can be. You will need to protect that amulet of yours, for one thing."

"What do you mean?" Iris responded, stifling a yawn. She hadn't realized until now what a long and tiring day this had been.

"Drake will recognize what it is—or, what it *was*—and he will want it," Auraltiferys revealed. "It was one of a few relics I was able to spare from his pillaging all those years ago, by the grace of God. Drake may have long since abandoned whatever plans he had for it, but if he sees you with it, he will undoubtedly wish to take it from you. You must protect it as your own, with your own spells, so that it becomes more difficult for the wrong hands to use."

"So you give me a relic Drake wants and then send me out there to face him," Iris recounted. "Isn't that sort of like smothering me with honey and dumping me in the woods with the bears?"

Auraltiferys snickered quietly as he shrugged nonchalantly. "I think you can handle yourself," he said encouragingly. "Now, go to bed," he instructed, "and prepare yourself to complete your training tomorrow, for the fire awaits you." Iris's short-lived good humor morphed directly into dread at the blacksmith's foreboding words. She tried to swallow, only to find her mouth painfully dry.

After a final brief but perspicacious look at her, Auraltiferys turned away and headed toward the hallway to his bedroom. As he left, he said, "I am grateful for the time we have had, short though it has been. You will not face your demonic adversary in the blindness of ignorance."

Iris watched him disappear through the doorway, nodding to herself as she reflected on his statement. She might not leave the mountain feeling fully prepared to engage a demon, but she would leave here readier than she had been—and that, hopefully, was more than Loomis Drake had bargained for.

9

Iris pulled her car into the office parking lot, feeling as heavy and dreary as the thick, gray clouds hanging low in the morning sky. A cold, pre-winter mist dampened the chill air, portending an early changing of the season. She did *not* want to be here for another day at Eden. Auraltiferys had sent her home after only her second full day with him, and although she had spent a productive weekend practicing some simple magic and reading the spell books he had given her, Iris had nonetheless slumped into a deep loneliness and a helpless terror, despite her best efforts to keep her mind from allowing it. She had only just met the holy blacksmith-priest on that otherworldly mountain, but she liked him, and she felt safe with him...and now she missed him terribly. She was accustomed to and perhaps even liked being alone, and missing someone other than her departed family was an unusual and unwelcome feeling that only compounded the misery of returning to her hellhole of a workplace.

She intended to park her black Dodge Challenger in her preferred and usual parking spot, but for some unknown reason, the boss had arrived early this morning and had squeezed his ridiculous, oversized pickup truck crookedly into the neighboring spot, with one of its big rear tires jutting over the white line and encroaching on the space Iris had used for her own car almost every workday for the past eight years. Usually, the asshole would drag himself to the office around ten or eleven, park in one of the designated handicap spots in the front, and then strut into the office like a rooster, expecting the receptionist to have his coffee ready for him with cream and sugar so he could grab it and walk straight back to his office, shut the door, then pretend to work for half a day before leaving. If he was at the office by eight in the morning, it probably meant there was an "important" owners meeting happening, and although Iris considered perhaps she should be impressed that he could show his face at work so early, his presence was actually just an extreme irritation for her on an already depressing day.

She glared at the truck and grumbled to herself as she found another parking place farther away. She got out of her car, slung her purse strap across her torso, grabbed her Starbucks coffee (the only positive aspect of the morning thus far), closed and locked her door, then walked across the parking lot, icy mist freezing the scowl on her face as she approached the building's entrance. For a fleeting instant before she opened the door, she glanced back at her boss's truck, imagining a number of damaging things she could do to it with nothing more than the thoughts of her mind. In the next instant, however, she envisioned a look of utter disappointment on the face of Auraltiferys, and she shook the angry, evil thoughts out of her head.

As she walked upstairs, Iris knew she would have significant difficulty focusing on her work today. In fact, she wasn't sure she would be able to focus on her work ever again, or at least not until Loomis Drake was properly attended to. Since leaving the mountain, she had lived in constant fear, imagining she would round a corner somewhere, anywhere, and find a specter-like Loomis Drake standing there ready to murder her and eat her soul, though she knew how unrealistic the thought was. Regardless, his voice on the phone yesterday, though smooth and genteel and handsome, had thoroughly frightened her. She had called his office, hoping to leave a message, and instead had been forwarded directly to his personal cell phone. He had expressed great sympathy for her experience on his jet, and he had intimated how relieved he was to hear she had survived the ordeal. She had explained to him how she had made it home with some good luck and the help of some miraculously convenient hikers who had found her. She had lied to a demon, and she had no clue whether Loomis had believed her lies...though she supposed it didn't matter. He had cordially dismissed her apology for having returned straight home instead of trying to meet with him after the plane crash, and he had told her, graciously, to take all the time she needed before rescheduling her interview with him, which, he had added, he fervently hoped she would do. Iris had paced her living room for the duration of the phone call with him, and after she had hung up the phone, she had sat nervously on her sofa for half an hour, expecting paranormal activity to overrun her house and drive her to the brink of insanity. Nothing of the sort had happened, however, and she had spent the rest of the day trying to convince herself that Loomis Drake was nothing to fear. Somehow, though, that beguiling voice of his was stuck in the back of her mind, beckoning like a siren and yet filling her with dread.

She sighed heavily before approaching the glass door to Eden's offices, mentally preparing herself for the receptionist's greeting and likely questions about her vacation last week. Iris never advertised her personal engagements at work, but scheduled absences were always included on a shared office calendar, so there was no hiding that she had been out, and each of her past vacations had taught her there would always be at least three people who would feel obligated to ask questions she didn't care to answer: *Where'd ya go? Did ya have fun? Are ya glad to be back?* Most of Iris's "vacations" from work consisted of staying home and doing nothing in particular—which she had always cited as one of her favorite things to do—and yet these idiots always asked, anyway. And if she told them she had gone somewhere, that would only prompt them to share some related story of their own. Either Iris was remarkably able to succeed in feigning interest, or her coworkers just didn't care that she didn't care.

"So, you're back!" the receptionist exclaimed in a cheerful sing-song. "Did you have a good vacation?"

Iris forced a tight-lipped smile and replied, "Yeah, it was fine, thanks." She kept walking past the front desk as she responded, only to have the receptionist swivel in her chair and keep talking. Not wanting to be overtly rude, Iris stopped in the walkway and faced her.

"So where did you go?" the woman asked, her face full of peppy eagerness to chat. How annoying.

"Oh," Iris shrugged, "I didn't actually go anywhere. Just took it easy, you know." She smiled as kindly as she could, hoping her vague answer would end the conversation.

The receptionist nodded in enthusiastic agreement and said, "Those are the best kinds of vacations! I would love to have that kind of vacation again, but, you know how it is with the kids and everything; it's just impossible!" Iris nodded silently, keeping a fake smile plastered on her face as she considered how dumb and unthinking it was for someone to say "You know how it is with the kids" to someone one knew had no kids. The receptionist continued talking, griping about how she now came back from all her family's vacations more tired than she had been before they had left. Iris continued nodding and smiling until, finally, the receptionist closed with a friendly, "Well, anyway, glad you're back," allowing her to proceed to her own office.

She set down her coffee and tossed her purse onto the desk,

then turned on her computer and plopped into her chair, no sooner contacting the seat than Matilda Gordon appeared in her doorway. *Oh, for the love of God*, Iris thought involuntarily. She mentally chided herself for it the following instant; she had left the holy presence of Auraltiferys only a couple of days ago, and she should be making more of an effort to emulate his graciousness, but damn, it was hard.

"Hey, girl!" Matilda greeted her excitedly, plodding into Iris's office with heavy, graceless footsteps and seating herself in the spare chair in front of Iris's desk. "Did you have a good vacation?" She was wearing a long, flowy black top over a pair of brightly colored, form-fitting leggings, topped by knee-high boots that Iris noticed zipped only three-fourths of the way up her doughy calves. To Iris's eye, she looked like a bulbous, poisonous mushroom.

With an expression that probably came out looking like more of a grimace than a smile, Iris replied, "It was nice; thanks for asking." She was not going to elaborate.

"Where'd you go?" Matilda asked, running her hands nervously down her thighs over and over as she sat there.

Iris shook her head slightly and answered, "I just stayed here; didn't do much." She leaned forward to log in to her computer and began clicking on emails, hoping it would prompt her unwelcome guest to leave, to no avail.

"Yeah, girl, I hear ya," Matilda said, scrunching her face into what was supposed to be a look of understanding. "Give me a glass of wine and a book and my pajamas, and I am set!"

Iris took a sip of her coffee and nodded in agreement, though wine and pajamas weren't exactly her personal idea of a perfect vacation.

"Anyway," Matilda went on, "I just *have* to tell you what happened to me last week!"

Spectacular, Iris thought sarcastically. She should have just gone straight to Loomis Drake. Whatever he might have done to her, it wouldn't have been half as miserable as this day at the office was already proving to be. She sipped her coffee, looking at Matilda over the cup and waiting for her to continue. Matilda, however, sat expectantly, apparently waiting for Iris to invite the story. After several awkward seconds, Iris finally gave in and asked, "What happened?" She didn't bother trying to keep a hint of exasperation out of her voice. If only this cow knew to whom she was speaking...

"Well," Matilda announced dramatically, "you know how I had to go to Denver for that training?"

"No," Iris answered flatly. She did know Matilda had gone to Denver last week, because it had been listed on that shared office calendar; she just didn't want to give the impression of caring.

"Oh," Matilda paused, slightly deflated but eager enough to continue her story that she recovered quickly. "Well, anyway," she continued, "I had to go to Denver for training, and you know how they had that snowstorm up there?"

"Oh, really?" Iris interrupted.

Matilda hesitated again and blinked several times in rapid succession, apparently surprised to have received a verbal response to her pointless rhetorical question, much to Iris's amusement. But, otherwise undaunted, she proceeded, "Yeah, it was a real bad snowstorm, like at least a foot of snow." Iris felt the hair standing up on the back of her neck as Matilda's drawling accent became more and more pronounced. The girl had managed to make "foot" rhyme with "putt," and, naturally, the word "of" had been abbreviated to only its vowel sound.

"Anyway," Matilda carried on, "I was on one of those little tiny puddle jumpers; you know, those little planes that just have one seat on one side and then two seats on the other side?"

"Mm-hmm," Iris mumbled, again responding to the wholly unnecessary "you know" question.

"Well," Matilda said breathlessly before taking a dramatic pause. "We got caught in that snowstorm," she announced theatrically, "and, oh my gosh, girl, I was terrified! The plane *literally* flew in sideways. I mean, one wing was basically on the ground like this." She stood up and pantomimed the scenario, twisting her ample form so that she could extend her arms out like the wings of a plane, indicating as closely as she could that the plane's wingspan had somehow been perpendicular to the runway.

Are you kidding me? Iris thought angrily. *'Literally' flew in sideways, my ass.* She had lost her patience, and she didn't even care that she had lost it. "If the plane 'literally' flew in sideways, wouldn't you have crashed?" she asked drably, unamused by Matilda's obviously exaggerated tale.

"Well, I mean, you know, not 'literally,' I guess," Matilda stammered, tripping stupidly over her own words. "But, like, I was thinking, 'Oh, Lord, this is it for me!' I mean, it was seriously scary."

"Yeah, I bet that was scary," Iris replied, her tone surprising even her with its coldness.

Matilda was either too obtuse to perceive the chill in Iris's voice or too absorbed in her own story to care. "I literally thought we were going to crash," she reiterated, obviously unaware of the misplaced modifier in her statement. "I mean, I never want to get on a plane again. It was the scariest thing ever!"

"Less scary than *actually* crashing, though," Iris rejoined bitingly. She was far less willing than usual to put up with Matilda's amateurish hyperboles and meaningless colloquialisms, and this particular story had triggered her anger in a very specific way, considering her own horrifying aerial experience less than a week before. She felt her usually exceptional self-control eroding with every passing fraction of a second.

Matilda had sunk back into the chair, unwittingly stroking her thighs again in anxious, useless movement. "Well, yeah," she acknowledged hesitantly, "I guess it would be scarier to really crash, obviously, but you know what I meant." Her voice increased in volume and strength as she finished her sentence; that was always Matilda's way of making herself sound confident after having been called out on the inanity of her words. That forced "confidence" was every bit as artificial as the girl's "interest" in Iris's weekends or vacations or work—it was a joke.

"How should anyone know what you mean?" Iris asked sharply. Matilda's puffy face went wide-eyed and thin-lipped as she continued, acerbically, "You misuse words and you blurt out ridiculous generalities, and you aggrandize all your stories to try to make yourself more interesting, but you're only succeeding in showing your ignorance. You're not the only person who's endured some turbulence on an airplane! No one cares! So until you've actually survived a *fucking* plane crash, why don't you either keep your stupid, exaggerated stories to yourself, or go share them with those other people out there who have less to do and are more willing to pretend to give a shit?"

Iris's heart was pounding in her chest as she spoke, partially from anger and partially from the adrenaline rush caused by saying things she knew she shouldn't say. She knew she was being mean, and part of her was appalled by the behavior, but...well, the other part of her felt suddenly and wonderfully free.

Matilda's cheeks colored a bright red, and her eyes blurred with tears, but she managed to contain them. She stood up and moved to leave the room, but, before departing, she paused in the doorway and apologized to Iris for whatever she had done to offend her. Iris watched as the girl walked away, at a faster pace than usual, probably heading straight for the bathroom so she could cry.

Iris smiled and took a casual sip of her coffee in the ensuing peace and quiet, amused beyond measure that she had just been a total bitch, while Matilda had been the one to apologize. How delightfully ironic! And, Iris thought, perhaps appropriate. She was, after all, a demon, and far more intelligent and powerful than Matilda or anyone else at this pissant office. She wondered if Matilda might file a complaint against her. At first, the thought was a scary one, but after a moment's consideration, she realized she didn't care. She had more important things to do than this job, anyway.

***

The day passed surprisingly quickly, and Iris was amazed by the amount of work she was able to get done. After her blow-up on Matilda, people had left her alone, and, remarkably, there had been no corrective action initiated against her. Either Matilda hadn't officially complained to anyone (at least, not to anyone with any actual authority; Iris was sure the girl had gone and told two or three acquaintances about her unwarranted snarkiness, likely embellishing that story, too), or no one had believed her or cared to do anything about it. Matilda was known to be rather sensitive, and Iris was known to be quite intense, to the point of seeming unfriendly sometimes. So even if Matilda had complained, management probably would have shrugged it off as a simple misunderstanding between coworkers. *Besides*, Iris considered, *what the hell would they do to me, anyway? I'm the best employee these assholes have, and they know it.*

Her mind had drifted occasionally to the billionaire demon she would eventually have to confront, but the stockpile of work amassed during her time off the week before had kept her busy and focused her attention away from him. By the end of the workday, Loomis Drake seemed like just a faraway daydream, and even the holy blacksmith Auraltiferys had become a distant memory.

The morning's overcast sky had broken into a mostly sunny afternoon, and although the air was still crisp, it made for a pleasant walk across the office parking lot. Iris got in her car, turned up her music, and sang as she drove home, feeling better than she had since her ill-fated plane ride. As she turned the corner onto her street, she had to stop momentarily to avoid hitting the children from the house on the corner, who were in the habit of playing various sports in the middle of the street. It had annoyed her a hundred times already since they had moved in, and more than once she had considered how nice it would be to run them over. It would serve them right, after all. It shouldn't take too many brains to know it was a bad idea for kids to play in the street, especially there at a corner. *Stupid little shits*, she thought as the oldest boy took his football and pretended to throw it at her windshield. *Ooh, careful there, buddy. You have no clue what you're messing with.* But that was kids these days...no respect for anything.

As Iris pulled into her garage, she noticed a sizable package sitting on the porch, near her front door. She parked, walked out to grab the mail from the mailbox, then went to inspect the delivery. It was mostly unmarked, except for a shipping label that indicated it had come from Portland, Oregon. Upon seeing that, Iris felt her sanguine attitude morph instantly into anxiousness. Part of her was excited to open the package; the other part was afraid to. Either way, the unexpected delivery was a sudden reminder of her new reality. She had made today just another day at the office, but that had been false security. She couldn't continue clinging to her past routines; Loomis Drake wouldn't wait for her forever.

She piled her mail on top of the box and carried the package back through the garage and into her kitchen, setting it on her dining table. She set the evening coffee to brewing, went to her bedroom and changed into shorts and a T-shirt, adding her plush robe over that for warmth, then returned to see what the mysterious box contained. For a brief moment before opening it, she wondered if it might contain some accursed object that would harm her, but that didn't make much sense. Loomis had been nothing but charming so far, and there was no reason for him to act any other way toward her—at least, not yet. As Auraltiferys had pointed out, he *needed* her.

She cut the packing tape and unfolded the cardboard to reveal a large gift basket, beautifully wrapped in sheer violet mesh and tied with gold cord—a much nicer display than the jejune cellophane-clad catalog orders typical of corporate gift-giving. She had to use both hands to pull the basket out of its shipping box. The basket itself was made of some kind of lightweight wood rather than wicker or plastic, spectacularly carved to look like roses. Untying the cord and carefully pulling away the mesh, Iris found the basket filled with a number of items she would have gladly gifted herself. There were two big bags of expensive ground coffee, one an Italian roast and the other hazelnut flavored; a dozen gourmet cookies; two fabulously scented candles; a rose-fragranced shower gel and a bamboo loofah sponge; three fancy and aromatic body lotions; and a trio of perfumed body sprays. Iris inspected each item individually, feeling as giddy as she had felt back when her family had still been with her to celebrate Christmas. Maybe even giddier. She couldn't remember the last time she had received a really lavish gift like this from anyone outside her family. In fact, the last gift she remembered getting was a five-dollar Starbucks gift card that Matilda had re-gifted to her something like two or three years ago—Matilda didn't care much for Starbucks coffee—and Iris had actually been pretty excited about that. This basket from Loomis Drake was exponentially more exciting, and Iris was astounded by how perfectly suited to her it was. She wondered if he had chosen these things for her himself. It seemed unlikely, but if he had...well, then it was clear he knew how to please her.

As she reached in to remove the box of cookies, Iris realized she had overlooked a single deep-red rose that had been situated among the gift items, a parchment envelope taped neatly to its stem, with

"Dr. Wakefield" penned across it in precise, elegant font. Curious, and nervous, she lifted the envelope away, then had to retrieve a letter opener in order to open it without damaging its intriguing wax seal. She seated herself at the table, removed the note inside and unfolded it, then read its brief message, written in the same beautiful script as the envelope, the pristine chirography of an intelligent and old-fashioned hand:

Dear Dr. Wakefield,

I extend to you my deepest sympathies and most heartfelt apology for the tragic event you have endured. I had hoped to make your trip to Portland a pleasant and memorable affair, and I feel personally responsible for its unfortunate outcome. Please find in this small gift a token of both my profound regret for your suffering and my great joy for your survival, and treat yourself to some indulgence and relaxation. When you are ready, I hope you will once again accept my invitation to your job interview. I eagerly await the pleasure of making your acquaintance.

Sincerely yours,

Loomis Drake

Iris read the note twice before setting it on the table and then mindlessly picking up the rose, admiring its beauty and fragrance as she considered the words she had just read. Loomis's note to her was thoughtful and kind, and not unprofessional, though there was certainly a personal and perhaps even romantic touch to it that seemed to penetrate the boundaries of their yet-non-existent relationship. She and Loomis had not yet officially met, and Iris was nonetheless feeling as though she knew him somehow. It was apparent he knew her. She twirled the rose gently in her fingers and grinned, imagining Loomis Drake could not possibly be the force of unmitigated evil that Auraltiferys had tried to make him out to be.

After a few moments, she stood and poured herself a cup of coffee, then dug through her "junk" cabinet to find a small vase for the rose Loomis had sent her. She placed the flower there in some water, then sat down with her coffee to enjoy one of the cookies. There were her two favorites to choose from, but she opted for the chocolate chip over the snickerdoodle. It was soft and flavorful, much better than anything from a grocery store, and even better than any cookie she had ever bought from a specialty bakery. As she broke little pieces away and savored them, she stared at the handwritten page on the table in front of her, and she let her thoughts stray toward the man who had sent her all these wonderful things. He must care about her; he seemed genuinely sorry for what she had gone through during her short-lived journey to meet him, and he seemed genuinely happy she had survived it. More than that, he seemed genuinely eager to meet her in person, and he had sent her a red rose, which must surely indicate at least a hint of a desire that their relationship, once it began, would be something more than just business. Iris could easily imagine Loomis sitting there with her, having just given her all these luxurious gifts for whatever reason, or for no reason at all, and the fantasy was a heady one. She pictured him sitting across from her, a grin on his face as he watched her enjoy a dainty little piece of a cookie. She would smile coyly at him but then quickly give up on her attempts to act unimpressed, and she would step over to him and seat herself on his lap, then pull his head toward hers for a racy kiss...

In her fanciful state of mind, Iris misjudged the distance to her mouth and dripped warm coffee down her chin and onto her chest, startling her out of her reverie. "Hell," she said to herself out loud as she jumped up and ran into her bathroom, hoping some dabs with a damp washcloth might prevent a coffee stain from making itself at home on one of her favorite shirts. She shook her head at her own reflection in the mirror as she wiped at her dribble. *Real sexy,* she thought derisively. *Yeah, you've totally got a real chance with a gorgeous, sophisticated billionaire like Loomis Drake. He probably loves coffee stains and dopey T-shirts.*

Feeling as cynical as ever, Iris sighed with exasperation, flung the washcloth into her laundry hamper, then headed back toward the kitchen. Golden rays of the season's early-evening sunset were filtering through the open blinds of her bedroom window and glinting off an object on her dresser, calling her attention to the amulet the blacksmith had given her. She had left it lying there, rather guiltily, not wanting to endure the interrogations that would certainly have arisen had she worn the amulet to the office. Her thoughts had been diverted from the mountain and from the blacksmith enough today to have made the whole experience seem like a bygone dream, but as she picked up the amulet and beheld it once again, she was reminded of the new reality it evidenced. This was a real, physical object that had come from a place not as sunken as the earthly realm; it was magical and blessed, given to her by a man who was centuries old and probably holier than the Pope. The amulet was undeniable proof that truth exceeded Iris's human imagination, and it was a reminder of her own personal place in that seemingly impossible truth.

She hooked the amulet around her neck and returned to the kitchen, staring for a moment at the rose sitting in its vase on her counter and at the gifts strewn across her dining table. What had she been thinking? The events of the day suddenly replayed in her mind with disquieting clarity. She was ashamed of how she had spoken to Matilda in the morning; she was ashamed of her focus on work and how easily she had put Auraltiferys and magic and even God out of her mind; she was ashamed of her bad thoughts about the kids up the street; she was ashamed of how ridiculously smitten she had become after receiving what was certainly an artificial expression of care from Loomis Drake, nothing more than a contrivance meant to lure her—which was exactly what it had done. Sinfulness was not relegated to physical acts, and Iris had spent her whole day in an evil state of mind, in one way or another. Practically every minute had been a victory over her for Loomis Drake, and she, like a fool, had traipsed along ignorantly, foolishly believing their game had not yet begun.

With a stony expression of defiance hard on her face, Iris grabbed the rose from its vase and focused her thoughts, watching as the flower turned to flame in her hand. She let the ashes fall into the kitchen sink as she vowed never again to be swayed by the fake romantic gestures of Loomis Drake. She would not be duped by a demonic spirit disguised in artificial charm and manufactured sex appeal—to hell with that. She dumped the water from the vase into the sink and rinsed the remnants of ash down the drain, then went to the table and hastily crammed all the gift items back into their decorative wooden basket, prepared to destroy it all with magical fire, but she stopped herself. These were nice things, things she would normally enjoy, and it would be shamefully wasteful to trash it all. What harm could there be in keeping the gifts and using them? Getting rid of them wouldn't get rid of Loomis; neither did keeping them mean she approved of his motives. She was mindful of him now that the amulet had helped her appropriately redirect her thoughts, and she wouldn't lose herself in his guile again. Coffees and cookies and candles and luxurious bath products were not evil, and she could enjoy them with a clear conscience, as long as she kept her head on straight. She realized, however, that her conscience was not clear right now, and she would have to rectify that before Loomis got any craftier. She would have to apologize to Matilda, of course, even if she had meant everything she had said this morning.

She would have to try harder to be patient with Matilda and everyone else at work, and with the kids up the street. And perhaps most of all, she would have to purge her thoughts of all those disgusting, foolish fantasies about Loomis Drake. Those kinds of thoughts were undoubtedly what he was counting on from her, and he had already from afar been able to plant those seeds in her head. If she couldn't correct her thinking while he was yet distanced from her, she would have no chance of succeeding in a stand against him when they would meet face to face.

She picked up her half-empty, now-tepid coffee cup and refilled it with warm coffee from the pot. She sat back down at her dining table, Loomis's gift basket in front of her, and she nodded thoughtfully to herself as she devised her general plan. There was no sense stalling any further; she felt ready now. She pulled her cell phone out of the purse hanging on the back of her chair and dialed the same number she had called just yesterday. A single butterfly in her stomach flapped its wings nervously, but Iris felt mostly calm as she waited for him to answer. She knew he would; she could sense it.

"Dr. Wakefield," he greeted her smoothly, his voice as abundant in charm as his bank accounts were in wealth. "I was just thinking about you."

I bet you were, Iris thought scathingly. If she hadn't reminded herself of his demonic nature, the cleverly shrouded suggestiveness of his almost-but-not-quite-too-personal remark would have shaken her, because some little part of her mind wanted to believe Loomis was a decent man with a real interest in her, despite everything Auraltiferys had told her. But now, once again cognizant of the demon's twisted, ulterior motives, she received the subtly flirtatious salutation as nothing more than an unamusing joke.

Deciding to play along for now, Iris smiled before replying, hoping it would sweeten her tone. "Oh, really?" she asked coyly. "I've been thinking about you, too. I just opened this amazing gift you sent me." She picked up the handwritten note with her free hand and glanced at it again before rolling her eyes and then tossing it carelessly back into the basket.

"It isn't much," Loomis answered, "but it comes with the most cordial of thoughts. I hope you are pleased with it."

There was something provocative layered within his words, and in a momentary lapse of focus, Iris saw in her mind a brief, flickering replay of her earlier fantasy before she regained full control of her wits. What the hell was that about? Surely Loomis didn't have the capacity to force those kinds of thoughts. No...demons couldn't control an unwilling person; she felt certain of that. She would just have to be careful to keep him out of her head.

"It's wonderful," she replied graciously. "You couldn't have given me a more perfect gift if you had asked me what I like," she added. It wasn't a lie. "It's as though you've known me for years."

Loomis responded with a low, decorous chuckle, then said, "It gladdens me to know I've delivered you some enjoyment. I had worried perhaps I was mistaken in the suppositions I had made about you, having had only your *curriculum vitae* to give me any insight."

"Well," Iris returned slowly, "either you're extremely perceptive, or I have common tastes and am far less unique than I once believed."

"Dr. Wakefield," Loomis returned with a hint of friendly chastisement, "I believe you are anything but ordinary. Let not my fortuitously accurate gift-giving convince you otherwise!" He went quiet for a second, then added, "I will admit to you, however, I have felt the strangest sense of familiarity as I've reviewed your background. Perhaps you and I knew each other in a past life."

Iris smirked at the comment, shaking her head, then she took a quiet sip of her coffee before answering, warmly, "It's a pity we haven't met in this one." She was amazed to hear the suggestion in her own voice. That must have been her own demonic nature aiding her, because her human person would never have made such a pointedly enticing statement, particularly to a potential employer.

"On that," Loomis replied confidently, "we agree."

Iris leaned back in her chair, impressed by the shrewd manner in which Loomis had fished her out of her blissful ignorance. His bait had been a new career, lathered with the enticing notion that the career might come with the bonus of romantic interludes with the handsome billionaire himself. The unforeseen plane crash had disturbed the calm waters, but only momentarily. Loomis had then tossed a generous gift to her and waited until her phone call divulged that she was hooked. Even then, in the course of this phone call, Loomis tugged at the line just enough to keep her interest, intending all the while to let her come to him. He knew she would. He must have done this thousands of times to thousands of people, using thousands of lures crafted individually to suit each of his victims. He must believe Iris would be just as easy a catch. He wasn't going to ask her to reschedule that job interview—he was going to let her think she was in complete control. It was a brilliant scheme, and it terrified Iris to think how successful the scheme might have been if not for her miraculous encounter with Auraltiferys. The only thing guarding her from Loomis's masterful temptations right now was her knowledge of the truth.

Loomis had allowed several seconds of silence on the phone as Iris had collected her thoughts. He had been waiting for her for a long time already; he had no reason to be impatient now. Finally, Iris said, "I'd like to reschedule that interview now, if the offer still remains." She imagined the statement must have brought quite an arrogant grin to Loomis's face. *Joke's on you*, she thought to herself.

"Of course the offer remains," Loomis answered, "though I should refrain from calling it an 'offer,' as that would imply some degree of generosity on my part. You see, Iris, in truth my motives are quite self-serving—I want you to work for me. I feel little need to interview you for a position as an employee; I've already deemed you to be someone I want on my side. So instead our meeting will be more an opportunity for you to interview me to determine if I meet your standards for an employer. I have, sadly, lost the chance to make a good first impression, considering the lamentable atrocity you were subjected to on your journey here last week, but I will certainly try to make up for it in any way I can."

Oh, that's good, Iris admitted silently, again astounded by his slyness. She was fully aware of his true nature, and she had at least some idea of his evil stratagems, yet she now found herself already entertaining the idea of joining him. He had advertised his desire for her; now he had deftly planted the suggestion that she should desire him, all under the guise of business…and Iris couldn't be sure his persuasion wasn't working. She knew he was speaking in words that carried meaning far weightier than their outward contexts would imply, and she would have expected that awareness to immunize her from his charm; instead, it was making him far more appealing.

"Last week was a terrible accident," Iris replied after her momentary internal reflection, "but certainly not your fault. It's over now, and I'd like to move on from it. Are you able to meet with me next week?" A part of her brain screamed at her as the question left her mouth, reminding her that Auraltiferys had suggested she stay away from Loomis as long as he would allow her to. It was too late to take it back, though, and besides…what further preparation should she need? Was she not every bit the demon Loomis was?

"I will make myself available as you desire," Loomis replied. *Good Lord*, Iris mused silently, hoping the informal petition to Heaven might pull her thoughts out of the gutter.

As Iris pressed her eyes shut and tried to remind herself that Loomis was her enemy, he went on to offer her yet another driver and private jet, which she politely declined. He understood, of course, and simply instructed her to pay for all her travel and incidentals with the company credit card she still had. She assured him she would do so, and after a final double entendre (she could practically feel him winking at her through the phone), he wished her a good night.

After their phone call was ended, Iris felt a flood of nervousness, and it angered her to feel that way. There was no need for fear; Auraltiferys had taught her that. And the blacksmith had told her she was stronger than Loomis, anyway. So even if she would be meeting Loomis sooner than her tutor might have suggested, surely it would not be problematic. In fact, it could be fun. As she considered the situation, she realized she did still have the upper hand. Loomis likely didn't know she had been alerted to the truth about him and about her own nature, and, even if he did know, he would still need her cooperation if he wanted to usurp Hell and complete whatever his evil intentions were. At least for now, there were no negative consequences Iris could foresee for herself. Loomis was going to get the worse end of the bargain, no matter what.

That thought was rather gratifying, and comforting, too. Iris picked up her coffee cup, grabbed a snickerdoodle from the gift box, and then relaxed back into her chair, contemplating, with a grin on her face, how different the week ahead now looked. She would apologize to that moss-brained coworker of hers, go to confession this weekend, and then meet with Loomis next week to discuss, first, her impressive expertise in behavioral psychology, and then, as a nice little surprise, her more recent research in the field of demonology. Cunning as he was, Loomis Drake was going to have a difficult time impressing Dr. Iris Wakefield.

10

Iris strode toward the large, brass-colored doors to which the man at the front desk had directed her, the heels of her dress boots clicking along the marble tiles with a satisfying echo as she approached the private express elevator to the top-floor office of Loomis Drake. A bright-eyed and ruddy young security guard stood dutifully by the doors to await her arrival, having been notified by radio that Iris was to be escorted directly to Mr. Drake's waiting area. He smiled and nodded respectfully, with distinctly militaristic chivalry.

"Good morning, ma'am," he greeted her in a strong, energetic voice. "You're here to interview with Mr. Drake?"

"That's right," Iris replied.

"Well, welcome! I'll take you up there," he answered as he pressed the button for the elevator. The doors opened, revealing a beautifully decorated interior: gleaming brass handrails; rich, textured burgundy walls; warm, recessed lighting; intricate, highly polished cherrywood wainscoting; and a large, gold-framed oil-on-canvas re-creation of Michelangelo's *The Creation of Adam*. Sensing Iris's surprise at the grandeur of the elevator, or perhaps simply assuming that any newcomer would be amazed by the sight, the guard laughed and explained, "Yes, ma'am, Mr. Drake has a real knack for the spectacular." Still smiling as he ushered her into the space, he added good-naturedly, "Guess you can do that kind of thing when you have all that money to blow."

"I guess so," Iris responded, finding it ironic that a man, or rather a *being*, such as Loomis would own and display such an obviously religious work. *You'd think he'd hate it*, she thought to herself disdainfully as the doors closed and the elevator began its smooth ascent.

"Yeah, but seriously, though, Mr. Drake's a great man," the guard continued, his tone deepened with sincerity. "I was in a bad place when I came back from Iraq, but Mr. Drake's veterans program saved my life. I owe everything to him."

Iris suddenly felt great pity for this young man, whose smile had faded at the bad memory only for a few seconds before gratitude for Loomis Drake had returned it to its full and genuine brightness. She also felt a great and sudden anger at Loomis for his nearly inescapable charm and practically limitless monetary resources. He could throw money at anything and everything, and the world would call it "charity," never even thinking he might have ulterior motives. It was clear to her—though, admittedly, it would not have been but for her divinely guided journey to the mountain and Auraltiferys's teaching—that anyone on the receiving end of Loomis's generosity effectively belonged to him. They loved him, and they felt indebted—a dangerous set of strings to have attached to oneself, particularly when the puppeteer in control was an inhuman force of evil who operated with invisible power. Loomis had many, many people across the globe practically eating out of his hands, ignorant of their ignorance. Most were probably decent people, but he could manipulate them in any direction he desired (which would certainly be toward sin and away from God), because he could do it with intelligence and subtlety that surpassed human thinking. So well-disguised was his treachery that no one could find outward fault with him; no one would suspect his words and actions might sway good people into bad things. Even Iris herself, almost always skeptical of the true motivations behind the supposed largesse of wealthy people in the news, had never really been suspicious of him. And, in all likelihood, even if she or anyone else were ever to question his apparent goodness, it would probably take no more than a genteel smile and a well-spoken word to mollify every concern. *Thank God I learned the truth when I did*, her internal voice exclaimed gratefully.

As they neared the top floor, the guard interrupted Iris's brief mental reflection, offering jovially, "Good luck with your interview! You'll do just fine. Like I said, Mr. Drake's a great man." Iris smiled and thanked him as the doors opened and he motioned her out. "You'll just take this elevator back down when you're finished," he concluded. "See you then!"

Loomis's reception area was every bit as grandiose as his elevator. This room had a dark, highly polished hardwood floor and expansive, opulent rugs that perfectly complemented the richly painted walls. Decorative pedestals in the corners held bronze statuettes, spectacularly offset by broad-leafed greenery set in large vases on the surrounding floor. After pausing momentarily to take it all in, Iris walked toward the desk in the center of the room, where there sat a sadly stereotypical stunner of a secretary—a girl in maybe her mid-twenties, with tanned skin and long, dark hair; big, dark eyes; and an enviable, petite hourglass figure. She wore a very tight, very low-cut, and very expensive-looking black dress that Iris guessed was probably very short, too. Had she been at this interview before having met Auraltiferys, still in her ignorance, she would have been extremely disappointed to see such a worn-out scene: the sexy multibillionaire and the undeniably beautiful but shallow and impressionable young plaything posing as his employee. Seeing it now, though, with her knowledge of Loomis's true nature, the scene seemed grimly appropriate...a perfect reminder of just how attractive sin could be made to appear. For an instant, Iris considered perhaps she might be jumping to conclusions; maybe the girl was an intelligent and strong woman who wasn't throwing herself at Loomis every opportunity she got, but...instinct told her otherwise.

The girl said nothing but gave Iris a long stare-down, her eyes scanning her from top to bottom, her face filled with contempt and judgment as she viewed the messy bun of Iris's hair, her modest gray turtleneck, her non-designer scarf, and her understated black leggings and knee-high boots. The girl's aloofness suggested she had somehow perceived Iris as a potential threat to her standing with the boss, though Iris couldn't explain why—this girl was much more physically attractive than she was, and besides that, she of course had no interest in Loomis, anyway—but she supposed perhaps she should be flattered by the assessment.

"I'm Iris Wakefield," Iris introduced herself. "Here to see Mr. Drake. He's expecting me."

The secretary's response was another disdainful stare, pursed (and perfectly glossed) lips, and a long sigh. She paused for several seconds as Iris stood there waiting, taking a casual look at her elegantly French-manicured nails before replying.

"Have a seat over there," she said curtly as she nodded almost imperceptibly toward a couple of wing chairs next to a small coffee table, offering Iris no invitation to the well-stocked beverage center along the wall just behind it.

Turning from the desk and rolling her eyes, Iris took a seat. The girl made no apparent effort to announce her arrival, but Iris suspected it didn't matter—Loomis was probably already well aware she had arrived. It might have been her imagination, but she thought she could sense him now. It was an uneasy stirring deep within her somewhere, more subconscious than physical, and if she could sense him, he could probably even more easily sense her. She hoped he still believed her to be oblivious of her spiritual nature.

If he had somehow discovered she knew what she really was... *It shouldn't matter*, she reminded herself. He needed her if he hoped to take control of Hell, and she was stronger than him, anyway. Still, though she had felt so ready for their meeting as she had sat there at her dining table after having bravely squashed all her fantastical thoughts about him, Iris couldn't help but hear Auraltiferys's steely voice cutting across the back of her mind, telling her to wait for Loomis to come to her, and she was becoming admittedly nervous, despite her best efforts. The blacksmith had cautioned her against arrogant trust in her divine superiority over Loomis, yet here she was, of her own free will, just outside the lion's den, still new to magic and quite unpracticed in it, while her adversary had existed in it and exercised it for practically an eternity. Now, she worried she might be undertaking an endeavor she was doomed to fail. In the heavy silence of the room, interrupted only by the distant rumblings of thunder outside and the occasional muted vibrations of the secretary's cell phone, Iris felt thorny tendrils of doubt creeping into her mind.

Several minutes passed and thunder rolled again, and still the secretary had done nothing but play with her phone while absently twisting a lock of loosely curled hair. Iris took a long, deep breath, closing her eyes and recalling the brief series of events that had brought her here. *God help me*, she prayed, trying to remind herself she wasn't alone. She did as she had been taught, clearing her conscious thoughts for a moment and letting spiritual feeling replace them. She reflected on what Auraltiferys had taught her; she recalled the magical amulet around her neck; she focused on the sensation of God's power as magic within herself, and it calmed her. Eventually opening her eyes, she finally heard the girl at the desk exhale with theatrical irritation as she shifted in her seat and pressed the intercom button.

"Mr. Drake? There's a woman here to see you..." She trailed off, released the speaker button, and shot Iris a pointed stare. "I'm sorry," she asked blandly, "what was your name again?"

Oh, please, Iris scoffed internally at the girl's immaturity. *What a joke.* "Iris Wakefield," she replied simply.

"Iris Wakefield for you, Mr. Drake," the girl finished into the speaker, in an overdone and synthetically chipper tone.

"Excellent," came the reply from the other end of the call. "Send her back, please. Thank you, Yvette." The familiar, richly mellifluous voice of Loomis Drake through the speaker was somehow completely unnerving now and not at all enticing, though Iris had all but melted upon first hearing it only a few weeks ago.

Yvette's voice reverted to its contemptuous monotone as she told Iris she could now see Mr. Drake. She remained seated as she indicated with an indifferent gesture that Iris should walk down the hallway behind her.

Iris pondered for an instant why she should be fearful now. This was demon versus demon, a fair fight. Yet her stomach sank heavily inside her, like a stone covered in swarming ants, and her thoughts slipped instinctively into prayer as she stood and began moving toward Loomis's office. She desperately hoped he couldn't hear her mind's pleading invocation: *Saint Michael the Archangel, defend us in battle; be our protector against the wickedness and snares of the devil...*

As she approached the next room, unsure whether she was truly ready to stand face to face with a fallen angel, one of the heavy doors was pulled open from the inside, held for her by the unarguably handsome and impeccably dressed Loomis Drake. He wore the slacks and vest of a well-tailored, dark gray three-piece suit and a lavender-colored dress shirt with a matching necktie, dimpled perfectly at the knot. Iris was no fashion maven, but even she recognized that Loomis's attire had probably cost him more than she had paid for her first car. His thick, dark hair was perfectly styled, slicked back from a stately forehead, and his goatee was expertly groomed, complementing his razor-sharp jawline and high, sculpted cheekbones to an almost painfully beautiful degree. Yes...he was even more attractive in person than on camera, though Iris hated to admit it, and he smiled in warm greeting as he extended his left arm toward the expanse of his *sanctum sanctorum*, bidding her to enter.

"Dr. Wakefield, how wonderful to make your acquaintance," he said pleasantly as he shut the door behind her and then offered her his right hand. She forced herself to look directly into his dark, deep-set eyes as she shook his hand with as firm and confident a grip as she could muster. She was simultaneously enchanted and sickened by his presence, but she managed a smile.

"Likewise, Mr. Drake," she answered, trying to ignore her sudden sense of déjà vu, a vague yet profound impression of having met him before. Replacing her smile with a somber gravitas, she added, "I appreciate your agreeing again to see me. I regret what happened the last time."

Loomis sighed and cast his eyes toward the floor momentarily. "Yes," he agreed, "it was truly heartbreaking to learn of the crash. A devastating tragedy. I consider all my employees as my family, so the losses were quite personal. And, naturally, I had assumed the worst for you as well." He placed a gentle hand on Iris's back and directed her toward the leather-clad seating area in front of his desk. She could smell the faint but appealing scent of his cologne—a masculine, woody, bergamot-toned fragrance she recognized as Montblanc Legend. She had smelled it once in a fragrance sample mailout and had liked it ever since. She wondered if that was a perverse coincidence or if, much more alarmingly, Loomis had somehow known this obscure fact about her and accessorized himself specifically for the occasion. "You haven't any idea how pleased I was to learn you weren't found among the wreckage," he continued. "I had fervently hoped you had survived, and I was so relieved to hear from you afterward."

Iris smiled understandingly as she set down her purse and coat and then took a seat beside them on the leather sofa. "It was a miracle. I don't recall much about the actual incident," she lied, "but I know I was terrified. I'm lucky to be alive."

Loomis had walked behind his desk and now stood there, giving Iris his undivided attention. "Certainly you must have been afraid," he acknowledged, "but you survived—in a cold, mountainous wilderness, no less! That speaks volumes of your resourcefulness and indomitable will. Attractive qualities, if I may be so bold." His eyes were locked with hers in a focused, probing stare, and Iris found it most disconcerting.

"Well, I've seen lots of action movies in my lifetime," she joked casually, brushing off his last comment. For now, on a human level, she was just a job candidate, and she couldn't let him change the game. Though she chuckled with mock nervousness at her own statement, just as a job candidate might do, her insouciant reply actually made her feel more comfortable. Loomis had assaulted her with a penetrating gaze and an insincere compliment, and she hadn't fallen for it. Moreover, his demeanor seemed to suggest he was yet unaware of her recently acquired knowledge of her true self, and that bolstered her confidence. She had the element of surprise. Although, she supposed cautiously, he could simply be toying with her.

If he was disappointed in her response to his compliment, he didn't show it. He simply chuckled and said in reply, "I suppose one might learn some survival tips that way, but I yet believe the majority of the credit must go to you." He turned and walked a few steps toward the bar along the wall. "Would you care for anything to drink?" he asked courteously. "We'll get down to business in just a moment, but I simply *must* indulge in my morning doppio before any shoptalk." He laughed quietly in feigned self-ridicule as he began operating a large, copper espresso machine, sitting among fancy accoutrements and an extensive selection of high-quality liquors. "I should be ashamed to admit it," he commented, "but espresso is perhaps my greatest vice." At that, he turned to Iris and smiled.

Greatest vice, indeed, she thought. Aloud, she replied with a small grin, "It may be mine as well. But I guess if that is our greatest vice, we're getting along more agreeably than some."

"That is certainly true," Loomis agreed. He had filled two demitasse cups and now brought them to his desk on a silver serving tray. He handed one cup and saucer to Iris, gave a genteel nod of his head in response to her thanks, then sat behind his desk with his espresso.

"I hope you enjoy it," he said, leaning back in his chair with casual grace. "I import the beans from Nicaragua. In my humble opinion, there is no better coffee to be found."

Judging by the aroma alone, Iris estimated he was probably right on that point. A cautious sip confirmed it. She lost herself momentarily in the drink's chocolatey and fruity undertones. It really was wonderful. And this was such an exquisite office. *I could get used to this,* she mused. *All the money in the world, all the best of everything...* She glanced again at her host, forgetting why she had formulated such an intensely negative opinion of him in the first place. Here in this lovely room, in this comfortable moment, he was a charismatic, charming, absolutely gorgeous man with perfect manners, refined taste, and a delightfully sultry aura. *I can have this, too. Loomis and I are no different. All he has, I deserve even more...* She suddenly realized her breathing had quickened. The man she had labeled her enemy sat across from her, elegantly sipping his espresso...and she wanted him. It wasn't only the thoughts of fortune and power enticing her...it was *him*. Never before had she found herself so completely and lecherously attracted to any man. There was palpable heat simmering under her skin, and she could feel her cheeks coloring, her blood flowing more freely now than if she had just taken the stairs up to this office. There was a most disturbing lustfulness coursing through her veins.

"Are you all right, Iris?" Loomis asked. He looked at her—into her—with the same intrusive, searching, and suggestive eyes he had turned on her before. His expression was one of slight concern, but there was an almost undetectable smirk on his lips that made Iris sure he knew exactly what he was doing, whatever that was. "Your silence makes me wonder whether the espresso failed to meet your expectations," he finished.

Iris swallowed hard and tried to slow her breathing as imperceptibly as she could. "Oh, it's wonderful; never had better," she said in a weak voice, as her inner thoughts cried in astonishment and self-loathing. *Dear Jesus, how did this happen? How the hell has he done this to me? Why am I so weak?* The warm, rich atmosphere of this room; the pleasing aroma and taste of the coffee; the melodic, soothing voice of Loomis Drake; his provocative demeanor and tangible sensuality, heightened by that intriguing fragrance she had always so enjoyed on a man...no wonder she was suddenly so enraptured. This place was a sensory paradise, a veritable temple of sublime hedonism. *God help me*, she thought again, hoping in vain that the booming voice of God might at once come careening into her mind and heart to set her straight. But, as was always the case, there seemed to be no voice at all. She *had* to break whatever spell she was under, whether the spell was literal or metaphorical. She had to remember why she was here, what she was fighting. But the way she had been so easily entranced by Loomis...she worried it was her demonic nature simply making itself known as it never had before. Maybe evil was what she wanted, after all.

Taking a deep breath, Iris set the empty cup on the small wooden table near the couch and raised her hand toward her neck, intending to remove her scarf, which had become unbearably hot.

Her fingertips found the heavy amulet hidden underneath, and she abruptly recalled what she had come here to do. She had come here to make a statement, to show Loomis she had learned her true identity, to reveal to him that his plans for his magical shadow-demon were about to be dashed, to prove to him she would refuse to become a pawn in his game of conquest over Hell and Earth and would instead become an obstacle he had never anticipated. She was here for the good of all humanity, yes, but for herself, too—she had recognized how Loomis had already tried to bait her, and she didn't like it. No doubt he had expected her to be an easy mark; his suggestive behavior already had proven he was completely sure of his ability to seduce her, and that was completely infuriating. No one had ever seduced her, and she wasn't about to let some impossibly handsome, elitist multibillionaire (who likely had a long history of too-easy success in seduction) be the first to do it, demonic or not. Reflecting on all this in the instant her hand brushed against the spellbound medallion, Iris felt her thoughts clearing, the fog of temptation gradually lifting as she recalled the advantageous position she currently held over Loomis. She was something he needed if he wanted his malicious plans to know success, but she would not be as easily taken as he had thought she might. The revelation would almost certainly ruin his whole day, and Iris enjoyed that thought as she forced her eyes back to her would-be employer, who was staring at her with startling intensity.

"It's warm in here," she commented, her hand still on the scarf. She unwrapped it slowly, then calmly folded it and laid it on top of her coat next to her. "I think I over-layered," she explained sweetly, adopting a much more relaxed posture as she leaned back into the sofa and crossed one leg over the other. "The rainy weather had me convinced I would be cold all day."

Loomis's gaze dropped almost immediately to the bronze shield medallion now exposed on Iris's chest. *Moth to the flame*, she noted with relief. Auraltiferys had been right—Loomis wanted the relic as soon as he saw it. His expression was stoically neutral but for the utter disbelief that flashed across his face before he quickly recovered himself and cleared his throat.

"That's a fascinating piece of jewelry," he said, pretending to squint so he would need a closer look. His confident bearing had shifted to a carefully hidden, mild agitation. To anyone else, the change would likely have gone unnoticed, but Iris could sense the subtle difference.

"This old thing?" she replied, looking down at the amulet with intentional indifference, lightly picking it up and then letting it drop to her chest again as Loomis rose from his chair and approached her. "I found this at a little vintage store in Boston when I was there for an internship years ago," she continued, wondering if Loomis had any idea she was lying. It didn't appear he did, and she was almost disappointed he wasn't demonstrating the vast intelligence she had been told he held. Surely he wasn't so dumb as to fall for this weak story; more likely, his sudden greedy, all-consuming desire for the relic had him believing what he wanted to believe—that Iris could not possibly have any idea of the true value of such an item. "I loved the look of it, but I think it's just a cheap piece of old costume jewelry," Iris finished, looking up with a self-deprecating grin at Loomis, who was now standing very close to where she was sitting.

He seemed to have regained his characteristic swagger. The unmistakable assurance had returned, and as a dazzling white smile accentuated his already perfect features, he gently placed a hand on Iris's crossed leg and lowered himself onto the couch, very close beside her. Iris wanted to be disturbed by it, but, in fact—damn her—she rather liked it.

"I have quite an eye for these things," he said, his voice now as entrancing as ever. *God, he smells good,* Iris thought as she felt her heart beating faster. "I don't believe this is a cheap costume piece at all," he continued, as his hand slid ever so slightly higher on Iris's thigh. *For the love of God, just reach for it already*, Iris screamed internally, suddenly worried her human nature would be too weak to overcome the temptation Loomis was so tantalizingly throwing at her. Thank God she hadn't worn a skirt today. She *really* wanted to feel him...in a very bad way.

"In fact," Loomis went on, "I believe this is an extremely rare and valuable artifact—"

Finally, his other hand reached for the amulet, subtly brushing Iris's chest as it did so. The electric sensation she felt from his touch was quickly subdued by the visceral reaction he displayed the second he touched the necklace. He inhaled sharply and yanked his hand away with blinding speed, instantly rising to his feet and taking a step away. He stared unblinkingly at Iris with a horrifying rage burning in his eyes. The effects of the protective spell had instantly revealed the truth—he now knew Iris knew what she was, and he knew she had deceived him.

Iris remained still, even as Loomis had been so forcefully repulsed by the amulet. She sat, legs crossed, looking directly into the eyes of a demon and feeling no fear. "What's the matter, Mr. Drake?" she asked in a syrupy voice, thoroughly enjoying the opportunity to mock him.

Loomis said nothing. He stood fully erect, his chest visibly rising and falling with quick, angry breaths. He had a twitch in his upper lip, like a wolf preparing to bare its teeth, and his skin had a dewy luster of perspiration forming on it. Veins throbbed noticeably in his neck and temples. Somehow, the sky outside had grown darker, and the thunder was now closer and louder, rumbling just outside the office's expansive windows. The lights in the room flickered slightly, and tension hung in the air like a guillotine blade about to fall, suspended only by the unseen hand of fate. Both demons had their human eyes fixated on those of the other, locked in an invisible power struggle. Iris was now seeing Loomis as she never could have before, with a perception that was completely new to her, and she could recognize the profound evil he was capable of. She couldn't know what he was seeing in her, but his gaze was a frightening and calculating one, and, for an instant, she feared she may have made an awful mistake in having come here.

After what seemed like a long time, Loomis broke the onerous silence, delivering his words in a deep, bone-chilling, otherworldly hiss. He spoke ancient Aramaic, but Iris inexplicably understood him: "My power will consume you."

Iris stood slowly and very calmly picked up her scarf and coat and purse, conscious of Loomis's eyes and unmitigated hatred still upon her. She turned her back on him and walked a few paces toward the door before turning again to face him, staring directly into him and responding in kind, her own voice now a low, foreign, beastly snarl coming from somewhere unknown within her, speaking also in Aramaic: "Your power is illusion. Thanks be to God."

At her words, Loomis's countenance darkened into a cold, silent, palpable fury. Only in her mind did Iris hear the loud, feral groan that could only have come from him. The overhead lights suddenly flashed and then shattered with a piercing echo, sending shards of glass onto the thick carpet and leaving the room in almost complete darkness. Illuminated by only the muted, overcast daylight and the sporadic bolts of lightning outside the windows, the shadowy figure of Loomis Drake became for just an instant to Iris's perception a giant monstrosity, an aberrant and frightful hybrid of a goat and a serpent, with hideous yellow-brown eyes that perforated the murky, gray dimness of the office. In the blink of an eye, he appeared again in his human form, nothing more than an attractive, well-dressed man. Iris met his eyes a final time, ignoring the seething detestation in them, then she turned and walked coolly through the door, closing it softly behind her.

***

It was a strange sensation as Iris left the umbral malevolence of Loomis's office. The bright light of the hallway and waiting area was somehow both comforting and unnerving. She felt safer in the light, but she also felt alarmingly exposed by it. As she proceeded toward the front, however, reflecting on the scene that had just transpired, she very quickly lost her momentary anxiety. She had tricked Loomis so well that he had literally lost control of himself, even if only for a split second. It felt good to have that kind of sway over him, or over anyone, really. A tiny smirk crossed her lips as she approached the front desk, now unabashedly pleased with herself for having so artfully emasculated Loomis Drake.

She entered the waiting area and immediately slipped back into reality upon seeing Yvette sitting at the front desk. *What do I do with her?* she asked herself. *I just pissed off a demon back there...he could take his anger out on her. Then again, maybe she deserves it.*

Her internal conflict was short-lived; she knew what her decision would be. She could imagine Auraltiferys speaking to her, could practically hear her parents and her sweet grandmother in her heart, all telling her to do what was right. So she glanced at Yvette, took a deep breath, and pondered what words might actually save this girl from the snare of evil that occupied the huge office behind her.

"Finished so soon?" Yvette asked before Iris could speak. "That didn't take long," she commented snarkily, facing Iris with a slight sneer.

"Yes, I'm finished," Iris replied, "and you need to listen to me. It isn't safe for you here. Loomis Drake is...a very dangerous man."

"Hmph!" Yvette snorted, with an expression of both contempt and confusion. "He isn't dangerous!" she exclaimed with great indignation. "I've never known a better man."

Iris sighed heavily, then answered her, "No, Yvette, you *really* don't understand, and you shouldn't tempt fate. He isn't the man you think he is. He got really angry at me just now, and I would hate for him to take that out on you."

With Iris having now bad-mouthed her object of affection (or lust, or whatever her feeling toward Loomis was), Yvette became visibly upset. "Don't talk about him like that!" she said forcefully, eyes blazing. "You don't know him like I do! You'll *never* know him like I do." There was a biting acidity in her words.

Shaking her head, Iris made one last attempt to convince the unsuspecting secretary. "It isn't safe for you to be here," she repeated. "You should leave, right now." She was looking directly into Yvette's eyes as she spoke, with grave sincerity she could see the girl almost believed, but Loomis's hold on her was simply too strong. Yvette stood up and moved closer to Iris before replying.

"*You* should leave," she hissed. "Mr. Drake doesn't need you, anyway. He wouldn't *want* you. So take your cheap bag and your frumpy outfit and just go. The elevator's that way, bitch." She tilted her head slightly, put on a sarcastic, mocking smile, and batted her long false eyelashes as she finished speaking.

Iris said nothing, but she shot Yvette a glare so black and hateful that the girl instinctively backed away from her. After a brief moment of sinister silence, Iris turned and walked to the elevator, taking her cheap bag and frumpy outfit with her.

***

Loomis had remained rooted in place for a long moment after Iris had so nonchalantly turned her back on him and closed the door. His anger had not subsided. His chest was still heaving, his breaths coming in shuddering, hissing pulses as his eyes and skin burned with actual physical heat brought on by the abysmal hatred that had engulfed him. He was sweating profusely now, and his bloodshot eyes were seeing nothing but red, even in the dim light coming through the windows. Finally, he clenched his teeth and tensed every muscle in his body, then opened his mouth and screamed in an animalistic bellow. He could make as much noise as he wanted to—that was exactly why he had had this office soundproofed, and there was no one on this floor but him and that slutty, dumb little secretary, anyway. With quick, long strides, he moved toward the bar and violently shoved the liquor bottles and glasses and espresso machine to the floor. He then picked up a side table and threw it into the opposite wall. A leather chair followed, dragging a Rembrandt to the floor with it. The crashing sounds emanating from his path of destruction helped calm his infernal rage, but they did nothing to abate the heat under his skin. He paused and surveyed the damage he had caused, breathing heavily. Physical destruction was one of the few human impulses that sometimes appealed to him, and, right now, it was well warranted.

After a moment, he collected his thoughts and replayed in his mind what had just transpired with Iris. He hadn't known she had learned her true identity. He had written off her survival of the plane crash as a "miracle" that happened to benefit him, but obviously something far more profound had occurred, and he hadn't recognized it until too late. Not only had Iris become aware of what she was; she had also obtained a relic and the resources and knowledge needed to place a protective spell on it, which could only mean she would be learning and growing stronger with each passing day. Nothing about this had gone according to his plan; Iris had come to his office in arrogance simply to mock him, and he despised her for it. *I will make her pay*, he thought. *Her suffering at my hand will be so great, even her father in Hell, the so-called Prince of Darkness himself, will cry for her.*

Admittedly, he would have to recalculate his next moves. He

had believed this exchange with Iris would be a simple one—and it would have been, had he known the full truth. But perhaps this was for the best. He could have hurt her. He could have done so many titillatingly vicious things to her. She couldn't possibly have discovered the true depths of her magical powers or her demonic knowledge in so short a time; he could have given her an indescribably painful and traumatizing display of *real* demonic power, and she would have been completely at his mercy. Instead, however, he had conscientiously made the most sensible and pragmatic move, allowing Iris to have this vapid little victory so he could regroup and continue his war. Iris had now shown all her cards, and in doing so, she had lost every future opportunity to hide from him. He would have his revenge. Unfortunately, confidence in ultimate vengeance did nothing to assuage his current passion of loathing. *How did I allow her to delude me?* His internal questioning reignited his anger. He reached toward his neck and roughly removed his tie, tossing it to the floor. He then ripped off the vest and the dress shirt he wore, scattering buttons as he strode toward his desk and shoved the intercom key on the phone.

"Yvette, get in here *now*," he said harshly. He ran his hands through his hair, firmly scratching his scalp in doing so, and then he stood there in his dark, disheveled office, beautiful and bare-chested, waiting for the prompt entry of the harlot who couldn't resist him.

As expected, Yvette entered almost immediately, and though she was clearly puzzled by the state of his office, she was soon utterly distracted and enthralled by his shirtless figure, glistening with sweat and radiating a wild, lascivious, bestial magnetism.

"Mr. Drake, what happened here?" she asked in an intentionally ditzy tone, trying so hard to be cute. Why did she bother to speak, the dumb bitch? It was nothing but an annoyance. He wouldn't put up with that now.

He advanced to where she stood, surprising her with his swiftness, and he noted the lustful little gleam in her eyes just before he seized her arm. She gasped at the strength of his grip, and suddenly the desire in her eyes turned to apprehension. He pulled her viciously toward himself, then turned and shoved her toward his desk. She stumbled off of her impractically high stiletto heels, twisting an ankle and falling into the table beside the sofa, grabbing it to prevent herself from going all the way to the floor.

"Mr. Drake, you're hurting me!" she whined as she pulled herself up.

That's the point, he thought sardonically as he once again approached her. He slapped her, his signet ring scratching her face and prompting an attempt to flee. But there was nowhere for her to go; he had backed her right up against his desk.

He looked down at her, pleased to see that her unease had become outright fear. He pushed her into the side of the desk, holding her in place with his legs, and he used both hands to wrench open the front of her tight black dress. His nails cut her chest as he did so, and the tiny droplet of blood that formed in its deepest part was most provocative. He ripped the dress the rest of the way so that it hung completely open. As he had come to expect, the whore was wearing no panties, so he simply clutched her bra between the cups and pulled it apart, too.

"Stop, Mr. Drake! Stop!" Yvette cried, tears rolling down her cheeks and small, feminine hands desperately trying to push him away. With a sneering grin on his face, Loomis picked her up by the hips and shoved her body down onto the desktop with a solid thud. He enjoyed the way her head whipped when it hit, so he leaned over, took her by the shoulders, and brutally pounded her into the desk a few more times.

Dazed by the blows to her skull, Yvette moaned softly, writhing feebly on the desk as Loomis removed his belt and unzipped his pants. He had to admit, he might actually be enjoying himself this time.

"No! Please...stop..." Yvette sobbed, still struggling ineffectually to extricate herself from his grasp. Funny, she had never before asked him to stop. She had always relished even the *thought* of having him inside her. Now the bitch was fighting him, and it was altogether amusing—and arousing. He yanked her thighs farther apart and drove himself into her, forcing a terrified and pained scream to emanate from her plump lips. Why should she scream now? She had so gladly taken him time and time again, in complete disregard for her supposed human dignity. The time had finally come for her to regret it.

Yvette was now sniveling uncontrollably, tears flooding out of her eyes and snot dripping from her nose, and her useless, pleading wails for help were inconceivably irritating. Did she really think he would stop? Did she really believe anyone could hear her? Stupid, pathetic fool. Hers was now the *true* face of humanity—weak and incompetent; ignorantly blissful and unthinking; pleased to wallow in guilty pleasures for a lifetime, then crying helplessly for mercy just as the executioner prepared to hurl them into final obscurity. Loomis felt his ire intensifying again as he stared at this worthless trash beneath him, recalling how he had just been tricked by the insufferable Iris Halcyon Wakefield—a woman, disgustingly corrupted by this stain of humanity and yet his equal in divinity. *Fuck her!* She had come here to his private office for no reason but to put his ignorance on display for him, to mock him, to evince for him her divine power and lord it over him...*FUCK HER, the loathsome cunt!*

In his redoubled anger, Loomis could no longer stand the sound of Yvette's infantile whimpering. He reached down and hit her face again, this time bloodying her nose and eliciting another loud and mournful cry.

"Stop...stop..." Yvette was now having significant difficulty formulating any actual words between her tearful, convulsive breaths. Loomis, still ruthlessly thrusting himself into her, now put a strong hand around her throat and started to squeeze. The previous terror in her face had been entertaining, but this new, ghastly panic in her expression was euphoric. He squeezed harder and felt a heightening of his pleasure as the tiny capillaries in her eyes began to burst. She shot her hands up to his, vainly attempting to claw his forearm and release his iron grip. How ridiculous and pitiable—her strength was nothing compared to his. Color was draining from her face and lips. Her coughing, sputtering gasps for air became less frequent and then stopped altogether as he further tightened his fingers around her neck like a vise, his arm a steel cable. Finally, he watched Yvette's arms fall limply to her sides as she surrendered. He locked his gaze into the girl's bloody eyes as he continued his merciless pounding between her legs, then, with acute, inhuman strength, he crushed her neck in his hand, reveling in the grotesque crunch of her cervical vertebrae as he watched the immaterial mortal life finally leave her. Amid his heaving breaths, he licked his lips and prolonged the stranglehold until the soft tissues in his hand became like pulp and blood welled up into the mouth of his victim.

His hands returned to the girl's hips, and he glared down at her with grim delight, allowing this profane vision to consume the mind and senses of his human body. How wonderfully rapturous this was, so thoroughly desecrating the image and likeness of God! Yes, some image *that* was—the pale, blood-stained face; the pulverized, bruised neck; the tanned legs spread wide for him. This was the race God had adopted and elevated to His right hand. Loomis laughed slowly and deeply in an alien baritone as he continued his depraved copulation, relishing the loose, rhythmic bouncing of the girl's breasts and the limp, bizarre movement of her lifeless head on its gelatinous, broken neck. What a pity...this was the most purely gratifying encounter the two of them had shared, and poor Yvette wasn't even present to experience it. Never mind; he would finish without her.

11

"I want that artifact found, and sooner rather than later," Marvin Whitakker squeaked as he took short, quick steps across the tiled floor of the lobby to meet the detectives at the door. He was a short, thin man, with unkempt, mousy brown hair, balding at the top, and a ridiculous mustache that made him look like a fair-toned Groucho Marx. The thick, round-rimmed frames of his eyeglasses heightened the resemblance. He wore an ill-fitting beige suit that appeared to have been slept in, and he had accessorized it with a bright red bow tie and a pair of red sneakers, one of which was on the verge of untying. Crane wasn't sure which part of the sloppy hipster outfit offended him most, but he was damn certain this was going to be a long, long day.

Marvin reached the detectives a second later, giving them no opportunity to speak. "Do you hear me, Detectives? I want the artifact found A-S-A-P," he reiterated. It sounded to Crane as though he were somehow projecting his voice through his long nose.

"Absolutely, we hear you, Mr. Whitakker," Crane replied, hoping he had successfully restrained any irritation in his voice. The guy had insisted on a face-to-face meeting at the museum to discuss the missing spearhead, even after Crane had assured him several times by phone that they had received all the information and photographs Whitakker had provided and were already looking into it, and then the pushy little twit had had the audacity to reschedule twice. Now, here he was, charging at the two detectives as though their presence was an unwelcome imposition and a waste of his time. Could he be any more of a jerk?

"It's *Doctor* Whitakker, if you please," the imp immediately demanded.

Yeah, whatever, Crane thought as he graciously responded, "Of course, *Doctor* Whitakker." What an arrogant little bastard.

"So what have you done vis-à-vis finding the stolen piece?" Marvin asked excitedly, blinking his eyes in rapid overabundance behind his glasses and somehow radiating the aura of an agitated chihuahua. *Who the hell talks like that?* Crane mused silently. *'Vis-à-vis'...what a stooge.* He was already beyond his patience threshold with this dweeb.

Crane cleared his throat and answered, "Well, Dr. Whitakker, to be perfectly honest, the investigation of Joshua Ellis's death is taking precedence over the missing spearhead. We haven't been able to rule out homicide." He noticed a cloud of disappointment descending onto Whitakker's face, and he was amused by it, though he was also shocked by the man's lack of concern for the deceased security guard.

Whitakker rubbed his hands together nervously and licked his lips several times under his bushy mustache, blinking excessively all the while. "That's simply not acceptable," he said. "I was told there was no evidence of any murder, so I see no reason to harp on that. Besides, it isn't as though you can do anything about his death. You can, however, find and return the missing artifact. We must move forward with what can still be done, rather than dwelling on things that cannot be undone."

Is this guy for real? Crane thought angrily. His expression must have shown his increasing rage, because Myron shot him a cautionary glance and replied to Marvin before he could.

"You understand, Doctor, we have an obligation to ensure the appropriate justice is served, in the event a crime was committed, and that's exactly what we're going to do," Banks stated authoritatively. This was the first time Marvin was hearing his voice, and Banks's brisk baritone clearly rattled him a bit. He seemed to take sudden notice of Myron's intimidating height and athletic build, and it gave him some pause.

Sinking further into the suit that was practically swallowing him, Marvin replied, "Yes, yes, of course; I understand. But *you* must understand my obligation is to this museum and the preservation of its exhibits, including the traveling exhibits, and I do not take my job as curator lightly. I don't want that spearhead lost forever because you two are hung up on the *possibility* of a homicide."

"We're going to do all we can, Doctor," Crane answered brusquely. It was time to take control from this pretentious dolt. "Why don't you take us through the exhibit and show us exactly where the spearhead was. We're going to have several questions."

"Very well," Marvin said, pivoting on the scuffed, white rubber heel of one red sneaker and leading the way to the museum's east wing. Crane glanced over at Banks with an eye roll as they followed the curator. Banks grinned slightly and shook his head in a silent reply. At least they had formulated the same negative opinion of this guy.

As they reached the entry room of the weapons exhibit, Crane slowed and then stopped. "Were these doors locked on the night of the incident?" he asked, indicating the east wing entry doors as he surveyed their handles and locks and frames with his eyes.

"No," Whitakker replied snappishly. "There should have been no need to lock them. The main entry doors are locked and secured by alarm. Fire exits are not accessible from the outside, and they are likewise monitored by an alarm system. All the exhibit display cases are locked. If I had any reason to doubt those security measures, I would have required these doors to be locked as well, but as it was, I believed I could trust the precautions we had in place. And that's why these doors weren't locked. But, believe me, we are already implementing new, stricter protocols." *Geez,* Crane thought as Marvin continued his excited rant, *I wasn't accusing you of anything; I just asked a simple question.*

Crane moved his attention from the doors and nodded his head toward the first exhibit room ahead. "All right," he said, "let's move on."

They walked into the cavemen room, and Crane felt a little pebble of anxiety drop into his stomach. It was daylight now, with no thunder or rain outside, which somehow assuaged the creepiness factor of the exhibit, but being back here brought that sickening vision of Joshua Ellis's ruined, blackened eyes to the forefront of his mind, and he could only hope he would be able to maintain the appropriate composure as this investigation continued. He wondered if Banks was feeling the same way. Obviously, Dr. Whitakker couldn't care less. He hadn't been forced to look into those God-awful eyes.

The detectives walked methodically along the periphery displays, then inspected the central display cases. After a few minutes, during which Dr. Whitakker stood with crossed arms and an impatient, tapping toe at the doorway to the next room, Crane addressed his partner, "See anything?" Banks shrugged and shook his head.

The trio proceeded into the next room, and the detectives continued their inspection as they followed the course of the exhibit. Whitakker, finally losing what little patience he had tried to show, interjected, "The spearhead was farther along, among the pre-Columbian tools. There's not a thing out of place besides the spearhead. I would know it immediately. You're wasting time."

Crane straightened up from the case he was studying and looked directly at Marvin with a dark scowl of final, decided irritation. He hoped the expression would say, *Piss me off one more time, dickhead, and you'll regret it.* Verbally, he said, "Do you want us to find the thing, or don't you? Let us do our jobs. We know what we're doing."

Marvin threw his palms up in an irenic sort of gesture, then turned away. *And stay quiet, dipshit,* Crane thought to himself. He and Banks, however, found nothing to argue the urchin's pompous statement of fact. There was, as best they could tell, nothing amiss. They finally reached the pre-Columbian section Marvin had referenced. The curator stood agitatedly near one particular display case and pointed.

"It was right here," he said emphatically. "Right here. This case was locked, and it was still locked the next morning. I'm the only one with the key."

Banks and Crane joined him at the display case and peered inside. There was, in fact, a small, blank space where the spearhead must have been, though its absence was not readily obvious to an impartial observer. This particular artifact had only a tiny identification placard within the case, and that was the only apparent evidence that a piece of history had once been sitting there.

"So the security guards don't have copies of display keys?" Banks asked as he and Crane circled the case slowly, surveying it in its entirety.

"Absolutely not!" Marvin exclaimed with reproachful-sounding horror. "This is my museum, and I hold myself personally responsible for its contents! Once items are catalogued and displayed, I allow no one any access to them. One simply cannot trust another."

"Is it possible someone might have taken your keys without your knowledge? Maybe copied them and replaced them before you noticed?" Crane suggested.

Marvin's eyes widened, bubbled even further by the heavy

prescription lenses of his Groucho glasses. "Are you *serious?*" he fumed. "What a ridiculous suggestion! I don't know how you run your own life, Detective, but I'm not the careless type who would leave keys to valuable items just lying around for anyone to take!"

Crane, thoroughly annoyed by the little insult Whitakker had managed to throw into his response, took a deep breath to soothe his anger and then answered, "I'm sure you're not careless, Doctor. You obviously run a tight ship here."

"Very tight," Marvin clarified sternly.

"Right," Crane continued, wondering how much longer he could refrain from punching this self-righteous cretin in his face. "I'm only asking if it was a possibility."

"It is not a possibility," Marvin replied decisively. "It is an *impossibility*. I keep my keys on my person at all times. If they were taken from me, I would know."

At all times? Crane wondered. He was tempted to ask, sarcastically, if that included periods of bathing or sleep, but, looking at Marvin's kooky appearance, he was afraid the answer would be an emphatic "yes."

Banks was leaning his face in close to the lock, scrutinizing it carefully. "I guess it could have been picked, but I don't see any evidence of it," he stated, standing up. "That lock looks new, not even worn from use. I don't see any scratching or anything."

"It is new," Marvin said. "The pieces in this exhibit were amassed by a group of the best historians around the world, and the displays were created by artists from the notable Madame Tussauds. This exhibit is extravagant in cost and spares no expense. It is funded by the very deep pockets of highly educated individuals. Do you think such great minds would overlook simple security measures? You think they would send these valuable assets across the globe with the same locks, so that everyone with a key in one city could just waltz over to the next location and take what they want?" His voice was excited, again, and full of condescension. He scoffed loudly, sending a tiny spray of droplets from beneath his mustache, then continued, "These cases have their locks replaced each time the exhibit changes venues."

Banks stared down at Whitakker as he rattled off his high-pitched tirade, with abundant displeasure evident in his eyes. Crane hoped his partner wasn't about to come completely unhinged, and he trusted Myron's composure with unruly interviewees, but he had to admit there was one corner of his mind that wanted to see Dr. Marvin Whitakker get bitch-slapped. In this case, it would almost be worth the paperwork.

"Anyway," Banks continued drably after Marvin's outburst, "we'll get the techs back out here to check for prints and inspect the lock again. Maybe something will turn up."

"Well, I don't want to tell you how to do your job," Marvin replied, "but have you reviewed the security footage? We have a dozen cameras throughout this exhibit alone, running twenty-four seven. We're fortunate we had the resources to install such measures, and I would very much hope you intend to avail yourselves of the information they can provide."

Crane answered him, sharply, "Of course we're checking the footage. We pulled digital copies of the recordings for the entire day and until the time we left the museum after our initial response. Unfortunately, it hasn't shown us anything."

"Well, what do you mean, it hasn't shown you anything?" Marvin scolded. "It shows you everything that happened here. Did you even look at the footage, or are you simply trying to placate me with a rote response?"

"Apparently there was a malfunction with the recording at the time of Joshua Ellis's death. The footage at that time was pixelated and grainy. We can't see anything for several seconds, and the techs haven't found any out-of-the-usual occurrences elsewhere," Crane replied, wishing he could instead simply roll his eyes at the obnoxious curator and leave this place. *Should have retired last year, damn it.*

"And you looked at the footage for this room? For *this* room?" Marvin whined again, accusatorily. "Or have you focused only on where the guard died?"

Crane, exasperated and now willing to show it, sighed and answered, as respectfully as he still could, "Listen, Doctor. We focused first on the potential homicide, and we are still focused primarily on that potential homicide, but, yes, we have reviewed the footage for this room, and I'm telling you, there is no evidence of anything unusual. We even re-reviewed the footage when you notified us the spearhead was missing. So unless the thing was taken sometime after our initial investigation here, there's no evidence of it." He felt his eyebrows scrunched tightly together, but he didn't care. What were a few more wrinkles going to hurt? If this one interview didn't kill him, the incessant, subsequent follow-up harassment from this egotistical little bastard almost certainly would, especially if they couldn't find his damn spearhead.

"We have techs working on the footage," Banks offered helpfully, obviously hoping to assist Crane in maintaining diplomacy. They both recognized they were on edge and dealing with an exhausting and unpleasant individual. Crane was particularly grateful for his partner in times like this—it was good to have someone he trusted watching his back and helping him stay in line. If not for Banks, he probably would have lost his temper with someone a long time ago, and he could have kissed his job goodbye.

"They're trying to salvage that portion that was corrupted," Banks continued smoothly, "and it might show us something useful, for both our potential homicide investigation and the theft. Detective Crane and I will review everything again as well. We'll focus on this area."

"See that you do," Marvin replied.

Fucking prick, Crane's internal voice exploded.

"And what about the other guard?" Marvin continued. "The one who was also on duty that night. Have you questioned him?"

Crane narrowed his eyes involuntarily at the curator's unfriendly query, which obviously held far more contempt than curiosity. The suggestion that he and Banks would have omitted such a basic aspect of an investigation was an outrage, and Crane could feel his blood pressure skyrocketing even as he forced himself to provide a levelheaded reply to Whitakker. "The other guard was taken to the hospital on the night of the incident, before we left," he said rigidly. "He was too upset for questioning then, and his doctors only cleared him for visitors late yesterday. We'll speak with him later, but, frankly, we don't expect him to have much more to add than what he had managed to share with the first responders."

Marvin's face was a portrait of utter disappointment and derisive repulsion. "Oh, I *certainly* understand, Detectives," he quipped with melodramatic sarcasm, driving his nasal voice even higher. "You *must* be sensitive to the feelings of your suspects!"

Crane blurted out, louder than he intended, "The man *isn't* a suspect! *Your* video footage proves he was in the security office just like he was supposed to be, until he heard a noise and found Joshua Ellis dead. He went right back to the office and called the police!"

"Well," Marvin rejoined, "you can't mark him off the list of suspects if you haven't even questioned him." His voice was so low that the remark almost sounded more like an under-the-breath insult than a reply to Crane's words.

"Listen to me, you jackass," Crane shouted unthinkingly. "There is no list of suspects right now, and even if there was one, the other guard wouldn't be on it! But I'll tell you who might damn well be on it: *You*, Doctor Marvin! *You* would be at the top of my damn list!" Crane felt his fists clenching inside the pockets of his jacket, and he was shocked by his own unintentional eruption. *Christ, I'll get reamed big-time for this one*, he thought with frustration.

Banks immediately stepped closer to Crane and put a calming hand on his shoulder, gently pushing him away from Marvin and placing himself strategically between them. "Easy, man," he said quietly. Marvin was already bleating out his great displeasure at Crane's behavior, lamenting his offended ego and threatening to call Crane's superiors and have him fired at once.

Banks apologized for the blowup and tried to calm Marvin, assuring him he was on no suspect list right now and adding that he and Crane had been working long hours on this case already and were admittedly a bit tense. Marvin was appeased slightly, or perhaps he was simply afraid to continue his ranting with Banks standing closer to him. Crane, meanwhile, had stepped several paces off to the side so he could breathe and mentally kick himself for his tantrum. After a brief minute, Banks glanced over at him, and Crane gave him a brusque nod to let him know he had cooled down enough to avoid further confrontation, at least for now.

Addressing Whitakker again, Banks suggested amiably, "Why don't you tell us what we need to know about the spearhead?" He opened his small notebook to write down pertinent information, which seemed to comfort the academically minded doctor.

"It is a pre-Columbian artifact," Marvin answered eagerly, "possibly from the Great Lakes region of North America. Its age is estimated at possibly around three thousand years. It is a simple, heavy copper spear point, but it is notable for its engravings, the meanings of which are unknown. At that time, such detailed decoration would have been exceedingly difficult and almost unheard of for something intended as a tool. It may have been decorative or ceremonial, although that is purely my conjecture." With his attention focused on the history of the piece, Whitakker was far less annoying. He obviously had a passion for his work.

"So what's the value?" Banks asked. "I mean, monetarily speaking. Is it one of the more valuable pieces in this exhibit?"

"Oh, no," Marvin replied, with a hint of sadness. "That piece, however remarkable, is actually among the least valuable items in this grouping." He had clasped his hands together and was absent-mindedly tapping his thumbs together. His eyelids, Crane noticed, had not stopped their infernal blinkfest. *If I could work my abs the way this guy works those eyelids, I'd have a six-pack*, he mused. Marvin continued, "The insured value on the spearhead is twelve hundred dollars. We have permanent fine art pieces here appraised at much higher values than that. Historically, the piece is interesting but fairly irrelevant by most standards. Personally, I disagree. I think the markings alone are cause for further study and could in fact shed a whole new light on pre-Columbian cultures, for North America and perhaps even South America, too!" The curator sighed dramatically. "But," he finished wistfully, "I am not in the majority with such thinking."

Banks finished jotting some notes and then looked back at Crane. "You have anything else, Detective Crane?" His eyes held a note of warning, hinting that Crane better not throw another fit.

"Why do you think someone would have taken just this one piece, then, if it's one of the less significant items?" Crane asked, staring impassively at Whitakker. The grubby little man was obviously irked that Banks had allowed Crane to address him again after his unfortunate flare-up.

"I haven't a clue, Detective," Whitakker responded stiffly. "But I do know I'm responsible for it, and I want it found. I do hope you'll not cast this investigation aside because the spearhead is not a high-dollar item." There was accusation in his voice, and Crane didn't like it at all. He didn't appreciate the insinuation that he would tackle this investigation any differently than he would a big-time bank heist. He was a good detective and a good man, and he wouldn't treat this case or this jackass Dr. Whitakker with any less attention than he would give to his own family, even if he couldn't stand the guy. For Whitakker to suggest he would do otherwise was a real kick in the balls, and he wanted to strangle the bastard for it.

"Thanks, Doctor," Banks concluded hastily, sensing his partner's growing indignation at Marvin's last comment. "That's all we have for you right now. We're going to take another look where the guard was found, if you don't mind, then we'll be out of your way."

"Fine, fine," Whitakker said. "Do see that you keep me updated vis-à-vis the investigation, please, Detectives. The guard on duty will let you out the front doors when you are finished." He turned on his heel, weaved his way back through the exhibit, and then was gone. Crane had to fight an urge to punch the wax figure of an Aztec warrior standing behind him just to release his pent-up rage.

Banks waited for Marvin to leave, then he turned to Crane. "Damn, man," he said, a concerned expression on his face. "What the hell?"

"Sorry," Crane apologized gruffly. "I don't know; he just really got under my skin," he explained, shaking his head.

"Yeah, I know," Banks replied. "Mine, too. Let's just hope he finds something else to focus on besides filing complaints on you."

"Yup," Crane agreed. "Let's go see the other area and then get out of here." He wasn't looking forward to being back where the body had been found, but he and Banks really needed to take another look. They shouldn't have bothered; there was, as they had already seen, not a thing out of place. No scuff marks on the floor, no toppled wax displays, no knocked-down stanchions, no broken glass, no blood...no nothing. However Joshua Ellis had died, he hadn't fought back. He had been alive one minute and dead the next, and whatever had happened in between had left no evidence behind.

12

The email had appeared on Iris's monitor not more than thirty seconds before Matilda bustled in, eyes wide and puffy cheeks reddened either by anxiety or by the physical exertion required to stomp that quickly down the five yards of hallway from her cubicle to Iris's office. Iris hadn't even bothered to read the full message yet, because she could tell from the all-caps subject line of "MANDATORY EMPLOYEE MEETING" that it was only going to piss her off, and because she was busy with two highly technical projects the boss had promised to a bigwig client in a nearly impossible time frame.

"Girl," Matilda drawled breathily as she beached herself in the guest chair. "What do you think that meeting is all about?"

She was trying to sound curious and conspiratorial, as if Iris might have some secret knowledge about the goings-on amid the trio of Eden's owners—which in itself was ridiculous, as Iris prided herself on staying out of the loop when it came to useless office gossip or time-wasting bullshit—but her voice sounded more panicked than she probably wanted to let on.

Iris refrained from vocalizing her mind's initial response of, *Girl, I heard they're going to fire you in front of everyone.* "What meeting?" she replied instead, choosing rather bitchily to play dumb. That always stunned poor Matilda, who simply couldn't understand how Iris could care so little about office happenings.

"They just sent an email," Matilda said, scrunching her eyebrows together as she puckered her lips in a deprecating look that seemed to say, *Really, Iris, what would you ever do without me to keep you informed?*

"Who sent an email?" Iris asked drably, continuing to type the paragraph she had been working on before Matilda's arrival. It wouldn't deter Matilda, of course; she had tried it a thousand times, unsuccessfully. And ever since she had apologized to Matilda for her profanity-laced blowup after the first of her recent vacations, she had found it even more difficult to shoo the girl out of her office once the threshold had been broken.

Matilda ran her hands down her thighs and answered, "They called a mandatory meeting."

If Iris had been truly unaware of the email, Matilda's responses certainly would not have provided any elucidation. She caught herself just before rolling her eyes, then sighed and opened the troubling email to read it. It said very little, indicating only that everyone should report to the large conference room at eleven.

"So, what do you think that's about?" Matilda asked again. She began fumbling nervously with the scarf around her neck.

"I have no clue," Iris answered with a shrug. "I'm sure it's nothing to worry about."

"Oh," Matilda chuckled anxiously, "I'm not worried. I just wonder what it could be about."

Iris looked at her blankly, wondering what Matilda's point was in being here. She shook her head, shrugged again, and said simply, "I guess we'll have to wait and see."

Matilda rose from the chair and repositioned her scarf again, but not before Iris caught a glimpse of the grease spot on her sweater underneath it. "Well," she said, "I just hope it's nothing bad. You know the oilfield is down right now. I hope they're not, like, laying anyone off."

Iris sat silently for several seconds as Matilda stared at her, obviously waiting for some response, though there seemed to Iris to be no response required. "They're probably not laying anyone off," she finally replied, forcing herself to sound as sweet and comforting as she could stomach. "This company has tons of clientele outside the oil industry. I'm sure everything is fine."

"Yeah," Matilda said, sounding relieved, "you're probably right." She stepped to the doorway, then turned back to Iris and, tucking a strand of stringy hair behind her ear, added, "Well, girl, guess I'll see you at the meeting then."

"See you," Iris echoed with a curt nod as Matilda finally left. *God, how annoying.*

Iris sighed and leaned backward in her chair, stretching her arms overhead. That stupid email, followed by her stupid coworker, had broken her focus, which up to that point had been razor-sharp. Now, she found herself dreading the meeting and whatever inanity it would hold, and she had no desire to be in the office anymore. She stood up, grabbed her coffee mug, and walked to the kitchen, hoping there would be no one back there just waiting for another body so they could start another what's-that-email-about deliberation. Fortunately, she was alone as she refilled her cup with the office swill. The damn line at Starbucks had been too long this morning, and she had made the painful decision to forgo the wait, opting instead to head straight for work. She was regretting it now. As she watched the mostly transparent liquid fill her mug, her thoughts drifted back to the top-notch espresso she had enjoyed in Loomis's office. The drink had been remarkable, but even that paled in comparison to the empowerment she had felt that day. She smiled to herself as she reflected on it. Loomis had been so sure he was walking on easy street, so sure his plan to trick her or tempt her into aiding him in his evil mutiny was infallible. Iris had given him a strong dose of a different reality. It was a difficult pill for such an arrogant bastard to swallow, and Iris found amusement in that. Drinking the nearly tasteless coffee at Eden now, however, she wished she could just give in and condone Loomis's wrongdoings. Then she could work for him and enjoy that expensive espresso—and other luxurious little pleasures—whenever she wanted.

She grudgingly returned to her desk and worked for about an hour, losing track of time until movement outside her door caused her to look up. It was a few minutes before the meeting, and the lemmings had begun their mass migration to the conference room. Iris stood and stretched, then sighed wearily and headed toward her door, nearly striding directly into Matilda's ample form as she reached the walkway.

"Oh, sorry, girl," Matilda giggled nervously as Iris stopped abruptly. "Are you heading to the meeting?"

Where the hell else would I be going? Iris thought sarcastically. Vocally, she replied with simple affirmation. Matilda joined her on the brief walk to the conference room, following uncomfortably closely at Iris's heels like a dim-witted puppy. She was whispering something Iris couldn't fully hear, though it was obviously another round of the same musings the girl had rambled off just over an hour ago, rehashed in even more excited tones. Iris led the way into the conference room, where practically all of the twenty or so employees were already seated at the several long, thin tables set up in the style of a classroom. Eden's three co-owners were at the front of the room, two of them seated in tiny swivel chairs as the third, to whom everyone else seemed to kowtow, for reasons beyond Iris's comprehension, stood beside them, chest puffed out and arms crossed. He glanced at Iris as she and Matilda entered, then turned his attention to the mass already seated in front of him, looking over them with an expression of something like haughty approval, just like a misguided dictator who believed all the success of his subjects was somehow his doing. What a dick. The only chairs remaining were at the front table, so Iris seated herself there and then shoved her chair farther to the side to make room for Matilda beside her.

"Oh, my God," Matilda whispered sharply. Iris turned and saw Matilda's eyes focused on the other door leading into the meeting room, opposite the side where they had entered. It took no more than a quick glance to realize what had so startled Matilda, who had barely managed to maintain enough composure to sit down without breaking anything.

"Is that...Loomis Drake?" Matilda continued in her hasty murmur. "Oh, my God, I'm pretty sure that's Loomis Drake!"

The man had just entered the room, dressed in an exquisite black three-piece suit, with a blue dress shirt and matching tie, and he was conferring quietly with the owners as the other employees obliviously continued their conversations among themselves. Iris didn't look at him for long before she dropped her eyes to the table in front of her. This was an unforeseen and deleterious development. Loomis was not here by accident; he had come here for *her*. She had announced to him—tauntingly, no less—that she knew what she was and what Loomis was and what he was after, and now he had no reason to maintain any pretenses. He was pursuing his prey, and there was nowhere for her to run. Shit was real now. Really real. Iris suddenly regretted having ignored Auraltiferys's advice. She should never have approached Loomis. She wasn't ready to face him head-on like this; what had she been thinking? Now, it was too late to turn back. She felt sick to her stomach, but she would have to hide it. Or at least try to. Loomis would be all too aware of her fear, and she didn't want to give him that kind of gratification.

Matilda startled Iris out of her terrified stupor by tapping her leg excitedly under the table. "Oh, my goodness, girl," she said frantically, annoyingly poking Iris's thigh, "you should hook up with him! He is HOT! And rich! Oh, my God, he'd be perfect for you! I'd take him myself, except I'm married!" Matilda paused for a quick breath and a theatrical pout before adding, "But you can go after him! You HAVE to! Let me live vicariously through you!"

Heat flooded over Iris as she listened to Matilda's frenzied goading. She was horrified and embarrassed, which she would have been even if the subject of Matilda's flagrant objectification had been just a man instead of a demon. She imagined Loomis could hear every word Matilda was speaking, including her mispronunciation of "vicariously," and Iris found the thought unimaginably awful. The last thing she needed was to reinforce Loomis's already firm belief that he would soon seduce her. Then again, she considered, perhaps showing fear was even worse than that. She needed to collect her wits and remain poised, and she needed to protect in secrecy the vile truths about her and Loomis.

With a wan smile, Iris looked at Matilda and replied, "Oh, I don't know about that. I really don't think someone like that would be interested in me."

"Oh, come on!" Matilda admonished her, slapping Iris's arm lightly with the back of her hand. "You're pretty, and you're smart; I'm sure he'd be interested! And besides, how can you not at least *try*? Look how gorgeous he is!"

Iris sighed tensely. "He's...okay, I guess," she answered hesitantly. Matilda's eyes got even wider, and her face was flushed with both the excitement of seeing the celebrity Loomis Drake and the rampant disbelief that any woman would describe him as "okay."

"Iris!" Matilda shrieked in a hushed voice. "*Okay?* How can you even say that?"

Iris shrugged. "Fine, I guess he's good-looking or whatever," she whispered, hoping her own quiet tone would calm Matilda down. "But, anyway, it doesn't matter. Whatever he's here for, I'm sure he won't be here for long. Just let it go."

Matilda opened her mouth to retort, but the boss interrupted her by calling for everyone's attention. The room fell quiet, and Iris hazarded a glance at Loomis. He was staring directly at her, a subtle smile on his lips and profound malice veiled in the cool gaze of his deep-brown, amber-dappled eyes. *Damn, he really is gorgeous*, she thought to herself. *How depressing.*

"I'm sure you're all wondering why we've called this meeting," the boss was saying. "We have some news, and it's good news. It's going to mean great things for all of us and for the future of Eden."

Blah, blah, blah, Iris scoffed silently. This guy was so full of shit. Why couldn't he just get to the point? It didn't take a genius to figure out where this was going. A few pseudo-emotional sentences later, her suspicions were confirmed. Loomis Drake had bought the company, which sounded like a great boon to everyone except Iris, who very decidedly did not want to be under his ownership. She had a feeling, though, that she was no longer an at-will employee, and like it or not, she was here to stay. Even if she could quit and go elsewhere, Loomis would just follow her. There would be no escape.

Her boss had ceded the floor to Loomis, who was now addressing the room with his easy, confident charm. "I thank Mr. Ruiz for that kind introduction," he said, nodding in acknowledgment toward Iris's boss. It was odd hearing the man referred to by his last name; everyone at Eden simply called him Rafe. "Many of you know who I am, thanks to popular media," Loomis continued smoothly, "but I assure you, such attention is not my preference. I'm a businessman and no different from any of you. I value success, and I believe in rewarding hard work and loyal service. Eden is successful now because of all of you, and I don't wish to interrupt that. I seek only to grow what you have already begun here, and to more amply reward the work you are all doing. This arrangement is an excellent opportunity for all of us."

Iris interlaced her fingers and rested her hands on the table, staring down at them as Loomis gave his short speech. He went on to say he would be in and out of the Eden offices over the next several weeks, getting to know everyone and finding ways to improve what was already a wonderful place to work, though he made it clear that no one should be fearful of any sweeping changes. It was a convincing little appeal, and only Iris recognized it as a load of total crap. She sensed everyone else in the room was fully on board with Loomis Drake by the end of it. She halfway expected them all to line up after the meeting to kiss his shoes, the fools.

Loomis concluded his address and then humbly inclined his head to a brief round of applause from Eden's employees. "Wow," Matilda whispered to Iris amid the clapping, "he's so nice! And even with all the money he has! I bet he gives us all pay raises."

"Mm-hmm," Iris agreed sullenly, saying nothing more.

After a concluding statement from Rafe, the short meeting was officially adjourned, and people began to filter through the meeting room doors and back to their workspaces. Most of them probably wanted to introduce themselves to Loomis, but he remained up front with Eden's prior owners, chatting quietly, and no one wished to interrupt him. Ironically, none of these people had ever thought twice about interrupting a private conversation anywhere else in this office. Perhaps they were deterred by the intimidation of speaking to an impossibly good-looking billionaire, or perhaps the idiots believed an impossibly good-looking billionaire was simply more deserving of uninterrupted conversations.

Matilda walked out in front of Iris, glancing over at Loomis but then quickly averting her eyes to avoid being caught staring. Iris pointedly ignored him altogether, knowing she was probably running out of opportunities to do so. She reached the doorway only to be summoned by her boss.

"Iris," he called, "come over here." *What a tool*, Iris thought. So many ways he could have asked her to join his little powwow, and he settled for the most dickish option available. Cavemen probably had better manners.

She turned and stepped over to join them, Rafe lightly grabbing her upper arm and pulling her in as she approached. Iris wanted to slap his hand away and then perhaps magically light him on fire, but she refrained.

"This is Iris Wakefield," Rafe said, introducing her to Loomis. "She oversees most of our permitting projects and compliance contracts, and she's my prime moneymaker. Iris, this is Loomis Drake." He smiled stupidly, nodding toward Loomis as he addressed Iris. *'Prime moneymaker'?* she thought with disgust. *What the hell does he mean by that?* The jackass made it sound like he was her pimp.

Loomis very graciously extended his hand toward Iris. "Iris," he repeated with a broad, flawless smile, "it is a pleasure to meet you."

Iris quelled her urge to vomit as she gently shook his hand. "Likewise," she replied flatly. She hoped Rafe hadn't expected her to convey any sort of giddy servitude toward Loomis; if he had, he hadn't learned a single damn thing about her in the last eight years.

"If you have questions about anything—what we do, how we operate—Iris should be your go-to," Rafe announced, standing uncomfortably close to her. He was wearing way too much cologne today. *Probably wanted to impress the new owner*, Iris thought sardonically. "She's been here a long time," Rafe continued, "and she knows all the ins and outs."

"I have no doubt of that," Loomis responded, not removing his eyes from Iris's. She was sure the comment sounded creepy only to her.

Rafe slapped Iris on her upper back and said, "Why don't you show Mr. Drake around the office for me? I've got to run some errands and make some calls, but he'll want to get acclimated and get a feel for everything that goes on here on a daily basis."

Iris felt her jaw tense at the suggestion. Loomis's secret demonic nature aside, she still had no desire to play friendly hostess for Eden. She had actual work to do, even if the work was practically meaningless in the grand scheme of things. It was more worthwhile, at least, than Rafe's errands and phone calls, which, if the truth were known, were almost certainly personal and not in any way business related.

Loomis, however, very courteously replied, "Oh, I've taken quite enough of Iris's valuable time today." He smiled at her, then added, "I'll make my own rounds this afternoon, then perhaps tomorrow morning, Iris, you might be so kind as to spare me a few minutes."

This bastard appreciates my time more than Rafe does; I have to give him that much, Iris reflected. To Loomis, she simply replied, "Of course," with a tiny, forced smile.

"Well, that's fine," Rafe said, clearing his throat and deepening his voice to mask his disgruntlement at having had his suggestion knocked down. "You two can work all that out." He glanced at his smartwatch, slapped Iris on the back again, then excused himself and left the office.

Eden's other two former owners had disappeared from the room at some point during Rafe's brief introduction of Iris, leaving only her and her demonic adversary in the conference room. She stared at Loomis, unamused, for a few seconds, during which he stared right back at her, much more amused than she was.

"What do you expect to gain by being here?" she finally asked.

Loomis simply smiled in response. It was a beautiful expression, with only the subtlest hint of a threat hidden within it. After a vexatiously long silence, he finally said, in a low, furtively sinister voice, "I'll see you tomorrow, Iris."

With that, he turned on his heel and walked away, leaving Iris alone to ponder all the awful plans he must have prepared for her. She had often thought this office was hell; now, her cynical opinion had been made objectively true.

13

"Hey, girl," Matilda whined on the other end of their internal phone call. "Can you send Rafe a copy of that audit report for the chem plant in Houston? He said he's been waiting for it."

Iris held the phone to her ear with one hand while flipping the bird in Matilda's general direction outside her door with the other. *For God's sake*, she thought. *I gave him that report, first of all, and even if I hadn't, how the hell am I supposed to know what you mean, you dumb cow? We've done work for at least six chemical plants in Houston recently. And why don't you just say 'chemical' instead of 'chem'? Are you really that damn lazy?*

Trying very hard to sound anything but bitchy, Iris responded, "I've done several Houston audits lately, and I've given all the copies to him already. What report are you talking about?"

"Oh, I don't know," Matilda giggled nervously. "He just told me to ask you for it."

"And that's how he phrased it?" Iris pressed. " 'Chem plant in Houston'?" She wanted to throw the damn phone out the window.

"I think he just means the most recent one, maybe," Matilda conjectured, her irritating southern drawl becoming even more pronounced as she anxiously tried to camouflage her ignorance.

"Whatever," Iris said coldly. "I'll check with him and see what he needs."

"Okay, thanks, girl," Matilda replied with fake sweetness. "Sorry I had to bother you."

Iris shook her head angrily and slammed the phone back onto its cradle. She had slept for only about three hours last night, having suffered a number of nightmarish dreams that would not allow her to rest, and once again this morning, the line at Starbucks had been a mile long. She was tired, improperly caffeinated, and in no mood to deal with stupidity. Besides all that, she had the threat of Loomis Drake scratching at the back of her mind. Her time apart from him was growing short; she knew it, and she was not looking forward to seeing him.

As if on cue, a gentle knock on her doorframe summoned her attention. While her heart dropped into her stomach, Iris raised her eyes from her computer screen to find Loomis in the doorway, looking dapper, as usual, in charcoal-colored slacks and a matching vest over a pale gray shirt and tie. She really wanted to hate him, but it was already proving difficult to feel anything but intrigued by him. He might be a demon, but he looked and acted the part of a gentleman far more convincingly than most human men could.

"Good morning, Iris," he said kindly, placing his hands in his pockets. "Might I impose upon you for a spell?"

The dual meanings in his inquiry were not lost on Iris, who, despite herself, found his phrasing rather entertaining. Knowing it was pointless to refuse him, and too tired to bother, anyway, she leaned back in her chair and said, "Whatever."

Loomis smiled slyly at her attitude-laced reply, as if to tell her she was playing precisely into his trap in their cosmic chess match. He strode confidently into her office and gracefully seated himself before Iris's desk. The door, untouched, closed quietly behind him, and Iris surmised he had shut it by way of magic.

"I'm certainly willing to make some allowances for you, Iris," he crooned soothingly, "but I *am* the owner of this company now, and I expect you to maintain at least a pretense of decorum with me while we're in this office."

Iris sighed. "Fine," she acquiesced grudgingly. Plastering a phony smile on her face, which required a surprising amount of mental energy, she asked, "Whatever can I do for you, Mr. Drake?"

Loomis reclined in the guest chair, with his hands clasped behind his head and his legs casually outstretched in front of him. "Your antagonism toward me is completely unfounded," he stated amicably. "I have nothing but the best intentions for both of us."

"Yeah, well, you know what they say about good intentions," Iris replied.

"Indeed," Loomis answered. "And what would 'they' have to say about someone like you?"

Valid point, Iris admitted to herself. Those who spoke ill of Hell would undoubtedly say any creation of Satan's belonged there and only there.

In her silence, Loomis continued, "Let us forget the animosity of our first meeting. You seem to have labeled me as your adversary, when no just cause for it exists."

Rolling her eyes, Iris responded, "There *is* a just cause for it. You have evil plans that will ruin humanity, and apparently I'm the one with the power and thus the responsibility to stop you."

"What do you know about my supposed 'evil plans'?" he asked. "How do you know you are not of the same mind I am? You seem to have an intense distaste for the human race."

Iris shifted nervously in her chair at Loomis's perceptive and accurate assessment. "Whatever my feelings are," she replied, "I won't just submit to your whims. You're wasting your time with me."

Loomis grinned. "I have nothing but time," he answered. "I can waste as much of it as I like."

Iris contemplated the gravity of his statement. It was true, of course; Loomis was an immortal being, and although Iris might have the escape of death to look forward to, she didn't relish the idea of living the remainder of her mortal life in the evil shadow of Loomis Drake, no matter how fine-looking a shadow it might be. Stifling a yawn and scrunching her forehead at the onset of a headache, she asked with exasperation, "What do you want from me?"

Loomis rose lithely from his chair and walked to the side of her desk, leaning himself nonchalantly against it, closer to Iris than she would have liked. "You assume I want something *from* you," he coaxed. "Why do you not ask what I want *for* you?" He picked up her coffee cup, still three-quarters full of practically undrinkable office coffee, then passed it to her with a smile.

Suspicious, but accepting the cup anyway, Iris glanced down at the liquid inside and took a tiny whiff of its aroma. It was no longer a weak approximation of a coffee-flavored beverage; it was the same exquisite espresso Loomis had served her in his own office at their first meeting. She looked up at Loomis standing next to her, his chiseled face drawn into an alluring grin and his brown eyes full of expectancy. Perhaps the appropriate thing to do, she considered, would be to throw the hot coffee back in his handsome face. But she was tired and very much in want of a good cup of coffee, so she held the cup to her lips and took a cautious sip, knowing Loomis would tally it as another win in his column. Fuck it; a cup of coffee never hurt anyone.

"See," he said smugly, leaning in slightly closer to her, "you're not *really* so opposed to me."

Iris took another sip, then lowered her mug and retorted, "Just because I drink your coffee doesn't mean I agree with you."

Loomis returned to his original posture, crossed his arms lightly across his torso, and shrugged. "Perhaps not yet," he suggested, in a tone that made readily evident he expected the ultimate outcome was inevitable. "Open that mind of yours, Iris, and you will find I offer much more than espresso to please your tongue."

Iris's eyebrows clenched together with disgust at Loomis's implication. She wasn't certain he had intended it in an untoward way, but...well, he was a demon, and he probably had. Shaking her head, she told him, "I'm not going to join you or help with your mutiny in Hell, or whatever your plan is."

Loomis had picked up a small plastic figurine from Iris's desk—a video game character she liked—and was examining it with marginal interest as she spoke. After her statement, he set the collectible back on her desk and returned his eyes to her. His gaze felt like talons lacerating her face, and Iris involuntarily leaned herself away from him.

"You believe your certainty is noble," he sneered, in a voice best described as a genteel hiss, "but soon you will recognize it as foolishness. I will deal in pleasure or in pain as you direct, and in the end, you will concede, either to satisfy your ever-increasing appetite or to end your excruciating torment." He lowered his face toward her again and finished, "All that befalls you now is your own choosing."

Iris could move no farther away from him and was immensely relieved when Loomis fell silent and withdrew from her. She swallowed and blinked, realizing she had done neither during his succinct but threatening oration. He moved behind her chair and stood with militaristic posture at her office window, looking out at the depressing parking lot and alley below. He clasped one wrist behind his back with the opposite hand, and although he had verily frightened her only seconds before, Iris failed to stop her eyes from ogling the attractive figure in front of her when she rotated her desk chair.

"That Matilda Gordon is a charming young lady," he commented randomly, all the edge gone from his tone and replaced with joviality. "I think I'll invite her to dinner with me tonight."

Stunned, and immediately indignant, Iris exclaimed, "Are you *serious?*"

Loomis turned to face her, a cheerful smile on his lips. "Of course I'm serious," he answered. "Why shouldn't I be?"

Iris sensed the unbridled disbelief showing itself all over her face, and she didn't try to conceal it. " 'Charming young lady'?" she repeated incredulously, her voice becoming louder and tighter than she would have liked. "I've eaten hamburgers that are smarter than she is!"

Loomis lifted his shoulders casually and replied, "Is intelligence the only measure of a person's value?"

"No," Iris answered slowly, trying to rein in her sudden emotion, "but I'd say it's a definite contributor, and Matilda is grossly deficient in it."

"Nonetheless," Loomis responded, walking toward the door, "I would like to know her."

Iris couldn't believe what she was hearing. She had nearly zero tolerance for Matilda; surely Loomis must have even less. This was insanity. "You do know she's married, right?" she asked stupidly, knowing a sacred vow meant jack shit to a demon. It meant jack shit to most people.

Loomis chuckled. "Her husband is on the road for two weeks at a time, and I very sincerely doubt he treats her as well as I can," he said, winking at the end of his sentence.

Iris scowled, both in reaction to Loomis's perverted innuendo and in frustration with herself. Why should she be bothered by this? She didn't like Matilda anyway, so if Loomis wanted to screw up her marriage, why should she care? She knew why, and she hated herself for it. The ugly truth was she didn't care about Matilda or her marriage to her overweight, immature dope of a husband; no, she was just made fiendishly jealous by the thought of Loomis and Matilda together.

Attempting to downplay her envious pique, Iris straightened up, realigned her chair at her desk, and turned her attention to her monitors. "Well, have fun," she said sarcastically. "I hope Bodey doesn't show up and pull one of his guns on you in a fit of jealous rage."

"Thank you for your concern," Loomis replied sweetly, "but I'm sure you must know how useless his firearms would be against me." He placed his hands coolly in his pockets and inclined his head slightly, flashing a mischievous grin. "I wouldn't fear his jealousy, anyway," he added. "I'm extremely charming and uncommonly persuasive, and it will be nothing for me to put him on his knees, making the same lurid supplications of me as his wife will be."

As his words registered in her brain, Iris could no longer focus on her computer. Utterly perturbed by the thought, she looked up at Loomis with a glower of repugnance. "You're disgusting," she said quietly.

With a smirk, Loomis moved to the door and laid his hand on the knob, pausing to make one final announcement before leaving. "*If* you really believe that, Iris," he answered, "then you are the only being this side of Heaven who thinks so. From my vantage point, your 'disgust' looks much more like intrigue." Smiling at her blank stare and speechless reply, he said, "Thank you for your time, Iris. I trust we'll meet again soon."

He departed quietly through the door, leaving Iris with a cold dread; a still-hot cup of fantastic coffee; the lingering, subtle fragrance of Montblanc Legend cologne; and a complete inability to concentrate on anything but him. She gazed vacantly at her keyboard for some unknown length of time, until the recognizable and intensely grating giggle of Matilda Gordon floated down the hallway to her ears. Suddenly angered to the very edge of her self-control, Iris slammed her office door with simple magic, not caring one bit if the loud noise had disturbed or startled anyone. A few seconds and three deep breaths later, she looked up and saw a crack in the drywall, radiating from the doorframe.

If anyone tries to make me pay for that, she thought furiously, *I'll kill them.*

14

It was 12:37 a.m. by the clock's orange digital display. Iris's room was dark and cool and quiet, but it offered no peaceful slumber. She was now once again lying awake after another startling dream had terrified her out of her sleep. Each time she closed her eyes, it seemed, hellish images assaulted her mind. They were extreme and vivid at the time, but upon waking, she could recall no details of the visions. She *felt* as though she had gone somewhere; she thought she had heard cries and screams; she remembered sensations of panic and dread and despair; she believed each nightmare had ended in freakish, bestial laughter, but then she would awaken to the calm of her bedroom, which should have been a relief but instead made her feel like the butt of some great cosmic joke. The tranquility contrasted so starkly with her racing heartbeat and her sweating chest and the agony in her mind, and the awful imaginings faded so quickly from memory that she wondered whether they had really occurred at all, or if perhaps she should simply begin cutting back on her caffeine intake after noon. Whether these were true visions or just bad dreams, they were keeping her awake, and this was at least the second full night of them. She needed sleep; she was backed up at work, and more importantly, she had Loomis Drake plotting who-knew-what to force her into endorsing his overthrow of Hell and whatever his ultimate dark plans were for the human race. She had to be fully alert at all times now. Rolling over in the bed, away from her nightstand clock, she suddenly regretted having drunk the espresso Loomis had so kindly magicked into her mug the prior morning at the office. How stupid she had been to drink it! All this sleeplessness was probably his doing. Of course it would be to his benefit to drive her to the point of exhaustion—it would make her an easier victim. *Oh, hell no*, she thought to herself. *I'll be damned if some demon's going to haunt me.*

She took a deep breath, closed her eyes, and silently prayed, *God, please help me defeat him.* It was a brief prayer, but she meant it—not only for herself, but also for the souls Loomis was going to rip apart if she couldn't stop him. She had something between general disinterest and marginal dislike for most people, but it didn't mean she wanted to witness their destruction or, worse, be partially responsible for it. So she kept her eyes shut and tacitly recited the words as a mantra until eventually she drifted into an uneventful and uninterrupted sleep.

Her alarm sounded at seven minutes before six. She opened her eyes and groaned, then reached and hit the snooze button, only to repeat the action five minutes later. At that point, she forced herself out of bed, tired but grateful for the few hours of sleep she had been able to enjoy. She made the bed, washed her face, then went to the kitchen for coffee. Ordinarily, the programmed timer on the machine should have ensured her morning joe was ready for her by this time, but she must have forgotten to set it the night before. She must have forgotten even to prepare it, because she could see there was no water level showing in the clear plastic on the side of the reservoir. *Not like me to forget that*, she thought, scowling at her own oversight. When she opened the lid a moment later to pour the water in, she discovered the filter and grounds were also missing. Now, that was beyond strange...prepping the morning coffee was part of her evening routine, and it was almost unheard of that she would have neglected it completely.

As she turned to the cabinet to grab a filter and a bag of coffee, she tried to recall all of her activities since returning from work yesterday. She had been pissed beyond measure as she thought about Matilda being out at dinner with Loomis; perhaps that had been enough to distract her mind from her usual customs. She remembered visualizing Matilda in a cheaply made black dress that showed way too much shoulder and arm skin to be flattering on a woman of her shape and size, with her stringy brown hair evidencing a poor imitation of some hair-curling trick she had seen on some dumb website. Her shoes, in Iris's imagination, were either an out-of-season pair of wedge sandals or a pair of "dressy" cowgirl boots; she hadn't fully decided which was more likely. Neither pair would have been flashy enough, however, to detract from the wayward black thread hanging from the hemline of Matilda's dress, made even more apparent by its contrast against her pale white skin. Loomis, on the other hand, had his tall, slenderly athletic form decked in the most expensive fashion, with a dark three-piece suit and whatever color shirt and tie he wanted to wear, because no one would give a second thought to his attire as soon as they laid eyes on the strikingly beautiful features of his face. He would be charming and debonair and flirtatious, and it would all be wasted on Matilda, who had maybe a total of six connected brain cells to begin with and would be as nervously excited as a chihuahua on adrenaline, effectively knocking her IQ down another fifteen points. That, of course, would not deter Loomis, who would simply substitute vapid, folksy idioms for his typically intelligent subtlety until he manipulated Matilda into whatever belief or action he wanted. Even the memory of the original imagination was enough to elevate Iris's blood pressure. She supposed it wasn't so far-fetched that she might have forgotten to prepare her coffee.

Shaking her head, and now fuming at the recollection of Loomis's "date" with Matilda, Iris placed a filter in the basket and unfastened the clip on the coffee bag. As she reached in to scoop the grounds, she heard a strange hiss, then suddenly the bag was wrested from her hand, sending coffee all over the counter and floor. She screamed and jumped backward, eyes wide and chest heaving with fright as she continued to stare at the counter in front of her. Writhing amid the spilled coffee was a black snake. It coiled and raised its head, facing her, its eyes appearing meaner and somehow more perceptive than any regular animal's. Iris was no herpetologist, but she didn't have to be in order to recognize the intimidating hood ornamenting the snake's head.

She wanted to close her eyes; she wanted to believe this was another nightmare, but she was too afraid. It all seemed very real, however impossible, and she realized perhaps she was much more fearful of snakes than a few visits to the laminated glass enclosures in the reptile houses of zoos had led her to believe. The cobra flared its hood and hissed loudly, staring at her with eyes that looked, at least to Iris, to be full of hatred. The sound was horrifying, and Iris was scared to move. She took a slow, shallow breath and focused her thoughts, fully believing this snake could be very dangerous if she couldn't manage to bring her own head out of its frightened stupor, and fast. It was Loomis's doing, of course; it had to be—no way was Starbucks bagging venomous serpents in their at-home coffee grounds. Besides, this snake was too big to have fit into that bag without the aid of magic.

The cobra raised its head higher, and the sound of its hiss increased to an unbelievable volume for such a relatively small creature. Its short fangs were bared, and Iris sensed this was the final instant before the serpent would either strike out at her or spray its venom into her face. Fortunately, her recognition of this as a setup by Loomis had transformed her initial fright into righteous indignation, allowing her to react with methodical precision rather than panicked flailing that might get her a vein full of snake venom. She met the snake at the midpoint of its lunge from the counter, using a magical spell to hold it motionless in mid-air. The hissing continued but decreased in volume and then subsided completely. Iris, though slightly unnerved by it, grabbed the cobra at the base of its head and released the spell. It gave one brief, irritated hiss as it wriggled in her hand.

"*Stop*," she commanded in her inhuman voice, holding the snake's head at her eye level as she spoke. If it were a normal, earthly serpent, perhaps her otherworldly nature would intimidate it; animals could be sensitive to things like that. If it were something different, something else that perhaps only *looked* like a snake, then maybe it would recognize in her the dominion she apparently had among the damned—the same dominion Loomis was aiming to manipulate away from her since he couldn't simply disobey it. The cobra immediately relaxed in her hand, its threat neutralized, leaving Iris with a stunning new problem: What was one supposed to do with a stray cobra found in a coffee bag? She couldn't just let it loose in her backyard...although placing it in the mailbox of the neighbors with the annoying kids seemed like a nice solution. *No*, she told herself with a sigh. *Can't do that either.*

She looked at the snake once again and then placed it in her sink, leaving it there as she cleaned up the spilled coffee grounds. She still needed her pre-work coffee and considered using what remained in the bag to brew a pot, but she soon decided it was too disgusting a thought. Magic aside, there had still been a snake in there. So she angrily dumped the remainder of the bag in the trash, making a mental note that Loomis was going to reimburse her for it whether he agreed to it or not, and then she pulled out her backup bag and finally brewed her coffee.

The cobra watched her placidly from the sink as she worked, and

Iris debated a few ideas for getting rid of it. Destroying it was within her capabilities, but she didn't have the stomach for that. Besides, in a mildly fearsome sort of way, the damn thing was actually kind of cute. She could send it by way of magic back to Africa or India or wherever such creatures called home, but she wasn't completely certain it was just a cobra and not something more malevolent, and she didn't want to risk unleashing anything truly evil on the unsuspecting world. Glancing at the clock, she realized she didn't have time for this right now. She decided, however bad the idea seemed, the best course would be to keep the thing, at least for the time being. She knew nothing of the proper care for a cobra, and it was probably illegal to have one as a pet, but she was short on options. She could hope it would survive the day here on its own until she could do some research and get some supplies. And if it wasn't a cobra at all...well, then it would probably depart from her on its own, magically, having realized its own ineffectiveness against her.

Iris grabbed some old newspaper from the garage and used it to line the bathtub of the guest bathroom, then she added a large plastic bowl of water. She flipped on the overhead heater, thinking a cold-blooded creature might need the additional warmth, then she removed the serpent from the kitchen sink and placed it in its temporary den, hoping the amenities would suffice for her uninvited guest for at least a day. "I hope you're not hungry," she said to it flatly, suddenly wondering whether Loomis had foreseen this strange circumstance. He had probably meant the cobra only to threaten her, or perhaps he had hoped it might hurt her—a seemingly unreasonable hope, considering he would need Iris alive if he wanted her to change her mind about helping him with his evil schemes—or maybe he had known she would react like this, ensuring his rather childish magical prank would become a daily burden to her. She lived alone and she liked it that way; now, thanks to Loomis, she was stuck with a pet she didn't really want but couldn't simply get rid of. His plan had either failed or been obscenely successful, and Iris had no way of knowing the difference. He was a sick bastard, but he was smart; she had to give him that. She didn't want to know what she was going to have to feed this thing.

She washed her hands, poured her coffee, then went back into her bedroom to fix her makeup and get ready for the workday. It was bound to be an eventful one, if her morning thus far was any indication.

She arrived at the office a half-hour late, but she didn't care. The disproportionate amount of shit she was sure to have to deal with would more than make up for her tardiness. As she walked in, she noticed the receptionist had styled her hair and applied her makeup much more dramatically than usual. She was wearing a dress, too, which was highly unusual, considering the casual nature of the office. She greeted Iris with only a smile and a cheerful hello—the concise and simple kind of acknowledgment Iris appreciated; however, this time, it seemed to be delivered thus not for Iris's benefit, but out of embarrassment, as though the woman did not want to call any attention to her atypically primped appearance. Iris stopped herself from complimenting the woman only to follow it up with the shaming remark that it must be on account of Loomis Drake's temporary presence. Better to say nothing at all.

Iris proceeded to her office, glad to see most of the employees were away from their desks, either out at other sites or screwing around in the kitchen. She removed her jacket, draped it across her chair back, then turned on her computer and sat down. She ignored the sixteen new emails sitting unread in her inbox and instead picked up immediately with the unfinished project she had been trying to complete yesterday. If she were left alone, she could probably have a draft to the client by the end of the day, but she didn't really like her chances on that.

A quiet, productive two hours flew by before she glanced at

the clock and was stunned by her good fortune. She hadn't seen or heard from anyone since arriving, and that was as pleasant a work experience as one could hope for. She stretched in her chair and yawned, then looked at her empty coffee cup and debated making a trip to the kitchen. Was crappy coffee better than no coffee? She decided it was, grabbed her cup, then headed to the door, only to be stopped by the sudden appearance of Eden's new bigwig.

"Hello, Iris," he said smoothly. "How fortunate I've arrived just in time to spare you the suffering of deplorably weak office coffee!" He gently lifted both of Iris's hands, cradling them in his own, with her coffee mug balanced in the middle, and, smiling, whispered, "Allow me." Iris stared at him with a stern expression (or, at least, one she hoped appeared stern) as an instant heat and inviting aroma emanated from her cup.

Don't drink it, she yelled at herself. *Don't fall for this shit again.* She should ignore him and go to the kitchen and swap this impossibly wonderful espresso for the cheap stuff that might taste like crap but at least came with no sinister strings attached. Indecision, however, made her slow to react, and before she could evade him, Loomis had shut the door and physically guided her back to her desk chair with a bewitching balance of tenderness and authority.

Iris sat and placed the cup on her desk in front of her, while Loomis stood behind her with his hands on her shoulders. It made her extremely uncomfortable, but she feared that was mostly because she almost liked it.

"Tell me," he asked slowly, pressing gently into her shoulders, "how are you, Iris? Has anything out of the ordinary popped up for you today?" He stressed his words in such a way that no question remained whether the cobra now in Iris's bathtub was his handiwork. It wasn't necessary, of course; Iris hadn't really doubted his involvement at all. He was just taunting her now.

Face hot and anxiety rising, Iris strove to maintain an appearance of indifference as she quietly, but bitingly, answered, "Nothing I can't handle." She hoped he had anticipated a different reply.

Loomis removed his hands, softly caressing her as he did so, then seated himself gracefully in the guest chair. "I'm glad to hear that," he said after a long silence. "I suppose, then, you won't mind the additional assignments I have for you."

Iris rolled her eyes and scoffed. "Is this level of direct involvement in your new acquisition really necessary?" she asked. "Shouldn't you just let the business continue to run itself and then take all the profit?"

"You would prefer to continue answering directly to Mr. Ruiz, then?" Loomis asked placidly. He sat perfectly straight in the chair, with his hands draped easily over the fronts of the armrests, looking completely demure yet unequivocally intimidating. Damn him. Iris wondered if the feeling she had now was the same one others occasionally had when addressing her. It would be nice to know she had that effect on people, but it wasn't too enjoyable being on the opposite end of it. "I didn't realize you had such a high opinion of him," Loomis continued, faint sarcasm beginning to color his tone, "but if you would like me to delegate these projects to him so that he can let them sit on his desk for three weeks before assigning them to you just before their due dates, I will be happy to do so."

Loomis had clearly ascertained her true feelings toward her current boss, and Iris didn't need much time for deliberation on the matter. In this particular case, she deemed Loomis to be the lesser of two evils. With a sigh and another eye roll, she replied, "No, please don't. Just tell me what you want me to do."

Loomis answered her with silence and a meaningful grin, and Iris immediately regretted her choice of words. She was about to clarify when Loomis said, laughingly, "There is hope for you yet."

"Oh, shut up," Iris snapped. "Give me these bullshit 'assignments' of yours and then leave me the hell alone."

Loomis chuckled affably and stood up, saying, "You should drink your coffee, Iris; you're really much more pleasant when you're enjoying a beverage."

His mocking provocation exhausted the last of her short patience, and practically without thinking, Iris picked up her full mug and hurled it at him. Loomis deftly caught the cup, but a significant amount of espresso splashed across his white shirt. He smiled wider, then reached over and set her mug in front of her, again filling it by magic. He glanced down at his stained clothing, then ran his hand smoothly down the fabrics, magically eliminating all traces of the coffee. Looking at Iris, he said, "If I were a man, I would instruct you to control your temper, and it would undoubtedly only enrage you all the more, but I am not a man, and you needn't control yourself around me. Do you not see the freedom that affords you? Upon whom else could you throw hot coffee without fear of consequence? I demand no apology; I expect no repayment." He paused to adjust the knot of his tie, then added, "And you should be especially grateful for my acceptingness now, because to replace these clothes would cost more than three of your usual paychecks."

In the brief moment while Loomis was speaking, Iris had calmed herself enough to recognize the shamefulness of her own behavior. She was aware of her deep-seated anger, but she had never displayed it to anyone outside her inner circle, and even when they had witnessed it, it had come in the form of loud tirades and unnecessary profanity rather than physical destructiveness. The anger had never been directed at her family, and they had known that, and although they had usually allowed her to vent her frustrations freely, they had also urged her to avoid letting things get to her so easily. Iris, however, saw no need to try curbing her rage. Around strangers or acquaintances or coworkers, she had always had what she believed to be immutable restraint. People very easily annoyed her; they almost as easily could make her as mad as hell, but aside from the occasional diplomatic and tactful statements of disagreement, Iris had never displayed flagrant animosity nor come unhinged with anyone. So why was it different now? First, there had been the slamming of her office door yesterday, leaving a crack in the wall; now, she had thrown a ceramic mug full of espresso at the multibillionaire who owned the company she worked for—not that he didn't deserve it, of course. Iris reflected on Loomis's words and realized what a good point he had made. She didn't have to exercise control around him; she could blow up on him and have zero regrets about it because he was, if not the epitome of evil, at least the penultimate evil, and he had no expectation that Iris should have to behave rightly when she was with him. It was a wonderfully pleasing freedom! *But that's the whole trick*, she thought with sudden horror. What Loomis offered was the freedom to sin without repercussions, and that was nothing but heresy and a one-way ticket to Hell. She knew better; she knew she couldn't become complacent in bad behavior, because once sin became comfortable, it became easier and easier to do. And considering her own demonic nature, she certainly needed to avoid making any excuses for herself. She thought of Auraltiferys, constantly striving physically and mentally for holiness, and she knew he would expect better from her than the childish tantrum she had just thrown. She needed to try harder. Loomis was beating her right now, and she hadn't even registered he was playing her.

Though her internal musings had spanned only a few seconds, they had been most edifying. Iris was calmer, better focused, and perfectly composed when she realized Loomis was staring intently at her, almost as though following her thoughts as she had them, though she knew he couldn't read her mind.

"No one can accept you like I can," he said in a low, chilling voice. "You can never be your true self around anyone but me."

Iris returned his stare as she replied quietly, "Then I'll just have to change my true self."

A look of disgust passed across Loomis's face, then he crossed his arms. "How noble," he said sarcastically. After a pause, he uncrossed his arms, checked the time on his Rolex, then placed his hands casually into his pockets and said brightly, "Well, Iris, I'm afraid I'm short on time; I have some important business to discuss with your supervisor, and then I plan to take Matilda out for an early lunch. I find I rather enjoy the pleasure of her company."

Iris managed, barely, to swallow her exclamation of "bullshit," instead replying to Loomis with only a dark look. That was enough, of course, to prove he had pushed another of her buttons again, and that was the only response he really needed. He grinned at her clear revulsion, nodded toward the edge of her desk where a neat, thick stack of file folders had appeared by magic, and he continued, "Those are copies of all the records I've been provided for six manufacturing plants my companies are in the process of acquiring. They are located in five different states and would mean substantial cost savings for my industrial subsidiaries. Unfortunately, I have been warned of significant deficiencies in these facilities' existing environmental permitting and recordkeeping and general compliance, and obviously I cannot allow such liabilities to exist under my watch. So, Iris, I want you to review the files, identify all the deficiencies, and then do whatever it takes to bring these facilities into full compliance with every state and federal regulation that applies."

Iris glanced at the nine- or ten-inch stack of document-filled folders now on her desk and then looked back up at Loomis. "Fine," she said flatly. "I can do that, but it's going to take a while."

Loomis shook his head, an insincere grimace of apology on his face. "The owners of these facilities have been made aware of the numerous violations they're committing," he explained, "and in exchange for my agreement to rectify the problems so that they may wash their hands of them, they have accepted my extremely low offers on purchase prices. The catch, of course, is that they want out quickly, and time is therefore of the utmost essence. You have one month."

"A month!" Iris blurted out, wide-eyed. "That's impossible!"

Looking at her impassively, Loomis replied, "I was told you are the best asset Eden has to offer me. Was that an incorrect assessment?"

Iris scowled, highly offended by the implied affront to her value as an employee. "No," she hissed, "that is a very accurate assessment. I'm good at what I do, and you would be hard-pressed to find anyone who works more efficiently than I do, but one month for an assignment of this scope is absolutely impossible."

"I'm sorry to hear that," Loomis answered grimly, his rich brown eyes suddenly sparkling with an energy nothing like his typical casual charm. The light in his eyes now was something threatening and chilling, something bright but simultaneously dark, like a forest fire sweeping its path of destruction with utter disregard for anything in its way. He propped his hands on Iris's desk and leaned closer to her. "You see," he continued quietly, "when these facilities fail to adhere to regulations, heightened dangers naturally exist. Normally, I realize such things would not concern you, Iris, but now, they will. Because if you fail to get the appropriate permits in place and the appropriate remediations under way in the time frame I have given you, there will be *catastrophic* consequences."

Anxiety twisted her stomach into a knot, but Iris purposefully maintained eye contact with the demon leaning in less than a foot from her face. "What do you mean?" she asked slowly.

Loomis retreated a step from her desk, crossed his arms once more, then answered, "*Accidents* will happen—the kind of *accidents* that result in environmental devastation and economic hardships and lengthy sicknesses followed by untimely deaths."

Iris listened, astounded by the terrible suggestion but also incredulous. Did Loomis have that kind of power? *Don't be stupid*, she silently answered her mind's own musing. *Of course he has that power.* Loomis was an ancient being with powerful magical abilities, and Iris could easily envision the "accidents" he could cause from afar, without any physical action...flaming chemical tanks, toxic gas clouds, disastrous oil spills, exploding nuclear power plants...none of them would be any real effort for him at all, and all the suffering that would follow would be her fault, because she was the only one with the power to stop him, either by magic or by caving in to his evil requests of her.

"That's not fair," she finally retorted. "Your issue is with me, not with anyone else. Leave innocent people out of this."

"No one is innocent," Loomis answered darkly. "And if you find my methods unfair, recall I have given you a choice. Say the word, Iris, and all this goes away."

Iris, feeling suddenly very human, sat in silence, wondering why she had so impetuously challenged him. Had she really expected an angel of Hell to fight honorably? Why had she acted so naively? There was no point in questioning her actions now, though; she had left herself with two bad options, and all she could do would be to choose the less costly path. After a long pause, she responded, weakly, "I'll get it done."

Loomis looked at her with narrowed eyes and a devilish grin. "While you're at it," he said smoothly, "I want you to take over some of Matilda's workload, too. She has a lot on her plate right now, and the poor girl really doesn't handle stress well. I worry about her mental health. I'll ask her to meet with you after our lunch outing so that she can explain whatever help she needs from you."

"No way," Iris objected, instantly resolute. "If Matilda is stressed about her workload, maybe that's because she spends half her time shopping online and chatting it up with the receptionist and anyone else who'll bother to listen. I'm not going to do her work for her." Having an impossible task set before her, with strangers' lives at stake, had made her feel nearly helpless and almost completely despondent, but the suggestion that she should assist Matilda in any way was infuriating enough to dispel her momentary weakness.

Loomis shrugged apathetically. "Of course, I cannot force you," he conceded, "but, should anything unfortunate happen to her as a result of all the stresses she is under, your stubbornness will be to blame."

"What the hell, Loomis?" Iris snapped. "Nothing *you* do is *my* fault; I'm not an idiot." Frankly, she wasn't sure she would care if something "unfortunate" happened to Matilda, anyway.

With a cold chuckle, Loomis answered, "Your guilt will be allowing evil when you have both opportunity and means to stop it. You're no longer betting with your own life, Iris. Others are at your mercy."

Iris felt uncomfortable heat in her face, and she hoped it wasn't showing. She wanted to argue; she wanted to throw her mug at Loomis again, or maybe start an all-out brawl with him right there in her office, but none of that would help anything. He was right—he had hinted at some nefarious plans, and he had given her the conditions under which he would abort those plans. If she did nothing, or failed to do enough, she would feel as guilty for the consequences as though she had committed the acts herself. For a few seconds, she wondered if the best idea might be to join him, to give him whatever permission he needed from her to overtake Hell and go on about his dastardly business. At least the only soul she'd lose then would be her own. But, no...Auraltiferys had warned her of potential devastation of the human race, of souls being lost if Loomis gained the rulership of Hell. Ultimately, she was going to be responsible for others' lives no matter what. It was a shitty situation, but she might as well fight until she either succeeded or failed. A fight to the end would be more honorable than surrender.

With a forlorn smile and a short sigh, she finally replied, "You won't break me like this. Give me whatever work you can dream up; I'll do it. I don't care. You'll get bored with it eventually. You'll get bored with that dumb new girlfriend of yours, too."

"You will lose your sanity long before I get bored," Loomis stated matter-of-factly, "and that will only make my work easier for me. And please, Iris, try to conceal your glaring jealousy of Matilda; it is most unbecoming."

"I'm not jealous," Iris countered as Loomis turned toward the door to leave. The statement would have carried less acidity in tone had it been true.

"My mistake," Loomis responded sarcastically as he opened the door and departed, flashing a final, haughty sneer.

Bastard, Iris thought angrily. Her jealousy of Matilda was shameful; that Loomis had created it in her and was fully aware of it only made it worse. She looked at the stack of folders next to her and wondered how in God's name she might be able to get all of it in order before Loomis started destroying the environment or killing people. It seemed impossible, and yet there had to be some way. She closed her eyes and took a calming breath, and in her mind's momentary stillness, she felt the same metallic hammering she had heard on the mountain with Auraltiferys. Anger and envy and worry faded away, and upon opening her eyes, she turned immediately to her purse beside her. She pulled out the shield medallion the blacksmith had given her and clasped it around her neck. Let her coworkers ask questions; let them all talk behind her back if they wanted to. Focus was what she needed now, and that's what this piece was fashioned to aid. She wouldn't be ashamed of it.

***

"Hey, girl," Matilda drawled shyly, lightly tapping on the doorframe of Iris's office as she peeked her head over the threshold. "Are you busy?"

Iris had been dreading this moment since Loomis had departed from her this morning. Already, she could tell Matilda was approaching in her insincerely apologetic manner, which, though completely unconvincing and an annoyance, was marginally preferable to her occasional forced-confidence displays. While Matilda had probably already developed a falsely inflated sense of her own importance on account of her new acquaintance with Loomis, it appeared, at least for now, she was going to make calculated efforts to avoid angering Iris. Of course, if Matilda's "calculations" in matters of social interaction were anything like her attempts at successfully completing mathematical computations, there was a strong possibility Iris was going to end up quite pissed off, despite Matilda's efforts to prevent it.

Iris took a deep breath, tried to focus her mind into an attitude of acceptance, and replied, "Don't worry about it; come on in." She could attempt to be patient and acquiescent, but she wasn't going to claim she wasn't busy just to make Matilda feel less guilty about interrupting.

Matilda walked in shakily on her high-heeled black pumps. She was wearing an uncharacteristically loud red A-line dress that would have shown a sickening amount of leg if not for the ankle-length black tights she wore underneath. She wore a black wool sweater over the dress, fastened at her rib cage by a single button that appeared to be struggling. *Dressing up for the new boyfriend*, Iris thought cynically. What was with these women at Eden? Every one of them but Iris was dressed up far more glamorously than was typical, all so obviously for Loomis Drake, and yet every one of them but Iris was either married or in a serious and supposedly committed relationship. Iris was appalled by the irony, but she realized she couldn't really pass any judgment. After all, she had intended to glam it up for her job interview with Loomis before she had known the truth. And perhaps wanting to look nice in front of a good-looking billionaire wasn't really so demeaning or terrible.

"Um," Matilda stammered, scrunching her forehead and cheeks together in an expression of reluctance, "Loomis told me to meet with you about taking over some of my projects."

Hearing Matilda call him by only his first name was an offense to Iris's senses. Her accent killed all the charm and mystery of the name, and it was just so *wrong* coming off her lips. Iris clutched at her medallion in hopes of dispelling the sudden, blinding rage of jealousy that rushed over her. There was no good reason for it, but she felt extremely possessive of Loomis all of a sudden, as though she should be the only one who could call him by his first name. Endeavoring to maintain a calm demeanor, she nodded brusquely and answered, "He mentioned that to me this morning. What do you need?"

"I'm SO sorry," Matilda responded, in lieu of providing a useful answer. "It was really all his idea, I swear!"

"It's fine," Iris said, almost impatiently. "Just tell me what you need."

"Okay," Matilda replied, "there are just, like, two things I need your help with. They probably won't even take you that long. It's just that, you know, I have all these other things I have to finish, and now Loomis wants me to start working on a new marketing project for the company..." She trailed off and sat there, staring at Iris with drab brown eyes outlined in way too much eyeliner and heavy false eyelashes, pleading for interest.

What, you want me to ask about your stupid new project? Iris thought to herself. *Get bent.* Out loud, she simply repeated, "So, what do you need from me?"

"I'll forward you the emails," Matilda answered. "Like I said, it probably won't take you very long. But, see, I'll be working on marketing for Loomis. He wants me to be in a commercial!"

Iris nearly rolled her eyes but covered by turning her head and glancing down at her desk. She happened to notice her coffee cup sitting there beside her keyboard, untouched from the second time Loomis had filled it with espresso for her in the morning. She had planned to pour it out, but she hadn't gotten around to it. There was still steam coming from it, as though it had just been served to her. *Well*, she mused silently, *if I'm going to be forced to listen to Matilda's story, I deserve something in return for it*. She picked up the cup and sipped from it. It was a damn fine cup of coffee.

Since Iris was now casually drinking coffee instead of reacting to her news, Matilda cleared her throat, shifted in her seat, and asked, "Can you believe that? Me, in a commercial!"

"Nope," Iris said, a little more acerbically than she should have. "That's crazy." She took another swig of espresso and wondered if Loomis knew she was drinking it. He probably did. She hoped he might keep the refills coming from wherever he was.

"Right!" Matilda exclaimed dramatically. "But, anyway, it's true! Loomis told me all about it last night at dinner!" She paused for a second, expectantly, but upon receiving no immediate reply from Iris besides a fake smile, she asked, "Did you know he took me to dinner last night?" She had obviously desired more of an excited reaction from her audience.

"No, I didn't know that," Iris lied. "How exciting for you." She felt her jaw beginning to clench and wondered how long she might be able to endure the boiling envy before exploding on Matilda. She would have to try, because she couldn't let Loomis win. At least, not so easily. She took another long gulp of coffee, hoping the action would mask any negative emotion that might be evident in her expression. This whole thing was a setup by Loomis to make her jealous or angry so that she would end up begging him to stop the torture, but her recognition of the scheme didn't make it any less successful. She was both insanely jealous and intensely angry right now.

"Girl," Matilda replied eagerly, "it *was*! I was so surprised when he invited me! He took me to that new Chinese restaurant; I think it's called Ban-kok. Ban...Bangkok? It was a weird name...I think that was it. Anyway, it's a *really* nice place! You should try it sometime!"

Although she wanted to point out Matilda's glaring ignorance of basic geography, and although she had informed Matilda on numerous occasions that she didn't care much for Asian food, Iris held her tongue on both points and instead forced another smile and gave a curt nod.

Continuing her story, Matilda went on, "Anyway, Loomis says he wants me to be 'the face of Eden'! I couldn't believe it! Honestly, I was surprised he didn't ask you first. I even tried to argue with him, but he's really persuasive. And, oh my gosh, Iris, you can't even believe how charming he is! He's so perfect!"

"I'm sure he is," Iris answered flatly.

"We're going out again tonight," Matilda added giddily, her puffy cheeks flushing.

"Hmm," Iris responded disinterestedly, with a mouth full of coffee. She swallowed, then added, "Seems like you two must have really hit it off. How does Bodey feel about that?" She stared hard at Matilda, who very quickly dropped her eyes at the insinuation.

"Oh, well, you know," she replied nervously, "we're just friends. Bodey doesn't care if I go out with coworkers while he's on the road."

In a split second before answering, Iris considered dropping the issue; after all, it wasn't her business what Matilda did with her time. But she also knew she couldn't simply let it go. She hated the idea of Matilda having any sort of relationship with Loomis, and while envy was her primary motivation, she could further justify her position by telling herself it was in Matilda's best interest to have nothing to do with him. Loomis would never end it, because it afforded him both the opportunity to drag another soul into sin and the chance to push Iris either into her own sin or into submission to him. So, if she cared for Matilda at all as a human person with inherent value, it was imperative that she do everything in her power to convince the girl to end her exciting new affair.

"Have you told Bodey the 'coworker' you're going out with is a famous billionaire you've been drooling all over since the first moment you laid eyes on him?" Iris asked pointedly. Her tone was openly accusatory.

"Well," Matilda said hesitantly, nervously playing with a bracelet on her wrist as she stared at her hands in her lap. "Um...no, I mean, I haven't really told him about it."

"Oh, well, I'm sure you have nothing to worry about," Iris said, in a suddenly speciously sweet voice. "From what you've told me, Bodey sounds like a really open-minded guy, and I'm sure he trusts you."

Matilda crossed and then uncrossed her legs, then began running her hands across the tops of her thighs as she answered, "Yeah, he's really open-minded."

Iris had to quell a snicker at the response. If her tone was any indication, Matilda herself didn't even believe the line of crap that had just come out of her mouth. A year ago, when she and Bodey had been dating for only a couple of months, Matilda had proudly told Iris a story about the two of them having gone out to a bar with some of Bodey's friends. As Matilda had described it, a stranger had come up and started flirting with her, and Bodey had gallantly stepped in to rescue her from the harassment by confronting the guy with some macho-talk that had ultimately escalated the situation to a profanity-laced shoving match that resulted in all parties being escorted from the premises. Matilda had been excited to tell the story, of course, because it wasn't every day a girl had two guys fighting over her. She thought Bodey had acted like such a man that evening; Iris, of course, had a far different opinion, believing instead that Bodey was nothing but an overgrown child with a short temper and the intellect of a caveman. Matilda had later shared other anecdotes that had only solidified Iris's initial opinion of Bodey Gordon. He wasn't open-minded, and there was no way in hell he would approve of his wife's outings with Loomis Drake. If he found out about it, Bodey's initial reaction would be to confront Loomis, either with his potbelly and his heavy, hairy fists or with a piece from his vast gun collection, even if he had no inclination that anything too terribly taboo had occurred. Matilda knew this, too, and she almost certainly had no intention of telling Bodey about Loomis. She just wasn't going to admit it to Iris, because it would make her look bad.

Iris said nothing after Matilda's insincere statement, and after several seconds, Matilda finally added, "Well, anyway, it really doesn't matter. Loomis is just a friend."

Iris smirked, then said sarcastically, "Right. Just a rich, handsome, charming, persuasive, perfect friend."

Shock was immediately evident on Matilda's pudgy face. Even her dim wits were bright enough to understand the implication. "Oh my gosh, Iris, you believe me, don't you?" she asked anxiously, her accent more pronounced as her voice edged into a higher pitch. Her cheeks were almost as red as her dress. "I'm not doing anything wrong!"

"I didn't say you were," Iris placated. "You're a *really* good person; you wouldn't do anything you knew was wrong. You'd feel too guilty about it."

"Yeah, I would," Matilda agreed emphatically. "I'd never do anything like that!"

"Of course you wouldn't!" Iris concurred jovially. Then,

immediately more serious, she said, "But are you sure *he* won't try to tempt you?"

Matilda opened her mouth to reply, then hesitated, pressed her eyebrows together, forcing her eyes into even narrower slits above her full cheeks, and stuttered, "Wait, what do you mean?"

Iris drank the last of her coffee and shrugged as she set her cup down. "I just mean you have to be careful," she said. "That's all."

"You mean with Loomis?" Matilda asked.

Catching herself before she rolled her eyes at the question that should not have been necessary, Iris replied slowly, "Yes, I mean with Loomis." *And stop saying his name like that, you bitch*, she screamed internally.

With an exaggerated shaking of her head that caused her cheeks to jiggle and multiple chins to appear at different angles, Matilda answered stubbornly, "He's not like that at all! He's not! He's a good guy. He would never!"

"I have a bad feeling about him," Iris countered in a deadpan tone, "and I think you should be careful. Don't you think it's at least a little bit odd for the new owner of the company to take a married woman out to dinner?"

Practically deflating before Iris's eyes, Matilda replied hesitantly, "I think...I mean, I think it was just business, you know."

"Sure," Iris agreed after a brief pause. She kept her tone consciously devoid of sarcasm, but she knew the simplicity of the concession would cause Matilda to question its veracity. The girl was clay in her hands.

"Anyway," Matilda continued, "I'm not even interested in Loomis that way. I mean, he's super good-looking; don't get me wrong...but, really, he's not even my type! Besides, he's, like, way too old anyway, even if I wasn't married." With a nervous chuckle as she began to play with the charm on her necklace, she added, teasingly, "That's why I thought you should get with him! I know how you like older guys!"

Iris forced as genuine a smile as she could. She didn't mind the teasing, but the joke had been beaten to death by this point. It had stemmed from a "reputation" she had developed after some high school friends noticed a trend among her celebrity crushes, and while Iris believed her preferences to be based on appreciation for talent and maturity, which she found quite lacking among the newer generations of male stars, everyone else attributed it to a fetish, and Iris had discussed enough movies with Matilda for her to have made the same erroneous connection. Ultimately opting to ignore that comment, however, Iris finally answered, "Personally, I think we should both stay away from him, but he's not interested in me. He's interested in you, so you need to be careful."

Matilda pouted and shook her head with feigned reproach as she stood up and straightened her dress, nearly losing her sweater button in the process. "Girl," she said affably, "you just don't trust anybody, and you worry too much! Loomis isn't bad, and we're just friends. So don't worry about me!"

With a tiny smile, Iris looked up at Matilda and answered, "You're right. I don't trust people, and I do worry."

Immediately apologetic, Matilda's eyes went wide and she waved her palms conciliatorily. "Oh, I didn't mean anything bad by that!" she gushed. "I'm sorry; please don't be offended!"

Iris gently waved off the apology, inwardly thinking how pathetic it was for Matilda to have such a need for people to like her that she was so quick to apologize for almost everything she said or did. "I'm not offended," she assured Matilda. "I should probably be a little more trusting of people, and maybe you're right about Loomis. Maybe he is just being friendly. But if I were married, I know how I would feel if my husband went out alone for a 'friendly' dinner with some rich, glamorous supermodel. I'd be jealous and hurt, even if I said I wasn't. And if I were married to a guy as special as Bodey, I wouldn't want to risk hurting his feelings. I wouldn't want some smooth-talking devil in a fancy suit to undermine my marriage, even if he didn't mean to." She paused and smiled at Matilda apologetically, then said, "Oh, listen to me! You're right; I worry too much. You said Bodey doesn't mind, so it isn't even a problem."

Matilda's furrowed brow and tightly closed lips suggested to Iris that her simple manipulation had succeeded. She was obviously troubled by the thought that her "friendship" with Loomis might hurt her husband. She had already had that thought, of course, which was why she hadn't told Bodey about Loomis in the first place, but, now, Iris had called her out on it, so if she wanted to keep going out with Loomis while Bodey was out of town, she was going to have to keep it a secret both from Bodey and from Iris. Matilda could be two-faced and fake, but Iris knew the root of that was just an endless desire to please other people. Worry about Bodey finding out about Loomis, combined with her guilt over keeping it a secret from him, would tear her up inside. Plus, the girl now knew she was showing up on Iris's judgment radar, which was a place she didn't want to be. She would give up on Loomis now—if not immediately, then at least soon.

"I still think you should get with him," Matilda announced at length, finally moving toward the door to leave. "Then you and Loomis can come over to dinner with Bodey and me one night, and I can still get to admire him from afar!" Her tone was cheerful and joking, but there was definite disappointment hidden underneath, and Iris found it most entertaining.

***

After only one or two uneventful hours of work, Iris found herself bending over the toilet with her hands braced against her knees, retching into the bowl until nothing more would come up. She took two shuddering breaths and pressed her eyes tightly shut, straining not to cry. The fringe of long bangs at the side of her face clung to her perspiring skin, and her arms and legs felt gelatinous and weak. She remained for half a minute in her retching position, waiting to see if another wave of nausea would strike her. Eventually convinced that her vomiting had ceased, she flushed the toilet and then moved shakily from the stall to the sink, terrified to look at herself in the mirror as she washed her hands. When she hazarded a glance at her reflection, she saw a startlingly pallid, sunken face with jaundiced eyes and pale lips. Her makeup had turned into a splotchy mess, and her hair was a damp, flat tangle on top of her head. She looked as good as she felt, and she felt like shit. *Thank God there's no one else in here*, she thought, immediately fearing the thought might somehow stir the universe to send someone into the restroom to join her, but no one came.

She rinsed her mouth with water, dampened a paper towel and blotted her face, then cautiously returned to her office, praying no one would pay any attention to her. She would have to go home; that was certain. It was particularly inconvenient timing, considering the impossible workload Loomis had dumped on her amid threats of chaos and destruction if she failed to complete it by his deadline, but she had no choice. She couldn't work like this; no one could.

After shutting down her computer and grabbing her purse, Iris rushed out as quickly as she could without drawing any unwanted observation from her coworkers, pausing only long enough to tell the office manager she was going home sick. She didn't bother replying to the feel-better-soon comment that followed; she simply wanted to be out of there as soon as possible, and she didn't care if she came off as rude in the process. It was better to ignore a canned response than to barf all over the office carpet, anyway.

She made it home just in time to run to her bathroom before

vomiting again. She had never felt so sick. She rarely came down with colds; she even more rarely experienced any other ailments that prevented her from working, and she had no idea what illness had now overtaken her. Whatever it was, it was awful. She finally left the toilet and was able to wash her face, which looked even more hellish with her makeup completely removed. She wondered if she should go to a doctor, but the idea was unappealing. She wanted just to lie down and sleep.

After changing into her pajamas, she went to the kitchen for water, thinking fluids would do her body good. She was startled by the cobra that had moved itself from the guest bathroom to her kitchen counter, lazily coiled and staring at her with marginal interest. She was glad the two of them had come to an understanding. She didn't mind its presence, and it didn't mind hers (or perhaps it just had enough sense not to mess with the Devil).

"I almost forgot about you," Iris said to the serpent as she filled her water glass. "You doing okay in there?" The cobra flicked its tongue briefly, and Iris decided to take it as an affirmative response. "You probably think I look like hell," she continued after taking a few small sips of water. "I feel like hell."

The snake raised its head and flared its hood a couple of times, very slightly. Iris never would have imagined herself standing in her kitchen speaking to a reptile like this, and if she had, she would have thought it was an indication of insanity. Oddly, however, she now felt as though her scaly companion was actually listening to her.

"Yeah," she went on, "I don't know what happened to me. I was just sitting there at my desk, finishing up that crap for Matilda, then suddenly I was all clammy and sick, and that's why I'm home early. I hope it's nothing serious. I really need to be at work right now; I have so much to do, and people will really suffer if I don't get it all done."

The cobra stared at her for a second, then uncoiled and slithered its way to the coffee maker, wrapping itself around the unit and then returning its gaze to Iris.

"No, thanks," Iris said with a sardonic snort, "I couldn't possibly drink any coffee right now." She tensed suddenly and felt her forehead gather into its furrow of suspicious thoughtfulness. *Coffee...Loomis...that's it*, she thought. *That bastard did this to me.* She was immediately convinced this was no illness, no infection, no gastric distress or parasite or food poisoning...this was the evil magic of a demon. Why had it taken her so long to deduce that? The cobra left the coffee maker and gave Iris one final stare before making its way off the counter by way of a barstool and then departing for its bathroom abode.

Feeling another bout of intense sickness coming on, Iris set down her water glass and closed her eyes, refusing to rush for the commode again. As she tried to focus her thoughts into magical healing, her body felt increasingly far away from her, weakened by its recent extreme regurgitations and being made even weaker by the convulsive gagging she was now trying to stop by force of magic. Her knees began to buckle underneath her, and she reached for the counter to try to steady herself. Her arms, however, were as useless as her legs, and she slid uncomfortably down the counter and the wooden cabinet doors beneath, ending in a heap on the floor. Fever erupted under her skin in a nearly unbearable heat; sweat was beading across her face and down her chest and back, and she felt herself losing the battle against her nausea, even with the aid of magic. If anything, her invocation was making the sickness worse.

"No, no, no," Iris groaned miserably as she brought herself to her hands and knees. She opened her eyes and ceased her spell, which seemed to provide a brief respite from the physical torment. *What has he done to me? How do I stop this?*

She reflected for a moment, wondering why she had been unable to heal herself. Loomis must be using powerful magic against her, magic she was yet unfamiliar with, and she knew he wouldn't tire of it. He was an eternal spirit, choosing to live in a human form on Earth but not tied to nor limited by the physical realm. He could prolong her torture in perpetuity, until she gave in and asked him to stop it...which, of course, he would gladly do—for a price. Her only other choice was to break his spells with her own, but so far, she was failing horribly at that.

Her feverishness had subsided a bit, and she felt a little more strength in her arms, so she brought herself upright on her knees, resting her backside on her heels. The hard tile of the floor caused a dull ache in her bones, but she didn't yet feel well enough to stand, and the coolness of the tile felt nice on her hot skin, anyway. After a few deep breaths, she closed her eyes again and recommenced her spells, this time trying different manners of prayerful thought, hoping the change would help her discern exactly how to save herself. As she had feared, however, the magic exacerbated her condition. Aches became excruciating pains; fever became an intolerable heat; bilious gags became spasmodic convulsions. She tried to endure it, tried to continue every manner of magical prayer she knew, but nothing seemed to work. Every spell she invoked seemed to be met by a counterattack of exponentially greater strength, as though Loomis were right there with her, recognizing and destroying every feeble attempt at defense before she even made it.

She shook her head, wanting to believe she was strong enough to beat this, but not convincing herself of it at all. Moaning in pain between involuntary convulsions, she considered giving up. She was sure there was a way to undo whatever he was doing, but the answer existed somewhere outside her realm of knowledge. Then again, all magic had once existed in that same faraway place unknown to her, yet she had discovered it. She could not give up so easily; it would be far better to endure physical suffering than to lose her own soul and the souls of countless others whom Loomis would destroy after gaining her consent or surrender. So, after resting her magical focus for a moment, Iris pressed her eyelids tightly together and began again, silently and pitifully weaving spells in her mind, each as ineffectual as the last and exponentially more painful to her physical body. *God, what am I doing wrong?* She pleaded for help from Heaven, believing she had opened her mind and heart in just the way Auraltiferys had taught her, but no booming voice or quiet whisper or comforting presence answered her. Suddenly, a terrible, squeezing pain assaulted her abdomen, and, as she gasped for the tiniest breaths of air, she felt fluid oozing up through her throat, choking her. She gagged and coughed, then vomited on the floor, opening her eyes to a terrifying pool of viscous, blackish-red liquid, splattered across her forearms, covering her hands, and ruining the tile.

My God, he's killing me, she thought with horror. *Why do you not help me?* Maybe this was the best course for humankind, after all. Maybe she should die, if for no other reason than to prevent Loomis from taking her inherent power as Satan and ushering in a new era of evil destruction. Giving up didn't necessarily mean giving in to Loomis's plan. If she continued her futile magic struggle against the wicked spell or spells Loomis was using on her now, it was sure to kill her mortal body; the dark, sickly blood on the floor beneath her was proof of it. Loomis had undoubtedly expected her to beg for his mercy long before she perished, but she would show him. She would keep fighting him with her useless magic until her body could no longer survive it. She would be no good to him dead.

With her mind made up, Iris shifted weakly from her knees to her rear, then scooted herself into the corner of the cabinets and rested there, pulling her knees in toward her chest and letting tears flow freely down her cheeks. Though the pain was far less intense now in the pause of her magical focus, she still tasted blood and bile in her mouth, and her stomach felt like it had been run through a meat grinder. She was exhausted and ill, hurt and scared, not wanting to die, but neither wanting to live only to fight a war she might lose, costing mankind dearly in the process. Briefly, she remembered Loomis's threat to her, how he would be the unseen force behind the "accidents" that would devastate many lives if she should not perform the tasks he had set before her. She wondered if he would follow through on that if she were dead. If he did, she could only hope God wouldn't count those lives against her. But she really had little choice. If people would suffer either way, then this was a game of numbers, and it would cost fewer lives if she preempted her possible failure against Loomis's grand plan with an early death of her own.

She took as deep a breath as she could, then she opened her mind again to the feeling of inhuman power flowing within her, and immediately her pains doubled. She tried spells of healing, spells of protection, spells of blessing; each one was recited silently beneath her outward vocalizations of agony, with no positive effect. She had to stretch her legs out in front of her to try to assuage the growing tension in her torso, then ended up on hands and knees again, gagging blood and raining tears onto the floor. After a minute, her arms were too weak to support her, and she fell sideways into her own blood, screaming and crying amid the gurgling of fluid still finding its way into her mouth. Her vision started to fade, and it became increasingly difficult to maintain the proper mindset for magic. She closed her eyes and tried to continue, reaching a lethargic hand to the shield medallion around her neck, hoping it would help her focus until the end, which must certainly be near.

The shield was strangely cold against her feverish hand, and in an instant, the distant hammering of metal echoed through her mind, beating like a foreign heart in her own chest. In the next moment, she felt her body lifted from the ground and carried for a short distance before being laid on a smooth, cool surface that was a wonderful relief to her burning skin. A deep, elegantly masculine voice reached her ears, praying over her in Latin. Her hand dropped away from her amulet, and her entire body relaxed. Slightly disoriented, she discontinued her magic and wondered if she had finally been successful in breaking Loomis's spells. Her body felt less like death than it had a moment before.

As the fog in her head cleared, Iris realized she was lying on the marble floor of the library on the mountain. Auraltiferys was kneeling at her head, holding it tenderly in his large, powerful hands as he prayed. Iris blinked several times, then breathed deeply, gladdened and immeasurably relieved by the cool air and the subtle aromas of incense and polished wood. The blacksmith fell silent and released her head, then gently lifted her by the shoulders until she was in a seated position. She wished she didn't look as bad as she knew she must, and she wished she hadn't changed into her pajamas before finding herself here with a priest, but she was still elated to see him.

"Iris," he said coolly, in simple greeting as he seated himself cross-legged on the floor in front of her. Iris immediately dropped her eyes to her lap, suddenly realizing she was now sitting before him as a failure again, only this time without the excuse of ignorance to rely on. She didn't even know what to say.

He removed his canteen from the pouch at his hip and handed it to her. She started with a small sip but had soon emptied the whole thing into her mouth. Auraltiferys crossed his muscular arms and watched her, sternly but not uncaringly, as she drank. Silently, he magically refilled the water for her, then he said, "It appears you have not heeded all of my advice."

Iris sighed, thinking briefly that it would have been easier had she died a minute ago. She wanted to make excuses for herself; she wanted to make all of this Loomis's fault, but she knew it wasn't. The blacksmith had told her to avoid him as long as he would allow it, and instead she had impulsively taken herself right to him. She couldn't bring herself to speak.

"I'm sitting before you with grave concern, Iris," he continued, "not with judgment. You may speak freely with me."

Meeting his steely, bright blue gaze, Iris hesitantly replied, "I...think I might be in over my head."

"You have acted impulsively and irresponsibly," Auraltiferys answered. "You should have let him come to you. There is yet too much you don't know."

"Yeah, I get that," Iris retorted, with mild irritation. "What happened to the 'no judgment' thing?"

"It is still in effect," the blacksmith answered stonily, "but it does not preclude me from pointing out your mistakes."

Iris lowered her eyes again before answering. "Wasn't something like this inevitable?" she asked. "Loomis wants my help; I won't give it; of course he was going to punish me for it."

Shaking his head, Auraltiferys countered, "This wasn't punishment. It was a sadistic temptation, and you might have handled it better if you had given yourself more time to learn."

"He bought the company where I work!" Iris exclaimed. "What was I supposed to do?"

Auraltiferys's eyes bore sharply into her as he replied, "You went to him first, Iris. You provoked him. He once believed you knew nothing of your nature; now he must test how much you do know, and he has found you know very little."

Feeling like a berated child, Iris answered, "I understand that now. I'm sorry."

"You don't fully understand," Auraltiferys said, cutting her with the edge of his voice. "Your actions now have immense consequences that extend beyond your own experience. Do you know what happened after you left Drake in his office?"

Iris looked up immediately at the question, suddenly anxious, but she said nothing. She didn't think she wanted to hear whatever might come next.

"Let me show you," the blacksmith instructed. He stared at her until his already penetrating blue eyes became sharper and hotter than the flames of a star. Opening her own mind to his, Iris was shown the terrible events that had occurred after she left Loomis angered beyond measure in his Portland office. She saw the young and beautiful Yvette answer the call to his office; she saw her brutally raped and murdered; she watched Loomis erase the entirety of his crimes with simple magic, some charismatic words, and some paltry sums of money slipped to the appropriate palms. She saw a family grieving for the untimely death of their daughter, granddaughter, sister, niece, and cousin, all made to believe the poor girl had sadly taken her own life, without any warning.

Iris stubbornly closed herself off, ending the vision, and Auraltiferys allowed her to do so. His eyes returned to their normal icy incisiveness, and Iris shakily asked, "Why would you show me that?"

"For the same reason God shows me," he answered. "It is so we recognize the evil we are fighting." His voice, though quiet in volume, was still powerful, seeming to echo within the stone walls of the library. "And, for you, Iris," he added, "so you never forget how your actions affect your brothers and sisters on Earth."

"I tried to get her to leave," Iris explained defensively. "I told her he was dangerous. She only insulted me."

"Well, then," Auraltiferys replied with a biting note of sarcasm, "she deserved it."

"I didn't say that," Iris argued. "But she did make her own choice. Besides, she was all over him long before I came around; it was totally obvious. It's not like she was completely innocent."

"Is anyone?" the blacksmith asked.

Iris fell silent, her mind clinging to her justifications of her actions but receiving no comfort from them. After several quiet seconds, she said, "It's still his sin, not mine."

"I agree," Auraltiferys answered. "Does that make you feel any better?"

"No," Iris admitted. She knew she shouldn't have provoked Loomis like that. It was immature and foolish, and it had cost Yvette her life.

Auraltiferys stared at her keenly for a moment, then inclined his head slightly and said, "I am glad to see you have not lost your humanity."

Iris looked down at the canteen she was still holding lightly in her hand, balanced against her leg as she sat. "I don't think I can handle this," she said quietly.

"No one is better equipped for it than you," the blacksmith retorted.

"I've screwed up everything already!" she blurted. "And it's going to get worse! Loomis has already threatened to hurt people because of me. Hell, he already killed Yvette because I made him so angry. He's horning in on one of my married coworkers; God knows what he'll do to her. And whatever he did to me today, I was completely powerless to stop. I can't beat him at this. He's too evil."

"You believe you are in over your head," Auraltiferys summarized, repeating Iris's words from minutes before.

"Yes!" she asserted vehemently.

"Do you forget what you are?" he challenged. "You are an angel, albeit a fallen one. You must not lose your humanity, but neither must you ignore your second nature, which is as great a part of you as is the other. You are capable of the same power Drake wields. Why were you so troubled by the spells he used on you?"

"Are you seriously asking me that question?" Iris asked in disbelief. "He was *killing* me! Nothing I did made it any better! Every spell I tried only made the pain worse."

"Then, had I not brought you here when I did," Auraltiferys inquired, "what was your plan?"

Iris looked away from him and sighed, not wanting to answer, though she expected he knew the answer anyway. "I was going to let him kill me," she finally stated, ashamed.

"It is by God's grace you were thwarted in such foolishness," Auraltiferys responded. "Drake would prefer you alive so that he can convince you to go along with his plans to overthrow Hell's throne, but your mortal death would not bring an end to his plot. From Heaven or Purgatory, you would no longer hold any rank in Hell, and Loomis would need only to find a way to take Satan's power from him, without you in his way. I have no doubt he could do it with relative ease, given his advanced knowledge in magic and relics. It would only take him more time than he would like. If your soul were damned to Hell, his task would be even simpler, for you would no longer have anything to lose. You would have no reason to deny him; you would have no care for humanity. No one would profit from your death but Drake."

Iris felt quite stupid for her lack of foresight, but considering the horrible suffering her body had endured, she was slow to kick herself too much for it. "Then why doesn't he just kill me?" she asked.

"Perhaps he will," the blacksmith suggested with a muscular shrug, "although I would expect him to exhaust all his temptations before he would do so. Mortal life is but the blink of an eye; he won't mind waiting if there is a chance he might lure you to his side before then." He finally uncrossed his arms and gracefully rose to his feet, reaching a hand down to help Iris up. "Furthermore," he continued as she stood with his assistance, "I suspect he enjoys the challenge you pose to him. You are a plaything for him, at least until he deems you to be a real threat."

"I don't want to be his plaything," Iris said with disgust.

"You needn't continue to be," Auraltiferys replied, retrieving his canteen from her and indicating that she should follow him. He led her through the door and outside into the cool twilight air. The crescent moon was already brightly visible against the dimming sky, and Iris was again astounded by the beauty of the mountain. She had always been enchanted by the moon, and here it was more beautiful than she had ever seen. She followed behind the blacksmith, striding quickly and purposefully toward his residence, his long, silvery-white hair reflecting the light of the sky. They walked in silence, and Iris didn't mind the quiet break in their conversation. It gave her a chance to enjoy the solace of the mountain, which she had so quickly forgotten after having departed the first time.

When they reached the house, Auraltiferys motioned her toward the dining table in the kitchen and invited her to take a seat. He sat in the chair on the adjoining side of the table and sighed thoughtfully. "Would you mind preparing us some tea?" he asked.

Iris, surprised by the request since the blacksmith seemed so naturally inclined to do things for himself, stood immediately and said, "No, I don't mind at all!" In fact, although she wasn't a particularly nurturing kind of woman, she found herself eager to serve him.

Auraltiferys stopped her with a gentle hand on her forearm. "From here, please," he said. "Magically."

Iris sat back down and looked at the blacksmith with some reticence. Not long ago, using magic had brought her very near death, and she now realized she was in no hurry to try it again. She felt safe here, and she trusted Auraltiferys wouldn't ask anything of her that would bring her harm, but a vestige of fear yet remained, and even if death were no longer a concern, Iris still didn't like the possibility that the magic might cause her to throw up on the priest sitting next to her.

She hesitated for only a few seconds, but Auraltiferys had already perceived her doubts. "You'll be fine," he encouraged her.

Iris focused briefly on the simple spells required for such a small task, and almost instantly, there was a kettle of hot tea and two full cups set on the table. The magic caused her no pain or sickness. She was tired, and strangely hungry, but she felt otherwise completely normal.

"Thank you," Auraltiferys said, pulling his cup toward him.

Iris smiled and shook her head, stunned by how simply the blacksmith had helped her. "How did you heal me?" she asked excitedly. "What was that magic Loomis was using? And how is this all so simple for you?"

After a tiny smile, Auraltiferys took a sip of his tea, then he set his cup down and answered, "I do have many years of practice, Iris. I've seen many things."

"That's exactly why it should be you fighting Loomis, not me," she interjected.

"Your human body is far less aged than mine," he replied, "but your demonic spirit is ancient. What I have learned in my lifetime is but a fraction of the knowledge your spirit holds. Anything I know, I am sure you already know, somewhere within yourself."

Iris stared at the dregs settling at the bottom of her teacup, suddenly frustrated and despondent. "How am I supposed to use what I don't know I know?" she asked sullenly.

"You're not trusting that you know these things," Auraltiferys said, "and I imagine that is your greatest obstacle. But you do have knowledge and power beyond what you believe, if you'll only get out of your own way." He paused for some tea, then sighed and continued, "Unfortunately, that is not something I can teach you. I myself am not an angel and cannot teach you how to exist as one."

"Should I really *want* to exist as what I am?" Iris returned.

The blacksmith looked at her with gentle reproach, which Iris believed was far more upsetting than a loud, scolding tirade would have been. "You should be grateful for your existence and the special purpose it serves," he said.

"Right," Iris replied quietly. It was a sincere agreement, devoid of sarcasm.

"I will continue to pray for you," Auraltiferys said, "and I will continue to make every sacrifice I can, asking that God will reveal your true nature to you at the appropriate time. I hope that time is soon."

"So do I," Iris concurred.

After pouring each of them another cup of tea from the kettle, Auraltiferys sat back in his chair and said, "In the meantime, I can explain what Drake did to you. It was, in fact, a common bit of demonic trickery, although Drake is far too artistic and arrogant to settle for the mundane, so he magnified his spells in a very severe way, almost certainly using a series of relics focused on such purpose. The deception always begins with a mild spell that induces sickness or physical discomfort, which is then made progressively worse until the victim turns to God for healing or solace. The demon will then employ other dark, offensive spells to exacerbate the pain or illness, relenting only when the victim's prayer ceases. The suggestion is thus planted in the victim's mind that it is the prayer, or in your case, the magic, that worsens the suffering. Ultimately, the demon's aim is to turn the victim away from a God they now believe is not listening to their pleas and will not help them. Since the suffering subsides when they ignore God, the victims are eventually willing to sacrifice their spirituality, which, of course, leads inevitably to sin and more sin."

With her eyebrows pressed into a look of disgusted interest, Iris responded, "So, Loomis was only trying to convince me to avoid magic?"

"Magic can be used without any actual reverence for God, if the user knows how to draw from that supernatural and omnipresent power," Auraltiferys answered. "Drake's goal is far more severe—to lure you away from God, away from goodness and righteousness."

"I was only using spells to try to counter his," Iris argued. "If he has no problem with magic, then why did he keep hurting me like that?"

"Your method of magic is likely too pious for his taste," the blacksmith replied. "You are a demonic entity as much as you are a human, but you don't realize it yet—not fully. You've learned to use magic in a humble way, not in an avaricious way, as is the preference of demons."

Iris reflected on the suggestion for a moment, but the idea yet left her with a feeling of insufficient understanding. "I still don't get it," she said at length. "I just can't believe he would already be willing to kill me."

Auraltiferys shook his head slowly, staring thoughtfully out the window behind Iris for a moment before returning his eyes to her. "I have no good answer," he admitted. "I don't believe he intended to kill you. I would guess he intended to break your will by causing you such great distress that you would surrender yourself to him in order to end the torture. Perhaps when you did not beg for his mercy as quickly as he hoped, he decided to double his efforts instead of admitting the failure of his plan. Your knowledge of magic right now may be rudimentary at best because you are limiting yourself to a singularly human nature, but the strength of your magic is already astounding. Drake almost certainly sensed that strength in you, and so he pushed you as hard as he dared. You, however, did not bend to his will, and you stubbornly prolonged your own suffering, to your own detriment." The blacksmith finished his tea, then added thoughtfully, "I imagine Drake is most infuriated with you right now, if that brings you any amusement."

With a tiny shrug, Iris admitted, "It kind of does...but it scares me, too. It...it didn't go well the last time I pissed him off."

"No, it didn't," Auraltiferys agreed solemnly, "but that was a different scenario. You approached him then in arrogance, revealing yourself to him as a challenge to be overcome. Tonight, however, you proved the strength of your humanity, refusing to submit to a demon."

Iris fell silent for a short time, then commented, "You said…my magic is strong?"

"It is," the blacksmith answered. Then, already deducing her follow-up question, he added, "Drake knows spells that haven't been used on Earth for thousands of years. Your demonic nature almost certainly knows the same spells, but you have not yet been able to unlock that part of yourself. Had you been able to do that tonight, you would have had no need of my assistance. If Drake prevails against you, it will be because of his knowledge, not because of his strength."

"If I'm as strong as you believe," Iris argued, "I would think it should be easy to 'unlock' my demonic nature. But even as I was inching toward death, I was nothing but human in my own mind, and God sure wasn't helping." She frowned and shook her head in frustration, then asked, "Do you think He wanted me dead?"

Auraltiferys stood from his chair and stretched for a couple of seconds, pressing his palms into the arch of his lower back, then he returned to his usual graceful-yet-authoritative posture and replied, "If God wanted you dead, I would not have been called upon to aid you." He picked up the empty teacups and kettle and carried them to the sink to wash and dry them.

Her mentor's response reminded her of a story a priest had once told during a homily, something about a shipwrecked man who was floating out in the middle of the ocean. The man, as the story had been told, had complete faith that God would save him. So strong was his belief that he disregarded offers of assistance from several boats that passed by him, telling all the people, "No, I don't need your help; God will save me!" Eventually, the man died, and then in Heaven, he questioned why God hadn't saved him. A question was posed to the man in reply, asking why he hadn't used any of the life preservers God had sent. Although Iris had asked the question mostly out of irritation and not out of actual belief, Auraltiferys's simple reply had made her feel foolish for asking it. She needed to work on being less temperamental and more aware of how God was working around her.

"Thank you for bringing me here," she finally said as the blacksmith returned to the table. "Thank you for helping me."

With a gracious inclination of his head, Auraltiferys answered, "I am grateful I was able to help you, and I will continue to help you as I can." He paused and looked at her very pointedly with eyes full of gravity. "But, Iris," he continued, his tone suddenly much more serious, "you cannot expect the same kind of assistance every time Drake approaches you."

"I know," she replied hastily, ashamed she had bothered the blacksmith at all, even if it hadn't been intentional. "I'm sorry."

"There is no need for apology," Auraltiferys responded. "I say this not because I wish not to be bothered, for that is not the case. I am willing to do whatever I am called upon to do. I tell you this because the future of humankind may rely on your ability to outlast Drake's temptations until you can put a stop to the dark creation he has begun. I fear you will not be able to do that as a human alone."

Iris had known this reprieve in the safety of the mountain with Auraltiferys would be a temporary one, but with Auraltiferys now speaking as though it was already drawing to a semi-permanent close, she felt suddenly nervous. With a tight chest and a stomach full of butterflies, she quietly replied, "You mean I have to work as a demon, too."

"I mean you must use every gift you have been given," Auraltiferys countered. "You will have to believe in the existence of your demonic nature in order to use it, but you have not yet fully accepted that as truth, and I cannot convince you of it. Defeating Drake will require more than an inhuman voice and ancient languages, Iris. You've used those spiritual abilities, probably because they seemed innocuous to you, but they will do nothing to stop Drake. You must match him in spiritual power before you can hope to defeat him in human existence. I sense you are afraid, and you may be justified in your fear, but at some point, you will have to acknowledge the unique creation you are and trust that God has not made a mistake in revealing all of this to you. He makes no mistakes."

"*He* makes no mistakes," Iris acknowledged, bitingly, "but *I* do. I already have. So, yeah, I guess I am afraid of my…other nature."

"I believe you have already proven you are not obligated to act like Satan just because he has cast his spirit into you," Auraltiferys stated with finality. "That spirit has always been there in you; it isn't new. Your *choices* will label you as good or evil; it is not the spirit within you that decides that. Be cognizant of your proclivities and be careful to avoid sin, and I believe you will both rescue humanity from peril and discover a deepness of faith you hadn't thought possible."

Iris felt some tears threatening to enter her eyes, but she stubbornly blinked them away. "If you say so," she said.

Auraltiferys softened a bit, relaxing slightly into his chair. "You told me Drake has threatened to hurt people because of you," he said, deflecting some attention from the sensitive subject of Iris's Satanic nature. "What did he tell you?"

Iris sighed, exhausted by just the thought of the metric crapton of work Loomis had insisted she must complete if she wanted him to spare lives. "He assigned months' worth of work to me and gave me a deadline of one month," she explained. "He said—well, he implied—that he would cause 'accidents' that would sicken and kill people if I don't finish everything in time."

"I see," Auraltiferys replied quietly, nodding gently. "Do you believe the task is impossible?"

"Yes," Iris answered. "I can't just make this stuff happen! Even if I did all of my part, which would be almost impossible by itself, the permits he has asked for would take months of processing by other agencies. There's no way."

To her surprise, the blacksmith's mouth curled into a tiny grin. His eyes glittered with an amused sort of concern, the same look a parent might have when a baby made a mess of food all over its face. "I've seen you make tea without lifting a finger," he said. "I've seen you move boulders with a bare hand. Is a stack of paperwork really too much for you?"

Iris stared blankly at him for a second, until she could no longer keep a grin away from her own face as his point dawned fully on her. "Okay," she said, "the paperwork, I can do. But how am I supposed to get permits in place? That's not under my control."

Auraltiferys ran one palm casually across the top of his silvery-white hair, then answered, "You are not limited to a single place or business, Iris. You must think more broadly, because that is how your opponent thinks. You can see to it that the pieces fall in place for the permits you need, in the time you've been allotted. I do, of course, caution you most strongly to do nothing that would negatively affect your conscience."

Iris's eyes narrowed, but she said nothing. She knew Auraltiferys would never suggest that she do anything immoral, although having a permit magically issued seemed like a questionable activity. The longer she considered it, however, the less angst she felt. It could be as simple as ensuring her applications, which would be thorough and free from error, were placed at the top of every involved party's priority list. Besides, there was no reason the applications would have to be complex. Auraltiferys was right—she had to think more broadly. If the run-down, outdated, unauthorized facilities Loomis had dumped on her would not be easily permitted, she could change them so that they would be. That was within her capabilities. And if Auraltiferys knew what he was talking about—if Iris really had just scratched the surface of her magical abilities—then such an endeavor should be not only feasible, but simple.

Iris roused herself from thought to find the blacksmith grinning at her, eyes sparkling. "That will be one problem solved, then," he said. Then, more gravely, he added, "Of course, you understand Drake is not the type to keep his word. You might meet each of his stipulations and still see lives lost."

The momentary optimism Iris had felt quickly departed her. "What's the point, then?" she asked.

"The point is that you do all you can to help those in need of your help," Auraltiferys answered strongly. "But this is all a game to Drake, and this task he has set for you now is nothing but a test. If you know enough magic, you can easily complete the work. If you rely on human power alone, you will undoubtedly fail. He is aware of both possibilities. If you succeed at this, he loses nothing and gains insight into his adversary. If you give up or fail, he will torture you with guilt over it until he convinces you to join him. Your best option, of course, is to complete his test successfully, then very quickly begin finding ways to destroy the evil work he has already begun. Otherwise, he will drive you to madness with countless other challenges, each more difficult than the last, and every one threatening the lives and souls of innocent people."

Iris took a shaky breath and nodded, wishing she hadn't called Loomis that night after receiving that stupid gift basket from him. If she hadn't rushed into all this, maybe she would have been better prepared to deal with his sick shenanigans. *Oh well*, she thought cynically, *too late to fix it now.*

"What do you plan to do about the married coworker you say Drake is threatening?" Auraltiferys asked after a brief silence.

Iris looked down at the table, then shrugged. "I tried to convince her to stay away from him," she said. "I told her I don't trust him. I told her she's a good person and her husband is a good person, and I mentioned it's weird that Loomis wants to take her to dinner and stuff, and she should be careful and whatever."

Nodding slowly and deliberately at Iris's flippant explanation, Auraltiferys crossed his arms. His eyes became like daggers of admonishment as she spoke. "I see," he said in reply, falling silent immediately afterward.

"What?" Iris asked defensively. "I'm not her keeper! She knows it's wrong to go out with him like that; that's why she isn't going to tell her husband about it. And she's stupid enough; she'll probably keep going out with Loomis anyway. But why should that be my problem?"

Concern darkened the blacksmith's patrician features, and he answered, "It is good you have tried to keep your coworker from falling victim to Drake's lurid temptations. What she does now is certainly not your problem. So then, to what shall I credit this sudden bad temper of yours?"

Iris realized her pulse had quickened. Thinking about Matilda and Loomis had immediately pissed her off. She forced herself to relax slightly, finding her neck and shoulders had tensed. After a breath, she said, "I don't know what you mean."

She regretted the evasion as soon as it left her mouth. Auraltiferys stared into her with stern reproach, and Iris knew she had just set herself up for an extremely uncomfortable exchange. She had played dumb, so now the blacksmith was going to call her bluff by answering his own question, to her great embarrassment. Because, of course, he knew *exactly* the reason for her sudden bad temper.

"You're jealous of her," Auraltiferys stated pointedly. Had he stopped with that comment, Iris could have lived with it, but, naturally, he did not. "Because you're attracted to him," he finished.

"I'm not!" Iris exclaimed. It didn't matter which statement she was replying to; the exclamation was an outright lie on both counts.

"Convince yourself of that before you try to convince me," the blacksmith answered, his tone as sharp as the blade he carried. "Your fight against Drake will be infinitely more difficult if you begin humanizing him. He is a demon, Iris; he is not a man, and you must not delude yourself into believing otherwise. And your jealousy is a terrible disadvantage for you; I see it may be your greatest weakness, and if I have recognized it, you can be certain Drake has recognized it. You *must* let that go; you must rid yourself of it. It will be a foothold for him; it will allow him to root himself in your mind and manipulate you."

Iris swallowed anxiously, embarrassed and angry at the same time. "What am I supposed to do about it?" she asked with irritation. "It's not like I can just turn off my jealousy! Yes, I'm easily made jealous; I know that. I have been since I can remember. But I don't act on it! It doesn't make me a bad person!"

"You *do* act on it," Auraltiferys answered, "though perhaps not in an overtly destructive way. It affects you, Iris. It changes the way you approach people; it changes how you feel about them, and not for the better."

" 'Not for the better'?" Iris quoted angrily. "How do you figure that? I tried to help her! I told her to stay away from Loomis! I was looking out for her!"

She felt hot as she tried to defend her actions to the blacksmith, whose cool demeanor and steady presence now opposed the heat and volatility of her ire. She knew he was correct in his assessment, and she knew it was her recognition of the weakness of her own argument that was fueling her hot-headed outburst. As she had often noticed and criticized among others, the least substantial words tended to be delivered with the greatest volume.

Auraltiferys's stern, noble expression and silent, icy stare compelled her to fall quiet. After several seconds, she had calmed down enough to feel the requisite shame for her behavior. "Iris," he said quietly, "you can tell me you were helping your coworker, and at the surface, that is true, but you and I both know her safety was not your primary concern."

Iris dropped her eyes toward her lap, numbly registering that her shirt and shorts and legs were still splattered with bloodied vomit from her wrangling with Loomis's spells earlier. "You're right," she finally admitted, her voice barely able to deliver the words without cracking.

"You are justified in trying to save your coworker and others from Drake's sinful traps," Auraltiferys continued, "but to do so for the sake of your own personal gain is truly regrettable, particularly when the 'gain' you seek is the singular affection of a demon."

Iris pressed her eyes tightly closed and shook her head emphatically, her chin still tucked toward her chest. "I don't want his affection," she said. "I really don't." The headshaking, she feared, was a subconscious attempt to convince her own mind of the truth of her words.

"I should hope not," Auraltiferys replied softly, "for he has no real affection to give you. His desire for you is no different than what a wild beast has for fresh meat."

Iris felt her eyes burning with fledgling tears, enough to blur the outskirts of her vision, but not enough, thankfully, to escape down her cheeks. She nodded gently, then sighed. "I know that," she said. Silence ensued, and though she was looking down, she was aware Auraltiferys was watching her. It felt as though he were wordlessly beckoning her to open her thoughts to him, and after a moment, she discovered she wanted to.

"I hate that I got jealous like I did," she confessed. "I hate that I'm...you know, attracted to him, or whatever..." Her voice trailed off, obviously trying to escape the embarrassment of the words it was being asked to convey. "I don't think I would ever *really* want...anything like 'affection' from him," she proceeded after a pause. "Actually, I know I wouldn't. But...it is difficult. He makes a very convincing human."

"His continued existence on Earth has required that," Auraltiferys replied. "You see now why he is so dangerous."

Iris hesitantly raised her eyes to meet the blacksmith's. "How do I fix it?" she asked. "How do I fix the jealousy? And the...the other thing?"

Auraltiferys's strictly authoritative air relaxed into a more comforting presence. "I doubt you will be able to 'fix' either of those things," he answered gently. "They will almost certainly be long-term struggles, though I must admit, your attraction to Drake escapes my understanding. I don't perceive you as shallow."

"I'm not," Iris stated, this time calmly and with genuine meaning. She found attractiveness in physical qualities like anyone else did, but those traits were not her measuring stick for anyone's value. She knew she valued substance more than appearance, and that did, in fact, make her attraction to Loomis even more confounding.

The blacksmith sat in quiet reflection for several seconds, then said simply, "Too many have already been fooled by his false charms; I hope you will not join them. You must pray; I should not have to tell you that. You must ask God's constant guidance and help, and you must confess your sins regularly, or Drake will grab hold of them and use them to drag you right into Hell with him."

"I went to confession when I left here the last time," Iris commented. "Didn't really seem to help me much."

Auraltiferys paused thoughtfully before responding, "It was probably that confession that allowed you to convince Drake you knew nothing about your demonic nature when you first went to meet him." As Iris considered the statement and realized, once again, that her tutor was almost certainly correct, the blacksmith stood and pushed his chair under the table. "It's a pleasant evening here," he said. "Let's sit outside for a moment."

She followed him to the porch, where they sat on the wood-and-stone steps, beneath a cerulean sky with a golden crescent moon. The stars were countless and bright, untouched by the miasma of humanity's fallen Earth. This mountain, in its holy place somewhere between Earth and Heaven, was truly beautiful, and Iris was glad she had been welcomed to it, though she felt shamefully undeserving.

Auraltiferys sat without speaking, and Iris was quite content sitting next to him, staring at the sky and reflecting on what she had learned in such a short time. All of this was beyond belief, yet it had become her reality. She was far from perfect, but somehow she had been deemed good enough to defend Earth against the onslaught of a very powerful demon. She owed it to all her human race to do a better job than what she had been doing so far.

"You know," Auraltiferys said after several minutes, "you may always confess your sins to me."

Instant terror sent Iris's pulse racing. She made a nervous, half-sighing, half-groaning sound before replying. "Umm...thank you, really," she said anxiously, "but...I'd rather not."

The blacksmith nodded his understanding, a small, compassionate smile brightening his face. "See that you confess to another priest, then," he insisted, "and work constantly to avoid sin, both in mind and body."

"I will," Iris answered. She wanted to mean it, but the reply sounded strangely weak to her own ears. She glanced at Auraltiferys sitting beside her, wondering if he might tell her he was unconvinced of her fortitude. His eyes, however, were directed silently toward the stars above them, and the moonlight fell so gracefully across his sculpted profile and his long, smooth mane of silver-white hair that Iris was moved nearly to tears by his beauty. No fortunate lighting effect could be given credit for such illumination; no, this was a man so holy and reverent that he radiated God's true, spiritual light. The moon and stars were but lending him their radiance, that his holiness might be made visible for a moment to Iris, who was both humbled and emboldened by his example. A brief glimpse at him was enough to fill her with purpose, with a true desire to complete the journey laid before her, however ugly the journey might be.

After a long moment, her mentor spoke again. "You will leave here soon, Iris," he said quietly, "and you will return to that realm on Earth where it is far easier to lose one's way. You have all you need to prevail over Drake, but you must learn how to employ it, and you must do so responsibly and in the right spirit. Move close to God and let Him draw you closer, because there you will be safe and strong. If you fall away, your opponent will pull you even farther, where he will more easily convince you his lies are true."

The nervousness Iris had felt a while earlier now returned with doubled energy. She swallowed and said, faintly and with tears stabbing at the backs of her eyes, "It sounds like you're telling me goodbye for good."

"No," he answered, turning to face her, "not at all. I hope you and I need never part for good. You were led by God to this mountain, and I will never keep you from it."

"You just think I need to fend more for myself," Iris suggested.

Auraltiferys gave her a tiny smile. "I would never suggest you proceed alone," he said in reply. "But the help you truly need is God's, not mine, and He is already present there on your battlefield."

"Auri..." Iris said hesitatingly, after a lengthy silence. "Can I call you that? Do you mind?"

"I don't mind," he answered graciously. His eyes danced with mirth, and Iris deduced he must be amused by the abbreviated moniker.

"Oh, good," she replied. Then, continuing her original thought, she said, "Auri, were you lying to me when you told me you're not an angel?"

The blacksmith actually rolled his eyes, more with cheer than with disdain or sarcasm. "I have never lied to you," he answered with a slight grin. Then, more seriously, he continued, "I am human, just as you are human. You, however, have an angelic spirit as well, and for that reason, I can offer you only so much as a tutor and mentor." He looked out at the sky once more and sighed heavily before concluding, in a somber tone, "There is another reason for which I must caution you against coming here more often than is necessary."

Concerned by the grimness of his last statement, Iris stared at him, tensely awaiting his explanation. The sudden knot in her stomach made her worry she might throw up again.

Auraltiferys paused, then set his sharp blue eyes directly into Iris's gaze and continued, gravely, "After Drake departed here the last time, so many years ago, I did everything within my knowledge and power to ensure neither he nor any other demon could set foot upon this mountain again. *Your* presence here I attribute to God's will, as you are a demon under unique circumstances, but I have gone to great lengths to keep Drake and the rest of them away, though I sincerely doubt any but Drake has the ability or desire to find this place. I have made it exceedingly difficult for him, but I cannot make it impossible. If he is watching you, he might learn from you the ways in which he can penetrate the magical defenses of the mountain. He might return here. My own safety matters not to me, but the protection of the forge and the relics and spells here are my responsibility. I barely survived him once; I do not know that I could fend him off again."

Iris swallowed and realized her hands were trembling slightly. "I'm so sorry," she said, her voice barely louder than a whisper. "I would never have come here if I knew I might be leading him back to you."

Auraltiferys shook his head and laid a strong hand on her shoulder. "You cannot lead him here directly without intending to do it," he answered, "so have no fear of that. But Drake is clever and perceptive, and if he recognizes you have found the mountain, he will read every trace of spiritual evidence it leaves on you, and he may, by those traces alone, be able to devise a method of safely returning here. The more you visit this place, the more he will learn."

Iris suddenly felt very much like an abandoned child, lonely and helpless and afraid. She didn't like the thought of leaving the mountain to never return. She hated the thought of never seeing Auraltiferys again. "Loomis would be stupid to come here," she said finally, her mind defiantly attempting to find a way to argue the blacksmith's concern. "You could too easily get rid of him."

He rose elegantly from the step and offered his hand to her, helping her to her feet. "I am humbled by the faith you have in me," he said, rather sadly, "but you overestimate my abilities." He flashed a warm, kind smile down at her from his lofty height, his eyes bright with wisdom and genuine feeling. "You underestimate your own abilities," he continued, "but I pray it will not always be so. Use your gifts, Iris, and direct them toward good. You will not be disappointed."

Iris felt an involuntary quiver in her bottom lip, and this time, she couldn't fully stop her tears. She restrained them to a trickle, though, and quickly brushed them away as she stared down at her feet. After a deep breath, she replied, "I'll try." She didn't trust her voice to say any more without causing a deluge from her eyes. She still had so many questions she wanted to ask; she had so many doubts she wanted her mentor to dismiss for her; she wanted his guidance and his comforting presence. Already, so much had gone wrong since she had first left him, and to leave him again, and to have to keep herself away, now seemed too painful to bear. He hadn't told her she couldn't come here, but he might as well have. If it endangered him, she couldn't risk it. She had already caused Yvette's death by her own foolish actions with Loomis; that alone was more guilt than she wanted.

Auraltiferys gently lifted her chin, bringing her out of her emotional reflections and directing her eyes to his. "Every mistake can be forgiven," he told her, "and every doubt can be answered with certainty. There is need of only one thing, and it has already been given to you, in spite of the fallen spirit that is your second nature. Choose the better part, Iris, and no demon can prevail against you."

Iris closed her eyes and nodded in reply. Though she wanted to thank the blacksmith for all he had said and done, she couldn't bring herself to speak. Somehow, though, she sensed he knew all she had wanted to say.

"It is goodbye only for now," he added softly. He placed his hand on her bowed head, said a blessing over her, then smiled sagely and turned away, disappearing into the house and leaving her alone on the porch.

After a last look at the most beautiful night sky she had ever seen, Iris focused her thoughts and instantly returned to her kitchen, the pool of stomach contents and blood there to greet her and to remind her how very near death she had come. With simple magic that now caused her no pain at all, she removed every trace of the evening's harrowing experiences, then she brushed her teeth, washed her face, and climbed into bed, thanking God for the blacksmith who had saved her and praying she would see him again, perhaps by then having already brought an end to Loomis's plans for the mass damnation of human souls.

You saw fit that I should exist as both demon and human, her thoughts spoke to God as she drifted to sleep. *Please, help me understand why. Please, help me to use it for good.*

15

Back at the office, Crane popped three aspirin into his mouth and forced them down with a swig of cold coffee from the breakroom coffee pot. He sat down and found a phone memo on his desk, informing him he had missed a call from that English lady he had briefly spoken with shortly after the museum artifact had been reported as missing. The note didn't say much, only that she had asked to speak with him as soon as possible.

"Hey, Banks," Crane addressed his partner, "why don't you see how the boys are coming along with the security footage? Maybe they've had some luck by now. I gotta return this lady's phone call."

"Will do," Banks replied, grabbing his notepad from the pocket of his jacket, which he had hung over the back of his desk chair. He walked away, and Crane picked up the phone and began dialing the number that had been left for him. It looked like a US phone number, which he was glad for, because he sure as hell couldn't remember how to dial international on these damn phones.

"Hello?" came the brittle, feminine voice on the other end of the line.

"Um, yes, ma'am," Crane began, "this is Detective Benson Crane—"

"Oh, yes, Detective Crane," the woman interrupted in her quaint British accent. "Thank you for returning my call. I've debated this for a while now since we last spoke, and I've decided I simply cannot bear to withhold this from you any longer. The artifact that was stolen from your museum, you remember, once belonged to my husband." As she spoke, agitation and unease entered her kindly voice.

Crane scrunched his forehead, wondering where on Earth she was going with this. "Yes, ma'am," he answered. "I remember."

"I *know* things about that artifact, Detective," she continued shakily. "Things I *must* tell you before you recover it, or before you halt your search for it, believing it lost forever. It is a treacherous thing, a loathsome thing, and you *must* find it...and you must *destroy* it." At her final words, emphatic conviction replaced the faint tremble in her tone.

Crane, as confused as ever, thought perhaps he had misunderstood. Or there was the possibility that he was simply speaking to a senile old lady who had too much time on her hands. Nonetheless, he couldn't just dismiss her if she claimed to have information related to the investigation, especially after his eruption with Dr. Whitakker at the museum earlier. Besides, she reminded him of his own late grandmother, and he felt obligated to treat her similarly. "I'm sorry?" he asked gently. "Did you say, *destroy* it?"

"I certainly did," she confirmed. "Detective, I know you must believe me a loony old kook, but I beg you to listen to my story and then do what I should have done years ago."

Crane massaged his forehead and replied, "All right, ma'am, I'm listening."

He sat silently on his end of the phone line as she narrated to him. A story spanning nearly three decades was told to him in a few short minutes, from the perspective of a wealthy widow who had moved from Bath in Somerset to New York City after her husband's sad demise twenty years ago, hoping to elude a series of awful memories and frightful events that had preceded her husband's death. The move had helped, but the news of the stolen spearhead had brought all the memories flooding back to her, carrying with them a heavy guilt for having donated the artifact to the museum in the first place, knowing what she had known. She had thought her storm had ended; she now realized the years of calm had simply lulled her into a false sense of security. Now, she was an elderly woman unable to put an end to the torment the spearhead had brought into this world, and she would have to rely on Detective Crane to do what she could not. The spearhead, she said, was haunted—an insidious, malignant, accursed thing that had changed her husband into a man she hardly recognized and had all but broken their family.

Five minutes after he hung up the phone, Crane made his way numbly to the IT room, where two technicians were reviewing a section of museum security footage with Banks. Upon his entry, Myron turned and began to say something, but he stopped abruptly when he saw the expression on Crane's face.

"What happened?" he asked, concerned.

Crane glanced quickly at the two technicians and then back at Banks, shaking his head slightly. "Nothing," he said stiffly. "Just a weird phone call. I'll tell you later."

Banks's eyes narrowed, but he took the hint. He took a deep breath and said, more cheerily, "Well, you gotta see this. These guys were able to salvage that part of the footage we had been missing." He leaned over the desk and rested his forearms on the tabletop beside the technician's keyboard. Crane walked over and stood beside him, leaning in toward the monitors from behind the tech.

"Go ahead and show him, Surge," Banks told the technician sitting at the computer. The kid's name was Sergio, but most of the department knew him fondly by his electronically inspired nickname. The other technician, standing on Surge's opposite side and intently watching the screens, was Max. Crane knew both of them to be good at their work, and he wasn't surprised they had been able to correct whatever had malfunctioned in the recording.

"Right," Surge replied, starting the video. "So this is the room where the guard was found, just before he enters from the left of the screen. I'll just let it play for you."

Crane watched the screen. He saw Joshua Ellis enter the room, likely headed back to the security office after completing a round. As he approached the Civil War display, something appeared to startle him, and he swiftly turned around and waved his flashlight behind him. Seeing nothing, he continued toward the front of the exhibit. Suddenly, something flashed across the screen, and in the next clear frame, the guard lay dead on the floor. Several seconds later, the older guard rushed in from the right-hand side, confused and frightened. The footage was better than what it had been before, but Crane wasn't seeing as dramatic an improvement as he had hoped for.

"We can't really get it any better than that," Surge said apologetically. "The digital file was awfully corrupted there."

"Yeah, but watch the frame-by-frame," Max urged, seeing what must have been some disillusionment in Crane's expression.

"That's where it really gets interesting," Banks agreed.

Surge restarted the segment, then paused the recording and began clicking through its frames individually, the room quiet but for his gentle, rhythmic keystrokes at the computer. Within the single still shots that created the video, it became more apparent—that momentary, blinding flash across the screen wasn't an *absence* of visible evidence; it was some kind of strange interference that almost-but-not-quite completely concealed a shadow that appeared in the middle of the frame.

Surge froze the image at that instant and zoomed in. The picture was poor quality, but Crane definitely saw something there. The dark shadow had a form, a figure—a head and arms and legs. It was grotesquely elongated and looked anything but human.

All four men remained silent for half a minute, staring at the creepy, demonic-looking shadow floating on the otherwise gray-white screen. Finally, Crane asked the question he knew they must all be thinking: "What the *fuck*?"

He didn't expect an answer.

16

Iris grabbed her purse, shut down her computer, and made a beeline for the front door. She couldn't believe how simple work had become, now that she had begun using magic to complete it. The workload she had been forced to accept from Matilda had been no effort at all, and even the seemingly impossible assignments from Loomis earlier in the week had proven far less challenging than she had assumed they would be. She had made it to the weekend having condensed months-long projects into the span of a few days, and her evening of sickness under Loomis's spells had nearly faded from memory. She felt stronger now; the more she utilized her magical abilities, the more natural it felt, and the more she liked it. There was wonderful, powerful freedom in it—she was no longer chained to the millstones of protocols or timelines; work was no longer work.

"Have a good weekend!" she told Matilda cheerfully as she passed her on her way out. The response she received was a droopy, asymmetrical pout and a mumbled "You, too." Iris continued on her way without hesitation, stifling her laugh until she had exited the office. Matilda had been a mopey sad sack ever since Iris had cautioned her about seeing Loomis outside of work, and Iris's impossibly fast completion of the tasks that would normally have taken Matilda a week or two hadn't helped the girl's mood. Iris had to admit, she found it hysterical. It had really made the office experience more enjoyable. Besides that, even Loomis himself had been strangely absent over the last few days, leaving Iris free from harassment. At first, she had been glad for it, but now, she was feeling almost eager to see him again. She knew he would return eventually to continue his torments and temptations, and she looked forward to disappointing him. She had begun to recognize the reality of an inhuman strength within her, and now Loomis would have no advantage over her.

She got in her car, turned her music up loud, and rolled out of the parking lot on screeching tires and the unnecessary but gratifying acceleration of her Challenger. A red light three blocks later spoiled her fun, but such was life. She sat there for a moment before inspiration suddenly struck her. *Why am I waiting for a light to turn green?* She forced the lights to change and slammed the accelerator to the floor, leaving behind a crowd of confused—and slow—drivers. She had no need to fret over the traffic ahead, either; she could see in her mind how everything was moving or not moving, and she could adjust her path accordingly. Come to think of it, she could adjust others' paths, too. The road was hers now; everyone else could deal with it.

In the span of only a few minutes, Iris was turning onto her street. The kids from the corner house were out enjoying the last remaining hour or so of evening sunlight, today bouncing a basketball in the middle of the street and shooting baskets at a hoop their parents had stupidly placed at the curbside entrance of their driveway. Apparently, they believed they had the right to usurp the public roadway and claim it as a personal basketball court for their bad-mannered, pea-brained spawn. Iris braked hard and honked her horn, then shot a dark look at the kids, who had clearly been startled by the sudden appearance of her car. *Good to know the little trolls can still be scared*, she thought to herself. In response to her clear displeasure, the oldest boy, who had an obvious attitude problem and complete disrespect for authority, grabbed the basketball out of the hands of his younger brother and bounced it as forcefully as he could off the hood of her car. It ricocheted off after a loud, metallic thud, leaving a visible dent on the otherwise pristine vehicle.

Iris narrowed her eyes and stared right at the boy, who insolently stared right back and then flipped his hands out in a what-are-ya-gonna-do-to-me gesture as the younger children ran back inside. Had anyone asked her before this moment what she would do to someone who intentionally damaged her car, Iris would have said she would repay the culprit with murder. She wouldn't have *really* meant it, because in no reality would she commit such a heinous act over something so trivial as a vehicle. But she was no longer the person she had once been; she had learned what she truly was, and now, in this moment of anger, she felt something break inside her. A torrent of vengeful wrath flooded over her, clouding her vision with a dark, blood-red haze and leaving little room in her mind for conscious human thought. Something told her, though, to bide her time for now, to refrain from any outward display of her rage. So she sat there in her idling car and watched the little imp pull his hood over his head, shove his hands into his jacket pockets, and walk smugly into his house. He probably hadn't even noticed how suddenly the sky had turned so dark.

When Iris pulled into her garage a few seconds later, she felt almost normal, except that it was not normal to feel almost normal after such an uncharacteristic and obviously inhuman onslaught of anger. She looked at the dent in the hood of her car, thinking perhaps she should be glad for it. The basketball that had caused that dent had dislodged whatever had been blocking her from really knowing the second nature that existed inside her. She had mostly believed the blacksmith when he had told her she was both demon and human, but now, she really *knew* it.

She repaired the dent with magic and went inside, where her cobra companion had pressed the button on the coffee maker for her so that it was already brewing. She nodded to it in greeting, but it didn't seem to want too much to do with her. It slithered off the counter and away to its den. Iris shrugged it off as typical reptilian aloofness, then went to her bedroom to change her clothes. She glanced at herself in the mirror and was startled by the reflection she saw. Outwardly, she looked the same as she knew herself to look, but there was a definite shadow in her eyes. Her face looked like the mugshot of a serial killer, just like those photos one might see on true-crime shows on television—the photos that were meant to prompt a viewer to think, *My God, what a vile and soulless monster!* It wasn't a look she had ever seen in her own eyes, and it alarmed her.

For a brief instant, she considered visiting Auraltiferys again, to confess to him what had just happened and to seek his counsel. But he had cautioned her against making too many trips to the mountain, and she had been there only a few days ago. *Don't be a baby*, she told herself. *Handle your own business.* It was easy to command herself to do that, but somewhat more difficult to know exactly what that meant she should do. She took a deep breath, and her hand involuntarily found its way to the shield medallion around her neck. She held it for a few seconds, then knelt down at the side of her bed and prayed. She hadn't really done the kneeling thing much outside of Mass since she was a child, but the display of reverence felt comforting now. *God*, she implored silently, *I know what that feeling was. It scares me that it didn't scare me. I don't want to be evil. Please, help me.*

She prayed for only a few minutes, but she felt much better afterward. She was planning to go to confession this weekend, just as her mentor had instructed her, and then she would go to Mass as usual. She would be fine. As Auraltiferys had pointed out, this demonic spirit wasn't new. There was no reason for her to become a different person just because she now knew the spirit was there.

She got up and went to the kitchen for her coffee, then she went in to visit her snake in the guest bathroom. She had practiced some of her magic by bringing in things from faraway places to make the snake more at home, and her bathroom had thus essentially become a tiny Asian rainforest. She was surprised she didn't mind it more than she did. Of course, it meant she could never entertain guests...but then, whom would she want to entertain, anyway?

"Sorry about earlier," she said to the serpent. "I know I looked kind of scary." The snake flicked its tongue and gently flared its hood, which Iris interpreted as an acceptance of her apology.

Now satisfied that her demonic nature was fully under her control, Iris moved back to the kitchen to finish her coffee, have some snacks, and watch some television. She sat on a barstool at her counter, reflecting during commercial breaks how nice it was to have the workweek successfully behind her and a weekend of relaxation and spiritual refocusing ahead. Her magical knowledge and ability had increased dramatically in a short time, and now she had also recognized the more powerful spirit within herself. Auraltiferys had been right—she was very strong, and now she could believe it for herself. The power was a wonderful feeling. Yes, it was naturally evil, but it could be redirected, and she would ensure it would be. She would keep herself on the straight and narrow. Whenever Loomis might pop up again, he'd be in for a real surprise. He would be unable to coerce her into doing anything, and even better, he would soon find himself having to scramble to try to pick up the pieces of his shattered plans for the world's damnation. Iris had caught a glimpse of her real strength, and Loomis was not going to be pleased.

As evening settled into night, Iris finally turned off the TV and moved to her bedroom, where she undressed and got in the shower. The water was hot, and it felt nice and relaxing against her skin. *Life's not so bad*, she thought to herself. *I'm glad I didn't die earlier this week.* How foolish that would have been, to have let Loomis kill her! She wouldn't make such mistakes anymore. As she lathered shampoo into her long hair, she closed her eyes and imagined how her next encounter with Loomis might go. He would show up, all gorgeous and charming as usual, and he would try to woo her with some suggestive words and some teasing, gentle touches that could be classified in no other way but tastefully naughty. Maybe she would even let him get away with it for a while—just a little while—before she would dash all his hopes. The blacksmith had chided her for being attracted to Loomis, but...was it really so terrible? She knew he was a demon; it wasn't as though he could trick her there. It wasn't her fault he had constructed such an appealing human form for himself. Why should she feel guilty for acknowledging that? What harm could there really be in enjoying a taste of it? She was, after all, going to save humanity from his evil clutches; didn't she deserve a little something in return? Loomis was initiating all of it, anyway; she couldn't be held at fault for his temptations. Besides, she could go to confession whenever she needed to. She would never let herself *completely* derail. In the meantime, it might be fun to let him think he was having some success with her.

She let her thoughts drift to only slightly devilish places for a moment or two before she became bored with the daydreams and started singing softly instead. She didn't have a great voice, but she could carry a decent tune thanks to years of various musical instruction, and the privacy to sing in the shower free from judgment was one of the perks of living alone. Thoroughly enjoying herself as she sang snippets from whatever tunes popped into her head, she cheerfully finished her shower and started in on "Midnight Train to Georgia" as she stepped out onto the bath rug to dry off. She wrapped herself in a towel and opened the door to the vanity area, where her casual singing was suddenly interrupted by a gasp of fright.

"Jesus!" she exclaimed, pressing her hand hard against the racing heartbeat in her chest. "What the *hell* are you doing here?"

Loomis was propped nonchalantly against the edge of her bathroom counter, clad in characteristically fine fashion, with dark slacks and a matching vest over a lighter-colored dress shirt. His sleeves were neatly rolled up, revealing well-toned forearms, which he had crossed across his torso.

"Tsk, tsk, Iris," he responded in feigned reproach. "Did they not teach you anything in Sunday school?"

Iris rolled her eyes, though she knew using the Lord's name as an exclamation had not been great form, especially in front of a demon. When she returned her gaze to Loomis a second later, she found him looking her up and down with overt suggestiveness, and she suddenly felt extremely vulnerable, standing there in front of him with wet hair and no makeup and wearing nothing but a towel. All the confidence she had felt a few minutes ago was gone, and all the not-so-nice thoughts she had entertained in the shower now sickened her. She didn't want Loomis; she didn't want him at all, but he was certainly going to try to make her want him, and that was terrifying.

"Why are you here?" she asked him, dropping her eyes to the floor and subconsciously tightening her towel around her.

With a small shrug, Loomis answered, "It's a Friday night. I thought you might like to celebrate the end of the workweek with some enjoyable company."

"You thought wrong," Iris answered sharply. She wanted to sound tough, but she was certain Loomis knew she was afraid.

Loomis grinned, staring at her in silence until she met his eyes. The angle of his head under the overhead lights resulted in a very handsome yet very sinister contrast of illumination and shadow on his face. "That hurts me, Iris," he said facetiously. "You haven't seen me for several days; I had believed you might be missing me."

"Nope," she replied.

He uncrossed his arms and turned to look at himself in the mirror, smoothing his vest and gently rearranging a few strands of hair. "So, then," he sighed, "I suppose you weren't fantasizing about me at all while you were in the shower." There was a strong undercurrent of accusation in his tone.

Iris hesitated, feeling extremely nervous and extremely disgusted with herself. "Gross," she finally said, quite unconvincingly.

Loomis turned again and leaned against the counter once more, this time closer to her than he had first been. "Well," he answered, his voice low and smooth and deep, "if you *had* been fantasizing about me, I wouldn't call it 'gross.' In fact, I would encourage it. There is no reason your mind shouldn't have whatever it desires. You could be totally freed from all that judgment, Iris. I don't know why you would choose to leave yourself in those chains."

Part of her brain thought he made a valid point, but Iris refused to let the idea take root. She couldn't allow him to set up shop in her mind. "Why don't you just say whatever you came here to say and then get out," she suggested with irritation. She then added, sarcastically, "Don't you have a date with your girlfriend Matilda tonight? Or is hubby back in town?"

Loomis grinned again and stood up from his lackadaisical post at the counter. "How funny you should mention that," he said as he turned and began inspecting the various lotions and perfumes on the countertop. "Matilda's interest in me seems to have waned most suddenly," he continued, "although it is readily apparent she was far happier when she allowed herself the indulgence of my company. I'm beginning to wonder if perhaps someone warned her to stay away from me." He looked meaningfully back at Iris.

"Maybe she just has a conscience," Iris proposed flatly.

Loomis ignored the statement but for an ever-so-slight grin and a pointed look of complete incredulity. He picked up the bottle of rose-scented lotion he had gifted to Iris, and she was suddenly ashamed by the fact she had used it at all. It was only lotion, yes, but the smug look on Loomis's face now upon seeing the half-empty bottle made her regret having ever opened it. He took the cream and moved slowly behind her, while she stood unmoving in an attempt to appear unperturbed, though a perceptive observer could see she was a block of pure, anxious tension. He dispensed a generous amount into his hands and slowly rubbed his palms together before he began massaging the moisturizer gently into Iris's bare shoulders.

"Iris," he said quietly into her ear, "you never had any reason to be jealous of her. It's you I want."

His hands were warm and strong against her skin, and the feminine fragrance of rose softly caressed the air as a pleasant and unfortunately arousing overlay to the masculine scent he wore. If she hadn't been completely horrified, Iris might have enjoyed letting him continue his seductive massage over every inch of her. Luckily, however (or unluckily, depending upon one's perspective), she *was* completely horrified. Holding her towel tightly closed with one hand, she slapped at him and lunged away, immediately turning to face him. His handsome features were set in a subtle yet undeniable expression of utter amusement. It was thoroughly infuriating, but Iris's thoughts were in such disarray that she couldn't readily decide how to retaliate.

"You're so talented in pushing people away," he stated with a rueful smile.

"Screw you," Iris hissed in reply.

"I say it without insult," he answered placidly. "It's only an observation, and I doubt even you would try to deny its validity."

"Whatever," she retorted angrily. She couldn't argue the point, but neither could she bring herself to acknowledge he was right.

Loomis sighed. "I have known your race for a very long time," he said gently. "So few can bear real solitude; they have an insatiable need for the affection of others. You seem to lack that particular weakness, and, in fact, I find it refreshing."

Iris was silent, her eyes focused in skepticism on Loomis as he spoke. She didn't disagree with him, but neither did she trust him or his motives. He slowly approached her again and took one of her hands in his, chivalrously letting her other hand maintain its guard of her towel.

"I didn't come here tonight to be confrontational," he continued, running his thumb lightly across the back of her hand. "I approached you in the wrong way, and for that, I apologize. You are so different from the rest of them. You're superior to them all."

Iris swallowed nervously and yanked her hand away from him, thinking it seemed the appropriate thing to do. Deep down, however, she hoped he would continue his thought. She wasn't hating the unexpected compliments.

"I could be the one you would never have to push away," Loomis went on. "I can give you everything you deserve, everything the world has failed to give you. Everything of mine would be yours, and, having only your company in the coming age, I would want for nothing more." He had, at some point during the brief statement, taken her hand in his once again. Iris was vaguely aware of it, but she no longer had any desire to pull away.

"I confess," Loomis proceeded, "I turned my attentions toward Matilda because I sought to make you jealous. I regret that I did it. She's an intolerable annoyance, and more ignorant than even I believed a human could be. She is nothing compared to you; what a fool I was to believe you'd be jealous of her! My worst mistake was my arrogance; I recognize it now. You don't need me. You don't even want me." He gently squeezed her hand, then slowly released it and asked, "Does it surprise you to hear that only makes me want you more?"

Only seconds had passed, but Iris had somehow become lost enough in her visitor's dark, amber-studded brown eyes that she hadn't even realized how close he had moved to her. Her wits suddenly regrouped when she felt his hands settle on her hips, holding her within a few heated inches of his body. She recalled the grotesque analogy Auraltiferys had used, likening Loomis's desire for her to that of a wild beast's desire for meat, and she suddenly had no desire to be the meat. Once again, she had foolishly proven she was as susceptible to Loomis's trickery as anyone else was, and that greatly annoyed her. *You're better than this*, her mind told her. Only a few hours ago, she had finally felt the true strength of her inhuman nature; how did Loomis so easily make her feel nothing but human?

In acute anger at her own weaknesses and at Loomis for so adroitly pointing them out, she focused an intense spell that shoved him hard into the wall behind him. His back struck against it with a solid thud, the impact causing a decorative shelf on the opposite side to drop its collection of trinkets with a loud clatter onto the desk in her bedroom. Loomis wasn't hurt by the spell, but Iris had expected him to be angered by it. Instead, he looked almost pleased. He adjusted his tailored vest as he regained his typical poise and then smiled maliciously at her.

"So," he said darkly, "you *can* use magic. I wasn't certain you could."

"Of course I can," Iris answered. "Surely you're not *that* stupid."

"Not all who are *aware* of magic are capable of *using* it," Loomis replied, surprisingly cheerfully. "Historically, such 'incompetents' have been willing to pay great sums for the services of magical attendants, who were once quite in fashion. They are much more difficult to come by these days, and they are inordinately costly. And they do breed such drama! I'm pleased to learn you are handling your own affairs. I expected no less, but, frankly, I was beginning to wonder about you."

With a scoff, Iris retorted, "Yeah, well, now you know. It's all me. Just another reason for you to stay away."

Loomis grinned and leaned himself against the doorway leading to the bedroom, looking completely relaxed and totally inviting, much to Iris's annoyance. "It's not *all* you," he corrected her. "You have help."

Something in either his tone or his eyes made Iris suddenly afraid. She hoped it was her imagination, but it was only an emaciated wisp of hope. If Loomis knew of her encounters with Auraltiferys, which seemed a strong possibility, then the blacksmith might already be in danger, for no other reason than his involuntary and unsolicited affiliation with her. It was an awful thought.

Loomis stared at her for a moment, his eyes bearing a remarkable resemblance in sharpness to the blacksmith's, as though he had stepped right into her mind. *He can't know your thoughts*, Iris told herself. *He can't.* But damn...it sure felt like he could.

"I believe I know who is helping you," Loomis continued, clearly enjoying the apprehension he sensed from her, "and I suppose I shouldn't be surprised, considering what an impossible creature you are. There are few who can appropriately direct a power such as yours."

Iris swallowed, as imperceptibly as possible. She wished she hadn't rashly assaulted Loomis as she had. His seductive approach had been uncomfortable, but this new direction was quickly moving somewhere she absolutely did not want to go. "I don't know what you're talking about," she said quietly, her jaw tight.

After several seconds of silence, which were excruciatingly tense for Iris, Loomis ignored the obvious lie and responded easily, "You must be so fond of him already! Who could fault you for it? As humans go, he is rather extraordinary; even I am willing to admit that."

He stood straight again and moved directly in front of her, stopping about a foot away and crossing his arms. He suddenly looked much more intimidating somehow, and Iris considered perhaps she had made a mistake in so rudely abbreviating that pleasant massage from him just a few minutes ago.

"He has made things difficult," Loomis said coldly, "but he cannot render anything impossible for me. I have stayed away because it has been my choice, not because of anything he has done." After a brief, thoughtful pause, he added lightly, "It has been so many, many years...perhaps it's time I pay him another visit."

Iris now felt totally helpless, with no clue how she might safely respond. Feigning ignorance would do no good; threatening him would be met with nothing but mockery. She wasn't even sure enough of her own power to make a convincing threat, anyway. If Loomis intended to reach Auraltiferys and harm him, it seemed very likely he would do just that. In a panicked instant, Iris realized how awful was the choice that had been set before her: Was her own salvation worth more to her than Auraltiferys's life?

Her thoughts drifted back to the mountain for a moment, and she pictured the ancient blacksmith prayerfully studying in the library as a dark, terrible cloud descended over everything, carrying the full, evil power of Loomis's demonic spirit with it. Auraltiferys would fight well, but he had said it himself—he was not as strong as a demon. Iris's imagination began constructing visions of what horrifying things Loomis might do to him, but the images were too painful for her to bear. She cleared them swiftly from her mind and found she was distressingly close to tears, while Loomis stood like an executioner in front of her, cold and emotionless but for the clear gleam of sadistic pleasure in his eyes. She couldn't let him see her cry. *God, help me*, she pleaded silently as she emptied her thoughts so she could focus on the feeling of the magical abilities within her. A strange sensation overcame her, an immediate disconnect from physical reality. It was as though time stood still and human limitation disintegrated. She wasn't certain what magic she was using, but she could now see her own body from outside it. There she stood in front of Loomis, as in a photograph on a wall, yet here she was, able to move about her bedroom while that picture remained unchanging. A dozen questions welled up in thought somewhere, but she knew this wasn't the time to consider the technical aspects of whatever ability she had just discovered. Drawn toward the shield medallion lying on her dresser, she placed a metaphysical hand on top of it and felt the relic's magic focusing her thoughts even more acutely. She felt the rhythmic, metallic heartbeat of Auraltiferys's work in the holy forge, and it immediately calmed her. Returning in an instant to the single location of her human body, she knew one thing with absolute certainty: Auraltiferys would not want her to sacrifice her soul to spare his mortal life.

Loomis's eyes narrowed as he stared at her; Iris assumed he must know she had used some magic, though he likely didn't know what it had been. Perhaps that human form of his limited him slightly more than he believed it did. She remained silent, and Loomis finally continued his baleful musings, saying, "That pious idiot undoubtedly believes God spared him from me the last time. It will be satisfying to prove him wrong. God didn't spare him; it was my decision to let him live then, and I had my reasons. I think by now he has outlived his usefulness."

Iris felt much more confident now, but the idea of an attack on Auraltiferys was no more palatable than it had been seconds earlier. Loomis might be bluffing; he might have no way of reaching the mountain right now. Still, she wasn't going to give him any more ammunition. After a deep breath, she asked him, "Who would be the more idiotic? The pious believer in God, or the demon who sends him to an eternity in Heaven?"

To her delight, she saw a flicker of irritation darken Loomis's countenance. He rolled his eyes and replied, "Steep prices are sometimes worth paying, if the benefit outweighs the cost."

Damn, Iris thought. *The bastard has an answer for everything.* Her confidence was, once again, rapidly waning.

"Don't worry about it just yet, my dear," Loomis continued, malicious joviality back in his voice. "I have more pressing issues to attend to first. But, do keep that pleasant little thought in the back of your mind." He winked at her, a gesture that looked ridiculous on most people but somehow looked very attractive on him. Iris dropped her eyes to the floor momentarily and adjusted her grip on the folds of her bath towel.

After uncrossing his arms and looking down at his Rolex with a dramatic sigh, Loomis stepped toward her and took her free hand in both of his. "It is late," he said sweetly, "and I have stolen enough of your time. When you reflect on the events of this evening, I hope you will focus on the pleasures I have offered you, rather than dwelling on the ugliness of hateful spells and vile threats. We needn't be opposed to one another, Iris. I believe, in time, you will recognize it. You have a unique strength that humankind cannot fully appreciate. *I* can fully appreciate you, however, and I could teach you so much more than any mortal man ever will. I could help you unlock powers within yourself that exceed human comprehension. Only with me will you become the true force you were meant to be."

With that, he lifted her hand to his lips and kissed it, then he slowly returned it to her, pressing it gently against her chest. Iris swallowed nervously, feeling very hot and very uneasy. Loomis smiled charmingly at her, and all she could do was blink dumbly.

She wouldn't expect her fantasies to have any place in reality, but would it really be too much to ask that she might have just a hint of the flirtatious feminine boldness of the fanciful, ideal counterpart of herself her mind always constructed? Loomis was a damn fine flirt, and Iris was no less a demon than he was. She hated how he so easily made her feel like a shy, delicate little girl. On the other hand, she considered, perhaps that was a good thing. Only Heaven could know what atrocious carousing might already have transpired if she acted toward Loomis in reality the way she did in daydreams.

Loomis turned and strode casually from the vanity area into Iris's bedroom, pausing at the foot of her bed to look back at her. "By the way," he said thoughtfully, "I noticed you have quite a nasty pest situation in your guest bathroom. You may not be aware, but extermination is one of my specialties."

The implication made Iris more irate than fearful. She felt a surge of hatred within her, and it was only a warning voice from somewhere in her mind that prevented her from undertaking an all-out magical attack on Loomis's artificial human body. With great effort of will, she restrained her anger and answered simply, "I have no pest and no need for your services."

Loomis smiled graciously. "Well," he sighed, "most people would consider that hideous serpent a pest. As you are so quick to defend its existence, I can only assume you have developed a strange affinity for it. I'm a bit surprised, but it is quite edifying to know you are capable of such...affection. I suppose we can attribute that to your human nature. Demons don't have such vulnerabilities." With darkened eyes and a cold voice, he concluded, "Let us hope you do not force me to take any extreme measures, with either your pet or your mentor."

Iris felt ire contort her face, narrowing her eyes and curling her lips into something nearing a snarl. "If you have any intelligence at all," she hissed, "you will preserve every object of my 'affection' from every evil within your power to thwart, because if any harm befalls them, you can kiss goodbye every chance you think you have with me. I've suffered enough loss in my lifetime to know I can endure it. You'll convince me of nothing that way; it would only solidify my opposition to you."

Loomis stared sharply at her as he listened, as if trying to measure the depth of her conviction. After a pause for thought, he answered, "Perhaps you are truly that stalwart. But grief can be a shockingly effective weapon, and I think you underestimate it. There is really only one way to know how you will react to it." He grinned nastily, like a psychopath who believed he had just outsmarted all the authorities. It was a look of incalculable evil.

"You're not going to take such a stupid risk," Iris retorted icily. "Don't forget, you need something from me."

"Ah, but you have no intention of giving me what I need!" he countered emphatically. "So, what would be the harm to me in making you suffer for your decision?" When Iris replied to him with silence and a hateful look, he tilted his head slightly and added with a sly grin, "Or perhaps your decision is not yet made, and we need not yet discuss such macabre affairs."

Iris thought for a moment, startled by the perverted logic in all that Loomis said. She believed she would never submit to him; she believed she would prevent him from overtaking Hell and from pillaging the souls of all humanity. But if she believed so strongly, then Loomis was right—it was pointless to try to tempt her, so inflicting pain would be the next best thing. It might even change her mind. Iris had always done everything she could to avoid pain; if she were honest with herself, that was probably one of the main reasons she had so few real friends and no romantic relationships. She didn't want to be tempted by Loomis, but she wanted even less to be punished by him. This was a bad situation all around.

Not waiting for her to reply, Loomis smiled handsomely and

said, "It is true, I need something from you. Equally true are all the offers I have made to you. We can serve each other perfectly. We will both be stronger as allies than we are as enemies." With another suave wink, he added, "We will enjoy far greater pleasures, too."

He turned his back and vanished. Iris slumped against the vanity and groaned, pressing one hand against her now-aching head while the other still unthinkingly clutched her towel wrap. She couldn't yet outguess Loomis Drake. He was charming and dignified and attractive, then perverted and threatening and terrifying, yet somehow, he always made a lot of sense to her. Either he knew her too well, or they had more in common than she cared to admit.

17

Slowly opening her eyes, Iris saw pleasant, golden sunlight filtering softly into the bedroom through the closed blinds. She remained in the bed, her face pressed against the cool satin pillowcase and her body feeling noticeably more comfortable than it ever had before. What a relief it was to have slept so soundly! She remembered having great difficulty falling asleep after Loomis's unexpected visit, but at some point, she must have found the ideal sleeping position, because she now felt more rested than ever. She closed her eyes again and breathed deeply, wishing to enjoy the comfort of her bed for just a minute longer. Was it her imagination, or was there the faintest trace of Montblanc cologne on her sheets?

The scent, though certainly not unpleasant, startled her, because it brought a vivid image of Loomis to the forefront of her mind, even though she had watched him leave last night after their exchange. It was probably just a remnant of his presence here, or perhaps it was a little joke of his, a reminder to her that she should think of him, cast to her bed by his magic from far away. Or it could just be her active imagination, her own thoughts of Loomis conjuring his scent from memory. If Loomis Drake had been in her bed...well, surely she would have known that.

Trying to put all fear aside, Iris wondered what fresh hell might await her today. Perhaps Loomis would stay away for a while, give her time to reflect on all the webs he had spun in her head, the promises of pleasure interwoven with terrible threats, all of which held at least some inkling of either appeal or logic. Or perhaps she would walk into her guest bathroom and find a dead cobra awaiting her. That was a distressing thought. *Only one way to find out*, she mused, grudgingly rolling herself to a seated position at the edge of the bed.

"You have *got* to be kidding me," she whispered aloud to herself as she looked around the room. This was not her bedroom at all. This was…she didn't have any clue what this was, but it was obviously Loomis's handiwork. It was a lavish bedroom, its most notable feature the large, extremely comfortable ebony canopy bed upon which she now sat, outfitted in expensive, gunmetal-gray satin sheets and sheer curtains that matched the deep indigo shade of the comforter set. The walls were a pristine, glossy black, outlined in elegant gold trim. Abstract canvases painted in blues and blacks and golds were hung around the room, bringing pops of color and light to the dark walls. Along the wall opposite where she was now facing, there was a large ebony dresser sitting below a huge, gold-framed mirror. Iris looked back at it only long enough to register what it was; she had no desire to see her reflection.

She stood from the bed, resolving not to panic. She was aware enough of magic by now to know this was nothing she couldn't handle. There were certainly far worse things than waking up in Loomis Drake's bedroom, assuming that was where she was. There was a beautiful, plush carpet beneath her bare feet, though it covered only the floor area beneath and surrounding the bed. Beyond the rug, the floor was a shiny, dark brown hardwood. Iris knew nothing about interior design, and she would have thought a brown floor with black walls was a bad idea. But in this room, it was actually quite spectacular. She might not have chosen these exact colors herself, but she found them very pleasing.

She glanced through a wide cased opening to see the vanity and bathroom areas, which appeared to be equally opulent and well decorated. Everything was wonderfully clean, and it was only then she realized how strangely unlived-in this place looked. She supposed that made sense; one wouldn't expect a spiritual being to create much of a physical mess. She wondered, with some embarrassment at her own thoughts, whether Loomis even had to do human things, like brushing his teeth or using the bathroom. His body lacked a soul, but...it probably required some physical maintenance, right? Or did he take care of all that with magic? Iris simply couldn't picture him ever excusing himself for a bathroom break, and, oddly, she was disgusted by the thought of it. Somehow, that human behavior seemed very far beneath him, and she wasn't sure if that was a good thing or a bad thing. Auraltiferys had warned her not to "humanize" Loomis, but now she was feeling a bit disgusted by her own humanity in comparison. Demonic existence suddenly seemed cleaner and more appealing than beastly humanity.

Ignoring her urge to rifle through the drawers of the vanity and the dresser, Iris left the bedroom and soon heard the gentle clinking sounds of a kitchen in use. Aromas of blueberries and vanilla and coffee greeted her, and though she knew who must be standing around the corner, she was so enticed by the pleasant smell that she didn't even dread seeing him. *Oh, God,* she thought in a sudden panic, her mental voice choosing the Creator's name as its irreverent exclamation, *I'm not even wearing my makeup!* It was ridiculous to have such a thought; Loomis had seen her without makeup just last night. And, well...of course she wasn't trying to attract him, anyway, so...her appearance before him shouldn't even matter to her. In the final second before she rounded the corner into the kitchen, however, she decided to let vanity win, and she added her usual cosmetic enhancements to her face by way of magic. Her long hair was down, which was not how she preferred to wear it, and it hadn't been brushed after she had slept, but when she had her makeup on, she cared a lot less about the look of her hair. Maybe the messy, slept-in hairstyle would somehow give her a wild, edgy sort of confidence. Besides, she didn't want to show up too "beautified" in front of Loomis...he might get the wrong idea. She flipped her head over and quickly tousled her hair, then she flipped it back and styled it haphazardly with her fingers before hesitantly entering the kitchen.

It was a clean, bright, modern-looking expanse of granite, tile, stainless steel, and glass, just like the luxury homes featured in magazines—the ones that always depressed Iris because she knew she'd never make enough money in three lifetimes to afford anything like them, even though plenty of people who were dumber and lazier and generally shittier than she was were somehow able to enjoy them. Loomis stood at an island in the middle, facing away from her, busy with something. He was wearing what Iris assumed must be his sleeping clothes: a pair of relaxed, silky pajama pants in a deep navy shade and a fitted black T-shirt that, judging by the apparent quality of its fabric, was probably the work of some famous designer and probably cost more than any one of Iris's regular outfits. It was hard to tell from behind him, but it appeared he was barefoot. Iris was surprised by the unassuming air of this new look. She had never seen him in anything but expertly tailored designer menswear. His apparel now was no less tailored and no less expensive, but, somehow, it made him look remarkably more human and far less off-limits. She looked at his figure for a lingering second, finding herself shamefully excited by the view. His form was a slender one, but he was lithely muscular, and the slim cut of his shirt accentuated the definition in his shoulders and upper back. He must know she was there looking at him (and enjoying it), but...well, at this point, who cared? She couldn't convincingly lie to him about his attractiveness, anyway; there was no point in pretending he hadn't chosen a completely intoxicating masculine form in which to dwell. He knew he had.

Saying nothing, Iris walked around the kitchen island and leaned over the side opposite Loomis, crossing her forearms on top of the cool, dark-colored granite and resting on them. From here, she could see Loomis was preparing a small bowl of icing for the pan of freshly baked scones that had apparently just come out of the oven and were cooling there on the counter between them. Even unfinished, the pastries looked fit for the display case of any professional bakery.

"Good morning, my queen," he greeted her in his pleasing baritone. "I'm glad you're awake; these will be ready soon." He smiled brightly at her as he whisked the ingredients of his glaze. "Your coffee is awaiting you," he added cheerfully, indicating with a gentle lift of his chin a cup of hot liquid sitting on the bar behind her.

Iris glanced at the coffee, but she didn't immediately move toward it. She wasn't sure what Loomis's angle was here, so she couldn't decide what reaction would be most appropriate. Should she express her confusion and irritation at this whole unexpected situation? Make some sarcastic retort to having just been referred to as his "queen"? Find a knife in a drawer somewhere and stab him with it just to make a statement? After only a second's hesitation, she decided just to play along for the moment. He wasn't threatening her, and he wasn't explicitly trying to seduce her, so there was no immediate danger or discomfort, and she knew he would make his purpose known eventually. So she seated herself on one of the two barstools and pulled the coffee toward her. She knew by aroma alone it was the good stuff.

Loomis finished the icing and drizzled it smoothly over the scones before placing the confections on a large serving platter. He set the platter in the middle of the counter and seated himself on the stool beside Iris. With quick and silent magic, the used baking dishes were removed from sight, and clean plates, cloth napkins, and gleaming silver utensils were set in front of the pair. Iris looked blankly at him, expecting some explanation now, but he offered none. Instead, he delicately placed a warm scone on her plate and nudged it closer to her with a subtle smile.

"I hope you enjoy these," he said. "It was quite an effort, but I believe I have finally achieved perfection. At the risk of sounding arrogant, I'll say you will not find a more delectable pastry anywhere." He placed a scone on his own plate and waited, watching Iris expectantly, his eyes bidding her to taste the fruit of his labors.

Rather reluctantly, not because she was uneager to try the pastry, but because she didn't want Loomis to think her too enthusiastic about it, Iris turned her attention to the scone and gently cut into it with her fork.

"They do smell good," she admitted, still holding the small bit on her fork over her plate.

"Mmm," Loomis agreed. There was no obvious suggestiveness in his wordless agreement, but the deep resonance of the sound from within him was oddly thrilling. "They're blueberry and vanilla," he continued amiably, "with just a hint of almond, and I added a touch of lavender to the icing. I think you'll be pleased."

Iris finally placed the bite in her mouth and had to mentally restrain herself from making any overt gestures of approval. Loomis already knew it had to be the best scone ever; he didn't need her to tell him so, and she didn't intend to.

"Well?" he asked hopefully.

Iris imagined she could see genuine expectancy in his eyes, though she believed it was only her own wishful thinking blurring her vision. After swallowing, she shrugged and nodded, then took a sip of coffee. "It's good," she said.

With a sigh, Loomis turned on his stool and took a bite of his own scone, then gently dabbed at the corners of his mouth with his napkin. "Honestly, Iris," he said ruefully, "why must you make me work so hard for the tiniest compliments?"

"I said it was good," she retorted defensively. "What more do you want?"

"You could be completely honest with me," he answered quietly. He looked at her with a keen stare and continued, his voice strengthening into its usual inviting smoothness, "You could tell me it's the best scone you've ever tasted. You could tell me you want more of it." He leaned away from her slightly, resting on his elbow farthest from her as he maintained his stare, and added with a grin, "You could tell me how aroused you are right now."

Iris rolled her eyes, but she felt her cheeks flush, anyway. "It's just a scone," she argued.

"You can't tell me you hate this picture," Loomis countered.

"What picture?" Iris snapped. "You mean waking up in a strange room to find you in your pajamas, baking for me and calling me your queen? Which I'm certainly not, by the way. Please." She shoved the plate several inches away and scowled, irritated that Loomis was so damn perceptive and had called her out on her forced disinterest. Most people were, if not easy to lie to, at least easy to withhold the truth from. But that was the problem—Loomis wasn't a human person. "What is all this, anyway?" she finally asked. "I don't like having someone else's weekend plans imposed on me without my consent."

"There is no imposition," Loomis replied pleasantly. "I just thought you might like to see what you could have."

"What I could have," Iris repeated. "And what exactly is that? I can get coffee and scones at Starbucks. It's expensive, but, to my knowledge, they're not yet charging people their souls."

Loomis smiled at her sarcasm. "I haven't asked for your soul," he replied coolly.

"Whatever," Iris answered.

"Really, Iris," he prodded. "What do you believe I want from you?"

Iris picked up her fork again and poked mindlessly at the scone still on her plate as she formulated her response. It still smelled amazing, and...well, as she had pointed out to Loomis, it was just a scone. So, though she had pushed it away just a moment before, she changed her mind and pulled it back toward her and took another bite, chasing it with a long draw of coffee before answering the question Loomis had posed to her.

"You want me to help you take over Hell," she eventually said. "You can't do it without me because I'm..." She trailed off for a split second, then finished, "Because of what I am."

"And you believe I need your soul for that?" Loomis chuckled. It was a cheerful sound, free of implied criticism or derision, as though he were about to suggest all the animosity between them had been some cosmic miscommunication that could be easily resolved and then laughed about in good humor.

"Souls are the currency of demons, are they not?" Iris asked.

"Hardly," Loomis replied. "They're practically worthless."

Iris's eyes narrowed at the statement, but she wasn't sure precisely why she reacted that way. It was probably more from surprise than from distrust. "Then why go to all this trouble to tempt me into sin or whatever you've been doing?" she challenged.

"I'm only searching for the surest way to elicit the response I desire from you," he answered breezily. "Sin and virtue are but arbitrary labels assigned by humankind to establish a false sense of order, but if virtue is so important to you, I will let you keep it. You will not have to burden your conscience on my account."

"Sure," Iris answered scathingly. "Nothing inherently sinful about forming an alliance with a demon."

"There doesn't have to be," Loomis assured her, "if you'll only redefine your standards." He paused briefly, then continued, "If you cannot disentangle yourself from the snares of your meaningless, self-imposed discipline, you should know the stars number fewer than the methods I have of manipulating you, and brute force is always a viable option. Luckily for you, however, I am not a brute, and I am gracious enough to offer you the freedom to choose me of your own will before I coerce you by manipulation. You should appreciate that choice. Were it not for our shared demonhood, I would not be so generous." He smiled handsomely, and for the briefest instant, Iris nearly forgot why she was arguing with him at all.

After a gentle shake of her head and another sip of coffee to help her refocus, Iris responded with another question. "Are you suggesting your antics until now have been something other than attempted manipulation?"

Loomis ate another piece of his scone, with perfectly refined etiquette. Iris thought with a rush of self-consciousness that she must look like a complete animal next to him. He followed the scone with a sip of his own coffee, then finally answered with a grin, "I would be more inclined to refer to my 'antics' thus far as courtship."

Iris hadn't expected that response, and it made her nervous—in more of an excited way than a fearful way. Her face turned warm, and she realized with minor indignation that she was now feeling once again like a shy schoolgirl on a playground, anxiously accepting a dandelion blossom offered to her by a charming little boy from her class. *Damn*, she chided herself silently, *how does he do this to me?*

"You're not going to fool me with that," she replied stonily, hoping to convince herself as much as she hoped to convince Loomis.

"I don't wish to fool you," he retorted. "What I seek from you is the power of your spiritual birthright, and you can share that with me if you choose to. In return, I will share with you all I have, and that is a substantial estate. As I have already told you, Iris, we are perfectly suited to serve each other. We will be stronger together than you can imagine."

Iris snorted. "So, you want to marry me, then? Throw a great big fire-and-brimstone wedding there in the underworld? Make it the event of the millennium?" She took an angry bite of her scone and then added, with additional sarcasm, "For the record, I'm sure as hell not signing a prenup. Forget that."

If Loomis was annoyed by her flippancy, he didn't show it. He looked, in fact, mildly amused. "If I did wish to marry you," he said smoothly, "I wouldn't be so crude as to reduce it to legalities."

"Right," Iris said acidly. "You're a true romantic."

"Let us desist with the sarcasm now," Loomis directed, with only a touch of impatience. "Demons have no romantic inclinations, and you are already aware of that. Neither do we marry. But the co-existence I imagine for you and me would not be altogether *unlike* a marriage. We would rule together, enjoying all the benefits of our shared powers, and we would answer to no one else. Just you and I over all the rest, Iris. If you tell me you're not enticed by that idea, I will not believe you."

Iris looked at him for only a moment, but it was almost long enough for her to become mired in the deep earthiness of his eyes. "I have no desire to be Queen of Hell, Loomis," she said simply, struggling to remain resolute. Rulership was not at all a revolting idea to her.

"Fine," Loomis replied placidly, taking a delicate sip of his coffee. "Choose whatever title you like, then. When I called you 'my queen,' it was more a term of endearment than a formal address."

"That's *really* not the issue," Iris pointed out.

Setting down his cup, Loomis turned to her with a challenging expression and rejoined, "You mean, you have no desire to rule over those inferior to you? You are content to dwell among the unintelligent and the weak, to be counted among the mindless and the inept? How many have put forth far less effort to be on equal or better footing than you? You live in a world where the foolish and lazy can steal from the wise and industrious, and where wrongdoings are left unpunished! Is that the existence you long for? You deserve better!"

Iris frowned as she listened to his short speech. As he delivered his words more and more emphatically, she became angrier and angrier. Not at Loomis, who was only speaking the truth, but at humanity, for all their hypocrisy and self-servingness, and for all the true injustices that went long unrecognized by so, so many. She agreed with him completely. People were, in general, shit. She was proud to be different from them.

Seeing she was considering his points, Loomis pressed her, "You would rule not only Hell, Iris, but Earth, too. There will be no one to take advantage of you, to use your work as their own. All will recognize the great power you truly are, and you will reign in whatever way you please, under whatever title you like—Mistress, perhaps? Lady? Duchess?"

A smirk crossed Iris's lips before she could think to stop it. "Duchess of Demons" had a nice and surprisingly satisfying ring to it. Clearing her throat, and trying to recall once more why she was obligated to deny Loomis's appeals, she asked, "Where exactly do you fit into all of that? Sounds like you'll just be riding my coattails."

Loomis raised an eyebrow. "I have certain character traits you might label as undesirable," he said, "but hypocrisy is not among them."

After momentary thought, Iris replied, "So, what do you bring to the table, then?"

Smiling enigmatically, he answered, "Is the pleasure of my company not sufficient?"

Iris grinned, despite herself, knowing the comment was facetious. "Can you do no better than that?" she asked. Her tone was upbeat, almost playful, and it sounded rather out of character to her own ears. She wasn't certain how Loomis might have interpreted it, but she realized with a little bit of unease that she might have just engaged in some unintentional flirtation. It was too easy to forget he was evil and inhuman.

"Well," he replied slowly, "technically speaking, your demonic birthright entitles you only to rulership of Hell. It is only by *my* work that Earth will be set at your feet as well. And I believe that will interest you even more in the immediate future than it will in long-term existence."

"And why is that?" Iris returned. Perhaps the better reaction might be to decline all his offers and get out of this place, but...well, she was genuinely curious.

"You have a human life to live, Iris," he answered her, his dark brown eyes sparkling with amber light. "I can make that life exactly what you want it to be."

Suddenly defensive, Iris challenged, "How would you know what I want?"

Loomis rose from the barstool and stood near her. He reached over with his fingertips and gently combed a section of hair at her scalp, tucking her long bangs behind her ear, smiling silently all the while. "I don't know," he admitted quietly. "I can make astute guesses, but only you can tell me what you really want. That's why I've brought you here."

His fingers in her hair had felt...shamefully good, and he was so *damned* attractive...Iris was feeling impulses she couldn't remember having experienced before. If she *had* felt such impulses before, it must have been far easier to repress them around everyone else she had ever known. Straining to refocus and gather herself, she grasped at the only portion of Loomis's last words that she could comfortably question. "Where is 'here'?" she asked.

Loomis had removed his hand from her but was still standing close enough that Iris would brush against him if she tried to turn herself on the stool. "It's nowhere, really," he answered. "This isn't a physical place, and we're not physically here. It's a magical construct I've created for us. Demons are often adept at creating these, though mine is, of course, particularly vivid and elegant because I have unique access to the physical world, thanks to the painstaking labors I undertook long ago." He surveyed the fancy kitchen around them, proudly, then returned his attention to Iris.

"You pulled me into some twisted dream?" she asked drably, feeling more focused and less airheaded than she had just a moment before.

"That's a barbaric way of looking at this," Loomis replied, "but I suppose it isn't wholly inaccurate." Iris thought she heard a note of disappointment in his voice. He sighed, then asked, "Does this *feel* like only a dream to you?"

Wary, Iris hesitated for a moment before responding, her forehead tightened in thought. "No," she admitted at length. "It feels real."

"Then, please, Iris," Loomis said soothingly, placing one hand lightly on her leg as she sat there beside him, "relax, and let me show you what your life can be. Stop questioning everything. Just enjoy this time I've given you here, in this place where there is no vice and no consequence."

"I don't trust you," she argued. No vice and no consequence sounded dangerously heretical, and, thankfully, she still had enough mindful presence to recognize that.

"You are free to leave if you wish," Loomis offered, stepping away from her and resting his forearms along the back of the barstool where he had previously sat. "I cannot keep you here against your will. Leave, Iris, and your body will wake in its own bed, alone, as you apparently like it. You'll remember this encounter only as an intense vision or a waking dream, one that felt remarkably real. But if you're so certain you will never want to join me, I would think you'd find no harm in letting me try to convince you otherwise."

She knew leaving would be the right thing to do. It wasn't smart to sit here in some magical ether, letting Loomis pick her brain to find all her deepest desires and then letting him show her how he could actually fulfill all those desires. Already, she had felt the pedestal of virtue eroding beneath her, and Loomis hadn't even yet done anything particularly tempting here. Still, if this *was* only a dream, and she wasn't *really* here...

"Are you not curious?" Loomis asked quietly, interrupting her thoughts at the most appropriate time. She was curious, and he knew it.

Iris waited for several long seconds before answering, letting conflicting voices yell at each other in her head until she grew weary of the tedious internal debate. "Just..." She stopped, closed her eyes and took a deep breath, then opened her eyes and finished, "Just show me what you want to show me." She was certain, if her pre-plane-crash self had been placed in this exact scenario, she would have left minutes ago with a solid "No, thanks." Why was she prolonging this now? What had changed? Maybe nothing had changed. Maybe she simply had a false idea about her former self.

There was no question Loomis was pleased by her response. He immediately took her hand and guided her off of the barstool, pulling her close to him with a wide, beautiful smile on his face. He wrapped his arms around her waist and held her for a moment, pressing his eyes into hers. Iris felt hot and tense, nearly in a daze. Her brain wasn't even functioning enough to register where her own hands were.

"You're fighting me," he whispered to her. "You're as anxious as you are in the flesh. Turn off that conscience of yours, Iris; it has no business here." His voice was quiet and deep and soothing, but Iris's heart only pounded faster. She felt Loomis move one hand to her head, drawing her toward his chest and holding her there, comfortingly. "This isn't real," he repeated. "You're safe in your bed, and I'm nowhere near you. This is only magic, touching your mind."

Iris swallowed hard. With her face pressed against his chest, she could feel the musculature of his human form, and she could hear a strong, steady heartbeat within it. He was surprisingly warm. She would have expected a demonic entity to be cold and lifeless and repulsive, but Loomis was none of those things. He even smelled good. *It's just a dream*, she thought, trying to calm her nerves. Loomis was saying something else, but she was only halfway hearing him—it was something about the direction of these virtual experiences, how he wanted to make them hers and not only his, how she was as much in control as he was. *Just a dream*, she repeated to herself. *Enjoy it. How many dreams do you get to control?* It was fantasy, projected images cast by magical spells...was a victimless crime a crime at all? For that matter, could anything done in the realm of dreams be called a crime? Was her curiosity a sin? If she wanted to know how it felt to be with Loomis...this would be her only chance. She would never allow it in the real world. Her human nature was, frankly, a sheltered bore of an existence. She was a demon, too; her anger at that neighbor kid had really made that known to her. And hadn't that sudden awakening of nonhuman power within her been utterly refreshing? If she were only human, Loomis would never have brought her here. He would never have given her any thought. He was looking for Iris, the demon, not Iris, the woman. The least she could do would be to show up. It could be fun. Harmless fun.

Forcing her body to relax, Iris brought her hand to Loomis's torso and gently nudged him away as she lifted her head. She met his eyes in the instant before she spoke, and that was long enough for her to see he already knew she had made a decision, and he was satisfied with it. Her voice came out in a breathy yet gratifyingly authoritative murmur as she smirked and commanded, "Impress me, demon."

He smiled in reply, then he took her by the hand and led her through the expansive home they were in, explaining it was all hers now, too. He took special care to point out the garage and its collection of vehicles, three of which he intended specifically for her: the newest generation of the Chevrolet Corvette, in yellow, with bright red brake calipers; a nice, smoky obsidian Mercedes G-Class SUV, presumably for her everyday, practical driving enjoyment, if practical driving became a hobby of hers; and, best of all, and perhaps most appropriately, a Dodge Demon, a rare and beautiful beast of a car, in gorgeous black that created a mirror finish under the garage lights. It was wholly unnecessary and obscenely extravagant, but Loomis obviously knew where Iris would permit such indulgences. She considered herself tightfisted elsewhere, but on coffee and cars, she was willing to pay for the best—within her means, of course. Clearly, though, with Loomis's grand fortune at her fingertips, she would have no boundaries when it came to expenditures. She could use hundred-dollar bills as tissues, and Loomis's financials wouldn't even feel the hit.

Eventually, Loomis suggested she get dressed so he could show her life outside the house. Iris knew it was all a virtual world, but the longer she remained in it with him, the more real it felt, and she actually felt giddy when he suggested they go out together. Somewhere in the back of her mind, she knew Loomis had no actual affection for her, but he made a convincing show of it. He took her for a pleasant afternoon outing at a museum, where he was perfectly genteel and charming, graciously following her lead with his arm around her waist and showing off a wealth of knowledge about literally everything. As he shared anecdotes about the various displays, Iris realized she could verify all his statements with her own learning, and she supposed that must be a benefit of her ancient demonic spirit. She hadn't recognized that breadth of knowledge within herself until Loomis had tangentially called it to her attention.

When they left the museum, they encountered none other but Matilda and her husband, Bodey. Matilda was obviously stunned to see Iris and Loomis together, and Iris liked that. Loomis greeted her, and she responded with complete awkwardness as she tried to introduce Bodey to him. Her chubby face was almost crimson with embarrassment or shame or jealousy, or some combination thereof. Bodey looked even more rotund and jiggly and disgustingly hairy than he had on the one occasion Iris had met him in person. His shirt was a wrinkled mess, and the button unfortunate enough to have been assigned the task of concealing the widest part of his belly had completely given up. It hung open, and although there was, most thankfully, a white undershirt beneath the button-up, it had a large enough hole in it to reveal a pasty, white stomach. Loomis didn't need any help in the appearance department, but seeing his expertly dressed and fantastically handsome form juxtaposed with Bodey Gordon's sloppy, drooping presence made him all the more spectacular to the eyes. *At least he really loves her, though*, Iris thought to herself briefly, looking from Bodey to Matilda. She might be standing on Loomis's arm right now, but there was no love between them. In the next minute, however, Matilda made some corny joke, as she was prone to do when nervously engaged in conversation, and Bodey snorted, announced boisterously to her that what she had said wasn't funny, and then proceeded to explain to Loomis and Iris how his wife was constantly saying dumb things. He laughed at his own comments for a second or two before the guffaws faltered into a mucus-laden cough, then he turned his head and spit on the sidewalk while Matilda stood there, red-faced. *Huh*, Iris considered, *maybe there's not that much love there, after all*. She shouldn't be surprised, really. People got married for lots of different reasons, and love wasn't always the first one. As if on cue, Loomis stated that he and Iris needed to be on their way, and he squeezed Iris affectionately with one arm, leaned down, and kissed her softly. Iris didn't miss the sad, asymmetrical pout that clouded Matilda's face as she watched the doting display. *Oh, honey,* Iris thought, *he never wanted you, anyway.* She almost laughed out loud.

As she and Loomis walked to his stunning black Maserati, they could hear Bodey hack and spit again behind them. Loomis appropriately commented about the vulgarity of the human race and told Iris she deserved better, and Iris couldn't disagree. Though not particularly prone to materialism or elitism, she appreciated good manners and gentility, and while neither wealth nor poverty could be credited or blamed for anyone's behavior, Loomis certainly presented a tempting package of both personal refinement and luxurious plenitude that far exceeded anything the average man could offer—particularly if the "average man" was accurately represented by the grotesque Bodey Gordon.

From the museum, Loomis took Iris to dinner at an intimate little Italian restaurant with candlelit tables and a pricey menu. Their server was a young man who looked completely unhappy to be there, with no intention of adding any pleasantness to anyone's meal. He brought the wrong drinks, sighed and rolled his eyes when Iris pointed out the mistake, then proceeded to disappear for a substantial amount of time before returning with the correct drinks and begrudgingly taking their food order. A little bad attitude from anyone in a customer service role had always gone a long way in angering Iris, and she had asked Loomis if she should say something to the kid. To her surprise, he had affably waved it off, telling her they were in no hurry and should just enjoy each other's company. Loomis did make an enthralling dinner date. By the time their food had arrived, Iris was talking to him as though they had known each other for years. She was so absorbed in him, in fact, that she didn't even feel hungry, and her practically untouched plate of spaghetti on the table as they were finally leaving made her realize with astonishment how easy and natural it felt to be with him.

When they exited the restaurant into the crisp evening air, Loomis led Iris away from the car, toward the rear of the building. She asked, with a brief flutter of suspicion, what he was doing, and he said he wanted to complain about their service now that they had finished their meal. Iris was confused until she saw their server leaning casually against the brick wall of the back of the restaurant, taking a smoke break. He was haloed by the yellow haze of an overhead lamp and a cloud of noxious fume. Loomis confronted him coolly, saying he didn't appreciate the attitude the kid had shown toward Iris. The response, naturally, was a disinterested "I don't give a fuck," and Loomis simply smiled, encircled Iris's waist with one arm, and led her back down the alley toward the parking lot. Iris, in disbelief at Loomis's apparent acceptance of such treatment, asked him why he wasn't angry. He stopped then, at the end of the alleyway, and placed a gentle hand on her face, directing her eyes back to the disrespectful youth. The tiny orange glow of the end of the cigarette suddenly burst into an intense explosion of flame, which was immediately followed by pained screaming and panicked flailing. Iris's initial reaction was horror, but it lasted only for a moment before a grin found its way to her lips. She chuckled as she commented to Loomis, "Maybe he gives a fuck now."

After a lengthy outdoor walk along uncrowded paths of a quiet park, Loomis took Iris back home. She had felt like a stranger when she had first awoken here, but now she felt like it belonged to her. They both changed into the more comfortable attire of their pajamas and then relaxed in the living room on a sumptuous, plush black leather sofa. Iris wasn't sure how it happened, but she ended up sitting sideways, legs outstretched and feet in Loomis's lap nearer the other end of the couch. She watched him as he sat there silently, massaging her feet. The dark windows showed it to be nighttime, but the room was dimly lit by a couple of warm lamps. Iris reflected on the events of the day, on Loomis's behavior and his treatment of her, and on all they had talked about, which had included not only pleasantly trivial but engaging conversation, but also detailed discussion of the grandiose benefits Iris would enjoy outside this virtual preview. She would no longer have to work among morons for the asshole management at Eden; she would never have to answer to anyone for anything, yet she would have everything she needed and wanted. While she knew the day had been only a magic-induced vision, it had felt remarkably and wonderfully authentic, and she realized she didn't want to leave it. No part of her real life was even half as nice as this dream had been, and she didn't want it to end. *It doesn't have to end*, she considered. *I could have this if I really want it.* So there was a little bit of a price to pay...didn't that only make sense? Nothing was free. But joining herself to Loomis didn't seem like such a terrible cost. He really wasn't *that* bad. Actually, he wasn't bad at all.

"You have beautiful feet," Loomis announced quietly, watching his hands work on her.

Iris smiled. Her feet were among only a few features she genuinely liked about her own physical appearance. "I agree," she replied. Her voice was huskier than usual, and she realized maybe she was enjoying the foot massage more than she had originally thought.

He didn't face her, but she could see him grin at her response. "Did you enjoy today?" he asked after a long silence. His hands inched away from Iris's feet to her calves, pressing firmly into her with slow, purposeful motions.

"Yes," she answered. Her breath seemed to catch in her throat, eventually escaping as a little moan of contentment. Ordinarily, that sort of involuntary physical reaction would have been grounds for an immediate attack on Loomis, because she didn't want his seduction. But *this* was only illusion...incredibly realistic, incredibly satisfying illusion...and she didn't want to stop it.

"I'm glad," Loomis replied, his low voice like another caress against her skin. Iris closed her eyes and leaned her head back on the armrest behind her, licking her lips as Loomis continued massaging her legs. Part of her brain still questioned whether this whole scenario was a sinful wrong, but it was easy to shut it up. Too much of her brain wanted this now. It would be different back in reality. She would never let Loomis this close to her there. But here? Well. She had told him to impress her, and he had. Why stop him now? In fact, this ever-nearing intimate encounter would likely make his greatest impression of all, and this would be the only opportunity she would allow herself to experience it. *Nothing but a dream*, she thought once more. *Have fun.*

Forcing the doubtful conscience into the shadows of her mind, Iris opened her eyes and looked back at Loomis, who was watching her intently, his warm hands now moving even more slowly as they stroked her bare legs. She grinned a little at him, not even realizing how she was biting her own lower lip. Playfully, she pointed the toes of one foot and ran them lightly up his thigh, never lowering her eyes. "How else can you impress me?" she asked suggestively, her voice a sultry whisper. She had never been so provocative with anyone, and though she felt a little dirty for it, her guilt was quickly replaced by desirous anticipation.

Loomis smiled but said nothing, and his mysterious, intriguing silence was much more arousing than any talk would have been. In the next second, he was leaning over her with one leg off the sofa and the other bent up next to her, pulling her head toward his with one hand while his other arm guided her leg outside of his. He kissed her seductively, and Iris enjoyed the warm fullness of his lips and the steady movement of his tongue teasing hers. She was frightened for a moment, thinking it had been a big mistake to invite this upon herself, but...it felt so good...she didn't want any chaste inhibitions to get in the way now.

She grabbed Loomis's head in her hands and held him there,

responding positively to his kissing. She felt his hand slide along her leg and into the loose opening of her pajama shorts, tunneling with ease under her panties and resting with a firm squeeze on the skin of her butt. He rushed nothing, instead securing her there with her legs around him as he pressed himself harder against her. Her heart was racing and her skin was hot, and though they were both still fully clothed, she knew Loomis could feel the desire radiating off of her as they kissed—as if her gasping moans between lip-locks wouldn't have given it away. She hadn't wanted to make it so easy for him, but...well, maybe he was just that good.

After a moment, Loomis started to move her body away from the armrest, and she didn't fight him. He could position her however he wanted to, as far as she was concerned; he was far more experienced in this than she was. She wouldn't have judged herself as the submissive type, but, to her surprise, she was thoroughly enjoying giving Loomis all the control. She looked at him on top of her in the dim light, during a brief lull in the buildup toward their sure-to-be steamy interlude. His usually impeccably styled hair was disheveled, and his skin was glistening with perspiration, but it made him, somehow, even more attractive. He smiled at her, eyes sparkling, as Iris reached down and eased her hands up under the bottom hem of his shirt. She began removing the garment for him, letting her fingertips glide across the hot, smooth skin of his abdomen.

Suddenly, a sharp, stinging pain racked her left arm, and Iris screamed involuntarily in response. The vision shattered in front of her mind's eye and was gone in an instant, and she found herself in her own bedroom, splayed out on her bed and staring at her ceiling. Her heart pounded in her chest, and she was drenched in sweat. She sat up immediately in a panic, wondering what the hell had happened. She tried to lift her arm to wipe wet strands of hair from her face, only to find that her arm wouldn't move as she wanted it to. Her other senses returned in short order from their dream-induced stupor, and she saw her cobra lying on the bed with her, hood flared and fangs exposed, its eyes full of vehement warning. Drops of venom glittered at the tips of its fangs, and Iris realized with horror what it must have done to her. She moved her gaze from the serpent to her own left arm. Just above the crease of her elbow were the pronounced bite marks of a king cobra. Blood drops had formed at the deep punctures, and the surrounding skin was a mottled splotch of black and purple. Already, the arm felt like a lead weight.

Her mind went blank with terror for an instant, but she forced herself to think logically. Why had she never educated herself on appropriate first aid for a cobra bite? Simple...she didn't *need* first aid. Refocused, she neutralized the venom with magic and then similarly healed the wounds in her skin. She wiggled her fingers to assure herself the danger had passed, then she sat on her bed cross-legged, with her head resting in her hands and her eyes closed as her breathing slowly returned to normal.

The cobra slithered away but then returned shortly, carrying Iris's shield medallion in its mouth. It dropped it on the comforter in front of her, flicked its tongue, then left the room. Iris looked at the relic and felt terrible shame for the choices she had made inside Loomis's vile magical construct. If the snake hadn't awoken her with its bite...she didn't want to think about it. She wondered how she could possibly confess that kind of thing. *Crap*, she realized suddenly. *What time is it?*

She turned to her bedside clock and was shocked to see it was after five in the evening already. She had never slept so long in her entire life. That stupid entrapment by Loomis had wasted practically an entire day. She had planned on going to confession and then to Mass today to get herself back on the right track. Too late for that now; she had missed confessions completely and had already missed a quarter of the vigil Mass.

She sighed and went to the bathroom to wash her face. She didn't wait for the water to heat up, and the cold felt extremely refreshing against her skin. When she closed her eyes, though, it didn't take long for that romantic rendezvous with Loomis to show up like a photograph in her head. He had really won that round; she had been played like a fiddle. She hoped he wouldn't say anything about it the next time they met in person, here in reality. Maybe he wouldn't...was he really the type to gloat?

She went to her kitchen, brewed some coffee, and ate a granola bar as she waited for the beverage to cool enough to drink. She sat at her counter and looked around, unwittingly comparing everything she had to everything Loomis had shown her. She wasn't living in opulence here, and her regular coffee and tiny snack bar were a far cry from Loomis's fine espresso and fresh-baked blueberry-vanilla-almond-lavender scones. Maybe the intimate encounter with him had seemed too guilty a pleasure, but the high-class living and untouchable status weren't looking too bad. She sat there contemplating for far longer than she realized, at times not thinking at all, and at other times, thinking about Loomis and all he had offered.

Eventually, the sun set outside, and Iris roused herself enough to take a cool shower. She could get up and go to Mass in the morning, at least...but she so enjoyed sleeping in on Sundays, and there would be a whole workweek to have to wake up early after that. Missing Mass one weekend wouldn't kill her.

She brushed her teeth, put her pajamas back on, turned off the lights, and got back into bed. She held her pillow tightly next to her, and she couldn't help but think of her handsome demonic adversary as she drifted back to sleep. She should have fought him harder; she shouldn't have let on that he was so tempting. Still, to his credit, Loomis hadn't forced anything upon her, either because he was too chivalrous to do so or because he lacked the magical strength on account of her spiritual birthright. Either way, he wasn't a *total* monster, and part of her hoped he would catch her up in another magical construct tonight.

18

Iris awoke with a scowl to the driving heavy-metal chorus of her Monday morning alarm, growling loudly as she slammed her finger against the snooze button on her cell phone. Usually, the anthem she had set as her wake-up call would motivate her and empower her, but today, the music was an unwelcome, grating annoyance. The weekend had teased her and then left her completely unfulfilled, and having to return to the bottomless abyss of moronic ineptitude that was Eden was therefore an even more disenchanting idea today than it typically was. She was already in a foul mood, and work sure as hell wasn't going to make that any better. In fact, strangely, she was looking forward to only one thing—the possibility of seeing Loomis. After the venomous bite of the cobra had broken her illusory rendezvous with him, she had initially hoped to avoid all contact with her demonic adversary for at least a time, but the following day had felt so empty and purposeless that she had found herself—she hated to admit it—longing for him. Not in an unseemly way, of course...but as a respected rival. Despite the setbacks he had created for her in their short game thus far, Iris knew she hadn't been the pushover Loomis had expected her to be, and she was eager for another chance to disappoint him. It was refreshing to have an equal with whom she could engage, and God knew no one else in that imbecilic morass of an office met that standard.

She stayed in bed a while longer than usual, then shortened her morning routine by way of magic, leaving plenty of time for her to eat a lazy bowl of cereal and watch some television before heading out. She hadn't allowed herself adequate time for a Starbucks run, but she stopped by for an Americano anyway, arriving to work about twenty minutes late. What could anyone really say to her? She had been a model employee for a long number of years, and her work had only gotten exponentially more spectacular now that she was supplementing it with unseen magic. No one would dare reprimand her, and even if they did, she happened to know the company's new owner was quite partial to her.

Checking her handwritten to-do list as she flopped into her desk chair, Iris smirked at the ease with which it could all be finished through a sequence of uncomplicated magic. *Hard to fill eight hours a day like this*, she thought to herself with a sigh. In fact, it was a damn shame she had to be here at all, and she couldn't help but entertain the notion that a life of idle earthly luxury with Loomis might be exactly what she wanted. She leaned forward lazily and crossed her arms along the edge of her desk in front of her keyboard as she allowed her thoughts to meander back to the black leather sofa of Loomis's magically constructed living room, where a mostly innocent foot massage had quickly escalated to a tantalizing satiation of erotic imagination—or, at least, as near to that as the slithering occupant of her guest bathroom had allowed. As much as she might like to fantasize about where that encounter would have ended without the cobra's intervention, though, Iris knew the workplace was hardly the appropriate place for it. Actually, there was no appropriate place for it; the idea was terribly seedy and wholly inappropriate for any place. She shouldn't even permit such thoughts in her own head. Her pet snake, she recognized, had exercised more virtuous fortitude than she herself had, and that was completely unacceptable. What was she doing, allowing Loomis to direct her mind to such unseemliness? Of course, that was precisely what he wanted. If she couldn't forcibly redirect her thoughts to godliness, Loomis would eventually prevail in his conquest of Hell and humanity.

Iris's eyes flickered to the photograph of her family, and the palpable weight of remorse settled instantly in her chest. What would they think of her right now if they knew? Missing confession, skipping Mass, showing up late to work—none of that conformed to her upbringing. And occupying an idle mind with lustful daydreams? Her family would be appalled! If they could know her thoughts, if they had seen how she acted toward Loomis (even though within a nonphysical, imaginary realm)... Iris closed her eyes and shook her head, upset by the idea. She couldn't bear the image of having the full truth laid open before her parents and her grandmother, and yet she knew that God, her Father and Creator, was already keenly aware of that same full truth, and the realization was like a punch to her stomach. She cradled her forehead in one hand, her elbow resting on the desk, then reached up to her amulet with her other hand, reflecting on Auraltiferys and all the guidance and warning he had given her. *God, forgive me*, she prayed. *I don't want to be like this; please, help me.*

After a moment, Iris roused herself and dutifully booted up her computer. As the blacksmith had told her, magic should not become a substitute for work; she needed to get back to doing things the old-fashioned way, with honest, hard effort and complete application of the intelligence and the aptitudes God had given her. Newly resolved, she took a sip of coffee to prepare for the day, just as her desk phone started ringing. Glancing at the identification on the phone screen as she hurriedly swallowed, she saw the call was coming internally from Rafe's office, and she rolled her eyes before she could stop herself. *Ugh*, she thought, *what the hell is he doing here this early, anyway?* If it was wrong to think such frustrated thoughts, she was going to have an impossible time trying to avoid sin.

After the third ring, Iris answered the phone and very nearly cracked the receiver with the white-knuckled force of her grip after her boss commented she should be quicker to pick up his calls. It was all she could do to maintain her composure on her end of the line as he proceeded to delegate a six-week backlog of his work to her, giving her an end-of-week deadline. Somehow, thankfully, she managed to grit her teeth and say "Will do" instead of losing control of her tongue. *Jackass*, she screamed to herself as she cradled the phone more forcefully than was necessary. *This crap has been piling on his desk for weeks...he could have assigned all of it a month ago if he had no intention of doing it himself.*

Iris sighed as she added the new tasks to her to-do list, then tried as hard as she could to ask herself what Auraltiferys would do in this situation. It wasn't an easy question to answer—she couldn't at all imagine a weasel like Rafe treating a man like Auraltiferys with the same complete disrespect he showed to his employees. In fact, she suspected a single look from the blacksmith's silver-blue, dagger-sharp eyes would send Rafe cowering into a dark corner. Alas, she did not have that same effect on people, and she would have to settle for doing the best job she could while trying to curb the anger, frustration, and utter dislike (perhaps it was, in fact, hatred) she was harboring for the useless dillweed who called himself her boss.

***

By midweek, Iris had made substantial progress on her newest assignments, but her other regular tasks were beginning to pile up, and though she had handled a far more daunting workload with relative ease not too long ago, she had to admit a certain amount of stress beginning to gnaw at her. She didn't want to rely too heavily on magic, but some augmentation of her natural ability would probably become necessary sometime soon, particularly given the time of year. The holidays were approaching, and Iris had no intention of letting valuable vacation time go unused as the year neared its end.

"Hey, girl," came a spineless, drawling voice through the open doorway of her office, followed shortly by Matilda's broad figure, clad in an unfortunately clingy sweater dress, a pair of tights, and heeled ankle boots that clomped on the floor like a Clydesdale's hooves. "Do you have a minute?" she asked nervously as she sat down in the guest chair.

Dear God, give me strength, Iris prayed as she looked away from her computer screen and forced a smile. "Sure," she said, hoping she sounded friendlier than she felt.

Matilda sighed deeply, then rushed into a frazzled series of sentence fragments riddled with antecedentless pronouns, several mispronunciations, and at least three separate acronyms Iris recognized as having certain letters transposed. By the end of it, Matilda's cheeks were red, and she was short of breath. Iris couldn't keep the look of judgmental confusion off her face; the effort was simply too much. She did, however, make some effort to help Matilda repeat herself in a way that was at least marginally understandable, and she deduced the poor girl had, not astoundingly, misinterpreted an important notice from a regulatory agency and had mistakenly believed she had extra time to complete a report that was, in fact, due today, and it was a report that Iris was mostly unfamiliar with, aside from a general knowledge of its name and purpose. It was Matilda, in fact, who *should* know more than anyone else at Eden about this kind of requirement, as it fell under the umbrella of the "certification" she had miraculously obtained earlier this year.

"Can you help?" Matilda asked breathlessly, nearing tears. "I honestly have no idea how to do this report, and I'm so afraid Rafe's going to fire me if he finds out."

Iris felt her eyes narrow as she bunched her eyebrows together involuntarily. "I can try," she suggested hesitantly, "but...Matilda, shouldn't you know more about this than I do? I don't work with those regulations on a regular basis, so I'm not sure what help I can be."

"But you're so good at reading and interpreting everything!" Matilda argued excitedly, not bothering to answer the question Iris had posed to her. "I bet you can look at the forms for five minutes and know exactly what to do."

That's probably true, Iris admitted silently. "Okay," she conceded. "Let me take a look."

"Oh, thank you, thank you, thank you!" Matilda gushed as she rose to her feet. "I'll email everything to you. Thank you SO much! Girl, I owe you big-time!"

With that, Matilda left the room, leaving an irritated Iris to wait for her email. She reappeared almost immediately after the message arrived in Iris's inbox, seating herself again and eagerly awaiting Iris's expert (though uncertified) opinion. In fewer than five minutes, Iris could tell the necessary submittal was much more involved than a form or two, and she found herself at least slightly entertained by having to give Matilda the bad news.

"There's a lot you have to submit with this," Iris said gravely before narrating an itemized list for her coworker, who deflated more and more with each requirement she named. It was a miracle the girl didn't implode upon herself and transform into a black hole right there in the guest chair. She did, however, dissolve almost immediately into a histrionic meltdown that involved teary eyes, panting breaths, and rapid successions of panicked oh-my-God's bookending the emphatic statement that she would be fired for this.

You should be, Iris thought cynically. *Certification, my ass.* Rolling her eyes as Matilda clamped her hands tightly over her face as if hiding from the world, Iris caught a glimpse of her family's picture, and she remembered having vowed only a few days ago to do better. Duteously, she tried to encourage Matilda, explaining that a late report would not be the end of the world and that all she could do now would be to move forward and get it done. The attempt at comfort, however, did not have the effect Iris had hoped for. She had hoped Matilda would buck up and then slink away to deal with the problem she had created for herself, but, instead, the girl remained in her chair and tearfully pleaded with Iris to help her get the report and all its required attachments done today.

Had the exact same situation arisen a couple of months ago, Iris would have laughed at the suggestion, as it was absolutely humanly impossible to do that amount of work in a single day. Given her more recently discovered abilities, however, Iris knew she could, in fact, put together an acceptable report by the day's end. Disgusted as she was by the thought of helping Matilda out of a jam (she had long desired for it to become undeniably apparent to everyone that the girl was an incompetent joke of an employee), Iris decided it would be wrong to withhold the aid that had been requested when she knew she could provide it. So, begrudgingly, she agreed to assist.

"I can take the last sections of the report, and you can focus on the first two," she proposed. "If we work fast, we should be able to get it finished before the end of the day."

"Oh," Matilda replied haltingly, finally somewhat calmer after her fit. Her expression morphed into a lopsided, guilt-ridden duck-face of a pout that Iris knew could only precede a statement that was going to piss her off. "Actually," she continued, rather fearfully, "I *really* need to focus on a different project right now, and…I'm *so* slow at those kinds of documents, anyway…you're so much faster than I am…I mean, I could *do* it, but it would take me longer, and you're so good at it…" Her voice trailed off as her still-red eyes met Iris's expectantly.

Iris felt a stone-cold mask crash over her own features as Matilda weakly stammered out her half-hearted excuses and revoltingly insincere compliments. Anger coursed through her, and she wondered if the rage was evident in her eyes. Even if it was, though, she had a feeling Matilda was too imperceptive to recognize it, and for an instant—just an instant—Iris badly wanted to demonstrate, physically, the depth of her disdain. With monumental effort, however, she restrained herself from an emotion-incited display of demonic power, and she simply responded, with a tight jaw and a stony voice, "I'll handle it."

Matilda, either truly unaware of Iris's extreme irritation or willfully ignoring it, heaved a big sigh of relief and stood from the chair. "Iris," she raved, her eyes wide as a deer's, "you are THE best! I will make it up to you; I promise! I'll bring you a Starbucks tomorrow!"

Iris tensed her face into something she hoped resembled a smile as Matilda plodded out of her office, but as soon as her coworker had departed, she bared her clenched teeth and seethed silently, balling her fists and shaking in her chair, her skin hot and her vision practically white from fury. After a moment, she was able to relax slightly, though she thought she might still be feeling engorged veins popping from her own neck. She had just agreed to do the impossible, for someone who, in her own estimation, didn't deserve any help, and she was livid. She had thought using her demonic abilities for good would feel better than this. The current reality, though, was that it was practically thankless and totally sucked. Evil was looking a lot more tempting.

Asking God to grant her patience, Iris waited for a silent moment, hoping, ironically, for an immediate answer. There was none, of course, but the simple act of praying, even for a few seconds, at least gave her an opportunity to regain more of her composure. With a sense of rightness, though also with extreme annoyance, she began reviewing the report forms and mentally plotting her magical course of action for completing everything. At some point, her mind drifted into a numb reflection on Matilda's promise of "a Starbucks," and she wondered with amusement whether that meant a coffee from Starbucks or an entire Starbucks store. The phrasing had left room for interpretation, after all. Even in jest, though, the question was wholly unnecessary; Iris had known Matilda long enough to recognize her promises were often hollow.

***

Driving home angrily after the end of the workweek, Iris blared her music at an inappropriate volume, not even listening to the lyrics that usually elevated her moods, trying to force from her mind the thoughts that seemed set on remembering every nuisance and every injustice that had befallen her in the course of five days. Her boss had been particularly needy and unbearable and completely unappreciative; Matilda had eagerly submitted the work Iris had done for her on the report she had almost completely missed and had then, naturally, failed to follow through on her offer to bring Iris a coffee in gratitude; and two other useless project managers had each successfully requested that their newest assignments be transferred to Iris on account of their staggering workloads, after which Iris had walked by to find them both reclining nonchalantly in one of their offices as they discussed the very important matter of whose college professors had been the most eccentric. Iris had, thanks to the acoustics of the hallway, overheard the entire forty-five-minute conversation as they reminisced about their college years, and she had wondered whether the supervisors who had been so quick to alleviate their workloads—to Iris's detriment, no less—had any idea how much time the asshats made a point of wasting every day. And, as if none of that had been enough, Iris had approached the front desk at just the right time to hear, with the aid of a bit of demonic power, Matilda complaining to the receptionist about the suggestions Iris had made regarding Loomis and the danger he might be to her marital relationship. It was their ultimate decision that Iris was just a "jealous little bitch," and that was why she had made such ghastly implications about Matilda's friendship with the company's wealthy and gorgeous owner. Iris had considered, for just a moment, lighting the whole building on fire with a spell and then casually walking away from it all. But for the weight of the amulet around her neck, reminding her of Auraltiferys and his fervent hope that she rise above the evil inclinations of her demonic nature, she might very well have done it, with not so much as a flinch from her conscience. She was growing infinitely tired of self-control for the sake of righteousness. No one else around her seemed too keen on acting justly; why should she?

As she turned onto her street, she was once again obligated to bring her Challenger to a complete stop as the hooligan adolescents from the corner house took a spitefully long time to pause their in-the-street basketball game and clear the road. The oldest one met her eyes again and smirked, and before she even registered her body's movements, Iris had thrown her car into park, opened her door, and exited her car, her eyes trained on the kid with a blazing fury. His eyes went wide with surprise or fear, and he involuntarily hesitated as Iris stepped swiftly toward him. As his siblings and friends jeered him from the sidewalk, the boy finally attempted to rush out of the street, but Iris was already too close. She grabbed him by the fabric of his T-shirt and held his squirming form in place as she took the basketball from him with her other hand, tucking it under her arm. The boy kicked her in the shin, but Iris didn't even feel it. Saying nothing, she shoved him backward, subduing her force just enough so the boy didn't fall. He was, however, sent several panicking strides away from her as he struggled to keep his balance. Iris took the ball from under her elbow and, utilizing only the smallest bit of power her magical ability gave her, deflated it between her two open palms, to the amazement and terror of the children. She was aware that the younger brother of the scrawny punk in front of her had run inside for his parents, but she wasn't concerned. She angrily tossed the flat husk of a ball at her victim, who was too stunned to catch it. The airless leather and rubber smacked against his chest and fell to the asphalt, and Iris smiled at the kid very pointedly before she returned to her car. She hoped her gaze had given him all the warning he needed, and she believed it had. He wasn't going to rat on her, and he was going to make sure his posse didn't, either.

She shifted gears and sped down the street to her own house, feeling much better than she had all week. As she pulled into her garage, she realized it had been just last Friday night when Loomis had caught her up in the magical construct he had crafted especially for her, to show her that glimpse of what her human life could be if only she would cooperate with him, and she remembered the laugh they had shared when his simple spell had engulfed that rude waiter in a pillar of flame. She couldn't deny it—it felt good to punish the misdeeds of others. Perhaps she hadn't done enough of it in her lifetime. She wondered what Loomis might say of her encounter with the kid down the street, and she imagined, with a subtle but unmistakable hint of pride, that he would approve.

She entered her kitchen to find her cobra coiled in a patch of waning sunlight streaked across the countertop. The quick-learning and ever-responsible serpent had already pressed the button on the coffee maker so that Iris's evening brew was ready for her to pour and enjoy.

"Hey, there," Iris addressed the asp cordially as she filled her mug. The cobra flicked its tongue toward her for a second or two, then languidly slithered away and disappeared through the doorway, likely to return to the solitude of its in-house jungle. *Guess it doesn't approve of me today*, Iris mused blandly. Strange how that would-be scare from Loomis had become her pet and was now far more judgmental of her behavior than it must have been of his (then again, the cobra probably hadn't been given the choice of participating in or refraining from Loomis's plan, so perhaps it had not been allowed the freedom of judging his behavior, either). Somehow, though, something in Iris's nature had commanded the serpent's respect, and now it didn't hesitate to point out to her, with cold-shoulder treatment, when she had done something unworthy of that respect. But what did the cobra know? It had things easy here—it didn't live among a bunch of insufferable morons whose existences were, at least in Iris's estimation, of questionable value.

The small house was quiet, and Iris seated herself at the dining table with her coffee, in the same chair where she had sat when she had opened that gift basket from Loomis, and she soon discovered she couldn't pull her thoughts away from him. The run-in with the boy at the corner, the aroma of freshly brewed coffee, the cobra which he had sent to her by way of magic—it all reminded her of the demon who was supposed to be her archnemesis but looked and acted a whole lot more like a handsome, faultless suitor, and though she would have liked to argue the fact, she had to admit there was a slight yearning eating away at her heart. Loomis had been noticeably and disappointingly absent all week, and she was missing him. It wasn't like her to miss someone, especially someone as infuriating as Loomis. In fact, aside from her departed family, Iris wasn't sure she could say she had ever truly "missed" anyone; yet, here she was, sitting at home alone and suddenly wishing Loomis would invite himself over and magically appear at her side. Auraltiferys, she knew, would lecture her most sternly right now if he could hear her thoughts. He would warn her again how dangerous it was to humanize Loomis, to let her human emotions color her perception of him, to think of him as anything but the demonic spirit he was. Iris would argue, of course, that the little pang of longing she was feeling as a result of Loomis's absence was neither a result of attraction nor an indication that she wanted anything at all from him. She was simply internalizing a ton of frustration and anger right now, and she desired to be around someone who was strong enough to handle an outburst of demonic power and feminine wrath without then burdening her with a slew of negative consequences and gnawing guilt. Essentially, she wanted a punching bag, and Loomis would make a good one. If only he would show up now, she could punish him instead of releasing potentially harmful steam on her human brethren. At least, that's how she was choosing to justify her current thinking.

By the end of her second full cup of coffee, Iris had given up all attempts to drag her thoughts away from the erotic scene that had nearly played itself out in the magical vision Loomis had shared with her a week ago. The metallic shield on her necklace had become a tiresome heaviness, and with some exasperation, she unclasped its chain and walked it to her bedroom, tucking it away in the top drawer of her dresser. What good was the thing, anyway? It certainly wasn't keeping her from anger or hatred. It wasn't making her want to help her human race. It wasn't helping her turn away from Loomis. She was no closer to God now than she had been before she had begun wearing it.

***

Halfway through the following week, Iris sat at her desk, staring emptily at the spreadsheets opened on her computer monitor and feeling a dangerous concoction of despondency and frustration and heartlessness simmering somewhere deep inside her. She didn't want to see anyone; she didn't want to talk to anyone; she didn't want to work. Basically, her current attitude was a big middle finger directed at the entire world. She still felt a twinge of guilt at having chosen to miss Mass again the past weekend, but she was quickly moving past that. She couldn't identify exactly why she had made the choice in the first place—until she had been forced into that day-long excursion with Loomis in his magical construct, she had never once left her Sunday Mass obligation unfulfilled—but something had kept her away. Part of that "something" was guilt for her thoughts and actions over the preceding week; another part, and maybe the bigger part, was perhaps her increasing pessimism toward humanity and a waning desire to thwart Loomis's dark plans for it. Whatever excuses she made, however, Iris knew the decision had been hers, and she had made it consciously. It was a sin, but…well, she would just add it to the ever-growing list. Frankly, she *was* a demon, after all—the embodiment of a rebelliously sinful spirit. Should she really expect that a human lifetime of virtue or good deeds would get her on Saint Peter's guest list at the end of everything? And if her demonic nature *could* be overlooked, and Heaven *was* a possibility, then surely an additional sin or two wouldn't compromise the deal.

The annoyingly cheerful musical notification of an incoming email drew Iris's attention back to work, and she sighed heavily as she pulled up her inbox. The new message had been sent by big-boss Rafe to everyone at Eden, with the subject line "Congrats on a Job Well Done." Iris rolled her eyes, then nearly choked on her coffee as she dropped her gaze from the subject to the body of the email.

You're fucking kidding me, she screamed silently in her head. The message, which was every bit as jejunely written as she had come to expect from her college-dropout supervisor, congratulated Matilda Gordon for her quick work last week to compile a very important report for a very important client. It described to everyone, in brief and rather puerile language, how Matilda had discovered a reporting oversight just in the nick of time and had worked fast and hard to put the necessary documents together and submit everything by the deadline, saving Eden's client from potentially significant penalties.

It went on to say that Matilda was exactly the kind of employee Eden needed and that management was exceedingly proud of her. It ended with the obligatory "we're proud of everyone" statement and an encouraging word about how all employees can make differences like this every day.

Iris's skin turned hot and her heart pounded with immense fury inside her chest as she forced herself to read the email. She clenched her fists so tightly that her arms shook with the effort. *God help anyone who comes into my office right now*, she thought. She wanted to destroy something, anything, but she knew it wouldn't do a damn bit of good. If she razed the entire office building right now, it wouldn't matter, because the world was full of people just like Matilda and Rafe and pretty much everyone else at this office, relying on the aid of others to hide their incompetence and never really recognizing the efforts of the workhorses who made their continued employments possible. *Fuck them all*, Iris concluded darkly. *Fuck them all.*

She slammed her door shut with a magical spell, halfway surprised Matilda hadn't already swayed into her office and prattled off a whole list of apologetic excuses that might explain why Rafe had believed she had done all that work, when she knew damn well Iris had done it. Most likely, Iris deduced with a bit of twisted pride, Matilda was feeling too ashamed and petrified to face her right now—and it was lucky for her she felt that way. Avoiding Iris was probably the only intelligent thing that useless cow would do today. Of course, she could only avoid Iris as long as Iris allowed herself to be avoided...

Near the end of the day, Iris sat in her office and waited, watching Matilda by way of magic. When the girl got up to leave her desk, with her ridiculously oversized purse on one shoulder and a travel mug in the other hand, Iris followed casually behind, at just enough distance to make her presence known and keep things awkward.

Matilda did what she probably thought was a subtle half-turn of her head, but it was totally obvious she was looking to see who was behind her. Iris purposely matched her pace for several steps as they neared the front door of the Eden offices, then closed the distance slightly just as Matilda was exiting.

"Good job on that report," she called out sweetly, obligating Matilda to stop and hold the door. Matilda was clearly nervous, but she forced herself to turn and look at Iris as she approached. As Iris followed her out into the hallway of the building, she added, "I don't remember the last time Rafe sent out such a glowing recognition about anyone."

"Um, yeah," Matilda stammered, her cheeks flushed. "I really didn't know he would do that. I told him you helped me; I don't know why he didn't mention you."

Iris paused at the landing just before the stairwell and smiled at Matilda, who was making a clear effort to appear cool and collected though she was absolutely bristling with anxiety. "Oh, that doesn't matter to me at all," Iris assured her. "The job is its own reward, you know?"

Matilda returned a half-hearted, sheepish smile, relaxing ever so slightly. "Right!" she agreed, with overabundant enthusiasm that betrayed her phoniness. "But, girl," she added, "seriously, thank you again for all your help." Iris shuddered internally at the girl's disgusting, drawling accent; "for" and "your" had come out as "fer" and "yer," and, amazingly, the word "again" had been drawn out into three syllables.

"Anytime," Iris replied graciously, carefully hiding her disgust. "Anyway, have a good evening," she concluded with a smile. "I'm going to stop by the restroom before I head out."

Matilda, looking more relieved than she probably intended to, smiled and wished Iris a good night, then turned toward the stairs as Iris continued in the opposite direction, toward the women's restroom. The unfortunate nuisance of a woman made it only two steps down the flight before the heel of one shoe inexplicably snapped off, throwing her broad form off balance. Even had Matilda been the paradigm of grace and poise (a laughable hypothetical, indeed), between her gigantic handbag on one arm and the mug in her other hand, she didn't stand a ghost of a chance at grabbing the handrail to right herself.

Iris listened with a satisfied grin as heavy thuds of diminishing volume echoed around the corner and finally ended with a solid pound, a cry of pain and utter embarrassment, and the clattering of personal effects falling to the tile of the first-floor foyer. Voices from the downstairs offices came a moment later, with a number of people coming out to check on poor Matilda. After waiting for a minute, Iris walked away from the stairs and exited instead through the rear fire escape, smiling to herself and wondering how Matilda would fare on the crutches she would inevitably need. Perhaps a magical sabotage of the building's elevator was also in order.

By the time she had reached the parking lot below, Iris was barely able to contain her laughter. She sat in her car and, with another spell, peeked in on the ongoing commotion just inside the office building's front doors. Matilda's face was as red and puffy as a beet, streaked with tears and eyeliner and mascara. Some good Samaritans had helped her to a bench, where she sat, breathing heavily, with her right leg extended out in front of her, her shoe removed and her lower leg revealed, already swollen and bruised. Whatever liquid had been left over in her travel cup had sloshed out across the front of her blouse, and one of the straps of her stupidly large purse had ripped during the fall. People hovered around her, asking if she was okay and offering whatever they could to help. The scene was entertaining for a moment—Matilda looked *exactly* like the pride of Eden right now—but, after a brief chuckle at the sheer perfection of the revenge she had invisibly claimed, Iris quickly lost interest. After all, she was off the clock now, and there was no point in wasting any unpaid minutes of life in the pothole-covered parking lot of Eden.

She started her engine and sped away, still grinning. Her only regret right now was that Loomis hadn't been there to witness her tastefully understated yet utterly delightful vengeance.

***

Her cobra greeted her with a critical flaring of its hood and a speedy departure from her sight. Iris pursed her lips, wondering why she cared at all about the opinion of a snake. Somewhere in her mind, calling out from a place growing darker and more remote by the day, she could hear the voice of conscience telling her she should be sorry, and she knew the voice was right. She hadn't been raised this way; she hadn't been taught this way; hell, she hadn't even been wired this way. She had once kicked a boy in the shin at school, but only after he had dared her to, and even then, she had been gentle about it. Violence was in her angry fantasies, perhaps (only as righteous, justified violence, of course), but it wasn't in her nature. Though his spirit was hers, too, Iris didn't *really* want to devolve into a monster like Satan. On the other hand, neither did she want to give up the undeniably pleasurable freedom that demonic power provided her—freedom to intimidate and to scare and to punish, freedom from every literal and metaphorical chain any other human might try to impose on her. Maybe it was wrong, but...it was *nice*.

She pondered, for a second, the possibility of returning to the mountain, to Auraltiferys, but she quickly erased the thought. She knew he could set her straight, but...well, it was dangerous for her to go to him. Loomis might be watching, after all, and she wouldn't want to jeopardize the safety of the mountain. It would be selfish for her to do anything but stay away. Besides, what need did she really have of the blacksmith? He wouldn't tell her anything she hadn't heard before—pray to God; ask forgiveness; seek His guidance, and all the answers will be given to you...blah, blah, blah. If she wanted intangible, valueless assistance, she could find it without the blacksmith's aid.

***

Another weekend had arrived, and Iris was feeling completely restless as she drove home from work. She had seen no sign of Loomis for two whole weeks now, and it bothered her. She recognized the strangeness of the sentiment, but she couldn't change it. She shouldn't want to see him; she should be glad for every minute he stayed away from her, because in theory, she should be getting stronger and smarter and better able to stand against his tyrannical endeavors. Instead, she was feeling ready to put him in his place, and now he was nowhere to be found. How could she be expected to fight an opponent who wouldn't show his face? But she knew that was only the less embarrassing of her concerns. In truth, the bigger question in her mind, shamefully, was why Loomis had shown her such a nearly perfect vision of what he could give her and then had disappeared from her life. If she were honest with herself, she would have to admit she was more interested in listening to Loomis than in fighting him, at least for now. She would do the right thing in the end, of course, out of Christian obligation, but...it seemed so uncouth to deny the demon a fair opportunity to state his case, and he had been so rudely interrupted by her serpent in that night of his magical construct...

She sighed, turned up the volume of her music, and tried to forget Loomis and everything he had ever said or done to her. Perhaps, she considered, this was for the best. Even if Loomis couldn't overtake Hell without her help, maybe he could go ahead and destroy the human race with his evil magic, and maybe the human race deserved it. It did, however, make her a little sad to think he might not need her after all.

Cold drizzle was misting the autumn air and pelting lightly against her windshield as she drove, striking her with a pang of nostalgia for the Thanksgiving celebrations she used to enjoy with her parents and her grandmother. This kind of weather inevitably made her think of the holidays, even if they were still a few weeks away, and even though the celebrations had died with her family. She suddenly felt very small, very weak, and very human...and she didn't like it. The callous attitude that had mostly taken her over of late was preferable to vulnerability, and she didn't want to retrogress into weakness. She silently worded a quick prayer for the souls of her family, hoping God might hear her on their behalf, even if she knew her voice didn't deserve to be heard, then she resolutely dammed the tears that had threatened to reach her eyes.

She neared home and, to her astonishment, found the kids from the corner house yet again playing out in the street, bundled in heavy jackets and beanies and happily throwing a football between them, straight down the middle of the roadway. Iris's eyes narrowed at them as she slowed her car and waited for them to move. The younger ones avoided eye contact and left the street immediately, but the oldest one had apparently recovered some of the cheekiness he had had before Iris's last encounter with him, and he met her gaze with an insolent smirk as he walked straight toward her car, slowly, before finally veering toward the sidewalk.

Iris laughed to herself, the sound reaching her own ears as a low, inhuman chuckle. She continued home without incident, knowing exactly what she would do next and loving that the punk-ass kid had no clue what was about to befall him. She parked in her garage and closed the door, entered her kitchen, poured her coffee, and seated herself at the dining table, opening her perception with magic and biding her time.

The kids blissfully resumed their game in the street while Iris watched traffic on the cross-street, waiting for an appropriate vehicle to approach. Cars wouldn't adequately serve her for this. She wanted one of those disgustingly massive pickup trucks that usually pissed her off in traffic and in parking lots, preferably an expensive one with a chrome cattle guard and a stereotypically over-compensating male driver who had never set foot on a farm, ranch, or construction or industrial site and might soon rethink his actual need for a giant "luxury" truck.

After ten minutes or so, an acceptable vehicle turned onto the cross-street, and Iris eagerly awaited its approach to her corner. Its driver was speeding, as so many did on that street, and the roads were slicked by the light rain...it was a disaster just waiting to happen, begging for just a little magical nudge...

Iris focused her spells and watched the "accident" happen. The pickup lost control on the wet street and, unfortunately, hydroplaned at unexplainable speed across the pavement directly toward the poor, unsuspecting children. The younger ones, miraculously, moved out of the way just in time, but, for some unknown reason, their arrogant leader remained frozen in place, eyes wide and mouth open in terror, unable to move. The driver couldn't do a damn thing; it seemed his eighty-thousand-dollar truck had sadly unreliable brakes and a suddenly unresponsive steering system. There were screams, then a squeal of tires as the brakes finally held and caused the truck to veer, and then a gratifying thump as the pickup spun and contacted the obstinate little shit who refused to play in his driveway instead of in the street. The side of the truck's bed slammed into the kid and tossed him like a doll, his crumpled body landing several yards away.

Iris didn't bother to watch the ensuing fuss. She had exercised at least some restraint in her evil—the kid would live, but he'd be in pain for a while. If she hadn't been able to magically correct the dent in her Challenger after he had thrown his ball at it a while back, his fate would have been worse. As it was, though, his unseen punisher had settled on a more merciful approach, simply teaching him a valuable lesson about the dangers of the world. Iris sipped her coffee and grinned, feeling powerful and completely untouchable.

19

It had been just over a week since Matilda's unfortunate mishap on the stairs of their office building, and although Iris hadn't missed her presence, neither had she enjoyed it as much as she had expected she might. Even while the prior week's "golden girl" had been out for her convalescence, there had been ample annoyance finding Iris at Eden, from being asked yet again to pick up others' slack on their assignments to having to endure endless small talk about how awful it was that poor Matilda had fallen and hurt her poor ankle. The work itself was nothing; a few magical spells here and there saw to that. There was, however, no easy cure for the irritation that *people* created, and Iris had soon realized that her injurious antics had done little to slake her distaste for others. In fact, she had felt some bits of remorse nagging at her conscience, and that had only made everything worse. It wasn't as though she could go to Matilda, or to the neighbors and their obnoxious kid, and apologize—she had a secret identity to keep concealed, and by all appearances, the happenings had been terrible accidents, leaving her with no culpability, anyway—so the knowledge of her wrongdoing was particularly insufferable, and she desperately wanted to silence that voice in her head that kept reminding her she was a better person than this. If Loomis had shown up, *he* would have told her there was nothing wrong with her actions; he wouldn't have been anything but supportive, and while Iris was still convinced she had no intention of aiding his grand scheme against mankind, she had to admit the approval would have been refreshing. As it was, however, Loomis had stayed away, so much so that even the rest of Eden had resumed their usual routines after having recovered from their starstruck dalliance. Iris could only hope he had been staying away from Matilda, too—the thought of her demonic rival seeing Matilda outside of work or possibly comforting her during her recovery was exceedingly infuriating.

Currently, however, Iris had a more pressing infuriation to deal with. She sat in one of two cheaply upholstered wing chairs that faced her boss's desk, staring disdainfully at the asshole sitting in the faux-leather chair behind it. He had called her back here and told her to take a seat, further commanding that she should grab the door on her way in. She had followed his instructions, wondering what bullshit he was about to concoct. Anyone else in the office would have been terrified to receive such a summons from the boss; he had a real knack for intimidation and control and manipulation, or so he believed. Everyone seemed to defer to him and to allow and accept his unprofessional behavior. Iris had once felt intimidated by him, too, when she had first started her job at Eden, but it hadn't taken long for her to see through his bravado. She had soon realized she was more intelligent, harder working, and just a generally better person than he was. He was a lazy, self-centered fast-talker who knew just enough about his field to get by, confidently sputtering out trite cliches or vapid idioms or managerially calling on others when he knew he didn't have the answers. How he loved the phrase "Well, I'll let Iris handle this one; she's my right-hand girl," like he owned her but was kind enough to let her speak sometimes, the dick! What he really meant, of course, was "Iris will have to answer that for you, because I don't actually know shit about anything."

Now, as Iris sat waiting for whatever reason he had called

her to his office, Rafael "Rafe" Ruiz was inconsiderately looking away from her, facing his computer monitor and leaning back in his chair, holding a cell phone to his ear and talking loudly and obnoxiously in Spanish to someone on the other end of the call. Iris stared at him, wishing she didn't have to pretend to be patient. God, she hated him. Before she had learned anything about her powers as a demon, the speaking-in-Spanish thing was something she had to tolerate because it was occasionally warranted, as Eden did have some non-English-speaking clientele. The boss, however, liked to use the foreign language far more often than necessary, finding it particularly useful when he wanted to mask his personal phone calls or shoot the breeze in the hallway with the cousin he had hired. Apparently the two of them shared both a deep love for the Spanish language and a deep distaste for doing any actual work. It had always annoyed Iris to no end. But now, able to draw from her innate ancient knowledge, she could understand every word of the conversation, and while it was still annoying, she did find some mild delight in knowing Rafe had no idea she knew what he was saying. She was tempted to address him in Spanish once he hung up his phone, but she would refrain.

She sat in silence, listening as he made plans with another cousin (the man must have fifty of them, at least) to meet up in Dallas the following weekend for a tailgate and a football game. The longer Iris stared at him, the more her anger increased. Rafe had gained a fair amount of weight after a motorcycle accident last year had excused him from the gym and regular exercise, and he was now even more disgusting to look at than he had been before. He was an oafish gorilla of a man, with beady eyes set deep in a square, hairy face; a thick neck with pudgy little folds of skin at the base of his skull; a blocky, slightly bowlegged physique; and a beer belly that was growing more prominent with each passing alcohol-laden weekend. He still walked around with an aggravating amount of machismo, swaggering like he was hot shit, but if he didn't get his fat ass back to the gym soon, he was really going to start losing some credibility there. At some point, looking "hard" required at least a little actual hardness.

Rafe laughed loudly and ended his phone call, casually lowering his cell phone toward his lap and replying to a text message before finally placing the phone on his desk and swiveling his chair to face Iris. She had rolled her eyes as he sent the text, irritated by the man's lack of professionalism, angered at his wasting of her time, and disgusted by his hammy little sausage fingers as they tapped out letters on his brand-new phone. This guy was a joke. But he was still her boss, at least in everyone else's minds. So by the time Rafe turned to look at her, Iris had made a grand effort to wipe the animosity off her face.

He looked at her for several seconds, blinking and pursing his chubby lips, saying nothing. It was one of his habits when meeting with employees, almost certainly intended to make them uncomfortable and to remind them of their place in comparison to him. On most people, especially women, it would often work. Iris, however, felt nothing but ire. She had no intention of speaking until spoken to, so she likewise sat in silence, meeting Rafe's eyes with hers and smiling fakely as she waited for him to get on with it.

At long last, he let out a hefty, dramatic sigh. "Well," he said, "we have some things we need to discuss." He interlaced his fingers together and rested his hands on his desk, slouching in his chair.

Iris very nearly rolled her eyes again, but stopped herself. Instead, she smiled sweetly and inclined her head slightly, lifting an eyebrow in invitation for Rafe to continue. She could tell her taciturnity was annoying him, and she was glad for it.

He scrunched his heavy eyebrows together and started nodding his head, moving his tongue around in his mouth so that his lips opened a bit and one cheek stuck out farther than the other—his signature look of put-on concern. Iris still said nothing, knowing he must be just about boiling inside by now since she refused to be ruffled by his supposedly intimidating presence. He finally put his tongue back in its normal place and said, "We have a big problem with those reports for the Stubbs-Lowe sites."

He kept his voice low and deep, trying to put a threatening edge on it. What did he expect as a response? Was he hoping Iris would gasp and go all wide-eyed and bewildered and apologetic? Stubbs-Lowe wasn't even one of her accounts, and even had it been, she would have remained as apathetic as she felt right now. Nothing could be screwed up so badly it couldn't be fixed, and the reports handled by this office were largely inconsequential, anyway.

Iris maintained an impassive expression and hesitated for several seconds, then shrugged and finally asked, "What's the problem?" She had already grown weary of this meeting.

Rafe sighed again and started to speak but was interrupted by the quiet opening of his office door. Iris turned with marginal interest but couldn't stop the involuntary fluttering of her stomach when she saw Loomis entering, his tall, lithe frame clad in dark slacks and a dark vest over a lighter dress shirt and complementary tie. Not even the sickly fluorescent lighting of the office could temper the handsomeness of his sharp features and warm-toned skin, so marvelously intensified by his dark hair and deep, amber-glittered brown eyes. Iris was unable to prevent her mind from immediately calling forth the memory of the day she had spent in his magical construct, when he had shown her what *could* be, if she would join him. She remembered all too well how unceremoniously it had ended, how close she and Loomis had come... *Stop it!* she yelled to herself, trying to dispel the image from her head. *This was probably his plan all along, to tease you and then make you miss him so you'd fall for his tricks later. Don't let him win!*

Loomis closed the door almost silently behind him, taking a

nonchalant pose against the doorframe, crossing one leg casually in front of the other and resting the toe of an expensive Italian leather shoe gently on the floor. He glanced briefly at Rafe and gave a slight nod, then he smiled broadly at Iris, flashing his brilliant white teeth and absolutely oozing charm and charisma. She smirked in a reply of forced indifference, then turned her attention back to Rafe, nearly laughing out loud at the sudden change in her boss's posture and demeanor. He straightened up and squared his shoulders, pulling his chair closer to his desk and clearing his throat. *No doubt who the alpha dog is here, huh, Rafe?* Iris mused. All it had taken was the entrance of Eden's billionaire owner, and suddenly the pretentious behavior had morphed into obsequious servitude. *Yeah, tuck that tail, you dumb piece of shit,* she thought. She hated Loomis (or, at least, she was actively trying to hate him), but at least he had some substance to him. He was smart and driven, even if toward evil purposes, and he was much better dressed and easier on the eyes. She was glad to see Rafe cower in front of him. She couldn't argue it even to herself —she hated Rafe more than she hated Loomis.

"Ahem, as I was saying," Rafe continued, his voice unnaturally and humorously deep, "the reports you did for the Stubbs-Lowe sites were all wrong." He leaned his head forward and squinted at Iris, clearly demanding an explanation.

After a brief, indifferent pause, Iris stated simply, "I didn't file any reports for Stubbs-Lowe. Matilda handles those."

Rafe glanced sideways toward Loomis, then focused once more on Iris. "Matilda told me you filed the reports this year," he challenged. "She said you were digging around in the files, and you told her she had messed them up before. She says you told her to let you handle all of their reporting from now on."

Iris had heard Matilda misinterpret correspondences and twist words before, but this was an outright lie, and she didn't bother trying to hide her aggravation. "That never happened," she said with clear irritation. "I don't know what she's talking about. I didn't touch those reports."

Rafe shook his head delicately and waved a hand in what Iris supposed was meant to be a calming gesture. "Look," he replied in a more jovial tone, "I don't care if you audit records from time to time. In fact, I think that's a good thing!" He leaned back a little, obviously having recovered from the anxiety Loomis's entrance had caused him. "We're not perfect, and I get that." He tapped his own chest with both hands and continued, "I'm not perfect!" *Yeah, no shit*, Iris thought. This attempt at a good-cop, bad-cop routine was another of his intolerable habits. Screw this guy.

Rafe sat forward again and proceeded, "But, listen, I do have a problem when you tell a coworker she doesn't know what she's doing. And then you try to take her assignments without asking me?" He paused and shook his head. "I can't have that."

Iris sighed audibly before responding. "I don't doubt that Matilda has fucked up her reporting more than once," she said, "and I know for a fact she has no clue what she's doing most of the time, but I've never said that to her. I have never audited her reports, and I never told her to give me any of her assignments. If the reports are messed up now, that's something she did." She paused and smiled, then, changing her tone, added kindly, "But I'm certainly willing to help you correct the issues if you would like."

"Listen, there's no need for profanity, Iris; that's just unprofessional," Rafe said. Iris's anger practically exploded inside her, but she said nothing. "Anyway," he continued, "this has really screwed us up with the client. Their CEO was contacted by a federal agency about all the errors in the reporting, and they don't trust us anymore. You had wrong facility names, wrong locations, numbers flip-flopped from one site to another...maybe it all could have been fixed. It would've taken a lot of man-hours, but...anyway, that doesn't matter. They've canceled their contracts with us, and not just for these reports—for everything we do for them. We've just watched a lot of money go down the toilet."

Iris looked at Rafe for a few seconds. She really needed to watch herself. She surmised the intent was to make her angry, and she was almost certain the situation must have been orchestrated by Loomis. This was just another of his attempts to make her life hell so she would agree to help him with his sick plans for killing the immortal souls of humankind.

"What would you like me to do, Rafe?" she asked placidly. "I never touched those reports. And if it's too late to correct them, then what would you like me to do?"

Rafe shot another glance toward Loomis, who was still standing quietly by as a casual observer. He had crossed his arms and turned slightly, propping himself against the wall with one shoulder. Rafe cleared his throat again and replied, "Well, there's nothing you can do. But this can't go without consequences, sorry to say."

Iris interjected, "Consequences for Matilda, you mean? Because whatever mistakes you're citing are not mistakes I made."

"Look," Rafe responded with obvious frustration, "it's her word against yours."

"And you trust her word over mine?" Iris asked, her voice louder than she intended. This was ridiculous, and she was pissed. "I've been here way longer than she has! And I've never done anything but a good job for you! You know that!"

Rafe opened his palms to her in a placating expression. "I know you've been with us a long time," he agreed, "and I think mostly you've done us a great job." *'Mostly'? What the hell does that mean?* Iris wondered with furious amazement. She bit her tongue to prevent an outburst, but she knew she couldn't control the hatred that must be showing in her eyes. Rafe, either oblivious to the look on her face or unfazed by it, continued, "That's why I want to come up with some creative solutions. Try to think outside the box. Put a square peg in a round hole, so to speak." *Put a square peg in your round hole, asshat*, Iris screamed internally.

"Because you *have* been here a long time, and because you *have* done good work, I'm going to stop short of anything rash like termination. I just don't think that would be fair to you in this case," Rafe stated sympathetically. *Termination?* Iris repeated internally. *You wouldn't dare, you prick. You can't fool me with this. I'm the best employee you have, and I know it.*

"Matilda has really stepped up to the plate in a big way lately," Rafe proceeded. "Like getting that certification earlier this year. We're real proud of that here." *Do the letters "PhD" mean nothing to you, you dumb fuck?* Iris's internal voice had gone beyond livid, and it was increasingly difficult for her to maintain control of her external behaviors.

"Anyway, what we're going to do," Rafe went on, "is put Matilda in charge of all reporting."

"Are you out of your mind?" Iris asked, no longer caring what came of this exchange. Why had she ever cared about it? She was superior to Rafe Ruiz in every way, and she certainly didn't need this stupid job in this stupid shithole. "Matilda is a dumb cow. She has no clue what she's doing, certification or not. But, you know what? If you want to throw shit right at the fan, you do it. I couldn't care less."

"*Hey!*" Rafe slapped his hand hard against the desktop as he yelled. He had stood up from his chair during Iris's brief tirade. Clearly, she had enraged him almost as much as he had infuriated her. "You don't talk to your boss like that! We're done making allowances for you and your attitude. You do good work, so we let you get away with some things, but that ends now!" He inhaled deeply and sat back down, apparently pleased by his masculine showing of authority. "I'm putting Matilda in charge of all reporting, and she's going to be your direct supervisor from now on." He pointed a porky finger at Iris as he continued, "You're going to help her with whatever she needs help with, and if I hear any reports that you're not being a team player, then you and I are going to have another sit-down discussion that you're not going to like."

Iris felt her hands quivering in rank outrage, and there was discernible heat coming off her skin. She stood up and stared at Rafe with eyes full of enmity. "Fuck you," she said quietly. "I won't work under someone so brainless and inept. I'm referring to Matilda and to you, too. I quit."

Rafe started shaking his head and once again donned his "concerned" look. "You can't quit," he stated, arrogance seeping off of his words.

"The hell I can't!" Iris screamed.

A cool, low voice suddenly emanated from behind her. "Iris," Loomis said, "do sit down and listen to what Rafe has to say. You may find you don't *want* to quit." He pulled himself away from the wall where he had been leaning and took an upright and commanding posture just behind Iris's chair, clasping his hands behind his back. Iris knew there was nothing but manipulative reason for him to take Rafe's side, but she felt oddly betrayed, anyway. Betrayal was a more painful feeling than hatred, though, so she narrowed her eyes and tried to redirect her own emotions into a vengeful wrath. She wouldn't allow Loomis to prevail over her like this; she would force herself to hate him, and it would render all his demonic tricks ineffective against her. For now, though, she could only bide her time, so, with a bitter expression still tightening her face, she sat back down on the edge of the chair, folded her hands on top of one another in her lap, and waited quietly for Rafe's next round of bullshit.

Rafe had lost the poker face he always liked to wear at the office. It was clear he had quite a distaste for Iris—a fact she had suspected from the first moment she had pointed out an idiotic mistake he had made in an email to a potential client. At length, he finally said, "Let me rephrase: You *can* quit. But if you do, you should know we will take legal action against you."

Iris didn't try to hide her confusion, making a pronounced gesture that very clearly though tacitly asked, *What the hell?*

"Playing dumb won't make this go away," Rafe said hotly. "We found evidence that you've been skimming money and pocketing it. For a long time."

"Ha!" Iris exclaimed. "That's ludicrous! I've never stolen anything in my life. Fuck you and your so-called evidence."

"I'm afraid he's correct, Iris," Loomis intoned from behind her. His voice made the hair stand up on the back of her neck, and Iris realized perhaps she was still more afraid of him than she wanted to let on. "You know I'm a businessman," he continued. "I purchased this company because I saw a money-making opportunity. It should come as no surprise that I had accountants thoroughly vet all the books here. Their findings are quite telling. I've discussed these findings with Rafe, and in fact, it was he who convinced me to allow you to stay, even after this most recent tragic error with the Stubbs-Lowe account."

Rafe beamed and puffed out his chest, obviously proud to have "convinced" Loomis Drake of something. "That's right," he said. "I told Mr. Drake we could work this out with you; you know, maybe solve this with some creative thinking, like letting you stay on with us, just in a more supervised role."

"And I think it's all a very good idea," Loomis added, verbally stroking Rafe's ego in disgusting fashion. "Rafe, please outline the long-term plan for her."

Rafe, now as confident and macho as ever, happily acquiesced. "So, Iris," he announced, "we'll put you under Matilda so you can assist her as needed and both she and I can approve all your work before it leaves this office." Iris felt her teeth grinding together inside her mouth. "And of course," he went on, "as we start seeing consistency and improvement there, we can think about maybe relaxing the supervision a little. Gradually."

Iris narrowed her eyes and stared with icy daggers at Rafe as he threw yet another conciliatory open-palm wave at her. He was so sure of himself, so egotistical. He didn't care how angry a face she might make at him, because he knew he would always be above her here. He was loving this chance to put her in her place, to remind her who was in charge. *This ignorant bastard still thinks he has real power*, Iris thought to herself. *I'll show him.*

"We'll be withholding part of your paycheck every two weeks until you've repaid the amount you stole from us," Rafe continued. "Mr. Drake's accountants have calculated it out to be nearly ten thousand dollars," he said with mock sadness, shaking his head again. "I just don't get it, Iris. Why would you do it? Was it really worth it? I mean, you could be in serious trouble for this. You better be grateful for this opportunity. We're letting you off the hook here. Turning the other cheek, so to speak."

What a tool, Iris heard her mind say. *'Letting me off the hook,' he says? No, they're making me pay back money I never stole! Does this jackass really think he's fooling me with this upbeat, I'm-still-on-your-side bullshit? FUCK HIM!* Her jaw was tight, and she could feel the veins bulging in her neck. Her blood was circulating with unnatural swiftness inside her, as hot and fast as wildfire. Outside the windows of Rafe's office, dense clouds in the sky grew and shifted, blotting out the sunlight that had moments ago been bright and cheery. Rafe paused for a moment and swallowed. He didn't seem to notice the graying of the sky, but he couldn't ignore the cold sweat that had begun to dot his forehead. He tugged at his shirt collar and swallowed again, trying to disguise any discomfort. He had to clear his throat and then cough before he could proceed with his speech.

"So, ahem, um...lastly," he stuttered, fidgeting with his collar again, "um, lastly, I'm going to need you to move from your current office." He turned his head and coughed loudly, turning red in the face after several seconds and gasping for air. He attempted to recover from the embarrassing display by swallowing a final cough and gruffly wiping the sweat off his forehead, but his performance was a pitiful failure, and he knew it. With eyes watery from the hacking, he bravely turned back to Iris and tried to talk again, though his words were broken up by humiliating, froggy gulps. "I'll put...ahem...I'll put Matilda...hmmmmph...I'll put Matilda in...in your office." He pounded a fist against his chest, hoping to clear whatever was causing his fit. "Anyway," he continued weakly, now clutching at his chest and struggling to breathe, "I'll put you at Matilda's desk." He practically choked on his final words. Iris stared at him impassively, her body coursing with vengeful fever and her heart void of all emotion. Rafe's face was now streaked with tears and sweat, and his usually tanned skin had taken on a pallid, purple-tinted hue. As the overhead fluorescents began to pulsate erratically, Rafe stretched out one arm to reach for his desk telephone, the other ape-like hand still seized up in a tight grip over his heart. He gasped and strained, unable to reach the phone and finding no one to offer any aid. He might have wanted to scream, to call for help, but he had no voice with which to do so. Finally, as he made an attempt to stand, his chair was suddenly pulled away from his desk by an invisible and mysterious force, toppling backward just enough to keep his body in the seat. When it came to rest, Rafe looked at Iris with teary, red, protuberant eyes full of confusion and fear. Iris looked back at him and smiled.

With his head turned toward the ceiling and one final pained, ineffectual breath, Rafe Ruiz slumped limply in his chair, a pathetic mound of useless flesh, just as he had been in life.

Iris studied the scene before her with a sort of amused disinterest. The lights regained their steadiness, and the clouds outside began to dissipate. She smiled when she recalled the weekend plans Rafe had made with his cousin in such eloquent Spanish not too long before. What a pity he wouldn't make it to that game! His favorite team actually had a decent record this year, the sorry fucks. Iris had always despised them and their fans.

After a minute, she took a deep, cheerful breath and stood from her chair, walking around it with the intention of leaving Rafe's office. Loomis moved into her path, facing her, his arms still held behind his back. There was a hint of a malicious smile on his handsome face and an obvious glimmer of approval in his dark eyes.

"What?" Iris asked sarcastically.

He remained quiet for several seconds, visually contemplating Iris and allowing his tiny smile to grow into a large grin. "That," he said, his voice its usual cool, manly, beguiling timbre, "was an impressive and, might I say, most erotic display of power." His gaze held no small amount of lust.

Iris shrugged. "The man had a heart attack," she said blandly. "Damn shame."

Loomis sneered at the insincere brush-off, then replied, "If you find yourself inclined to engage in a few sins of the flesh, Iris, there will be no better time than now."

God, he was attractive. And so damn charming...Iris debated internally for an instant, really, *really* wanting to know how it would feel to let him ravage her. But, sadly, that might give him at least some slight advantage over her, and she couldn't allow that.

"Loomis," she sighed, "you are so, *so* tempting." She reached out and lightly brushed the side of his face with her finger. "But you know what they say—one should never mix business with pleasure." She stepped around him and headed toward the door, halfway hoping he would stop her, but he made no move to do so. When she grabbed the doorknob, though, his voice arose quietly from behind her, caressing her with enticing sensuality and stopping her in her tracks.

"I don't think you know," he said slowly, turning her to face him and gently pulling her hips close to his, "just how much *pleasure* I can give you."

Iris had never felt fear in this office before, but she certainly did now. It had been nice for a moment, letting her wrathful, arrogant demonic inclinations take control and allowing herself some teasing flirtation, perhaps, but now her physical, human body was absolutely screaming at her to give in to temptation, to let Loomis have his way with her, while her demonic sense—and maybe in some smaller way, her human conscience—was telling her she was in grave danger if she didn't resist him. She swallowed and tried hard to conceal her perturbation.

"Physical pleasure, yes," Loomis continued. "That goes without saying. But that is only the *beginning*, Iris, and perhaps of the least interest to you, though I know you are interested. *Very* interested." His face was close to hers. She could feel his cool breath on her and could smell the pleasing scent of his cologne, and she could feel her own heart racing inside her chest. Why had she allowed herself to fall into this position again? Sooner or later, he was going to break her. *No*, she told herself. *No! You're stronger than he is.*

"Think about it, Iris. Think about all I can give you," Loomis went on, his hands sending waves of heat and desire through each of her nerves. "Wealth greater than you've ever dreamed of; power in any career you like, or no career at all, if that is what pleases you; fame or anonymity as you desire..."

With every word, Iris could practically feel her opposition to him caving in right beneath her. She remembered all he had shown her before, and she couldn't help but consider all he had yet to show her, and...well, frankly, being bad had felt quite good. Loomis moved his hands up to her face, placing a palm against each of her cheeks and staring unnaturally, immortally deep into her eyes. "And that is just on Earth," he concluded fervently. "Let me show you what I can give you in *Hell*."

With that, Loomis released Iris's face and guided her to the office window with a firm hand. The parking lot, the cars, the neighboring buildings...all earthly surroundings had passed away, and Iris witnessed before her a vast expanse of jagged, cracked obsidian, surrounded by a moat of fire and mottled by pools of acrid flame. Thick, caustic smoke hung heavy in the air all around, yellowish green like bile. There was no sun, but the brightness of the flames reflecting off the glassy obsidian and refracting through the dense particles of sulfuric haze cast a dim, jaundiced light throughout the wasteland, illuminating with grim sharpness the scenes of graphic horror therein. Iris saw what her mind recognized as human beings, though without their complete earthly forms. While their shapes were identifiable, they lacked skin or hair or bone, existing instead almost as vapor, held intact by some thin, sinewy substance drawn painfully tight into their shapes, to the point of translucence. All were shockingly emaciated, and their gaunt faces had no lips or eyelids or teeth. Their eyes were cloudy spheres of matte black, like slate in a visibly gaseous form. There were courses of these damned throughout this endless void, all prisoners held in eternal torment at the hands of demons. There were souls drowning in the moat of fire, screaming out in anguish, surely knowing there would be no rescue. There were souls nailed to crosses of ragged iron, with flames set beneath them and hordes of demons whipping them mercilessly with brutish, flailing weapons. Huge, crooked black trees dotted the obsidian island, their rough, dead boughs stretching out like bolts of lightning from trunks as large as skyscrapers. Their branches held still more souls, perforating their taut coverings like barbed wire into flesh, heinously penetrating their forms where their human orifices would be. At the trees' bases were winding messes of snake-like roots, with yet more souls hopelessly entangled among them. Elsewhere there were souls trapped within large, rough wheels of dark stone, chained by their necks to iron axles, sentenced to tread for eternity on the stone devices. Demons stood guard nearby, ready to punish any who might succumb to fatigue. The turning wheels operated enormous pulley systems of heavy chain, which seemed designed to suspend another plane above the sulfur clouds. There were scores of the wheeled apparatuses throughout the expanse, each with a dozen wheels or more and no shortage of souls for turning them.

The souls numbered more than Iris could count, more than the stars she had seen on the clearest earthly night. Their wails were constant and ghastly, loud and raspy and dry, rife with agony and dire hopelessness. She could see and hear them all vividly, her mind having been opened beyond what her physical senses could perceive. *So these are the damned*, she thought. *These are the proud and the envious, the wrathful, the lustful and greedy and gluttonous and slothful.* She wondered for a moment how she should feel upon seeing them and hearing them. Should there have been pity or compassion there inside her? There was none. Instead, she heard only one prevailing thought: *They deserve it.*

As she numbly drank in all the horror playing out in her mind's vision, she felt herself drawn upward through the stinging brimstone haze to the level that sat above. The ground appeared as a smoky glass, with the tormented souls below visible through the smoke as it rolled and thinned in places. Demons stood idle all around, some glancing through the floor with disinterest, others pacing without purpose or mindlessly picking at the sick-looking weapons they held. The place was a cold, lifeless desert. Even these demons, who clearly enjoyed the higher ranks of Hell, had no fulfillment, no joy. Each one was apart from the others; none showed any concern for another. Their eternities had become pointless, loveless existences in the absence of God, and the long starvation of their once-angelic natures had corrupted and mutated their spiritual forms as well. They appeared as hideous, monstrous patchworks of various earthly beasts, but with a murky translucence that physical bodies would have lacked. Iris could recognize among them similarities to dogs, hyenas, goats, lizards, snakes, birds, bats, and even insects. Some were bipedal; others walked on four legs, as their grotesque deformities necessitated. Most had at least two ash-covered, moth-eaten wings that slumped with heaviness, tokens of onerous burden rather than symbols of freedom. *Is this what I am?* she wondered. *Is this what I look like?* She was momentarily disturbed by the thought; she had never considered it before.

Near the center of the glassy domain was a huge stepped pyramid of obsidian. Loomis directed her vision toward it now, and Iris sensed a frigid oscillation all around her as they neared it. Climbing metaphysically one step at a time, she could see the pyramid was hollow inside, with dark but diaphanous exterior walls. Inside were innumerable human souls, piled miserably in a writhing, crying heap, those nearest the walls pressing against the panes as if futilely gasping for air. Four demons guarded the pyramid, one on each face at the narrower steps near the peak. These four appeared similar to one another, with horned, horse-like heads set on winged though humanoid bodies that devolved into goat-like legs and hooves. They held heavy, black iron shields and various metallic weapons that resembled long, rusty nails or dirty, serrated hatchets. Iris was led above them, to the top of the pyramid, and in the middle was an empty throne, seemingly wrought of iron and adorned with large but lusterless cut stones that looked like dried blood.

Iris heard Loomis speak inside her mind now, though she couldn't see him. "Now you have seen Hell," he said, a biting cold sharpening his voice. "It is filled with the pitiful damned, wicked angels and sinful humans who have imprisoned themselves here without direction or reason. You and I, Iris, we are not like these. We are *leaders*; we are powerful and rightfully ambitious, masterful authors of our own destinies! We heed no one, and we will be subject to no one." His words came to her with penetrating conviction.

Suddenly, Iris stood before Hell's throne with Loomis beside her, overlooking the underworld and all its pathetic, worthless inhabitants. "We can *lead* them, Iris," he said. "We can be their compass; we can give them purpose. See how they will serve you," he continued, making a sweeping gesture with his arm. As he did so, the demons below them fell into ranks, lining up with punctuated immediacy like expertly trained soldiers. Facing the pyramid, they knelt and bowed their heads. Iris was amazed at the sight. Where she had just witnessed apathy and aimlessness, there was now militaristic servitude—and that servitude was directed at *her*. She could feel the authority she held. She could sense the power in her hands; a wave of a finger would send a horde of demons wherever and to whatever end she pleased. It was a heady feeling.

"They will do our bidding," Loomis went on. "Help me to complete my magical creation, and we will command them to unleash it upon the Earth. You and I will feed upon the souls of the destroyed. We will consume all the power that exists within them, all the divinity they are too ignorant to use, and with every imbibition thereof, we will become stronger and stronger, until you and I are gods. *Gods*, Iris! At the end of this age, we will be two gods commanding a limitless army, and we will have plentiful might to defeat the vanguard of Heaven, to prevent the creation of a 'new earth' and instead claim the Earth as our eternal dwelling, all its denizens bowing in worship to us!" Iris listened silently to Loomis's monologue, inebriated by this sensation of almost infinite authority and intoxicated by the idea he was visualizing for her.

He pulled her close to himself and took her face in his hands.

They were not in a physical realm, but the action still tangibly affected her, even in this dream-like mirage Loomis had constructed, not unlike the earthly vision he had shown her before. His eyes were ablaze with dark, dancing fire. His face was aglow with the reflection of the flames of Hell below, and her closeness to him enveloped Iris with a pleasing heat that contrasted sharply with the bitter cold of the obsidian ziggurat beneath their feet. Loomis was fathomless desire and insurmountable passion, a being obsessed by a fantasy he firmly believed he could make real...and, as Iris stared into his eyes, she believed it, too. He was intelligent, resourceful, creative, and patient—to nearly impossible degrees that set him far apart from those whom he would make subject to himself. If anyone could usurp the power from God in Heaven, it was Loomis Drake.

Is it? Iris heard her mind ask. She could still sense Loomis's presence in her head, could still perceive the vision he had created for her, but from another corner of her mystic perception, her own voice was coming to her. *He can't do it alone. He needs you. All his fateful plans fall to ruin if you resist him. All his power, all his drive—they are meaningless but for your consent. Why is this throne empty? Where is Satan in this vision he has shown you?*

Iris had accepted what Auraltiferys had told her of her dual nature; she recognized she was both demon and human, and she knew she was powerful in both magic and demonic sense. Until this moment, however, she had failed to recognize the true significance of her duality; she hadn't *really* considered what a high station she held by virtue of the evil essence with which she had been endowed by her evil creator. *Remember who you are*, her inner voice implored her.

Suddenly, Loomis released her from his divination, the vivid scenes of ice and flame and torment disintegrating like vapor as earthly reality reclaimed its place. He still held her face close to his, an earnest hunger burning in his eyes. Slowly, he lowered his palms and brushed them gently down her arms, taking her hands in his.

"Are you ready now?" he asked softly. "Join me, and have what you *deserve*. The wicked must be punished, and *you* can be the one who punishes them. Is that not what you most desire? To become a force of *true* justice? You can reign over them. You can have all creation at your feet," he finished, tenderly squeezing her hands.

Iris looked at him silently, relishing for a moment how spectacularly attractive he was in his false human form, particularly in this affectionate denouement from the lusty prelude and covetous climax of his latest temptation. If not for the words that had whispered to her from the recesses of her own demonic consciousness, she might have submitted to him now. What a fool she would have been!

A slow smile spread across her lips as she formulated her response. Finally, she replied to Loomis in a voice as quiet and easy as his had been. "You know me well, Loomis," she acknowledged. "It *is* what I most desire—to punish the wicked, to rule with divine authority."

"Then you will join me? You will let me give you all I have promised?" he asked, pulling her hands expectantly toward his chest.

Iris chuckled slowly, then allowed her chuckle to become a menacing, growling laugh. It was her demonic voice that answered Loomis as she said, "What can you give me that isn't already mine?" She noted with satisfaction how an almost imperceptible flaring of his nostrils evidenced for her that Loomis was shocked by her reply. He released her hands immediately.

"Have you forgotten who I am?" Iris continued, her words becoming louder and faster. "Or were you hoping *I* had forgotten? I AM the one who punishes the wicked. I AM the one who rules over them. I AM the one who rules over *you!*" A hard mask fell across Loomis's expression, as though a set of iron bars had slammed down in front of him. He intended to hide any emotion, but Iris noticed how he took an unprompted step away from her before she continued.

"*I AM* the Prince of Darkness," she said, "the same substance in a different form! You would try to sell me my own throne, for a price greater than I paid for it, for in your dream I have but half the throne and all the same damnation! You are a wretched imbecile, Loomis Drake! You have grandiose plans that cannot be realized without my consent. *I* can realize your plans myself, without your aid. You have tried but failed to use me for your own devices, and your hubris will be punished." She cocked her head tauntingly.

Loomis's eyes narrowed, and he radiated a flagrant hatred, but, impressively, he kept his voice low and controlled as he responded, "You will never be able to do what I can do, Iris. You will never be able to realize my plans; you will never truly be able to rule in Hell." He swallowed and took a quick, shallow breath, then proceeded through clenched teeth, "You are inherently flawed. Your human conscience will never let you tear yourself from God."

Iris rolled her eyes and yawned dramatically. "You know as well as I how easily a human conscience is ignored or broken," she said, her voice now returned to its earthly tonality.

Loomis looked at her with a rueful sort of disgust and frowned. "Not yours," he said acerbically.

His response momentarily forced Iris's thinking back to its human level, and she was confused by it. Should she be ashamed of what she had just done? Of all the less-than-holy things she had done after all of Auraltiferys's warnings? Should she be proud that a demon (and a very strong one, no less) had just admitted that her conscience was not easily broken? Should she beg forgiveness from God and refuse to engage in any battles of will or struggles for power with this fallen angel, even should he make her a martyr for it?

Iris didn't like the doubt that the simple statement had caused her. She didn't like this sudden questioning uncertainty and the weakness it brought with it. She had just felt unmitigated strength, had just sensed inarguable and irrevocable dominion within herself, and she much preferred that to this feeble, human humility. She would put the moral dilemmas out of her mind; there should be no place for them there.

"Well, now I'm confused, Loomis," she said coquettishly. "Do you *want* me evil, or do you want me good?" She let out a campy little sigh and shook her head in artificial sadness. "I'm beginning to think I'll simply never satisfy you either way." She smiled at him before speaking again, this time without the histrionics. "You know, it really is a beautiful irony you've designed. I never knew what I am, *who* I am, until you called me. It was because of you that I learned of my nature and realized my innate powers, and now I shall be an eternal thorn in your side, put there by your own hands through your greedy, prideful scheming."

She smiled again, stepped toward Loomis, and ran both her hands delicately through his thick, dark hair before resting her palms against the sides of his face, gently pulling it close to hers. "Perhaps you should have let sleeping demons lie," she whispered.

After a silent moment there near his face, she lightly kissed him on the cheek and then moved casually for the door of Rafe's office, shooting one last meaningful, taunting glance at Loomis before taking her leave.

***

Loomis watched with silent irritation as Iris closed the office door behind her, casting on him a final teasing sparkle of her gold-green eyes as she did so. A human man would have interpreted it as a flirtatious come-hither look, one that said, *Not here, darling, but follow me, and I'll give you what you want*, which, of course, for a human man would mean physical conquest of Iris's feminine form, a chance to enjoy her submission to him and to gratify his animal desires. Loomis, however, was not a human man, dwelling as they did in their shallow little pools of egotism and convincing themselves they could ably satiate the lustful hunger of anyone. No, Loomis knew Iris's look had a far deeper and much more sinister meaning for him. She had said, with nothing more than a glance, *Now you've finally convinced me, darling, and you'll regret it. I'll give you exactly what you deserve.* He had succeeded in pulling her on board with his grand plan, but unfortunately, the conniving wench had immediately threatened him with mutiny, and even more unfortunately, she had ample means of making her threat a reality.

He stared at the closed door for a few seconds, gathering his thoughts, then he turned and rested his elbows on the back of a wing chair, one hand slowly rubbing his chin as he reflected on this recent and unexpected turn of events. He had not forgotten what Iris was, of course, but he had admittedly formulated the mistaken belief she would always favor her human nature over her demonic one. It would have been preferable. Iris was certainly a challenging woman, annoyingly headstrong when it came to refusing his tempting advances, to refusing her body the sensual indulgences he knew it desired—so unlike the other women of these earthly times—but he would have seduced her, eventually. He would have crafted a romantic scenario so perfectly tailored to her deepest fantasies that even she would have no choice but to give herself to him, even if he had to go so far as to pretend he loved her. He was a *very* convincing actor, after all, and humans were so foolishly inclined by nature to seek out love.

But, lamentably, he had lost that opportunity now. He had impatiently abandoned his focus on lust and had instead so expertly preyed upon Iris's human envy and pride that he had driven her straight from human sinfulness to spectacular Satanic wrath. *I'm too evil for my own good*, he thought with perverse approval. *Damn me.*

Iris had jeeringly asked him whether he wanted her to be good or to be evil. It was, irksomely, a valid question. What he needed from her was something in between: a human willing to sin and a devil willing to submit. He now realized he had grossly underestimated the complexity of such a task. Iris was capable of sin, yes, but she had to be properly motivated to it, and, unluckily, her most sensitive triggers were the same ones that had always most incited Satan to evil. In prompting her to sin by attacking her pride or her envy, he was also stoking the flames of evil that fed the demon she was, and that demon was characteristically most unwilling to relinquish any authority to another. He shouldn't have been surprised by Iris's reactions to him. Even as a woman, she was decidedly disinclined toward submissiveness; that she was also the essence of Satan only compounded that aggravating trait.

For the first time in ages, Loomis wondered whether he had made a mistake. Should he have "let sleeping demons lie," as Iris had suggested? No, no...he would simply find another way. He had tried the path of lesser resistance, and he had found it a dead end, but he would never resign himself to failure. He would relentlessly pursue more esoteric knowledge and ancient arcana; he would experiment and discover until he could do away with Satan altogether. He was already able to steal human souls (a feat all the rest of Hell would have labeled impossible), and he had already formulated the intense magic that would allow him to devour their very essences, consuming their power. He would soon bring that part of his plan to fruition, and from there, it would be but a little stretch to imagine he could find a way to destroy angels, too—even ones as powerful as Satan and his bastard offspring, Iris Wakefield. It would be more work and a longer time of waiting, but in the end, he would have what he wanted. He would rule Hell and Earth for all eternity, because there would be no one to stop him. Perhaps, in fact, his success would be even sweeter this way—doing away altogether with that obnoxious devil-woman *was* an attractive thought.

Looking across the desk in front of him to the flaccid body of Rafael Ruiz, sagging lifelessly in the inexpensive vinyl executive's chair that Iris had made his final resting place, Loomis felt a malicious smile creep across his lips. He reflected on how masterfully she had demonstrated her wrath. She had wielded her magic seamlessly, her demonic power emanating from her invisibly but unquestionably, completely eclipsing every human limitation that had once restrained her. She hadn't even flinched as she had watched Rafe's pained, gasping, fearful struggle while she supernaturally strangled the human life out of him, and then she had nonchalantly waved off the whole incident, in wanton disregard of her own human conscience. Such an entertaining display! He couldn't deny having found the scene an exhilarating one. He was a demon—a spiritual, nonphysical being—but he had experienced quite an electric sensation in his loins as Iris had removed her veil of humanity and engaged in that violent, carnal act of pure and naked vengeance. It was such a shame she hadn't accepted his subsequent offer of fleshly gratification; they both would have enjoyed it immensely.

Alas, she had denied herself that enjoyment, and in doing so, she had left him with an unsatiated appetite for something he shouldn't even desire. He had dwelt too long in this false human body. He was used to the upkeep it required, to the physical yearnings it experienced, but clearly those yearnings were beginning to creep through the body and the mind to his demonic spirit. For so long, he had worn this self-created mask of humanity, and now he realized it had become a parasitic worm, gnawing at him and threatening to overtake him. He had toiled for so long to make it a reality, and he alone of all the damned had succeeded in it. He was able to dwell on Earth in a vessel he had created himself, without the nagging heaviness of a human soul chained to it, and he much preferred this existence to the drudgery of Hell. But Iris had just made it apparent that he had developed some weaknesses, had lost his once clear and razor-sharp focus on what he truly wanted. He would have to return to Hell now for a time, to restore his concentration and to find for himself exactly what he needed in order to destroy the contemptible wretch who was standing in his way. It would be done. He should have begun it already; he should not have wasted time trying to lure Iris to his side. At the moment she had first revealed to him her awareness of her true self in that enraging and taunting little ostentation of hers back in his office in Portland, he should have known she wouldn't be tempted. Why had he even tried? And, worse, why had he kept trying?

As Loomis considered his lack of appropriate judgment, he once more directed his attention to the morbid tableau that Iris's demonic passion had artfully designed, and he suddenly understood...and he hated it. He had first tried tempting her because he wanted the challenge she presented, and he had, perhaps too arrogantly, believed he might succeed; for that error, he was willing to excuse himself. But he should have changed tack then, should have accepted he would have to remove the obstacle in front of him. Instead, he had kept trying to convince Iris to consent to him, even after she shunned him over and over. The reason was unthinkable and atrocious, but it would only make him weaker if he refused to acknowledge it: He *respected* her. He respected the power and the authority she had, and he respected her ability to refuse him. It had made her *desirable*, and that was a disgusting realization. He had no longer wanted to trick her into sanctioning his plan so he could take the throne of Hell; in fact, he truly wanted her to rule *with* him.

The admission made him angry. That sort of weakness was inexcusable and unallowable, and he would have to correct it. Iris was a human woman, and he would not be made weak by any human woman. So she was also a separate manifestation of Satan; what of it? Satan was an angel, no different from Loomis himself, and no more deserving of Hell's throne. Loomis had given Iris every chance he was going to give; she had refused them all, and now he would end her.

As he stewed in his ire, he sensed a doubtful thought in the back of his mind: *Should I be afraid of her?* He felt his jaw tense and his hands begin to shake just a little. *NO*, he screamed silently to himself. She had threatened to punish his hubris. She had once again torn him down in dignity through an unexpected exhibition of so-called power. Never mind it. Let the woman have her little ego trip. Her power was different, perhaps, but not superior to his. And, he thought, perhaps this was for the best. She was a being of two natures that were inherently contradictory, and the nature that had been subdued for so long had just shown itself in a most decisive fashion. Satan had created this form of himself thinking it would be the antithesis of Jesus Christ, but God had spat upon the Devil's arrogant plan. Where Christ was both God and man, made in the image and likeness of God, Satan's Iris was a demon in a human shell, which God had then stolen for Himself by giving her His own breath. She was the bastard begotten of two fathers, the substance of one and the adopted of the other. She was incongruous duality that could not exist indefinitely. Her two natures would attack each other, would struggle inexhaustibly with one another until she submitted to one or until both were destroyed. Either way, the resultant aftermath would be a ruined, shattered mess of whatever power or glory she once was. Perhaps he wouldn't have to destroy her at all. Perhaps her own internal impossibility would consume her first. Regardless, her end was determined. Whether by his doing or through her undoing, Loomis would eventually claim his rightful throne.

20

At the conclusion of what had been a tedious day, Dr. Marvin Whitakker ascended the stairs from his office in the museum basement, locking the door behind him, and wished a curt "Good night" to the guards working tonight's shift. They let him out the front doors, and he strode briskly to his station wagon, thinking with great delight how wrong they were to believe they were securing the museum behind him.

Marvin entered his car and drove six short minutes to the trailer park where he resided. It was already after dark, owing both to the hour and to the season, but he wasn't going to skip his evening ambulatory. He parked his car and began walking, toward the rear gate of the park and out into the empty field behind it. He whistled a cheerful tune as he went, mindless of the cold air around him and the overgrown, yellowing weeds and brush beneath him. He carried his hands in the pockets of his sport jacket and surveyed the night sky with casual interest, well aware of how tiny and insignificant the Earth is on a cosmic scale.

Finally, he reached the spot he knew so well. Hidden at the base of a tangle of feral shrubbery was an old manhole cover. His crowbar was nearby, cleverly concealed in a notch he had carved in a low-hanging, dead branch of a maple tree. He removed the bar and lifted the manhole cover with some effort, then dropped the bar into the hole and lowered himself after it, stepping onto the rusted iron bars of a ladder leading downward. He slid the cover carefully back into its place above him. It was always a bit of a challenge due to the weight of the metal, but he had practiced it for so many years, he knew it could no longer best him.

Climbing down into the darkness, he felt for his crowbar and carried it with him down the long tunnel. He had no light by which to see, but he had no need of such luxury. He moved with haste down the damp and slightly noxious mold-covered passage, letting his feeling guide him, until he reached an out-of-place aluminum ladder set along one wall. This was his exit.

This passage was a defunct sewage tunnel that had been removed from the city's sanitary sewer lines during a separate expansion project decades ago. Few, if any besides Marvin, even realized it was still accessible, leading from a vacant piece of land behind a trailer park to just below his museum. It had taken hours of study, poring over historical city plans and museum blueprints, and countless more hours of physical labor for Marvin to carve out an access point from the museum to this tunnel, but he had done it, and he was proud of that.

He climbed his ladder and exited the tunnel, stepping out into a dark, concrete-lined bunker. This room had been part of the museum's original construction, which had begun shortly before American involvement in World War II. At the time, it had been a well-equipped bomb shelter; now, it was Marvin's private abode beneath the museum he adored. He could come here whenever he liked, and he could study all the pieces in storage or undergoing conservation. The bunker's top entry was a cellar door located in the floor of the museum's large storage room. After several modernizations had taken place, like the addition of a new storm shelter, and after asbestos had become suddenly passé, the bunker's stairs had been removed and its door had been sealed and covered by shelving, but those things could not stop Marvin Whitakker. He had rearranged the obstructive storage shelves and had built his own steps from his secret bunker to the room above. Now, he exited the cellar and walked through the storage room to his office, where he unlocked the door and retrieved his worn-out duffel bag full of supplies. He could move about freely down here; only the door from the main museum to the basement was secured by alarm.

He took his bag and retreated to his bunker. Pulling out a large flashlight, he walked to the shelves where he had placed several artifacts of particular interest to him. One, of course, was his special pride and joy. He seated himself on a wooden crate near the shelves and set the light on another crate facing him. He reached over excitedly and picked up the copper spearhead, admiring its intricacy and loving the sensation of power that emanated from its metal into his fingertips.

Maybe those ass-brained detectives would find the copper spearhead that had gone missing, and maybe they wouldn't. Marvin Whitakker couldn't care less either way. He had recognized this piece and its value the moment it had fallen so spectacularly into his lap, and he had worked very hard to replicate it for the exhibit. He had completed it not a moment too soon, for, just as he had expected, someone else had come looking for it. Little did they know, Marvin Whitakker had already outsmarted them.

21

The door opened as Iris approached, Loomis standing there behind it to greet her with a silent, brusque nod of his head. He was dressed in his usual impeccable style, this time sporting expensive black slacks and an expensive black tailored vest, worn over a pale pink shirt. Iris almost always hated to see a man in pink, but Loomis wore it very well. He had forgone a necktie, and the slightly opened collar of his shirt revealed just a hint of his clavicle, which Iris found most agreeable. He was every bit as handsome and inviting as always, but to Iris's perception, something about him seemed off. Was it her imagination, or did he seem nervous?

"Thank you, Loomis," she said with a confident and flirtatious smile as she entered. Ever since she had realized and accepted the true depth of her demonic identity, she had been a paragon of self-assurance and unabashed sensual magnetism. It was a contrast to her solely human personality, and she had to admit, she wasn't hating it.

Loomis closed the door and locked it behind her, then turned and asked dully, "May I take your coat?"

Iris, though a bit disappointed by his deadpan tone, grinned, unzipped her leather jacket, and handed it to him silently. He opened a well-camouflaged closet beside him and hung the jacket inside, then motioned with his hand for Iris to proceed into the living area. His place was a large, beautiful Victorian manor, with modernized amenities but an interior decor that still effectively captured the classic, antiquated elegance and romantic opulence of a bygone era, much like his office in the city, where Iris had first met him. Dim lights were on overhead, softly supplementing the illumination coming from a fire he had prepared. The wide stone hearth breathed gold and amber flames that filled the room with a warm, pulsing glimmer and a pleasantly woody, erogenous aroma. Iris seated herself facing the fireplace on a plush, exquisitely upholstered loveseat of dark walnut wood with scarlet-and-gold jacquard. On the coffee table in front of her was a sterling tray that held a large French press filled with fresh coffee and two serving cups on saucers. Loomis followed behind her and sat on the edge of the loveseat, pouring coffee for each of them.

As he turned and handed a cup and saucer to Iris, he asked, in a low and serious tone, "Do you know why I have asked you here?"

Iris accepted the coffee and thought for a moment before responding. She had been curious when Loomis had requested that she meet him at his estate outside Portland—enough so that she was willing to make the simple magical journey here—but, truthfully, his reasons for wanting to see her no longer mattered. Whatever he said or did, she would always have the commanding authority and the final word. Loomis was, at this point, not much more to her than an enjoyable diversion that she was, for now, willing to entertain.

"Well," she answered at length, "since you've finally realized I have no need or desire for you, I can think of only two reasons you might want to meet with me. Either you're ready to admit defeat and end your campaign for Hell's throne, or you believe you've discovered some new and sure method of obliging my forfeiture of it." She took a delicate sip of the coffee and then continued, "You're not the capitulating type, so I'm guessing you're about to tempt me in some new way to join you, or to tell me how you plan to destroy me."

Loomis had poured himself a cup of coffee, but he left it sitting on the table, turning instead to Iris and looking straight into her eyes. Oddly, Iris noted, his gaze held a businesslike sobriety and a rather unsatisfying lack of hedonistic invitation.

"Do you know where I've been?" he asked quietly.

Iris sighed and drank some more coffee. It was, as should be expected of anything material from Loomis Drake, of utmost quality, and she took an intentionally long time to savor it before answering the question he had posed. Eventually, she said, "I assume our last encounter sent you limping back to Hell to lick the wounds I inflicted upon your pride." There was no small amount of derision in her voice, and she noted with approval that a pained expression briefly flickered across Loomis's face before he could hide it.

He turned away from her and stared into the fire for a moment. "I did return to Hell," he admitted. "I intended to expand my knowledge and my abilities so I could develop a way to exterminate you." After a brief silence, he turned to face Iris again, finding her leaning comfortably back into the thick cushions of the loveseat, nonchalantly sipping the rest of her coffee, one leg crossed lightly over the other and the toe of her leather boot nearly touching his leg. She looked at him impassively and waited for him to continue.

"I have discovered something I believe you will want to know," he went on. "Something about the one who created you, and what he plans to do to you."

Iris wondered briefly where Loomis might be going with this. "I was *begotten*," she corrected with a mocking smile, "not *created*. But, do go on."

Loomis moved closer and took the saucer and empty cup from her hands, set them back on the serving tray, then turned back to her, resting one hand near her knee and the other forearm along the back cushion of the sofa. "Iris," he said fervently, "he intends to take back from you the essence of himself he gave you. He is planning to pull his spirit from you, and he has already designed the magical spell that will do it." He paused and penetrated her eyes with his as if searching for a response. Iris returned his stare but said nothing. What he was saying seemed impossible, though not altogether unbelievable, and that was somewhat concerning. Not so concerning, however, as to justify any disclosure of anxiety to her demonic host.

"Does this not anger you?" Loomis asked, his tone sharp.

"I don't believe it can be done," Iris replied flatly. "But even should he have a spell that will take his demonic spirit from me, he is mired in Hell, whereas I roam freely on Earth. His magic is far weakened by the time it gets to this physical realm. Mine, as you know, is not," she said, stabbing him with a taunting sneer.

Loomis shook his head slowly. "He has only to find a human vessel he can use," he argued. "It won't take him long."

Iris sighed. "There are many human beings willing to lose their souls to evil, but you know most of them are useless when it comes to possession," she said, her voice drab with boredom. "Those who could effectively be used to perform any powerful magic are few and far between, and even those will always be weaker than I am, because I'm fully demon *and* fully human, rather than a possessed soul."

"They won't need magic," Loomis returned condescendingly. "Satan needs only to bring you to himself. A competently possessed human being can easily kill your mortal body. And, as you are undoubtedly aware, your sins are grave and scarlet. Your soul is bound for Hell, and the end of your earthly life will send you there. Then he can do with you as he pleases."

A fleeting chill coursed through Iris's body as she recalled her Catholic upbringing and her almost lifelong practice of it. Her human heart was terrified of Hell, and of course Loomis was right about her soul. There would be no redemption if she died at this very moment. She ignored the cursory human musing; it was silly. She was too far gone for saving, and besides, she was a ruler in Hell. She was, by divine nature, stronger than the rest. She had nothing to fear.

Replying with a broad smile, Iris said confidently, "I'm not too far from completing the creation you yourself began. While you were playing around in Hell trying to plot my demise, I made a number of changes to the magical work you had started here, and I now have full claim of it. By the time Satan comes for me, *if* he comes for me at all, I'll already be holding far more power than he's aware of. It won't be easy to kill me." After a thoughtful pause, she added, "Besides, it would be self-destructive for him to take anything from me, especially once I've finished what you started. Only with my continued existence can he enjoy total and unchallenged dominion over both Hell and Earth." She leaned forward slightly and grinned, tilting her head nearer Loomis in goading. "Have you again forgotten he and I are the same?" she asked pointedly.

Loomis's expression was dark, though his face was quite attractive in the dancing firelight. "Have *you* not yet recognized you are different?" he rejoined, a definite bite in his voice. His question and its acute, almost desperate delivery caught Iris by surprise. How long had it taken her to realize she was Satan, even after being told? And now, the demon who had known her identity long before she had was telling her she was, what? *Not* Satan? Was this Loomis's fresh idea? To ruin her from within through a cancerous identity crisis he would initiate? *Whatever you're up to,* she thought, *it won't work. I know what I am.*

Loomis had gone quiet and had trained his eyes blankly on the fire again, though his hand remained on Iris's thigh. She couldn't be sure, but she imagined he must be debating with himself how to continue. "You are strong now," he finally said, his voice very low. "And you are stronger than he, *because you are different.* I have finally understood it, and I don't enjoy making you aware of it, but knowing as I do that he can, in fact, take all your power from you, I believe my telling you this is the only way to thwart his plan." He stopped again, seemingly collecting his thoughts. Iris stayed quiet, wondering why the hell he was acting so strangely.

He removed his hand from her leg but remained in place near the edge of the couch, facing halfway between her and the fireplace. He leaned over, resting his forearms on his thighs and interlacing his fingers, letting his hands hang naturally between his knees. "You are the begotten of Satan, manifested in a separate form," he proceeded slowly. "That is true. You believe it was your unforeseen humanity that made you able to think and act separately from him. But, you see, Iris..." He trailed off and sighed with indignant exasperation. He lowered his head briefly, clearly reluctant to continue and unconcerned with trying to conceal his hesitancy. Iris, though increasingly nonplussed by his atypical behavior, forced her muddled thoughts into the back of her mind, where it was easier to ignore them. The most advantageous strategy for her now would be to hear Loomis out. All his words and actions would be inconsequential, anyway. She was superior to him in strength and in station; she might as well let him show her all his cards now, since that seemed to be his agenda for the evening. It would make it easier for her to determine his motivations and then apply the appropriate punishment for whatever convoluted scheme he was trying to set up for her.

"It isn't just the free will that separates you from him," he announced after a long silence. "You were *changed* when...when humanity was put on you. Still the spirit of Satan, yes, but...*enhanced.*" Again, he fell silent, looking at the floor with heavy gravitas.

Iris was quickly losing interest in this painfully slow buildup. "You flatter me," she said sardonically. "Make your point, Loomis. So I'm *Satan 2.0*, bigger and better. Doesn't that just prove I'm right *not* to fear my counterpart down under?"

Loomis didn't appreciate her sarcastic levity, and he finally snapped, turning toward her and very forcefully grabbing her upper arm to pull her out of her casual reclining posture. Iris's eyes widened for just a second at his sudden physicality, but she quickly recovered and gave him a darkly cautionary scowl. Loomis, now acting much more in character, ignored the hateful expression and glared right back at her.

"You don't understand, you ignorant bitch," he hissed. The insult ignited an instant, burning anger in Iris, but she refrained from any outward display of wrath. He continued, sharply, "When you were stolen from Satan, when you had humanity put upon you, you were *hidden* from him. You have his spirit, his power, all his inclinations...but he has none of yours. You are both the same substance, but the link between you is a one-way conduit in your favor. He never sought you on Earth because he couldn't *see* you. Your existence was made known to him; it was shown to him that his own separate self had been ruined by the stain of humanity, and then you were torn from his vision. He decided it didn't matter, because he expected you to end up back in Hell with him, as it would be only fitting that a human with a demonic spirit should be eternally damned. It was always his plan, even from your beginning, that he would reclaim that part of himself he had given you. It was never a gift freely given; it was a loan that would be repaid, even if you hadn't also been made human. That irritating little joke just affirmed the necessity of his reclaiming you. But, you see, Iris, you are *different!* You are *completely separate*. You are fully divided from him. You can exceed him in every way! He is blind to your knowledge and your actions; you have his power with or without his consent, and he is incapable of changing that. You already have all that he is, but you don't have to stop there. Everything you learn beyond what you already know, every magical skill you hone and master in excess of his ability, is yours alone!" He paused and swallowed. He had been speaking quickly and earnestly, and his chest now rose and fell in swift tempo.

After several seconds, he added, more calmly, "I've only just discovered this truth about you, but I don't doubt its veracity. I had often wondered why Satan didn't try to use you. I assumed he had disowned you for your humanity, but I could never explain why he would so easily give up on a chance to possess your soul. Now, I understand."

Iris reflected on this revelation for a moment, considering how much more powerful this made her than she had already known. It meant she could pull everything from Satan, all his knowledge and strength and evil, while giving nothing back to him in return—if it were true, of course. If it were true, it would explain why he had never appeared to her or tried to possess her or otherwise convince her of her demonhood. It would explain why she had never heard his voice, even after realizing her identity and then using her powers for evil. The story was not inconceivable. After all, she had been made a mockery of Satan. He had intended her as a clone of himself to carry out his will on Earth, and instead she had become a renegade superior to him and then masked by Heaven from his view. Of course he should want to destroy her! And it was altogether probable he had in fact intended it from the start, anyway, the sick bastard.

After mulling over Loomis's words for a short while, Iris asked skeptically, "If I'm so invisible to him, how should he expect to find me now? And why bother, if Hell will have me in but a short time, anyway?"

Loomis leaned forward, picked up his yet-untouched coffee cup, and drank the entirety of its contents before replacing it on the table. He poured two more cups from the French press and handed one to Iris, giving her a hard stare as he did so. She took the cup with a tiny smile and reclined back into the sofa cushion, once more crossing one leg over the other knee, this time lightly dragging her toe down Loomis's nearest leg. It was refreshing to see him return to his usual arrogant and enticing demeanor.

He left his coffee on the table and slid back into the loveseat, turning his torso and bringing one leg onto the seat so that it rested against Iris's. He held the back of the sofa with one hand and gently grasped Iris's thigh with the other. Though her demon's mind was wary of him and his preternatural aptitude for deceit, Iris's human person still felt a nervous thrill each time he acted suggestively. Perhaps in time she would allow herself to succumb to the temptation he presented, but until she could be absolutely sure of her preeminence over him, she would have to abstain from such pleasures.

He looked at her with dark approval. "You have *killed*, Iris," he said icily, "and in magnificent, diabolical fashion! That kind of magic leaves an indelible mark on the very thin veil that exists between here and Hell, and there are not many here who are capable of it. He has seen the evidence and recognized its meaning, and now he knows of you and the power you are wielding. It is, so he believes, *his* power, and he doesn't fancy sharing it. He was once complacent, willing to wait for your damnation before he consumed you, but now..." He shook his head slowly and dramatically, with a sneering grin. "Now," he continued, "he sees you are a threat to him. He sees you are stronger than he imagined. He has been forced to recognize his folly in bringing you into existence...*and he hates it*."

Loomis chuckled with sadistic merriment at his own statement. His vitriolic laughter brought a delightfully villainous glow to his face, and Iris found it rather arousing. As she watched him, she couldn't help but grin. It was a humorous picture he had painted, of Satan in Hell, pissed off at something he had done and yet unable to rectify it. Should she be offended? Was he laughing at her when he laughed at Satan? No...Iris believed all Loomis had told her tonight. She had thoroughly searched him for any subconscious indicia of trickery or deception, and she had found none. She now knew her identity to have a fascinating new depth; she was not just Satan; she was a second Satan, the New Satan. She had accepted what she was given (and that was a great and evil power), but now she knew the Devil could lay no claim to whatever she would take for herself. There would be no more questioning her own supremacy. There was, however, one nagging question lurking in her mind, and it wiped the grin from her face.

"Why are you telling me all this?" she asked, her tone quite accusatory. If Loomis was plotting something, which he almost certainly must be, she needed to decipher it. To her surprise, his expression quickly lost its nefarious mirth and became more serious and, astonishingly, somewhat less confident. He looked at her for a short time, then turned away again, moving away from her ever so slightly.

His reply was hesitant and quiet. "I don't want to see him take your power," he said slowly. After a breath, he continued, "I don't intend to abandon my quest for Hell's throne, but..." He allowed his sentence to disappear into the warm air before the fire. Iris watched as a hard aspect fell across his countenance. She interpreted the look as one of extreme reluctance under a thin veneer of anger, or perhaps disgust. "If I should never have the throne," he finally concluded, "then it is either you or he who will have it, and I would rather it go to you."

Iris scoffed. "Why? Because you think I'm the easier one to dethrone?" After all he had just revealed to her about her nearly limitless demonic nature, surely the imbecile must know he would never defeat her, especially if she took the throne. Yet why else would he want her as Hell's ruler? She chugged the remainder of her coffee, irritated, then uncrossed her legs and leaned forward, setting the cup on the tray with a harsh clank.

Loomis didn't answer immediately. Iris straightened up and crossed her arms in front of her chest, narrowing her eyes in slight confusion and in great suspicion of his behavior. She could postulate that Loomis would perhaps always believe her to be weaker than Satan, even if he stated otherwise, simply on account of her feminine humanity, but she would have expected him to corroborate that assumption with a malicious sneer or something of the like. It was most unlike him to miss an opportunity to advertise his pompous theory that he would eventually claim the throne.

"I believe you to be the more deserving ruler," he finally stated coldly, his eyes still lost in the flames across the table from him.

Iris uncrossed her arms and curled her fingers along the edge of the seat beneath her, dumbfounded. It was a tall order—no, an impossible order—expecting a demon to pay a genuine compliment, yet that was exactly what she believed she had just heard. He hadn't looked her in the eye when he said it, but she had been staring at him as he spoke, and, at least on the side nearest her, there had been no mannerisms she could label as subconscious evidence of subterfuge. Maybe her humanity was simply making her want to believe Loomis had developed an actual respect for her. The endorsement was simple and devoid of embellishment or romance, but its apparently painstaking delivery from its consummately evil writer gave it an intensity and depth that pierced Iris's demonic indifference and grazed the surface of the human emotions she had buried inside herself. She shoved the feeling deeper and quelled a revolting urge to hug Loomis. The sly bastard was acting almost human, but she couldn't allow herself to be duped. Her mind instantly generated a list of skeptical thoughts that might explain his strange affectation, and she soon settled on the most probable.

"You believe I'm the one more apt to share the throne," she said cynically, hoping the submission to her demon nature would completely hide the human disappointment she felt. Loomis turned to face her, and that in itself was confirmation of her suspicion—he wanted to rule alongside her.

"I have given you all this," he said gravely. "I've told you about your *true* power." His voice regained its often-sinister edge as he spoke louder and faster. "I have revealed to you a part of yourself you didn't even know! And it is *that* part of you that distinguishes you from him, makes you superior to him! Without me, Iris, you would not be what you are or what you can become. You *owe* me," he finished, with caustic punctuation.

Iris felt a slow simmer of choler beginning in her veins. *I 'owe' you?* she thought angrily. *You should be grateful I allow you to continue existing at all, you impotent fuck!* She said nothing, but she stared at Loomis with virulent contempt.

"Satan came to me," Loomis went on, having subdued the malice that had entered his tone. "He enlisted me to seize you, to bring you to him. I refused," he said genteelly. Iris blinked hatefully in reply. Unperturbed by her silence, Loomis proceeded in polite charm, "You see, I could have destroyed you. I could have let you fall victim to his dastardly plan to ruin you. I rebuffed the Devil himself, and in doing so, I have already chosen your side." He looked at her with a plain expression, as though he believed his simple logic would convince her to accept him.

Iris smirked as she replied, "Ah, Loomis, you don't burn the bridge before you've successfully crossed it!" There was unveiled ridicule in her articulation. "How foolish of you to shun the Devil of Hell believing the Devil of Earth will receive you! *I don't want you,*" she said, softly though emphatically. "You've lost both Hell and Earth now." After pausing momentarily, she stood up to leave, and in an excited and derisively facetious fashion, she suggested, "I know, Loomis—why don't you try knocking on Heaven's door?" She flashed a beaming, mocking smile at him in conclusion.

Loomis, spurred immediately to anger in customary Loomis fashion, arose instantly and snatched Iris's arm. "You will not turn me away," he spat, eyes gleaming with acrimony and ablaze with the reflection of the flames from the fireplace, his grip tightening.

"I know the spell he intends to use on you. You will lose the spirit that gives you your power. You will feel it hacked away from you as you moan in anguished, defenseless paralysis until you are nothing more than a worthless, damned human soul, rotting in Hell for your eternity!" There was startling exigency in his words, but Iris ignored it. Loomis suddenly seized her other arm and pulled her closer to himself. "Do you want me to show you?" he yelled hotly.

Iris, unable to prevent the brief ripple of terror that permeated her humanity, swallowed hard and tried to slow her breathing. She hadn't noticed how rapid it had become. Her mouth was dry, but she managed to reply stonily, "You can do nothing to me."

Loomis released her arms and glared at her. For an instant, Iris thought perhaps he had lost his nerve, or perhaps he had been bluffing all along. But then she heard his demonic voice; or, rather, she *sensed* it, for the sound was almost inaudible, but the coldness in her bones was pronounced. As Loomis intoned low, barreling words she didn't readily recognize, she felt a frightening prickle throughout her body, as though millions of stinging ants were swarming on the underside of her skin. As seconds passed, she felt a gnawing in her chest and a lurch in her stomach, and she had no voice with which to scream. Conscious thought was quickly becoming a whirlpool of nearly unintelligible ideas, like dark water of an angry, alien sea swirling above a giant cosmic drain. Iris recognized her thoughts would soon be taken from her, and in frantic instinct toward self-preservation, she tried to step away, but the loss of her spirit had already weakened her physical body, and her legs could no longer support her weight.

As she started to fall, Loomis reached out and caught her, his strong arms a welcome anchor. Iris watched him as he continued his imperceptible chant, thinking she was finally ready to give up. She felt weak, empty...*Not yet*, she heard a drowning thought in her mind cry out. *Use what is left; remember what you already know!*

Iris listened and forced her thoughts to follow her mind's voice, ignoring the pain in her body by what willpower she still held. If Satan knew this spell and had planned it for her since her beginning, then she already knew it, too. Her mind's own whisper meandered through an eternity of knowledge and magic until it found what she needed. Desperately fighting to hold on to the remnants of her own spirit within her, she began the spell, uttering it with focused energy in her mind. She pulled some of her power back from Loomis, and she saw in his eyes a flicker of surprise. *Good*, she thought. *Show him how powerful you really are.*

She repeated the spell fervently but silently in her mind, feeling its success as her physical distress subsided and her demonic power returned. Loomis, seeing what she was doing so ably, let go of her body and stepped away from her, allowing his shock to rest unconcealed on his face. Iris, having now regained her complete strength, smiled. *Now it's my turn*, she mused.

She licked her lips and let her demon voice resound from within her as she continued her incantation. Every bit of her Satanic power converged on Loomis, and she knew he was weaker than she. In a moment, she felt his spirit being pulled out of him and into her. It was a stimulating sensation. With every enunciation of the spell, she drew more and more new and impassioned strength inside her. This strength—Loomis's strength—was decidedly foreign. It was textured differently but beautifully, and enveloping it with her skin was an aphrodisiac delight. She continued her onslaught, pleased to see Loomis was looking rather faint. She pulled him closer and then shoved him onto the loveseat next to them and mounted his lap. Internalizing her magical words, she sustained the spell silently, taking still more and more of Loomis's being into herself with each rapid breath. She pressed her hands against his shoulders and drove her eyes deep into his, enjoying the undeniable fear she saw there as she writhed in pleasure over him.

Finally, with a final, hard tug at his being, Iris felt the fullness of Loomis's power inside her. Her back arched with his entry, and her eyes rolled involuntarily in extreme euphoria as she savored the moment of unparalleled energy she received from the taking. The fire behind her had grown wild, its flames extending out of the fireplace, licking the air of the room and heating it to an uncomfortable degree. After a few seemingly interminable seconds, Iris ran her tongue across her lips and dropped her head back toward Loomis's now pitifully vulnerable yet still handsome face.

She closed her eyes dramatically and then reopened them, then slowly brushed her long bangs away from her forehead, now drenched in sweat. She breathed heavily and smiled at her victim. "Oh," she said in a prolonged sigh, "you *are* strong, Loomis." He looked at her in dumb horror.

Sensing the fire and the temperature returning to normal, Iris relaxed a bit and briefly searched the expanses of her supernatural knowledge until she found another spell, returning Loomis's spirit to him. "I'll let you keep your power," she said with an amorous and teasing grin. "You need it more than I do."

Loomis's color returned to his skin, and the empty, horrified look in his eyes was replaced by a shineless despondency. He swallowed, but he didn't try to speak.

Iris, still straddling his legs with hers, leaned in and kissed him quickly but passionately on his lips. When she pulled away, she said conspiratorially, "You've been right about one thing all along." Lowering her mouth close to his ear, she whispered, "It *does* feel good having you inside me."

With those evocative words and a brief, iniquitous giggle, Iris stood from the sofa and moved to leave, hesitating before she did. She turned and looked down at Loomis, sitting stiff and forlorn on his expensive Victorian couch, and she grinned again. As an afterthought, she picked up his now-cold second cup of coffee, sucked it down with a few large swigs, and then replaced the cup on the table.

"Thank you for *everything*, Loomis," she said sweetly, knowing he would taste the poison in her undertones. "This has been an exceptionally *pleasurable* evening."

She moved to the entryway, removed her jacket from the closet, and then departed, leaving Loomis in stunned solitude to suffer the residuum of his debasement.

***

Through monumental effort of will, Loomis maintained a statuesque immobility as he unwillingly accepted Iris's unsettling, innuendo-laced words of gratitude. He remained unmoving as he listened to her footfalls upon the rug and then the hardwood, then he waited for the calm void that descended around him to confirm her departure.

Upon her exit, he finally allowed his artificial human body its desired physical reaction. Shuddering tremors coursed through his limbs, leaving his hands unsteady and weak. His breathing raced and his jaw quivered. His thoughts were an involuntary endless replay of what Iris had just done to him, and though he wanted desperately to leave the body and return to Hell in his natural demonic form, he found himself too apprehensive to remove his spirit from the relative safety and security he suddenly felt inside the earthly vessel. It was a weak form, but at least it provided some shelter from the eyes of those in Hell who might witness in him the aftereffects of Iris's unwanted violation of his spirit and then ridicule him for it. The greater comfort, however, was that remaining in the body meant he wouldn't have to trust his own magical abilities right now and potentially discover Iris had kept some part of him in herself. That was the most terrifying thought—that whatever she had returned to him was just a vaporous shadow of what he had always known himself to be.

Anxiety had settled in his stomach like a spider's eggs, and he could foresee what would happen when those eggs hatched. He attempted to stand and move for the bathroom, but his legs were shaky and proved most inutile. After a step and a half, his weight became too burdensome, and he slipped to his knees after failing to regain his balance by grabbing the coffee table and nearby wing chair. The dormant anxiety exploded within him, sending nausea like a swarm of arachnid legs crawling fast through his gut, leaving in their wake ripples of acidic bile. He leaned over and retched, fetid regurgitation cutting up through his chest and throat like a laser and leaving a repulsive taste in his mouth.

He rested himself on his heels after he vomited, still on his knees at the edge of the mess he had left on his antique Persian rug. The heat and light from the fireplace in front of him were now breathing a hellish ambience onto this pitiful, grotesque scene in which Iris had left him alone. Suddenly, all his heavy, opulent furniture and abundant, lavish decor became a suffocating miasma all around him, exacerbating his sickness and leaving him oppressed and claustrophobic there on the floor. As he stared down at the ruined carpet, his thoughts registered only the latent vision of Iris Wakefield on top of him, sucking his power, his *spirit*, into herself and enjoying every moment of exponential horror it had caused him. He could still feel her weight writhing in perverted ecstasy like a serpent in his lap; he could still feel her arms holding him solidly in place while his own body became, in his absence, too weak to fight her; he could still see those devilish green eyes, all dilated with insatiable lust, staring down into him, watching with ineffable satisfaction the fear he was unable to hide. Why was this human brain able to remember it at all, and, worse, so vividly? Why had it not just shut down when Iris had taken him? Had she purposely left just enough of his spirit there to keep the body active? Had she known its senses would be imprinted forever by her molestation, so they could then replay for him *ad nauseam* the painful and terrifying rapine?

He breathed heavily and tried to force the memory from his mind. He shakily pulled himself onto the edge of the coffee table and sat there, hunched over with his elbows on his knees and his hands holding his head. He tugged hard at his hair, hoping the physical pain would trounce his emotional one, but it was useless. He felt tears welling in his eyes, and though he was disgusted by them, he had no desire to resist their onslaught. They overran his eyes drop by drop until they rolled in tiny rivulets down his face and into his goatee. Outrage and confusion at his own weakness compounded whatever had led to the tears, turning thin streams into heavy, choking sobs. He cried for a few minutes, simply allowing the impotent, sniveling lamentation to run its course. He wondered briefly with horror if Iris might show up again at this moment, ready to deride him for this vile display of frailty, but, thankfully, she did not.

Finally, after the tears had slowed, he was able to close his eyes tightly and take some deep breaths through gritted teeth, and the deluge of remorse, or sadness, or grief, or whatever other fragile human emotion this was, was finally dammed. He rubbed his eyes roughly and then indelicately dried his face with his sleeve. This was another unexpected and most unfortunate predicament Iris had created for him. He couldn't know what effects her violation of his spirit would cause him, but perhaps this flooding of foreign emotion was one of them. He had spent practically the full duration of human existence tempting souls away from God, and he had never experienced any second thought, any regret or shame or guilt. What Iris had just done to him in spirit, he had done to hundreds in their thoughts or their bodies, with nothing but evil amusement and deviant pride. Now that he had just proven himself susceptible to the same victimization, he wondered if he might be feeling some hint of contrition for the anguish, both ephemeral and eternal, he had caused so many.

He shook his head in reply to his own silent musings. They were ridiculous thoughts. There was a stark difference between his actions against humanity and Iris's act against him—humanity *deserved* what he gave them. His defilement of them was a just punishment for their faint-heartedness, their inability to shun evil and choose righteousness; in all cases, they had willfully submitted to his temptations in one way or another. What Iris had done to him...that was an unsolicited and unwarranted attack, a barbaric pillaging of a spirit that was equal to hers in dignity. They were both demons, notwithstanding Iris's bastard human soul; simple propriety would ordain there should be some level of mutual respect between them. But, no; Iris had shown him no respect. She had rebuffed him and then stolen his plans for Hell's throne, and now she had forced herself on him and torn his own spirit right out of him, laughing as she did so. There had been no temptation, no proposal; she had left him no chance to fight back; she had simply taken by brutal force what was his and only his, what he would never have willingly given her. She had corrupted him and left him sulking in the debased ruins of a once-powerful self that was now full of doubt. She had left him questioning his decisions and his actions; she had left him questioning who and what he was. Worst of all, she had left him feeling *human*.

The truth was there before him, appalling and loathsome, but unequivocal. He had underestimated not only Iris's power, but also her capacity for evil. She was stronger than he, and she was stronger than Satan; she was also more evil than either of them might have imagined. He doubted even Satan could now succeed in removing his spirit from her. All of Hell should tremble at her presence, for hers was a power still growing and a darkness more consuming than any Satan could have hoped to achieve. That she would have the throne was inevitable, and Hell would rue that day.

Unless, of course, someone could yet stop her. No one demon would be strong enough to do it, not even Loomis himself, but perhaps if they united against her...he scoffed hatefully at the thought. Fuck all of Hell; they deserved the ironclad domination that was coming to them. If he had to submit to Iris's will, so, too, should the rest of them be subjugated.

But Iris had said she would let him keep his power. Surely he still had all of it; he still had his earthly presence. The war was not yet ended for him. He would simply have to strategize differently. There would be no coaxing Iris to join him; that ship had long since sailed. It seemed she had no inclination to let him rule with her, and why should she? There was nothing he could do that she couldn't do herself. What option did that leave him?

Loomis bit his lip and sighed. He turned his head and saw the coffee cups sitting there beside him with the French press on the silver serving tray, and he trembled with hatred and poignant misery as he recalled Iris's fingers and lips on them—the same fingers and lips that had then turned on him—and with a sudden, agonized and angry scream, he swept his hand hard across the table, sending the tray and its contents flying over a side table and into the drapes on the window across the room, finally crashing with a metallic clang and the tinkling of broken Italian porcelain on the floor below.

With his jaw firmly set and his chest heaving with unwanted, lingering emotion, Loomis reached a vexatious decision. If he wanted to save his existence in Hell from the rule of a tyrant, he would have to cajole Iris Wakefield back to Heaven.

22

Iris stood near the edge of a small copse of mesquite trees, their thorny and nearly bare branches offering just a hint of shadow from the pale glow of the rising moon. It was a cold night following a cold and rainy day. The clouds had poured themselves out and then dispersed, leaving in their wake clear skies and muddy ground. Iris, though normally quite repulsed by the thought of dirtying her boots, had no reason to pay it any mind tonight. She was here on important business that simply had to be done, mud or no mud, but, of course, it was nice to know she could command the ground beneath her to be dry under her feet, and it would obey.

A short distance across the field in front of her, people were gathering in front of a poorly maintained wooden farmhouse and barn. The farmhouse was dimly lit from within, several of its first-floor windows filled with a warm, citrine glow. The people outside stood chatting with one another in small groups, clustered in the circles of light offered by a handful of rickety lanterns hung on wooden posts lining the dilapidated stone walkway leading to the farmhouse from the property's long dirt-and-gravel drive. Iris watched them indifferently, patiently awaiting tonight's action, whatever it would prove to be. She had come here with a simple goal and, therefore, a simple plan. If her human nature were steering now, she would be bogged down in a swamp of insignificant details, trying to plan for every contingency and finding it intrinsically impossible to do so. Her human nature would fear repercussions or failure and would almost certainly abandon the idea. However, it was not her human nature that was in charge now. Iris had realized the breadth of her powers as a demon—as Satan himself, no less—and she was quite confident her demonic nature could wing this one and enjoy an overwhelming, and hopefully entertaining, success.

Still staring at the figures as they waited for the arrival of their leader, Iris smirked to herself. *How ignorant they are*, she thought in amusement. She knew nothing about these people individually, but she knew enough about them generally to know she didn't have to be here as a demon to outsmart every last one of them. This group came from two dozen or so families who lived in this backwoods rural area. They were poor chicken farmers, mostly, with properties that had been handed down for the last few generations, deteriorating with every passing year. Some of the wealthier ones, though still far from wealthy by urban standards, might own one or two bony horses or possibly a lice-infested cow. They earned their incomes by peddling eggs, homegrown vegetables, and handmade goods at nearby farmer's markets. At least, that was the source of their above-the-table income. Below the table...well, now that was where their story got interesting.

Many years ago, a two-bit dairy farmer in the area, who at the time enjoyed better success than his distant neighbors, fell suddenly ill with an unknown ailment and joined the company of his already-bedridden wife, who suffered from a myriad of inexplicable aches and chronic infirmities. His sudden sickness forced his business and the care of both him and his wife onto his teenaged son, a relatively bright and genuinely good young man. The boy had always applied himself in all things—in his homeschool studies, in his work with his father's dairy cows, in his daily attendance of his sickly mother—and while he had never complained nor advertised any desire to move beyond the life he had always known, he dreamed of greater things. He wanted to know success—real success—and move to the city; he wanted to study at a university and learn alongside intelligent, cultured people; he wanted to see the world that existed outside his country upbringing. But, of course, his father's unexpected malady made it all impossible for him. He loved his parents and was a willing caretaker to both of them, but their constant complaints and groanings and demands eventually became a painful and jading thorn in his side. His father, in particular, pressed upon him to keep the dairy business afloat, but he would moan incessantly when attention was diverted from his own needs for too long. The boy, quickly losing his desire to help his parents and soon finding his nighttime dreams overrun by visions of murdering them, began devising plans for extricating himself from the prison his home had become. Running away seemed the most obvious and cleanest solution; perhaps he could return after a few weeks and find his parents dead, and then he would sell everything and move on with his own life. He had nearly convinced himself to do it one night before a wave of guilt drowned him and washed away the idea.

The following morning, a knock at the door brought a welcome visitor. It was a girl he had known since childhood, who lived with her uncle about two miles up the road. She was plain and homely, and simple and naive, but kind, and she had come to bring him a small basket of freshly baked bread, having heard of his parents' sickness. Her uncle, she said, had been outraged when she left with the bread—he was a mean man when sober and outright abusive when drunk, which he often was. Scared to return home, she asked if she could stay for a while, and the young man was smart enough to know the opportunity when he saw it. He offered that she could stay as long as she liked, if she would assist with the daily care of his parents. Caring by nature, she accepted the invitation, glad to help her friend and his parents and glad for the respite from her uncle's volatile temper and tyranny. The arrangement worked well for a time, until the girl's uncle stormed in through the front door one evening with a shotgun, a cold-blooded ultimatum that she return home immediately, and a threatening demand for money in payment for both the bread his niece had brought and for all the nursing work she had done.

Though angry at the intrusion and concerned for the girl's safety, as he had developed quite a fondness for her, the boy reacted with intelligent restraint, sensing another opportunity being laid at his feet. He calmly pushed the girl behind him, standing between her gasping sobs and the two barrels of her uncle's gun. He told the man he kept his money hidden in a canister on the kitchen counter, and he could have all of it if he would then leave. The uncle had asked how much it was; he estimated it at around sixty dollars. Overt greed flashed instantly across the man's teary, drunken red eyes. *It's just behind you, there, in the kitchen...*

The man lowered the gun and grunted as he turned to head into the kitchen. The boy, much more agile and surer-footed than his unwelcome and inebriated guest, lunged toward the man and shoved him from the back into the doorframe of the kitchen, grabbing the shotgun with one hand. The uncle, stunned by the surprise attack and too tipsy to react in time, tripped and lurched forward, inadvertently releasing his gun and stumbling headfirst into the rickety dining table in front of him. The boy wasted no time with internal thought or debate. He readied the gun, pointed it steadily at the loathsome man who had come to take his money and his girlfriend from him, and he pulled the trigger. The first blast killed him; the second was purely ornamental.

Amid the girl's frantic, incoherent cries, the young man backed out of the kitchen and turned down the hallway to his parents' bedroom, where two more shots rang out in swift succession, leaving the bed a bloody knoll, a silent testament to the freedom the young man had just purchased for himself.

He returned to the living area, where the panicked girl sat quaking in terrified disbelief, her face and eyes red and soaked with tears. She had managed to silence her screams, or perhaps the emotional trauma had rendered her speechless and paralyzed. The young man set down the gun, knelt on the floor in front of her, and tried to calm her. He explained they were free now—free from his parents and their infinite neediness, free from her uncle and his liquor-laced abusiveness, free from all that imprisoned them in this godforsaken Podunk. He told her they had everything they needed, and all the world was open to them now. He painted for her an idyllic scene of their future life together; his words were the flawless brushstrokes of a masterful artist. Eventually, she was ready to trust his lead, and she quietly asked what they must do now. Her question dealt a hard blow of reality onto the young man's free-spirited high, and he realized he would have to devise some plan for cleaning up this mess.

As his mind rambled through various possibilities, he heard a sharp rap near the front door, still hanging slightly ajar from the blow the uncle had dealt it. The sudden sound startled the children, but the young man quickly answered it, knowing he must keep any prying eyes away from what he had just done. He took the shotgun with him to the door, intending to use it again if necessary. He peered through the small opening between the broken door and its frame to the porch, where a tall figure stood robed in shadow. When he asked the visitor's identity, a mellow voice with a strange accent replied, *I am the help you seek.*

The young man, his curiosity piqued and his guilty paranoia instantly abated, opened the door and let the stranger in. He was a tall, slender man, dressed in a black woolen suit, a white high-stand collar, and a deep-red silk tie. A black wool cloak was fastened at his collar and draped over his shoulders, flowing with elegance in gentle pleats nearly to his ankles, its scarlet lining adding an imposing color of confidence. His black shoes were shiny and clean, showing no evidence of the dust he must have had to walk through to get onto the porch. His face was quite handsome—intense and mysterious, with olive-toned skin, dark eyes, and a neat black goatee. Atop his black hair sat a black top hat, encircled by a scarlet silk band. He carried a strange-looking ebony dress cane with a decorative pewter handle. His attire was foreign but bore the look of great wealth, and that was certainly of interest to the young man. But even beyond his apparel, there was just *something* about him, something that made the young man believe this stranger could help him, something that made the young man *want* to trust him.

The visitor glanced over at the brutal scene in the kitchen, then turned his eyes on the young man and said, *In the end, they all get what they deserve, and those who administer justice shall be administered justice themselves.*

The young man and the girl, who had curiously though cautiously joined his side when the stranger entered, stood in confused silence, marveling at the man's exotic appearance and cryptic speech. He continued by asking the young man what he desired. It was a simple question that lacked a simple answer, and the boy didn't reply immediately. With a tiny smile, the man removed his thin black leather gloves, pocketed them, and then detached the headpiece from his walking stick. From within its base, he extracted a heavy silver ring with an engraved bezel and a small ruby inlay, and he placed it on his finger, saying in his strange but soothing voice, *Desires unnamed will be left unsatisfied. Only those of us who can name our desires will find the power to fulfill them.*

With those enigmatic words, the man turned and walked to the dead body of the girl's uncle, lying eviscerated on the kitchen floor, the children following closely behind him in anxious curiosity. He held his adorned hand over the body, staring at it with a focused intensity. In an instant, the body was engulfed in bizarre red flames. The girl let out a shocked little gasp and grabbed the boy's arm. He, though startled by the fantastic scene, with rapt attention watched the flames—if they were, in fact, flames—as they consumed the body but brought no harm to anything else. After a few seconds of bright, crimson-colored light, the uncle's body was gone, no smoke or ash or blood or bone left as evidence of his demise. Simply gone.

Eyes wide with amazement, the young man looked from the floor to this strange, wonderful man who had just erased every hint of the life he had so brutally taken. His young girlfriend was dumb with stupefaction, but he, being of greater intelligence than she, could still feel the wheels of his mind turning. He had a perfect idea; he would tell this man his desire, and this man would fulfill it for him, and by fulfillment of this one desire, he would unlock for himself all his other dreams. He would use one wish to demand infinite additional wishes from the genie, so to speak. Pleased with the unquestionable cleverness of his own thinking, the boy told the man, *I want your power.*

The man smiled understandingly and nodded, then he removed the ring from his hand and offered it to the boy. *Then it is yours,* he replied. *But you must know your power is only borrowed, and the one who lends it to you may just as quickly withdraw it. Forget not your master, for to him you will repay with interest what you have borrowed.*

The boy nodded mindlessly in acceptance of the terms and put the ring on his finger. He looked inquisitively at the man, who gave him a slight nod and a smile, and then he ran to his parents' bedroom and stretched out his hand to them. To his astonishment, the same crystalline red flames appeared under his hand and effaced every indication of his parents' murder. Empowered and confident like never before, the young man returned to where the girl stood waiting for him. The front door was shut, its previous damage magically erased, and the strange man was nowhere to be seen. The girl handed him a small book, explaining the man had instructed her to give it to him, and then he had departed.

The young man studied the book and used the magic it taught him, creating some semblance of the life he had always envisioned for himself, with the girl following by his side. With his magic ring and his clever thinking, he built a modest wealth for himself and his wife, and he invited all around him to follow him and reap the benefits of his power. He sometimes thought about what the man had said to him that night—something about remembering who gave him his power. He knew it couldn't have been God, because there was just something too strangely sinister about that man. A human being couldn't give out that kind of power, so that left only one logical conclusion. That strange man had been Satan, and he had chosen him to wield his magic powers. The fact didn't really bother him, and he went through life unafraid of any consequence. But, in order to ensure the supply of magic never ran out, he coordinated regular ceremonies of worship to the Devil, over which he presided, with all his brethren in attendance. That, he believed, would keep the Devil happy.

It was an amusing story, really, Iris reflected. That young man had thought himself the sly one, but, of course, it was his dark and mysterious "savior" who had pulled all the strings. The boy had been chosen, all right—chosen as a patsy. He had been set up from early on, his mother tormented by a demon since shortly after the boy's birth and then his father stricken by the same demon's spell, creating a soul-sucking hellhole that drove the boy nearly to insanity, until he finally snapped and did what he knew to be wrong. And then had come the offer of power, of gratification, and it was no wonder the boy had greedily accepted it, ignoring all future fallout.

Just like that, a less-modern and less-Americanized Loomis Drake had coaxed another soul from God, and by this one well-placed piece, he had checkmated all the other simpletons who would join the ranks of this cult over the next generations. Perhaps some of them were truly ignorant and might have hope of redemption, but most of them did freely make the conscious decision to accept that their power, or rather, the power of their leader, came from Satan and not from God. How stupid of them! Neither Satan nor Loomis Drake cared anything about them or their insipid little displays of so-called servitude to the Devil. Their self-serving worship was as vacuous as their minds. They were simply a punchline, fools tricked for amusement and then forgotten, but, of course, they would never have the judgment to recognize it.

And the "power" the cult held? That was a joke, too. The ring Loomis had given the young man was practically worthless as a magic tool. It enhanced the natural abilities of the wearer, but nothing more. What the boy had done that night was not his doing at all, but Loomis's, and every spell he learned afterward from that little book was an inconsequential scrap of arcana. Iris had to admit, though, Loomis had chosen his prey very well. The young man he bewildered had been trapped so long in a needfully selfless position that the opportunity for easy self-advancement had gone straight to his head. He had become, as Loomis had almost certainly expected, a greedy snot, and he had kept to himself most of what little magical knowledge he had. Even to his own son, who was to follow in his footsteps, he had imparted only a fraction of what he knew. He thought it was the smart thing to do, so that the power would never be used against him. His son, likewise, withheld certain spells from his son, and so it had continued for generations, such that what existed now was an irrelevant sect of supposed Satanists whose leader, the great-great-great-grandson of its founder, possessed a watered-down, infantile repertoire of magic. In fact, aside from a few parlor tricks, the cult's leader had only one reliable ability, which was, luckily for him, what enabled the sect to fund their unimportant existences. He could turn any metal into gold, and it was enough of an ability to keep his followers under his thumb. He would send them out to their peddler's shows or farmer's markets, and they would sell their goods or steal what they could, and they would return their coins and other metallic wares to him for his "divine" alchemy. Those who brought the most received the most in return, though inevitably what they received was far less than what they had given. But, of course, it didn't take much to make beggars happy. All the members of the cult were discouraged from outward displays of wealth, anyway, as it would draw unnecessary scrutiny. It had been the practice from the sect's early days—another brainchild of its founder. Conveniently, however, the self-imposed seclusion also minimized outside influence that might bring with it any fragment of actual truth, just as Loomis had predicted from the beginning.

I wonder, Iris thought, *if Loomis would have done all this had he known I would one day use it all against him.* She was glad things had worked out this way; it was a delicious little treat to be able to use Loomis's own creation against him in order to, ironically, use another of his creations against him.

Iris saw the cult's current leader emerge from inside his outwardly slovenly hovel of a farmhouse, and the dimwits standing outside bowed their heads in greeting. The leader proceeded down the porch steps and led the way to a large cellar entrance in the ground. Two of the cultists opened the cellar doors and watched their leader descend, with all his lost sheep following him. Then they entered the cellar themselves and closed the doors behind them.

Iris smiled, knowing what was about to happen. For so long, these people and their ancestors had prayed they might continue sharing in Satan's evil abundance. Tonight, they would have what they prayed for, and they would surely regret it.

23

Sixteen-year-old Levi Kohler was both nervous and excited for this evening's events. Life hadn't been especially kind to him thus far, but certainly that would change with his full initiation tonight. He finished styling his curly, pale blond hair, glanced briefly at his reflection in the bathroom mirror and nodded to himself with as much approval as he could muster, then walked back down the short hallway to his tiny bedroom. He knelt on the worn rug near the foot of his bed, in front of a small trunk, a narrow box of about two feet long and a foot deep, made of cheap particleboard covered with a thin, beaten-up layer of dark-colored veneer. It had warped slightly with moisture, such that its hinged lid no longer opened or closed without some effort, but Levi had been opening and closing it nearly every day since the past summer had begun, and he knew the exact touch it needed to make it obey. He was proud of this chest and its contents, which he had earned through hard work and skillful pilfering. He opened the lid and peered inside, knowing what he would see but wanting to check one final time. It was a sizable donation, he thought, and he hoped it would be enough to impress the vicar. It would be nice to be recognized and accepted for once. That wasn't to say he had never been accepted; Levi's parents had already heaped great praises on him for his work over the summer, and they had been very supportive of him today through his qualms and last-minute bouts of anxiety as he wondered whether his trunkful of coins and scrap metal would make an acceptable pledge of his allegiance to the cult. But to have people outside his family know him and like him would be an even more satisfying feeling.

Levi had been in foster care since before he could remember, juggled from house to house and family to family as the system saw fit, and he had known more than his fair share of trauma because of it. He had lived with neglectful mothers, abusive fathers, hateful brothers, and manipulative sisters, and he had never felt at home among any of them. There had been some good people, too, but it seemed every time he began to warm up to someone, the boat would capsize and send one of them drifting away. Levi had tried to convince himself it wasn't his fault. He tried to believe he was a good person who deserved to be loved, but the world always seemed to argue...until he met the Kohlers.

It had been a little more than a year ago, shortly after Levi had been pulled out of a foster home and moved to a group home after his then-foster parents were arrested for some fraudulent scheme that involved artificial multiplication of government subsidies and chronic tax evasion. Levi didn't understand all the details, and he didn't much care, because those people had been nothing but mean and selfish, just like so many others. The group home wasn't an ideal place, either, but at least there was one nun there who would chide the other kids when they made fun of him. She didn't always catch them, but she cared enough to speak up on his behalf when she did witness any harassment. And, occasionally, she would sneak Levi a few pieces of hard candy after dinner—always those little yellow butterscotch discs, which were Levi's favorite. So life there was tolerable, but Levi knew he wouldn't be there long. It was a temporary placement, and he fully expected to get shipped off to some new foster home where he would have to start from scratch again trying to fit in. Instead, the universe had finally smiled on him. After about two weeks, a lovely couple arrived for an interview with him, and everything had gone beautifully. The Kohlers were modest and quaint-looking people, but they were very kind. They were in their forties and lived on a rural property about sixty miles or so outside the city, which was an exciting thought for Levi, who had always had a great love for animals and the outdoors. They had brought photos to show him, and he was ecstatic when they told him he could learn to care for the horses and ride them. How much better could life be? He would be away from the crowds of strangers in the city, away from people who made fun of him, away from the stupid public schools he hated. Even from the start, he had believed he would enjoy living with the Kohlers, which was a new feeling for him.

 Levi didn't know what the Kohlers may have had to prove to the agency in order to adopt him. In his mind, if they all agreed on it, he should be allowed to go with them. But whatever they had to do, it hadn't taken too long, and things had worked out just as Levi had hoped. He moved with the Kohlers to their farmhouse, which looked old and maybe a little sloppy but had everything a house needed. Levi had his own little bedroom and a bathroom that no one else really used, and he felt comfortable following the Kohlers' directive that he should make himself at home. He had no misgivings about living here, and it didn't take him long to acclimate. He enjoyed waking early and helping his dad feed the horses and the chickens. He enjoyed helping his mom in the kitchen and doing his school lessons with her. He enjoyed spending his afternoons with the horses, riding them around the property and then brushing them. The horses liked him, and it was a joy to be around them. They would eat from his hand and nuzzle him, and they never once commented on his pale skin or his pale hair or his pale eyes. They never pointed out how skinny he was or how much acne he had developed. In all, the horses were the best friends Levi had ever had.

Levi also enjoyed those evenings on which the Kohlers took him down the road to the vicar's property for the cult meetings. The first visit had been a bit strange, but Levi had grown accustomed to it. He had never really been taught any religion, unless one counted the witnessing of rampant hypocrisy as a religious lesson. He had known plenty of people who would yell hurtful things at him or send him to bed hungry or even slap the daylights out of him, all while wearing a cross and holding a Bible. Some people, like that nun he remembered, may have been genuinely faithful, but so many more had been nothing but hypocrites. They would tell him to believe in God, believe in Jesus, say his prayers, be good...but they couldn't have really meant it. Levi had matured quickly, and he wasn't dumb. He saw how they lied, how they stole, how they disrespected others, how they put themselves first always, even at the expense of others. He still remembered one awful night when a terrible nightmare had awoken him and sent him to the bedroom of a foster mother, where he found her in a compromising position with some man who was not his foster father. He was maybe ten years old at the time, but he had learned enough by then to know what was happening. At age sixteen, he had already witnessed the breaking of all Ten Commandments, and so it was only a little blip of uncertainty that had crossed his mind when the Kohlers introduced him to their religion. Having grown up around so-called Christians, he did feel a momentary trepidation when he was told they worshiped Satan. But the Kohlers had explained to him all that the vicar did for them—how he was generous to them and kept them safe, and how he had helped them adopt Levi and keep prying eyes away from him. They explained how the vicar's gift for alchemy came from Satan, and how the cult's ongoing worship of the Devil would ensure none of the members had any reason to fear Hell, in contrast to all the untruths the world tended to teach on that subject. It seemed logical to Levi, and besides...what had God ever given him?

The Kohlers hadn't forced their religion on him, but he had really taken to it nonetheless. Levi saw how gifted the vicar was, and he saw how he used his gift to take care of all his flock, and he understood how the cult's rules protected them from unwanted scrutiny from people who couldn't be expected to understand. He saw sensibility and prudence in the cult, and he appreciated the secluded, rural lifestyle it enabled and the wealth it brought, even if that wealth had to be kept underground. The cult members were extended family, and now, Levi was old enough to become a full member of this family. If his offering tonight was sufficient, the whole community would know him and respect him.

A gentle call from his mother down the hallway roused Levi from his musings. It was time to leave for the vicar's house. After closing his trunk and fastening the clasps, Levi stood from the floor and donned his coat, then proudly lifted the box and its heavy contents. He sidled out of the bedroom and met his parents, waiting for him by the front door. They smiled, opened the door for him, and followed him outside. It was a muddy walk on a cold night, but Levi didn't mind. He proceeded onward in silence, with a smile on his face and gold in his eyes.

24

Iris waited for a minute after the cellar doors had shut and locked, then she walked slowly toward them. By now, the cultists would have enrobed themselves in their ridiculous, outmoded hooded cloaks and performed their meaningless Chant of Gathering. Vicar Horatio Grady would be about thirty seconds into his presumptuous announcement of tonight's meeting agenda, which, of course, he didn't know would include a meeting with the cult's supposed Divine Authority. This was going to be fun.

Iris approached the doors and stopped, listening through them. Her human hearing would have had difficulty making out the words coming from underground, but her demon sense was well able to interpret. *My brethren,* she heard, *tonight, you will once again witness the power of Satan, our lord, who works through me to bring us the wealth we enjoy! I, as his Chosen One, will take the scraps you have brought and give them real value, and you, as my flock, will reap the benefits of my gift!* Iris rolled her eyes. This prick sure was full of himself. Of course, that sort of came with the territory. Satan didn't tend to attract humble followers, nor did he tend to care about those who did follow him. He couldn't care less about this cult or Vicar Grady and his alchemist's power, and the vicar probably knew it. Or, at least, he expected Satan had more important things to do than attend a cult meeting, which was why he had never feared these worship ceremonies and had so boldly labeled himself as Satan's "Chosen One" without circumspection. Even if he believed his power came from Satan, which it didn't, Grady wouldn't really have any interest in thanking him or worshiping him for it.

Grady's dramatic pause was a perfect cue, and Iris transported herself down into the cellar without touching the locked doors. The cellar was as she had seen in her meditations—an expansive room set deep underground, with a high ceiling of at least twenty feet, a stone floor, and walls lined with sand-colored clay brick. It was set up like an underground amphitheater, with a large, stepped dais in the front and long, curved risers that rose gradually higher toward the back so the full assembly could stand and witness the work of Vicar Grady at the altar up front. A fresco had been painted into the wall behind the altar, a poor interpretation of *The Last Supper*, modified, of course, so that the cult's leader (most likely the Vicar Grady's great-great-great-grandfather, the cult's founder) stood in place of Jesus, raising his arms over the table and turning everything atop it (not food, in this case, but metal wares) into sparkling gold, to the amazement of all the hooded cultists at the table with him. And, in further contrast to the apparent poverty of the property sitting just above ground, the cellar was equipped with electric lights, climate control, and ventilation. It was a well-hidden little testament to the glamor of evil, the tacky fresco notwithstanding.

Iris had placed herself on the riser farthest in the back, at the end of a row of cult members, leaving herself an unimpeded walkway down the steps and to the altar. The room was quiet, still hanging on the last words of Vicar Grady as he had announced to his flock how they would soon reap the benefits of "his" gift.

"The 'gift' is not yours, Vicar Grady," Iris declared loudly, her voice cutting the silence like a knife and clearly startling everyone present, including the vicar. She began walking down the steps toward him, smirking as she felt the great surprise of all the eyes on her, a stranger inexplicably attendant in their midst, daring to speak out of turn and daring to approach the vicar with her head held high and no cloak or hood to cover her out-of-place attire. "You only borrow the power, Grady," she continued, "and you borrow it from *me*."

Iris arrived in front of the dais, placing herself halfway between its bottom step and the nearest row of cultists, amid befuddled gasps and incoherent murmurings behind her. She looked up at Vicar Grady directly before her. His expression was both confused and angry, bringing a red color to his fat cheeks and a damp sheen to his bald head.

"Who are you, and how dare you enter here where you are not welcome?" Grady bellowed. The cultists stood in nervous silence.

"Do you not know the one you claim to serve and worship, Vicar Grady?" Iris asked in response. "I am Satan."

The vicar glanced briefly out at his assembly, who were clearly on edge as they waited to see how their leader would react to this alarming anomaly. He furrowed his eyebrows and wiped his forehead with a chubby hand, staring at Iris with rage. She had stolen the spotlight from him, and he didn't like it at all.

"You're a blaspheming harlot!" he yelled. "Satan works through me, and he has worked through my father and my grandfather, and through his father and grandfather before me! He chose our lineage as the embodiment of his power, and no *woman* will claim it from us! You desecrate the name of Satan, and for it you will be punished!"

Iris ignored the vicar's tirade and ascended the steps onto the dais, nonchalantly surveying the altar and the trunks that surrounded it, no doubt full of the cult members' offerings of metal to be turned to gold. Two men, previously standing behind the altar, had slowly approached and now stood on either side of her. She looked at each of them in turn, sizing them up. One was a burly man with a shaved head and a long, frizzy, pointed beard on a permanently angry-looking face; the other was a tall, thin man with surprisingly intelligent brown eyes and a calmer disposition. The first was obviously a bodyguard; the second, most likely Vicar Grady's right-hand man. Iris noted with amusement the manservant had a gleam of eagerness in his eyes, as though he were hoping perhaps she really was Satan and was about to de-throne the vicar and put someone more deserving in his place. No question he believed himself to be the appropriate choice for successor.

Iris finally turned to face the congregation, with Vicar Grady and his navy-robed potbelly right in front of her, and she responded to his last comment, saying, "If I choose to 'desecrate' my own name, what concern is that of yours?"

"HERETIC!" Grady screamed, his face and balding head now a bright crimson. He looked immediately to the hulking man beside him and commanded him, "Remove this lying bitch at once!"

The man dutifully stepped toward Iris, believing he would easily overpower her. Instead, Iris focused unspoken magic on him, shoving his big body off its feet and ramming it into the wall about thirty feet away. He fell to the floor in a stunned, winded heap, and the whole room erupted in unison in a terrified gasp. They had seen Iris remain in place, unmoving, while the vicar's bodyguard was cast brutally aside, as if by magic. Vicar Grady's eyes were wide with terror now, and as Iris stared at him with merciless condescension, he unthinkingly backed away from her. His attendant, meanwhile, made no move to hasten to his aid.

"What...what *are* you?" the vicar asked breathlessly as he retreated. He had never witnessed a power like this. Taking another step, so that he now stood below the highest platform of the dais, he said, "Take whatever you want and go. Leave us in peace."

Iris chuckled slowly, then allowed the chuckle to devolve into demonic laughter. With her chilling, inhuman voice, she replied with a sneer, "How generous of you, *faithful* servant, to return to me what is already mine!" Looking down at Grady, she saw his hands were now trembling, and his breath was coming to him in rapid, shallow inhalations. She extended her open hand out toward him, opting for a needlessly theatrical display of magic as she raised her arm and, with it, Vicar Grady's short, plump form.

The cult members were now beyond confused and afraid; they were edging on frantic. There were gasps and tiny screams as most of them clustered near the back of the room, watching with horror as their leader was suspended helplessly in the air above them, struggling in a futile physical attempt to extricate himself from a nonphysical grasp.

"You have disappointed me, Grady," Iris said coldly.

"Please," Grady cried, "please! I'll do anything! Please let me go! Please let me go!" Tears were rolling down his cheeks. *What a pitiful excuse for a man*, Iris thought.

"It is far too late for that, Grady," she replied. "If it was mercy you wanted, you should have chosen a heavenly god."

"I'm sorry," Grady implored from above. "I'm so sorry, my lord! Please, have pity on me!"

"Very well," Iris teased, her voice low and icy and frightening. "Here is my pity."

With that, she swiftly raised her other arm, closed both fists, then threw her arms down to her sides. It was all for show, of course; no hand gestures were necessary to effect the magic, but it was wonderfully entertaining this way. With her demonic power, Iris tore Vicar Grady's body open from mouth to anus, sending a sickening wave of blood and viscera splashing onto the cellar floor. She let his ruined form fall to the ground with a fleshy thud, smiling as she listened to the horrified screams of the cultists, most of whom were scrambling toward the passage door in hopes of escape, shoving their so-called brothers and sisters in vicious instinct toward self-preservation. Humans were such a loving family, weren't they?

"Do you all desert me?" Iris asked sternly, after watching the frightened mob for several seconds.

"I do not, my lord," came a quiet but avid response from the vicar's former manservant, who still stood near Iris. He dropped to one knee and bowed his head when she turned to face him. *Wow*, she thought. *Groveling fool. He's as useless as Grady was.* Though she had to admit, it was a real pleasure to be worshiped—even if she suspected that worship would last only as long as it resulted in profits for the worshiper.

She did not reply to her newfound loyal minion but instead addressed the assembly, in a disturbingly cheerful tone, "Return to your places, brethren, for there is still much to be done!" Most of the group turned from the door, glanced very briefly at Iris, and returned slowly to their places, obviously afraid, yet unwilling to disobey. For those who still hesitated in uncertainty and distrust at the locked passage door, Iris added, more sinisterly, "There will be no escape until I allow it."

With the cult members now back on their auditorium risers, avoiding the swath of area that had been painted red by the innards of their former leader, Iris had fully regained control of the room. She took the opportunity to survey the people gathered here, looking from one frightened face to the next, determining which of these poor, oblivious souls would best serve her purpose. Most of the women, who numbered significantly fewer than the men, were too upset to pull their gazes from the floor, and they stood huddled near their husbands or fathers or brothers, trying to conceal their sobs and sniffling. It was not surprising; five generations under a concentrated patriarchal hierarchy, sheltered from outside influence and focused on the necessity of a single man's power and of his followers' submissiveness to it, didn't tend to create strong, independent women. Some of the men would hazard a quick glance up at her, but never for long. They, too, were weak and afraid, though they were somewhat more reticent to show it. Even the vicar's former bodyguard was among these, unwilling to face her eye to eye for more than a second or two, though perhaps he had a good excuse; she *had* manhandled him rather roughly. Iris wasn't impressed by any of them as she analyzed them. They were all clear followers, too unmotivated or too stupid to do what she needed done.

Then there were those few who had never tried to escape after the vicar's brutal demise. They looked right at Iris as she looked at them, and she did not approve. They were prideful men, not unafraid of her, but able to hide their fear, and they obviously believed their brave facades might gain them some favor. Or perhaps they still refused to believe Iris was who she claimed to be. Either way, they needed to be taught another lesson. At least the brown-noser on the dais beside her had the good taste to feign some humility.

"As you see," Iris announced, "your small sect is now in need of a new leader. Who among you believes himself to be worthy of my power?" Iris wondered with an internal laugh which dumb, arrogant bastard would be first to sign his own death warrant. There were a handful who might do it, but it would take a great deal of pride to come forward in front of everyone, especially after the events that had already transpired.

For several awkward seconds, no one spoke. Iris waited patiently, then sighed snobbishly as she removed her leather jacket and tossed it casually onto the altar behind her. Turning back to the crowd, she continued, "If no one here believes himself worthy, then neither shall I believe you worthy. You will all be destroyed."

Naturally, at the threat, a pompous, self-appointed hero emerged. He was a heavyset man, though not astonishingly fat, with beady blue eyes and a round face topped with a thin tuft of gingery red hair. He was almost certainly related to the late vicar; there were notable similarities in their features. He was likely a younger brother who had been cut out from the magical practice for whatever reason the family had, leaving him disappointed and unfulfilled and angry. He approached the dais steps, clearing his throat as he moved past the rent carcass of his brother. He stood before Iris and said, "I am worthy. I am of the same lineage you chose from the beginning, and I will succeed for you wherever my brother has failed." Iris sensed an almost imperceptible snort from the attendant beside her, and she smiled with genuine amusement at the drama she was so easily directing.

"What is your name, my *worthy* servant?" she asked jeeringly.

"Ivan Grady," he replied, making his voice artificially deep.

"Well, Ivan," Iris said with a smile, "you will certainly succeed where your brother failed." A self-pleased smirk placed itself on Ivan's face before she continued, "Because your brother failed to teach his flock that I find arrogance most distasteful." The smirk sank into a concerned confusion. "Your brother," Iris proceeded, her voice growing colder and darker, "failed to inform you all that I alone decide who is worthy of my power, and that I believe none of you worthy of it. I allowed him to borrow from me, and he repaid me with artificial gratitude, believing I would never take from him what he owed. And now you, Ivan, approach me with the same arrogance, hoping to receive something from me and give me nothing in return, for what do you have to offer?"

She paused. The electric bulbs in their alabaster sconces and hanging frosted-glass lanterns went dim, and the cellar air became as cold as the night outside. She descended to the bottom step so that she stood just inches above Ivan, then she gently grabbed his shoulders and turned him around to face the assembly.

"Here is what you will offer me: You will be another example, Ivan," she said with quiet malice. "You will be the example your brother failed to be." As she still held his shoulders from behind, she felt him try to pull away and run, but of course he had nowhere to go, for it was not Iris's hands alone that held him in place. Releasing him, she stepped back onto the upper platform and watched the cult members' wide-eyed petrification as the man in front of them was engulfed in a sea of red flame. He screamed in hysteric pain and dumbly ran forward toward the congregation, who dispersed as he approached, leaving him alone near the middle of the room. He stopped in place and flailed around, ineffectually trying to remove his cloak and impede the flames, eventually falling to the ground and shuddering frantically like a dying cockroach until finally his agonized screams dissipated. The flames grew brighter and hotter, then suddenly were gone, and the charred, unrecognizable body of Ivan Grady joined that of his brother in a pool of blood, entrails, and ash on the stone floor. The lights returned to their full brightness, and the chill in the air disappeared as quickly as it had arrived.

Half of the members had now fallen to their knees, and the rest quickly followed suit. Not even the haughty wished to remain standing before Iris now. Whether it was out of respect for her power or divinity, or simply out of fear, they would not dare defy her.

Iris turned to the man beside her, on his knees with his eyes averted in deference. She reached down and gently tilted his chin up to face her. "Stand," she told him, "and tell me your name." She sensed a thrill rush through him, as though he knew she was about to deem him her worthy one. His brown eyes were full of a hopeful hunger for power, though he was smart enough to know such power would require sacrifice of his own pride. He, unlike the Grady brothers and their ancestors, understood only the humble would be exalted. Unfortunately, however, he was too wise for his own good.

He slowly stood upright, bowing his head so that he was not as much taller than Iris as he otherwise would have been, and he replied, "My name is Solomon Priest, my lord." He gently held an open palm against his chest as he introduced himself, then bowed.

Iris didn't know from where he had come, but he was certainly much more eloquent and cultured than the rest of these inbred hillbillies. And, of course, he was well aware of it, which was exactly why she couldn't use him for what she needed. It was also exactly why he would be so enraged by what she was about to do. She smiled at him. "I see you are a wise man," she said, "humble and willing to learn from the mistakes of those before you. So, tell me, Solomon, who do you say is a worthy leader, and a worthy wielder of my power?"

Solomon, as Iris expected, didn't miss a beat. "You alone are the one who knows, my lord," he replied.

Iris looked back out at the cultists, still on their knees but now watching with rapt attention the dialogue occurring on the dais in front of them. Smiling broadly, Iris moved toward the altar, a large, heavy table of beautifully carved rose-colored marble. She stepped onto one of the large chests set around it and lifted herself lackadaisically onto the tabletop, seating herself with her legs crossed daintily over the edge. It was a shamefully inappropriate action to perform on an altar of worship, but, as she was the subject of this particular altar's worship, she felt inclined to do whatever she liked on it.

"He has answered rightly," she announced with a grin. "Learn from your brother Solomon, for he does indeed have wisdom to share." The expectation emanating from Priest was quite palpable now. He was sure she was about to name him as her vicar and the leader of this sect. Instead, Iris searched the faces of the congregation one last time, making her final decision. There was one among them who she believed would perfectly suit her needs. He seemed like a smart young man, though almost certainly not particularly well educated academically, which meant he could ably learn without asking too many far-thinking questions. He seemed shy and quiet and submissive, though Iris sensed in him a longing for recognition and acceptance. He had the aura of one whom the world had beaten down and left in the dirt, but he had not lost all hope of being picked up, dusted off, and made into something shiny and new. Tonight, he would have his hopes fulfilled.

She pointed at the young man, who was nearer the front of the group than he probably would have liked. "You," she said, beckoning with her finger, "come forward." She glanced at Priest as he looked to where she was pointing, and she was quite cheered by his expression of stunned consternation.

The boy, startled, looked to the eyes of those around him, unsure of what to do. A man behind him, perhaps his father, nodded to him and then shoved him gently in the back. The boy rose from his knees and hesitantly approached the dais, stopping with uncertainty at the base of its steps. Solomon looked down at the boy and then back to Iris with grave though unspoken concern. Iris pointedly ignored him. She stared at the young man whom she had called forward, a skinny kid of maybe fifteen or sixteen. He was quite unfortunate-looking, with ivory skin, pale blue eyes, and whitish blond hair both on his head and for his eyebrows and eyelashes, such that the acne mottling his face was practically the only real color on him. She questioned, fleetingly, whether her human nature might have felt sorry for this boy, but she quickly cast the thought aside.

"What is your name?" she asked him gently, leaning forward as she sat on the edge of the altar.

The young man swallowed, then replied shakily, "Levi, ma'am. Um, my lord." He was staring down at his shoes.

"Ah," Iris exclaimed jovially, "Levi! A Biblical name, and, delightfully, an anagram of 'evil'! I like it!" She smiled at him as he looked up at the approving comment. "And never mind the titles, Levi," she continued. "They matter not to me, so long as you know who I am. Do you know who I am?"

"You are Satan, the Prince of Darkness," he said quietly, keeping his head down.

"Do you wish to serve me, Levi?" she asked.

Levi hesitated, obviously scared to death he might say the wrong thing. Little did he know, he could say nothing wrong. Iris was going to use him as her patsy, regardless of his answers to her meaningless questions.

"Yes," he said finally. "I will serve you."

Iris hopped down from the altar and walked toward him, stopping just in front of him. "Why do you wish to serve me?" she pressed. The young man swallowed again, clueless as to where this conversation was leading and terrified he might soon suffer the same fate as the Grady brothers. He didn't know how to answer.

Iris prompted him kindly, saying, "You can be honest with me, Levi. Lies are transparent. So many have said they serve me because they respect me, they worship me. They are liars. They serve me only because they wish to use my power, because my power brings them all they desire in this world. I allow them to lie to me, when it serves my purposes. Inevitably, Levi, they all kneel before me in Hell. It's so hard to find good help, you see."

Levi looked at her with confusion. She rephrased her question to him, asking, "What is it you most desire, Levi?" She watched him in silence as he thought for a moment, then she started prodding him for clues. "Is it wealth? Elite status? Curses upon those who have hurt you?" His jaw tensed ever so slightly at that one. She paused again, then asked, "Perhaps you desire to gratify your flesh in the company of a woman?" Levi's face flushed at the suggestion, and Iris scoffed internally at the ease of it all. Of course the young man lusted for attention and pleasure; he was not attractive by society's standards, and undoubtedly the world had shunned him for his entire young life. Iris had not lost how he had glanced at her from among the congregation before she had disemboweled the vicar, how he had unknowingly let his face convey his thoughts that she was a beautiful woman. The inexplicable power she had subsequently displayed would only have attracted him more, as he was still practically a child, submissive to authority and seeking a guiding hand. And of course he desired ill for those who had hurt him; very few honest human beings didn't.

Iris smiled, not forcing Levi to answer her questions, and she gently pulled his face close to her breasts, holding him there near her for a moment as she ran her fingers easily through his hair, then she held his chin, lifted his face, and kissed him lightly on his lips. His whole body had gone rigid with nervous shock and guilt-laden timidity as he tried to conceal his enjoyment of her touches. He had never been treated in such a manner, and certainly never by an older woman whom he found to be quite attractive, and certainly never in the view of fifty or more other people who knew him.

Iris pulled back tenderly and said, "Relax, Levi. I *want* you to use my power. I want you to lead this flock."

Solomon shifted uneasily on his feet and looked at Iris. "My lord," he interjected, "he is a child! Surely there must be a better-qualified leader among us?"

Iris shot him a cold, hard glance. "Do you question me, Priest?" she asked, her voice teetering on the inhuman.

Solomon bowed his head in reverence born of fear and replied quickly, "No, no, of course not, my lord."

"Good," Iris returned. She then addressed the entire congregation, "If any of you questions my authority, do speak now." Silence answered her. "Then know I have chosen Levi as your new leader," she continued, "and his directives are to be followed without question. He will have my powers as I allow him to use, and you will all benefit from it, at only the cost of your souls."

She then turned directly to Levi and said to him, "This position does not come to you freely, Levi. I have a test prepared for you, and only with its successful completion will you enjoy the use of my power. If you accept these terms, then your remaining business here tonight will be to complete what the Vicar Grady is no longer present to do. You will turn these metallic offerings to gold." She indicated with a small wave the trunks at the base of the altar behind her, then continued, "And you will then distribute the bounty as you see fit. You and I, Levi, will then have much to discuss, *in private*." She knew her final words would immediately draw Levi's mind to thoughts of lusty intimacy with her away from the eyes of his cult followers. Poor kid. He was so naive.

Levi bravely swallowed once again and then replied, with as strong a voice as he could, "I accept your terms."

Iris held out a hand to him, which he grasped limply, then she led him behind the altar. She instructed Solomon, much to his irritation, to open the trunks surrounding the altar and dump their contents. He obediently complied, though his jealousy of the new vicar pro tempore was all too apparent, then he moved to the side of the altar and waited, probably hoping Levi would fail to perform the alchemy successfully.

With the coins and metal spread on the floor below the altar, Iris stood behind Levi and whispered in his ear what he should do. Levi nervously but submissively followed her instructions, raising his hands and repeating the words she gave him.

As the cult had come to expect, the pieces of iron, steel, copper, and silver became solid gold before their eyes, glittering under the cellar lights. Those who were still kneeling now stood and applauded for Levi, who beamed with great pride at what he had just done. They formed a line to come forward for their portions, as was their custom. The dead bodies of Horatio and Ivan Grady lay forgotten in the middle of the floor, their services no longer needed.

Iris watched from near the fresco reredos as the cultists took their gold pieces and left for their aboveground homes. Solomon stood to the side, a dark expression on his face as Levi doled out the abundance. As the line became shorter, he quietly moved toward the late vicar's body, darting his eyes around to ensure no one saw him, though Iris did. He bent down for a brief moment; when he rose, he was just removing his hand from within his robe, where Iris suspected he had just pocketed the vicar's antique ring. *Clever*, she thought. She believed young Levi would, with her help, succeed in procuring the relic she needed him to bring her. She also believed she had sentenced him to an early death, because Solomon Priest had just become an envious man, and now he had a magical relic in his possession and was already formulating a plan for mutiny.

25

The sun was setting on another foggy, early-winter day, and Levi Kohler was taking no joy in the evening meal set before him. His stomach was a pit of bundled nerves, twitching with ungrounded electricity. His mother had made him his favorites—pot roast with potatoes and carrots and brown gravy, and a strawberry rhubarb pie for dessert. His father had even opened a bottle of red wine for him, believing it a harmless libation that would bolster his confidence and make him feel more grown-up as he prepared for his work tonight. After all, Satan would be giving him all the power he needed; what harm would there be in some alcoholic influence?

His parents had brought him this celebratory dinner and had told him how proud they were, then they had wished him good luck on his endeavor and had left him alone as they returned to the vicar's house. They had already taken some belongings and begun setting up their places there since the residence had fallen into Levi's hands as a benefit of his new title. Levi, however, refused to move to his new abode until he had completed the test Satan had set for him, not wanting to take his vicarship for granted. He remained by himself with the horses and chickens here in the house he had come to call home, feeling nervous and isolated, while his cult family joined together at the vicar's cellar, where Satan, in a woman's form he called Iris, had instructed the group to remain in fastidious worship as they awaited Levi's successful return from his quest.

Levi took tiny, tasteless bites of food that brought him no joy as he reflected on last night's terrible events. He had been ready for full enlistment in the cult, yes, but he had never dreamed he would, in the same night, be put in power by the Prince of Darkness himself. Or herself. It was all so confusing. The woman was older than Levi but definitely younger than his mother, maybe thirty or so, and stunningly beautiful, with wonderful curves and a pretty face and full lips and green eyes and nice brownish-red hair. When she had been alone with him after the Gathering, she had pulled her hair down from where it had been tied in a messy updo on her head, and Levi had been very excited to see how long it was, cascading nearly to her low back in shiny waves, made kinky by the hair tie that had held it up before. He could smell it as she shook it out with her fingers. It had a sexy, spicy kind of rose scent that he had found most appealing, and when the woman had pulled him close to her and held his face in her hands while explaining what she needed him to do for her, he had had some very ruttish thoughts indeed. Nothing about her seemed evil. Her skin had felt nice and warm against his; her face had appeared patient and kind; her voice was intelligent and soft and beckoning. He had wanted her to hold him and touch him, and why would he desire those things if she were the Devil? Shouldn't the Devil be a frightening monster? A big, red, brutish gargoyle with black horns and yellow eyes and goat's hooves, who would speak with a terrifying, bellowing rasp? Yet the woman Iris had astounded everyone at the Gathering with her unprecedented power. She had said she was Satan, in no uncertain terms, and then she had proven it. So Levi might be confused by it, but he had to accept it. He had met the Devil, and he was fiendishly attracted to her.

He was lucky Iris had chosen him for this. She was going to give him power beyond what Vicar Grady had known, and she told him that, if he succeeded in the mission she gave him, he, as the cult's new vicar, would be right to enamor any of the cult's members as he desired, for it would be an honor for them to serve his every inclination and longing. It was a wonderful thought, to know he could have his way with anyone he liked. Well, almost anyone. Levi had felt some disappointment when Iris limited his options to cult members. Most of them were men, and most of the women were his mother's age or older, and quite homely—nothing like the exotic beauty Iris was. But there were some Levi had noticed as being reasonably attractive, and besides, Iris had assured him, after sensing his disappointment, that after he first experienced the satisfaction of a carnal hunger, he would no longer care so much about attractiveness. She had also reminded him he would have power to expand cult membership as he liked; he could tempt whomever he wanted to join his cult, and he would be limited only by his own shortcomings as a salesman, which, of course, he could improve over time.

Levi suspected, though Iris hadn't actually said it, that if he did well enough tonight to be named officially as the vicar, and if he continued to do well as the vicar—better than the Grady family who had apparently failed her—maybe eventually Iris would let him have his way with her. She was just too tempting to be completely off-limits. He would just have to work for it really, really hard. But he was letting his mind get ahead of him. First, he would have to succeed tonight and return to Iris the relic she had enlisted him to procure for her. He had felt confident about it before, believing when Iris told him she would help him as he needed, but as the time was now nearing, Levi was no longer so sure of himself. He had to admit, however gorgeous he thought Iris was, he was truly terrified of what she might do to him if he failed this task.

The food was nothing but an onus to chew, so Levi pushed his plate aside and poured a glass of the wine his father had left for him. He knew nothing about wine, had never tasted it, but the guilty feeling of drinking alcohol at his age gave him a nice tingling sensation. He looked at the burgundy liquid in the glass and realized he was a man now. He took a sip of it and gagged. It was pungent and vinegary, and it burned his throat. He stood to pour the foul stuff down the sink, but he hesitated as he thought what the cult would think of him if he couldn't even drink wine. "He's just a child," they would say, just as that snarky Solomon Priest had been so quick to point out to Iris at the Gathering last night. He would never earn anyone's respect if they all thought of him as a boy and not a man. So he carried the glass and the bottle back to the table, seated himself again, and took a deep breath. Holding his nose, he sucked down the contents of the first glass. *Screw you, Solomon Priest*, he thought. *I'm as much of a man as you are.*

Levi then took the bottle in his hand, readied himself with another deep breath, and swallowed every last drop of the vile drink. Pressing his hand over his mouth after he finished, forcing his body to keep the liquid down, he stood up, threw the empty bottle against the kitchen wall, picturing Solomon's uppity face there, then grabbed his jacket and backpack and the keys to his father's pickup truck. It was time for him to head out. He was going to do this, and Solomon Priest was going to hate it.

***

Levi couldn't see her, but Iris could see him. His young mind was fully malleable; she had easily convinced him to do her bidding. He would have been useless by himself, but his simplicity and his eagerness had made it easy for her to set a magical link between them. The boy was clueless, of course, but Iris had attached herself to him in what was essentially a mild form of oppression. She couldn't read his thoughts or control his body, but she could whisper right into his head whenever she needed to, and of course Levi would listen, because he wanted nothing more right now than to succeed in the work she had set before him. She had told him to ask for her help when he needed it, and she would hear him and help him, if he would listen to her and trust in her. Child's play.

She snickered as he gulped down an entire bottle of wine and then petulantly threw the bottle. He had nearly poured it out but had changed his mind; Iris guessed the he's-a-child comment from Solomon Priest last night had perhaps cut a little deeper than Levi had first realized. He would be drunk and sick, which was unfortunate, but Iris's nonphysical attachment to him should yield enough of a presence to allow her to heal the effects of the alcohol with simple magic. If not, she would find another grunt to do the work. She didn't enjoy having to rely on others to get things done, but there was simply too much scrutiny around this particular relic because of the spectacular way in which Loomis's shadow-demon had stolen it for him, and the last thing she needed was to become embroiled in some criminal investigation. No human system could truly inhibit her, of course, but it would mean wasted time and unwanted attention. If she could find someone to take care of it apart from her physical presence, that would be ideal. She still felt confident in the boy Levi, though his immaturity was as annoying as it was useful.

She watched him as he climbed into his father's dilapidated old truck and steered it down the long caliche drive and onto the dirt road leading to the highway. He had about a forty-minute drive ahead of him to the potter's field where Malachi Grady, the cult's original founder, had been buried. Malachi had journeyed up that way in the early 1900s, intending to gain some new membership to his cult by way of his magical power, but instead he had suffered an untimely heart attack and had been found dead on one of the town's streets. No one knew him, and no one claimed him, and thus the potter's field had become his final resting place. It was there Loomis had aptly chosen to conceal the final relic, in testimony to a cult he had built through his effortless temptation of a young man in need of aid. Loomis had taken the time and put forth the extra effort to create a gate to Hell there where Malachi was buried, just so he could leave the relic there and still use it as he needed to effect the full power of his evil shadow creation. He had believed no one would find it—or, at least, no one would care if they did find it—as it was a practically valueless location for a Gate, sitting in the middle of, now, an abandoned, unpurposed piece of land in today's downtown area of the city. Records had not been well kept, and eventually a hotel had been built on top of a portion of the old burial ground. It hadn't fared well, having quickly gained a reputation for being haunted, and had soon been shuttered and abandoned until eventually it was demolished. The land had gone through a few different owners and then was sold back to the city, and nothing had since been done with it. Iris suspected Loomis had interfered with the property at opportune times so that it would be left untouched in case he had deemed it worth using sometime later, which he now had. He might have expected her to find the new Gate eventually, but he must have believed it would take her much longer than it had. Then again, he hadn't expected her to...*know* him in the way she had known him. That experience had been both pleasurable and elucidating.

Levi drove for a mile or two before the wine really got to him. Iris saw him pull off the road, stop the truck, then stumble out of the driver's seat and into the barren field beside him, vomiting a runny, purplish emulsion. Iris rolled her eyes where she sat in her bedroom, then closed them and magically watched Levi until he had completed his ejections. She then forced her voice into his head, saying, "You're wasting time, Levi. Why do you linger here?"

She could see her voice startled him, but he accepted its presence and answered her hoarsely, "I'm sick, my lord. I think...I think I drank too much." There was an inebriated drawl in his words, but it didn't fully conceal the fear in his voice. He was afraid he had already failed her.

Iris had expected such a reaction, and she used the opportunity to strengthen his trust in her. "Never mind that, Levi. I pass no judgment on a little bit of gluttony," she whispered gently, in a good-natured, conspiratorial tone. "Do you want me to remove these effects from you? Or do you enjoy them?"

Levi tripped back to the truck and balanced himself against the hood as he walked around it and back to the driver's door. He seated himself and closed the door, sitting in the cold darkness of the cab and listening to Iris's voice inside him. "Please, my lord, take it away from me," he pleaded weakly. "I don't enjoy it."

Iris focused her thoughts and transmitted a silent spell through her spectral form near Levi. It wasn't a simple task, practicing magic away from one's own body; for most, it would be impossible. She was pleased, though not surprised, to see how effectively she accomplished it.

Levi straightened up in his seat and looked through the windshield to the road in front of him. The fog in his head, at least, had cleared, and now he had only to brave the misty shroud of night as he continued on the charge Iris had given him. He fastened his seat belt and started the engine, then proceeded back onto the road and toward his destination. "Thank you, my lord," Iris heard him say. "I won't fail you."

Sometime later, he approached his target. He did as Iris prompted him, parking the truck a few blocks away and walking to the field, his small bag of supplies strapped on his back. A chain-link fence had been erected along the field's boundary, but Levi had no trouble pulling himself over it. Moonlight was being dispersed by the fog, casting plenty of glow by which he could find his way. He walked quickly to the remnants of a building that had once stood there, and he rested there against a piece of an old brick wall, watching his breath come out in tiny white puffs and trying to remember exactly how Iris had taught him to find the correct site for his dig. There was a drastic difference between standing alone in this cold, open field and being held in Iris's warm hands while she explained to him how to locate the relic. Now he wasn't sure he could do it.

To his credit, he called straight to Iris for assistance. She smirked at his humble pleading and then guided him, as she had fully expected to have to do. This was the most challenging part, in fact, for she had to divine the magical impulses of the relic underground, in a spectral form away from her own body. Luckily, Levi was simpleton enough to be no obstacle, and Iris's powers were stronger than even she had dared to believe. She found the burial place, about seventy yards or so from where Levi had called out to her. Unfortunately, there was a sheet of badly cracked concrete still overlying this portion of the property. Loomis Drake had the power to bury a relic beneath concrete and earth without so much as lifting a finger; Levi Kohler did not have the same abilities. Iris sighed as she watched the youth's childlike despair and then waited for his supplication.

"What do I do, my lord?" he asked in a slight panic.

Iris was growing tired of holding his hand, but she made a conscious effort to hide her irritation. Since things had happened this way, and since she had become impatient, she would need Levi's total submission now. "It's a challenge to be overcome," she said to him, "and nothing more. I can unearth the relic for you, Levi, but you must let me have you—*all* of you. Give me control, and do not fight me. Then, I will leave you, and you must complete your task without further aid. Do you understand?"

Levi nodded resolutely, then replied, "I understand, Master. Do what you must with me."

Iris projected herself through the realm of spirit and placed herself inside the young body of Levi Kohler. She felt his soul inside him, as weak and mutable as his mind, searching for its true happiness and settling instead for the promises of instant gratification and earthly power. It was easy to quarantine, and Iris had full possession of Levi's form. After appreciating the strange new sensation for a moment, she began to work, breaking apart the concrete with a single magical word and leaving the shattered pieces levitating above the ground. With another spell, she pulled a column of compacted earth out into the luminous, damp air, exposing its layers and various contents. Among some bones that must have belonged to the original Vicar Grady, she found the copper spearhead. She grabbed the relic from its resting place and waved the earth and concrete back to their places with a simple reversal of her initial magic, leaving no hint of any upheaval, and, finding no desire to prolong her stay inside Levi's body, she returned control to him. He regained full consciousness to find himself on his knees on top of the concrete, with the antique spearhead in his hand. Befuddled and amazed, Levi stared at the relic and prodded it with his fingers, brushing dirt from it and tracing the lines of its carved runes.

"Take it, Levi, and return to the cellar at once," Iris commanded him, more sternly than she intended. "Your flock awaits you."

The implication of his official nomination as vicar gave Levi renewed eagerness, and he promptly placed the spearhead in his backpack and ran for the fence line. The boy had succeeded after all—with Iris's ready aid, of course. The hard part was finished, and now Iris could take her physical self to the vicar's cellar to retrieve her relic and give Levi his full commission as Cult Leader. She prepared for her magical relocation, paying little attention to Levi's actions, but suddenly a separate figure in her mind's vision caught her interest. Levi had returned to the truck without incident, but he found someone else there in the shadowy passenger seat waiting for him, a silver dagger glittering in his hand.

"Give me the relic," the figure demanded. His was a quiet and intelligent voice, not particularly authoritative or commanding. The knife, however, was quite imposing.

Iris winced, recognizing first the voice and then the figure as it lifted its hood from around its face. It was Solomon Priest. She was perhaps as taken aback by his presence as Levi was. He couldn't have known the plans she had given the boy unless Levi had told him, and that seemed improbable. She questioned for an instant how she should handle this. Should she possess Levi once more and kill Priest? Should she wait to let the drama play out naturally? Would the soon-to-be vicar have presence of mind enough to ask her for her help, or to handle the situation himself? Almost certainly not, on that final count.

As she considered her options, she heard Levi reply, timidly, "Solomon? What...what are you doing?" *Yes, Solomon,* she thought. *What are you doing?*

"I am taking what should rightfully be mine," Priest responded, waving the dagger. "Give it to me, and you can return with me to the cult. I am going to hand over the relic, and I will be vicar. Everyone wins this way, Levi. You're young, and you don't realize how difficult it is to be the cult's leader. You won't enjoy it. I'm helping you."

As he moved the knife, Iris noticed its carvings. It was undoubtedly the work of a magical blacksmith. She could not readily identify the dagger or whatever specific power it might have, but she knew it hadn't come to Solomon by chance. Someone had given it to him—and she had a good idea who had done it. Priest likely didn't have too much magical knowledge, but there was no way of knowing how much he might have been taught in a short time, and there was no telling how strong he might be in it, especially if he had the late vicar's ruby-studded ring anywhere on his person. This could prove problematic. The simplest solution would be to instruct Levi to give up the relic and allow Solomon to return it to her. She didn't care who took over the cult, so long as she had the spearhead.

"I...I can't do that," she heard Levi say nervously. "I want to be vicar. She chose me as vicar."

"*She* is just using you," Priest said harshly. "*She* doesn't care about you." True as that might be, it wouldn't do to have Levi hearing it, particularly if he might start believing it. If he didn't shut up soon, Iris was going to have to silence Solomon Priest.

"You're wrong!" Levi exclaimed. "I'm not too young or too dumb or whatever else you think I am! You're jealous because she chose me and not you!"

Iris actually smiled to herself at the boy's retort. He had certainly called that one correctly. Plus, admirably, he had not lost faith in his devil-savior. Unfortunately, he had also escalated an already volatile situation.

Priest suddenly exited the truck and went to the driver's door, pulling it open before Levi's fumbling hand could lock it. He dragged the boy out with one hand and snatched the backpack from him with the other. Priest was not a strong man, but Levi was a scrawny sixteen-year-old, and it didn't take much to overpower him. He held the dagger against Levi's throat and tossed the backpack onto the hood of the pickup. "You're going to leave now," he hissed in Levi's face. "You're going to run away and never come back. Let *her* take care of you."

Iris had to make a decision now; there was no time left. The situation was about to explode. She ended her magical link to

Levi and transported herself physically to the place where he and Solomon were.

"I intend to take care of him," she said coldly from behind Priest. Levi's eyes widened with surprise and elation at her sudden appearance out of nowhere.

Solomon, though also surprised, had a more subdued reaction. He turned to face her, repositioning himself so that he blocked Levi into the cab of the truck, and he pointed the dagger toward her as menacingly as he could. "Do you know what this is?" he asked. Despite his best efforts, Iris noticed his hand was trembling slightly.

"No," she replied unenthusiastically. "Should I care?"

"Yes, you should care. It can kill you. It is meant especially for killing demons. It will send you straight back to Hell," he announced, his voice edging higher.

"Is that so?" Iris asked, with overt disinterest.

"You're not the only one with power, you know," Priest continued. "Others have it. I don't believe you're the Devil. You're just some demon in a human's body. I've been told the truth, by one who is stronger than you, and he won't let you ruin this cult. He has given me what I need to destroy you, to put you back in your place. I was going to do it at the Gathering, but since you've come all this way, I'll do it here."

Priest began an incantation Iris recognized as a binding spell, intended to prevent movement of its target. It was a simple spell, and Priest executed it well, likely aided by the late vicar's silver ring on the chain around his neck. Iris stood motionless, and once Priest was convinced he had bound her by his magic, he lunged at her with the dagger. She moved at the last possible second, having undone Priest's spell even as he recited it. Finding no solid object where he had expected one, he tripped to the ground with a surprised grunt.

Iris casually walked over and stood next to Levi, nudging him playfully in the ribs and nodding at the man on the ground in front of them. "He *almost* got me," she said jokingly, and both she and Levi started laughing.

Enraged, Priest pulled himself off the ground and faced Iris. "You *bitch*," he snapped.

"What you believe or don't believe about me will not change what *is*," Iris replied coolly. "You believe another has told you the truth; I tell you, he lied to you. And he has sorely under-equipped you for a grappling with me. He knows it. He simply wants to thwart my plans, and he cares not what happens to you in the midst of it."

Priest hesitated, considering her words. He was clearly unsure whom to trust, but Iris had chosen Levi as the new vicar, while his other mysterious benefactor had almost certainly promised him more power and wealth than he could ever need. He would, as most did, listen to the words he wanted to hear.

Iris offered him a final chance, saying, "Stand with me, Solomon. There is room enough in this cult for both you and Levi." They were empty words. She knew Priest's arrogance and envy were far too great already. The only thing that would bring him back to the cult would be Levi's refusal of the vicarship, and the teenager had already been too enraptured by the promise of power and authority for that to happen.

"Get rid of the boy, then," Solomon replied. "You know he isn't a fit leader."

Iris might have replied in a way Solomon would have liked, knowing it would be easier to deal with a disappointed Levi than an unsatisfied Solomon, but she didn't have the chance. Levi, emboldened by Iris's presence next to him, strode directly up to Priest and slapped him in the face. "I *am* a fit leader," he yelled angrily, "and she's already chosen me!"

Priest lost all composure. His eyes blazed with sudden anger as he grabbed Levi by the hair and threw him to the pavement. He dropped to his knees on top of the youth's back and jammed the dagger into his flesh. Levi screamed in pain and horror, wriggling uselessly on the ground beneath Solomon's weight. As Priest withdrew the blade and then stabbed him again, over and over and over, Levi soon went quiet and finally still, a pool of blood oozing out in shining scarlet around his torso. Priest finished his violent tantrum and remained on top of Levi, breathing heavily into the cold night air and letting the dagger fall to the ground beside him.

Iris, for the flash of an instant, was appalled and saddened by the horrible crime she had just witnessed, all of which had come about because of her meddling. Her human nature threatened to make an appearance with a sick stomach and some tearful remorse, but she shoved it back deep inside herself. No sense being weak now; the problem had solved itself. She picked up the dagger and stood behind Solomon Priest, still panting on top of Levi's dead body. He knew what was about to happen...and he probably knew he deserved it.

Restraining him roughly by his chestnut hair, Iris slid the blade through his throat, sending a spray of blood in an arc onto the street. She let his body slump on top of Levi's, then she wiped the stained dagger on his cloak and reset its switchblade. She yanked the chain and the silver ring from Priest's torn neck, grabbed the backpack from the hood of the truck and stuffed everything inside, then returned to the comfort of her bedroom, not bothering to destroy any of the scene she left behind. Let the police find it; let them see once more just how evil human beings could be.

***

Back at home, Iris tossed the backpack onto her desk chair and turned to sit on her bed. She hadn't bothered to flip on the overhead light, but enough glow from the streetlamp outside filtered in through the blinds to reveal a figure already sitting there.

She sighed. "What are you doing here?"

Loomis willed the nightstand lamp on with unspoken magic, then rose gracefully from where he had been sitting at the foot of her bed and faced her, arms crossed across his chest. He looked handsome, as usual, in an expensive, crisp white shirt and black vest and slacks, but he seemed just a tad low on the animal magnetism he usually exuded.

"Has your excursion been a success?" he asked in response, inclining his head slightly toward the backpack in the chair. His expression was solemn, his tone somber.

Iris scrutinized him, trying to analyze his motive for being here. She removed her jacket and pitched it lightly onto her bed before replying. "I have what I need," she said simply.

"I believe you have exactly what you *don't* need," Loomis responded, lowering his arms as he walked toward the bedside table, studying the small crucifix hanging on the wall above it.

"Don't you get tired of being so cryptic?" Iris asked impatiently. "I'm not giving you the relic, if that's why you're here."

Loomis turned and stared at her from the opposite side of the bed, his hands in his pockets and his face nicely contoured by the lamplight. "You've already taken all the other relics I had so carefully amassed and oriented," he said placidly. "What need would I have of this one?"

"None at all, unless you simply want to spite me," Iris answered.

"I wouldn't dare," he replied.

Iris shrugged and turned to the chair beside her, fishing the obsidian-handled dagger out of the backpack. "I believe this is yours," she said icily, tossing it to him across the bed. "Be careful with that," she added as he deftly caught it. "I hear it's dangerous for...*people* like us."

Loomis pocketed the knife and prompted her, "Shall I assume from your harsh tone that perhaps the night did not go as you planned?"

Iris felt her eyes blink once in an involuntary tell. The pointed question had brought the violent replay to her mind, and once again she felt a gnawing sadness for the boy whose life had been so brutally taken from him by a man made envious by her sinister games. Either her eyes or her hesitation in answering must have given away her thoughts.

"How do you feel right now, Iris?" Loomis asked quietly. There was a strange softness in his tone, as though he actually cared. For the breath of an instant, Iris wanted to break down and cry. Her mind could almost imagine Loomis might hold her and comfort her now. She had to force such daydreams aside; she knew what an able liar he was.

She recovered and hardened herself. "I feel nothing," she replied, hoping her eyes looked as dark as the color of her voice. They must have, because Loomis dropped his eyes from her gaze. He turned and sat on the edge of the bed near the nightstand, his back facing her.

"I think you *do* feel something," he said softly, staring at the closed bay window in front of him. Iris said nothing, but her mind was abuzz with curious thoughts and unsolicited emotions. Damn human nature...was Loomis purposely appealing to it? She remained standing at the opposite side of the bed, contemplating her adversary from behind and crossing her arms. Whatever he was up to, it wouldn't work.

"What happened out in the potter's field tonight?" Loomis asked.

"You must know what happened," Iris retorted with a snap.

"I wasn't there," he answered.

Iris scoffed loudly. "Whatever, Loomis," she said with exasperation. "You sent Solomon there to screw with me. I came back with the spearhead anyway, so your plan failed, although I shouldn't really call it a 'plan.' You must have known he wouldn't have any chance in hell at stopping me. Frankly, I can't see what you stood to gain by doing it. I know you couldn't care less about that cult or its leadership, so putting Solomon in charge wouldn't have made any difference to you."

"You're right, of course," Loomis replied. He inhaled deeply and slowly, then exhaled in similar fashion. He arose from the bed once more and turned toward her. "I have no concern for them," he proceeded, "but...I am concerned for you."

Iris lifted an eyebrow quizzically, not bothering to conceal a bit of surprise. She could hear her own thoughts asking if he could possibly mean it; she could also hear a cacophony of arguing responses to her internal questioning. Perhaps it was her destiny to suffer forever, or at least for the remainder of her mortal life, from such inward debate and dichotomy of self. After all Loomis's temptations and lies and evil plots and schemes, here she was, still wanting to believe him. *Don't buy it*, she told herself. *He's a demon; all he does is lie.*

An idea suddenly struck her, a way to shove Loomis right off of whatever kindly, morally upright pedestal upon which he was pretending to stand. She unfolded her arms and rounded the bed, putting herself right next to him. He stiffened slightly in discomfort at her approach but stalwartly faced her anyway. She took his hands in hers, and even Loomis Drake couldn't disguise his disquietude.

"Loomis, darling," she coaxed slowly, with a small smile, "have you developed such tender feelings for me because of our *intimate encounter?*" She interlaced her fingers with his, drawing out the diminutive movement for as long as she could. His whole body was almost as rigid as marble, though he was still desperately trying to veil his angst. Iris looked up into his eyes and pulled him closer, until their bodies were touching and her lips were nearly on his chin. He returned her gaze as best he could, but his head involuntarily turned upward ever so slightly in an attempt to move away from her. He seemed to be holding his breath, too, and Iris found his anxiety quite amusing. Finally, she concluded, "If so, darling, I do hate to tell you our rousing tête-à-tête meant more to you than it did to me, even as wonderfully satisfying as it was."

She practically breathed the words into his goatee, and Loomis finally abandoned his forced stoicism. He exhaled sharply and stubbornly withdrew his hands from hers, stepping backward into the nightstand as he did so, with a tiny squeak of expensive leather against polished wood. Iris sneered at the nauseated look that passed across his face. She knew his artificially constructed body was immune to human illness, but unfortunately for her demonic rival, it was not immune to physical symptoms of emotional pain. She stood in place just before him, refusing to allow him any additional, comforting physical space. *Time to pull out the knife*, she thought. *He wants to pretend he has a heart; I'll leave it bleeding.*

"What's wrong, Loomis?" she asked revilingly. "You want me to leave the room so you can cry? I don't mind. But I would ask that if you're going to puke your guts out, please do step into the bathroom."

She made no move to leave, instead rooting herself in place and staring at the victimized demon in front of her. He had likely wondered whether she had seen his reaction after their interlude that night; now he knew without doubt that she had, and it hurt him. For a moment—just a moment—she regretted her words. Loomis had what appeared to be genuine sadness in his eyes. Iris had never before seen him so exposed and helpless, and though her humanity screamed at her to apologize, her demonic predilection for evil would not allow it.

Loomis looked at the ceiling and clenched his jaw, then returned his focus to her. "It is not easy for me to face you after that," he said, in a voice almost as low as a whisper and as tremulous as a dry leaf caught in a cold wind. He swallowed, then implored, "Could you not show me even the slightest hint of compassion?"

Iris looked down at her feet before she consciously registered what she was doing. She felt suddenly ashamed of her behavior. Yet, she considered, why feel shame for treating a demon so badly? If she should be ashamed of this, what must she make of all her other devilish dealings? No...shame was a slippery slope; best to stay off that trail. She looked back up at Loomis and answered, "Compassion isn't really in my character, is it?"

He seated himself on the bed again and replied, "I believe it is. I *know* it is. I've seen your human conscience. I've seen how you so staunchly refused my lurid temptations, how you championed for your human race even though you are different from them, even though you have such righteous anger for their hypocrisy and transgressions. Perhaps I succeeded in driving you toward evil after all, but...I believe I was wrong to do it."

"Ha!" Iris exclaimed. "Of course you were wrong to do it! We demons delight in wrongdoing, do we not? Do you hope I will actually believe you're feeling remorse now?"

"I don't know what I'm feeling, if I am in fact feeling anything at all," Loomis admitted. "I *shouldn't* be feeling whatever this is, and trust me when I tell you, I don't enjoy it. You have...you have made rather a mess of me."

Iris was thoroughly confused. She felt humanity clawing at her insides like an animal buried alive. *No*, she yelled silently to herself. *He's acting weak so you'll do the same. He wants you to mimic him. Don't fall for this.*

"Well, never mind it," she told him. "It doesn't bother me that you drove me to evil, although I do hesitate to give you all the credit for it. I've never been stronger than I am now, and it's my evil nature that has made me so. So, if you *are* feeling guilty for having goaded me into darkness, I extend to you my sincerest forgiveness." Her tone was flat and uncaring.

Loomis remained quiet for a second or two, then asked, "Does the crucifix not bother you?" He nodded subtly in reference to the Saint Benedict's cross on the wall above the nightstand near him. Iris, still standing beside him, darted her eyes to the crucifix, briefly, and then back to Loomis.

"On the contrary," she answered drably, "I rather enjoy the irony. *Vade retro, Satana!*" She chuckled mirthlessly. "Funny, no?"

Loomis was unamused, shaking his head with reproach. "Iris, please," he admonished her. "When will you finally understand you are *of* him, but you are not Satan? How long will you continue living this lie? Your human conscience will eat away at you, and rightfully so. It is as much a part of you as your demonic nature is. You cannot escape it. You shouldn't *want* to. It is what makes you different, and special, and...wonderful."

He had spoken his words with solemnity and earnestness, and Iris felt suddenly more human than she had felt in some time. She was momentarily moved by Loomis's speech, and she quietly seated herself on the bed a short distance apart from him. Could this be reality? Was Loomis truly feeling this way about her? Was he feeling respect for her? Possibly even...dare she think it...*love* for her? *Listen to your own thoughts, you fool! Do you not hear the absurdity of it all? Hell is the absence of love and respect, the abode of self-serving evil, and Loomis Drake is its most exemplary tenant.*

Iris stiffened once the shock had worn away and been replaced by sensible thoughts. She knew Loomis was after something; there was no other reason he would act this way. He wasn't capable of genuine respect or love or any other pleasant emotion toward another; damnation was the active choice of the alternatives of all those things.

"Once again, you flatter me with your compliments," she finally responded, "and again, I question your motives. You and I, as demons, are no different from one another. We behold the human race with contempt and disdain. I can't believe you would view my humanity any differently. You certainly haven't before." She crossed her hands in her lap, reflecting on every untoward provocation and enticement Loomis had offered her in the past, and it reminded her how weak she had been then, before she had fully embraced her demonic nature. She couldn't allow him to make her that weak again.

"I did, at first, consider your humanity a defect," Loomis answered. "Now I have come to realize it is what gives you power that exceeds my own, power that exceeds even Satan's. And...I respect it." Iris swallowed, wondering how many more sensitive words she could handle before breaking down into human sympathies.

"If your human soul is damned to Hell," Loomis continued softly, "you will lose that unique part of yourself. I fear you will become no different from me, or from the one who created you and then hated you. It is not too late for you, Iris. You have a mortal life to live, and the opportunity to repent and be absolved of your sins. You have a chance to save your humanity, to preserve it for eternity, and I fervently hope you will." His dark, amber-dusted eyes were staring deeply into hers, not with any of the lustful baiting or fearsome penetration she had seen in them before, but with openness and compassionate urging. Iris found herself questioning whether he was even a demon at all. *Even his eyes lie*, her evil sense yelled to her.

Shoving her clamoring humanity back into its tiny place within her, she replied, "Worry not about my human soul, Loomis. It's already covered in sin, yet you see I'm still powerful. I'm doing just fine."

"Even after tonight?" he asked, standing from the bed and looking down at her where she sat. *So he does know all that happened*, she thought. "You hear your own conscience," he pressed. "I know you must. You feel it tearing away from wherever you've tied it inside yourself; you feel it pining for release and freedom. You will not ignore it forever! Do you not believe you'll hear that boy's pained screams in your dreams tonight? Do you not expect to see visions of his parents crying and wailing at his loss? Do you not fear you'll wake to find his blood staining your hands?" His voice had grown stronger and more ardent.

Iris felt her expression turn hateful. "I didn't kill him," she growled through gritted teeth. "That was *your* doing. You enlisted that obsequious, big-headed prick, Solomon Priest, and you convinced him to doubt me, and then you gave him that blade and a few magic tricks and sent him on his way. You had to have known what he would do. You knew he couldn't kill me."

Loomis considered his words carefully before replying. "Of course I didn't expect him to kill you," he said. "Neither did I expect him to kill the boy. I expected he would steal the relic and return it to you, in exchange for vicarship of the cult, and then he would deny you at the Gathering, and you would be compelled to demonstrate your power once again." He crossed his arms and continued, "I planned to have this discussion with you then, hoping you would have seen enough bloodshed for your lifetime. I underestimated the boy's devotion to you. I expected he would be convinced to give up the spearhead, either by Priest's words or by his threat with the dagger." He paused again, thinking. "I shudder to think what you must have done to coax that boy to your side," he concluded.

Iris stood up angrily, her face hot. "Oh, fuck you, Loomis," she countered bitingly. "I've done nothing you haven't done. Don't judge me. Don't patronize me. Don't pretend to give two shits about my soul. And don't act as though you care anything about that boy."

Scowling, she added, "His name was Levi, by the way." She heard a hint of ruefulness in her own words as they exited her mouth.

A sympathetic expression rested on Loomis's face, and he answered in a calm, quiet voice, "You cared for him, didn't you? You liked him. You wanted to protect him, to help him. You can't fully hide it, even from yourself. You regret that Levi has lost his life."

"He lost his life because of *you*," Iris replied, her human compassion threatening to well up and overflow as tears. She firmly held them back. "I promised him wealth and the fulfillment of his desires. You sent after him a wolf, envious and already suffocating on his own ego. His slaughter came by Solomon's hand under your influence. I'll not accept his blood on my hands."

Loomis shook his head slowly. "There is more to sin than murder," he said. "You know you were wrong to persuade a child to follow you. You were wrong to promise him anything. You were wrong to prey on his emotions. You were not his executioner, but you led him to the slaughter. And you did it while convincing yourself you didn't care. But you recognize it now, do you not? You do care, and you are right to care, because you are *human*."

Iris glowered at him and then answered, with quiet, icy venom, "Fuck my humanity."

"Do not profane your human nature!" Loomis retorted swiftly and sharply, like a strict disciplinarian to a child. "I have dwelled among human souls for a very long time," he added more softly, "and I have never denied myself an opportunity to profane them, because they are ugly to me. But yours, Iris...yours is truly beautiful."

Iris blinked in amazement, stunned by the admission and stirred by the plea evident in Loomis's eyes. He must really mean it; he seemed so genuine, so different from how she had known him to be. But why? Why this change in him? She was being duped; she had to be. Unless her deviant tryst with his spirit had impacted him in some way she couldn't understand...that was a possibility. She was at a loss for words.

"Go to confession, Iris," Loomis implored gently. "Repent and be freed from your sins, and live as you were meant to live." He smiled rather sadly, then concluded, "He adopted you for a reason. He loves you, and He longs for you. Go to Him, Iris. You were meant for Heaven. Hell does not deserve you."

She felt the tears straining behind her eyes. Guilt erupted within her, threatening to overwhelm her composure and leave her sobbing on her knees at Loomis's feet. A whisper of a warm flame flickered in her human heart, and she wanted nothing more at that moment than to run to a priest and be healed. Not even Loomis doubted God could forgive what she had done. Even he believed she deserved Heaven over Hell.

But that's not what he said, came her demon's voice to her mind. *'Hell does not deserve you,' he said. He cares not if you go to Heaven; he only wants you to stay out of Hell. He fears you.*

As suddenly as the feelings had arisen, Iris crushed them with her own Satanic force. She set her face like stone and returned to Loomis a gaze that was grim and menacing and quite unlike the soft, supplicating concern in his eyes.

"You almost convinced me this time," she hissed, watching his face cloud with disappointment and nervous uncertainty. "I actually *wanted* to believe you, you lying piece of shit! But I'm not so easily tricked anymore. I see what you want. You want me anywhere but Hell, even if it means sending me to Heaven."

She could sense the fear in him, even if he masked it in his countenance. He did, however, take one small step backward, though it was of no avail. Iris stepped toward him with fierce intimidation.

"I'll have whatever eternity I choose," she snarled quietly, clutching Loomis's hair and pulling his face roughly toward hers so he couldn't escape the fire in her eyes. "And *you* will not steer me either way, because you are too impotent to sway me."

She released his hair with a stiff shove, noting with sick pleasure how the smell of dread very nicely complemented his masculine cologne. For a tense handful of seconds, the two stood facing one another in foreboding silence. Finally, Iris spoke once more.

"Fear is a tantalizing scent on you," she jeered. "It pleases me, and you're right to wear it, because if I choose Hell, you will finally know *true* misery, in endless suffering of torments you cannot yet contemplate, naked and alone in the midst of all in Hell who hate you and will revile you and bludgeon you with their mocking laughter, all while you cry out to me for reprieve, for an infinitesimal quark of the human compassion you've tried to kindle in me tonight, and you will find none." Her voice had become a low, acidic growl to match the merciless wolfishness of her black expression. "I promise you, Loomis," she finished, "my private rape of your spirit will be for you a *fond* memory."

She watched his eyes as they lost their gleam. He doggedly pulled all emotion from them, but she sensed his anguish at the painful reminder of his spiritual molestation. He might stand there resolutely, but his posture wouldn't fool her. His spirit was a broken reed in her hands.

After a moment, Iris turned and went to her desk, where she fished the silver-and-ruby ring from Levi's backpack. She threw it at Loomis, who let it hit him in the chest and fall to the floor. He showed no intention of picking it up.

"That's yours, too," she said coldly. "Take it and go. You may find it comforts you, although you know I return it because I am yet more powerful than what it helps you to be."

Loomis closed his eyes for a moment, then bent and took the ring from the ground, placing it in his pocket. He straightened and leveled his eyes with Iris's for a final time. She saw in them an echo of the honesty they had held just a few minutes before.

"I meant what I said," he declared slowly. "Whatever my motives, which you are justified in questioning, I have finally been honest with you."

"Says the liar," Iris added provokingly. She pulled the spearhead from the backpack and turned it over in her hands, running her fingers along its edge, then she finally waved it nonchalantly at Loomis. "If you'll now excuse me, Loomis, I have work to do."

Loomis glanced at the relic, looked down at the floor with a small, despondent shake of his head, then turned and disappeared from her room.

***

Having returned instantaneously to his home in Portland, Loomis seated himself in darkness on the loveseat upon which Iris Wakefield had vilely abused his spirit, leaving him a sobbing, retching wreck of the demon he had been. She had apparently then watched him suffer the physical atrocities that followed the return of his violated spirit, and that horrible realization was exponentially worse than the original torture.

He had pulled his dagger and centuries-old ring from his pocket before sitting and had thrown them onto the table in front of him. He now leaned forward and picked up the ring, twirling it slowly and mindlessly among his fingers as he remembered how he had used it so long ago to bait a young man and plant the seeds of a cult that would grow and inveigle generations of souls toward Hell. It had been a simple, profitable scheme, requiring little effort but returning decent dividends. He had thought himself safe to hide the final relic there with the bones of the cult's founder. That sect was an insignificant group with minimal power. They had never even summoned a demon to join them, so great were their ignorance and ineptitude. He had not expected Iris to take any interest in them or in his history with them, so it had been with some disappointment in himself that he had realized she had discovered the cult and located the relic so quickly. That she then so ably enlisted a cult member to procure the relic for her was an unnecessary additional sting, but he could appreciate the sinister beauty of the plan. Even so, he wished things had worked out differently. He had thought it good fortune when Levi had provoked Solomon and been savagely victimized, for it gave him some additional leverage with Iris in his attempt to nudge her toward Heaven and away from Hell. He knew the human conscience within her could not be totally silenced; he knew she must feel something, and he was right. Iris was affected by the boy's murder, though the demon nature in her was deplorably evil and frighteningly strong, allowing her to conceal her human emotions and stifle her human conscience. His appeal to her soul and its natural thirst for redemptive love had nearly succeeded, but Iris had once again, and perhaps finally, now, strangled her own human nature with her spiritual serpent's tail.

He sighed and magicked a fire into the fireplace across from him, then threw the ring into its roaring flames. Iris had told him to take it, had told him it might comfort him. She knew what it was—a magnifier of the wearer's innate skills and powers in magic—yet she had no doubt her natural power was still greater than his, even under magnification. He, likewise, had no doubt of it. The ring was useless to him, and even were it a remarkable boon that would somehow give him a ghost of a chance at becoming stronger than Iris, he wouldn't be caught dead wearing it after her taunt. He wouldn't be made a bitch.

Loomis leaned back into the sofa and closed his eyes. Iris had the final relic now, so it would be only a short time before she would be able to gain control of his shadow-demon. She would have it at her beck and call, to do with as she pleased. Whether she sent it on a rampage or acted more subtly, the human race was going to pay dearly. He had himself commanded his creature only once, and that was to steal the spearhead that should have completed the creature's dark power. It had come into being and was powerful without that final relic, already having the ability to steal souls and drag them to Hell, but the spearhead's particular magic should have been the puzzle's final piece, the one that would let the creature's master consume the spiritual power of a soul. Reflecting on it now, knowing Iris was preparing to take his creation from him, he considered again where he might have gone wrong. He had worked at the science of it for so long; he had studied countless histories and pre-histories; he had tinkered with spells and runes and magical formulae for thousands of years in Hell, knowing all along his plan was extremely long-term, for it would take ages to effect the appropriate conjuring and then to convince those above him in Hell to allow the plan to take its life breath. He had thought the overthrow of Satan would be the simple part, especially after Satan had so stupidly attempted his own earthly incarnation. The Devil had borrowed that science, partially, from Loomis, but he had not paid close attention to the vital details, and he had ended up creating Iris and then letting God stake a claim in her, thereby exacerbating both his own Hell and Loomis's.

Iris was already a domineering entity; if she began consuming souls, she would become a flagitious tyrant, the likes of which perhaps God Himself had not foreseen. It was the blackest magic Loomis had initiated, magic that had taken unbelievable patience and intelligence, a feat of which God should not have expected any of His creation capable. Likely not even Iris could have done it alone, for she lacked the indefatigable patience it had required. Now that she had stolen his work, however, all that remained for her was to find whatever mistake he had made along the way, for he knew he had made one. He had placed the final piece, yet he was unable to consume a soul. If Iris should find his mistake, whatever it was, and correct it, her apotheosis would begin. He had searched his own work dozens of times and failed to see an error, but somehow he doubted Iris would reach the same conclusion. She was smart, and she was driven by hatred to outdo him. She would reign over him soon, and she would make his existence a wretched affliction, just as she had promised.

Loomis opened his eyes and contemplated the burning flames of the hearth. It seemed almost certain now that Iris would choose an eternity in Hell to torment him. Staring into the fire, he could see just one chance for peace, but of course it was an utter impossibility, one his intellect shouldn't even have conjured as a worthwhile thought. He was too far gone for saving.

He stood and walked numbly to his bedroom, feeling empty and exhausted and completely forlorn. His weak human vessel needed its rest; that was the most plausible explanation for all these sensitive feelings he was experiencing now. He lay on his back beneath the canopy of his bed, not bothering to undress. He closed his eyes and prepared to leave the body and take himself back to Hell, hoping its fires might purge him of all the confounding humanish inclinations that had acutely infected him. He would try to appreciate his visit this time, for his Hell might soon be transformed forever into something truly unbearable.

26

Iris sat alone at a two-person table near the window in the corner of a crowded Starbucks, a fresh venti Americano steaming in its cup next to the empty one she had finished half an hour before. Caffeine had been the majority of her diet for the past thirty-six hours or so, and although her stomach felt hungry, she ignored it. She had one leg crossed over the other, and her toe was twitching with rapid, mindless movement as she stared out the window at the parking lot and the street beyond. Her mind registered very little of what she saw; she was too deeply mired in thought to pay attention to earthly happenings.

It didn't make sense. She knew Loomis must have made some mistake as he had constructed his complex series of spells and relics, intending to create a quasi-demonic entity with the power to remove human souls from their bodies and feed those souls to its master. He had succeeded on the first count but not on the second, and it was unlike him to fail wherever the science of magic was concerned. She knew the shortcoming must have caused him great consternation, and that made the possibility of her success with it so much sweeter. She had perhaps been overly confident in her own abilities, though, because she had toyed with the relics and spells herself for hours now, and she was succeeding no further than

Loomis had. The shadow-demon, which Iris had facetiously nicknamed Boris, though it had no personality or independent thought or action, was effectively under her control, but its power was not complete. She had tested Boris on three different souls, letting him prey on homeless individuals in three separate cities as she made various tweaks to his design. He had stolen their souls, but Iris couldn't consume their power. She had hypothesized it might be due to her human nature or, by extension, her physical existence outside of Hell, but the theory didn't hold much water. Boris carried the souls within his own form, and he had been magically manufactured to move between Hell and Earth. That fantastic ability, in particular, was an impressive scientific formulation Loomis had figured out. It was the same magic that allowed him to move his own fabricated human body effortlessly in the same way, and Iris was glad he had put in whatever tedious work it must have been, because she knew she wouldn't have had the patience. She didn't fully understand its workings even now, with the end result laid out in front of her eyes. Regardless, with the arrangement as it was, it shouldn't matter whether Boris brought a soul to her on Earth or in Hell; she should be able to consume whatever he carried, yet she was not.

Loomis had saved the copper spearhead for his last relic. That may have been simply a stroke of nostalgia, a little artistic flourish that he couldn't help but stamp onto his work, especially since the relic's physical proximity to one of his cults had allowed such an opportunity. Or it may have been more deliberate; maybe the spearhead itself was the relic meant to unlock the final stage of Boris's power. Or it could be nothing but a wild goose chase. Perhaps that was Loomis's intent all along, a security measure in case someone did try to steal his work—amass the relics in meaningless order so that, if he did make a mistake, no one else would know where to find that mistake. But, no...Loomis might be completely distrusting of others, but he wouldn't have anticipated any failure on his own part.

So Iris had settled her caffeine-addled brain on the idea that there was something wrong with this last relic. Of all the relics Loomis had used, this was the one she was most unfamiliar with. She knew not its origin nor its intended purpose, and she realized that might be part of her problem. It was a displeasing thought, but she knew what she would have to do. She would have to take herself back to the mountain to see Auraltiferys—if she still could, in her sin-laden state. And if she did make it to him, her skills as an actress would have to be spot-on. She didn't relish the thought of standing in front of him. The man was a living, breathing icicle, with eyes that could see the heart. If she was unable to fool those eyes, he would not only refuse to help her, but also likely try to kill her. *Oh, well*, she thought. *Let him try.*

Having made up her mind, Iris turned her attention to her coffee, sipping tentatively at the hot liquid and attempting to fortify her will for the disguise she would soon have to wear very convincingly. An eruption of nasal laughter startled her from her thoughts, blasted from a group of four college-aged dipshits at the table next to her, two girls and two guys. She darted a sideways glare at them, but of course they were oblivious to it. Glancing around, Iris saw most other patrons were wearing headphones, engrossed in their own laptop or tablet screens and paying no one else any mind. These four next to her were loud and obnoxious; she must have been so lost in her musings that she had somehow ignored them. Now that her brain had jumped back to temporal reality, she found them completely unacceptable.

She stood and shrugged into her purse strap, put on her sunglasses, then grabbed both of her coffee cups. The first was empty, and the second was half full, but before she had stepped over to the offending table, both cups were magically filled with extremely hot fluid. It didn't bother her hands too much, but few others could boast of having a demon's tolerance for pain. On her way to the door, she stopped at the offending table and set the drinks down, saying with a smile, "Here, you all have these; I've had enough coffee today, and I think you deserve it."

The four looked at her with indignant confusion before Iris continued to the door, ignoring the "Uh, no thanks!" comment yelled to her back by the young man who appeared to be the prime douchebag of the group. She was already in her Challenger by the time the surprise wore off and the kid reached for the two cups. She couldn't see them physically from her car, but the eyes of her demon's mind were able to watch. At her magical invocation, the cups exploded inexplicably as the young man touched them, sending scalding liquid over the hands and arms and faces of all at the table. They jumped back in pain and panic, and they almost certainly tried to scream, but they discovered very quickly that, although their mouths were moving, no sound was coming out. Alas, there was to be no further vocalization from any of these four young college students for the rest of their lives. Unless, of course, they happened to learn some magic. Or maybe eventually they would have the bright idea to visit a priest, and maybe a blessing from God would help them. Regardless, they would certainly remember from this day on to use their indoor voices wherever propriety mandated. Pleased to have done the world this small favor, Iris drove home and readied herself for another trip to the mountain and its saintly inhabitant.

* * *

The Empyreal Hounds looked at her with suspicion, but thankfully they remained silent as Iris walked past them up the path toward the blacksmith's home. She wanted to believe she had fooled them and would as easily fool Auraltiferys, but a feeling in her gut told her otherwise. This visit would almost certainly end badly, but she had made it here to the mountain, so she had to trust her power.

Doubt was pawing at the back of her mind somewhere, though, especially with the unusual ominous gray and brisk chill hanging over this holy place.

The front door opened as she approached, and soon framed in the doorway was the imposing figure of Auraltiferys, clad in thick tights, heavy knee-high boots, and a loose-fitting, long-sleeved shirt, cinched by a leather belt. His hefty blade was strapped to his thigh, and Iris felt her eyes dart involuntarily toward it before she forced them to meet the icy blue gaze of the blacksmith.

"Iris," he said, inviting her in. His cool, steely voice was a dagger to her heart, but she maintained her composure as she entered.

"Hello, Auraltiferys," she replied, forcing a smile. "I need your help."

He closed the door quietly behind her, then turned and stared at her as he answered, "Very well; have a seat. Would you like some tea?"

Iris averted her eyes as she seated herself in front of the fireplace. "No, thank you," she responded, thinking her voice sounded a touch nervous. She'd have to correct that, and soon. There was no reason for such anxiety. Why was she having such difficulty remembering Auraltiferys was just a human? His power would be nothing if matched against hers. All she had to do was remember that.

The blacksmith sat gracefully in the chair next to her and asked softly, "What help do you need?"

Iris pulled the spearhead from her pocket and handed it to him. "I stole this relic from Loomis," she explained. "I discovered he had used it as part of his shadow-demon. I want to repurpose it so he can't use it any longer, but I don't know much about it, and before I do anything disastrous, I need to know exactly what it is. Do you recognize it?" She swallowed, hoping the blacksmith would fail to recognize her pretense.

Auraltiferys turned the spearhead slowly in his hands, studying it. For almost a minute, he seemed lost in thought, then he roused himself and set the relic on the table in front of him with a deep sigh.

He turned his silver-blue eyes on her and asked, stabbingly, "Why do you *really* want to know about this relic, Iris?" His tone was sharper and more threatening than the blade at his hip.

Iris straightened instantly, knowing he had already sized her up correctly. She let her expression turn dark as she returned his gaze. "Do not fight me, Auraltiferys," she said coldly. "Tell me what you know about the relic, and I'll be on my way."

The blacksmith shook his head almost imperceptibly. "I will not help you, demon," he practically whispered.

Iris stood hastily from the couch and replied, with hateful anger, "Then you will die."

Auraltiferys also stood, towering over her in height and physical strength, with his hand on the hilt of his knife. "This isn't you, Iris," he exclaimed forcefully. "This is *not* who you really are. Do not give in to evil; do not forsake all you believe in! You can confess your sins to me now, Iris, and be healed of all of this."

Iris laughed. "Why would I want that? I've never been stronger," she answered.

"Your strength will never be greater than when it is used to serve God," Auraltiferys retorted, with profound sincerity. His voice resonated in Iris's human heart, but she promptly smothered it with her demonic nature.

"Shut up, *priest*," she growled in her demon's voice. "Tell me about this relic, or die keeping its secrets. You will not stop me either way, but I give you this one final chance to save your life."

Auraltiferys said nothing, but he pulled his blade from its sheath in defiant response. Iris immediately focused a spell on him, intending to drop him to his knees; instead, she was stunned when her own body was thrown backward, over the couch and through the thick wood of the front door. Outside, where it was now raining, she caught her breath and started to her feet, enraged and now prepared to hold back none of her power. She may have underestimated the blacksmith's magical abilities for a moment, but she was still superior to him.

Before she had regained her full balance, Auraltiferys was already standing in the doorway. He shoved her backward again with a powerful spell, throwing her off of the porch and onto the cobblestone path through the clearing in front of the house. Stunned again, Iris rushed to get up, finding the blacksmith on top of her even as she did so. He swung at her with his blade, but she was able to deflect it with a spell in the instant before it struck her. Suddenly realizing how foolish she was being, she projected herself a few yards away, positioning herself behind her adversary. He must be manipulating time by fractions of seconds, which was an impressive feat, especially considering the man was only human; Iris was unsure even she could do the same if she tried. As astounding as his skills were, however, she would put an end to this. Her ability to relocate herself should help; if it didn't, she'd have to start bi-locating, which would be thoroughly exhausting. She worried this might become an epic test of endurance, and, unfortunately, she hadn't faced any real challenges since learning of her true potential. The blacksmith, meanwhile, had spent the last two thousand years disciplining himself, teaching himself, preparing himself for any battle that should arise, and for the briefest moment, Iris wondered if she may have bitten off more than she could chew. *Don't be ridiculous*, her demon's mind yelled at her. *Human strength alone will never exceed your power!*

Convincing herself she could defeat him, and having positioned herself advantageously behind him, Iris uprooted a pine tree from the edge of the clearing and propelled it trunk-first into Auraltiferys's chest, knocking him directly to the ground, where he was pinned momentarily by the weight of the tree. She opened the ground beneath him as deeply as she easily could, sending his body falling into the deep fissure with the pine on top of him. It would hold him for at least several seconds, hopefully.

Iris paused where she stood and closed her eyes, focusing her concentration on a spell that should have enabled her to command lightning from the clouds above. A terrifying cry interrupted her, and her eyes opened to see six Empyreal Hounds gathering around her, teeth bared, golden flames blazing in their eyes, and their silvery-white fur, though wet from the rain, seemingly illuminating the air around them.

Oh, hell no, Iris thought. She quickly refocused, finishing her spell and drawing purple daggers of lightning into three of the Hounds, who howled and whined as the power struck them. They dropped to their sides, wounded and paralyzed by the shock. The three she had missed, however, converged on her in an instant, and she was trapped beneath their heft. She felt her skin being scratched and torn before she was able to relocate herself. When she moved, she found she was bleeding badly in several places, and the claw marks and bites of the Hounds were painfully hot. She took a moment to heal the worst injuries, then, infuriated beyond belief, she called more electricity from the sky, faster this time, eradicating—or at least postponing—the threat from the remaining Hounds. Their unfortunate interference had distracted her from Auraltiferys, who had now thrown the tree off of himself and had emerged from the crevasse in the mountain. Whatever injuries he must have sustained, he had already been able to heal. He stood near the precipice, knife in hand and ferocious purpose set like stone in his face.

Iris transported herself directly to where he stood, materializing her physical form as a propellant so that they both fell into the crag. Auraltiferys absorbed the fearsome blow of the landing for a second time, and Iris was glad his muscular body had cushioned her fall. She was also quite pleased to hear the foul cracking sounds from several of his bones as they struck the granite depths. She allowed herself to relish the momentary victory as Auraltiferys lay unconscious beneath her. He had dropped his magical blade, which now lay just a couple of feet from where they had landed. Iris was incensed at seeing the knife, remembering how she had once tried to pick it up and the blacksmith had so boldly, so arrogantly, stated only he could lift it, and he was immune to its blade. *Fucking arrogant bastard*, she thought to herself. Perhaps no other human could wield that knife or use it against him, but she was not just any human, and she knew exponentially more now than she had known then. A demon as powerful as she could break the blade's protective spells; of that, there was no question.

She moved from the prone form of the blacksmith and tugged at the knife. She sensed how it fought her, but, by concentrating on the specific vibrations of the magic flowing through it, she could see in her mind how to undo its spells. It was tedious, but eventually her hand pulled the hilt from the ground. A second later, she stood upright, holding Auraltiferys's robust blade.

Turning, she saw the blacksmith had awoken and had brought his torso upward slightly, leaning on a strong left arm propped behind him. His right arm hung limply near his lap, and his legs appeared to be useless to him. His right leg, at least, was jutting out from beneath him at an awkward angle. His eyes had lost some of their vigor, and he breathed heavily. Though his face was brave and full of fortitude, it exuded exhaustion and pain. Seeing Iris now towering above him with his knife, he closed his eyes and waited in silence.

Iris laughed demonically. "Do you now *pray*, priest?" she hissed vitriolically. "It will not save you."

Auraltiferys opened his eyes slowly, then answered, annoyingly, "It already has." His voice was low, but still powerful.

Iris, thoroughly provoked by his pious reply, kicked him savagely in the face with her boot. His head snapped backward, and he fell back to the ground with a grunt. Iris dropped to her knees on top of his muscled abdomen, smiling at the blood from his nose and mouth.

"It doesn't have to end this way," she said, with mocking sympathy in her tone. "You have lost, Auraltiferys, but you have fought well, and I respect that. Let it not be said I am incapable of mercy. I'll give you this final opportunity—tell me all you know about the spearhead, and I will let you live. It is but a small price to pay."

Auraltiferys, struggling to breathe under the weight of both his injuries and Iris on top of him, responded, "I will not help you, Iris. Not now; not like this." He paused for breath, then continued, "Please, take *your* final opportunity—repent of your sins. You will be forgiven, and you will know the power of God. Let not damnation be your eternity; succeed where the Satan of Hell failed."

Iris felt the smile wiped from her face by the blacksmith's unsolicited preaching. "I *will* succeed where he failed," she replied drably, "and I don't need forgiveness to do it." Ignoring the clear and genuine sadness in his expression, she jammed the blade down into his chest. He grimaced in pain and closed his eyes. Consumed by infernal malice, she pulled the knife out and stabbed him again, a second and then a third time.

Suddenly, she felt a sharp pain near the base of her ribs, and she screamed in horrified agony as a plasmic heat engulfed her from within. Her vision went blindingly white, and she heard whispering voices just before she lost all consciousness. *You were taught better than this*, she thought she heard them say.

***

Iris's senses slowly began to awaken. She felt cold, soaking water around her; she heard a distant rumble of thunder; she felt a warm pain in her abdomen. She opened her eyes and found she was lying on her back, looking upward at a crack of pale gray sky high overhead. She fumbled in her mind for her memory and eventually recognized she was still inside the cavern she had opened in the mountain. The rain had stopped, but not before flooding the fissure with a few inches of cold water. Things felt calm and placid, at least.

In an instant, she recalled the vicious atrocities she had committed against Auraltiferys. She didn't know what had happened to her, but she remembered kicking him and stabbing him. The nausea of absolute horror overwhelmed her, and she feared she might vomit. She started sobbing uncontrollably, terrified to look around her and find his dead body there, brutally murdered by her wicked hands. *No, God, please! No, no, no,* her frantic mind pleaded. She didn't want to look. If she had killed Auraltiferys, she should die right here and never be forgiven.

A tiny splash from somewhere impelled her to raise her head. Her ribs hurt from the sudden movement, but she forgot the discomfort as soon as she saw the holy blacksmith kneeling beside her. She rolled over stiffly, unable to stop her own crying.

"Oh, my God," she sobbed, "I thought I had killed you!" She tried to bring herself to her own knees, wanting to hug him, but her body was weak and limp.

"I will live, Iris," Auraltiferys said quietly, his voice a soothing balm of gentle grace. "Do not try to move yet," he urged softly. "You're badly hurt."

"What?" Iris questioned dumbly, trying to stifle her sobs. She remembered the pain near her ribs and looked down, seeing her own blood seeping out from a gash in her right side. With slight panic, she looked back to Auraltiferys, who had moved closer and was now chanting a healing prayer under his breath. She had nearly taken his life; now he was saving hers. He laid a strong, gentle hand across the wound in her side, and she felt an easy, pleasant heat there.

"The bleeding has stopped," he said, "but you'll be weak for some time. Let us go." He stood and held a hand out to her.

"But what about you?" Iris asked, taking his hand. The blacksmith's chest and face were covered in blood, and the sight made her sick. How had she allowed herself to become so depraved?

"I have healed," he replied simply, supporting Iris with a muscular arm as she stood shakily beside him. It was his right arm, the one that had broken so nastily in their fall down here, and while Iris was grateful to God just to see him alive, she was truly amazed to see how fully he had already recovered. "Can you get us out of here?" he asked, his voice mild and not uncaring, but tinged with a hint of wariness. "I am quite exhausted, I'm afraid," he finished.

Iris felt a brief jolt of anxiety at the prompting. What if she no longer had any magical abilities? What if whatever had happened to her had taken away her power? *Have faith, you fool*, her mind urged her.

An instant later, both she and Auraltiferys entered the den of his home. Iris paused in the doorway and surveyed the destruction she had caused, appalled by the aftermath of her own demonic inclinations. Everything here had been so beautiful, so peaceful, so holy; she had stained it with her evil and brought ugliness and chaos to it, and now she was filled with regret. She was able to repair the effects of her dark uses of magic, sealing the ground and replanting the pine tree and replacing the wooden door, and somehow Auraltiferys had survived her violent assault and had healed; she knew it was all by the grace of God, and she was truly thankful for such blessings, but they didn't erase the horrible guilt she felt for having come here with evil intent in the first place. As she stared for a moment out at the clearing God had allowed her to restore, she remembered with dismay what she had done to the Empyreal Hounds. There was no evidence of them out there, but she prayed they had lived.

She finally turned inside and closed the door, then joined

Auraltiferys at the coffee table. He had created a fire in the hearth, filling the room with comforting warmth, and had seated himself in his chair. He was reclined with his back and head resting against the upholstery and his sizable arms relaxed atop the armrests, unconcerned that his hair and clothes were still soaked from the rain. His eyes were closed, and though he appeared to be sleeping, Iris sensed he was fully awake and very deep in prayer. She smiled sadly as she admired his refined, patrician features and watched his chest gently rise and fall under his torn shirt, ensanguined with the blood that had nearly made him a martyr. A tear rolled down her cheek, and she roughly wiped it away. Her mentor had seen enough of her tears.

After a few silent, peaceful minutes, Auraltiferys opened his eyes. With a deep breath, he shifted to an upright posture and turned his eyes on Iris. "How do you feel?" he asked.

Iris felt a sudden, inexplicable, overwhelming joy upon hearing his voice again, and she couldn't help but smile. She wanted to cry again, too, but she managed to refrain. "I'm fine," she answered decidedly. "Don't worry about me. How are you? I almost killed you," she continued, her tone devolving into one of tremulous anxiety.

Auraltiferys gently dismissed her comments with an easy wave and replied, "I am prepared for my death at my appointed time, which has apparently not yet come. I am alive, Iris, and I will be fine, for as long as God allows me to be. Now, we need to take care of you. You may not realize it, but...I very nearly killed you, too." He lowered his eyes and pointed to Iris's bloodstained shirt. She had seen herself bleeding while they were still out in the cavern, but she hadn't noticed then how extreme the injury was. Blood had radiated from the puncture in her side and had run all the way down her leg. Her chest, too, was spattered with blood, though she guessed that belonged to her would-be victim. Regardless, it appeared she had indeed lost a lot of her own blood, though it was difficult to tell for sure, considering how wet and muddy she was. She felt tired, but mostly normal otherwise.

"What do you mean?" she asked. "What happened?" She poked gingerly at the area of her wound, then added, "I think you healed me. I don't hurt."

Auraltiferys stared at her with concern for several seconds, then replied, "I have healed the physical wound in your mortal body, but I admit I know nothing of what other effects you may suffer from it."

Iris narrowed her eyes with hesitant curiosity. "What are you talking about?"

Auraltiferys opened the leather pouch at his belt and pulled out what appeared to be a splinter of wood. He held it in his open palm and, with silent magic, returned it to its true size. It was a jagged piece, sharp and splintering at the edges, about nine inches long and three inches wide, and it was dyed with blood.

"I used this against you," he said quietly, "and God forgive me for having done it." He held the wood reverently, and his voice, though strong, held heavy sadness. He extended it toward Iris, nodding gently at her tacit request for permission to take it. She studied it carefully, but there were no distinguishing features on it. It was, by all appearances, just a piece of unfinished wood, damp with rain and stained with scarlet.

"What is it?" Iris asked, handing the piece back to the blacksmith.

"This," he answered as he carefully accepted the fragment back from Iris, "is a piece of the cross upon which our Lord was crucified."

Iris felt her breath leave her momentarily. When it returned a second later, she blinked and shook her head, then stammered, "Um...wh...what?"

Auraltiferys did not reply immediately. His eyes were fixed with sorrow on the wooden piece cradled lovingly in his hands. Finally, he looked up and answered her, "This, Iris, is the wood of the cross, and until I stabbed you with it, the only blood upon it was that of Jesus Christ." He nodded understandingly at Iris's dumbstruck expression, then continued, "I have desecrated this by weaponizing it, and I pray I'll be forgiven for my transgression. At the time, I could think of no other way to stop you."

Iris closed her eyes and massaged her temples, then looked back to Auraltiferys, trying to organize her muddled thoughts into coherent sentences, but words escaped her.

"What do you remember?" the blacksmith asked.

Iris reflected for a moment, then answered, "I remember stabbing you." She shuddered, even though the fire had already removed the chill from her. "I was killing you, and then...I'm not sure. There was a pain in my side, then terrible heat and overpowering white light...the next thing I remember is waking up down there in the cavern," she explained.

Auraltiferys nodded slowly and thoughtfully. "I hoped you would survive it," he said. "I knew the injury to your body would not kill you, but in truth, I knew not what would happen to your spirit. A demon alone would be weakened immediately by such holiness, such that it would be compelled to return directly to Hell. You, of course, are not just a demon, but you had subdued your human nature to such a small degree, I feared the relic might hasten your eternal damnation. It seems it has not, and that is cause for great joy. I believe you have endured a purifying fire, and you have been not weakened, but strengthened by it." He paused again in contemplation, then he smiled. It appeared a heavy weight had been lifted from his broad shoulders. He looked at Iris and added, "I suppose I should not be surprised. You have consumed the Body and Blood, Soul and Divinity of our Savior. You are both a holy child of God and an unholy creation of Satan, but I believe we have witnessed today which of your natures is the true source of your power. Your human life from God will not be outdone by your demonic existence from the Devil."

Iris considered her mentor's words. They were, as should be expected, full of wisdom. It made sense, as outlandish as it seemed on the surface. She had always been a demon, even if she hadn't known it, yet she had participated in the Church's sacraments for most of her human life. Then she had strayed and followed the vile inclinations of her demonic nature, letting it choke the life from her humanity. The holy relic had therefore caused her abundant discomfort, because she had let the demon's spirit take control. Undoubtedly, the Eucharist would have had the same effect, had she tried to consume it in the state she was in. Now, she had been purged of her sins, and her heart and her mind were hers again, to turn in the direction she chose.

Auraltiferys allowed her to sit in silence, knowing she had much to reflect on. Finally, he rose gracefully from his chair, the fragment of the cross in his hand, and walked to the mantel above the fireplace. He opened a small, hidden door in the decorative scrollwork, revealing a tiny compartment lined with cushioned white cloth. He placed the relic inside, affectionately, then closed the door and genuflected.

Iris watched his movements with a loving wonder, yet overwhelmed by the man's saintliness. God had created great beauty in him. God had created beauty in all of humanity, she supposed, but it was so much easier for her to recognize the face of the Creator in this man.

He turned and found Iris staring at him and determined she had finished her musings. "I will not force you, Iris," he prompted, "but I would suggest you make a full confession now; let God complete the spiritual healing that has begun in you after your physical purification by the holy relic."

Iris felt an anxious palpitation in her heart, which somehow fell to her stomach and settled there like a lead weight. Going to confession was never fun; it was even less enticing when it was to be a screenless, face-to-face confession with a priest one knew well enough to have just tried to kill. Iris hadn't even enjoyed confessing to a parish priest when all her sins fell in the venial, human category. Now she had the mortal sins of a demon to confess, too, and she was going to have to speak of them out loud in front of, arguably, the holiest man in all the sub-Heavenly cosmos. She would rather confess her sins to the Pope. But she recognized now, in the gore staining Auraltiferys's chest, how desperately in need of healing she really was. So, though incredibly nervous, she smiled shyly at her mentor and nodded in reply to his prompting.

Auraltiferys was, not surprisingly, an excellent confessor. He listened intently and then advised benevolently and wisely. He assigned Iris an appropriate penance and helped her when she couldn't recall the Act of Contrition (ironically, she could find the words of thousands of magical invocations in her mind, but this simple prayer eluded her). When he granted her absolution, she felt intrinsically changed; it was as though, having finally availed herself of reconciliation after having once completely submitted to her second nature, she had made her first full and true confession and had reconciled both her natures with God.

After hearing her confession and absolving her, Auraltiferys returned to his chair and stared thoughtfully into the fire for a moment. Iris, too, watched the flames, remembering the vision of Hell she had been shown by Loomis, and how very nearly she had chosen it for her eternity. She would have been damned if not for the strength and grace of Auraltiferys—or, more precisely, if not for the strength and grace of God, whom the blacksmith allowed to work through him so fully.

"I don't know about you," Auraltiferys finally said, his cheerful tone elegantly carving its way through the tranquil silence, "but I could use something to drink." His blue eyes sparkled as he smiled, and Iris was amused by the joyful emotion evident in his face. She had never seen him so jubilant, and she supposed it was on account of her recent penitence. She had nearly murdered him in cold, evil blood, yet he rejoiced with her in her conversion.

"Do you want me to make tea?" she offered.

Auraltiferys stood as she spoke and walked to a set of built-in cabinets near the largest bookcase. "No," he said, pulling a squat, round glass bottle out of a cabinet, "I think today's events have called for something a bit stronger."

Seeing the bottle and the amber liquid inside, Iris asked in shock, "What? You *drink*? Like...*alcohol*?" She couldn't explain to herself why she had assumed the man would have eschewed such potables.

He chuckled softly at her exclamation. "Yes, I drink alcohol, Iris," he stated with a grin, "in moderation on special occasions. I believe the last time I opened this bottle was about, oh, eighty years ago. I hope you do not think less of me for it."

"No, of course I don't," Iris answered hastily. "I'm just surprised; that's all." Her surprise had initially stemmed from the discovery that the blacksmith would imbibe; after she processed his response, the surprise settled on the eighty-year sobriety he had mentioned. It was so easy to forget how ancient he was.

He set the bottle on the table and moved into the kitchen for drinking glasses. "You don't have to join me, if you don't wish to," he called from the other room. Iris, peering at the bottle on the table, realized the copper spearhead was still lying there, and the sudden recollection of her original reason for being here distracted her from answering immediately. "I will be happy to make you tea," Auraltiferys added, having already returned to the den with two small glasses in hand.

"Oh, no," Iris answered, rousing herself. "I'll try whatever this is. So...what is it?"

"It's a liquor I prepare in small batches from time to time. I believe you would liken it most closely to bourbon," he explained.

"Bourbon is my favorite," Iris replied, eager to try the drink.

The blacksmith poured two small portions, perhaps a generous shot in each glass, then took both from the table and handed one to Iris. He raised his glass slightly and said, "Let us give thanks to God for the blessings He has bestowed on us today, and especially for your reconciliation. May He guide you upon your new path, your right path, and may He work through me to help you in every way I can."

"Amen," Iris concluded with a genuine smile. She sipped the drink carefully and found it quite palatable, though extremely strong. It was fiery, with an oaky sweetness.

They sat in silence for a few minutes, sipping their drinks, until Auraltiferys finished his and picked up the copper spearhead from the table. He inspected it in detail, his eyes narrowed in careful deliberation.

"I suppose I can help you with this problem of yours now," he said. "I trust you no longer have any intentions of furthering Drake's evil plots, either for his ends or your own." He looked with grave sincerity at Iris, piercing her with his icy eyes.

"I'll put an end to all that," she answered resolutely. "You don't even have to tell me anything about this relic if you believe it's safer not to."

Auraltiferys scratched his head and smoothed his hair, then replied, "There is no harm in knowledge. This, however, is not a relic." He tossed the spearhead carelessly onto the table.

Iris felt her forehead tighten in consternation. "What do you mean?" she asked skeptically. "This was the final relic Loomis needed for his shadow-demon. It was to provide him the power to consume human souls. He stole it from a museum, killing a guard in the process, and he opened a gate to Hell out in the middle of nowhere in order to be able to use its magic both in Hell and on Earth. What do you mean, it isn't a relic?"

Auraltiferys listened to Iris's brief narrative, then laughed. Iris was startled by his reaction, but he offered a quick explanation. "It isn't often a demon as intelligent and motivated as Drake makes such an amateurish error," he said. "He must have gotten careless or impatient. This piece," he continued, picking up the spearhead once more, "is an imitation of a very powerful relic, one that was cast specifically to exhaust the spirits of its targets."

"How do you know that? How can you tell it isn't the real relic? And who could have made a replica? And why would Loomis not have recognized this?" Iris's confusion embodied itself in myriad excited questions.

"I know it isn't the real relic because I have studied and maintained the records of all relics created by the Knights of Heaven's Forge," he answered, his tone somber. "This particular relic, the true one, was created a little over a thousand years before I was born. It enrages me every time one of our creations is used against humanity, but it has also proven impossible to collect every relic created by every Knight over thousands of years of human history. Our works were intended to be used *against* the forces of evil, not *by* them." He sighed, then proceeded, "Regardless, I know the specific spells that were alloyed into the actual spearpoint. This replica does not resonate with those same spells. It is cloaked with similar spells, but not imbued with the true ones. Drake may not have known the specific resonance he needed for his demonic creation. He may have learned only theoretically that this relic should have had the correct potency. In appearance, it is exactly like the original, and that could explain why Drake didn't know the difference. To answer who could have created such a replica, I can only hypothesize. It wasn't a Knight; I am certain of that. The most likely culprit would be a demon, because a demon would have the necessary magical knowledge. Humans, generally speaking, lack both the necessary magical abilities and the knowledge of such ancient arcana, particularly when it is as ancient as this."

Agitated, Iris stood from the couch and walked around it, arms crossed and forehead rumpled in concentration. She paced as she theorized aloud, "What if Loomis did this himself? Maybe he created the replica and replaced the real one, then stole the replica in a visible way so attention would be diverted and I would end up with a useless copy of the true relic."

"He would have had no motive," Auraltiferys said, shaking his head. "Drake never imagined you would requisition his work. He would not have constructed his monstrosity to its penultimate degree and then waited to place his final piece."

"Right," Iris agreed, deflated, realizing how stupid the idea was. "So, who then? I'm the only other demon I know," she continued. "Besides Satan, but he's in Hell. Wait...are there *other demons* living up here? On Earth, I mean?" *Of course there are*, she screamed at herself. *Why else would the Church need exorcists?*

"Drake is the only one I know of who dwells on Earth in a fully human form," Auraltiferys replied. "But, as I know you are aware, Iris, any demon can coerce a person to certain actions or possess a human's soul. In such manners, they can walk the Earth with you, though not as ably or freely as you and Drake can."

"How will I figure out who did this, then? I have to find the real relic, or else it's left out there for Loomis to find. Whoever made this counterfeit had a reason to do it, which probably means he or she stole the original," Iris responded.

Auraltiferys remained unspeaking for a moment, eventually standing and picking up the liquor bottle and both empty glasses.

He set the bourbon in its cabinet and placed the glasses in the kitchen sink, then returned to the den and leaned his arms against the top of the chair back, looking over at Iris. "You mentioned the spearhead was stolen from a museum," he suggested. "That means it was discovered at some time after its original use and treated as a historical artifact. The replica could have been created only after discovery of the original, and since the spearhead was handled as a piece of history rather than being taken straight to Hell or used immediately for nefarious purposes, I am inclined to believe a human found it. It may have gone through a number of hands, but I imagine the true relic was replaced by its copy at some time during its museum days. That may have been recently, or it may have been hundreds of years ago."

"Great," Iris replied sarcastically.

The blacksmith smiled, stood upright, then smoothed the top of his long, silvery-white hair. "Iris," he said with amusement, "you are quite impatient. If you wish to locate the true relic and find the creator of this paltry imitation, I recommend you begin at the most recent museum and then trace it back as far as you need to."

"It might not matter, anyway," Iris said, her tone darkened by ample pessimism. "I may be able to destroy what Loomis created so far, but he can probably do it all over again with different relics. He may even find another that will serve his purposes even better than this spearhead would have."

Auraltiferys's expression became immediately serious. His blue eyes focused on Iris, and she saw penetrating admonition in them. "You're right," he said sternly. "It may not matter. You may stand and fight against the legions of Hell for all your mortal life and never see a victory. If you fight for Heaven, however, your victory is already assured, whether you witness it on Earth or after all the old things have passed away. Will you give up, Iris, just because you fear Drake may best you after all? Even should he do so, his triumph is vanity;

his prize remains eternal damnation. After what you have already been through and survived, after the temptations you have already fought, after the redemption you have experienced today, will you now give up?"

Iris ducked her eyes as the blacksmith heaped his earnest reproach on her. She knew there was truth in his words, and she was ashamed her recent reconciliation with God had not made her a more faithful servant. Holiness was truly a marathon, and Auraltiferys was right—she was impatient. She also hated the idea of losing.

"Of course I won't give up," she said quietly.

Auraltiferys softened. "For what it's worth," he said gently, "I have faith in you."

"Thanks," Iris replied with a tiny smile. "For everything," she added.

The blacksmith indicated his understanding with a gentle, humble inclination of his head. "Now," he said, "we are both in need of much rest after today's evils. If you can spare the time, I suggest you remain here overnight so I can ensure you will have no lingering side effects, physical or otherwise, from your encounter with the holy relic."

Iris nodded in agreement, in no hurry to leave the peace of the mountain, anyway. She headed toward the room where she had stayed before, but hesitated as a memory struck her. "Auri," she asked uncertainly, "did the Hounds survive my...attack?"

Auraltiferys turned to face her, having paused in the doorway on the opposite side of the den. He smiled and replied, "Yes, they did. The Hounds cannot be killed, Iris, not even by a demon."

"Oh, good," she exhaled, relieved but also confused. She still didn't know exactly what the Empyreal Hounds were, but she had asked plenty of questions for one day. She turned away from her mentor, then stopped herself and faced him again. "One last thing," she added, rather sheepishly. Auraltiferys showed no sign of irritation at the further interruption, though it was apparent he was exhausted, both physically and mentally.

"Yes?" he inquired placidly.

"I'm sorry I tried to kill you," she stated simply.

He prodded at his injured chest with a slight grimace, then replied, "All is forgiven, Iris. My body will be sore; my soul shall not be. But please, do strive to refrain from such evils from now on. Now go and do those parts of your penance you can now do, and sleep well. I will see you in the morning."

Iris nodded, wished him a good night, and then returned to her room, where she slept soundly.

* * *

She awoke in the early morning to the metallic heartbeat of the mountain, knowing Auraltiferys must already be hard at work in his forge. She waited for him in the den, reading from a few of his ancient tomes. When he entered, covered in soot and sweat, he was carrying a hefty, dual-bladed axe of exquisitely burnished bronze. Intricate runes graced the edges of each blade. He extended the weapon to her, and she accepted it with cautious uncertainty. She was amazed at its weight and astounded by its beautiful craftsmanship, but she had no idea what Auraltiferys intended it for.

"It's yours," he said, as if in response to her thoughts. "It has been revealed to me you may need a weapon, and the Spirit has directed me in this way." He nodded at the axe now in Iris's hands.

She gently waved the axe around for a few seconds, then reviewed its inscriptions again and looked at her mentor with questioning eyes. "It's a gorgeous weapon," she admitted, "but...what do I do with it? And what do these inscriptions mean? Isn't this character the mark of Satan?"

"It is," the blacksmith replied, brusquely wiping his face with his forearm. "I was reluctant to inscribe it, but it is not for me to question the Holy Spirit that guides me. There is no need to fear it. The mark of Satan is not evil, and neither is it prudent to pretend the Devil does not exist. You, likewise, are marked by Satan, but you have chosen to direct your nature back toward your true Creator and his. Perhaps this piece will be to you a constant reminder of that fact." After a brief pause, he recalled Iris's first question and continued, "As for its purpose, it is a magical weapon. You are to use it in your battle against evil. It is similar in magic to my own blade, but it has particular unique powers. I trust you will discover those on your own, however." His eyes glittered with mirth at his intentional mysteriousness. "Carry it with you at all times," he added, with sudden seriousness in his tone. "You will not know when it will be needed."

Iris sighed. "It's easy for you to carry a weapon everywhere," she answered in frustration. "You don't live in the same physical realm I live in, Auri. I can't just walk around out there with an axe sticking out of my purse or strapped on my thigh, although I admit I would love to do that." She couldn't help but think how badass she would look if that were a viable option.

The blacksmith grabbed the axe and looked down at her from his towering height with disapproval of her exasperation. In silence, he magically resized the weapon to no larger than a charm for a necklace or bracelet, then offered it back to her on an open palm. She accepted it graciously, with her eyes lowered and a smile on her lips. Without saying a word, Auraltiferys had reminded her how little she really knew and how much she still had to learn.

27

Armed with the results of a brief investigation and committed to the decisions she had made after all she had learned since her most recent excursion to the holy mountain, Iris placed herself inside Loomis's lavish Portland office, not bothering to knock. He was standing at the opposite side of the large room, staring out the expansive windows to the overcast sky and the view below, his hands clasped behind his back.

Sensing her entry, but not turning to face her, he said, derisively, "Well, do come in, Iris. Of course there is no need for you to knock. Please, make yourself comfortable."

Iris seated herself on the couch in front of his desk, recalling how nervous she had been the last time she was here. She knew so much more now, and she felt no fear. Loomis returned to his desk chair as she sat down, and he surveyed her with dark gravity in his expression.

"You seem...rather *holy*," he stated blandly.

Iris flashed him a small, humble smile and replied, "Holier than I was, maybe, but nowhere near where I need to be."

Loomis shifted rather uncomfortably in his seat, rolling his eyes, then asked, "What brings you here?" Iris guessed he was glad to see her so-called holiness, as it could signify safety from the eternal torments with which she had threatened him, but he was too proud to show it.

"I have a proposition for you," she answered.

Loomis reclined in his chair and threw his feet onto his desk, crossing his ankles. His meticulously polished shoes reflected the same luxury as his furniture. "If you are suddenly striving for sainthood, should you really be making deals with demons?" he asked tauntingly. How nice it was to see he hadn't completely lost all his evil charm.

"It isn't much of a deal, I'm afraid," Iris replied. "I don't expect you to keep your word, but I will ask for it anyway. That sounds foolish, I know, but..." She paused for effect, then continued, "I *am* willing to trust your fear of me. You should know, I will not allow you free rein on this Earth, and if you choose to breach the terms of our contract, I will punish you, severely."

Loomis blinked, subconsciously disclosing a hint of uneasiness. The agitation was hidden from his expression in an instant, however, and his features set in hard seriousness. "If I ever feared you," he said, with a tangible bite in his voice, "I see no further need of it now, as you have obviously cast away your Satanic inclinations."

Iris returned his gaze steadily, feeling her own arrogance simmering somewhere inside her. She wanted to hurt him again, to remind him of her strength; instead, she fought to remind herself all power was only borrowed, and she had vowed to use it rightly.

"I may endeavor to avoid all sin as best I can, Loomis," she said evenly, "but what I am, I am. You *know* what that is. I have chosen to spare humanity that evil, with God's help. The denizens of Hell do not enjoy that same security and should therefore tread with utmost caution and at their own peril." A drop of venom had entered her voice as she spoke, and Loomis pressed the matter no further.

"Tell me your proposition, then," he prompted dryly.

Iris leaned forward, setting her elbows on her knees, and responded pointedly, "For your part, I want you to leave me alone, for good. No trickery, no temptations, no asking me for help; none of that."

"How very trite," Loomis commented, with another eye roll.

Iris stared at him with unamused, cautionary coldness. After a lengthy pause, she continued, "You are to leave the human race alone, too. I realize I can't stop you from tempting people from God, but I can tell you to cease all physical harm to them. And, obviously, you will dispense with the shadow-demon idea. I've already removed it from Earth, and I expect you to leave it that way. I care not what you do in Hell, but if you choose to continue dwelling on Earth, you'll be subject to my governance."

Loomis chuckled mirthlessly. "I do hope whatever you're offering me in return is something of incalculable value, Iris," he said, "for it sounds as though you intend to take from me the only things that bring any joy to my existence."

"Well, sadly, I can't help you with that," Iris answered. "You've shunned the only source of true joy." She leaned back into the couch and added, "But you're industrious. Maybe you can find a different hobby."

Loomis stood from his chair, walked to his espresso machine, and brewed himself a cup, all without emotion and without speech. Iris allowed the lingering silence as he finally returned to his desk, having offered her no coffee.

"What *do* you offer me," he finally asked, "if you are prepared to request such lofty sacrifices on my part?" His dark eyes stared down into the cup in his hands rather than looking at his visitor.

"Knowledge," Iris replied simply. He lifted his eyes to meet hers briefly, then focused on his coffee once more. "I know how you appreciate knowledge," she proceeded, "and this revelation in particular will be of great interest to you, because it will answer the question you've been unable to answer for yourself with regard to your shadow-demon. You must want to know why it never worked as you intended."

Loomis looked up at her again, this time setting his cup down on the desk and straightening in his chair, arms crossed and eyes narrowed.

"That's not all," Iris added. She leaned forward again, stared intently at Loomis, and said, "Someone tricked you, and I know you must want to know who did it."

Loomis held her gaze for a discerning moment, as if searching her expression for any hint of treachery. He eventually looked away, staring straight ahead of him with empty eyes, obviously far away in thought. Even should he distrust her, Iris knew he would be enraged by just the possibility someone else had deceived him somehow. He would have to accept her deal; he would be unable to bear the idea of having been hoodwinked. He might complain of the "sacrifices" Iris was asking of him, but he would, of course, almost certainly fail to uphold his end of this bargain. Iris would simply execute justice upon him then as required. There was, effectively, no downside here for either of them, really; if Iris recognized that, so also would Loomis recognize it. *And who knows*, she wondered. *Maybe he really will keep his word, after all.* That would make her life a lot easier, but she wasn't going to hold her breath for it.

Loomis sat quietly for what felt like a long time, though it was perhaps only a minute. Finally, he stirred and uncrossed his arms, leaning forward so that his elbows rested on the desk. He interlaced his fingers in front of him and directed his attention back to Iris, anger glowing like embers behind his eyes. "I will accept your terms," he said stonily, his voice low and cold and unfeeling.

As she looked at him, Iris felt a terrible pang of sympathy. It was an emotion not completely foreign to her with regard to Loomis, but she had allowed the Devil in her to drive those feelings away each time she had felt them before. She knew he was not a human man, but he was certainly a convincing imitation of one, in both appearance and action, and she was suddenly saddened to think what he must have been, once. The demons had all been counted among the Heavenly host before they had rebelled. Iris wished he had made different decisions, not because it would have made her existence an easier one, but because she now recognized Heaven had lost something wonderful. She questioned whether she would feel the same way if Loomis had created for himself a less gentlemanly, less handsome persona. Perhaps her human nature was simply being deluded by this demon's outward, earthly appearance. After all, he had chosen Hell for himself; it wasn't as though God had forced it upon him. There was really no reason to feel sorry for him.

Iris eventually realized she had fallen silent after Loomis's statement, temporarily straying into the metaphysical realm of thought and emotion. She found Loomis still staring at her, but a hint of puzzlement had entered his expression.

"Did you hear me?" he asked sharply. "I said I will accept your terms."

Iris sighed softly and rose from her seat. "Yes, I heard you," she answered with a touch of sadness, walking around his desk to stand beside him. Loomis swiveled his chair as she approached, so that he could continue to face her from a slightly more comfortable distance. She pulled the spearhead from the pocket of her jacket and held it out to him. He looked at her distrustfully but then accepted the relic from her, waiting for her to impart her new wisdom. "This isn't a true relic," she told him. "It's a counterfeit."

Loomis inspected the spearpoint with cursory interest, then set it beside him on his desk. His face remained emotionless, but a slight pulse of a vein in his neck made it evident he was angered by her statement.

"It's identical to the true relic in every way except substance, which is, of course, why it couldn't do what you wanted it to," Iris went on. "This copy was cloaked with spells that mimic the original magical alloy of the spearhead, but the maker of this replica couldn't fully imitate the magic that was cast into the original by the Knights."

Loomis allowed disgust to descend across his elegant features as he shook his head. "I should have recognized it," he murmured acidly, as if to himself.

"You couldn't have recognized it, unless you had known the exact spiritual resonance to expect from the spearhead," Iris replied. "Very few, if any, outside the Knights would know that." She thought briefly, then added quietly, "I do believe the true relic would have worked for you. The science in your plan was, I hate to say, flawless, if that is any consolation."

Loomis seemed to find no comfort in her supportive remark. "You know who created this worthless imitation?" he asked after a brief silence.

Iris nodded. "Dr. Marvin Whitakker," she said. "The curator of the university museum from where your shadow-demon stole the spearhead. He's a demon. Well, not a demon exactly...more of a super-possessed human soul. I can't exactly describe the relationship I witnessed in them, and I won't even claim to understand how it came about. A demon seems to have, um, *borrowed* some of your research. He couldn't create a human body for himself like you did, but it turned out he didn't have to. Marvin Whitakker was a man so strangely kindred to that particular demon's spirit that he gave the demon free use of his body. They have a sick sort of mutualism going on in there. The demon has full control, but Marvin is right in there with him, not subjugated or tormented, but loving his life. He gets to enjoy the knowledge and power of a demon without having to work or feel any pain, at least until his body's earthly death, and his demon gets to enjoy a human life here on Earth, in a career field he apparently has taken great interest in." She shrugged, then added, "I guess it would be inspirational if it weren't so twisted. Anyway, he knew the significance of the piece when it fell into his lap as part of that weaponry exhibit. He took the real relic and made that copy. I don't know for sure if he expected you to come for it, but he certainly knew the intrinsic value of the relic, and he wanted it for himself."

Loomis scowled, then asked, "How do you know all this?"

"I visited the museum," Iris answered. "Thankfully, the answer was right there and not buried somewhere back in the relic's decades-old history of ownership transfers. I posed as a doctoral student studying pre-Columbian history, and Dr. Whitakker was all too happy to discuss the topic with me. I'm fortunate he has such enthusiasm for his work, because it made him quite oblivious to my true natures. I was able to study him rather easily during our conversation, and I was immediately certain he—or, more accurately, the unnamed demon inside him—was the culprit. After some simple reconnaissance, I discovered the little abode he's created for himself under the museum. He had the original spearhead hidden away down there in his rather impressive collection of pilfered history."

"You already found the true relic?" Loomis asked, with mild interest and a touch of surprise.

"Yes," Iris asserted. "I've repurposed it and moved it, of course, along with all the other relics you had amassed; I would not otherwise share this information with you. And I will need the replica back. I'm going to help the police with their investigation of the museum theft. I'll have to return this copy to Marvin's hideaway before sending the detectives there."

"And what of their investigation into the dead security guard?" Loomis asked. "Do you plan to assist them with that as well?"

Iris stared impassively at him for a moment, then answered

slowly, "That crime, I'm afraid, is to remain for them unsolved in this age."

Loomis looked at her steadily, understanding the tacit meaning in her words. She was giving him Marvin Whitakker practically free of charge, but for the stipulations that he leave her alone from now on and avoid future physical harm to humankind. She had no intention of revealing to anyone Loomis's true identity or his involvement with the museum theft and the unexplained, mysterious death of the guard.

He finally lowered his eyes and turned toward his desk. He grabbed the counterfeit relic from beside him and stood from his chair, turning to face Iris, a frown on his face. She was close enough to him to smell his cologne, and the fragrance carried her mind back through memories of their previous interactions, those times when Loomis had tempted her and those times when she had made him regret it. For an instant, she imagined she might be truly sad if she never saw him again. He silently offered the spearhead back to her. She took it in her hand and returned it to her jacket pocket, not removing her eyes from his.

After a long, heavy minute, Loomis finally spoke, his voice subdued. "Do you require some physical ratification of our deal?" he asked. "Perhaps you want me to sign something in blood?" His tone held some disinterested-sounding sarcasm.

"No," Iris answered him, surprised at the sorrow in her own tone. "I will accept your word alone."

"Then," Loomis replied, "I suppose this is goodbye."

Iris, suddenly very reluctant to leave him, stopped herself just after she had started to move away. "Loomis," she said gently, hesitantly, "I was excessively harsh in my evil toward you. You're a demon, but...that doesn't give me license to torture you. I don't know if you can feel real pain anymore, but...if I have caused you any real pain, I'm...I'm sorry." She felt heat in her cheeks and a tear threatening to escape her eye, but she managed to maintain her composure.

Sadness darted across his dark eyes only for a nearly imperceptible instant. Iris saw him swallow inconspicuously, then he answered her only by saying, "Goodbye, Dr. Wakefield."

She stood unmoving for another few seconds as Loomis turned away from her and returned to his post at the window, standing there with impeccable posture in his impeccably tailored slacks and vest and dress shirt, arms clasped behind him.

***

When Iris transported herself back to her bedroom an instant later, she felt numb and empty. She sat on the edge of her bed, looked to the Saint Benedict's cross above her nightstand, and recalled vividly how Loomis had brought himself here not long ago to goad her back toward Heaven when she had let her demonic nature derail so treacherously. She shook her head, straining to keep herself from crying. There was just something about him she couldn't quite identify, something that had always prevented her from *truly* hating him. Something that, judging from her feelings now, she had actually grown to like about him. She stopped short of calling it love, because that was a terrifying and painful thought. But she couldn't stop the whisper in the back of her mind, telling her there was more to Loomis Drake than met the eye, telling her there was something more for her to know about him.

***

Loomis remained motionless in front of his window for a minute after he felt Iris leave, staring out at nothing in particular.

Eventually, he turned and walked numbly to the bar at the side of his office. He opened a bottle of sixty-year-old scotch and poured himself a generous glass of it. He drank it quickly, then threw the glass into the sink, shattering it. There had been a time he almost enjoyed that drink; now it had no taste at all.

He leaned against the counter, clenching his fingers tightly around the edge of it. He closed his eyes and gritted his teeth, trying to force real anger into his mind. He would have his vengeance against Marvin Whitakker, of course, and that should be his focus now. That insignificant, nameless demon bastard inside him had not only stolen some of his work in order to gain tangible access to Earth and find a human vessel in which to dwell, but it had then recognized the copper spearhead as the powerful relic it was and had tricked Loomis out of it before he had even known the difference. Marvin would pay dearly for that deceit.

But the promise of revenge felt void and meaningless, and Loomis knew exactly why, though he didn't want to admit it. He had found an equal in Iris Wakefield, another being who could challenge him and give some new purpose to his otherwise monotonous existence, and now she was gone. Had her effect on him been solely the presentation of an obstacle to overcome, the proposition to which he had just agreed would not have been such a difficult one. But, unfortunately, Iris had somehow changed him. Perhaps it was the strength of her demonic nature, the fact she could match his own power, that had caused him to respect her, even *like* her, both of which were uncharacteristic sympathies for him. It would be the most palatable explanation, but it would be only a partial truth, if there were any truth in it at all. Iris was a dual being, both demon and human, and he could not give credit or blame for her effect on him to either nature individually. In fact, it was her human nature in which he had recognized something that scratched at the deepest recesses of his memory, the part of his existence that lay so far back in temporal reality that he had believed it erased. To have these particular memories awakened was a painful torment, though he could not fault Iris for that. He had made his decisions. He had to continue existing with the consequences of those decisions. That realization was evidence in itself that he was different now, that Iris had transformed him, even if only slightly; what demon should even consider the consequences of his own actions?

He shook his head vigorously and then slammed both fists into the dark marble countertop of the bar, rattling the espresso machine and other various bottles and glassware upon it. Iris didn't matter now. Nothing mattered, except holding Marvin Whitakker accountable for his misdeeds.

And what after that? he heard his thoughts nagging him. *When Marvin has been dealt with, then what?* He grimaced and tugged at his hair as he walked to his desk and flung himself angrily into his chair. That was the worst part of all of this, and it was unavoidable. Dealing with Marvin would be but a temporary reprieve, and after that was done, Loomis foresaw nothing but drudgery for his existence. Iris wanted nothing to do with him, and she had forbidden him from harming the human race. Temptations were too easy; they were as flavorless now as that pricey Scotch whisky. Tormenting demons was a worthless endeavor. Even Hell's throne seemed overrated now. What good was ruling Hell if he could not then send his armies to overtake the Earth? He would be about as powerful as a child wearing a paper crown.

He took a shuddering breath and closed his eyes, leaning his head against the back of his chair. It wasn't ideal, but if he preferred existence with Iris in it, then he would have to renege on the word he had just given her. The thought of dishonoring their agreement actually made him feel sick—not out of fear for what Iris might do to him, but because he actually wanted his promise to her to have meant something real. When she had expressed her belief that he would never maintain his end of the contract, it had made him want to prove her wrong. Now, however, faced with the melancholy reality of an endless existence without any purpose, he would be forced to submit to his own selfish desires. Iris would punish him, as many times as he could claw his way back from Hell, but maybe one day she would slip up, and he could try once more to win her to his side.

28

Crane slammed the phone into its cradle with a loud thud of plastic on plastic, missing the appropriate placement on the first attempt and having to repeat the angry action twice more before succeeding.

"God *damn* it!" he bellowed. "I'm sick of this!"

Banks had jerked slightly in his chair at the slamming of the phone and now was staring at his partner from across their desks with wide eyes and extreme concern. "Holy hell, Crane," he said furtively, his eyes darting sideways at other officers who had briefly turned their attention toward the commotion. "Calm down, brother; what's up now?"

Crane sighed heavily and looked around the room apologetically. "Yeah, yeah," he addressed the others. "Sorry, everybody. Go back to your work." Turning back to Myron as he roughly rubbed his eyes, he sighed again and answered, "We got another weird one. Vandalism and possible arson at that old cotton gin downtown."

Banks was already standing from his chair to put on his coat. "Shit," he replied. "Is this another one of those cult things?"

There had been two other bloody deaths after the museum incident, one a young kid and the other a middle-aged man in a hooded cloak, both found together in the middle of the street near a vacant lot in the shabbiest part of the downtown area. After some asshat in the media caught wind of it and referred to it as a possible "cult killing," all sorts of weird shit had started. Most of it had turned out to be the work of no-good teenagers with absentee parents and too much time on their hands, but a couple of incidents had been more than that. In one instance, they had received a timely tip and managed to arrest some guy who had claimed to be a Druid priest just as he was setting fire to a young woman in some ritualistic sacrifice in front of a group of fellow "pagan" onlookers, all of whom were nutcases. The girl had been rushed to the hospital and had third-degree burns over a quarter of her body, but she was alive. That, Crane now realized, had been just about the only success story he and Banks had enjoyed since that late-night call to the museum. The museum case and the double-murder downtown remained unsolved, and the detectives had been unable to determine whether those crimes were related in any way. Neither of them had known a moment's peace since they had first laid eyes on poor Joshua Ellis in that museum.

"Christ, I hope not," Crane answered, shaking his head and standing to put on his coat. "Guess we'll see," he added somberly. "The patrol that called it in said there appeared to be some animal sacrifices and strange symbols drawn in blood."

Banks snickered bitterly. "Would it be too much to ask for just a plain crime? Remember when we used to get those?"

"Yup," Crane sighed, "I remember. Who'd have thought we'd call those the good old days?"

Banks shook his head as the pair began walking toward the front of the station. "We have to catch a break soon," he said, "because I'm seriously worried about both of us. This is...I don't know, man. Everything since the museum has been tough."

As the pair neared their exit through the doors of the reception area, they were stopped by an officer at the front desk. "Detective Crane," the young man called, motioning for Crane to come back. Crane grunted and mindlessly smoothed his mustache, then shot a glance at Banks, who stepped to the side of the doorway to await his partner's return.

"Yeah?" Crane asked, returning to the front desk. The officer was speaking with a young woman, maybe early thirties and reasonably attractive, who was now facing him and standing patiently with her hands inside the pockets of her black leather jacket. There was intensity in her face, though Crane couldn't readily identify what made him think that. Maybe it was the combination of the knee-high boots and the leather jacket and all their zippers and buckles. Not a biker look, exactly—that description would have too negative a connotation. She looked dignified and intelligent, but also tough somehow. He didn't doubt this girl could handle herself in a fight.

"Detective Crane, this is Iris Wakefield," the officer stated. "She's come here with some possible information on the museum case."

It was an unexpected statement, and Crane felt his eyebrows press together before he could stop them. He was suddenly suspicious of the woman, though she didn't look like a criminal. He cleared his throat and addressed her as he fished a business card from his wallet. "Well, uh, Ms. Wakefield," he said, handing the card to her, "why don't you take my card and leave a report with this officer here, and I'll follow up with you later. My partner and I are headed out on a call, so now isn't a great time, I'm afraid."

The woman took the card and glanced at it, then stuck it in her pocket and replied evenly, "I'm sorry, Detective, but I'll speak with you only in person. Your colleague here suggested I do as you say, but I've been most stubborn with him." She smiled at the officer at the desk, then returned her focus to Crane and continued, "To his credit, he's been nothing but gracious and understanding, but I'm sure he would appreciate it if you'd spare me ten minutes of your time so he never has to deal with me again."

"Oh, no, ma'am," the officer piped up cheerfully. "It's no trouble at all, really. I'm happy to help you."

Crane had to hide a flicker of amusement from crossing his face. *Yeah*, he thought, *can't wait to help out when it's a pretty lady at the desk.* How many times a day did officers complain among each other about the creeps and freaks and busybodies that came in here all the time? *'Happy to help,' my ass.*

"Well, all the same," Iris proceeded, "I'll be happy to set an appointment if you can't meet with me now, but..." She paused and gave him a pointed look. "You look like a man who could use a break in this case," she continued, "and I see no reason your highly competent partner can't get started out there without you."

Her gold-laced green eyes held something particularly convincing. Crane wasn't sure what it was, but she had made a decent point, and he was inclined to accede to her request. He thought silently for a second, then he said, "All right, sure. Give me a sec." He walked over to Myron, who had been watching from near the front doors.

"Listen, can you head out there without me? I'll meet up with you. This girl says she has info on the museum theft," Crane said as he tore a page out of his notebook and handed it to Banks.

Banks, surprised, took the note, glanced cursorily at the few things written on it, and replied, "Sure thing. You think she can tell us anything useful?" He lifted his eyebrows toward the young woman.

Crane scratched his head. "I don't know, but, frankly, I'm willing to pick at any hint of a lead right now." As Banks nodded in agreement, he added, "Anyway, shouldn't take me long. I'll be out there right after I hear whatever she has to say."

Banks wished him good luck and proceeded out the doors, and Crane returned to the woman waiting for him.

"Follow me," he invited her, rather gruffly. "You want a water or soda or anything?"

"No, thank you," she replied, following him to his desk.

Crane pulled Myron's chair to the side of his own desk and waved for Iris to sit down, but she hesitated, glancing around the room and all its desks and personnel.

"Is there a more private room where we can talk?" she asked. "I'm not the trusting type."

Ugh, here we go, Crane thought. *This lady's going to turn out to be one of those crazy paranoid types who see shit on the news and then get the bright idea to go to the police with useless information.* Aloud, after a brief and rather awkward silence, which seemed to bother him much more than it bothered Iris, he suggested they could use one of the interrogation rooms. He led her that way, and several seconds later, the two stood in the quiet of a closed room.

Iris seated herself in a metal chair on one side of the table in the center of the room. Crane noted that she placed herself with her back to the two-way mirror, opposite where they would seat a criminal suspect. He stood with his back to the door for a moment, then cleared his throat again and sat down across from her, pulling his notebook out and readying his pen. "All right, Miss, um, Iris," he began.

"Wakefield," she responded helpfully, recognizing Crane's memory lapse. "But it isn't important."

"I have to record my sources and everything," he said, with a mild touch of frustration. "We have protocols to follow."

"This case isn't going to resign itself to your protocols," Iris replied gravely. Something in her tone prompted Crane to raise his eyes from where he had been writing her name on his notepad and look at her. Her expression was dark and serious, and he was strangely creeped out by it. He opened his mouth to respond, only to find he had no clue what he wanted to say. Iris, though, had clearly not expected a reply from him and continued, "Detective Crane, I know who stole the artifact from the museum. I know how the security guard was killed. I can explain it all to you, and you may find peace in it, but the information I offer cannot be written into your reports nor made any part of a case file. Once you hear the truth, however, I doubt you will even *want* to document it."

Crane was stunned by her assertiveness, but also irritated by it. "Listen, Ms. Wakefield," he answered decidedly, "I don't know who you think you are, coming in here like this, but you're either crazy or you've been watching too many cop movies. We follow protocols, and that's how it's going to be in this case, too." It wasn't until after he had finished speaking that his brain registered she had claimed to know how the security guard was killed. That was suspicious. This whole scenario was weird and uncomfortable.

Iris had listened to his little soapbox proclamation with either disdain or disinterest in her face; Crane wasn't sure which. She let a hush fall over the room after he finished, then responded, "You're a good man, Detective Crane, and I respect your work ethic. Do take all the notes you need to; I shouldn't have suggested otherwise." Her voice was steady and not uncaring or recognizably disingenuous, but there was an odd sort of coldness to it.

"Fine," Crane answered, suddenly nervous, as though he had asked permission from this woman to take his notes and had very nearly been denied such permission. "Uh, go ahead and tell me whatever you wanted to share."

"The copper spearhead was stolen by the museum curator, Marvin Whitakker," Iris stated simply.

Crane wrote nothing and instead looked at her with a furrowed brow. He knew Whitakker couldn't have taken the spearhead. There was no evidence of it in the security footage. "Ms. Wakefield," he said, attempting to lean back in his chair before recalling it was bolted to the floor. After adjusting his seated position with a sigh, he continued, "We've checked him out already. There's no evidence he stole the spearhead."

"You'll find the artifact among a cache of other stolen relics in a hideout Marvin has created for himself under the museum," Iris replied. The woman didn't *look* crazy, but her words were proving she was.

"What?" Crane asked. "You realize this sounds ridiculous, right? Don't waste my time."

"This is nothing but the tip of the iceberg when it comes to ridiculous," she retorted. "I warned you, you wouldn't want to document the truth once you heard it. Do you want to know the truth about Joshua Ellis's murder?" She maintained a calm, poised demeanor, with a soft but confident voice.

Crane, stupefied, answered, "What do you know about that?"

Iris returned his gaze with her intense, green eyes. "His soul was torn from his body by a demonic entity that has since been relegated to Hell," she asserted. "That's why you find degraded security footage and no trace of physical evidence. It's why Joshua's body was so cold, why his heart appeared like stone, why his eyes were so grotesque and inhuman…and why good-hearted people can hardly stand to look at the aftermath."

Crane felt his body going numb as he listened. The pen fell out of his fingers, and anxiety settled in his gut as his mind instantly recalled the matte, black eyes of the dead young man. Nothing had been reported to the press about the strange findings during the autopsy, especially those eyes. Nothing official, anyway, and he hadn't caught wind of any rumors being strung about, except for the whisperings that the spearhead had been haunted. That little anecdote had somehow leaked…had the strange, disgusting appearance of those dead eyes leaked, too? There was no other way she could know…

He shook his head slowly from side to side, mindlessly, completely at a loss for words. He wanted to believe Iris's statements, but...they were just so ludicrous, so unbelievable. And yet she was so serious. She must believe her own theories, and that would make her either insane or right. And there had been no shortage of inexplicable shit in this case—the awful, dead eyes; the indeterminate cause of death; the screwed-up videotape and that creepy shadow in its frozen frame...Crane realized after a long silence that he had neglected to blink. He roused himself and rubbed his tired eyes, then sighed and decided to follow his gut instinct. He just couldn't convince himself Iris Wakefield was insane.

"Okay," he said, his voice gritty from having dried out while his jaw hung open in shock. "Say I want to believe what you're telling me. How...how do you know these things? Are you a psychic or something?" He would try to keep an open mind here; God knew nothing else had worked in their investigation so far.

Iris didn't respond immediately. She sat still, looking at Crane and obviously thinking. He couldn't help but feel he was being analyzed, and it made him nervous.

"Detective," she finally answered, slowly and quietly, "are you a churchgoing man?"

Crane lowered his eyes and shifted apprehensively in the hard chair. Clearing his throat, he replied, "Um, well, not really so much anymore. What does that have to do with anything?"

"Is that because you stopped believing in God?" Iris questioned in reply.

"No," Crane answered, "I just...I don't know." He fell silent and wondered why he was even engaging in this conversation with this stranger, but somehow, he just felt inclined to confide in her. Sighing again, he continued, "Life happens, you know? And somehow the idea of having to go to confession is just...really unappealing."

Iris's lips moved into a very slight smile, one full of understanding. "Detective Crane," she said, "you have to forgive yourself for what happened all those years ago. The only thing keeping you from the Church is your own self-blame, and that comes from the Devil."

Crane felt a sudden, shameful heat in his face, as though Iris had peered right into his past and found the skeletons there. He argued with the emotion as soon as he sensed it; there was no way she could know his past. If she was one of those self-purported psychics, she was used to reading people and spouting off generalities that could apply to pretty much anyone. He couldn't let that fool him.

Iris spoke again before he could respond. With her eyes piercing hard into his, she said, "When you were in high school, you fell in love with a girl in your class, and the two of you had planned to marry and have a long, happy life together. She became pregnant during her junior year, and you panicked. You loved her, but you were only a teenager yourself and not ready for a child of your own. You encouraged her to have an abortion, which she ended up doing. She was so racked with guilt over it that she committed suicide three months later. You remember her to this day, and you still suffer the thoughts of the child—your child—whom you never knew. You love them both, even now, and you blame yourself for their deaths."

Crane was stricken by grief and pain as Iris narrated for him. His hands trembled, and tears came out before he could even try to stop them. He rose hastily from the chair and backed away from the table, leaning himself against the wall and putting as much distance as he could between Iris and himself. How in God's name did she know these things about him? Christ, his own wife didn't even know. He had never told anyone, not a parent or a sibling or a priest or a counselor—no one. By the time Iris had finished speaking, he was breathing heavily, with tears streaking down his hot cheeks.

"Who...or what...are you?" he asked shakily. He was ready to believe just about anything, because the words that had just escaped this woman's mouth must have come from God Himself.

Iris stood from her seat but remained on the opposite side of the table. "You will not believe me if I tell you," she answered, in barely more than a whisper.

"Try me," Crane replied, wiping tears from his face.

"I was intended to be the human incarnation of Satan," she responded flatly, after a lengthy pause. "God intervened and gave me a human soul and free will, and now I am both demon and human."

Crane, dumbstruck, stared at her for a long, tense moment, then swallowed and shook his head. "No," he said. "No, no...I don't know who you are or how you found out those things about me, but you need to leave, right now."

Iris, with no emotion evident in her expression, remained unmoving. "What Satan knows," she said, "I also know. And I know he has tormented you about your past for long enough. God's mercy is infinite; I myself am evidence of that. You need only ask for that mercy, and you should be unafraid to do it. You stumbled upon a dark and unholy plot with this museum case, and you have stepped very close to powerful evils you're not aware of. You should thank God for having seen you safely through it."

Crane, suddenly enraged, yelled, "Get out of here, now, or I'll have you removed!" He had no reason to be angry, but it was a simpler emotion than all the others that were threatening to overwhelm him now. When Iris made no move to leave, he pulled out his handcuffs and started purposefully toward her. "Fine," he growled. "We'll do this the hard way."

Iris helpfully held out her wrists in front of her as he approached. Crane slapped the cuffs on her and turned to lead her toward the door, but the metallic clink of the cuffs dropping onto the table stopped him. When he looked back at Iris, she was picking them off of the table.

"You'll need something more durable," she remarked casually, holding the cuffs out in front of her on one outstretched index finger, "if you want to restrain me."

Suddenly, inexplicably, the cuffs began to melt away from where she held them, silvery ooze dripping from the bottom cuff and then off of Iris's finger, until nothing was left of them but a puddle of molten metal resting on the tabletop.

"What the *fuck*?" Crane exclaimed, stepping away from her.

"Do you need more parlor tricks, Detective Crane, or are you now prepared—fully prepared—to believe me?" Iris asked.

Crane hesitated where he stood, his mind as useless right now as those handcuffs. He pressed his back against the wall. Should he pull his gun on her? Should he reach for the door two long steps away and call out for backup? Or should he simply believe her, trust her? If his eyes had not deceived him and Iris really had just melted those cuffs somehow, psychically or magically or spiritually or whatever the fuck else it could be, then couldn't she have already killed him if that's what she wanted? In the passing instant in which his thoughts raced, he began to feel light-headed and nauseated. The room started to spin around him, and blackness started to creep into the edges of his vision. He began to faint, feeling his body give out under him. Iris stepped swiftly toward him and balanced him before he fell. Somehow, though Crane was at least three or four inches taller and probably fifty pounds heavier or more, Iris upheld him with seemingly no effort, and she walked him gently to the chair in which she had been sitting.

"Relax, Detective," she said soothingly. She placed a cool hand on his forehead, and the dizziness and queasiness vanished even more quickly than they had appeared. She removed her hand and squatted beside him, resting one hand on the table and the other on the back of his chair. Looking up at him, she asked again, "Do you believe me?"

Crane leaned forward and placed both elbows on the table, then rested his face there in his hands. After a few seconds, he pulled his hands away, sat back, and then looked down at the young woman next to him.

"Yeah," he said with a sigh. "Yeah, I think I believe you."

"Good," Iris replied. "What I have told you about your case is true. Marvin Whitakker did steal the copper spearhead, and a demonic creation did kill Joshua Ellis. I can help you find where Whitakker has hidden the relic away, but you will find no evidence beyond that. You might try to arrest him, but I don't like your chances of success in a trial. And, obviously, the shadow-demon that killed Joshua will never submit to human laws."

Crane, still in shock but now actively trying to wrap his mind around Iris's words, answered, "Right. I...I get that. So, um, what do we do?"

Iris stood up and crossed her arms. "You'll have to leave Joshua's cause of death undetermined and let the case go cold," she began. "That's no closure for his family, but it will do less harm than telling them the truth. As for Marvin, you can arrest him for the theft. Maybe the discovery of his little collection of stolen artifacts will be enough to convict him." She shrugged, then added, "I admit, Detective, I don't know much more about criminal law than one learns from television. Maybe it isn't worth the effort. But if you do choose to pursue Whitakker about the spearhead, I must set one condition for you, and it is to be followed without deviation."

Crane scrunched up his eyebrows again, then consciously tried to relax them before asking, "What condition is that?"

"Do *not* go after him unless I'm with you," Iris urged, her expression stony and her voice sharp. "He's...dangerous."

"What do you mean, 'dangerous'?" Crane asked suspiciously. "And how the hell am I supposed to explain my taking a citizen along to make an arrest?"

Iris pursed her lips as she thought for a moment. "I guess you're not supposed to explain it," she admitted. "The best thing is for you to leave Whitakker alone. I can bring the spearhead back to you, and you can return it to the museum, and that can end your involvement with it. You can just say it was returned anonymously, or something like that."

Crane considered the suggestion, realizing what a crappy position this was. "Damn," he mused out loud, "I've never believed there was a case that couldn't be solved. And I hate the idea of letting that prick get away with this, especially knowing he had the damn artifact the whole time and then acted like a complete dick to Banks and me for the entire investigation." Remembering his outburst at Marvin in the museum and the bullshit lecture he had endured afterward on account of it, Crane felt a strong desire to punish the little troll. With an inspired thought, he asked, "Did Whitakker have anything at all to do with the guard's death?"

"No," Iris answered flatly.

"Damn," Crane repeated. He had hoped he could blame that on him, too, even if there was no substantial evidence. He deliberated for a moment, then looked at Iris again. "I guess you're right," he conceded, disappointment in his voice. "If you can return the spearhead, then…I guess we'll just let it be."

Iris nodded. "It's for the best," she replied. "I'm sorry you found yourself embroiled in this. Earth is no place for these antics. At least this will be some resolution, even if it won't be what you had wanted."

"That's fine," Crane said regretfully. "We were losing our minds with this case, anyway. I think we'll just be glad to get rid of it." He stood up from his chair and pushed it under the table. Turning to Iris and finding his brain prickling with disbelief all over again, he asked, "Is that everything, then?" He hoped to God it was, because he was struggling enough with the supposed truths that had been told to him in the last several minutes. He still couldn't believe this woman claimed to be the Devil.

"What will you tell Detective Banks about me?" Iris asked pointedly. The question caught Crane off guard; he hadn't even made that consideration yet.

"Uh, well..." Crane stuttered, his voice trailing off into oblivion.

Iris interrupted, thankfully. "You know him better than I," she said. "I suppose you should trust your judgment with him. But I'm a shrewd judge of character, and there are reasons I chose to speak with you and not with him. I surmised you would be more apt to believe me, and, besides that, you're stronger than your partner in terms of spiritual fortitude."

"How do you figure that?" Crane asked, surprised. He hadn't been to Mass except for Christmas and Easter for the last twenty years or so, and he hadn't been to confession since his confirmation. But, he supposed, Banks wasn't the spiritual type, either. At least, he had never known Myron to be particularly spiritual.

Iris held his gaze steadily with her green eyes, full of seriousness. "You've been away from your Catholic upbringing for some time," she said, "but at least you've had the sacraments of initiation. Your partner has never been baptized."

"What, really? I guess I didn't know that," Crane acknowledged. "But he's a good guy. And he had his two girls baptized, I know that."

"His goodness isn't in question," Iris replied gently. "But I believe he had his girls baptized only because his wife insisted upon it. His belief in God is not as strong as hers, or as yours, for that matter, and that makes him vulnerable. You have both come very near the forces of Hell, unknowingly and without adequate preparation. It has been a far more dangerous situation than you could have imagined, and you should be grateful to have been protected throughout it. See to it, Detective Crane, that the case ends for you with my anonymous return of the spearhead. I won't keep you waiting too long. Detective Banks may want to investigate further. He may want to delve into it all again, and that would be even more treacherous now than it would have been before. Keep him away from Whitakker."

Crane listened quietly and then nodded his firm assent. The disbelief had been replaced by a sort of numb fascination and then an instinctive trust. Iris Wakefield might be the Devil, but she spoke more like a nun. He had a sudden urge to go to the chapel and pray. "I will," he finally answered her. His voice was heavy with resolve and with residual sorrow and guilt from the things Iris had said before.

Iris smiled understandingly, recognizing the pain in his tone. "I'll leave you now, Detective," she said. "I'll be back soon with the artifact, and you can put this behind you. You can put many things behind you."

She moved around the table toward the door to leave, but Crane stopped her with a clearing of his throat. Trying not to choke on his own words, he inquired shakily, "Do you know...do you know if...if they're okay? I mean, my...are they...are they in Heaven? Or in...?" He couldn't finish the final phrase, because it was too horrible to imagine. He hoped Iris knew what he was asking, because he couldn't be any clearer without breaking down into tears.

Iris grimaced slightly, empathetically. She knew what he was asking. "It hasn't been granted to me to know the particular judgment of any man or woman or child," she answered softly. "I have seen souls in Hell, but I know not their names nor their mortal bodies. I do know God's mercy is boundless, and He loves all His creation."

Crane brusquely wiped his eyes then put his hands on his hips and nodded, saying nothing further. Iris gave him one last meaningful glance and a tiny, sympathetic smile, then opened the door and exited.

Crane stood alone in the interrogation room for half a minute, praying he'd be able to keep it together once he found himself out there in the real world again. Finally, he walked back through the station and toward the front doors to get in his car and join his partner. The officer in the reception area stopped him again.

"Hey, Detective," he said as Crane approached the front desk, his eyes glancing around, probably searching for Iris. "Is Iris not with you?"

Called it, Crane thought to himself with an internal eye roll. "No," he answered. "She already left."

"Oh," came the dejected response. "Well, hey, did you happen to get her phone number? I was going to ask her for it. I've been watching for her; I swear I didn't see her leave."

"What the hell you want her phone number for?" Crane asked, playing dumb.

"Come on, Detective, don't bust my balls over it," the kid answered. "I'd like to ask her on a date. I felt a connection, you know?"

Crane actually smiled as he heard the words spoken. It was a funny thought, considering what Iris had just revealed herself to be. "Uh, yeah," he replied with a drawn-out breath and a shake of his head, "I really don't think she's your type."

"How would you know my type?" the officer questioned.

"Okay, I don't," Crane admitted with a chuckle. "I'm just trying to be polite. Truth is, she wouldn't be interested in you."

The officer smiled and shook his head. "You're an asshole," he said laughingly as Crane walked to the door.

"Yeah, yeah," Crane called back to the desk, jovially waving off the comment. He opened the glass door and stepped out into the brisk winter air, feeling suddenly more alive than he had felt in weeks.

29

Myron slung himself into his desk chair, causing it to roll a few inches so that he had to pull himself back toward his desk. "Well," he said with relief, "at least this one was easy enough."

"Yep," Crane agreed, seating himself heavily in his own chair. "Too bad for those poor cats though." Their most recent call out to the old gin had been a simple crime to solve. The fire marshal had determined a trio of Molotov cocktails to be the cause of the fire that had practically destroyed the abandoned, dilapidated building. Along the brick walls that still stood, crude pentagrams had been inartistically drawn in a combination of spray paint and blood. A half-dozen feral cats had been killed and left nearby; there was a plenitude of them in that area. Crane and Banks had been lucky enough to find an eyewitness, a homeless man who frequently set up roost behind the office buildings nearby, who had noticed a couple of teenagers climbing the chain-link fence that still stood along the edge of the gin's old parking lot. In their survey of the area, Banks had found a bloody pocketknife with initials carved into it, which would have been great evidence in itself, but fate had been even kinder than that—one of the kids had lost his wallet while scaling the fence, and the driver's license in it made it easy to locate at least one of the suspects. They visited the address and questioned the kid in front of his extremely angry parents, and the kid had sung like a canary. He confessed his own involvement and gave the names of every one of his fellow conspirators, claiming it was meant to be just a prank. Crane hoped they would all do time in jail, but they would probably get off easier than that. What kind of sick asswipe would kill a bunch of cats and call it a joke? The heathens would probably end up becoming serial murderers.

It was nearing eight o'clock in the evening, and Crane was tired and hungry, even though the simplicity of the recent investigation had been a pleasant and welcome change. He looked at Myron, who was staring at his computer screen and typing, and he shook his head. "Come on, Banks," he said. "It's late. Don't you want to get home to your girls?" He turned off his own monitors and stood up, ready to head home.

Banks tapped a few more keys, then checked his watch. "Whoa, you're right," he replied. "Yeah, I guess it's quitting time. I forgot what it's like to have such an easy case; I guess it inspired me." He chuckled as he shut down his computer and stood up, then he suddenly looked at Crane quizzically, tilting his head slightly to one side. "Hey," he said, "we were on such a roll out there today, I didn't even think to ask—what did that girl tell you earlier? About the museum case?"

Crane felt suddenly anxious, remembering the warning Iris had given him about Marvin Whitakker and keeping Myron away from him. He cleared his throat and shrugged. "Oh, that turned out to be nothing. She didn't have anything useful," he lied, turning away from Banks and starting toward the exit.

Banks followed him but didn't let the subject drop. "Well, what did she say? She had to have some theory," he pressed.

"No, not really," Crane grunted, finding it extremely uncomfortable to keep the truth from his partner and friend. Myron wasn't going to buy such a weak reply. "Well," he added, "I mean, she had a theory, just not a useful one. She suspected Dr. Whitakker had stolen the spearhead."

"Oh," Banks responded. He thought for a second, then asked, "Why'd she think that? Does she know him?"

Crane inhaled deeply, nervously, and tried to formulate some way to end the questioning. "I think maybe the girl reads too many mystery novels," he answered nonchalantly. "She just had it in her mind that the curator would have the best access but might seem like an unlikely suspect. I guess she thought we wouldn't have checked him out."

The two had exited the station into the chilly night air and were now standing near their cars under the yellow-orange light of a parking lot lamp. Crane wanted nothing more than to get in his car and get home to a sandwich and a beer, but he could tell from the thoughtful expression on Myron's face that he was going to keep poking at this. He couldn't fault his partner for wanting to press the issue; he'd be doing the same thing if their roles had been reversed.

"You know," Banks mused, "I've been thinking about that guy, Dr. Whitakker. He rubbed us both the wrong way, and I wonder if it's not our instincts trying to tell us something."

"I think the guy's just an asshole," Crane countered.

Banks shook his head, his eyebrows drawn together in deep thought. "I just don't know," he replied. "Yeah, he's an asshole, but...the more I think about him, the more creeped out I get. I think there was something off about him."

Crane sighed, hinting some exasperation in hopes of deterring further theorizing from Banks. "I wouldn't be surprised if the guy is a creep," he asserted. "He's probably got some kinky fetish or something, but come on, Banks. You know and I know he couldn't have taken the spearhead. We would have seen it on the security tapes.

The thing was there when the exhibit opened, and it was gone after the guard died. There's just no way he did it, even if he is a freak."

Banks looked down at the ground, then answered dejectedly, "Yeah, I guess you're right." He turned toward his car, then hesitated. "Let's go talk to him again tomorrow, just in case," he suggested. "We can tell him we just have some follow-up questions, and it'll give us a chance to feel him out some more. We have good instincts, Crane. If something's up, we'll know."

Crane reached a hand behind his head and scratched it, not from an itch but out of an anxious need to move. "I don't think it's a good idea," he said slowly. "I blew up on him last time, and—"

"Aw, come on, Crane," Banks interrupted with a broad, white smile. "You don't even have to say anything this time. I'll be bad-cop."

Crane fell silent, except for a grumble of displeasure from deep in his throat. Banks, undaunted, told him to sleep on it, then got in his car with a cheery "See ya in the morning." As Crane opened his own car door and sat stiffly in the driver's seat, watching Myron pull out of the lot, he had an unsettling certainty that his partner would feel no differently in the morning, and Iris's words came echoing back into his head. *Do not go after him*, she had stressed. *He's dangerous*. Crane now realized she had never told him why Marvin was dangerous, but...if she was what she had claimed to be, and what Crane himself felt compelled to believe she was, then it would be a foolish move indeed to ignore her warning. Yet he feared Myron might leave him no choice.

***

Banks approached his desk a little before eight in the morning, two large coffee cups in his hands. He extended one cup to Crane, who accepted it gladly, then he set his own cup down near the edge of his desk and reached into his coat pocket, retrieving a small paper bag, which he then also offered to Crane.

"What's this?" Crane asked as he took the bag and peeked inside.

"Coffee cake," Banks answered. "Figured I'd better sweeten you up before dragging you out there to visit your buddy at the museum."

Crane, at first excited by the promise of pastry, immediately lost his perkiness as Banks finished his comment. He dropped the bag on the desk disinterestedly and leaned backward in his chair with a scowl. "Come on, Banks," he pleaded. "I'm begging you: Let that go."

Banks stood there with his hands in his pockets, having not yet sat down. "Crane, I know you're not itching to see Dr. Whitakker again," he said. "I'm not, either. But when you mentioned that girl suspected him, too, well...I don't know; I just got this eerie feeling about it. You know there's a ton of weird stuff with that case, anyway. I don't think we should let the security tapes try to tell us the whole story. I mean, you were there when the guys reconstructed the file; you saw that shadow thing on the video. Who knows? It could have been Whitakker. He might have tampered with the recording somehow. There are possibilities we haven't considered, right? I mean, there must be, because we haven't solved any of it."

Crane bunched his eyebrows tightly together as he looked up at Banks. The man was right, of course, and if Crane hadn't been visited by Iris Wakefield and her startling information, he would never in a million years argue with his partner's line of thinking here. It put him in a terribly awkward position.

Having received no quick response, Banks shrugged and said, "I'm going with or without you, man. You want to tag along, or don't you?"

Crane could see in Myron's eyes he wasn't going to change his mind, and that left him only one choice. He stood up, pulled on his coat, then grabbed his coffee and the bakery bag. "You're gonna owe me more than coffee cake for this one," he ribbed.

"Yeah, yeah," Banks replied, picking up his own coffee and turning to leave. "Tell you what—just don't throw any punches at Marvin while we're out there, and maybe I'll buy your lunch."

As they walked toward the doors, Crane wondered if he should try to call Iris and tell her what they were doing. By the time he had entered the passenger seat and fastened his seat belt, however, he had decided it was an unnecessary precaution. After all, he and Banks had spoken to Marvin before, mostly without incident. It wasn't as though Myron would barge in guns-blazing and cause a scene. How dangerous could it really be?

***

The detectives pulled into the museum parking lot shortly after eight. The museum wouldn't open to the general public until ten, but staff and appointed visitors often arrived as early as seven o'clock on weekdays. Crane and Banks were buzzed in by a security guard and then waited on a bench in the dimly lit lobby as the same guard went down to the staff offices to announce their visit to Dr. Whitakker. Crane slouched over with his elbows on his knees, looking at his feet. A speck of something in the lower part of his peripheral vision caught his attention, and he tucked his chin further to find a few bits of coffee cake on his chest. He brushed them away roughly and suddenly wondered why he hadn't made more of a point to stay in better shape. The zipper on his jacket appeared to be struggling more than it used to.

He glanced over at Banks, who was tapping one foot impatiently against the tile floor. "How exactly do you plan on handling this?" Crane asked him.

Banks shrugged. "We'll play it by ear," he answered. "If we think he's hiding something, we can try to rattle him a little." Crane had started to feel more confident in the car on the way over here; now, he felt a nervous writhing in his stomach. *God, help us*, he found himself praying.

Off to their side, a door opened and then clicked shut behind the slight, sloppily dressed figure of Marvin Whitakker. "Detectives," he squeaked, approaching with quick, short footsteps. "Have you found my spearhead?" *Damn, his voice is irritating*, Crane thought.

Banks stood up as Whitakker approached where they sat, and Crane followed suit. "No, we haven't yet," Banks answered him. "But we have some follow-up questions for you. Is there somewhere we can talk privately?"

"Privately?" Whitakker repeated nervously. "What need is there of privacy? Can we not talk here?"

"How about your office?" Banks suggested, his tone more authoritative than friendly. Crane had to admit, if Banks was going to intimidate the little prick, it could be an amusing show. The guy didn't look like much of a threat; maybe Iris had been overly cautionary.

"My office? Well, I'd rather not," Whitakker answered, wringing his hands and rocking back and forth on the rubber soles of his nearly untied sneakers. "I have quite a lot of important documentation piled up, and I'm cramped for space—"

"We won't touch anything," Banks interrupted. His delivery made it evident, even to Whitakker, that it would be easier to acquiesce than to argue.

"Well, I should hope not," Marvin replied, a touch of anger in his nasal voice. "You should have already been put on warning after your last visit here," he added, with a pointed glance at Crane. *Yeah, screw you, you nerdy bastard*, Crane screamed internally. He immediately recalled how Iris had urged him to return to the Church and the sacraments, and he regretted his angry internal monologue. Whitakker was an asshole, but that didn't mean Crane had to think or act the same way. Unfortunately, he was rather set in his less-than-holy ways.

The detectives followed Marvin through the door he had appeared from, down a rather narrow flight of cement stairs, and to another door secured with a keypad. Marvin entered a code and then opened the door and led them into a large warehouse-type room, crammed with shelving and crates. Crane marveled at the expansiveness of it; he had no idea the museum had this much space, and he had never guessed that space was filled with such a vast collection of pieces, most of which had probably never been displayed. The room had a dusty sort of scent, like the antique shops his wife liked to drag him to sometimes. Oddly enough, Crane noted, the same creepy vibe he felt in many antique shops seemed to be lurking in this room, too. The feeling reminded him of the phone call from the woman who had donated the spearhead from her late husband's collection, and he found her claim that it was haunted to be far less inconceivable now. A chill tickled the back of his neck, and he had to suppress an urge to tug at Myron's arm and tell him they should get out of here. They walked along the front edge of the warehousing area until they neared an oversized open doorway. The route took them right past a terrifying specimen of taxidermy—a huge Kodiak bear standing on its hind legs, jaws open and claws out—and Crane wished he had stayed in the car. Whitakker had to be a freak to work in such a spooky place and think nothing of it. Even Banks had glanced up at the bear and instinctively distanced himself from it.

The trio proceeded out into a separate hallway, with a bare concrete floor and soul-sucking, yellowy-beige walls. A series of closed doors adorned the wall opposite the warehouse side, and Marvin led them to the one that secured his own office. He opened it with another keypad code and entered, not attempting to hold the door for either of the detectives. Banks caught the door and shot an irritated glance back at Crane before entering the office himself. It was a disgusting excuse for a workspace; towers of paperwork covered all but enough room for a laptop computer and a telephone on the desk, and the walls were lined to shoulder height with dusty cardboard boxes and piles of file folders. Most of the visible wall space was decorated with a multitude of display boxes containing the unpleasant mountings of various insects, their wings and legs and antennae throwing frightful shadows behind their glass cases. A cheap metal shelving unit behind Marvin's desk was packed with various artifacts, all covered with dust. Crane glanced at the items he could see, thankful for anything that could draw his attention away from the nasty bugs on the walls. There were two or three sets of carved earthen vases, a half-dozen African or South American tribal statuettes that left no part of the human anatomy to the imagination, a metal lamp that looked like appropriate housing for a genie, a patina-covered sundial, a small brass scarab beetle figurine, and an ornate but upsetting gilded statue of a cobra with its fangs bared. The fluorescent lights situated among the yellowed tiles of the ceiling cast an appallingly greenish glow over the whole mess, and the room reeked of dirt and something rancid, like moldy cheese. Crane wondered, with a modicum of amusement, whether Myron might be regretting his decision to bring the meeting into this repulsive little room.

Marvin seated himself in the only chair in the room, which was placed behind his desk. "Fine, Detectives," he said with irritation. "Here we are. I have quite a lot of work to do, so please go ahead and ask your questions so we can hurry this along."

Banks, instead of pulling out his notebook, crossed his arms across his chest and cleared his throat authoritatively. "Dr. Whitakker," he began, "we've been unable to find any evidence that the spearhead was stolen."

Marvin interrupted with a nervous, petulant giggle. "It was there, and then it wasn't," he stated sarcastically. "What 'evidence' do you need?"

Banks grinned slightly, then replied, "We have plenty of evidence that the spearhead was removed from the weapons display; we just don't believe it was *stolen*."

"What are you talking about, Detective?" Whitakker asked, his tone suddenly colder and darker than it had been before. Crane felt a little tremor of unease in his gut.

"I'm talking about the impossibility of someone else removing the piece from the museum," Banks answered Whitakker. "I'm talking about a suspicion we have that maybe someone here took it."

Whitakker said nothing, but he peered at Banks with angry eyes from behind the thick frames of his glasses. Crane could see tiny beads of sweat dotting the little man's broad forehead. *Iris must have been right*, he thought. *This guy is definitely hiding something.*

Banks allowed a few seconds of silence, then realized Marvin did not intend to respond, so he continued, "Dr. Whitakker, we need to look at the very real possibility that a museum employee removed the spearhead, and since you're the only one with the appropriate key to the display case, I think we need to start by looking at you."

Marvin stood up and furiously straightened his bow tie, then pulled a stained handkerchief from the pocket of his wrinkled, too-big tweed suit and dabbed it across his brow. "Detective, this is ludicrous," he exclaimed with a loud squeal. "I do not have to put up with this kind of harassment from you! I want you to leave now," he whined, brushing past Banks to get to the doorway. He pointed a finger down the hallway and repeated, "I want you to leave!"

"We're not leaving until we get some straight answers," Banks replied stonily as he turned to face Whitakker behind him. "And if you don't settle down, we'll arrest you for obstruction of a criminal investigation."

Crane's nervous stomach twitched again. He wouldn't normally mind if Banks heaped some melodrama into an interrogation in order to elicit a truthful or at least a telling response, but he was growing increasingly uncomfortable around Marvin as he heard Iris's voice replaying in the back of his brain. Banks obviously sensed no danger from the museum curator, and neither would Crane if he had never met Iris, which made her strange warning even more alarming. What was so dangerous about the man? Why had she told him to keep Banks away?

"Obstruction?" Whitakker bellowed. "I'll have both your badges for unwarranted harassment! You'll both be out of a job!"

"Listen, Doctor," Banks responded, raising his own voice to match the volume of Whitakker's. The loudness was much more intimidating when colored with Myron's deep tone. "If you did take the spearhead, we can work it out. We've seen things like this before. Maybe you were working with one of the insurers; maybe you get a cut of the payment. Whatever it was, it's best for you to admit it now so we can work with you." Banks had added some amiability to his voice. It had proven in several prior cases to be an effective tactic, implying some suspicion and then offering appropriate help, but in this case, Crane had a sinking feeling it would do more harm than good.

Whitakker stood in the doorway, wringing his hands. His upper lip was twitching, his greasepaint-free Groucho Marx mustache wriggling atop it like a caterpillar. He thought for a few seconds, then answered Banks, "I have nothing to do with the missing spearhead, and you can't prove otherwise."

Banks sighed audibly and shook his head slowly, staring at Whitakker the whole time. "See," he said with mock disappointment, "that's not what we hear. We had a witness come to us with information. That witness tells us you stole the artifact yourself and then tampered with the security tapes to hide it."

"A *witness?*" Whitakker squealed. "Who? This is impossible! I demand to know who accused me! I know my rights!"

"You need to help us first," Banks answered. "Is it true? Did you take the spearhead?"

"Absolutely not!" Whitakker asserted, blinking his eyes unnecessarily fast and nervously pressing his glasses higher on his nose.

Crane put his hand on Myron's shoulder and stepped around him so that he could face Marvin directly in the doorway. Banks looked wary for an instant, but said nothing. It was time to get out of this oppressive, nauseating room, and Crane figured he had a way to do it. He did, after all, have knowledge that neither his partner nor the curator knew he had. "So," he addressed Whitakker gruffly, "you didn't take the spearhead from the weapons exhibit. Is that what you're telling us?"

"Yes, of course that's what I'm telling you, *Detective*," the curator replied, pointedly enunciating each syllable of "detective" so that it came out like an insult instead of a title.

Crane should have left it at that, and he knew it. He knew he should just thank Marvin for his time and then coax his partner out of the museum and wait for Iris's anonymous delivery of the copper spearhead. But he couldn't do it. He and Banks both suspected it now. They both believed Whitakker was involved, and Crane knew it for a fact. He couldn't let the offensive little geek get away with it.

So, against his better judgment, Crane opened his mouth again. "Just so I understand," he said, "you're telling us you *didn't* take the spearhead and store it in your personal collection of stolen artifacts, which you have tucked away in a little hideout below this museum?"

Crane sensed ample surprise and confusion from his partner beside him, and the sentiment was reflected momentarily in the wide-eyed, frazzled expression on Marvin Whitakker's face. The ensuing quiet stillness lasted only a fraction of a second before Whitakker turned out of the doorway and took off down the hallway, opposite the direction from which they had come. Startled, Banks sprinted after him, with Crane following as closely as he could. *Shit*, he chided himself. *Now I've done it.*

The detectives were only a couple of seconds behind Whitakker and his baggy suit, but the impish little curator had enough of a head start to enter a security code on another door at the far end of the hall and slip through it, pressing it closed behind him. Banks arrived at the locked door first and tugged at the handle, to no avail. Judging from the door's placement and the objects visible through the door's four-inch-wide window slit, Marvin had just entered the rear portion of the museum's storage room. The only other unlocked opening at this end of the hallway appeared to be a flight of stairs back up to the museum's ground floor, meaning the detectives' likeliest chance of catching up to their suspect now would be to cut through the warehousing area, hoping it would open into the other storage area somehow. Banks assessed the situation as quickly as Crane had, if not faster, and they both sprinted back to the open doorway through which they had entered. They took a hard left past the Kodiak, rushing down a narrow aisle that carved a path among wooden crates, antique furniture, and metal shelves and all the crap they held. Some of the items were too long or wide for the shelving and encroached on the walkway, making it a treacherous run. Banks's jacket sleeve caught the end of a resin cast of a fossil, pulling it and a dozen other items around it to the floor just in front of Crane's feet. Myron turned his head to check on him, but Crane waved for him to continue on as he stumbled over the mess and then tried to catch up, weaving his way among the clutter.

Another loud racket from deeper within the room reached Crane's ears, and he panicked, thinking perhaps Banks had reached Marvin and there was a scuffle. "Banks!" he called out. "Where are you?" This room was a maze of useless historical shit. He kept working his way roughly in the direction of what should be the back of the room as he anxiously awaited a response.

He heard clanging and scraping of metal, punctuated by dull thuds of wood and plastic being thrown to the ground. It was nearer than the first crash had been, and Crane was relieved to finally hear his partner's voice not too far away from him. "I'm here," Banks yelled. "Get over here; help me move this!"

Crane followed his partner's voice and found him struggling to drag a large shelving unit across the floor. The space they had reached was even more dimly lit than the primary storage area was. It appeared this part of the room was rarely visited, even by museum staff. Crane rushed to help Banks move the shelves.

"He pulled this whole thing down," Banks grunted as he strained with the cumbersome rack. "There's a door in the floor below here," he continued, breathing heavily. "He went down there. I have no idea how he pulled this down like he did."

The weight of the shelves would not normally be any problem for the two men together, but the plethora of large items that had adorned them, in combination with the other bulky pieces stored in this rather tight area, made it almost impossible to move with any haste.

"Set it down," Crane instructed as he stepped into an empty space between shelves. He attempted to pick up one of three heavy bronze urns that were contributing to the problem. "Here, let's get rid of these."

He and Banks lifted and moved each of the urns out of the way and were able to clear enough path to pull the shelves away from the door, which was well camouflaged in the floor. In the dim lighting and all the shadows of the museum pieces, the door's handle was nearly impossible to see. Crane eventually found it and pulled, expecting Whitakker to have locked it behind him, but the door opened easily.

The detectives listened for a few seconds at the open passage, but they heard nothing. Darkness enveloped whatever this belowground space was. Fortunately, both Crane and Banks were accustomed to carrying flashlights. They turned them on and peered down, seeing a short set of wooden stairs leading into a room that was probably once used as a storm shelter. There was no sign of Marvin.

Banks wiped sweat off his forehead with the back of his hand, then pulled out his gun and looked at Crane. "I'll go first," he said, readying both the gun and his light.

"Be careful," Crane said gravely as he drew his own weapon. "I'm not sure we know what this guy is capable of."

"Yeah," Banks agreed. There was a tinge of nervousness in his voice.

Crane pointed his own flashlight down the stairs and pulled out his gun, carefully watching the portion of the cellar area he could see from here. Myron descended the stairs and surveyed the room, then called out, "It's clear."

Crane joined him a second later. They glanced around with their flashlights, finding a set of shelves which, interestingly, held a rather sizable collection of artifacts, although the copper spearhead was not readily identifiable among them.

"Damn," Banks said, walking over for a closer look, being careful not to touch anything. As he studied a couple of the pieces, he asked, "How did you know about this? Did that girl tell you about all this? How did she know? And why didn't you tell me?"

Crane groaned as he approached the shelves, surprised that Iris's statement had been accurate after all, though he couldn't explain to himself why he was surprised by that. "Too many questions for now, Banks," he deflected. "We'll talk about it later."

A sudden slam from above them caused both detectives to turn quickly and point their lights and guns at the doorway. The cellar door had closed, and in the same instant, a terrifying chill filled the room. Banks darted his light around as Crane ran back up the steps and tried to open the door. It was useless; the thing wouldn't budge.

"What the *hell*?" Banks cried. Crane turned from the door and saw his partner staring at the wall opposite the artifact collection, and for good reason. Opened up in the wall was a black, gaping hole, its edges aglow with ruby flame. Standing in front of the maw was a disheveled Marvin Whitakker, eyeglasses and bow tie gone, shirt unbuttoned to mid-torso, and a hateful, alien look in his eyes.

"Oh, my God," Crane heard himself whisper. Time seemed to stand still for a moment, then he saw his partner lifted from his feet and thrown roughly into the shelves behind him, all while Marvin Whitakker stood unmoving in front of the hole in the wall.

***

Iris rubbed her eyes as she waited for her coffee to finish brewing, while her cobra dutifully shoved an empty mug toward her from its place near the sink, readying it for immediate filling. Apparently, even her serpent companion recognized what an awful night she had had. At least, thankfully, she had left Eden—not that she really had much choice after going full-Satan and causing her boss's demise. Of course, no one imagined she had anything to do with that unfortunate incident, but she would have found it far too awkward to stay there after that, even had she wanted to. She would have to find another job eventually, but the thought of working at a normal job right now was wholly unappealing. She had just recently been rescued by Auraltiferys from the precipice of eternal damnation, and she had even more recently had her final interaction with Loomis—unless, of course, he failed to keep his word that he would wreak no physical havoc on the human race. Her thoughts right now were muddled, and her emotions were even more so. She had believed she would feel free once Loomis was out of her life. Instead, she felt sad and somehow lonely. She almost hoped he would fail to keep his word, just so she could see him again, even if only to punish him. She had cried herself to sleep last night, like a stupid teenaged girl who had just been dumped by her boyfriend and believed the whole world would end because of it. She resented herself for feeling that way. She and Loomis had never been in any relationship but a twisted, demonic tug-of-war, and it was illogical to feel anything but relief from having ended it, but logical argument with her own mind hadn't stopped the tears.

Then, there had been the dream. She hadn't had that dream in years, and she had almost forgotten it. It was a hazy, golden vision of an angel, a warm and beautiful dream that had once brought her comfort each time she saw it in her mind. This time, however, it saddened her. It felt like nothing but false hope for an unattainable goal. She was sure it was her subconscious thoughts about Loomis and about her own demonic inclinations that had prompted it; her brain was probably searching for comfort in something that had once provided mental succor, but, unfortunately, Iris had grown in age and wisdom and experience, and now the gilded angel in that old dream was just a painful reminder of how easily lost Heaven was.

She yawned as she leaned over her kitchen counter, wishing the coffee would brew faster. She toyed with the idea of using magic, but Auraltiferys had warned her not to become complacent in that way. Magic was not meant to replace work, he had told her. She was trying to follow his advice.

Finally, enough had brewed so that she could pour her first cup, so she pulled out the carafe and tipped the coffee into her mug. As she replaced the pot, her eyes snapped wide open, and she froze. Something was calling to her from within her own mind. She sensed sinister darkness much nearer than it should be, and as her heart started racing, she felt her thoughts drawn directly to Detective Crane. Something was terribly wrong.

Forgetting her coffee and her self-pity, she readied herself with quick magic, then she focused her thoughts on the detective and transported herself to where she found him.

***

Crane ran down half the stairs and propelled himself over the banister once he neared the bottom, aiming his gun and flashlight at Whitakker the instant he regained his balance. The curator had not moved, but it seemed he didn't need to. Crane's mind was flooded with conflicting options—he could try to arrest Whitakker, though that seemed doomed to fail, or he could just shoot the bastard, but that was against protocol and almost certainly a lawsuit waiting to happen. He heard Iris's words again in his mind: "This case isn't going to resign itself to your protocols." *That's right*, he thought to himself. *Fuck protocol.*

In the instant before he pulled the trigger, Crane felt his gun wrenched from his hand, and then he heard it clatter against the farthest wall on the other side of the stairs, while Whitakker simply stared at him with a crazed expression and a disgusting, twisted smile.

"Crane!" Banks yelled from behind him, prompting Crane to look back. He had recovered his breath after having been smashed into the wall and had managed to extricate himself from the mess of shelving and strewn-about artifacts to draw his own gun on the lunatic. Crane moved immediately to the side, and with a flash of light and two loud blasts, Banks sent two bullets hurtling toward Whitakker's chest.

The nightmarish scene should have ended there. Banks was an excellent shot; he could definitely hit a target much smaller than Marvin Whitakker at that short distance. But as the detectives regrouped in the center of the cellar, looking around in surprise and confusion, it was clear Whitakker had not been neutralized. The man had disappeared, leaving the room a cold den of tension and suspense. Gone, too, was the strange black hole in the wall.

"What the hell is happening?" Banks whispered, slowly turning in a circle with his flashlight and gun readied in front of him. Both he and Crane were panting in shallow, rapid breaths.

As Crane opened his mouth to answer, an invisible energy exploded between them, sending Crane crashing painfully into the wooden handrail of the stairs and throwing Banks into the opposite wall. Crane heard his partner's gun fall to the cement floor, and he knew one of them better recover a weapon before Marvin showed up again. The guns had proven useless so far, but there would be no other way to defend themselves against this man, or whatever he was. So, dazed and hurting, Crane tried to pull himself up from the splintered wood beneath him. He reached for his light a few feet away, but as his hand neared it, he felt a presence that froze him. In the dimmest extremity of the flashlight's beam, he saw Marvin Whitakker, teeth bared animalistically under his ridiculous mustache, staring right at him with hateful, jaundiced eyes that looked anything but human. Crane didn't try to hide his fear. He wasn't ready to die, but that was exactly what was about to happen. Marvin must have known that, too, and he must have enjoyed instilling such fear, because after holding Crane's terrified eyes for a moment, he grinned. It was a joyless, pernicious curling of his lips, and it was utterly sickening. Slowly and dramatically, the curator raised his hand and snapped his fingers, and all the light in the room was gone. *God, forgive me*, Crane begged silently. It was all he could ask from the Creator he was about to meet. Icy air embraced him in the darkness and settled around his throat, constricting it like a python. He gasped and groped at his neck, but there was nothing physically there.

Suddenly, the cold fell away, and Crane could breathe freely again. He heard footsteps very near him as a voice commanded, "Unhand him, Marvin."

Light filled the room, from no apparent source. Crane turned to see Iris Wakefield standing beside him, her intense eyes shooting daggers at Marvin in front of them. He had never been so glad to see someone. He carefully stood up, sensing it was safe to do so with her there.

Iris, not removing her gaze from Whitakker, quietly but authoritatively instructed Crane to check on Banks. He jogged to the opposite wall, giving Marvin a wide berth, and knelt beside his partner, who was slumped unconscious on the floor. He checked Myron's pulse and thanked God he was alive. He moved him so that he was lying flat, then tapped him gently but briskly as he urged him to wake up. After several seconds, Banks's eyes fluttered open, and Crane was able to help him sit up.

Banks quickly spied the strange scene in front of him and asked again, "What the hell is going on, man?" He rubbed gingerly at the back of his head and grimaced.

Crane found Banks's gun a couple of yards away and retrieved it, handing it to his partner as he replied, "Don't worry about it. We need to get out of here. You able to stand up?"

Banks accepted Crane's offered assistance and stood shakily. He gradually took on his own weight and regained his balance, then answered, "Yeah, I'm fine."

The detectives walked cautiously toward the base of the cellar steps and then paused, astounded by the uneasy stare-down Marvin and Iris were engaged in. Marvin seemed unwilling to disobey whatever Iris's eyes must be demanding.

Addressing the detectives without looking at them, Iris said, "I've opened the cellar door. Go, and don't come back here for anything. Do you understand?"

Crane saw Banks open his mouth as if to speak and immediately grabbed him by both shoulders and forced him toward the stairs. "We're going," he announced, both to Iris and to his partner.

"You'll go nowhere," Marvin squealed. His voice had a distinctly inhuman tone, and Crane instinctively stopped moving because of it.

"Marvin," Iris retorted, her voice low and full of warning, "do not defy me. You will succeed only in making your existence more unbearable."

Marvin thought for a moment, then smirked. "I've outsmarted others who think they're better than me," he said with a jeer. "I'll take my chances with you."

He disappeared from view, and suddenly the detectives were shoved off the stairs through the broken banister by the inhuman strength of an invisible hand. They fell together where Iris had stood a second earlier, but she had somehow moved. She muttered something under her breath that lifted both Crane and Banks into the air before gently setting them along the wall behind her. "Stay there," she charged them.

Crane watched in awe as Marvin reappeared, floating in mid-air. The little man waved his hand toward Iris, who took two steps backward but then somehow, invisibly, sent Marvin crashing into the opposite corner of the cellar. Was he dumb? Iris was clearly stronger than he was.

Marvin disappeared again, then showed up right behind Iris, who was already turning to face him even as he manifested there. He suddenly seized, seemingly prompted by something Iris was doing in her mind. The curator appeared paralyzed, though fully conscious, as Iris forced him into the wall where the hole had been.

"I warned you, Marvin," she growled, invisibly holding him in place against the wall, inches above the ground. "You've outsmarted no one, and trust me when I tell you, you have a punishment coming that is far worse than anything I would do. I could have helped you, if you had only listened to me. But now, you will face that punishment alone."

Marvin started to yell something in a foreign language, maybe Latin, when suddenly Crane saw the red flame return to the wall behind the panicked curator, opening into the same yawning void they had seen before. Iris seemed momentarily surprised by the appearance. She released Marvin, letting him fall to the floor, and screamed, "What have you done?" Marvin's only response was maniacal laughter.

The welcome light Iris had brought to the room was suddenly squelched, leaving only the eerie red glow from the wall to illuminate the cellar. Cold filled the room again, and Crane pulled Banks with him into the corner as he watched Iris reach down and pull out a small item that had been tucked into the laces of her knee-high boot. When she stood and dropped her hand, she held a large, double-bladed axe. Marvin stood up and tried to lunge at her, but he was suddenly pulled into the hole in the wall, legs kicking and arms flailing.

Even as the curator was sucked from the room, Crane heard Iris chanting quietly in a strange dialect he didn't recognize, her words coming out in fervent haste as she stared at the hole. It started to close, but then opened again, apparently fighting whatever she was doing. Suddenly, a black, smoky figure emerged from the red halo. Crane couldn't even focus his eyes on it before it drove itself through Iris and disappeared, eliciting a frightened yell from Crane as he watched the young woman drop to her knees. He rushed over to help her, sensing Banks right behind him with his gun drawn to cover them both, assuming a gun would be any help to them at all. Iris was stunned but otherwise unharmed, except that Crane could see by the light of the red flames that her eyes had gone almost completely black. Only tiny bits of white were left in their corners.

Crane grabbed her by the shoulders and forced himself to stare into her eyes, which had been made terrifying by whatever had attacked her. "Hey!" he shouted in her face, shaking her gently. "Are you okay?" Banks stood beside her with his gun ready, watching for a possible return of the evil shadow.

Crane caught Banks's eyes for the briefest instant, both of them concerned that something awful had happened to the woman who had come to their aid. When Crane returned his eyes to Iris's, he discovered they had returned to normal, and relief settled upon him for a passing second before she screamed "No!" It was an urgent, petrifying cry that seemed to slow the passing of time. The word had not fully escaped her mouth before she shot to her feet and turned toward Banks, shoving him with one arm and throwing the axe from the other with deadly speed. Crane saw her target and fired his gun, too, but they were both too late.

Myron shrieked in terror as the shadow approached him; in the subsequent nanosecond, the shriek became a sickening gurgle and then an awful silence. Crane watched his partner's body go immediately limp and collapse, his own heart dropping into his stomach as Banks fell. He ran to him, no longer seeing his surroundings nor caring what was happening in this godforsaken cellar. He felt for a pulse and tried to revive his friend, all while crying and repeating the word "no" over and over. He knew, though he couldn't bear to accept the thought, that Myron was gone. The detective's body was colder than ice and as rigid as a statue, and worst of all, his eyes were wide open and solid, matte, inhuman black.

"Dear God, no," Crane sobbed, kneeling beside Banks's body. "No, no, no...please, no..." Tears flowed freely down his face, and drainage seeped from his nose into his mustache, and he couldn't care less. This was all his fault. Iris had warned him, and he hadn't done enough to listen.

"Detective," Iris urged quietly. "Detective, calm down." She tried to pull him by his shoulders away from Myron, but Crane roughly brushed her hand away, barely registering her words or his own actions. His mind had practically broken beneath the weight of all his emotions.

Iris grabbed him more forcefully and turned him toward her, slapping her hand hard across his face. "Detective!" she yelled dominantly. "Pull yourself together! Listen to me!"

The sting of her slap roused Crane momentarily. He shook his head, ran his hand over his face to wipe away his tears, and tried to catch his breath between sniffles. He now realized Iris had been able to restore the light to the cellar, and the hole in the wall was gone again. He looked at her silently and searchingly, feeling utterly like a child.

With her hands firmly on his shoulders, she spoke evenly but urgently to him. "I'm going to get him, okay? I'm going to try to bring him back."

"Huh...how?" Crane stammered, his chest heaving and his eyes still welled up with tears.

"That doesn't matter," she answered definitively. "Stay here, and pray for him," she continued, removing her hands from his shoulders and turning to retrieve her axe from where it had somehow lodged itself in the cement wall. After pulling it out, she moved to where the void had opened, then she faced Crane one last time.

"Pray for him," she repeated earnestly. "Pray that God will deliver him from this, whatever happens. Do you hear me? Do you understand?"

Crane nodded, though his brain instantly questioned whether he would know how to pray correctly, whether the wrong words would mean his partner was gone forever, whether the right words might bring him back somehow. And what did Iris mean, "whatever happens"? Would she be able to save him? What was she going to try? And what if she didn't succeed? Then what? How could he ever explain this to Myron's wife, or to his two little girls? He imagined trying to explain Myron's death to his daughters, with their puffy twin buns drawn up high on their little heads, colorful plastic barrettes adorning them, and he started crying again.

As thoughts and emotions stampeded through Crane's mind, he saw Iris turn to the wall and heard her intoning a series of strange words. Bizarre symbols suddenly appeared like glowing, red snakes, and the dark circle opened again. Iris tightened her grip on the handle of her bronze axe, then she stepped into the blackness, leaving nothing but a cement wall behind her.

30

The air was a stifling mephitis of heat and sulfur, which burned the nostrils and suffocated the lungs even more than its noxious yellow haze offended the eyes. Iris coughed and gagged, unprepared for the assault to her senses. She hadn't known what to expect as she entered the gate to Hell, but she hadn't thought twice about doing it after seeing Detective Banks fall victim to the shadow-demon she had believed she had safely locked away in the netherworld. Myron wasn't baptized; she had known that in her Satanic mind. But he was a kind and decent man, as was his partner, Detective Crane, whose emotional display at his partner's violent murder had thoroughly wrung Iris's human heart. If there were any way she could free Myron's soul from its unsolicited and untimely damnation, she had to try. Even if she should prove unsuccessful, the attempt was worth the effort; besides, she knew she'd be unable to live with her own conscience if she were to let it go. She felt at least partially responsible for all the detectives had just endured, and she was infuriated she had been too late to spare Banks from the shadow-demon's strike.

Finding it increasingly difficult to breathe, she formulated a prayerful spell she hoped would guard her physical body while she was here. It was not, after all, a place meant for the living. The spell seemed to work, and she was able to breathe again, though there was nothing she could do about the smell. Her eyes had teared from the stinging onslaught of caustic air, and she had to blink the moisture away and recover her composure before she could take visual note of her surroundings. She was standing on an island of craggy, ash-covered rock in what appeared to be a deathly black valley surrounded by jagged obsidian mountains veined with rivers and pools of fire. It was not unlike what Loomis had shown her before, when he had tried to convince her to share Hell's throne with him. She was seeing it now firsthand, however, and with limited, human eyesight. The place was expansive and hideous, and it echoed with the wails of the pitiful damned, whose disembodied souls crowded the vast domain. There were demons everywhere, too, their once-angelic and now horribly mutated and disfigured spirits branding nightmarish visions in her memory. If God allowed her to leave this place alive, she might never sleep again. *My God, help me*, she prayed. The empty feeling the words left inside her made her wonder if God had even heard. Only then did she fully recognize this was a physical reality, not a vision or a dream. She was truly in Hell, human body and human soul and Satanic spirit—and probably God had not heard her. God was not present here.

A thud and an agonized cry emanated from something close beside her, and Iris turned to see the body of Marvin Whitakker impaled on a glassy stalagmite of obsidian. He was facing upward, with the volcanic dagger penetrating his back and jutting out through his rib cage. Blood pooled beneath him, and the body was dead in an instant. Its human soul and its demonic coinhabitant fell to the rock below, only to be immediately enchained by a spell cast by Loomis Drake, who stood there in his human form, as well-dressed and nonchalant as if it were just another day at the office.

"I wasn't expecting an audience," he said casually, turning slowly from the trapped victims at his feet to look at Iris. There was a vague hint of surprise in his visage. "I do hope your recent foray back into holiness hasn't weakened your stomach," he added, "because the torments I have planned for these two are quite wicked."

"Loomis, you bastard!" Iris exclaimed angrily. "I told you, no physical harm to humankind! You gave me your word, you worthless piece of shit!" She took a wrathful, intimidating step toward him, clutching her axe in her right fist. Loomis stepped backward and held up his hands in appeasement. He narrowed his eyes in both confusion and anger.

"You allowed me my revenge on Marvin Whitakker," he reminded her coldly. "It was practically the only concession you made to me. I've done nothing to violate the word I gave you."

Iris shook her head, not believing him. "I'm not talking about Whitakker," she said acidly, "and you know it. You sent your shadow-demon back through that Gate, and it stole a human soul."

"I did no such thing," Loomis answered calmly.

"Give it up, Loomis," Iris chided with ample disgust. "I don't believe a word you say." He stood his ground as she approached, but Iris sensed some unease in him as she neared. She stopped just in front of him, staring at him with hate-filled eyes. The previous night, she had cried at the thought of seeing him no more; now, she suddenly wanted to hurt him. It must be the evil of this place, beckoning the evil in her nature.

Loomis returned her gaze, letting confusion edge out all the anger that had at first entered his expression. His voice was quiet and even as he answered, "I swear it to you, Iris. I pulled Whitakker through the Gate he himself had opened, and that is all."

Iris found no evidence of trickery in him, but the shadow-demon was his creation. If he hadn't released it again, who had? "I saw the shadow-demon take a soul and return through that same Gate," she explained, her voice sharp with distrust. "I had locked it down here, and I had removed its ability to take human souls. So if you're not responsible for its resurrection, then who is?"

Cold suddenly swept across them, temporarily silencing everything in their immediate vicinity, with the only exception of a sad whimpering coming from Marvin's soul. Iris had her eyes still trained on Loomis, and she didn't have to turn to know who had just joined them. She could feel it inside her, underneath the goosebumps and the fear that erupted below her skin.

"I AM," came the icy reply, delivered in Hebrew. Switching into Iris's native English, the voice continued, "What a pleasant surprise it is to finally see you, daughter."

Iris swallowed and squeezed the handle of the weapon Auraltiferys had forged for her. She had a strong suspicion she was really going to need it. A fleeting look of panic in Loomis's eyes bolstered that suspicion.

After a few stupefied seconds, Iris slowly turned to face the Devil standing beside her. It would be foolish to be afraid; after all, she was stronger than he, was she not? A terrifying thought suddenly clawed its way into her mind—what if she had been deceived from the beginning? What if Loomis had convinced her of her superiority to Satan only to lure her here to him in an unwise decision born of false confidence?

"Ah, look at the two of you," Satan jeered. "I have often wondered why Loomis would have chosen to spend the majority of his existence in that disgusting human body when he could have been my most trusted and well-paid servant here in Hell. When he refused to deliver you to me, Iris, I marveled all the more. But now, seeing the two of you together like this, I think perhaps I see it."

"Neither of us has asked for your opinion," Loomis interrupted. Iris shot him a sideways glance, stunned he would speak thus to the Prince of Darkness. Then again, why should she be surprised? He had sought to mutiny for quite some time; it wasn't as though he respected Satan's leadership.

The grotesque monstrosity towering in front of them grinned with malice. "You'd like to fuck her, wouldn't you?" he said, his voice a disgusting hiss. "Admit it, Loomis—you want to fuck my daughter's nice little cunt."

Iris, thoroughly repulsed by Satan's unparalleled vulgarity, fought the sudden urge to throw her axe at him, sensing it wasn't yet the appropriate time. Loomis, however, apparently equally offended, was far less subdued in his reaction. With pure hatred evident in his face, he vocalized a spell that struck the Devil with a painful blow of energy. These were spiritual beings, but they had forms here in Hell, and magic could inflict physical pain on them just as it could on mortal humans on Earth. Satan made a dull, grunting sound and stumbled backward.

"Don't speak that way about her," Loomis growled. "And she is *not* your daughter."

The Devil regained his balance and approached again, this time raising a deformed, bony, hand-like appendage and snapping what would be his fingers. Four horse-headed demons descended immediately upon Loomis, shoving him to his hands and knees. Iris stepped away from their attack, but their focus was not on her at all. They tore at Loomis's body with their crude iron weapons and kicked and beat him. Loomis didn't appear to fight back, to Iris's great disbelief. He must be unable to fight, for whatever reason, because he would never willfully submit himself to a beating like this when he was so powerful in magic. Most likely, the weapons entrusted to these four guardian demons had been cast with dark power that protected them from magical attack and weakened the abilities of their victims. After all, they would need such heavy magical armor if they were to convince Hell's lesser demons of their strength as the Devil's Chosen. Iris knew they couldn't kill an immortal being, but their brutality terrified her. The momentary anger she had felt toward Loomis upon her entry to Hell had vanished, and she couldn't stand to see him abused in this way. In her slowness to react, though, the demons had wrested his spirit from the human form he wore, and Loomis's demonic being was now curled up in a defensive position at their feet, accepting their blows with pained groans.

"Enough," Iris commanded, her demonic voice echoing through the caverns of Hell. She had believed she'd never speak with that voice again after having been stabbed by the Cross of Christ, but it felt quite natural and even invigorating here, and she was glad her Satanic nature was still there inside her. She had directed it toward goodness and light, but that had not weakened it in the slightest, and the substance was still the same. She was still an incarnation of Satan, and that gave her power and status here.

The demons paused, recognizing Iris's authority as equal to Satan's. They backed away from Loomis as she stepped toward them, turning their hideous heads from her to Satan with great confusion. Obeying the order of a human was a foreign concept to them, and yet from the woman before them had emanated the voice of their evil ruler.

"You fools!" Satan yelled, shaking Hell's stone walls so that they belched smoke and fire amid the cacophony of alarmed screams that erupted at his distress. "She is a *human*," he spat. "You do not follow her! She's an imposter, a fraud! She is not a *true* demon! Tear that soul from her now and lock her away, or be sentenced to the gravest punishment at my hand!"

Iris had stopped near where Loomis's demonic form lay battered and torn amid the Devil's guards. She looked down at him as he painfully labored to bring himself to the knees of his strange, demonic form. Shreds of skin-like matter hung from his torso and arms and legs, the wounds leaking a glassy, pearlescent violet-black ooze—not exactly blood, but certainly a physical representation of excruciating spiritual torture. At the instruction of Satan, his guards now closed in on both her and Loomis, readying their weapons. Iris's eyes dropped to Loomis again, who was weakly balanced on his hands and knees, his head down. She had seen him only once before in his demonic form, after she had infuriated him in his Portland office during their initial meeting. It had been for only a passing instant, but Iris thought he looked quite different and somehow less monstrous now. She was moved with pity for him, greater than those similar inclinations she had felt before, for only at this moment did she finally understand what she had been missing in her assessment of him. Suddenly enraged by the idea that she and Loomis should be subject to the unholy will of Satan, she snapped her eyes toward the nearest demon guard and silently invoked magic that wrenched its horse-like head nearly completely from its shoulders. The guard fell immediately with a revolting, anguished bleat that froze the other guards where they stood. Consumed with feverish anger, Iris then cast another spell that struck the remaining guards with force enough to tear their arms from them as they were launched backward, two collapsing hard into stone outcroppings about thirty yards away and the other landing among a crowd of wailing souls in a lake of flame. She scanned the area for Satan, but he had disappeared. *Coward*, she scoffed to herself.

Having created at least a momentary peace, or the nearest semblance of peace one could find in Hell, Iris knelt on the sharp rock in front of Loomis, who had yet been unable to stand. She dropped her axe beside her, took his head gently in her hands, and lifted it to face her. Some of the animalistic deformity was gone from what she had seen in his demonic shape before. His face, though it still had a serpentine appearance, more closely resembled a human's than a beast's. His inhuman eyes, like oblong pieces of amber-colored glass, reflected the eerie light of the rivers of flame around them. He looked her in her eyes only very briefly before he forced his head down to hide his face, but it was enough to confirm for her what she had thought she had finally recognized in him minutes before.

She let him draw his face away from her, but she extended one hand and placed it between the strange, iridescent, goatish horns on his head and then closed her eyes and focused healing spells on him, hoping her intentions would allow the spells to work on him now, though they were typically used on wounds of the flesh. After several seconds, she opened her eyes, sensing Loomis had in fact regained some of his strength. She picked up her axe, stood and brushed the ash from the knees of her jeans, then reached down and offered her hand to Loomis, who accepted her help as he rose to his full height, which was much greater outside his human body. That body, Iris now realized, was lying several feet away in a bloody heap, having been tossed away by the horse-headed demons after they had beaten it and removed Loomis from it. As he now went to retrieve it, Satan reappeared, descending with frightening haste from somewhere above them. His giant form made the ground quake, but Iris had lost all fear of him.

"How very *tender* of you, daughter," he mocked, "but you are even more foolish than I expected if you believe Loomis Drake reciprocates those human inclinations of yours. He is a demon, the embodiment of evil, and if he has pretended to care for you in any way, it has been only to tempt you to follow his own evil will. I assure you, the tenderest emotion he can have toward you is indifference." Satan stared at Iris as he hissed his words at her. She made a conscious effort to maintain a blank expression. The Devil's statements were nothing she hadn't told herself before, on more than one occasion, but hearing them delivered to her aloud by a separate entity did scratch at her heart. She hoped Satan couldn't recognize it. She hoped her soul was as masked from him here as it had been on Earth.

As she tried to focus her thoughts into a response, a deluge of terrifying, bestial laughter burst from the Devil, and she jerked involuntarily at the sudden echoing noise. "How sad this must be for you to hear!" he taunted. "After all those years, you finally meet a man who recognizes your unique abilities, a man who appreciates you and respects you, a man who understands you in ways no one else can...and he isn't even a man! His human mask has expertly deluded you; everything you have believed he might feel for you is nothing but a wicked lie!" Satan laughed more, the sound pounding painfully in Iris's ears and cutting deeply at her human sentiments.

His words were true, at least to some degree. For a long time, Iris had endured the occasional questions and comments from people she had met, at work or at the gym or at church. They'd ask if she was married or if she was seeing someone, then they'd ask why she wasn't, then they'd tell her she needed to "find a man," then sometimes they'd even offer to find one for her. Iris had written off such exchanges as best she could, but they always took an emotional toll, especially as they built up over time. She had never really gone actively searching for any "significant other," and she never really felt like she was missing out because of it, but it didn't mean she was opposed to the idea of a serious relationship. Those you-need-a-man comments were hurtful, even though spoken with genuinely good intentions, because they implied her personal value was somehow less than what it should be because she wasn't attached to some man. At least, that had been Iris's take on them. And, yes, she had fantasized about romantic possibilities with Loomis, but that had been before she knew what he was, and before she knew what she was. Once she had learned the truth, Loomis had never *really* been able to fool her with his lies and his ulterior motives. Her feelings toward him were no longer any sort of simplistic human longing...were they? She did believe Loomis respected her and even understood her; she had wondered if he loved her, even knowing he was incapable of it. Why had she lost sleep and shed tears at the thought of being done with him for good? Was she really made weak by her human nature and its yearnings? Had he truly tricked her after all?

Even as the questions crossed her mind, Iris could hear her inner voice arguing the other side. Humanity didn't make her weak, and her feelings toward Loomis, though perhaps she could not fully explain them, were not some fairy-tale romantic ideal, especially after the realization she had finally made as she looked into his real eyes, his demon eyes. No...Satan was wrong. Iris knew he couldn't read a human's thoughts, and she, in particular, had always been specially shielded from his view. He couldn't know anything she didn't tell him either by word or by expression. He was guessing at her emotions to elicit a reaction so he could twist those feelings and confuse them. *Not today, Satan*, she thought to herself, with a tiny internal chuckle at the irony and a significant boost in confidence. The Devil would not trick her today.

"I saw a pitiful creature in need of assistance I was able to give," she finally answered flatly, explaining her actions toward Loomis the moment before. "His opinion of me is immaterial, as is my opinion of him."

Satan fell silent, the shineless iciness of his malformed, perverted eyes boring into her. Iris suspected he was unconvinced by her reply, but that didn't matter. He turned toward Loomis, who was now standing over the victimized human body he had created, and said, "It would seem you have her exactly where you want her, Loomis. You're not even in your human form, yet she practically *drips* with desire for you." Another eruption of fiendish laughter punctuated his statement.

Loomis's demonic spirit departed from sight, and his human body arose stiffly and achingly from where it had lain. It was badly lacerated and bruised; its eyes were swollen and bloodshot, and its jaw hung crookedly from its ears. Iris wanted to cry at his disfigurement and the physical agony it evidenced, though she knew the body was nothing but a mask Loomis wore. He had recovered enough to begin healing it, and as soon as the worst injuries had been addressed, he replied with exhaustion to Satan, "She wants nothing to do with me, just as she wants nothing to do with you."

"I don't believe that's true," Satan responded in a low, rumbling growl as Loomis walked with slow, difficult steps back to Iris's side. "If it is true, then you've lost your most profitable ability, for never before have you met a woman you were unable to tempt. Do you mean to tell me my daughter has made you impotent? I have noticed your *conversion* numbers are down lately."

Loomis stared at Satan with disillusionment. "I have been busy with other things," he answered woodenly.

"Of course," Satan replied. "You mean your intricate plans to overthrow me and claim rulership of Hell. Did you think I was unaware of your machinations? I have allowed you to continue on your quest because I have always known you would fail. And, after all, you have contributed significantly to the fullness of my kingdom's bowels; that is why I have so long allowed you to dwell in that physical form on the Earth, when no others here enjoy such entitlement. I have given you far more than you deserve."

"You allow me to dwell on Earth because you lack the knowledge and the ability to preclude me," Loomis answered, dark derision coloring his tone. "You *give* nothing. I *take*."

A cold pall descended upon Iris and Loomis, originating from Satan's oppressive figure. The Devil remained unspeaking for several seconds, then he hissed, "You haven't *taken* my daughter, and you cannot *take* my throne."

Loomis scowled, then answered with a shrug, "I have no desire for either."

A guttural cackle began somewhere deep in Satan's form, growing until it was a dry, demonic hammering of mirthless cachinnation.

"Oh, you lying little fuck!" he exclaimed. "You have the strongest desires for both, and you shall have neither! Only with my daughter's aid would you have the ability to usurp my authority; that is written immutably in stone. I would say perhaps you might yet tempt her, but it wouldn't matter, for I am going to destroy her."

At the threat, Iris tightened her grip on the axe in her hand. She hoped she would know the right time to use it. For now, she sensed she should let the Devil continue. She glanced sideways toward Loomis and saw him watching Satan with disgust, his face still bruised from its beating. The screams of the damned adorned the tense air in the pause.

"Yes," Satan proceeded, carefully examining the reactions of the two human forms in front of him, "my daughter might yet submit herself to you, for having seen her now, I do believe she has grown fond of you, owing to that repulsive humanity of hers. You gave up on her far too easily, Loomis; you resigned yourself from tempting her, and when I gave you a specific chance to redeem yourself by delivering her to me, you refused. I had wondered why; I have since determined you simply spent too long in that ridiculous human body you created. You lost yourself among the wretched human race, there in the temporal and the physical. Man's desires started to seep into you, demon, and my daughter is the only other being in all of creation who can possibly commiserate with you in such experience. You let her make you soft! You actually *enjoy* that disgusting human tenderness she shows you, don't you? Happy you would be to suckle the warm, feminine affection from those breasts!"

Iris felt her stomach turn at the horribly uncomfortable suggestiveness of Satan's words, and she felt her face flush with heat that could not be attributed to the lakes of fire surrounding her. She imagined Loomis must feel the same way, but then she realized he probably didn't. Either he was just an indifferent demon who had acted in certain ways toward her to achieve his own goals, or Satan was correct and he really did feel some attraction to her. Iris wasn't sure which was worse. She did recognize, however, Satan had suggested two extremes, and truth was more likely somewhere in the middle. If Loomis felt anything for her, surely it could be something affectionate short of any desire for...suckling. Loomis seemed to shift rather uncomfortably on his feet beside her, but Iris supposed that could be from lingering physical pain in his human body.

Before either of them could respond to the Devil's comments, he added, rather thoughtfully, "I should destroy you both; it is in my power to do it. But you may both prove useful to me after all, considering the twisted web of supposed emotion that has entrapped you together. Let me propose a deal to you, Loomis: I will give her to you. You will no longer be allowed to dwell on Earth, but you may keep your human form here in Hell, and you will have my daughter here with you, to do with as you please for all eternity. Defile her in whatever ways bring you the greatest pleasure, demon! And she will enjoy it." Iris swallowed nervously, hoping Loomis wasn't actually considering the offer. How would either of them keep her here against her will, anyway?

Satan turned to Iris directly and addressed her, "You, daughter, will accept what I have graciously offered, for you will be allowed to feed every one of your most secret, sensual desires, free from judgment."

Disgusted, but also nervous, Iris retorted, "I'm really not a particularly sensual woman."

The Devil laughed plentifully, then went quiet and answered, "I will not ask, then, whether you've fantasized about him, about his passionate kisses or his gentle touches or his warm caresses or the teasing flicks of his tongue as he eases his way inside you." Iris involuntarily looked down at the rock and ash beneath her feet, her cheeks hot and her heart racing. She wished she had never had such thoughts about Loomis, but she couldn't deny them. And even if she *hadn't* had such untoward thoughts before, she was certainly having them now. Satan had wormed his way into her head; she hadn't even realized what he was doing. She closed her eyes and swallowed again, struggling to refocus her mind. The lurid ideas the Devil was planting were not in fact what she wanted for herself or for Loomis; she knew that.

During her anxious silence, Satan continued, "If lust will not convince you, perhaps the threat of alternate punishment will. You have already seen I have taken Loomis's shadow-demon and programmed it for my own use. If you do not willingly relegate yourself to Hell, I will unleash it upon the Earth, and it will steal human souls for me with unprecedented haste. Ask yourself, then, are you willing to condemn your human race to such suffering? All you must do to save them is accept my proposal. Remain here, with your darling Loomis Drake beside you, and know you have prevented the massacre of souls. Of course, you and Loomis are both demons, and you will be expected to lure souls here; that condition should not have to be told to you." He paused, looked from Iris to Loomis, then addressed them both, saying, "There; the proposal is set before you. You will both enjoy an eternity only dreamed of by the other denizens of Hell. What do you say?"

Loomis sighed, and for an instant, Iris was afraid he would capitulate and accept Satan's distasteful terms. Instead, he said simply, "I don't have time for your imbecilic game. I have other items of business to attend to." He turned around as if to return to where Marvin's human soul and demonic possessor were chained to the ground, but an impulsive stomp from the claw-like foot of Satan suddenly cracked the rock upon which they all stood, cutting it deeply enough that a narrow capillary of fire opened up within it. Iris was startled and thrown off balance but recovered quickly with the aid of magic. Loomis stopped in his tracks but left his back facing the Devil.

"You have no other business," Satan hissed, his voice reverberating at extreme volume, drowning out the background wailing of the underworld. "You have refused me again, Loomis, and this has been the final time. I will give you one last opportunity to earn your keep here; if you fail me, I will destroy you, and your eternal existence will be no more."

Loomis turned slowly to face his ruler. The air, eternally laden with heat and odor, was now oppressively weighted by tension. Iris focused on the encounter playing out in front of her, certain that things were about to go bad. Here were probably the two most arrogant creatures in all the cosmos, who had coexisted for so long only because Loomis had found a way to enjoy some degree of freedom by inhabiting Earth more often than Hell. Iris's arrival here had changed the status quo; having witnessed for himself the inexplicable connection she and Loomis seemed to share, Satan had new ammunition and a new reason to remind Loomis of his place. If he did destroy Loomis, Iris would feel completely responsible for his demise. She couldn't allow it, especially considering what she now knew. She calmed herself as best she could, hoping she would be able to prevent unnecessary spiritual bloodshed in the coming moments.

With a slight grin, Loomis quietly answered Satan, "You cannot hope to destroy me. I have toiled endlessly for knowledge and have sought greater power, while you have lazed upon your throne, content with the wasteland and all its indifferent inhabitants at your feet. I am superior to you."

Iris expected a beastly tantrum; instead, Satan, in silence, reached the skeletal talon of his hand to an area in his own chest. The strange, opaque vapor that acted as his skin opened, and he pulled from inside his form a small, gem-like object with rough edges and a smoky burgundy hue and the luster of dirty glass. As a human, Iris would not have known what it was, but her demon's mind recognized it instantly as the relic that gave Satan his authority in Hell. Just after his rebellion against God and Heaven, before his separation from his Creator had taken its full toll on his spirit and form, Satan had created this relic using his own power (or, what he thought of as his own power, though, of course, all magic was from God alone) and a tiny fragment of Heaven's banquet table, which had been damaged during the demons' uprising. He had managed to steal it (more accurately, God had allowed him to take it), and with its power and the magic with which he had endowed it, its presence within his now utterly unrecognizable form was the force that prevented any other from taking his place. Iris had never before had reason to pull this ages-old knowledge from within herself; now, she understood why Loomis had truly needed her assistance. Only she, as the same substance as Satan, would be able to remove that relic from the Devil and put a new ruler on Hell's throne.

When Satan extended the relic out before him with a gnarled hand, Loomis's expression went completely dark. It was a look of unmitigated hatred, but it couldn't completely mask the fear underneath. The relic began to glow with a dim, pulsing light, and suddenly, every wail and cry in all of Hell went silent. Iris felt nothing, excepting her increasing human tenseness, but Loomis groaned softly, then dropped to his knees. He closed his eyes, and his body began to quiver. Iris sensed him straining with magic to fight off the effects of the Devil's relic, almost certainly knowing it was a futile exertion.

Loomis grabbed his head with both hands, shaking it from side to side and tugging roughly at his human hair. He groaned more loudly, until the agonized sound became a harrowing scream, and then he shouted, "NO! No...no...please..."

It was the only time Iris had heard Loomis plead, and it sparked an inferno of hatred within her for the one who was hurting him this way, whatever this particular hurt was. She was now prepared to attack Satan, but in the instant before she acted, he ended his spell. Loomis, on his knees, relaxed slightly, though distress still covered his face. Iris wanted to drop beside him and hold him, but that kind of human reaction could only make things worse here. She had acted too humanly toward him already.

"Oh, I forgot," Satan croaked in a demonic singsong voice, his words soaked with mockery, "you do not enjoy having your spirit crushed inside you! You know, no one else here seems to mind it quite as much as you do, Loomis. I suppose we must attribute it to all that intelligence and knowledge you have. You do not wish to lose it, yet you know I can take it all away from you. I can turn you into another mindless, purposeless, meaningless mass of spiritual indifference, just like all the rest of them. And so will I do, unless you do as I command you."

Loomis, his human chest rising and falling with quick breaths, remained kneeling silently as he looked up at Satan, awaiting his command. Iris realized she was slowly shaking her own head, not wanting to believe Loomis would submit himself to Satan's rule like this. But, she supposed, what choice did he really have?

"Stand," Satan commanded Loomis. "Take from my daughter the weapon she has brought here. You are going to kill her with it."

Iris went rigid as she heard the Devil's words. She stared at Loomis, her eyes wide with disbelief as he stood and turned to face her. Surely he wouldn't do this; surely he would choose her side over Satan's. After all they had been through... *What am I thinking?* Iris suddenly asked herself. What had she and Loomis really been through? A demonic chess game that had included some seductive words and some failed trickery and a little bit of collateral human damage? Stupidly, she realized, she was still humanizing him and believing he felt something not demonic for her. Did she simply want to believe it so badly that she had convinced herself? But then...what about that visionary revelation she had experienced here, the recognition of that part of Loomis she had failed to see before? There had to be truth in that...

Loomis approached her slowly, stopping just in front of her. He looked at her briefly, then opened his mouth as though he wanted to say something, but he refrained. Iris returned his gaze, then, with great sadness, slowly lifted her hand to offer her axe to him. He seemed surprised at her simple acquiescence, and for a long second, he didn't move. When he finally reached for her weapon, Iris knew what she had to do, and she wasted not an instant.

With focused magic to contravene the normal passage of Hell's perceived time, she reclaimed for herself fractions of the second before, then threw the axe with blinding speed and devastating accuracy into the chest of Satan's demonic form. At its entry into him, he froze in a solid, black mass, a statue of living, ebony marble, with the haft and one blade of Iris's bronze axe protruding from his torso. The engravings of her weapon were lit with a purple glow, and Iris recognized what it had done to the Devil. It was temporary, and she couldn't guess at its duration, but the axe's penetration had broken her target's ability to use any magic whatsoever.

Loomis, briefly taken aback by the sudden turn of events, turned from Iris and gazed for a moment at Satan's paralyzed form, then looked back at her with subtle approval.

"That's quite a weapon you have," he said simply. He didn't really show it, but Iris thought she sensed relief in his voice. She wanted to believe the relief stemmed from the fact he hadn't had to kill her after all, but perhaps he was relieved simply by the fleeting peace brought to Hell by Satan's loss of magic.

"You're nothing like him, Loomis," she told him quietly, shaking her head. "You could have so much more than this. You're better than him."

Loomis stared at her, nearly expressionless but for a vague inkling of suspicion at the impulsive compliment she had given him, then he answered drably, "You have now witnessed the injustice firsthand, then. I am better than he, yet he is the one on the throne, and there is not a damn thing I or anyone else here can do to change it. You have seen how he puts us under his feet. This is my existence, Iris. You alone have power to rectify it, but, of course, I'll never again attempt to coax you to my side; I gave you my word." He looked at her for a short moment longer with cold eyes and a tightened jaw, then turned to walk away.

"You'll no longer have to coax me," Iris replied. At the words, Loomis stopped abruptly, turned, and stepped aggressively back toward her, ruthlessly penetrating her eyes with his.

"What do you mean?" he demanded. His voice had a bite to it, as though warning her not to try misleading him.

Iris sighed and glanced briefly at the temporarily powerless statue of Satan, then she directed her eyes back to Loomis. "I think our opposition to one another has been nothing but a shortsighted exercise in poor judgment," she stated cryptically. "I think we have both been confused for a time, but...now I believe we both desire the exact same thing, and it isn't this." She gestured with mild disdain at their surroundings, then added, "I hope you arrive at the same conclusion."

Loomis lifted his chin slightly, peering down at Iris with wariness, but he said nothing. After a brief silence, Iris shrugged at him and concluded, "I guess it doesn't matter what conclusion you arrive at for yourself. I don't want him to hurt you anymore. This place isn't what I want, and I don't think it's really what you want, but if my being here is the only way to spare you additional torture, I'm willing to submit to it."

Loomis crossed his arms and scowled. He had healed his body almost completely, but the expensive clothing on it remained tattered and bloody. His pose somehow drew Iris's attention to the amount of skin she was seeing on him. It was far more than she was used to, and the echo of the Devil's earlier words taunted her again. She had to close her eyes for a self-deprecating second; there was no acceptable reason she should have to continue reminding herself what Loomis truly was, especially now.

"I have endured his rule for a very long time," he responded darkly. "I have no need of your protection or your aid. I am not the soft, pitiable creature he would have you believe I am. If pity for me is the motivation behind your sudden submission, then I will not accept it."

Iris rolled her eyes, thoroughly irritated by his habitual arrogance. "I find you neither pitiable nor soft," she said. "I know the opposite to be true. Why would I listen to his words at all, when I know you so much more deeply than he does?" The question caused Loomis's eyes to dart away from her for an instant. "Don't misunderstand my decision," she continued. "It isn't motivated by pity; it's motivated by a desire to change what *is*, and by a fervent hope you will finally admit to yourself you share that same desire."

She went quiet, swallowed, and verified that Satan was still held immobile and powerless by her axe. Loomis remained silent, too, so she continued, "You may accept my submission, or you may reject it; I won't force you either way. But I think you and I both sense an impending fork in the road, and your decision will have to be made before we reach it. Think about it, Loomis. Think about what it is you *truly* want, and let your decision not be limited by what you believe possible or impossible, and let it not understate your inherent, remarkable value."

Loomis's eyes narrowed as he stood rigidly in place, arms still crossed. "You seem to believe I may want something different from what I have proposed to you before," he replied, "but if you will share Hell's throne with me and allow the execution of my original plan for the conquest of Earth, there is nothing else I need. Is it to this end you are offering me your surrender?"

Iris let a tiny, sad smile settle on her lips. "If that's all you want," she answered slowly, "that's all you shall have." She shook her head gently and sighed, wondering if she had altogether misinterpreted the vision she thought she had seen. Maybe Loomis was just a pathetic, arrogant, bastard demon, after all. "There are greater things, Loomis," she added despondently, "and I believe you could share in those greater things, if you would only recognize how narrow-minded and vacuous is your plan for Hell's manifest destiny. But I may have misjudged you. Maybe you are worth no more than the throne of Hell." With another shrug, she finished, "The decision is yours. Decide what you want; whatever is in my power to give, you can have, but I'm telling you, there are powers mightier than I, and if you settle for me, you've sold yourself far short of what you could have had."

Loomis turned, took a few steps away, and stared emptily at Satan's frozen spirit, evidently deep in thought. Iris could only pray he would understand the meaning of her words and recognize the possibility of which she spoke. If he didn't, then Hell would be her eternity, too, because she simply couldn't let the Devil do any more harm to him. She had seen Loomis in a light that had changed her attitude toward him, and if he wouldn't rid himself of all his torment, then she would do what was in her power to assuage that torment, even if it meant damnation. Whatever Loomis would decide, though, she still had business to attend to; it was time to retrieve the detective's soul, if she could, and get out of here.

Loomis had drawn himself out of his short reverie, but he still faced the Devil's unmoving form. Addressing Iris, he asked, "How long do you leave me to make my decision? And am I correct to assume your surrender has stipulations?"

Iris stepped over to join him, standing by his side and likewise staring at Satan. The glow on her axe, she noted, was dimmer than what it had been. The Devil would be free again soon.

"I do have stipulations," she answered, sensing Loomis stiffening in agitation beside her. "I came here to rescue the soul that was just stolen by the shadow-demon," she explained. "Detective Myron Banks. I ask that you help me find him, because my human eyes can't identify the souls here. Find him for me, and release him from this place, and let me take him back. Let him face his particular judgment as his appointed time."

"Is that all?" Loomis asked blandly.

"Pretty much," Iris replied. "I'll leave you whatever time you need to make your decision. I only ask that you not arrive at it lightly." She considered the ramifications of her words, finally realizing the true heaviness of what she had proposed and wishing in some part of her mind she had never suggested such a thing. Knowing it was too late to retract her words, though, she stalwartly proceeded, "When you've made up your mind, come find me on Earth. I'll be expecting you. There is one final thing I will want to discuss with you, and then you will have my agreement to whatever you have decided."

"Fine," Loomis agreed in a stony voice. He moved a few paces away, muttered a spell in Aramaic, and disappeared. He reappeared after a short time, materializing in his own human form with a soul in his arms. To Iris, it looked like every other damned human soul here, sinewy and emaciated and unrecognizable, and she wondered, with sudden horror, if Loomis would be so consummately evil as to give her a soul other than Myron's to take back to Earth and put in Myron's body.

"That is the soul you seek," he said, dropping the dreadful form to the rock at Iris's feet.

She knelt down, sickened by the appearance of the soul, and gently touched the part of it that resembled a humanoid face. She closed her eyes and concentrated her demonic vision until she was convinced this was, in fact, the poor detective's illegitimately damned soul. Standing again, she looked at Loomis and nodded gently. "I'll be going, then," she said. "You should return to Earth, too, before I retrieve my axe. It won't be safe for you here."

"Have no concern for me," Loomis answered coldly.

Iris wanted to be angry at the comment, but she felt only hurt from it. It was unlike her to show this level of concern for someone in the first place, and to have it returned to her so unappreciated was a blow to the heart. She had never been the type to accept such abuse. If the subject had been anyone but Loomis, she would have waved off the glacial retort with a "screw you, then," and she would have hoped the bastard got whatever he had coming. Unfortunately, she had lost the ability to adopt such a cavalier attitude toward Loomis now, and she still wasn't sure whether that was a positive development or a lamentable new handicap.

Saying nothing, she bent and picked up Myron's soul, which was far lighter than the size of its apparent form had suggested. With him over one shoulder, she began the spell to reopen the Gate. She would call her axe back to her just as she departed through it, and Loomis could subject himself to the Devil's ensuing tantrum, if that's what he wanted to do.

Before the Gate appeared, however, Loomis took two long and ferociously quick strides toward her and grabbed her upper arm, roughly turning her to face him. His face was inches from hers as he hissed, "See that you are not planning any tricks for me, Iris. I will not be made a fool by you again."

His grip on her arm was uncomfortably tight, but Iris did nothing to oppose it. Instead, with her other hand, she reached up and tenderly brushed the side of his face, contemplating him through the lens of the visionary revelation she had experienced—a revelation Loomis couldn't know she had been given. He must believe she could see him only as either a human man, which was a lie, or a demon, which was really only a portion of the truth, but she was seeing something else, and it was exceptional. Resting her palm against his cheek, she gave a tiny shake of her head and whispered, "No tricks."

Loomis hastily shoved her arm from his grip and angrily forced her hand away from his face, taking a step backward. He watched with an ominous expression as Iris finally turned away, opened the Gate, magically drew her axe back to her hand, and departed.

As she moved from Hell back to Earth, she hoped Loomis would do as she had urged him. She hoped he would consider the one possibility he had almost certainly deemed unattainable. Even more desperately, she hoped the possibility truly existed in reality and not just in the fancies of her own mind.

31

Detective Crane had lost all concept of time as he knelt on the hard concrete floor of the old bunker, beside his partner's lifeless body. His knees were aching, but he was afraid to move, as though changing position might be irreverent to God. The tears had stopped, but the heavy iron jaws of despair still clamped on his stomach like a vise. He was shocked and numb and disbelieving, and he felt empty and dumb and terrified all at once. He struggled to focus his thoughts on prayer as Iris had instructed him. He wanted nothing more than to help Myron out of this if he could, but he couldn't completely prevent the rambling of his mind upon the twisted pathways of distracting questions—stupid questions, like what would he say at Myron's funeral, or what kind of flowers should he and his wife order, or why hadn't he just heeded Iris's advice? None of it mattered now. If Iris failed to rescue Myron's soul, then there would be a funeral and there would be flowers, and neither of those would mean a damn thing, because Myron would be gone and that was the bottom line. And as for having heeded Iris's advice...well, there wasn't anything he could do now to change that. If she didn't save his partner, though, Crane would spend the rest of his miserable life beating himself up for this. It was no different than what had happened so long ago, a terrible mistake that had hurt other people, only this time it was worse, because this time he should have known better, and this time he probably wouldn't have nearly four decades to soothe the pain.

"Dear Jesus, help him," Crane muttered, shaking his head and burying his face in his hands. He didn't know what else to say. If he could speak frankly with God, maybe he would ask why the hell He would allow this. He might ask why God hadn't let the shadow thing take him instead of letting it take Myron. But, somewhere deep down, Crane was afraid to be angry at God, so he just kept on pleading for help, wondering if God was even listening. He couldn't stand to look at the ruined eyes on his friend's body, so he kept his own eyes tightly closed, and he hoped he was only imagining the increasingly cold draft coming from the soulless form lying near him.

It was an internal feeling more than an audible sound that prompted him to open his eyes. The dim light Iris had left for him was tinted momentarily by a garnet glow, drawing Crane's attention to the wall where the hole had been. By the time he focused on it, the void and its red aura were already gone, leaving only a wall of intact concrete with Iris Wakefield in front of it, rising to her feet from her knees. The menacing axe she had taken with her lay on the ground beside her, and after she dusted black ash and dust from her clothing, she bent down, picked it up, somehow shrank it, and tucked it back into the laces of her boot. Crane stared at her hopefully, wondering if she had Myron's soul with her. He didn't know what a soul would look like or how someone would carry it, but it appeared, much to his dismay, that Iris was alone.

As she approached from those few yards away, Crane realized she was looking down at Myron and not at him. Following her gaze with his own, he hazarded a cautious glance at his partner. To his surprise, Banks's eyes were no longer the horrifying black orbs of death they had been moments before. His eyelids were closed, and he lay peacefully as though asleep. Crane could see him breathing.

Iris knelt by Myron's opposite side and met Crane's eyes for a second, giving him a gentle, confident nod. She took Myron's shoulder in her hand and squeezed lightly. "Wake up," she said quietly. Her voice sounded hoarse and strained, and she looked paler than she had before. Crane saw her face and hair were covered with ash, too, and he noticed she smelled not unlike the arson scene he had investigated less than twenty-four hours ago.

Crane watched in awe as Myron's eyelids blinked several times and then opened, revealing the detective's normal, deep-brown eyes. He looked around in confusion and then started to sit up, aided by Crane on one side and Iris on the other. "What happened?" he asked slowly, pausing for almost a full second between the words.

Crane, overwhelmed by the relief he felt rushing upon him, couldn't help but laugh. He slapped Myron amiably on his back and then hugged him. "You were dead, man," he replied to him. "I thought you were gone for good," he added, having to rub his eyes to prevent any overflow of tears as he released his embrace of Banks and gave him some room.

Banks sat on the floor, legs straight out in front of him, looking from Crane to Iris. "I died?" he asked, running one hand absentmindedly over the smooth dome of his head. "How?"

Crane rose stiffly to his feet and held a hand down to help Banks up. "You don't remember?" he asked in response. "That shadow thing attacked you, the same thing that killed Joshua Ellis."

Banks rubbed his head and sighed. "I'm not sure," he said. "I don't know if I remember."

Iris had now stood as well, and Myron was looking at her quizzically. "Wait," he exclaimed, pointing at her. "You were there, right? I saw you there. What...what was that place?"

Crane waited silently for Iris's answer. "That was Hell," she stated simply.

Banks just stared at her, forehead scrunched as though he hadn't understood what she had said. "I...I died and went to Hell?" he finally asked, horror evident in his muted voice.

Iris smiled wanly. "Not exactly, Detective," she answered. "You had your soul stolen from you and taken to Hell, and that caused the death of your body. It was unnatural and untimely, and it should never have happened, but evil *is* allowed to play around like this on Earth, at least for now."

"You brought me back from Hell?" Banks questioned, his voice shaking slightly. It looked to Crane as though he might be on the verge of tears.

Iris reached a hand up to the messy knot of hair that had fallen slightly from where she had tied it. As if realizing now how unkempt it must look, she removed some bobby pins and pulled out the hair tie, revealing an astonishing length of auburn hair. She shook it out, dust falling from it in little ashy puffs, then tied it high on her head in another informal bun as she answered, "I was only an instrument in it. It was God who saved you from that place."

Banks let his eyes fall to the floor and stood apparently lost in thought, slowly and gently shaking his head. After a long, silent minute, still staring at the floor, he whispered, "I never really believed in any of that before."

Crane reached out and squeezed Myron's shoulder encouragingly. "It's all over now, Myron," he said. "You're here, alive, and that's what matters. We've all been through some hard shit today, and it's gonna be a while, maybe a long time, before we sort ourselves out, but we'll get there. It'll be okay." He finished in a confident tone, nodding to himself.

"I can't go back there," Banks mumbled quietly. Crane noticed his partner's breaths were starting to come in quick, shallow whiffs, and his eyes had taken on a wild, terrified look. "I can't ever go back there," he repeated. "It was awful; it was so awful..."

Crane, now doubly concerned for Myron's state of mind, put an arm around his partner's shoulders and tried to calm him down. Banks had derailed onto an incessant, panicked mantra, and Crane's words were useless. The episode lasted only a handful of seconds before Iris stepped toward Myron and laid her hand gently against his forehead, muttering either a prayer or a magical spell; Crane wasn't sure which it was, but it immediately pacified the hysterical detective. His eyes closed and his breathing normalized, and Iris somehow moved his tall, athletic frame to a seated position against the nearest wall, effortlessly and without Crane's assistance.

"He's asleep now," she stated. "We should get him out of here, and I recommend you have him checked out by a doctor. I don't know how the separation of his soul from his body might have physically affected him. Of course, the emotional and spiritual traumas are likely going to prove far worse. In a single day, he's gone from 'not really believing' to experiencing his soul's complete and utter deprivation of the God he never understood was a part of him. He'll have a lot to sort out, as you said." She paused for an exhausted sigh, then added, "It may be a difficult recovery ahead, but I think he'll be okay. You'll be there to help him."

Crane nodded vigorously. "Of course I will," he affirmed. Then, since Banks was resting peacefully for the moment, and because he was curious to no end about it, he asked, "What was it like?"

Iris thought carefully, then replied, "Imagine the deepest despair you've ever felt, magnify that by a thousand times, and even that would not begin to compare to the misery. At least here, you can find God if you seek Him. There is no God in Hell."

The words were delivered as a matter-of-fact, unembellished attestation of truth. Crane reflected silently for a moment, recalling how he had questioned whether God was hearing his desperate prayers for Myron. Even if he hadn't been sure about it, at least he had been able to maintain the hopeful belief that God was listening. He tried to imagine how it would feel to *know* God wasn't there, and he couldn't do it.

"Come on, Detective," Iris prompted through his musings. "Let's go." She had squatted down and picked up Myron's slumbering form before Crane could step over to him. It looked quite comical, amazing though it was, seeing a woman of Iris's rather average build effortlessly carrying a sleeping man who was over six feet tall and probably at least two hundred and twenty pounds of muscle. Crane figured she was using some supernatural power of hers, but it made him feel awkward nonetheless, letting her carry his partner.

"Here, I'll get him," he suggested, extending his arms. Iris didn't argue, and once he was holding his younger and sturdier colleague, he regretted having offered. Iris smiled a little, almost certainly aware of his struggle to support Myron's weight, but she said nothing and instead simply led the way up the cellar steps. Crane grimaced and grunted, but he successfully carried his partner back to the cellar door. Thankfully, Iris took Banks from there and rested him gently against the marble pedestal of a Greek goddess statue, then helped Crane and his stiff, bruised limbs out into the museum warehouse.

Seeing the hodgepodge of historical junk, Crane suddenly remembered what had brought him and Myron here in the first place. "Hey," he asked, "what happened to Dr. Whitakker?"

Iris shook her head and shrugged. "He got what he knew was coming to him," she responded.

Crane furrowed his eyebrows at the enigmatic reply, but he didn't press the issue. "Well," he replied slowly, taking nearly two full seconds to complete his introductory word, "what do we do about this whole...incident?"

Iris made some silent considerations, placing her hands on her hips and staring at the floor. Her dark eyebrows were pressed together much like Crane's often were. At long last, she took a deep breath and admitted, "I don't know, Detective." She unzipped a pocket on her jacket and removed the copper spearhead Crane recognized from the photos Whitakker had provided at the investigation's onset. Handing it to him with an encouraging nod, she continued, "You can still pin the theft on Whitakker. You can tell some of the truth. You came here with follow-up questions; there was a scuffle; you chased him into an abandoned cellar beneath the museum. All those things can be reported. You'll just need to rewrite the rest of the story. Say Whitakker escaped. There is, in fact, an alternate exit down there that leads through an old tunnel to a field near the trailer park where he lived. He used it often. So you lost him, and he disappeared, but you recovered the artifact. That's all anyone will really care about. I'm sure the museum staff had about as high an opinion of their curator as you did."

Crane nodded as he listened, casually inspecting the spearhead in his hand. He snorted at Iris's last statement. "Yeah," he agreed, pulling out a handkerchief and cleaning the relic before wrapping it and placing it in his pocket. "No one's going to miss that guy."

"Probably true," Iris answered. "At least, no one here on Earth will miss him." Crane winced as he understood her implication. Damn, he was inconsiderate. The guy was still a human being with value. *Or was he?* Crane decided it didn't matter. Whatever Whitakker was, or had been, God had made him, and maybe God missed him.

"Anyway," Iris continued, "Dr. Whitakker stole the artifact and then escaped from the police. That's part of the museum case solved. Sadly, Joshua Ellis's death will have to remain a mystery." After a momentary hesitation, she added, "I don't know how to direct you regarding Detective Banks's traumatic experience. For now, I think maybe you call for paramedics and have them check him out. Tell them there was a confrontation. The details can all be sorted out later. I doubt his memory of it all will ever return completely."

"I don't like it," Crane grumbled. It felt so wrong, trying to weave this web of deceit.

"I know you don't, Detective," Iris answered. "I don't like it, either, but we both know the truth will only scream of insanity." She sighed, then said, "You do what your conscience tells you. Maybe ask for some guidance from a power greater than me. Everything will fall into place as it's supposed to."

"Right," Crane muttered, unconvinced but striving to remain hopeful as he looked down at Myron, still fast asleep like a child. Had he not just witnessed the miraculous today? If God could send Iris into Hell to rescue Myron's soul, then God could concoct a believable story out of something less than the full truth. Crane realized it was his own ability to listen that was really in question.

He looked at Iris and found her smiling slightly at him. "You're going to become an example to your partner now," she said quietly. "You won't be his only example, but you'll be an important one. Detective Banks has suffered the one true Hell, a horrifying reality not meant for a living soul. So his most significant religious experience so far has been complete separation from a God he doesn't really know. How strong a faith do you want him to see in you?"

Crane closed his eyes and took a deep breath, trying to ensure the tears didn't come back. He opened his eyes, mindlessly smoothed his mustache, and nodded silently in understanding.

Iris glanced at Banks one last time and then returned her gaze to Crane. "I guess I'll be going now," she said. It sounded to Crane as though she were reluctant to leave. "Good luck with everything," she finished.

"We'll see you around, won't we?" Crane asked hopefully, prompted by the note of finality in Iris's voice. He knew very little about her, but for some reason he liked having her around. Besides, the three of them had been through a really harrowing experience together today, and Iris had saved the detectives' lives, especially Myron's; it would be nice if they could all remain friendly. "You would be a great example to us both," he added, borrowing a few of Iris's own words.

With a muted, sad kind of smile, Iris answered, "I don't know, Detective. I...might not be around."

Without another word, she turned and walked away, soon disappearing among the clutter of the storage room. Something in her tone had caused a heavy dread in Crane's stomach, and he had the odd, terrifying thought that maybe the rescue of Myron's soul had come at a great price. He pressed his eyes shut and rubbed his forehead, forcing tears away as he pulled out his phone with his other hand. It was time for him to call the paramedics and get Banks attended to.

32

"I'm here," Loomis announced dramatically, extending his arms out to his sides as he approached with his usual swagger. He had parked his sleek black Maserati across the street, giving himself plenty of room for a theatrical entrance as he strode toward Iris, where she waited on the corner of the sidewalk for his arrival. His masculine frame was silhouetted by the reddish glow of the setting sun behind him, cutting an impressive, intimidating, and inarguably sinister form that sent Iris's heart sinking into her stomach. Considering his current attitude, she surmised there was very little possibility this meeting's end would be anything but the one she had hoped to avoid.

Once he had entered the same dim light of the streetlamp under which she stood, he placed his hands in the pockets of his long overcoat, gazed at Iris with a deep stare and a contemptuous grin, then commanded sharply, "Whatever it is you wanted to discuss with me, do get on with it."

"Hello to you, too, Loomis," Iris answered sarcastically, fully aware that her forced confidence didn't completely hide the nervousness she felt in her gut. Why had she hoped he might have shown up here with an open mind and a willingness to entertain some notion other than evil? He was obviously here to listen to her only because she had stipulated it as a term of her surrender; it seemed all too clear he had already made up his mind, and the result would be her damnation.

He narrowed his eyes at her response, and Iris's thoughts were momentarily swept back to her first meeting with him, when she had seen in his expression a hate more profound than she had believed possible. In the next instant, though, she thought she saw a flicker of something else—perhaps the subtlest trace of regret?—and she hoped it wasn't just her feminine emotions blurring her vision. Maybe, just maybe, Loomis might still change his mind.

"If you will recall, *Iris*," he said acidly, "you have already agreed to whatever I would decide, and I have now decided, which means however amusing I have found our past escapades, I no longer feel obligated to endow you with my patience. I will hear whatever you have to say to me now only because you required it as a term of your surrender. So get on with it, and know I will *absolutely* destroy you if you attempt to withdraw your white flag. You have no idea how powerful I will soon be."

His voice was the same smooth, low tone it always was, but it had a distinct chill to it, much colder than the winter air surrounding the two of them now. Iris couldn't help but recall the times she had wondered if Loomis might actually care for her somehow, including most recently when he had stood up to Satan for her in Hell, and she realized with great sadness that those inclinations had been nothing but empty, unwarranted, stupid hope. Or, if they had been even the least bit true, Loomis had now thoroughly obliterated them. He was ready for Hell's throne, and he would have her right there beside him, damned for eternity simply because she wanted to protect him however she could from the torture of the Devil. From a distant corner of her mind, she heard the wrathful thought, *He could never destroy you; you're stronger than he is. Don't let him forget it.* She dismissed it, however, knowing she couldn't bring herself to hurt Loomis after what she had finally seen in him, even if he acted like a jerk for all the rest of eternity.

When she replied to him after a second of contemplation, her voice was drawn and tired. "I don't intend to repeal my surrender," she said, desperately searching Loomis's eyes for some hint of remorse or reconsideration, but finding none. With a sigh, she continued, "I've asked you here because…"

She trailed off inadvertently, suddenly realizing how ridiculous she was going to sound. She'd be lucky if Loomis responded with anything other than hysterical laughter, and even if she were so lucky, she wasn't likely to get the true answers she had been hoping for. Loomis's expression, though, surprisingly, showed more curiosity than amusement at her stuttering. His eyes were slightly narrowed, still probing her own gaze with a disquieting depth, but he said nothing, instead tacitly prompting her to continue, or to try to continue.

Iris took a deep breath but remained silent for another couple of seconds. Finally, after looking down at the sidewalk and then back to Loomis, she simply said, "Walk with me."

Loomis rolled his eyes. "Iris, my dear," he sighed, "you bore me. This is a waste of my time and yours."

"A waste of time?" she snapped, genuinely aggravated by his statement. "What the *hell*, Loomis? You've waited since practically the dawn of humanity for this, and you'll have an eternity to gloat over it. Don't tell me I'm wasting your time! You can spare twenty more human minutes, can you not?"

He raised an eyebrow at her outburst, his expression tightening, and with his handsome face framed by the high collar of his coat, he exuded a most imposing aura. "For a being teetering so precariously on the cusp of complete nonexistence, you have quite the attitude," he admonished her.

Iris stared at him quietly for a moment before replying. "You're curious what I have to say," she challenged. "You've enjoyed toying with me, and you've enjoyed the difficulty I've given you, so I know you must want to know why I've finally ceded myself to you."

Loomis heaved a melodramatic sigh of exasperation and responded, "You are an insufferable annoyance, but, though I loathe to admit it, I must say you understand me quite well." He smiled at her with a beautiful but menacing display of teeth, devoid of warmth or humor, then said, "Lead the way."

Iris turned away and started walking. She knew where she was going, of course, but she felt lost and alone. The two walked in silence for a few minutes until, finally, Iris began her story. She knew Loomis would listen. He would listen because of his curiosity, and then...well, in all likelihood he would laugh and then kill her with great pleasure.

"I had this recurring dream as a kid," she stated. She wasn't looking at Loomis, but she could practically feel his eye roll. Undaunted, however, she continued, "It was always hazy and indistinct, but it was bright and warm and safe. I could make out only a single figure in the dream, and only vaguely, but it was always the same figure. I never knew what meaning to draw from it." She turned a corner and proceeded down the next street; Loomis followed but said nothing. "I never told anyone about it," she went on. "It eventually stopped, and I thought nothing of it. But then I remember one day, quite a while later, sitting in a Sunday school class and recalling that dream, wondering if that figure in it had been my guardian angel." She chuckled sheepishly, wishing she could read Loomis's thoughts right now. He remained quiet.

They walked around another corner and for another brief stretch before she led Loomis across the street and to the parking lot of Saint Augustine's Church. He followed without complaint through the parking lot to the stone steps leading to the entrance of the church. Iris took one step up and turned to face him, the shallow stair raising her to about his height.

He stared back at her, disdain and boredom on his face. "Was this your grand scheme, Iris?" he asked. "Bore me nearly to death with some insipid story of your childhood as you lead me to some holy place where you think I'll be somehow weakened?" He leaned closer so his nose nearly touched hers, then said bitterly, "There is nothing here to stop me from burning this church to the ground and dancing on the ashes."

His voice was lower and colder than before, leaving his mouth and striking Iris's skin as a threatening sibilation. She forced herself to remain where she stood, fighting her human instinct to back away from him. Striving to keep anxiety out of her voice, she answered quietly, "I believe that. I bring you here only because this is where I want to be before you take me, and I tell you the story not to bore you, but...to elucidate you." Her gaze had fallen to her feet at some point, and she had to make a conscious effort to raise it again to meet Loomis's stare.

His tense posture relaxed slightly, and he moved back just a bit, leaving Iris with some breathing room. He casually replied, "I fail to see how this is to elucidate me." *He's still curious*, Iris thought. *Good.*

"I had that dream again, not long ago," she explained, speaking more confidently, "only this time, I could see it. I could *really* see it; I could *feel* it. I saw the figure clearly, and I saw all that was happening, and I finally understand it now. It fully dawned on me when I was down there in Hell." As she recalled the experience, her words became more impassioned. "It wasn't a *dream* at all," she stated with certainty. "It was a *vision*. Not a prophecy, not a foretelling, but an echo from the past—like a photograph of what used to be."

Loomis stood before her, listening attentively but wearing a stony, opaque mask of neutrality. She stared at him for a long moment, wishing she could read his expression.

"That figure was you," she finished simply.

Loomis still stubbornly withheld any verbal response, but Iris interpreted his demeanor now as an unadulterated, hateful darkness. She felt tears beginning to burn behind her eyes as she reflected on the majesty of the vision she had seen. Now as she looked at Loomis, having seen the image of what he once had been, she could no longer feel any animosity toward him. If anything, she pitied him, and she ardently desired an explanation. It was clear to her she could no longer keep her emotions out of this, so she allowed herself to continue with a small voice, addled with sadness, anger, confusion...and the desperation that Loomis might finally explain to her what she couldn't understand.

"Loomis, *I saw you*," she proceeded, her jaw beginning to quiver as emotions overtook her. "You were...so *beautiful*. So strong, so noble, so dignified. So...perfect, and glorious..." She stared at him, seeking a reply but receiving none.

"You were a seraph," she continued, her voice increasingly tremulous. "More powerful than the archangels! I saw you kneeling at the foot of the throne. I couldn't see *Him*, but I heard what was happening. You were given a divine vocation, a sacred duty to protect the human race from the temptations of the Evil One, and you accepted that call with solemnity and humility. You loved God and all His creation, and you swore to protect it. You were so *loved* by Him!" She felt some tears escaping her eyes, but she found no shame in it. Let Loomis see her cry; what harm was there in displaying weakness now? She blinked and wiped the tears away with a gloved hand, just to clear her vision, then she sniffled and shook her head as she met Loomis's gaze. It was evident he didn't yet intend to reply.

"*Why?*" she begged him, truly dismayed to have seen his former glory after witnessing the horrid aftermath of his fall from grace. "Why did you leave? Why did you betray Him? Why would you follow Satan? Loomis, tell me *why!*"

Her speech ended on a clear note of anguish. It was nothing to witness the everyday sins of humanity, for she had never seen their glorified forms. They had always been sinners, as far as she had seen. But to have beheld what Loomis had been, in awesome splendor and perfect glory, with full knowledge of what he had become after a descent into sin and decay and self-inflicted damnation...it was true agony for the heart. Silence ensued for a long moment. Iris continued to stare at him, an interrogatory plea manifest in her eyes. He remained fixed in front of her, maintaining eye contact, anger somehow radiating from an otherwise impassive expression.

When Loomis finally responded, his voice was a deep, biting hiss. "I owe you no explanation," he asserted vehemently, "but, lest you think I am some pitiful creature in need of redemption, I will tell you what the One who showed you this *vision* failed to include. Yes, I vowed to protect the human race. As the most powerful of the angels, I was to lead the Heavenly host in their guardianship of God's creation. I was also given a personal ward—Eve, the mother of all the living. It was my duty to guard her from the wickedness of the Devil, and I would stop at nothing to do it. Yes, I loved God, and I loved her, in the purest and most chaste manner that can be conceived." As he spoke, his words became faster and angrier, imbuing his story with terrifying ferocity.

"You know what happened," he continued, practically spitting out the words. "Eve sinned. She betrayed what she knew to be right, at the prompting of a *serpent*. I never blamed her, though the sorrow she caused me was more profound and more harrowing than your feeble mind can imagine. I blamed myself. I believed I had failed my ward, and I had failed my God and all His creation. But I wasn't allowed to interfere with her free will. I *had* to let her make her choice; on that, I had no choice. So I cast the blame and all abhorrence on Satan. *He* had lured her away, tricked her into careless rebellion against her Creator. In doing so, he had won a victory over me, and over the Lord."

He paused, glaring at Iris with dagger-like sharpness, but she could formulate no reply. She was stunned by the emotion so tangible in his speech, and she was paralyzed with rapt attention to his words. Was there not a hint of regret in his tone? Would a demon recount his past with such feeling? Would the eternally damned even be able to recall true love or a once ardent desire for righteousness? Her mind was abuzz with questions she couldn't yet answer, and although Loomis's passionate retelling of his past was frightening, she desired nothing else but for him to continue.

"So I made his destruction my mission," Loomis proceeded, his words now a bit slower and slightly less acidic. "I would descend into Hell and vanquish him so he would never again turn mankind against their God. I confronted him in his own so-called Kingdom of Darkness. He showed no fear. If anything, he was amused, and I hated him for it. He asked the reason for my anger and my hatred, though of course he was already well aware of it. When I told him I'd not allow his treachery to impose anymore upon the human race, he asked me why." He paused again, his anger seeming to have subsided into something else, something resembling indifference, though Iris wondered if it might be well-disguised shame.

"I left silence before him, for I saw no reason to reply," he continued. "He asked me then whether I *really* knew the human race. He asked me if I deemed them truly worthy of Heaven, of the plan God had for them. I answered him as any holy one would— that God's plan was perfect, that His creation was perfect, that any incapacity of understanding on our parts was inconsequential. He told me it was folly, a mistake to follow so blindly. He told me he knew the weakness of humankind, how they were incapable of true divinity because of their limited understanding and their foolish desires and curiosities, and yet this was the race God planned from the beginning to adopt and to elevate to the seat at His right hand, making them greater than the angels. I didn't want to listen to him. I argued with him, but I had no retorts other than the same points I had already used: God's perfection and our inability to comprehend it because we are less powerful than He. By then, those words had begun to sound ignorant and weak, even to me."

Iris had inadvertently lifted her hand to cover her mouth as Loomis narrated. She was beginning to see where his story was going, and she was appalled and sickened by it. A pale, drawn look on Loomis's face made her wonder whether he felt the same way.

He breathed deeply and audibly before speaking again. "So he proposed something to me," he went on at length. "He made a deal with me: If I would tempt one man or woman to sin and he or she should resist my temptations and remain true to God's commandments, Satan would abdicate his throne as Prince of Darkness, and he would never again meddle in earthly affairs. His wicked snares would never again entrap the human race. I considered his proposition for but a moment. Even after Eve's grave error in judgment, I still believed in the perfection of God and His creation. I believed Satan would be proven the fool. And so...I accepted his proposal."

Iris felt a tiny gasp escape her lips as tears once again began to well up behind her eyes. She couldn't believe what she was hearing, but she knew in every fiber of her being that Loomis was telling the truth.

"Do you know what I found?" Loomis asked abruptly, his tone suddenly rife again with fiery animosity and his face pressed close to Iris's. She trembled slightly, involuntarily. She did, of course, know what Loomis had found, but he hadn't intended that she should reply.

"I found the *real* truth," he said in answer to his own question, his voice low and dark. "I found hypocrisy, lust, greed, envy, pride, wrath, corruption, vanity, ignorance." He had begun slowly, but the words came faster and faster as he spoke, accented with palpable disgust. "I found a race unashamedly willing to sin. It was *easy*. *Too easy*. And the more of them I lured, all the easier it became." Loomis now had a ghastly snarl on his lips, his teeth bared in animalistic malignance. After another short pause, however, he relaxed somewhat. When he continued, it was with a flat and uncaring attitude.

"I found Satan had been right," he stated. "Humanity was a base and idiotic creation, a mockery of the divinity of Heaven. They didn't deserve such splendor. They couldn't appreciate it. They couldn't uphold that kind of dignity. They wouldn't fight for it or defend it. I realized the greatest service to Heaven would be to purge it of humanity. And so I pulled them away. I pulled so many away." He had once more adopted the erect but casually confident and entitled posture Iris had so often seen in him. He smiled. "I've pulled away so many more than has Satan himself," he finished with twisted pride. "Much more artfully, too. And I've *enjoyed* it."

The conclusion of his story left Iris shaken and ill. Her hand fell slowly, numbly, away from her mouth as she stared in incredulity at the immortal being standing before her, so seamlessly masked as a human man. His tale had brought her immense despair—she much preferred stories in which good prevailed over evil—but she understood it. She wasn't completely unsympathetic to Loomis's motivations. As scary as the thought was, she had to admit she might not have done anything differently herself. She and Loomis were not unalike, but there was one very significant disparity: Iris had a true human nature. She *should* want more than anything for humanity to be welcomed into Heaven, yet she could imagine herself having acted exactly as Loomis had.

Regaining her senses and trying to rein her wild thoughts into some showing of logical debate, she took a deep breath and swallowed hard, then heard a flood of words start spilling out of her own mouth. "But you *must* have found people who were good," she argued emphatically. "People who resisted temptations to sin! There have been saints and martyrs—"

"And they have all been sinners," Loomis interrupted.

"Yes," Iris admitted, "but they've been forgiven! We've all been forgiven. We aren't expected to attain perfection here, Loomis. We have only to strive for it, and when we fail, we trust in the abundant mercy of God!" She paused, feeling suddenly uncharacteristically forgiving of the hypocrisy and sinfulness she herself had so often witnessed and hated.

Loomis glared at her. "Spare me the ridiculous sermon, Iris," he charged. "Don't *preach* to me. Your God's mercy is weakness. Impotence. An unwillingness to admit a mistake. A race that cannot earn their divinity should not have it freely given to them."

"Did *you* earn your divinity?" Iris asked pointedly in response.

He was quiet for several seconds. When he finally replied, his voice held no small amount of venom. "I *deserved* it," he said. "I would not have betrayed it."

Iris shook her head, her mind finally clearing. "But you *did* betray it," she asserted. "You were no better able to fight the Devil than Eve had been! You allowed yourself to be tricked by him, just as she was. How can you not see that now? How do you not recognize how he so easily lured you away and then started using you? Manipulating you to serve his own devices? You were stronger than he was! He knew that. He would have been powerless against you but for trickery, and you fell for it!" Sensing herself yet again nearing the verge of tears, she paused and collected herself before continuing. "You say you 'deserved' Heaven," she went on, "but you know Heaven can't be *earned*—it can only be *given*. And it was given to you, freely. You disowned it."

She shook her head again, not in disapproval or judgment, but in profound sadness. She longed for some final reply from Loomis, hoping perhaps some word of hers might have been prompted by the Holy Spirit and might have touched him, might have spurred him into some sudden recognition of his transgressions and made him repentant, but he was as cold and unmoving as a statue, and Iris sensed finality in his attitude. She desperately wanted things to be different for him. After she had fully recognized him as the glorified seraph from her vision, she had truly believed she had seen a remnant of righteousness in him, and she had truly believed he might yet seek an eternity outside of Hell. She wished he would beg for forgiveness and be welcomed back into Heaven, assuming that was even an option God might give him at this point. If God's mercy truly was infinite, then why *couldn't* a demon be made holy again? Unfortunately, possibilities or impossibilities aside, it appeared Loomis had made his choice, as inconceivable as it was. He had given her what she asked, an explanation of his forsaking of God for the Devil, and now there was nothing left for her to say or do but to await her fate at his hand.

"I'll be inside," she announced despondently into the frigid silence Loomis had left for her. "Just...come get me when it's time." She turned and walked slowly up the remaining steps toward the church doors, hoping he would give her at least a moment of peace before the end.

From behind her as she reached for the door, Loomis's low, demonic voice taunted, "Prayer will do nothing for you now."

Iris looked back at him one final time, a strange and unexpected calm descending upon her. "I won't be praying for me," she answered quietly. She turned and entered the church in silence.

The lights were off inside the gathering area, except for dim security lighting near the doors. Iris walked through the space and turned toward the sanctuary entrance, removing her gloves as she did so. She found the dimmer switch on the wall beside her and turned the lights to their lowest setting. The heavy, engraved wooden altar at the front of the church was beautifully lit by recessed bulbs, and the brightest lamps shone on the elevated gold tabernacle and the large, intricate crucifix hanging high on the brick wall behind it. Small alcoves near the entrance where she now stood were flickering with the mild, yellow-orange light of tiny votive candles in their decorative wire racks at the feet of painted resin statues of the Virgin Mary and the Holy Family. Iris walked forward to the holy water font before her, dipped two fingers, and crossed herself before moving down the center aisle of the church toward the steps leading to the altar. How many times had she entered this church, or churches just like it elsewhere, having crossed herself the same way? How many times had she stared at the image of Jesus on the cross, bloodied by thorns and nails, a gaping hole in his side? How often had she genuflected before the tabernacle and the altar? How many Masses had she attended? And yet as she stood here now, in a cold and empty room, she felt a strangeness, a newness to all the motions. It was as though she were *feeling* the sanctuary for the first time, like every time before had been just a thoughtless practice in a virtual setting. *What a waste*, she thought with shame. *Why did I waste a lifetime taking all this for granted?*

 She removed her coat and set it on the front pew, then fell to her knees beside it, in the center of the aisle, a short distance from the foot of the altar steps. She stared past the altar to the tabernacle, the red sanctuary lamp burning beside it to signify the presence of Christ. She bowed her head and prayed in silence. She had nothing left to ask for herself, because she had already resigned herself to the only two options Loomis seemed to have left her for the end of her mortal life—either eternity in Hell with him, or the complete destruction of her spirit after he gained the power of Hell's throne. She did, however, have much to ask for Loomis, even though he was about to kill her. Had she never seen that vision of him in divine grace, and had there never been sparked in her the thought that he might still have goodness within him, she would have continued fighting. She would have opposed him with all her power and with every prayer and every magical rune and spell she could learn. She would have persevered until either he surrendered or she was vanquished. Now, though, she didn't want to fight him at all. She wanted to save him. She had seen him in a new light, in a serene and beautiful image of glory and nobility and love, and the vision had displayed for her the unmarred splendor of God's creation. She had been shown what existed behind Loomis's human mask; she had been shown his beginning and his purpose—what God had intended for him. And if God had intended it for him from the beginning, would He then withhold it from Loomis now, if Loomis would only ask for it? And why would God have shown her this, if not to suggest to her that perhaps Loomis *could* be redeemed? Iris didn't expect to receive any answers to her lingering questions now, but she implored the Lord to help Loomis, if there should be any seed left in him of the holiness he had once held.

After an indeterminate amount of time, she felt Loomis enter the sanctuary behind her. She rose stoically from her knees and turned toward him, watching him nonchalantly remove his coat and drape it across the back of a pew. He carefully and methodically rolled up the sleeves of his dress shirt, then turned his eyes on Iris. She wondered what he saw when he looked at her. Her eyes still saw him as a handsome human man, but her heart beheld him now as a once-glorious angel of God.

As he approached, he broke eye contact just long enough to cast a disdainful glance at the crucifix behind her. When his eyes met hers once more, he spoke in his smooth, human voice. "You've had time," he said, "for whatever purpose you believe the time may have served you. You realize, however, after this patronizing little display of yours tonight, I no longer have any intention of letting you exist in Hell. I will kill your body here and I will take your soul with me, and I will torment it with such vile brutality, you will be *begging* me to destroy it. And when I'm finished, that is *precisely* what I will do." His tone had sharpened as he spoke, and Iris found herself truly afraid, despite the inner voice that tried to challenge everything he said. Though her strength and demonic status exceeded his, it no longer mattered; she couldn't bring herself to use it against him anymore—not when something else inside her still suggested he wasn't completely, hopelessly evil.

"I suppose, though," he continued thoughtfully, "you *have* been a rather enjoyable plaything for me in our brief affiliation, and since you're now such a proponent of mercy, I'm willing to show you some, if you desire it." He flashed a brief, malicious smile, then added, "Not that you *deserve* it. You've been every bit as tedious as you have been amusing, but I'm not the graceless and impolite barbarian that Satan is, and I'm willing to let you fight for your existence."

"I won't fight you, Loomis," Iris responded somberly.

"Come now, Iris," he answered enthusiastically. "Perhaps I'm weaker in this holy place!" He extended his arms on either side and took an exaggerated turn where he stood, looking around the room before turning a black expression back on Iris, putting himself very close to her. "You've said you find me neither pitiful nor weak," he snarled, "so prove it. Fight me now, no holds barred, and if you defeat me here on Earth, I will allow you to remain with me in Hell."

Iris shook her head, feeling her expression tensing into one that must have resembled disgust. The sadness she felt for him was morphing into righteous anger. "What do you gain from this?" she asked indignantly, defiantly returning his stare. "Why do you *want* me to hurt you? If you're concerned that I've become too 'holy' to drag to Hell, forget about it. I told you I would join you, and that's what I'm going to do. That's the choice I've made. I thought you might choose something different for us both, and I guess I was dumb to hope for anything like that from you, but I've seen what you were, and what I believe you could still be. I've seen the perfection of what God created in you, and I won't harm it. So if you're going to kill me now, just do it. Do whatever you want. I won't try to stop you. For the record, though, I do find you both pitiful and weak now. You could be something so much more spectacular, so much more wonderful, yet you're stuck right there under Satan's thumb. So, really, you're not worth a fight."

Loomis pulled his face away from her and stood glacially still for a moment, darkness pervading the amber-flecked brown depth of his eyes. "Very well," he said placidly. Then, with lightning quickness, he snapped his left hand across her face, striking her with his signet ring and unbalancing her.

Stunned, Iris turned from the blow, only to be shoved to the ground by Loomis's strong arm. From the floor, she could hear him above her, urging, "*Fight me*, Iris! You're not the type who plays the victim. You want to defend yourself."

Moving to stand, she shook her head and answered, "I won't do it." She was saying it not only to Loomis but also to the voice in her own head that was screaming at her to hurt him, to put him in his rightful place beneath her own demonic power.

He grabbed her hair and viciously pulled her to her feet and held her there as he punched her several times with his right fist. Iris screamed unintentionally, feeling her eyes flood with tears as blinding pain engulfed her nose and cheek and jaw. She felt blood seeping from her nose and lips, and she could taste it on her tongue. Loomis surveyed with an evil grin the damage he had done to her face, then he threw her again to the floor. She breathed heavily and watched crimson droplets speckle the carpet beneath her, feeling dazed and sick and very much inclined to unleash her Satanic wrath, though she steadfastly restrained herself, even as a sudden, sharp kick to her side sent her sprawling closer to the altar. She tried to pull herself up, but Loomis kicked her again, the savage blow making a cracking sound as her rib broke with a radiating pain. Her natural reflex was to draw her knees and elbows together to protect herself, but Loomis's inhuman strength made it a futile effort, and her unwillingness to use any magic against him left her with no choice but to submit to the beating. He kicked her arms away and sent his foot right back to her rib cage for a third and then a fourth blow. With the last one, Iris gasped and cried out, hearing a nauseating crunch from inside her body that rendered her suddenly unable to breathe. She lay on the floor with her mouth agape, desperately trying to suck air in but succeeding only with shallow, gasping breaths that sent fire through her chest. The metallic warmth of blood in her mouth was more poignant now, and it made her sick to her stomach. She wanted to stand, hoping at least to take from Loomis whatever perverted satisfaction he might enjoy by gloating over her badly beaten body, but the pain in her side as she moved made the process slow and tedious. Loomis stood nearby, watching her feeble endeavor to rise. After a few lengthy seconds, he reached down, grabbed her under her arms, and pulled her savagely to her feet. She moaned in agony as she was lifted, laboriously struggling to breathe. At least, she considered dismally, she was succeeding in fending off her own demonic instinct to retaliate. She wouldn't cave to Loomis's goading—not after she had already promised him too much.

When Loomis released her, Iris immediately doubled over in pain, grabbing her side and wobbling on her feet. He lifted her from the ground, her weight like nothing to the otherworldly musculature of his physical form, and then Iris felt her body thrown like a rag doll, flying seemingly weightlessly in the air for several feet until her back and head struck the front of the altar with an echoing thud. Too exhausted from pain and heartache to care anymore, and with her head now swimming in confusion and murkiness, she allowed herself to slump down the altar into a bloody, broken heap, trying to find Loomis with her eyes but seeing only hazy, dancing lights and indistinct shapes before her. She blinked a few times and finally saw him move in front of her, seating himself casually near her on the altar steps.

"Ah, Iris," he sighed campily, "I am, in fact, glad you chose this way of doing things." He leaned in closer to her face and gently raised her chin with his finger. "It has been quite pleasurable for me," he concluded with an ominous whisper. His hand moved to his pocket and withdrew an engraved obsidian handle that Iris recognized even in her half-stupor. As she distantly watched him reveal its gleaming silver blade, she felt somehow glad the end had come.

With a sudden jolt that startled and confused her, Iris saw her attacker rise quickly to his feet, his focus completely redirected. After a surprised instant, she recognized why Loomis had shifted so suddenly. The ground beneath them was shuddering, a slight tremble that rapidly became an apocalyptic quake. Iris moved herself painfully as a crack opened beside her, her body just able to crawl sideways for the necessary distance as the maw grew wider, opening from the base of the altar and spreading into spidery veins across the sanctuary floor. The rift had separated her from Loomis, who now stood slightly unbalanced on the opposite side. A rolling, thunderous clap from above rattled the ceiling, and several of the hanging lights fell to the floor and shattered, with bits of sheetrock and clouds of dust following them. A blindingly white light swallowed the entire room, prompting Iris to close her eyes and instinctively shield her face. Then, in a breath, it all seemed to disappear, fading into a calm silence outside her closed eyes.

Slowly lowering her hand and hesitantly opening her eyes, Iris saw the light had dimmed from its piercing brightness but still had the church enveloped in astounding luminescence. As she blinked and tried to recover her normal vision, she heard a masculine yell from a short distance away, and her pulse quickened with the acute fear of what might be happening to Loomis. When she could finally see him a second later, he was on his knees, his back perfectly erect and his face raised toward a figure standing in front of him. His arms were being restrained behind him by another figure. Iris's eyes widened at the breathtaking sight. The figures were large and imposing but inexplicably beautiful, with silvery, eagle-like wings on their backs. Their bodies were not unlike a man's in shape, but they were glassy and translucent in appearance and much sleeker, without skin or hair or clothing, having an iridescent, pearly glow about them. Their faces likewise bore some resemblance to those of men, but they were far less defined, smoother and more aural, with only slight protrusions where humans would have a nose and cheekbones. They had eyes like large gemstones, set aglow in their glass-like visages, illuminated from within by the same pearly, white fire that seemed to radiate throughout their forms. The one standing before Loomis held a long, golden sword, its glittering, hefty blade for now pointed only at the floor but still very threatening in the hand of the one wielding it. Iris had never seen these figures before, but in spirit she recognized them now as Saint Michael, who held the sword, and Raphael, who restrained Loomis.

She felt her body suddenly lifted and carried nearer to the three by a pair of strong, warm arms. She looked up and beheld another angel holding her, this one with sapphire eyes. Gabriel, she sensed. As he held her, she felt a comforting warmth moving through her body. The repulsive taste of blood left her mouth; the excruciating pains of her broken ribs and punctured lung disappeared; she felt the swelling and bruising in her face and arms and torso fade away until her body felt nothing but invigorating vitality. Her thoughts and senses became clear and alert, keener and more perceptive than she had ever experienced. Gabriel laid her gently on the floor and stood protectively behind her, allowing her to watch whatever was transpiring with Loomis, whose expression of defiance and anger was tinged with a pallor of weakness and a masked but incompletely hidden fear as he was held kneeling in the presence of these three holy ones. Iris rose from her supine position to her knees as Michael turned his garnet eyes toward her and then toward Gabriel. He inclined his head in some almost imperceptible signal, at which Iris felt Gabriel from behind her lean down and touch her ears before standing once more.

The silence was finally broken by a resonant, echoing voice as Michael spoke something to Loomis, who snarled some demonic invective in reply and writhed ineffectually in Raphael's grasp. Iris heard the sounds of their voices but could make no sense of their words, which came to her hearing in a babbling stream of muddled gibberish, without discernible structure or form or cadence. Confused and concerned, she could only watch the exchange and wonder at the meaning of it. A magical spell might have allowed her to understand, but the thought never even crossed her mind.

Loomis ceased struggling, but his face and eyes were dark with loathing. It appeared his demonic powers were useless at this moment, and that, in itself, would certainly have been enough to infuriate him. Iris found her mind teeming with questions she wanted to ask and statements she wanted to make, but she had the clear impression her presence here was allowed only as that of a lowly observer, and in humility and fear, she couldn't bring herself to speak. Besides that, she believed her words would be of no consequence now. Loomis was, without question, completely at the mercy of God, who had sent these powerful archangels as His servants and His soldiers, either to justify Loomis or to condemn him once and for all. Iris was only guessing at the meaning of the scene before her, of course, but she imagined it must be a final opportunity for Loomis, that fork in the road from which one course would end in eternal torment, while the other would return him to his former station and his former glory. From her perspective, the choice should be easy. Loomis, however, had his own motivations and had already spent millennia in a temporal world that had never been made for him, sinning and leading others to sin. While Iris still hoped he might choose redemption, she knew neither she nor the archangels could force him, and God Himself would not force him. Loomis was free to choose damnation, and the hostile gleam in his eyes convinced her he had done so.

Michael said some final words, and in the ensuing silence, a funereal gloom filled the sanctuary. Iris's heart felt like stone inside her, and the cold, empty grief of a terrible loss overwhelmed her. Not even when her parents or her grandmother had died had she felt such grave sorrow. From the archangels, too, issued a somber, unspoken melancholy. The brightness of their presence turned dim in bereavement. Loomis alone appeared unmoved by his own decision, still kneeling stoically before Saint Michael, held in place by Saint Raphael, unblinking and unspeaking. Iris shook her head faintly in sadness and disbelief, wondering if Loomis recognized how the holy ones mourned for him. If he did, he showed no sign of caring.

The quiet lasted for a few long, tense seconds, then Saint Michael swiftly raised his sword, his strong arm outstretched on the side where Iris knelt, poised to swipe the blade through Loomis's human body. Unthinkingly, Iris leaped up and grabbed the blade, screaming "*No!*"

The blade sliced into her right hand with razor precision and crippling heat, but she couldn't immediately withdraw her hand. She wailed in pain as fire seemed to engulf first her palm, then her arm, and then her entire body, and she fell back to her knees amid the banshee-like sounds of her own cries. Her vision was gone, with nothing but impossibly radiant white left in front of her eyes. She finally released her grip on Michael's sword and slumped onto the floor, still screaming and crying from the heat inside her. Her body was lifted again and moved, though she now had only a halfway-conscious awareness of what was happening. She thought she caught a glimpse of Loomis still kneeling, with Michael having lowered the blade, leaving him unscathed. She felt Gabriel lay her down and run a gentle hand across her face, and everything went dark.

When she opened her eyes, drowsily recovering her grasp on reality as if waking from a deep slumber, she saw she was still inside the sanctuary of Saint Augustine's. It was cool and quiet and dim, with only the few spotlights shining on the altar area, just as they had been before. The red candle still burned by the tabernacle; the crucifix still hung on the wall behind it. There were no gaping crevices in the floor, no shattered lamps, no dust or debris. She was lying on the floor to the side of the altar, near a set of large candle stands and a decorative floral arrangement of evergreen branches, poinsettias, and winter berries that was adorning the church for the upcoming Christmas celebrations. She pushed herself to her knees and tried to remember how she had come to be here. It had all felt so real, but...could it have been a dream? No, no...she was certain she had just witnessed something real. Heaven had torn the veil and come down to this place, to her and to Loomis...

In a startled panic as she remembered her adversary and how she had seen him awaiting his executioner's blade, Iris quickly surveyed the room with her eyes, searching for him. He was on his knees in front of the altar, slumped over so his chin was almost touching his chest. Upon hearing the faint rustle of Iris's movement, he snapped himself to an upright posture and glared at her. Iris could feel the abysmal hatred emanating from his eyes. It frightened her in a way she had never before experienced, as though she had never felt true fear before—and, considering she had journeyed into Hell not long ago, that was saying something. The loathing evident in his expression was so profound and consuming, it practically pulled her breath out of her, like the gravity of a black hole crushing anything that would cross its event horizon. There could be no denying it now—Loomis was pure and unadulterated evil, by his own choosing, and he was terrifying.

He turned and searched the floor around him, quickly locating his runic switchblade. He picked it up and moved with astonishing haste toward her, then grabbed her by the fabric of her shirt with his free hand and dragged her a few feet before dumping her roughly on her back in front of the altar. He straddled her hips and held her torso solidly with his left arm, placing the knife in his right hand with the blade against her throat.

"Did *you* do this?" he asked sharply, his anger unbridled to the point where his words came out dripping with spittle. "Was this all part of your plan? Did you think you would save me?" The dagger pressed harder into Iris's neck as he continued his tirade. Iris shoved her head back into the floor as far as possible, keeping her breaths shallow in an attempt to prevent the blade from cutting her, knowing it was a vain survival instinct. It wouldn't matter; Loomis was going to kill her.

"I've told you, Iris," he growled, "I don't *need* saving! I don't need your pity! I don't need salvation; I don't need mercy! I have *no need* of your God! Why should I serve Him who is too weak to punish the sins of His human race? I would far rather rule in Hell!"

Iris shook her head as much as she could without slicing her neck. Tears she hadn't known had formed were falling from the corners of her eyes and rolling down into her ears and hair. "Do you hear it, Loomis?" she asked rhetorically. Her voice came out small and gravelly as the knife pressed into her throat. "Do you hear how Satan laughs at you? *Rule* in Hell, you say? It will never be, even if you have my help. You're nothing but his court jester. He has you in chains you can't even see, and the throne isn't going to free you. He's given you only enough slack so you can dance for him." Both anger and sorrow colored her words.

Loomis snarled and replied through gritted teeth, "I *will* have his throne, and I *will* rule Hell and Earth, but you won't be there to see it. He is weaker than I am, and time will reveal it."

"Oh, you idiot!" Iris cried, too irritated to care that she was millimeters away from physical death. "*Are* you stronger than Satan? *Are you really?* Because from where I am, it looks like you're his fool! He tricked you into betraying your calling, into becoming a sinner just like Eve, and then he kept you trapped in darkness for all these ages, for so long you can't even remember the holy place you had reserved for you by a God who loved you—who *still* loves you! You don't even recognize your own imprisonment!" She paused and took a shaking breath, feeling her nostrils flaring at the passion in her words. With scoffing disdain, she concluded, "Satan's smarter than you, and that makes him stronger than you."

Loomis shoved his blade deeper into her neck, not cutting, but applying enough pressure to choke her. "I *am* stronger," he argued acidly, "and smarter. I have dragged so many, many more souls to Hell than he—"

Iris cut him off, making her voice as strong as she possibly could under his suffocating press. "And how many of the seraphim have you dragged into Hell?" she asked. At this, Loomis released the tiniest bit of pressure on her throat, and he leaned back ever so slightly.

Accepting the opening he had allowed her, Iris continued her debate. "Satan's lured at least one," she said, "and he has *kept* him, locked him away for thousands of years as a demon. And that one he lured has now chosen to stay with him in Hell, of his own free will, even when invited back to Heaven by the archangels sent by God to offer him a chance at redemption. So, tell me again, Loomis, how many human souls you've corrupted! Tell me again how proud you are to have turned sinners into worse sinners, to have pulled away the already fallen and imperfect. Satan has taken with him the angels, the pure and unblemished spirits who had known nothing but the love of God and of one another, with you among them." She stared into Loomis's eyes as she spoke, seeking to find some glimmer of hope still left in them. She couldn't be sure she saw any, but her heart yet wanted to believe she did. Loomis, in reply, remained silent, still pressing his weight into her and locking her into the floor, but listening to what she said.

"You're the most pitiable of all creation," Iris stated ruefully. "Men and women have been welcomed into Heaven, and many more still will be. They'll survive the time of great distress, having washed their robes in the blood of the Lamb, having thanked God for his infinite mercy. So many of the human race will sit at the eternal Heavenly banquet...and where will you be, Loomis, Destroyer of the Human Race? You'll be in eternal, unquenchable fire, without peace or love or hope. You'll have no true life and no true power. And if there's any justice at all, one day you'll remember the chance you had for forgiveness, and you'll regret not having taken it. You'll be forced to exist forever under the weight of your mistakes, when so much of humanity has had their mistakes purged and forgotten."

Loomis still said nothing, and his expression was still bleak and angry, but the pressure on Iris's neck had subsided slightly more. The once-cold blade had warmed from having been held against her skin, so it felt less threatening now, but she was still keenly aware of its nearness to her throat.

"I wish Heaven could laugh at you," she finished quietly, in an irate sort of despair. "But, as it is, the holy only cry for you, for the loss of your spirit to Hell." Her eyes had dried as she had spoken, but new tears were now prickling the backs of her eyes.

Loomis's voice was tight and raspy when he spoke. "I resent this 'divine' machination you've played out here tonight," he announced. "I won't make a success of it for you." He shoved the knife into Iris's throat, preparing to cut her.

"*My* divine machination?" Iris exclaimed, wriggling slightly under Loomis and his blade. "Loomis, I *swear* I had nothing to do with what happened here tonight! That was all for you, and it was no doing of mine." She paused for a second, then added in an almost inaudible voice, "I wish you had chosen differently."

Wincing at the memory of the incident, Iris closed her eyes and took a cleansing breath, as deeply as she could with the blade at her neck. When Loomis didn't immediately reply to her comments, she concluded, "If you're still planning on killing me, get it over with. Take my soul, torture it, destroy it; I don't care. You've just caused me a grief so unbearable, I have no fear of whatever else you can do to me."

Loomis narrowed his eyes at her with a look of hateful consternation, then his gaze darted away for a fleeting glance at her hand, lying limply on the floor beside her. Keeping the dagger at her throat, he grabbed her wrist with his other hand, lifting her arm and turning it so he could see her palm. Iris hadn't even thought to look at it after what had occurred, and she felt no pain from it anymore. She wondered if the archangel's sword had left any mark. It should have, as excruciatingly painful as it had been to touch it, but Gabriel had healed the injuries her body had suffered during Loomis's beating, so perhaps he had healed the wound from the sword as well.

Loomis stared at her hand for what felt like a long time. His face was expressionless, and his eyes became distant, as though he were looking at something far beyond Iris's palm. Iris lay motionless underneath him, hardly daring to breathe, allowing him to hold her wrist without movement or complaint. She couldn't read his thoughts or discern the emotions written in his countenance, but whatever this was, it was preferable to his vengeful fury.

Finally, Loomis blinked a few times and inhaled deeply, exhaling very slowly. He tossed Iris's arm away from him, and Iris let it fall to the floor, yet unaware of whatever he might have seen in her hand. He met her eyes once more, flared his nostrils, then gradually removed the knife from where it had left a red indentation in her neck. He dropped it languidly beside him, then gracefully rose to his feet. Stepping over her, he walked down the altar steps and proceeded with impeccable posture down the center aisle of the church. He grabbed his coat from the pew as he passed, swinging it around him so he could insert first one arm and then the other, never breaking stride. Iris watched him buttoning it as he exited elegantly through the sanctuary doors, leaving her lying alone and confused, but unharmed, in front of the altar.

She remained where she lay for a moment, marveling at how Loomis had left her alive. *He might still have a chance*, she thought, despite the shocking malignity she had witnessed in him only moments before. She closed her eyes and reflected on the events of the night, and she was soon submerged in a deluge of emotion she couldn't control—sadness, confusion, anger, hope, astonishment. She had never been prone to bouts of extreme emotion like this, preferring to internalize her feelings and control them, particularly when in the presence of others, but now she was alone and the floodgates were open, and she found herself powerless to stop the surging sentimentality. She sobbed audibly, convulsing with labored breaths. Burying her face in her hands, she suddenly remembered her seizure of Saint Michael's sword, and she wiped her tears away and blinked, swallowing further sobs as she extended her right palm out in front of her. Even in the dim light of the church, she could see the scar that had been left there. Where her skin had touched the blade, there was a glassy, garnet-colored slash that faded into a golden luster at its edges. She ran the fingers of her left hand gently across it. It felt like no earthly physical scar. There was no open gash or messy gore; there was only a smooth, translucent, gem-like substitute where once her flesh had been. She tested the motion in the hand and found it was unchanged, free from pain or stiffness. As she stared at the mark, she finally smiled a little, in genuine thankfulness and a humble sort of pride. It was beautiful.

33

Auraltiferys was kneeling in the soft, deep-brown soil of his garden, carefully planting a new row of vegetable plants beneath the quiet, peaceful afternoon sun of the mountain. Iris approached him in silence, not wishing to disturb the halcyon scene. The fresh, natural smell of clean earth wafted to her on a gentle breeze of cool air as the sun warmed her face and forearms. It was a pleasant feeling, and if she hadn't been wearing the same outfit from last night's meeting with Loomis, she might have been able to put that whole astounding and awful scenario out of her mind. Unfortunately, however, Loomis's violence had caused the loss of the two buttons she typically fastened on her overshirt so that it was now hanging loosely over the tank top underneath, its fabric fluttering open as a constant reminder of what had happened at the church. She wondered what Auraltiferys would have to say about it. She desperately hoped he might be able to speak some words that would console her, because right now, she was feeling grief unlike any she had ever known, and it was so profound and painful, she wasn't certain she wanted to go on living. When her parents and then her grandmother had died, she had felt sad and angry and empty, but she had recovered. She had healed. But it had been easier to understand with them—they had always anticipated physical death, and although that death seemed to have come to them too soon, Iris could accept it as a part of life, something that was hard, but meant to be. For Loomis, though...he was freely choosing something far worse than physical death, even after being offered a way out of it. Iris couldn't understand it or accept it.

The blacksmith stood abruptly as Iris neared him, not bothering to brush the dirt from his knees. He stared at her with marked concern, but he said nothing. Iris opened her mouth to speak, but seeing her mentor filled her with such overwhelming relief that she couldn't get any words out. Tears rolled out of her eyes, and she stepped quickly toward him and embraced him. He reached down and hugged her silently, letting her cry there against his chest, and Iris felt as though she were being held by the Savior himself. She had long found it difficult to recognize the presence of God in humankind, but in Auraltiferys, it was particularly easy to perceive divine grace, and she was grateful for that, especially now, when God felt so far away.

Eventually, she gathered herself and eased away from him with a sniffle and a shuddering breath, wiping her nose and her eyes. "Sorry," she said quietly. He had let her end the embrace, but his strong hands still rested gently against her upper arms, holding her at a short distance.

"Let's go inside," Auraltiferys replied softly, "and you can tell me what has happened."

He led her through the garden to the rear porch, through a portion of the house she had never seen, and eventually to the living room where she had first awoken to meet him. Iris sat on the sofa, and her mentor seated himself beside her. She clasped her hands in her lap and looked down at them, wondering where to begin the story. Much had happened since she had left the mountain the last time. Auraltiferys didn't prompt her; he knew she would talk when she was ready.

"I...I don't know where to start," Iris admitted sheepishly.

Auraltiferys smiled understandingly. "Well," he said, "when I last saw you, you had brought with you a false relic. What has come of it?"

Iris collected her thoughts and then began her story, beginning with her discovery of Marvin Whitakker as the culprit who had recognized the copper spearhead relic in a traveling exhibit and had replaced it with a forgery before Loomis's shadow-demon had shown up to claim it. She told him how she had collected and repurposed all the relics Loomis had amassed, banishing the shadow-demon to Hell, and she explained the deal she had made with Loomis afterward, offering him knowledge about the flaw in his plan (and an opportunity for appropriate vengeance against Whitakker) in exchange for her peace and for the physical safety of the human race. Until that point in her narration, Auraltiferys had sat quietly, listening with rapt attention and watching her with keen interest, but he tensed visibly when she mentioned the truce.

"You made a deal with Drake?" he asked, his deep voice taking on its knife-like edge.

Iris gave him a rueful grin. "It's not like I was bargaining with my soul, Auri," she answered. "Loomis got nothing out of it, except the knowledge of why his grand plan didn't work."

The blacksmith silently accepted her justification, albeit with a tight jaw, and waited for her to continue. Iris proceeded to relate the darker events: the ill-advised challenge of Whitakker by the two detectives investigating the death of a young museum security guard; Whitakker's even more ill-advised opening of a gate to Hell in the museum basement; the unfortunate re-emergence of the shadow-demon, its theft of the soul of Myron Banks, and Iris's own subsequent descent into Hell to save him. Auraltiferys's silver-blue eyes widened, blazing with paternal concern, but he refrained from making any comment. Iris knew she had approached the part of her story where her kindly mentor was almost sure to disagree with her every decision.

She recounted the events of her visit to the underworld with great detail, hoping the account would convince Auraltiferys that there was, indeed, goodness left in Loomis. She included the vision she had seen—of Loomis as a seraph in Heaven, before his descent to Hell—and how she recognized it fully only when she had seen him outside his human form after the beating ordered on him by Satan. Auraltiferys remained silent and impassive, and while Iris doubted her words were making him any more sympathetic toward Loomis, she was glad he allowed her to speak without argument, at least for the time being. Finally, though, she admitted to the blacksmith that she had been prepared to spend eternity in Hell with Loomis just to protect him from further torture at Satan's hands, and that statement immediately dispelled Auraltiferys's stoicism.

He stood abruptly and turned toward her in utter disbelief, his long, silvery-white ponytail whipping over his shoulder and his usually icy eyes now aflame with the same blue-white heat of a celestial body. He grabbed her firmly, but not roughly, by both shoulders and stared into her eyes, with clear, desperate hope that she had reconsidered. "Iris," he urged, his voice cutting through her like a blade, "tell me you have not chosen this!"

Iris smiled sadly and shook her head. She reached up with her left hand and placed it reassuringly against his. "I'm still here," she said simply.

He inhaled sharply, then let his breath out slowly, released Iris, and sat back down next to her. "For now," he replied, his tone weighted with seriousness.

"Auri," Iris answered quietly, "if you could see him as I do, and if you had the powers I have, you wouldn't want to leave him there alone in Hell, either."

Auraltiferys shook his head. "Hell is what he has chosen," he argued. "You have a good heart, and it is right for you to be moved with pity when another suffers, but you mustn't forget *it was his choice*." He paused, sighed heavily, then added, "Your presence in Hell won't end his suffering, Iris."

"Satan can't hurt him if I'm there to stop him," she said weakly. The discussion was leading her to the verge of tears, again. She knew her statement would be easily contradicted, but the words came out anyway.

"Only God could end his suffering," Auraltiferys replied, softly but precisely, exactly as Iris had expected. "He doesn't want God."

Iris closed her eyes and swallowed, unwilling to submit to her urge to cry. After several seconds, she asked, falteringly, "What if...what if he did?"

Auraltiferys's eyes narrowed, and he leaned back slightly, thoughtfully considering Iris's question while remaining wary of it. "What if Drake wanted God?" he clarified. Iris nodded. "At the risk of sounding uncaring," he answered slowly, "I say if he wanted God, he wouldn't have chosen Hell."

After a brief silence, Iris said, "I don't think he really *chose* Hell. I think...I think he just...sort of lost his way."

Auraltiferys appeared completely unconvinced, and Iris could understand why. Loomis wasn't a poorly informed traveler who had taken a wrong turn on a foreign street; he had always known the difference between right and wrong. Why, then, was she still so convinced he belonged in Heaven and not in Hell? She would emphatically condemn any human man who had even a tiny fraction of Loomis's sins on his own record, yet for Loomis Drake, the demon responsible for tempting countless souls into damnation and for causing much of her own recent suffering, she wanted Heaven.

She sighed wistfully, recognizing that the remainder of her story, amazing though it was, would probably not sway Auraltiferys's opinion. Her eyes drifted away from him, and she found herself staring at the empty fireplace before eventually lifting her gaze to the mantel above, where Auraltiferys kept the relic of the Cross of Christ—the same relic that had drawn her blood after she had wandered far into demonic sin; the relic that had rescued her, at least for a time, from certain damnation. If not for the blacksmith, she would have lost every chance she had for Heaven. Was her redemption so different from what she now wanted for Loomis? Admittedly, her situation and Loomis's were not the same, but, ultimately, was the root of this debate not the possibility of God's grace extending to a demon? Was that grace not exactly what she had experienced firsthand? Iris knew what Auraltiferys would argue, though—she was not just a demon; she was also human, and that was enough to place her among those saved by Jesus Christ. She was *different*, and that would be the end of the discussion. For a moment, she questioned whether she should have come here at all. She wasn't sure she wanted to finish her narrative. She suddenly feared her tutor would tell her exactly what she didn't want to hear—that there could be no redemption for a demon, that it was too late, that Loomis would never again see Heaven. Then again, she thought, perhaps that was what she *needed* to hear, even if it hurt.

At some point during her despondent reverie, Iris realized Auraltiferys was watching her intently. "There is more to your story," he prompted gently, after allowing her ample silence for her inward reflections. "Please, continue. I will strive to remain as open-minded as I can."

Iris told him about her meeting with Loomis at the church, relating Loomis's story about his own descent into Hell after the serpent had tempted Eve into sin, then she described the angry beating she had willingly suffered afterward as she refused to fight him.

Auraltiferys nodded slowly as she spoke. "I sensed you were in danger," he said quietly. "I prayed earnestly for you, but I was warned not to intervene."

"I wouldn't have wanted you to," Iris replied gloomily.

The blacksmith's expression was one of complete neutrality, but Iris imagined she could sense the slightest hint of disappointment emanating from him—disappointment that she had fallen victim to Loomis's treacherous appeals to her heart. He said nothing more, however, and Iris proceeded with the most incredible part of the story, telling him about the appearance of the three archangels there in the church. His eyes sparkled with clear fascination and obvious reverence as she described the scene.

"I don't know what they said to him," she explained. "Gabriel prevented me from understanding it, but I really believe they were offering him a chance to return."

Auraltiferys crossed one arm over his ribs and rested the opposite elbow on top of it, pressing his thumb against his jawline and his finger thoughtfully across his lips, and he sat silently for several seconds, his eyes far away. "And?" he asked finally, bringing an abrupt and simple end to the long silence. There was no bite of sarcasm in it; he asked it elegantly and graciously as a brief invitation for Iris to finish her tale.

Iris hesitated, afraid to convey the ending. It would only solidify the blacksmith's belief in what Loomis had chosen for himself. She looked at her mentor, and the great expectation in his silver-blue eyes compelled her to continue.

"Loomis...he...he just knelt there," she stammered, her jaw beginning to quiver as she replayed the scene in her mind. She remembered the terrible gleam in Loomis's eyes that had prompted Saint Michael to ready his sword for execution, and it immediately intensified her sadness. She paused and breathed heavily, pressing her eyes tightly shut and swallowing hard to prevent a flood of tears. She felt Auraltiferys place a strong and comforting hand on her shoulder as he patiently waited for her to finish.

"I guess he had made his choice," she finished sadly. "Saint Michael lifted his sword to strike him, but...I reached out and grabbed it."

She opened her eyes and looked down at her right palm, then she turned slowly and showed it to Auraltiferys. He took her hand gently in his, staring at the glistening, gem-like scar with genuine deference. He ran his thumb lightly across it before Iris could give him any warning, but he was unaffected by the contact. She had feared the scar might cause the same blinding pain the blade had caused her, but either the mark was innocuous, or Auraltiferys was pure and holy enough to touch it without incident. After a few seconds, he slowly released her hand.

"Extraordinary," he remarked in a hushed voice.

Iris looked at the mark again and couldn't help but smile. "It was terribly painful," she finally commented, with a tiny, rueful laugh.

Auraltiferys smiled understandingly. "The scar is a vestige of an angel's blade," he told her. "It can cause great agony for the impure if they should touch it. You will have to keep it covered."

Iris furrowed her brow but nodded her agreement. "Okay," she replied. She was disappointed to have to hide it from the world, but she certainly understood it.

Auraltiferys recognized her disappointment and was somewhat amused by it. "To boast of it would only cheapen it," he offered encouragingly. "Let the experience and the memory be yours alone, and let them bring you constant hope and joy." He straightened up and quietly cleared his throat. "Now," he said, "do tell me what happened to Drake."

Iris shrugged. "He was still there in the church with me after the angels left," she explained. "He was angry—accused me of having set the whole thing up. We talked. I told him I wished he had chosen differently. I told him he's been outsmarted by Satan, and Satan will keep laughing at him for all eternity, and that's pitiful." Sighing wearily, she continued, "Loomis finally looked at my hand and saw the mark. He stared at it for a while and then just...left. Grabbed his overcoat and walked out of the church. I don't know where he went."

The blacksmith interlaced his fingers behind his head and reclined into the sofa back with a thoughtful exhale. "It is a remarkable story," he said matter-of-factly, his eyes staring straight ahead.

"Auri," Iris replied imploringly, "I know all the teaching. I know about free will and Heaven and Hell, and I know, at some point, it really is too late; there's no going back. But...I just can't believe that Loomis is meant to be in Hell."

Auraltiferys searched her eyes for an instant, then answered grimly, "He was made for Heaven; we all were. Neither Heaven nor Hell is forced upon any of us." He squeezed Iris's shoulder with an encouraging hand, then stood and headed toward the kitchen, pausing in the doorway to look back at her. When he continued speaking, his tone was gentle, but his words were sharply precise. "I see you are deeply troubled by Heaven's loss of him to the netherworld, and I see how fervently you desire his redemption," he said, "but it sounds to me as though his choice has been made, and more than once. Grieve as you feel you must, Iris, but I urge you not to dwell on this. He has the eternity he has chosen. I pray you choose differently." He shot her a meaningful look, then gracefully disappeared into the kitchen to make tea as Iris waited in silence, knowing she would be unable to drop the issue.

He returned a couple of minutes later with two cups of hot tea. He set them on the table and seated himself in his usual chair.

"He didn't really *choose* Hell," Iris immediately blurted out upon the blacksmith's return. "He wasn't cast out of Heaven! He went to Hell because he was angry at what Satan had done, tricking Eve into sin. It was righteous anger, and he descended out of love for the human race, not out of arrogance against God!"

"And do you imagine God sanctioned that revenge he sought?" Auraltiferys challenged. His voice was neither loud nor angry, but there was such conviction in it that Iris felt suddenly small and insignificant, like a peasant who had foolishly addressed a king. Her posture straightened involuntarily, and her chin dipped so that her gaze fell to her lap as Auraltiferys continued his argument. "God is love, not vengeance," he said. "You must recognize that Drake followed his own will, not God's, when he chased after Satan. And if you believe it was only Satan's trickery that kept Drake in Hell, then Drake has succeeded in clouding your judgment and your ability to discern Truth. He has always known right from wrong; he has made his own decisions. He didn't lose his way; he *chose* a different path, and it was one that led away from God. Drake isn't a victim—not a victim of anyone but himself, that is."

Iris stared at the tea on the table in front of her, sending its little tendrils of aromatic steam into the tranquil air of the den. Gloom rested in her stomach like a stone, and the solace she was accustomed to feeling while with Auraltiferys on this mountain was notably absent. She hadn't really expected him to tell her anything different from what he was already saying, but she had hoped to hear him speak of something less than hopeless finality for the demon whose former glory she had now witnessed. She could feel the blacksmith's eyes on her, and she felt true care and concern for her in their gaze. She knew he believed his words and spoke them only to help her, not to hurt her, but still she didn't want to accept them. She was silent for a long time before she spoke again. Auraltiferys sat quiet and unmoving, regal and dignified and statuesque as he waited for the conclusion of her contemplations. He was a cool and calm presence, and though he had a stern and disciplined manner that commanded respect, he was yet gracious and welcoming. Iris knew he was waiting for her arguments, and she knew he would listen with an open heart, even if he disagreed with her. He wanted to guide her rightly, and that was what she needed.

"I know how I must sound," she finally said. "I know I sound like a girl who's fallen victim to Loomis's charms. But...I can't convince myself I'm wrong about him. I see goodness in him still."

The blacksmith leaned forward to retrieve his tea, sipped it thoughtfully, then sat back in his chair and crossed one ankle over the opposite knee. "Perhaps goodness remains," he mused, "even if buried beneath a multitude of sins. I suppose that is possible, and maybe even fitting. Even demons were once good and pleasing to God."

Iris shook her head. "It's not just that," she replied. "He's different from Satan and from all the rest in Hell. I've *seen* them, Auri. I know what I'm talking about." She glanced at him for a reaction, but his expression was unreadable. His eyes, however, beckoned her to elaborate. After a sigh, she continued, "I saw Loomis's demonic form that day I met him in Portland. He didn't look the same when I saw him in Hell."

"You were shown a vision of him in glory," Auraltiferys suggested. "That vision likely changed your perception of him."

"Maybe that's all it is," Iris admitted, "but I really don't think so. I know he's done terrible, unspeakable things to humankind. I know he wanted even worse things for them, at least for a time...but I think he has changed somehow. I don't believe he really wants that anymore."

"Iris," Auraltiferys answered gently, "assuming your interpretation of the events at Saint Augustine's is correct, you witnessed him declining an invitation from the archangels to return to Heaven. Even if God would allow such a marvelous thing to happen, Drake doesn't want it. How can you believe he has changed? How can you believe he wants anything but Hell?"

"I don't know," Iris replied, her voice like that of a child trying to convince a parent that there was a monster in the closet. "I just...I just *believe* it. I can't explain it, but Loomis...he's never treated me as badly as he could have."

"Only because your demonic spirit outranks his," Auraltiferys retorted, his tone heavier and sharper than before.

Iris balanced her elbows on her knees and rested her face in her hands, closing her eyes and rubbing her temples. She was finally feeling the fatigue from her inability to sleep last night, and her head was beginning to ache from anxiety. She was worried about Loomis; she was worried about herself; now, she was worried she was going to turn her mentor and her most trusted friend and ally against her by arguing the virtues of a demon.

"You don't know him like I do," she said after a long hesitation. She was out of points for her debate, and she could see it would end in a stalemate. Auraltiferys couldn't be convinced of Loomis's goodness; she couldn't be convinced of his unmitigated wickedness.

"That's certainly true," Auraltiferys returned quickly and pointedly, the swift blade of his voice signifying quite clearly that he remembered what Iris had confessed to him, what she had done to Loomis's spirit. She felt her face flush with embarrassment and shame. Sharply, he continued, "It is also true *you* don't know him as *I* do. Remember, I've had my own personal encounter with Drake, and I have witnessed the depth of his depravity. If he has treated you better than he has treated others, it is only because he needed something from you that he couldn't take by sheer force. And, by the sound of it, his tactics have been successful, for you've now told me you would submit yourself to damnation to be with him. You would choose him over God, and that is all he needs from you."

Iris chuckled forlornly. "I don't want damnation," she insisted grimly. "I don't want Loomis over God; I want him to return to God. Is that so wrong?"

Auraltiferys sighed heavily, then set his empty teacup back on the table and relaxed slightly, leaning his arms on top of his thighs. "No," he said quietly, "that isn't wrong. The desire to unite God's creation with Him is never wrong." Seeing tears welling in Iris's eyes, he moved nimbly from his chair to the sofa beside her and wrapped a muscular arm around her shoulders. She leaned against him and let the tears fall out soundlessly.

"I see Drake as a demon, and I cannot see him otherwise," he went on, holding her caringly. "I can't share your sympathy for him, and I'm sorry, because I see how deeply this has affected you. But you will have to let this go, Iris. You can't save him."

After a shaky breath, Iris whispered, "I feel like I was supposed to. I feel like that was my purpose with him. I think I failed."

Auraltiferys squeezed her tenderly. "You were supposed to protect the human race from an unforetold dark age," he told her, "and you have done that. You will continue to do that for as long as the threat remains. You will follow God, and in that, you fulfill your purpose. God would not have tasked you with saving a demon from Hell; He will not drag anyone toward salvation."

Iris stayed in the blacksmith's embrace for a moment, then eventually eased away and wiped her eyes. Auraltiferys withdrew his arm and looked at her with a small, kind smile and eyes full of compassion.

"Do you believe I'll ever be in Heaven?" Iris asked.

Auraltiferys seemed marginally surprised by the question, but he answered simply, "Yes, I do."

"Even though I'm a demon?" she asked further. "Even though I'm the same spirit as Satan?"

"Your spirit may have come from the fallen," Auraltiferys replied steadily, "but it has been redeemed by the perfect. And you are also human, with a soul created in the image and likeness of God, and you are a member of the Body of Christ. You are indeed a unique creation, Iris, and admittedly, one that cannot be classified by our current understanding. But I believe Heaven is as open to you as it is to me or to anyone else on Earth."

"If it's possible for me, then," Iris answered, "why is it not for Loomis?"

"I can't tell you it's *impossible* for him," Auraltiferys admitted. "That the archangels appeared to you both is, in itself, miraculous, and your story does seem to speak of at least a *possibility* that Drake might have had an opportunity to return to grace, which I would have believed impossible if not for the events you described. Beyond that, however, you already know everything I will say to you on this: You're not like him; you have not followed the same path he has followed."

"But you believe in the infinite mercy of God," Iris prodded.

"Of course I do," the blacksmith replied. His eyes, however, flashed a cautionary warning, as though he knew where she was going with this, and he knew she wouldn't like the response he would have to give her.

Iris looked at him for a few seconds, then she smiled and relaxed a bit. "I won't prod you any further on it than this," she said, finally picking up and sipping the tea he had brought for her. "If Loomis *asked* for God's mercy," she continued, "do you think he would have it?"

Auraltiferys returned her steady gaze for what felt like a long time, then he inclined his head slightly, graciously, and answered, "I suppose he might."

Iris continued drinking her tea, feeling once again comforted by her mentor's presence in the holy place of the mountain. She knew there were other thoughts behind his words, thoughts that he had chosen to withhold just for her sake. She knew he believed it was too late for Loomis, and maybe he was right. But he had acknowledged the limitations of human understanding; he had stopped short of arguing impossibilities. And for Iris, for now, it was comfort enough to be left with the *hope* that infinite mercy might even reach as far as Hell.

* * *

After brewing a second pot of tea for Iris, Auraltiferys had left her alone in the den and had disappeared into some other part of the house, telling her he would return with something for her. Iris was content to sit in silence, drinking tea and reading through a couple of the blacksmith's ancient tomes. Their locks could no longer keep her out, and though she now knew all the magical spells they described, she found them fascinating nonetheless.

Auraltiferys returned after a short time, carrying a small piece of dark fabric with him. "Here," he said, extending it to her. "Try this on."

Iris took the fabric and realized it was a glove for her scarred hand. It was fine, burnished black leather, fingerless, with an opening that would expose the back of her hand in the shape of a cross pattée, embellished in the center by a small pewter stud engraved with her initials. It fastened at her wrist with a thin leather band and a metallic snap, and it fit her perfectly. She inspected it approvingly, then rotated her hand and moved her fingers, all with a smile on her lips. The blacksmith obviously knew her taste.

"This is perfect," she told him with a grin. Though "perfect" wasn't the first adjective she had wanted to use, she thought it might be more appropriate than "badass" in present company. She wouldn't mind at all having to wear this particular article at all times.

Auraltiferys smiled, his eyes dancing with amusement. "It suits you," he replied.

"You know," Iris commented cheerfully as he sat down, "if you lived out there with the rest of us, you could make a ton of money making and selling things like this. And your metalwork, too, obviously. This is high-quality stuff."

He chuckled. "Thank you for recognizing that," he said, leaning back in his chair. "But money seems like a dreadful onus. Besides, I wouldn't want to create things to sell to just anyone."

"Only for the worthy, huh?" Iris replied, her tone playfully accusatory. "That's not particularly generous or merciful of you."

The blacksmith smiled broadly and shrugged as he answered, "Perhaps that's why God has put me here and not out there with you. Saving me from myself." His eyes were bright and mirthful, and his chiseled, scarred face was creased handsomely by the grin on his lips. Iris looked at him and couldn't help but smile in return.

"Hey, can you make boots, too?" she asked, genuinely excited by the sudden idea.

"Of course I can," he answered. "In fact, that isn't a bad idea. It's obvious to my well-trained eye that the bootmakers in your realm are...inartful, at best." He lifted an eyebrow and nodded toward the knee-high boot on Iris's crossed leg.

Iris laughed. "I like these boots!" she exclaimed. "These are my favorite pair!"

Auraltiferys inclined his head slightly and made a conciliatory motion with his hands, grinning all the while. "I could do much better," he said jovially.

"I believe it," Iris answered smilingly.

After that brief period of levity and a momentary silence, the blacksmith's expression turned more serious, and he moved to the edge of his seat and leaned forward. "I must ask you a difficult question," he stated heavily, instantly sending Iris's thoughts into a whirlwind of panicked curiosity. She straightened up and felt immediate tension in her neck and shoulders.

"Okay," she said rigidly. "What is it?"

His eyes pierced hers for several seconds before he asked, "Where does your loyalty lie now?"

Iris blinked several times and felt her forehead tense. "If you're asking whether I will choose Loomis over God," she replied stonily, "the answer is no. I'm loyal to God and to humanity."

Auraltiferys did not relent in his penetrating gaze. "Are you certain of that?" he asked. "Can you continue to deny Drake if he continues to threaten the human race?"

"Yes, of course I can," Iris answered, flustered.

"You no longer wish to fight him," he challenged.

Iris looked away and exhaled wearily. "That's true," she admitted. "I don't want to fight him or hurt him, but...I guess if he insists on being evil, he leaves me no choice." She absentmindedly rubbed the back of her neck, the leather of her new glove groaning quietly as she did so. After another sigh, she added resignedly, "I'll keep him in check."

Auraltiferys pursed his lips. "You don't intend to join him in Hell?" he asked.

Iris met her mentor's eyes again and answered evenly, "I don't believe he really wants me there."

"Iris—" Auraltiferys began advisorily.

"I know I said I would stay in Hell to protect him," she interrupted, "but I didn't expect him to follow through on that deal, and he didn't."

"No," Auraltiferys returned, "but he severely brutalized you and then renewed his commitment to damnation. If he now demands that you honor your word—"

Iris scoffed and shook her head, cutting him off. "Please, Auri," she begged, "I don't want to argue this with you."

"It is not a conversation I want to have, either," he replied, cool precision in his tone. "But I would be failing my vocation if I didn't press you on this. I need to know you are on the right footing when you leave here."

"Loomis won't demand anything of me," Iris answered flatly. She believed it, but it was clear Auraltiferys remained unconvinced, and she knew she had no convincing evidence to offer him.

"He will not have forgotten the offer you made to him in Hell," he warned. "And, worse, he now knows your true feelings toward him. He will prey upon those sentiments. He has you exactly where he wants you to be."

Iris shifted uncomfortably. "I'll be fine," she said. "He didn't accept the offer at the time, and the offer no longer stands. As far as my 'sentiments' are concerned, I'm...I'm better now. I was emotional before, but you and I have talked now, and I think I can let it go." She finished speaking and glanced back at the blacksmith, sitting like a dignitary on his throne, a somber expression darkening his noble features.

"You can accept that Drake has chosen Hell?" he prompted. "You will recognize the evil power he is?"

Iris hesitated, looking down at the floor in front of her. A momentary pause lengthened into an awkward silence. She finally met her mentor's eyes once more, and she saw disappointment cloud them as he interpreted her reticence. He sighed, closed his eyes, and shook his head.

"Listen," Iris implored, her voice beginning to crack, "I know you have your opinion of Loomis. I know you believe he's nothing but evil, and I know you believe it's too late for him and there's no hope for redemption. I just *can't* believe that! I don't believe he *wants* to spend eternity in Hell. I don't believe he's pure evil and nothing else. I *see* the glory of the seraphim in him still, and I believe he could return if he wanted to. In fact, I believe he wants to! I think he's afraid, or he thinks himself unworthy now. I think all the anger and darkness he showed me last night were forced, like he was trying to convince himself he's something he's not. But, whatever the case is, I won't stop hoping he finds his way back." She paused and breathed. Her words had come out quickly and emphatically, leaving her slightly winded. Her mouth was dry and her face was hot. After composing herself, she continued, "I do understand it isn't my choice to make. I understand I can't save him. And if I have to fight him, if I have to send him back to Hell over and over to preserve the human race, I will. But I can't pretend it won't hurt me."

Auraltiferys stared at her as she spoke, his eyes narrowed and gleaming with acute perceptiveness. When she finished, he lifted his chin slightly and stared at her for one moment longer, then, finally, he nodded once, in approving silence. They both sat quietly for some time after that. Iris imagined seeing Loomis again, and she realized how difficult it would be to follow through on what she had just avowed. Each time she pictured him now, she saw not an enemy, but a creature in desperate need of her help. She hoped her emotions weren't obscuring her judgment. She didn't believe they were, but...there was yet a part of her brain that shared the blacksmith's concerns.

"I'm proud of you," Auraltiferys eventually said, his low voice gently disrupting the stillness.

Iris looked at him quizzically. "For what?" she asked. "You think Loomis has made me weak."

"On the contrary," he replied, "I believe he has strengthened you, though I am certain that was never his intention. I don't share your opinion of him or your belief in him, but I do recognize your conviction, and I know you stand on Heaven's side. You are just and merciful, much more than I am, for you mourn the loss of Drake's spirit to Hell, whereas I consider it an appropriate punishment. I hope at my judgment God will be as merciful toward me as you have been toward him."

Iris sat motionless, stunned by her mentor's words. After some hesitation, she felt a tiny smile on her lips and a stirring of tears behind her eyes. "Auri," she answered quietly, "I...I don't even know what to say to that. You're...so wonderful, so holy. I see God in you. You're the example I've followed. If not for you, all of this would have ended so differently. I thank God for having named you as my teacher." She tried to hold the tears back, to no avail. They trickled slowly down her cheeks as she stared at the blacksmith.

He smiled knowingly. "And I thank God for all He will yet teach me through you," he said gently. He stood up, in his usual graceful manner, and extended his hand to Iris, genteelly helping her up from the sofa. "I don't know about you," he said lightly, "but I'm quite hungry. Would you like to help me with dinner?"

"Of course," she answered with a grin. She followed him into the kitchen and leaned against the counter, waiting for instructions.

As Auraltiferys began removing various ingredients from the refrigerator, a sudden, terrifying sound from outside startled them both. Iris remembered that sound, and she knew Auraltiferys was all too familiar with it. She looked toward him with wide, confused eyes, but the blacksmith was already moving swiftly to the front door, his magical blade drawn from the sheath at his thigh. Iris focused her thoughts and immediately followed him, pulling her axe from the strap on her boot and enlarging it to its useful size. It felt warm through the leather of her glove.

The blacksmith threw the door open with a spell, and he and Iris exited onto the porch. There, they stood side by side, momentarily held motionless by the shock of the sight before them. Six Empyreal Hounds, howling in loud, unearthly cacophony, encircled an unwanted visitor, standing unperturbed among them with a slight, placid grin on his lips.

Iris felt the sudden cold that emanated from Auraltiferys beside her. It was a hateful, vengeful cold, and she realized with instant terror that she would have to choose a side right here and now.

34

The Hounds went quiet shortly after Auraltiferys and Iris reached the porch. For a moment, all the mountain seemed suspended in time, everything still and silent; then, reality descended upon it again like a heavy curtain, and the brief emptiness that had swallowed Iris's thoughts was replaced by tense indecision. She didn't want to act rashly, but neither did she want to wait for a bloodbath.

"Do call off these dogs," Loomis said smoothly. "They are most unwelcoming."

Iris glanced from Loomis to Auraltiferys. She saw his hand tighten on the hilt of his blade, but he made no movement toward the demon just yards away.

"The Hounds remain, Drake," Auraltiferys answered, his voice colder and darker than the stone of the mountain. The Hounds maintained their formation like statues, their eyes glowing like fire.

Loomis smiled and shrugged, then crossed his arms and turned his gaze toward Iris. "Perhaps my darling Iris will oblige me, then," he cooed.

As Iris looked at him, the incredible encounter at Saint Augustine's replayed in her mind, and all the grief she had brought here struck her again like a freight train. She remembered how Loomis had been ready to kill her before seeing the mark of the angel's blade in her hand, and how he had then left the church in silence. She was certain the experience had affected him; it must have. Why had he come here now? She knew how difficult Auraltiferys had made it for all demons but her—the journey must have drained Loomis of much energy. Why would he bother? Had he changed his mind? Was he seeking redemption now? His demeanor did seem slightly off; he seemed to be forcing his appearance of impassive confidence. Iris wanted to trust him, but she sensed a tacit yet unignorable warning from Auraltiferys beside her.

"Why are you here, Loomis?" she asked him. Her voice was tight, and she felt a sudden urge to throw up. She would have to protect one of these two from the other; it was only an ever-shortening matter of time, and the thought of having to make that instantaneous decision was terribly nauseating.

"He's here for destruction, Iris," Auraltiferys interjected quietly. "Trust nothing he says."

Loomis glared briefly at the blacksmith, then returned his eyes to Iris. "Everything I needed from here," he announced, "I took long ago. I'm not here for destruction, Iris. I came here only to speak with you."

Iris blinked. "About what?" she asked. She felt Auraltiferys tensing more and more with each passing second.

Loomis shifted uncomfortably on his feet and dropped his eyes to the ground with a sigh. After a hesitation, he answered simply, "Forgiveness."

Iris felt a surge of incredulous joy sweep through her chest, the same feeling one would have when reviewing the lottery numbers and believing he had won big. She had never been particularly trusting of such feelings, however, because she knew that sort of optimism would only lead to greater disappointment if a mistake were made. She wanted to believe, but she also wanted to verify.

"He's lying to you," Auraltiferys stated coldly.

"I'm not lying," Loomis said quietly but ardently. He looked desperately at Iris, his rich brown eyes blazing. "Iris, you were there with me," he pleaded. "You know what we've been through together. You have worked so hard to make me see what I couldn't recognize on my own! Will you now turn me away?"

Iris felt her pulse racing. She couldn't believe this was really happening, but there seemed to be genuine earnestness in his eyes and in his words.

Auraltiferys kept his eyes trained on Loomis, but he knew exactly what thoughts were running through Iris's mind. "Don't listen to him, Iris," he hissed, his voice like the point of a knife being dragged across stone. "You *must* let me take care of this, though I know it will pain you. Go back inside, and stay there until I return."

"*Take care of this?*" Iris repeated scathingly, in agitated offense. "What will you do to him?"

"He cannot be allowed to remain here," Auraltiferys answered. The veins of his forearm were more prominent now than Iris had ever seen them. She remembered her first encounter with the blacksmith, when he had been prepared to kill her because of her demonic nature, and she recognized that same readiness in him now. Loomis wouldn't leave this mountain alive unless she did something to stop her mentor.

"Auri, no," she said. "Don't hurt him."

"Iris," Auraltiferys returned sharply, "go inside! He is *not* here for your help or forgiveness. There is still much here that he can take, and the world may be plunged into eternal darkness if he succeeds. I *must* protect this mountain and all the relics upon it, and I will do just that!"

"Just let him talk," Iris begged. "He can't do anything while I'm here; I won't let him!" She shot a black look at Loomis, just to let him know she was serious about it. Loomis's expression was sedate.

"I can't trust you to stop him," Auraltiferys replied flatly. "You're compromised; you're too emotionally involved; you can't even recognize his lies. Now go back inside; I won't ask you again."

Iris's eyes widened with shocked fury. "You won't *ask* me at all!" she exclaimed. "You can't command me!"

Auraltiferys finally turned his face and looked down at her, his silver-blue eyes like lasers cutting into hers. "Please," he said earnestly, his voice low and urgent. "Please trust me. Drake is here for nefarious reasons, and I must send him back to Hell. I'm running out of time, Iris. Getting here cost him much energy, and that is why the Hounds are able to render him incapable of magic for now. But he is regaining strength with every passing moment, and I can already see you will try to stop me from harming him, even when the Hounds are no longer able to protect me. I cannot fight you both."

"Iris," Loomis called to her, "you *can't* let him send me back there! Please! Satan will know I've been here to see you; you *know* what he'll do to me!"

Iris turned to Loomis as he entreated her, and her heart was moved with pity for him. She couldn't forget how frightened he had looked there in Hell, as Satan had threatened him with his spirit-crushing relic. She couldn't forget how he had screamed and begged and writhed in agony as the Devil had tortured him. Those weren't reactions that could be faked. Loomis was right—she couldn't let Auraltiferys send him back to Hell. She looked back at her mentor, and she realized he had known the choice she would make even before she had made it. She was too late.

The blacksmith was on the porch beside her in one instant; in the next instant, he stood behind Loomis, in the midst of the Empyreal Hounds, his towering height and muscular build making the demon's human body look rather small by comparison. Iris recognized what he was going to do, but she couldn't even react with magic in time to stop it. She stood as if frozen, unable to do anything but watch as Auraltiferys pulled his heavy, silver blade solidly through Loomis's neck, sending a gruesome spray of blood across the cobblestone path and the soft green grass of the clearing.

She covered her mouth with her free hand, stifling a scream as Loomis's blood-soaked body fell limply to the ground. Her axe dropped from her grip, but her dazed thoughts hardly registered it. Practically mindlessly, she walked slowly toward Auraltiferys as the Hounds dispersed silently into the recesses of the mountain. The blacksmith hurried past Loomis's crumpled form to intercept her. He had returned his knife to its sheath, and he grabbed Iris firmly by both shoulders.

"I'm sorry," he whispered, "but it had to be done."

Iris shook her head emphatically and shoved Auraltiferys off of her. Though she used no magic, and the blacksmith easily could have overpowered her minor physical assault, he released her immediately and let her push him away. She dropped to her knees beside Loomis's body and gingerly touched its face. It was warm but completely lifeless, and while she knew his spirit hadn't been killed, the death of his body still brought her infinite sorrow. She pictured him back in Hell, in his demonic form, already suffering again at Satan's hand.

"Why?" she asked quietly, her vision blurred by tears.

Auraltiferys stood beside her, a looming and imposing figure. "He would have killed us both," he answered. "He could have taken the whole mountain. I couldn't allow that. With his body here now, he will have to go to extreme efforts to return to Earth again, and to even more extreme efforts if he wishes to return here to the mountain. This has spared humanity much suffering, at least for a while."

Iris remained silent for a minute, staring at the empty, bloody vessel lying in front of her and hearing Loomis's urgent plea echoing through her brain. He had begged her to save him from Auraltiferys; she had failed him, and it was her fault he was back in Hell. She stood and looked up at the blacksmith.

"I don't believe you," she said coldly.

Auraltiferys narrowed his eyes. "What do you mean?" he asked, a note of suspicion in his tone.

"I don't believe Loomis was here to kill us," she answered, her voice almost low and gravelly enough to be called a growl. "I think you just wanted your revenge."

"Iris," he replied evenly, "that isn't true."

"No?" she asked acidly in response. She could feel her own eyes flashing with intense anger at the blacksmith's sudden betrayal. "You've lived here alone because of him for how many hundreds of years? You've hated him ever since. You wanted to be the one to fight him! You wanted to send him back to Hell! You did this for your own sake, not for Earth or humankind!" By the time she finished her thought, her voice had crescendoed to an infuriated yell.

Auraltiferys shook his head calmly, trying to mollify her growing rage. There was a faint trace of something like distrust, or perhaps fear, in his eyes. "This was not revenge," he maintained steadily, keeping his voice low and cool. "I didn't do this for myself; I did this to protect the secrets this mountain holds. I didn't *enjoy* doing it, Iris. I know how it has hurt you. But he was here for evil, not for good."

"You don't know that," Iris retorted vehemently, although at a lesser volume than her prior outburst. "What about all that bullshit about mercy just a little while ago? What about that? You didn't even give him a chance!"

Auraltiferys exhaled heavily, an almost pleading expression shadowing his usually fortitudinous visage. "I *saw* what he planned to do—" he declared solemnly.

"You saw what you *wanted* to see!" Iris interrupted.

"No, Iris," Auraltiferys answered forcefully, suddenly impatient with the argument. His voice descended upon her like an anvil, cold and hard and heavy, and she bowed her head before she even realized what she was doing. "I *wanted* to see in him what you see in him. If he desired to be saved from Hell, and if God allowed him to return, then I would want to help in whatever way God would use me, for Drake's sake and for yours. But that is *not* what I was shown. I see as you cannot see."

Iris stared silently at the bloody grass at her feet for several seconds before finally lifting her eyes. "And I see as you cannot see," she replied, quietly and wistfully. "You've sent him back to suffering he doesn't deserve."

Auraltiferys searched her with his trenchant gaze, then shook his head almost imperceptibly. "What are you going to do?" he whispered. Though posed as a question, the words came out more like a statement, as though he already had a pretty good idea what she was thinking.

"You see so much," she responded flippantly. "I'm sure you don't really have to ask."

"Please," he urged, "don't act on this right now. You'll do something you'll regret. Please, let it go. Stay here and pray with me."

Iris scoffed. "Prayers don't help demons," she asserted, her voice like ice. "Prayers don't work in Hell, and Hell is where demons belong."

"Iris—" Auraltiferys entreated.

"I'm only going where I belong," she continued, ignoring the blacksmith's interjection. His eyes widened with concern.

"No!" he exclaimed. "You must not do this! Choose rightly, Iris. This isn't what you want; this isn't you!"

"Yes, it is," Iris answered, in her demonic voice. She watched a veil of sadness fall across Auraltiferys's face before she began the magical incantation to open a gate to Hell. The sadness was immediately replaced by alarm, then fierce resolution.

"NO!" he bellowed, quickly pulling his blade from its sheath with a metallic swish. "You can follow Drake to Hell, but you *will not* open a Gate on this mountain!"

Iris suspended her spell. "Stop me, then, priest," she hissed, nodding toward the blacksmith's knife. She could see indecision in his eyes and a faint tremble in his usually steady hand. It would be far more difficult for him to do to her what he had done to Loomis.

After a suspenseful moment of silent tension, Auraltiferys let his armed hand drop to his side. He shook his head slowly and ruefully, saying nothing.

"It was so easy for you to kill Loomis," Iris jeered inhumanly. "Why can you not kill me?"

The blacksmith held her gaze steadily, but she recognized a mixture of deep emotions stirring in them—despair, dread, doubt; it seemed not even Auraltiferys was immune to the soul's dark night. He was searching desperately for the right guidance now, but no one was answering him.

Iris smiled with malice. "Where is all that faith of yours now?" she rasped.

She saw him swallow hard, and she recognized he was stubbornly holding back some tears. The image caused her to falter momentarily. She suddenly wanted to embrace the beautiful and holy man who so desperately wanted her to follow the path of righteousness. She wanted to apologize for her behavior, to tell him she would stay—tell him that Hell wasn't what she would choose and that everything would be okay. But, instead, she forced the sentimental thoughts from her mind. It was too late for those affectations now. The blacksmith was surely destined for Heaven, no matter what she did. Loomis was the one who needed her.

Submitting herself completely to her demonic spirit, which was the only way to ensure her good tutor could not pull at her heartstrings and cause her to reconsider, Iris commanded him, "Do your duty, priest, and send me back to Hell!" She cast a spell, and the clearing of the mountain erupted into violent flames, leaving only a small circle of safety for her and Auraltiferys and Loomis's ruined, inanimate body.

"Iris, please..." Auraltiferys implored. All his attention was on her, and the intense, roaring fire seemed to cause him no distress at all. He yet held his blade, but it hung low at his side, wielded by an unnerved, unwilling arm.

Iris growled out her disdain with an animalistic, guttural spitting sound. "You're as weak as the rest of them," she spat. In a split-second decision, she focused a series of spells on the blacksmith, and she knew she had caught him off guard. As she stood unmoving within the ring of fire, she forced his arm into position and pulled him instantly toward her, shoving the full blade of his knife through her own heart, his hand still fastened to its hilt.

She heard a deep, agonized cry amid the flames and smoke as her vision faded away and she descended into darkness.

***

Dismal cold enveloped her as the passing void was replaced by the crowded expanse of Hell. It was familiar, but different somehow. The hot, pungent air was an annoyance, but Iris had no trouble breathing it. Wails and cries still resounded throughout the cavernous space, but they reached her more as sensation than as sound. Her perception had completely changed—there was no limit to her vision. All the souls in perpetual torment now had distinguishing features; they had identities. She was seeing as a demon now, not as a human. Her physical body was gone, and her form now was one of spiritual substance. Sudden, hopeless isolation bore down upon her, and she instantly recognized, with exceptional horror, the permanence of the decision she had made. Her soul had become an orphan, and it cried painfully from within her like a lost and abandoned child, with no one and nothing to console it. She knew there would be no end to that grief now. The eternity looming in front of her was as black and immovable as the cragged stone encasement of this realm of the damned, and yet she would have to bear it, for it was what she had chosen.

Only her Satanic spirit would have any modicum of peace here, and that false contentment would be preferable to the inconceivable suffering of a soul removed from its source of life. So Iris focused on the power of her demonic spirit, burying human thought and feeling beneath the arrogance and hate of the fallen angel whose substance she shared. It brought no real comfort. She could not separate her two natures; she could not choose to exist as one or the other. Her humanity would not be silenced, and her demonic spirit would never be fulfilled. Hell was hers now, and it was more awful than anyone had ever taught her it would be. She remembered Auraltiferys begging her to choose rightly, doing everything he could to keep her out of this terrible eternity. The memory was too unpleasant, too grievous; she couldn't allow it to linger in her thoughts. Anger would be far easier, and she knew where she could appropriately place that emotion. Why had she come here in the first place? It wasn't her own Satanic nature that had brought her here—she had lived as a decent, moral person, even with a demonic spirit in her, and Auraltiferys had helped her even further after she had learned her true identity. He had never written her off as a lost cause; he had tried desperately to lead her toward Heaven and away from Hell. She had made a foolish decision in the end, perhaps, but she had made it with good intentions. No...only others could be blamed for her damnation now. If goodness yet remained in Loomis, she might still find some hint of purpose and fulfillment here, in what she had once offered to him: protecting him from the needless torments of Satan. She could spend eternity angry at the Devil, and that might at least assuage her grief. Or, if Auraltiferys had been right about Loomis all along...well, then her anger would rest on Loomis alone, and she would find purpose and fulfillment in making him suffer for having tricked her into this endless abyss. Either way, wrath would keep her from completely drowning in misery.

There was no time here, but Iris could still organize her perception in a linear fashion, and from that perspective, she needed only a moment to adjust to her new existence. With her seemingly limitless vision, it was easy for her to find Loomis, even among the countless inhabitants of this wasteland. He was alone in a deep cave of obsidian, carved out in one of the mountainous islands that floated in the lakes of fire. It was a large space, dotted with jagged columns of black glass and lit by a thin rivulet of garnet flame that began as a fiery pool within the cave's recesses and then meandered through the cavity and out onto the harshly cracked stone of the island, seeping down its side like incandescent blood. Iris guessed Loomis must have created this place for himself as his own personal refuge and workroom. He must have spent most of his time in Hell here, studying magic and relics and devising all his evil plans and schemes, all while avoiding the rest of the damned as much as he possibly could. A number of relics sat on shelves carved into the wall, with a dozen or more gilt-edged tomes among them. She had a pretty good idea where they had come from, and it made her sad. Auraltiferys and the holy mountain already seemed so far away as to have been nothing but a reverie. Although, she considered cynically, perhaps that was for the best. She could never return there; she would never see her mentor again. The sooner she forgot him, the easier her existence would be.

Loomis's demonic form seemed much smaller and less imposing

than she remembered, perhaps because Iris was now seeing him from a different form herself. She didn't want to know what she must look like now, outside her human body. Loomis was still quite clearly demonic—a goatish, serpentine head affixed to a beastly, humanoid body—but Iris recognized the faint glimmer of an angel's form in him, though she couldn't readily identify what it was in his appearance that gave her that idea. Maybe it was the dim glow of iridescence beneath the outline of his form, which seemed the slightest bit less murky than that of the other demons; maybe it was the more glassy and less leathery "skin" that gave him his shape; maybe it was, in fact, his shape, which more closely resembled the archangels' figures than did any of the other animalistic monstrosities dwelling here. Or maybe it was the nearly imperceptible trace of light she believed she saw in his amber eyes, struggling desperately to shine through the smoky, ashy patina that dulled them. As she looked at him, she felt once more the desire to help him. She felt he didn't belong here. But then, neither did she belong here, really. It wasn't her choice—or, at least, it wouldn't have been her choice but for him. Auraltiferys had been right—Loomis had been offered a chance to repent, and he had declined it. Hell was what he wanted, and Iris had been too sentimental or too stubborn or too foolish to accept it, to the point of her own damnation. There would be no help for either of them now, and it was all Loomis's fault. She should hate him for it. She *would* hate him for it. Any other emotion would be only a weakness here.

"I'm surprised to see you here," Loomis commented indifferently. His demonic voice seemed to resonate from within Iris's mind rather than traveling as sound through the sulfuric air. "I thought you had other plans for yourself."

"I did," Iris answered coldly, momentarily startled by her own voice. She had spoken with her demonic voice before, but it sounded different—and much more terrifying—without the veil of a physical body.

Loomis looked at her, expressionless. Iris felt a wave of anger crash over her, brought on by his lack of appropriate interest. It was his fault she was here for all eternity; the least the bastard could do would be to ask why she had followed him.

"Why were you on the mountain?" she asked him, wrath completely unhidden in her tone.

A strange contortion, like a smirk, settled on his visage. "That doesn't matter now," he replied cockily.

In immediate fury, Iris focused a powerful spell that sent Loomis flying backward, his form crashing through two thick obsidian pillars, leaving shards of black glass strewn across the floor of his little hideout. He had been too slow to try to defend himself, and while Iris found it amusing, she wished he had proven somewhat more challenging. Even magic felt different here—she sensed it the instant she had focused her spell. As powerful as she had been on Earth, trapped in a human body, she was exponentially stronger here. She could *feel* it, and it felt wonderful. Loomis had made a good point; his purpose on the mountain was inconsequential now. But his impertinence would have to be punished, and severely so. She had asked him a question, and the insolent fuck was going to give her an answer, whether it mattered or not.

As Loomis stood from where he had fallen, Iris attacked him again with additional magic. He was better prepared this time and attempted to fight her, which made her effort much more gratifying. She was fully aware she was stronger than he was. She let him defend himself a while, intentionally weakening her own offensive as he cast paltry spells back at her. Then, with sudden intensity, she forced him to his knees at the edge of the fiery pool. He squirmed within the death grip of her magic, and she felt his fear as he recognized his own comparative weakness. He knew he couldn't overpower her, and he knew she was pissed as fuck. This must be exactly what he had hoped to avoid, she reflected, back when he had tried to coach her toward Heaven. Sadly for him, he had failed at that.

Iris stood beside him and watched as her magic effortlessly effected her will. She brutally shoved his head into the magmatic well and grinned as his arms clawed ineffectually at the cruel stone floor, trying to find a position from which he could remove himself from the fire. Though his face was submerged, she could hear his tormented cries as the flame scalded his demonic form. After a moment, he gave up his struggle, and she released him from her spells. He emerged from the basin but remained on his hands and knees with his head bowed, his entire form heaving spasmodically in agony. Iris reached down (with an arm that looked completely alien to her) and grabbed him roughly by one of the broken horns on his head, tilting it back so she could see his face. It was a repulsive sight. He was practically unrecognizable, looking more like an abstract or surrealist painting than any legitimate being. His face and eyes seemed to have melted and fused into a glassy mess, thin lines of blackened amber splayed across an almost shapeless violet-black canvas of charred demonic skin—the stuff of nightmares. If not for her Satanic spirit, Iris was sure she would have been appalled. As it was, however, she was rather satisfied by the aftermath of her onslaught.

"You will answer my question," she hissed. "Why were you on the mountain?" She pushed Loomis backward as she spoke, causing a grotesque cracking sound from his ruined face.

Loomis crawled a short distance away from her, the mutated wings of his demonic form pressing heavily upon him as he moved. He supported himself against another pillar as he struggled to rise to his feet. After a long silence, he said, emotionlessly, "I was going to kill you both."

For an instant, Iris felt her Satanic ire replaced by the immeasurable despair that had plagued her after Saint Augustine's—the grief for a once-good spirit lost to Hell, now made infinitely more painful by the utter hopelessness of a godless eternity. The blacksmith had been right all along; Loomis didn't want any forgiveness. While she had still lived, she could at least have held on to the *hope* he might one day seek to return to grace; she could pray to God and know her prayers were heard, even if the only result had proven to be her eventual acceptance of Loomis's self-imposed damnation. Here, however, she could feel no hope, and it left her soul like a dead weight within her, pleading for consolation that would never come.

"Why?" she asked him unthinkingly, not even realizing she had allowed her human voice to do the talking until after she sensed the weak and pitiful sound of it. It startled her; the last thing she needed now was vulnerability. She doggedly quelled the sadness with another bout of anger, reminding herself that Loomis was the reason for her death, and that he had never had any intention of asking for mercy or redemption. He had tricked her; she had lost their game in the end...and she didn't like losing. She would listen to Loomis's answer since she had already asked the question, but his explanation wouldn't matter. Whatever it was, his fate was sealed.

Loomis had begun magically repairing the damage to his form, but it was still evident the brief torture to his spiritual being had inflicted a great deal of pain. "You were never going to join me," he said coldly. "You would only continue trying to change me; you would have become an insufferable, pious, nagging bitch, and I had no intention of subjecting myself to your constant sermonizing. There are other ways for me to take the throne—more difficult, yes, but not impossible. I expected you to prevent that sanctimonious priest from attacking me, and I expected I would have regained my strength enough by then to finish him. Then it would have been easy for me to end you, considering your supposed unwillingness to hurt me. The mountain and all its wealth of hidden knowledge and relics would have been mine, and nothing could have kept me from ruling Hell and Earth." He paused, then added, rather more gently, "I didn't anticipate you would end up here."

Iris felt a sneer settling across the face of her spiritual form. "Sorry to have disrupted your plans," she replied acidly.

"Why *are* you here?" Loomis asked, his demonic face nearly returned to its normal appearance. Iris thought she saw another timid flickering of light within his eyes, and she felt a fleeting stab of regret for what she had just done to him. It wasn't so long ago, after all, that she had been begging Auraltiferys to show him some compassion. How could she have transformed so quickly into a force of aberrant hate? *It doesn't matter*, she told herself. *Put it out of your mind; there's no goodness in him. There's no goodness in you, either.*

"I don't answer to you," she countered stonily. There was an atrocious conflict of emotions happening inside her right now, and she no longer wanted to participate in this conversation.

"Iris—" Loomis prompted her quietly. He added nothing further, but the manner in which he had uttered her name nearly brought Iris to her knees in sorrow. His voice had brushed across her like a comforting breeze, carrying a soft supplication she couldn't ignore, no matter how much her Satanic nature wanted to. It sounded demonic, but it *felt* anything but wicked, and she suddenly believed there was something more benevolent than selfish interest hiding in the question he had asked.

"I didn't want you to be left alone here," Iris admitted, after a long silence. Loomis stared at her, deadpan, and she immediately chastised herself for her momentary sentimentality. Of course he didn't *really* care why she was here; he was upset by her presence only because of how it might negatively impact him. Letting her demonic spirit take over, she added angrily, "I was weaker on Earth.

I won't make those mistakes again. I will spend my eternity making you suffer, and that is well worth the damnation."

Loomis stood like a statue in front of her, occasional reflections of garnet flame darting across the amber facets of his eyes. Iris thought, for just a moment, she saw him shaking his head in a nearly imperceptible intimation of sadness, and her human soul screamed inside her again, threatening to drown her once more in the forlorn grief that defined this realm. The damned thing *knew* there was no hope, and yet it pleaded in vain. She cut it off with another suffocating bout of wrath, focusing her spirit into cruel magic she found somewhere in her vast expanse of demonic knowledge and turning it on Loomis with extreme prejudice. She recognized it as the same magic she had witnessed Satan using against him when she had been here before, both shielded and limited by her human body. The Devil had needed his special relic for it; Iris was pleased to discover she didn't share that same impediment.

Loomis dropped instantly to his knees, futilely clutching at his head as though it might prevent the horrifying dissolution of his spirit within her inescapable magical vise. He fought in every way he could, knowing it was useless, and Iris could only laugh at his impotence. She was crushing the thing he most valued—his individuality. She knew every fissure she caused in his spirit anguished him. She knew he could feel himself eroding from within, could feel himself becoming just like all those he despised—mindless and unmotivated and unthinking. If she maintained the magic and refused to reverse it, Loomis would soon be no different from any other demon under Satan's rule.

"PLEASE!" he cried, his demonic voice cracking wretchedly as he felt himself weakening. "Please, no...Iris, please!"

Iris was unrelenting, enjoying the pitiful display in front of her. Here was the one who had believed for so long he would outsmart her, would take from her whatever he wanted. Now he could do nothing but cry like a little bitch at her feet.

A sudden, thunderous blast echoed through the caverns of Hell, and the roof of Loomis's hideaway was torn off amid a cloud of smoke and ash and crumbling stone. Iris ceased her magic, leaving Loomis in a sad, contemptible heap on the shaking floor. A dark and easily recognizable figure appeared at a short distance beside her, and she pointedly refused to turn her attention toward it.

"Well, well," Satan greeted them sarcastically. "Surely you two lovebirds aren't bickering?"

Iris's rage toward Loomis was instantly supplanted by an even more profound hatred. *Lovebirds, my ass*, she thought. The Devil was such a fucking tool.

"Loomis," Satan cooed demonically, "I've *never* treated you so badly. I simply cannot understand what it is you see in my daughter. Perhaps now you will finally recognize how necessary it is that I destroy her."

Loomis lifted his head slightly. The color was completely gone from his eyes, and he looked as gaunt and stooped as the other demonic drones enslaved by Satan. "You can't destroy her," he replied hoarsely. "She's stronger than all of us."

Iris was somewhat surprised by Loomis's admission, and she felt an impulse to reverse the spiritual damage she had just done to him. But she also knew any compliment from him might be nothing but bait in a trap. So, instead, she simply waited, turning her gaze from Loomis to her evil creator.

"You must convince yourself of that," the Devil replied to him, "for otherwise, your failure to either tempt her or defeat her is nothing but your own fault." He laughed slowly and mirthlessly, in a low snarl, then said, "Let me show you how weak she truly is."

Iris remained unflappable; she wasn't the least bit afraid of anything Satan might try. He lifted a crooked, bony hand to his chest and opened the vaporous substance of his skin. She had seen this gimmick before; did he really think it would do anything to her? With dramatic slowness, the Devil removed from inside his form the rough, burgundy-colored relic that established his rulership.

Loomis stood up, with impressive agility for a creature that had been so viciously tormented, and moved closer to Iris, placing himself just in front of her in a protective sort of stance. Iris knew she hadn't completely deadened his spirit, but she was stunned by the vivacity he was showing. He seemed to be focusing every free thought he still had into defending her now.

"Don't," he said, with cold simplicity.

"You still defend her?" Satan asked incredulously, immediately bursting into cacophonous laughter. "Your stupidity amazes me!"

"Why *do* you defend me, Loomis?" Iris asked suddenly, quietly, in a voice more human than demonic. He turned slowly toward her.

"I suppose you and I both have had untimely revelations," he answered enigmatically. He gave her a long look, and although her Satanic attack on him had all but broken his individual will, Iris clearly recognized in his eyes the conviction of a warrior, glowing dimly but certainly within a spirit hardened and jaded by millennia of sin and suffering. She understood now why Satan had allowed Loomis all the comparative freedoms he had long enjoyed—even the Devil knew no relic could kill that fortitude. Had he ever *really* backed Loomis into a corner, had he tried to subject him in the same way he had subjected the others who had followed him, Satan would have found himself hopelessly outmatched. The veils of the Devil's lies had obscured Loomis's vision, or maybe Loomis had simply believed for so long that he had become unworthy of his Heavenly rank that he could no longer see it in himself, but Iris recognized it very plainly, and with complete certainty now—the spirit of a seraph burned within him still.

As Loomis returned his focus to Satan, Iris reversed her spell against him, freeing his spirit from the magical restraint she had constructed. She thought she sensed gratitude from him, though he made no outward sign of it. Whether he was grateful or he wasn't, Iris knew she had done the right thing—and even in this horrid place, left alone by God out of respect for the free wills of His creation, doing the right thing brought her a whisper of hope. Her soul clung to it with dire urgency, filled with joy at this remote and slight chance that its God might still be present here, in some form. The feeling refreshed her spirit, and she felt stronger and more confident than when she had first arrived. In fact, she felt alive.

"How very sweet and utterly sickening," Satan growled loudly, his speech echoing over the endless squall of damned souls as he recognized Iris's reversal of her Satanic spell. "I see my daughter yet has a weakness for you," he continued. "Tell me, Loomis, do you share that same feebleness? I expect that kind of thing from a human woman, but I have always believed us to be far superior to them. Have I misjudged you?"

Loomis stood resolutely, in an aura of cold unbendingness. "One of you has misjudged me," he replied stoically. "I'm inclined now to trust her judgment over yours."

Satan snapped the bony protrusions that acted as his fingers, still holding his relic in his other claw-like hand. His four horse-headed guards descended promptly from above, strategically surrounding their lord and his two unruly subjects. They appeared to have recovered from the abuse Iris had administered to them on her previous visit to the underworld. She laughed demonically, knowing the reason for her laughter did not have to be vocalized.

"Laugh while you can," Satan announced angrily at her amusement. "You will find them much more imposing after I take my spirit back from you." Iris's silence after the remark enraged him more, but he withheld any action against her and instead turned his attention back to Loomis.

"So, you side with my ungrateful bitch of a daughter," he snapped at him. "How much are you willing to suffer for her?" He screamed the question in an irate, high-pitched bellow that violently incised the air, raising his relic toward Loomis as he spoke. The rough, jewel-like object pulsated with dim light, silencing all the wails and moans of the abyss. He wasn't going to wait for an answer.

Loomis fought the spell immediately, to no avail. He dropped again to the harsh stone floor and screamed as he once again felt his spirit being crushed against his will. *He can't even see he has the power to fight it*, Iris thought with pity. She quickly intervened, using her own power to counteract Satan's magic. She sensed at once that the relic was a potent one, but the Devil wasn't as adept a user as he believed himself to be, and she had little trouble warding off the spell. The glow faded from the relic, and a sudden explosion of fire from the lakes below illustrated just how angry Satan was at this turn of events. Loomis rose hesitantly from the ground and stood silently beside Iris, both of them staring at the Devil and waiting for the tantrum that was sure to follow.

"Oh, you insolent, fucking *bitch*!" Satan yelled, his whole ghastly form shaking with excessive rage. Iris felt his words vibrating through her, but she was unafraid. She was certain she was stronger than the Devil, and she was equally certain Loomis would not betray her again. Whatever had been the "revelation" he had referenced so mysteriously, it seemed to have changed his thinking. His abiding goodness was now abundantly evident to her, and she believed she could safely trust him. "I should have thought you'd *like* to watch him suffer, after all his treachery toward you!" Satan continued. "He tried to take from you what is rightfully yours! Tried to trick you into giving him power he shouldn't have! And you've been foolish enough to fall for it! You don't deserve my power; you never have! That fucking human soul of yours is an abomination. You disgust me."

"I'm not particularly fond of you, either," Iris answered contemptuously.

Satan ignored her retort and moved his cold, black eyes to Loomis. "And you," he growled, "you have always thought yourself better than all the rest of my subjects; what can you say for yourself now? You rely on a human woman to save you from my wrath! You're the weakest of any here!"

"Am I?" Loomis asked. "If I have her to aid me in my weakness, am I truly weak?" Iris felt her soul moved with compassion toward him. Had she yet been alive, in a human body, she was sure she would have been unable to refrain from hugging him. His response held abundant wisdom and inherent humility—something one could expect from an angel, but not from a demon. *God, bless him*, she thought, remembering only after her mind had uttered the words that she had abandoned God to be here.

Satan lifted the chin of his gaunt, goatish face, staring at Loomis with lifeless eyes that embodied pure hatred. The roofless obsidian chamber went still and silent as it was enveloped with an invisible shroud of frigidity. The chill wasn't a physical one, and although the sensation was much the same, it was far more agonizing. This cold froze the soul and the spirit.

"Do you hear that, daughter?" Satan addressed Iris, surprisingly calmly. His skeletal arms rested at his sides, one mangled hand still holding his currently inert relic. "He uses you. What he cannot do for himself, he is content to let you do for him. He has made you his servant. He brought you here for his own security, knowing the fondness you have for him. And now he will expect you to serve him for all eternity. You're nothing but a tool to him, a means to his ends."

Iris felt her form go rigid at the suggestion. Was her idiotic human soul still clinging to sentimental fantasies and making her blind to reality? It must be. Why else would she yet be hoping for something other than fire and brimstone and gnashing of teeth forevermore? This was Hell; there would be no going back, no return, no redemption. Her soul would wish otherwise forever, but that wouldn't change her circumstance, and that was precisely why damnation was such a torment.

"That isn't true," Loomis said quietly to Iris, turning to face her.

"You planned to kill me," she challenged him, her demonic voice colored with paranoia and grave warning. She didn't like being tricked or used, and she certainly didn't have to put up with that down here. She would torture Loomis again right now if not for her soul's desperate plea that she should still believe in his goodness.

"Yes," Loomis acknowledged, inclining his head, "but I believed you had chosen a different end for yourself."

Satan snorted. "Daughter, listen to his lies no more," he said. "Crush him, just as he would do to you, were he not the impotent bastard he is."

An abrupt eruption of anger heated Iris's entire spirit. "I'm not your daughter," she screamed. Her internal conflict was tearing her from inside, and she couldn't stand it any longer. She could put both Satan and Loomis under her feet now; neither of them was a match for her in magical power, and their subjugation would be the only way to ensure she was not being manipulated by either of them. "I'll break both of you," she exclaimed. "You're both powerless to stop me!" The horse-headed guards shifted in their places when she screamed, recognizing her voice as Satan's. Apparently, the spirit-disintegrating magic of the Devil's relic had detrimental effects on intelligence as well.

Satan made a guttural snarling sound, full of loathing. "I created you," he bellowed. "I can even more readily destroy you!"

"Try it," Iris urged him.

Loomis immediately moved in front of her, concern emanating from his being. "Iris, stop," he cautioned. "You don't understand—"

"What's left to understand?" she asked hatefully. "You're both full of lies, and I know how strong I am. Neither of you can challenge me."

Satan snapped his fingers, and two of his guards descended directly on Loomis, striking him with their heavy iron weapons and forcing him to the ground. The Devil threw all three of them aside with his own spell and then jumped in front of Iris, causing the stone of the island to quake beneath them. He placed a clawed hand on her head, and, despite her confidence in her strength, she felt fear permeate her spirit for an instant.

"No!" Loomis snarled. With monumental effort of will, he knocked the demon guards off of him. The guards were stunned; their dark weapons usually protected them from the magic of other demons, and they weren't at all accustomed to having their victims fight back. They had just learned Loomis had greater strength than what he had previously displayed. Loomis disappeared briefly, then materialized right at the Devil's side. He invoked another spell and shoved Satan harshly away from Iris.

"It's not the same here," he said rapidly, grabbing Iris tightly with two glassy, strangely humanoid arms. "He'll take your spirit from you; he'll absorb you. You don't have a body to shelter you here; the magic is exponentially stronger—"

"I'm not afraid," Iris interjected casually.

Loomis tried to say something more, but Satan cut him off by slapping him across the side of his face with his sharp talons. The skin of Loomis's demonic form tore from the attack, hanging in limp shreds as viscous, pearlescent fluid oozed from the wound. The Devil then assaulted Iris in the same way, slashing across the plane of her vision. She had been distracted by Loomis's injury—probably owing to her humanity's emotional millstone—and hadn't expected the hit. If she could have described it in a physical way, she might have said it felt like dry ice stabbing the eyes while a hot razor slashed the skin. That pain, however, might have been preferable to this.

She fell to the jagged rock below, hearing the Devil's raucous, malicious laughter from above her. "Not so almighty after all, are you, *daughter?*" he hissed.

Iris wasn't looking at him, but she could see in her demonic mind what he was doing. He stood over her and stretched out his hand, his relic glowing again with its magical light. Angry at the weakness she was showing, she immediately focused on the magic she had used before to disable the relic. Her spell seemed just as effective against the relic now, and she rose cockily from the ground to face her attacker again. She didn't remain upright for long. She heard Loomis yell at the Devil to stop; then, as she felt her form drop again to the stone below, perception fell away from her.

There was suddenly nothing around her but emptiness, as though she had been sealed in a vacuum. A frightening sensation rapidly engulfed her, beginning as something like the gnawing of maggots, then quickly escalating to something like the thrashing bite of a shark. It was all internal; she was feeling her demonic spirit and her human soul literally tearing apart, and she could neither see nor hear the spell that was causing it. This was a different and more terrible incantation than what was used simply to deaden the spirit; the excruciation chased her thoughts away with great swiftness, and she knew she would have little time to try anything to stop the dark magic. Her spirit was already being wrested from her.

She focused all the energy she could into the same spell she had used against Loomis when she had visited his Portland home, when he had warned her what Satan had planned for her. She could only hope she hadn't begun her fight too late. It had been one thing to reclaim her spirit from Loomis when he had previewed the dark spell for her on Earth; it was proving infinitely more difficult just to keep her spirit out of the Devil's grasp here in Hell. If he had already taken too much of her power...Iris didn't have any idea what her existence would become, or if she would even have an existence. As she fiercely repeated her magical defense and let the power flow through whatever was left of her, she felt her soul involuntarily crying out, *God, help me.*

After a torturous moment, she sensed a change in the stasis of the battling Satanic spells. Strength started returning to her, and with every quark of spirit she regained, the power of her own magic increased, making it easier to fight the Devil's attack. Sound, or the feeling of sound, returned to her first, and she realized she was not combating alone for the integrity of her spirit. She sensed near her the vigorous substance of Loomis's being, and she heard his voice chanting the same invocation against Satan, tugging the Devil's spirit away from its focus on hostile absorption of Iris's demonic essence. With his help, Iris was soon able to pull her spirit back to herself. When she recovered her perception, she was kneeling on the ground, with Loomis standing beside her, continuing his magical offensive against the Devil until she could stand and join him. Satan had either backed away or been forced away and was perched inelegantly atop a mound of broken stone on the opposite side of the stream of garnet flame, clutching his now unlit relic as wrath and hatred resonated from every perceivable spiritual atom of his form. His guards surrounded him, holding their weapons in a particular array that might have protected their dark lord from other demons but would certainly prove useless against Iris and Loomis together. But for the macabre and gruesome deformity of their beings, it was a rather comical sight.

The Devil placed his relic back inside the miasmic sinew of his form and suddenly grabbed the guard nearest him, placing one gnarled hand on its horse-like head and another inside its torso. The demon cried out in terror, then Satan wrenched its form apart and threw both halves into the fiery lake far below. Its weapon fell with a metallic thud at the Devil's feet. He magically lifted it to his own hand, then struck down his three remaining guards with a single swipe of the blade. Their forms vaporized, leaving only disembodied squealing and the clattering of their dropped weapons as evidence of their existence. The noise faded into the general babel of Hell as the Devil retrieved the other iron instruments. Iris and Loomis watched in silence as he amalgamated the pieces into a single nightmarish torture device.

"You two have seen only a fragment of my real power," Satan announced, his voice seeming to come at them from every direction, rattling the walls of the underworld. "I am finished with these games." As he spoke, his right arm merged with the weapon he had just assembled. The blades and cudgels took on the misty, leathery look of his demonic form and then were illuminated from within by a baneful, yellow aura. The Devil jumped down from the pile of rock and moved immediately in front of Iris and Loomis, his form appearing twice as large as it had before. Iris wasn't particularly afraid; if she and Loomis had successfully fought against his reclamation of her spirit, then surely the Devil could do nothing of lasting consequence to them. She noted, however, with some anxiety, that Loomis did not seem to share her confidence. His fear was tangible.

With a raspy, insidious chuckle, Satan reached down with his comparatively normal left hand and lifted Loomis's face toward his. "Of course you're afraid," he said scathingly. "You believed you knew everything. You believed you had seen all of my tricks. Now you see I have powers you hadn't dreamed of. You will not fare well against an opponent you do not know."

Iris instantly realized the peril of this development. Satan was speaking the truth now—Loomis was completely unfamiliar with whatever complex magic the Devil was building up to, and that left him helpless against it. Iris would have to fight this alone. Whatever Satan knew, she also knew; she had only to find the answer within her own Satanic spirit.

The Devil released Loomis's face and took a long stride backward, giving himself more space. "Perhaps the best way to punish my daughter," he mused darkly, "is to destroy you in front of her." He turned his deathly black gaze to Iris and added, "Unless, of course, she wishes to spare you by submitting herself to me."

Iris returned the Devil's stare in silence. Loomis replied to his statement instead, saying, "I wouldn't allow it."

"The demon cannot speak for you, daughter," Satan told Iris. "His wishes are inconsequential. But you see he doesn't even care enough for you to let you save him; he doesn't care if your eternity is filled with endless grief for his destruction."

Iris's mind was rife with running thoughts. In this inhuman, metaphysical existence, she could focus on a multitude of things simultaneously, without distraction. She was listening to the words being spoken even as she searched her spiritual ken for the key to preventing Satan's upcoming ambush, and the Devil's arrogant need for dramatic prelude had given her all the time she had needed. She remembered how Auraltiferys had explained relics to her; she recalled how they were originally forged for specific users. She remembered the feeling in her own human arm as she held the axe the blacksmith had crafted for her—how the two magical, bronze blades seemed to become an extension of her being, their magic increasing her abilities as her spiritual power fueled their magic, a strange and wonderful symbiosis of the physical and the supernatural, not altogether unlike the union of flesh and spirit that defined humanity. And humanity was something Iris knew much more about than Satan did.

"I will neither submit myself to you nor watch his destruction," she answered the Devil.

He responded with a deprecating snicker. "Whatever you say," he chortled in a biting, demonic singsong, moving his gaze to Loomis. He recited some Hebrew words, invoking a spell that bound his victim in place. It was a spell Loomis undoubtedly knew how to break, but he made no attempt to. Iris knew, and likely Loomis had induced it, too, that freeing himself from the binding would be meaningless. The coming blow from the Devil's strange and ancient weapon would reach him wherever he was. Even if Loomis were a formless phantasm, the magic would strike his spirit. Freezing his victim before the end was but a nod to Satan's appetite for theatricality; his ultimate malevolence, which he obviously considered this weapon to be, would never rely on such an unreliable bit of simple magic.

In an instant, all the fires of Hell went dark, and every loud lamentation went mute. The only perceivable light was the intensifying, jaundiced glow of the Devil's engorged reliquary of an arm, bright enough only to encircle Satan and his two would-be mutineers. He readied himself to strike, sending a frighteningly black magic through the essence of his weaponized appendage as he raised it high above Loomis.

Iris had already begun preparations of her own, however. Relying on her memory of her mentor and the relic-weapon he had forged under divine inspiration specifically for her, she directed a flow of magic into the form of her own right arm, conscientiously matching it to the same feeling, the same resonance, as the bronze axe she had used against the Devil before. As Satan's sulfuric luminescence reached its brightest, her arm ignited with a purple radiance. In the blink of a magical spell, she was directly in front of the overgrown form of Satan, penetrating his chest with her arm before his sinister weapon could complete its evil work. The Devil howled in horrified indignation as her attack bluntly truncated his magic. The light in his arm went instantly dark, and his form returned promptly to its typical size. The crude iron parts of his relic dropped from his thin, airy skin, noisily striking the stone floor as the separate pieces typically wielded by his guards. Flames and cries returned to the abyss, and Satan stood immobile, magicless and weak and humiliatingly exposed.

After a significant period of silence between them, Loomis finally turned to Iris. "It seems I will forever be in your debt," he said quietly. His tone was a casual facetiousness, but Iris discerned genuine gratitude beneath the flippant veneer.

Iris ignored his remark and asked, "What now?"

"Now," Loomis answered, refocusing his gaze on Satan's trapped form, "you should take what is rightfully yours."

"I never wanted his throne," Iris retorted bitingly. Why did Loomis's reply fill her with such leaden disappointment? Had she hoped for something else? She would have been stupid to expect anything else.

"Iris," he urged, "the rulership should be yours! See how you have so swiftly set him beneath you! Do you really intend to dwell in servitude to him forever?"

"I didn't *intend* to be here in the first place," she replied. Her voice was clearly human.

Loomis stared at her, the amber gemstones of his demonic eyes still showing the faintest hint of illumination from within, at least to Iris's perception. "But," he said evenly, "you *are* here. This is Hell, Iris. Nothing that happened before matters any longer. This is the eternity you've chosen." Iris returned his gaze but said nothing. Her soul was in exceptional pain.

"Make of it what you can," Loomis exhorted her, recognizing she was not going to answer him. "Take the throne, and be subject to no one. You deserve that more than he does."

After a prolonged hesitation, Iris asked, in rueful and scornful disbelief, "Is that really all that matters to you? The throne of Hell?

Even now, knowing I don't want to rule this godforsaken abyss, you still press me to take Satan's place?"

"It is the only comfort you will possibly know," he answered, his demonic voice strangely weak.

"And the only comfort *you* would know," Iris snapped. "You only want to share my authority; you don't care about my comfort."

Loomis bowed his face, shaking his head slowly from side to side. "No," he replied, "I wish to spare you the suffering I have known. You are not like me—you are superior; you do not have to submit to it. My advice to you now comes without cost. Take your rightful place as ruler, and do to me whatever you wish. I'm asking nothing from you."

Iris listened to him and felt her entire being crying for what might have been. She didn't want to be here, and despite all his arguments to the contrary, she believed Loomis truly regretted his own presence here.

When she offered no prompt reply, Loomis added, "The throne has no price for you anymore. You have nothing else to lose."

The statement triggered in Iris a consuming, bitter remorse for having chosen this end. She couldn't believe she had opted for damnation out of some misguided notion that she could save Loomis from Hell. His words were true—infinitely sad, but true. She had nothing to lose; she had already lost everything that mattered. And for what? For love of a demon? What a ridiculous sentiment! For all her human intelligence, she had certainly ended up a total fool.

She looked at Loomis for a moment, then turned to Satan, still powerlessly frozen where she had left him, his disfigured, dark form still breathing a dim, purple echo of her magic. From somewhere within her spirit, inspiration struck her—not hope, exactly, nor anything like joy, but a rebellious whim that whispered of freedom, or at least of the nearest approximation of freedom one might know in Hell. Both Loomis and Satan had their ideas about how she should spend her eternity; she wanted to surprise and disappoint them both, even if it should bring her eternal torment. After all, what *did* she have to lose?

"You're right," she said to Loomis after a thoughtful moment. "I have nothing to lose. But you do. And he does." She nodded her head toward the Devil, then continued in a voice as cold as the obsidian expanses of the wasteland, "The way I see it, I'm here because of the two of you. I've lost everything that ever really mattered to me, and I won't accept all the blame for it. You were the ones who led me here. So, now, I'm going to take what very little the two of you have left. If I have to be miserable forever, so should you be."

Loomis stiffened beside her, clearly wary of whatever she might do next. Satan had already surprised him once, and if anyone else was capable of doing the same, it was certainly Iris. Satan remained uncharacteristically quiet, the unknown duration of his current magical impotence giving him substantial cause for worry. With his powers disabled indefinitely, even the typically overly confident Devil knew he was incapable of preventing whatever fresh hell his "daughter" might be intending for them all.

Iris moved in front of Satan and stared harshly into the bleak, colorless eyes of the fallen angel who had first brought her forth as a clone of his own evil spirit. She recognized in those eyes not even a shadow of herself, though she knew beyond doubt that her spiritual essence and his were the same. Perhaps her mortal life truly had been enough to transform her into something completely different from him. Although she had ended up here in Hell with him forever, she had lived better than he had. She had known forgiveness and virtue and grace, and the memories of those now-forsaken gifts would have to become the only droplets of sustenance and relief she would ever enjoy in her eternal damnation. She hoped their succor would be enough to last her for infinitude.

The Devil stared back at her, his hate and rage not completely disguising his discomfort. He might not believe Iris could do anything of consequence to him, but he was uncertain enough to have lost some of his bravado. He said nothing, and after a lingering moment, Iris placed the hand of her spirit's form onto his chest, the sheer, inhuman parchment of his "skin" rippling at her touch like the surface of a windblown pond. In an instant, his true fear became palpable.

"NO," Satan commanded coldly. He spoke with authority and intimidation, but Iris wasn't fooled. There was a childlike terror masked in his tone; he recognized what she was about to do. "Leave it with me," he charged. "I am the one who knows how to use it. You have proven yourself to me now; you are my daughter, and it is fitting that we rule together. My kingdom is your kingdom; I will share it with you proudly. We are the same spirit; let us not be opposed."

"I'm not your daughter," Iris answered evenly, "and you're not a king." She reached into his form, just as easily as Satan himself could, and removed the crude, blood-colored relic that had so long ensured his power over the realm of the dead.

"Stop!" Satan screamed. "The throne is mine; you cannot take it from me!"

"I just did," Iris replied apathetically. "Maybe you shouldn't have relied so heavily on a simple relic for your authority. And maybe you shouldn't have been so arrogant as to seek your own incarnation; it hasn't worked out well for you."

"You villainous cunt!" the Devil roared. No flames erupted at his outburst; no clamoring spirits fell silent at his words. He had become a nonentity, with no relic and no magic to justify him. "Stop her, Loomis!" he growled, turning his gaze toward his once-profitable servant, who appeared to be completely unmoved by his ruler's misfortunes. "Stop her, now," Satan continued urgently, "and I'll free you from your servitude! Hell and Earth will be completely open to you, without rules, without expectations, without consequences! I give you my word: I shall never torture you again! You will no longer have to serve me!"

Loomis listened indifferently to Satan's vapid negotiation, his eyes fixed on Iris as she approached him. Without looking at the Devil, Loomis answered him flatly, "I believe Iris has already relieved me of any obligation to serve you."

To Iris, his voice sounded (or rather, felt) lighter, as though a heavy burden had been lifted from him. He was, however, still unsure of her intentions, and he hadn't so quickly forgotten she had threatened to take something from him as well. He watched from behind the amber eyes of his spiritual form, quietly and patiently waiting for her play. She stared at him for a long time, yet unable to understand why he had chosen this end for himself. Not that she could really fault him for it—she had done the same damn thing. They may have had different reasons, but their results had been identical. Even so, Iris believed she would absolutely take a chance to leave here if it were offered to her. Loomis, however, had been offered that chance and had chosen instead to stay. It was already beyond time for her to accept that.

"You've always been different from the others here," she told him. "You never bowed to his authority; you never fell into complacency like all the rest did. You have ambition and purpose, and those traits separate you from everyone else here."

Loomis watched her as she spoke, an air of tense curiosity radiating from his inhuman form. "Thank you for recognizing that," he answered drably. Iris could tell he was wondering where she was headed, and his aloofness was a defensive tactic.

"That's really all you have now, isn't it?" she asked. "Ambition, I mean. It has driven you for a long time; it has allowed you to maintain your hold on your own mind. Satan never had half the ambition you have."

Loomis's eyes flashed with...something. Fear? Warning? Pride? Iris wasn't sure, but he was obviously unnerved by the direction of the conversation and his inability to forecast it. He said nothing.

"Maybe Satan didn't need ambition," Iris mused. "He had everything he wanted."

"He was a complacent fool," Loomis returned stonily. "He has no idea what real power is."

"Neither do you, anymore," Iris replied cuttingly, "and maybe you'll never remember. But if that memory ever does return to you, it will grieve you forever. You'll know then the torture that Hell really is." Pangs of agonized sorrow ripped through her spirit as she spoke the words. Loomis straightened ever so slightly, like a soldier reprimanded by a commanding officer. Maybe he had already remembered more about real power than she had believed.

"Here," she continued, holding the Devil's relic out toward him. "The key to the throne you've sought for so long. Take it. Have your power; have your authority."

Loomis didn't move instantly, and when he finally did reach for the relic, he did it slowly and uncertainly. As Iris dropped the relic into his hand, she said, "See the end of all your ambition, Loomis. Rule over Hell, try to claim the Earth...it won't matter. You'll end up with no worlds left to conquer, and you'll be every bit as unfulfilled as you are right now. Ambition gains you nothing when you seek vanity."

Loomis looked down at the relic in his palm, its smoky, craggy facets dimly and brokenly reflecting Hell's flames. Iris felt her soul desperately hoping that maybe he didn't want the relic anymore, that maybe he had finally realized the emptiness of his desires for evil dominion. Those damn human emotions were such a painful burden now. She tried to ignore the feelings, focusing instead on reality. Loomis wanted Hell; he had chosen it more than once. Maybe now, at least, with his lofty goals so near attainment, he would finally realize he should have chosen better. It wouldn't change anything, but Iris hoped it would make him regret his mistakes. If it didn't, then Hell really didn't have much consequence for him, and that seemed completely unfair.

"Return the relic to me, Loomis," Satan urged from his immobilized, magicless form beyond the garnet stream of flame. "She's tricking you! The throne cannot be held without cost. If you wish to keep your ambition, keep your desires, then you must let me keep the relic and the throne. Do you wish to end up as I did, a 'complacent fool,' as you say? The throne will make you so, but my offer to you still stands. Stop her from doing this; it is the only way we will both keep what she tries to steal from us. Surely you'll not choose this lying bitch over me! Surely you'll not let her take your freedom from you!"

Loomis ignored the Devil's warning and moved his attention from the relic in his hand to Iris. "Do you believe the throne will make me like him?" he asked her quietly.

Iris scoffed. "Of course not," she answered callously. "The throne is as meaningless as existence has become for all of us here. It won't make you anything you're not. But you're only fooling yourself if you still think you're any better than he is! You've already ended up just like him, and not because of the throne or because of any stupid relic. You *chose* to be here; you chose to stay. You oppose what gives life and meaning to the spirit. So, Loomis, you're no different from him. I wanted to believe otherwise, but I'll blame that on weak human sentiment. I'm past that now. So claim your throne and have everything you ever wanted, and know that it's nothing." Her voice was a strange union of demoniac hissing and disembodied human speech. She was both insanely angered and inconsolably saddened by her own words.

Loomis stared again at the relic, remaining silent for a long time. "It doesn't have to be nothing," he replied, in a practically soundless voice. "I'll share it with you," he continued, looking at her. "We can have each other, at least. That's something, isn't it?"

Iris found herself in nearly complete disbelief at his suggestion. There was definite light in his eyes now; she was sure of it. There was some part of him that was still pointed rightly, a part that still sought love when demons should seek only misery. She knew in truth she was only the penultimate object of that love; Loomis, somewhere within himself, still desired the love of God, and perhaps Iris yet retained enough of God's image, somehow, to remind him of that desire. Could it be there *was* hope, even now? *No*, Iris told herself. *It's too late. He had his chance, and now we're both stuck here. Let it go.*

"I don't want any part of this realm," she answered stoically. "I never did, and I still don't."

"See how she rejects you!" Satan called out, chuckling grotesquely. "She hates you, Loomis. She wants you to suffer. You don't have to give her what she wants! Don't let the woman manipulate you."

Ignoring Satan's urging, Loomis shook his head and began to say something to Iris. Suddenly, however, his voice was interrupted by a faint, faraway, metallic beat that Iris felt buried within her spirit. It was slow and distant, but perceptible, like the vibrations of sound through deep waters. It startled her enough that she thought she had completely missed whatever Loomis was trying to say to her, but she soon realized he had never actually begun speaking.

"The priest is trying to revive you," Loomis finally said, looking at her almost wistfully. "Do you hear it?"

Iris, stunned both by the call of the mountain and by Loomis's statement, could barely formulate a response. "Yes," she whispered, quite humanly. "How do *you* hear it?"

"I don't know, and it doesn't matter," Loomis answered. His hand still held the Devil's relic, but it hung limply at his side. After a moment's hesitation, he added, almost pleadingly, "You don't have to go back. You could stay. We can rule together, or I'll rule alone, but you can stay with me. If it still matters to you, I'll leave humanity alone. I'll spare the Earth and everyone in it; I'll let them make their own decisions, without temptations or manipulations..."

He stopped himself and chuckled forlornly, shaking his head at his own proposal. When he spoke again, his voice was stronger, and the note of hope in his tone was completely gone. "No," he said resolutely, "you don't belong here. You don't want to be here. I won't try to convince you to stay."

Iris knew what she had to do, but her spirit felt torn nonetheless. If she had a way to leave, she had to take it; she wanted to take it. But leaving Loomis alone in Hell after having recognized his still-present desire for love, for goodness, for life...that seemed inconceivable and heartless.

"You should go," Loomis stated somberly, noting her hesitation. "The opportunity won't last forever, and you won't have another chance."

Iris shook her head ruefully. "And you know all about taking chances that are offered, don't you?" she asked despondently. After a sigh, she added, "But you're right. I don't want to be here." She stared at Loomis for a moment, as the hammerfall of the mountain's heartbeat seemed to grow closer to her. Finally, she told him, "I wish there had been some way to convince you. I don't deserve this opportunity any more than you did; it will always be my greatest sadness that you chose to stay here." Feeling her spirit reaching for a pinprick of white light somewhere within her perception, she looked at Loomis's demonic form one last time, then she said, with finality, "Goodbye, Loomis."

Sight and sound and all perception receded instantly as she surrendered her spirit to the invisible power that had called her back from the damned. When her senses returned, she found herself back within the confines of her human body, lying face-up on the plushy grass of the holy mountain, silver-white moonbeams brightening a velvet, indigo sky overhead.

"Praised be God," she heard Auraltiferys's quiet, graceful voice whisper in humble thanksgiving beside her.

35

From his place on his knees in the grass beside her, Auraltiferys reached out and took Iris's face in both of his hands, gently lifting her head and turning it so he could see her eyes. Feeling numb and confused, as though she had just awoken from a particularly vivid dream within the deepest sleep, Iris had to blink several times before she could clearly see the blacksmith's eyes staring back into hers, his scarred but elegantly handsome face illuminated by the soft glow of moonlight from above. It was hard to tell in the dimness, but he appeared to have been crying. Even if he hadn't shed any tears, his features were still tensed with worry or grief, and as she looked at him, Iris felt her thoughts slowly slipping into focus. She remembered what had happened before she died (rather, before she had foolishly killed herself using the blacksmith's blade), and she understood how much pain she must have caused her gracious mentor. He must have believed her gone forever, but he hadn't completely given up hope.

Iris reached up and lightly squeezed Auraltiferys's hand. "Thanks," she said. Her body felt tired and weak, and she felt strangely limited within it.

Auraltiferys released her face and gave her enough space so she could sit up. Iris propped herself up with both hands on the ground behind her, but a wave of dizziness stopped her from moving any further. She closed her eyes for a few seconds and breathed, surprised by how foreign yet wonderful that involuntary action felt to her now. When she opened her eyes again, she felt much better. Auraltiferys watched her with an expression of both concern and awe. Iris couldn't help but smile at him.

"I'm okay now," she told him. "You don't have to worry about me anymore. You saved me."

The blacksmith shook his head slowly. "I healed your body," he said, his voice as comforting as a warm blanket. "It was all I could think to do. I certainly don't have the power to bring a soul back from the dead; that was God's work, and a miracle I'm humbled to have witnessed. I can't say I even truly believed it was possible, so weak was my faith."

Iris smiled. "Your faith is anything but weak, Auri," she replied. "We just have to be reminded sometimes how little we really understand."

Auraltiferys nodded thoughtfully. "I have certainly been reminded of that tonight," he answered quietly. He rose gracefully from his knees and offered his hand to her. As he helped her to her feet, he asked, "Can you tell me what happened?"

Iris sighed, realizing how distant her less-than-permanent damnation already seemed to feel. Perhaps that made sense, though—it wasn't an experience a living human mind could fully comprehend. "I can try," she suggested, "but words can't really describe it."

"You were...in Hell, though?" Auraltiferys asked hesitantly, expectantly.

"Yes," she replied gravely.

The blacksmith shook his head again, his arms crossed and his eyes staring off into a distance beyond the pine trees at the edge of the clearing. He stood silently, deep in thought, for at least a minute. Iris was content to stand beside him in the peacefulness, the cool, clean air and the quiet reverence of the mountain a marvelous contrast to the horrid abominations her spirit had endured in the underworld. After a long moment, he stated, wistfully, "I didn't believe it was possible."

Iris slipped her arm through the crook of his bent elbow. "Yet, here I am," she said cheerfully. "And I have to say, I am *so* happy to be alive."

The blacksmith gave her a tiny smile. "I'm happy for that, too," he replied.

"Will you join me in the chapel?" she asked him. "I have an overwhelming urge to be there right now."

"Of course," he answered. He began walking with her toward the path that wound around the house and led to the church and library. Iris released his arm after a few paces and jogged the short distance to the porch, retrieving her bronze axe from where she had dropped it after watching Loomis's gruesome demise. Auraltiferys waited for her to return, watching her magically shrink the weapon and tuck it into the strap of her boot before she rejoined him.

"You know," she said, "this axe has really come in handy."

Auraltiferys smiled broadly. "Has it?" he asked.

"More than once," Iris answered, "and in ways that would surprise you." She glanced at her mentor as they continued on the path, and something in his expression told her he actually wouldn't be surprised at all to hear how the weapon he had forged for her had proven useful.

"I'm glad," he replied simply, humbly inclining his head.

They walked in silence for a while, until they were about halfway to the chapel. At that point, Iris could no longer contain her curiosity; as soon as she had seen her axe glistening under the moonlight, the question had popped into her mind.

"What did you do with the body?" she asked, expecting there

was no need to be any more specific in her question. Auraltiferys stopped immediately and turned to her with an almost suspicious gleam in his eyes. She returned his gaze calmly; she knew he would find no duplicity in her.

Once his searching had assured him she had no ulterior motives, Auraltiferys sighed deeply. "The body was created with powerful magic," he answered. "It is not a creation of Heaven's Forge, but it is a relic nonetheless, and I cannot rightly destroy it without divine guidance to do so, though my personal inclination would have been to obliterate it." He sighed again and looked at Iris, likely trying to ascertain her reaction to his confessed "personal inclination." Or perhaps it was for some other reason. Iris pursed her lips but said nothing, waiting for him to continue. Finally, he said, "I placed it in the relic room of the library and locked it with six magical restraints. It should be safe there, until it is revealed to me what should be done."

Iris nodded ruefully. It still hurt her heart to know the end Loomis had chosen, even though she knew she had done all she could to convince him otherwise. She hoped now, with a second chance at life after a taste of true Hell, she could finally accept it, even if she could never understand it.

"I know you were right," she announced as they proceeded to the chapel. "Loomis had come here to kill us and take the mountain. You did what was right. He chose Hell; he keeps choosing Hell. I wish I could have accepted it sooner."

"Do you accept it now?" Auraltiferys asked. There was no sarcasm or accusation in the question; he was merely asking for an honest response.

"It's what he's chosen," Iris replied with a shrug. "I don't understand it, and I don't believe it's really what he wants. But...it is what it is, I guess."

"Maybe you weren't so wrong to hope for him," Auraltiferys

answered, to Iris's surprise. "You chose Hell and returned." He fell quiet and looked skyward as he walked for several more steps. Eventually, he spoke again. "Iris, when you...died," he began, obviously pained to recall the event. He cleared his throat, then continued, with a stronger voice, "When you died, I knew where you were headed; I knew what you had chosen, and it broke my heart. I couldn't accept that Hell was your end. Even knowing it was your choice, and believing there could be no return from it, I still hoped there was hope for you, and I begged God that He might allow you to reconsider. I prayed for what I believed to be impossible, and now here you stand, alive again, by the grace of God, and I realize I was wrong to be so certain of Drake's damnation. I understand now that desperate hope you had for him. It's easier for me to see goodness in you than in him, but you have a greater perception than I have." He took a deep breath, then concluded, "Even had a thousand years passed, I still would have been hoping and praying for your return. God and the angels exist beyond our human time; maybe Drake might yet change his mind."

Iris didn't realize she was crying until she felt a warm tear streak down her cheek. She brushed it away and asked, "Do you really think so?"

"I don't know," Auraltiferys admitted. "But you boldly defended him to me. You were convinced of his goodness. You argued that to me, even knowing my extremely negative feelings toward him. Has anything changed your mind?"

They had reached the chapel. Auraltiferys stood to the side of the great wooden entrance door and opened it with magic. Dancing, golden candlelight and a beautiful fragrance of leather, wood, and roses emanated from within, mingling with the night air of the mountain under the arched stone canopy of the entrance, and Iris felt her heart suddenly cradled in serenity. The blacksmith looked at her, patiently awaiting a response to his question.

"Nothing has changed my mind," she answered softly. "If anything, I'm more certain of his goodness now than I was before."

"Then," Auraltiferys replied, gesturing for her to enter the chapel, "let us not give up hope."

Iris stepped inside and froze, so overwhelmed by the invisible but sure presence of God that all human thought failed her, making physical movement practically impossible. She had been here once before, when she had joined the blacksmith for his evening prayers after one of the early days of her training. She had found it remarkable then, too, but setting foot in the chapel now after two journeys into Hell, the latest of which had been the fullest experience of death a spirit could know, she could only gape in awe at the spiritual resplendence around her. It wasn't a particularly ornate room, but it was filled with unquestionable holiness. The chapel was relatively small, with perhaps a dozen short, glossy wooden pews situated in rows on either side of a central aisle lined with the same violet carpet as the library. Three of the walls were made of stone, decorated with heavy tapestries that beautifully depicted the Stations of the Cross. Gleaming golden candelabra had been built into the marble floor, situated along the walls so that the light of their magical flames would illuminate the entire space. The front wall, behind a small wooden altar, was plastered and painted a deep ruby color, so lustrous as to appear almost like glass. Within a recess carved into the wall at a level just higher than the altar was a large gold tabernacle.

Auraltiferys remained motionless beside her for some time. He could only imagine what Hell was like, but he believed Iris had experienced it completely, and he was gracious enough to recognize how death must have transformed her perception of and her appreciation for God's presence. Iris's awareness of his company eventually returned to her, and she was glad for his quiet and humble example. She knew he was standing there appreciating the nearness of God just as profoundly as she was, though he had probably entered this chapel daily for over two thousand years. He never took God for granted. Away from the mountain, there in the midst of a fallen world and a fallen race, people seemed to have so little humility, so little reverence. They would walk into a church as casually as though it were an auditorium or a lecture hall; they would socialize and gossip, or they would grumble about having to be there; some might listen to a message from their pastor, but almost all would miss the point of it, assuming the pastor had any valid point to make. They would sit there, distracted and uninterested, wearing their shorts and T-shirts and flip-flops, evidencing in physical appearance just how little true spiritual respect they had for their Creator and their King, whom they claimed to be going there to worship. Iris had wondered if her observations would be valid elsewhere, or if perhaps the generalities she had formulated after years of membership in the Catholic Church and years of increasing jadedness were applicable only to American, so-called Christians, but she expected there was no shortage of lacking faith anywhere, in any religion, and not even she herself had been innocent of that. It used to make her mad; as she thought about it now, however, she was atypically forgiving of the human race. *It's a journey for each of us*, she thought to herself. One couldn't expect all of humanity to share the ancient blacksmith's reverence; one couldn't expect all the living to recognize how God had saved them from the dead—even Iris had truly recognized that only after her own literal physical and spiritual death. So instead of filling her with anger now, these reflections made her particularly grateful—grateful she had a tutor with such pure reverence and wisdom, and grateful for her own experiences, which, though painful and terrifying, had given her a new and special perspective on matters of faith. She would have things easier now than most did.

Seeing that Iris had recovered from her awestruck paralysis,

Auraltiferys motioned for her to move forward. She walked to the front row and genuflected, then entered the pew and knelt in silent prayer. The blacksmith similarly entered the pew on the opposite side of the center aisle. Iris closed her eyes in the silence and soon lost conscious thought. She was praying differently now, not speaking words in her mind, but simply *existing* in thankfulness and praise for the God who had seen fit to let her return from certain and eternal damnation. After a time, she felt her gratitude had been appropriately conveyed, and she let grief take its place. She remembered, in a dream-like replay, how Loomis had defended her in Hell, how he had even then urged her to accept the chance to return to life from death. She remembered how vulnerable he had appeared when he had asked her to stay. She knew it wasn't her personal existence or presence that comforted him; it was God's presence in her that made him feel that way. And how could a demon feel anything but disgust at God's presence? It was abundantly clear to her that if Loomis continued into eternity as a demon, it would be only because he refused to accept the mercy of God. So she voiced both her grief for the loss of his spirit to Hell and her hope that God might yet give him another chance for redemption, in His time and if He willed it.

Iris had no idea how much time had passed when she finally reopened her eyes and ended her prayers. She sat back into the pew and glanced toward her mentor, who was yet kneeling, his head bowed and his entire body as still as a statue. Iris couldn't even be sure he was breathing, though she knew he must be. She dropped her eyes and realized, for the first time since returning, that her shirt was still torn and covered in her dried blood. She shook her head, recalling how she had forced the blacksmith's knife into her own chest, not even allowing him the freedom to refuse participation in the awful act. How he continued to put up with her extreme antics, she couldn't fathom. She watched him for a moment, contemplating him with a tiny smile on her lips. He had made such a striking impression when she had first met him, with his tall, muscular physique; his kingly features; his clear, sparkling ice-blue eyes; and, of course, his anachronistic garb—the tights, the tunic, the leather vest and belt and boots, the hefty blade sheathed at his thigh. She had been intimidated by him, even afraid of him. She was glad that hadn't lasted long. He had become for her a steady, sure guide, a calm and comforting presence. *A father*, she realized, with mild surprise. It hadn't occurred to her just how expertly Auraltiferys was living his vocation. He was a priest, after all, and a saintly one at that. He acknowledged himself as a humble servant of God; Iris wondered if he recognized himself as the dauntless and mighty hero she knew him to be. She still had trouble believing his age, though. That long, silver-white hair of his was the only apparent physical sign of his longevity, and it really only made him look wiser, not older.

At some point in her contemplation, Iris closed her eyes again, silently thanking God for Auraltiferys and asking abundant blessings for him. Unknowingly, she drifted off to sleep, not having realized how exhausted her body had felt. Her eyes fluttered open sometime later, awoken by a sound or a stirring nearby. She was still in the chapel; across the aisle, her mentor was rising from his knees. His eyes met hers, conveying recognizable concern.

"Something's happening," he said quietly, walking swiftly across the aisle and down the pew behind where Iris sat, headed for the side door of the chapel, which opened directly into the library.

Iris roused herself immediately and followed. Once Auraltiferys had exited the chapel, his swift gait became an all-out sprint, and Iris maintained his pace only with the aid of magic. There was, without question, something happening. They were halfway down the length of the library when the Empyreal Hounds began baying outside. There was a terrible, onerous tension hanging in the usually peaceful air, and the marble floor and stone walls seemed to vibrate as the pair neared the relic room. When they descended the steps down into the grotto-like reliquary, the vibrations became drastically more intense, and the blacksmith hurriedly cast a few spells to prevent the relics from falling out of their caches.

On a new granite slab near the farthest end of the grotto, Loomis's body lay intricately tangled in heavy, solid gold chains fastened by six oversized padlocks, each with a runic inscription instead of a keyhole. Though the chains held the body tightly to the stone, the body was convulsing within what little give it had been allowed, violently straining against its imprisonment with a loud, shaking metallic rattle. Completely unsure what was happening, but fully aware it had to be stopped, Iris quickly approached the body, her mentor right beside her. As they reached the slab, a sulfuric stench wafted up to them, and a shrill cacophony of screams suddenly ripped through the room at a disturbing volume. Iris recognized it immediately, and she was certain Auraltiferys did, too. Even a non-believer could have guessed what was happening, so clear were the signs—Hell was opening into the mountain, straight through Loomis's body.

The smell of sulfur was soon joined by the odor of rotting flesh, and the heavy air, weighted by the arrival of insidious evil, became suddenly so cold that breath became visible. Iris had no idea what time it was, but, if there was any daylight outside, it was not reaching the floor of the relic room. The only illumination now was the ambient light from the torches in the library above, leaving the grotto area in dim shades of blue and gray and black. The screaming took on additional voices, so jumbled and intertwined with one another that no words could be discerned, assuming there were any actual words being uttered. Auraltiferys was speaking in a low voice, probably reciting some incantation, but Iris couldn't hear him above the din. He touched the chains around Loomis's unused vessel as he spoke, and the inscriptions took on a blue glow. Apparently satisfied the restraints would continue to hold, at least for now, the blacksmith then turned his attention to the body, his bright, silver-blue eyes searching somewhere beyond the physical for some clue as to what needed to be done.

Iris called forth her own demonic spirit, now ready to put an end, once and for all, to whatever new scheme Loomis had contrived. The body was his creation; he couldn't leave it alone. He had obviously orchestrated this uprising of the damned, and Iris was angered by it. She had suffered for him; she had grieved for him; she had prayed for his return to grace; he had continued to oppose it all. If God wanted to save him, let God save him. As far as she was now concerned, her only lasting obligation to Loomis was to ensure his failure in dragging Earth into eternal oblivion. She had given him the throne of Hell, but she wouldn't let him take this mountain and its secrets. She owed that much and more to Auraltiferys. She hadn't needed any relic to make her stronger than Satan; she wouldn't need it now to make her any stronger than Loomis.

With inhuman perception, she could hear the individual speech of the voices resonating invisibly from the underworld to the holy mountain. There were at least a dozen demons bellowing at once, each growling out a magical spell in a different language, seemingly working together (though such collaboration was practically unheard of among demons) to enable their passage to the mountain through the relic Loomis had created. Amid the spells were the wordless cries of souls in torment, wailing so desperately that Iris could visualize their emaciated, bodiless forms clawing at the veil between Hell and Earth. The mountain was even farther out of reach for them than Earth was, but the dark magic being cast by the group of demons was bringing them ever nearer.

They're using the body as a conduit, Iris spoke demonically to the blacksmith, confident he would recognize the soundless voice as hers. *There are at least twelve of them.*

"These chains won't hold against the strength of twelve demons," he answered her aloud. His voice was even and precise, but it held a certain undercurrent of concern. "We must exorcise them as quickly as possible."

As if threatened by the possibility of quick expulsion, the demons redoubled their efforts to reach the mountain. Auraltiferys had already begun a rite of exorcism, but the demons' presence grew stronger. The ground began to quake, and creaking sounds, like bones about to break, started to emanate from the marble pillars of the grotto. A couple of them cracked from their bases, veins of damage branching up their glossy sides. The skylights far overhead suddenly shattered, sending shards of glass cascading down around them, and Auraltiferys had to turn all his attention to the magical protection of the building's integrity, ignoring cuts on his face and arms that the plummeting glass had caused. Loomis's body, by this time, had seized so fiercely against the chains that they had loosened. It now had more freedom of movement, though its appendages were still entwined, and it looked quite grotesque as its back contorted sharply back and forth, its motions powered by the demons trying to gain its full control. The shoulders and head were still fairly solidly strapped to the slab; if not for that, Iris was certain the skull would have been completely ruined by perilous bashing against the stone.

Iris continued the exorcism where Auraltiferys had left off, finding the knowledge somewhere within her personal spiritual arcana. As she recited a prayer, she heard—*felt*—Loomis's voice, whispering in her head.

I've tried to stop them, he said urgently. *There are too many. They've found my spells; they're trying to use the body as a portal to the mountain. You MUST keep them out...*

As his voice abruptly cut off, Iris felt a gut-wrenching pain in her spirit, her heart. She focused all her attention on the feeling of the whisper that had ceased, and she sensed Loomis was under attack. She thought she heard a small, pitiful groan before he spoke again.

I tried to get there first, he insisted. *I tried to keep them away. Satan has incited them all against me; I can't reach the body...*

Iris noted, with an odd combination of sorrow and self-satisfaction, that it seemed Loomis's claim of Hell's throne had not gone as magnificently as he had always believed it would. She instantly hated herself for the serves-you-right thought that ran across her mind. She couldn't forget the image of the glorious seraph whose desperate voice was now crying to her from Hell, and she wanted to help him, despite her depleted patience for his seemingly incessant vacillation between nearly complete evil and nearly tangible goodness.

Auraltiferys, having subverted further physical damage to the relic room for now, returned to a recitation of prayer, trying to force the demons back to their realm.

He won't succeed, Loomis told Iris, genuine earnestness in his voice. *They're already too close.*

In evidence of Loomis's statement, Iris saw the blacksmith suddenly slapped across his face by an unseen force, powerful enough to drop him to his knees. She moved immediately to his side and helped him up, though he didn't really need her assistance. The blow may have surprised him, but it hardly fazed him, even though it had left three substantial, inflamed scratches in his skin. His prayer had paused for less than a second, if at all.

Iris focused her own magic against the spirits she sensed nearest full apparition. She struck at them just as she had struck the Devil's guards, sending them reeling, but only for an instant. As the first demons were pushed back, the others pressed forward, and Iris quickly recognized it would be an exhausting cycle. She wondered, with brief uncertainty, if she would even prevail.

The blacksmith continued his prayers, invoking Christ's name against the entities threatening the holy mountain. He removed a small vial from one of the leather pouches of his belt, opened it, and splashed some of its contents across the stone slab. It had a pronounced effect, causing a series of tortured screams and a violent whiplash in Loomis's body.

With a terrible, hissing laugh, a single voice became stronger than all the rest, clearly enunciating its words to Auraltiferys, in Latin: "Water will not save you, priest!"

Iris knew it was Satan's voice, but she didn't sense his presence to be particularly near. It seemed he was projecting his voice through the portal the other demons had worked so hard to open, while keeping himself far away from the possibility of any actual run-in with the power of God. *Classic Satan*, she thought with irony.

Human rites won't stop them, Loomis called soundlessly to her. *Get me into the body, Iris, and I can force them out.*

I can't trust you, Iris replied to him, instantly recalling his last nefarious trip to the mountain.

Please, Loomis answered. *Please, don't forsake me now.*

Another, clearer cry of pain reached Iris from his spirit, and she forced her doubts aside. As Auraltiferys valiantly persisted in his priestly rite, Iris began the foreign incantation to draw Loomis's spirit toward her. With some subtle nuance, she could direct his spirit not into herself, as she had once done, but into the body Loomis had created. Auraltiferys either heard or sensed the spell as she cast it and immediately turned to face her, startled enough to have temporarily ceased his prayers.

"What are you doing?" he asked her sharply, his voice a veritable blade slicing the air and penetrating into her. He was suddenly distrustful of her motives, and Iris couldn't blame him. He was likely unfamiliar with the actual casting of the spell, but, as a Knight of Heaven's Forge, he would readily discern what its purpose was, able to judge the magic as it was used in his presence. Iris already knew he was completely against any use of it, even if he hadn't yet recognized what the spell would do. She had confessed to him her use of it against Loomis, in as little detail as she could conscionably provide, and he had been most adamant that she must never use it again. It was an unnatural and dangerous practice, he had told her, to manipulate another's spirit, and even more so if that spirit was demonic. Iris imagined, although her good mentor and confessor had remained rather unflappable as she had listed her sins to him, he had been truly appalled by that particular confession. She had marveled then at how irreproachable a priest he was. He had listened to the sins of the incarnate Satan and had never passed any judgment, but neither had he sanctioned any behavior contradictory to God or to the Church's teachings. He had been a stern but gracious director; he had made no special allowances for her or for the demonic spirit that was as much a part of her as humanity was, yet he had, in his own noble and aloofly warm way, made sure she knew everything he said or did was said or done with great love. Now, here she was again, using practically the same perverse spell, right in front of her mentor and confessor, but her conscience wasn't troubled by it.

"What I do," Iris answered, her human voice speaking even as her demonic voice continued its incantation, "I do for the glory of God. You've taught me well, Auri. Trust me."

The blacksmith's blue eyes were as bright as flame as he stared at her with the keen gaze of a righteous clairvoyant. She nodded to him, slightly, and after a momentary indecision, Auraltiferys returned the gesture, even more slightly, his eyes warning her to be careful. He turned away and resumed his fastidious prayers and his magical defense of the mountain. Iris focused on Loomis's spirit and drew him toward herself, chanting the spell in a hushed and rapid flow of ancient words, too quiet and too swift to hear. She felt his spirit growing closer, and for a fleeting instant, she recalled the extreme, euphoric sensation of having had his spirit enveloped by her own, and she had an intense but, willfully, short-lived desire to pull him into herself again. She resolutely ignored the depraved and lustful thought and continued her spell, directing Loomis magically toward the body he had used for so long.

With a sudden, brutish lurch, Loomis's body sat fully upright, breaking free from the granite slab from the waist up. Thankfully, the arms remained in one last magical restraint, and the legs were still pinioned to the stone by three of the gold chains. The eyes snapped open, revealing two inhuman, black orbs that seemed to suck even the dim, bluish glow of the relic room into nothingness. They reflected no light, and they were definitely not Loomis's eyes. The mouth opened into a wide, toothy snarl, and a demonic laugh emanated from it, coming out partially from the mouth and partially from the horrid slash that still existed across Loomis's neck, the one from the blacksmith's blade that had nearly beheaded the body, killing it and forcing Loomis back to Hell, at least temporarily. Iris, only by her own demonic nature, could recognize the laugh as belonging to one of the multitude of indifferent, wayward demons that crowded Hell, a being whose name Satan neither remembered nor cared about. It couldn't be too strong on its own, but the uncharacteristic unification of so many fallen angels was giving them all a power they had long forgotten they held.

"You won't bring him here," the demon said through Loomis's body, turning its disgusting eyes toward Iris. "You're not stronger than all of us together, and he is even weaker." It laughed again, gratingly, then continued, "We all saw how you tried to help him. If you want to help him now, you will let us take his body."

She suddenly felt Loomis's spirit being ripped out of the grasp of her magical aid, and she angrily refocused her efforts to help him to his body. She felt a series of awful blows to his spirit, and she heard him groaning with agony as he withstood them.

It's too late, Loomis called to her. *They've taken too much of my power...*

"Feel how we make him suffer now, you traitorous whore!" the demon yelled, before bursting into a fit of hysterical laughter.

"Leave him alone!" Iris exclaimed, dumbly, in her human voice. She struggled to keep Loomis's spirit within her demonic magical reach.

"Do *not* engage with it," Auraltiferys commanded her harshly. He recognized her attempt to reunite Loomis with the body was failing, and he knew, with her well-meaning and powerful but still immature wielding of magic, she might inadvertently make things far worse. Protectively, he stepped toward her and forcibly moved her away from the stone slab, placing himself between her and the demon-controlled body.

From behind the blacksmith, the demon cackled loudly. "You think you can protect her, priest?" it shrieked.

There was a clattering of metal, then one of the broken gold chains was suddenly draped across Auraltiferys's neck. The body remained at its bizarre, upright angle, conveying the laughter of its uninvited demonic guest as the spells of the other demons continued invisibly around it. The chain was pulled tight and then hoisted a few yards into the air, floating without any support as Auraltiferys strained to breathe against it. His muscular arms tugged at the gold links cutting into his throat, and his strong legs kicked purposefully as he tried to free himself from the metallic garrote. With continuous and amazingly disciplined magic, the blacksmith maintained the ability at least to endure the attack. A magicless victim would have perished within seconds under the violent, supernatural strangling.

Simultaneously enraged and petrified by the attack on her mentor, Iris unthinkingly screamed in her Satanic voice to the demon possessing Loomis's body. "Unhand him, demon," she ordered authoritatively.

The gross, black eyes blinked tentatively, then the demon answered her, "You have no authority over us here." Its voice was far less sure of itself than it had previously been.

Iris didn't reply. Instead, she unleashed her own demonic spirit on that of this particularly irreverent aggressor. Her physical vision was limited to that of her human body, but in her Satanic perception, she could see its spirit's ugly, animalistic form having its head slowly broken away from the rest of its spiritual body. It screamed and cried, then lost its form completely. Loomis's body slumped back to its granite resting place for a moment, eyelids and mouth all closed. The chain fell away from Auraltiferys, and the blacksmith gracefully lowered himself back to the ground with flawlessly executed magic. He appeared to Iris as resolute and confident as ever; there wasn't a trace of fear anywhere in him. He grabbed the two broken chains and immediately moved to replace them across Loomis's body and over the slab, but he didn't have enough time. Another demon almost instantly claimed control of the body, jerking it upright before the blacksmith could restrain it. Its dead eyes were as repulsive as the other's.

"You won't stop all of us," it said acidly, kicking against the chains still holding the body to the granite. "We are too many."

Iris looked helplessly at Auraltiferys. She was inclined to believe the demon at this point; nothing she nor Auraltiferys had done had succeeded in anything more than delaying what seemed to be inevitable. To her great distress, Auraltiferys returned her look with one of stoic, defiant resolve—the same expression Iris imagined a great number of martyrs had worn in their last moments. He shook his head and shrugged, then pulled out his knife, preparing to fight more physically. Loomis's body was still dead; it was nothing but a vessel. The demons vying for it now didn't really desire to possess or use it as Loomis always had, as a dwelling on Earth. They were simply using its particular magic as a doorway onto the mountain, and they had already drawn nearly enough power that they would be able to exist here in their own forms, using their magic directly instead of having to cast it to a separate realm. Iris realized, with horror, that Auraltiferys must have witnessed something very much like this before, when Loomis had been granted magical access here by a misguided Knight.

"No," she whispered, shaking her head, "we can't let them in."

"They've drawn too much power from it already," Auraltiferys answered stonily. "I don't believe we can stop them from entering. It is, as it has always been, in God's hands."

Time seemed to stop as Iris returned the blacksmith's steady gaze. *In God's hands*, her mind repeated to her. She dropped her eyes to the floor.

Stop them, Iris, she heard Loomis's voice crying to her from far away. *Destroy the body; it might weaken them.*

Iris, suddenly decidedly sure of her actions, ignored Loomis's suggestion and quickly removed the black leather glove from her right hand. She approached the body and placed her scarred palm on its forehead. Purposeful, demonic voices became tortured, high-pitched wails of pure anguish as the spiritual echoes of the archangel's blade radiated through the body Loomis had created with his scientifically precise magic. The floor shook violently and then cracked, and the sounds of spiritual excruciation became so painfully loud that even the surfaces of the marble pillars fractured into shallow, web-like fissures. Iris watched in amazement as the body went completely still beneath her hand and then returned to the handsome appearance with which it had been so carefully designed. The mortal wound to the neck was healed, and the body appeared as serene and beautiful as an innocent child in slumber. Only the copious amount of blood yet staining the expensive attire upon it remained as evidence of the body's grisly fate.

Within seconds, the relic room returned to its typical quiet tranquility. The air remained cold and dim, but the fetor of death and decay was dispelled, and the restrictive weight of Hell's evil presence disappeared. Iris pulled her hand away from Loomis's face and mindlessly replaced her glove on it as she stared with sadness at the relic she would always associate with only him. The body had been an untoward endeavor, created solely by painstaking magic, wholly separate from human procreation and God's natural law, but it would always be to her the earthly image of the demon whom she had somehow come to love, whose damnation she would never understand. It may not have been created by God, but it was every bit as intricate and beautiful as each one God had created, and, as she looked at it now, she couldn't hold back her tears at the awful reality she knew existed. This body appeared to be at rest, at peace, and that made the truth even more difficult to bear, for the spirit that had dwelled within it was as far from rest and peace as one could ever be. For just a moment, she hoped somehow the eyes would open and Loomis would be there, out of Hell and changed for good, but she knew it was a futile hope.

Auraltiferys lit the magical torches around the periphery of the grotto, bringing wholesome, golden radiance and warmth to the room. Iris composed herself and turned away from Loomis's body to assist the blacksmith in repairing the damages the demons' magic had wreaked. The two worked in silence for a few minutes, ensuring the library and its contents were safe. Auraltiferys then picked up the broken chains and glanced briefly at Iris, his eyes seeming to say, *I'm sorry, but you understand I have to do this.* Iris blinked and nodded at him, and he replaced the golden fetters around the body, strapping it securely again to its granite slab. He whispered a spell over them, and the locks' runic inscriptions glowed with blue light for an instant. Iris turned away and stared at the floor, holding her arms close across her ribs, feeling tired and chilled and numb from the hellish encounter on the mountain and still deeply, sickeningly grieved by Loomis's refusal of the archangels' offer to him. She moved to the nearest marble pillar and seated herself at its base, resting her back against it as she hugged her knees into her chest. After he locked Loomis's body on the stone, the blacksmith created a magic fire on the floor a short distance in front of her, then sat next to her against the pillar, moving as silently and lithely as a cat. The fire needed no fuel to burn; it would neither grow nor die unless commanded by magic; it generated no smoke and left no ash. It only gave off a pleasant, comforting heat, and Iris was soothed by it.

"How are you?" Auraltiferys asked quietly.

"I'm fine," Iris answered with a sigh, not really feeling too fine. She shifted slightly and crossed her arms on top of her bent knees, then rested her head on them, facing the blacksmith. "What about you?" she asked him. "Are you okay? They roughed you up a little bit."

Auraltiferys smiled. "Scratches," he answered, with a dismissive wave of his hand. "I've survived worse; don't worry about me. I was really asking how you are *internally*—emotionally, mentally, spiritually."

"Oh," Iris replied, turning her head again and balancing her chin on her folded arms. "I'm fine."

"I know you care for him," the blacksmith prodded. "I know this can't have been easy for you, especially after you hoped so fervently for his redemption."

Iris shrugged. "I can't save him," she said. "I know that now. That's between him and God, and I'm going to leave it there. But...you know Loomis didn't do this." Her mentor's eyes narrowed, tacitly asking her to explain.

"Those were other demons," she expounded, "being commanded by Satan, trying to use Loomis's magical spells and the power of his body to transfer themselves here. Loomis tried to stop them, and they were torturing him for it."

Auraltiferys thought carefully before hesitantly responding, "You realize, Iris, all of that could be trickery."

"Couldn't it just as easily be the truth?" she asked, in a tired reply. "Auri, he was speaking to me, and I could *feel* his spirit being beaten by them. I could *feel* it. That can't be faked."

Auraltiferys took a deep, thoughtful breath, the reticent sort of inhalation that always came just before something one didn't want to hear. Iris cut him off before whatever statement he was going to make.

"There's something else," she told him. "Something I haven't told you yet." The blacksmith stiffened beside her, but he said nothing. Iris looked at him and said, "I gave him the key to Hell's throne."

Auraltiferys's eyes widened. "You did *what?*" he asked, horrified.

"I took it from Satan and I gave it to him," she answered flatly. As the blacksmith opened his mouth to speak again, she silenced him with a gesture and a shake of her head. "I don't think he kept it," she added defensively.

Auraltiferys massaged his forehead with the palm of one strong hand as he considered for a moment. "If Drake had all of Hell's power at his control," he mused, "getting here to the mountain might have been an easy task."

"Exactly," Iris agreed, relieved that her tutor was amenable to discussion. "And he wasn't speaking as a ruler would," she continued. "He spoke like someone condemned as a traitor."

The blacksmith looked at her thoughtfully, piercing her with his eyes. "You believe, then, he had no part in this...attempted infiltration?" he asked.

"Yes, that's what I believe," Iris replied. "And I believe he tried to fight it."

"If he fought it," Auraltiferys argued somberly, "the likeliest reason is that he didn't want any other demon to have use of the body he created. He's very possessive of his work; most demons are."

"No," Iris stated positively. "He actually suggested that I destroy the body."

The blacksmith's dignified brow furrowed in curiosity and skepticism, his eyes alight with keen intrigue. "He suggested that?" he asked, incredulously.

"He did," Iris answered. "Just before the end."

Auraltiferys sighed and leaned his head back against the pillar behind him. "I suppose," he considered thoughtfully, "Drake might be so desperate to keep his creation out of other hands that he would have asked you to destroy it, though that does seem unlikely. He has always taken great pride in his knowledge and his magical science. That body, in particular, was a nearly impossible feat. He wouldn't want another to use it, but neither would he want it destroyed forever."

"See, Auri?" Iris asked, suddenly impassioned. "It doesn't make sense! If Loomis were ruling Hell right now, he could have come here himself and then summoned the others. If he's not ruling, and if they did unite against him for access to the body, it would serve him better to let them use it as a conduit here and then reclaim it for himself later. The others didn't want to dwell in it; they were only using its particular power to pave their way out of Hell. Either way, Loomis hasn't acted like the perversely intelligent and insidiously patient force of consummate evil you believe him to be."

"His behavior is...rather baffling," Auraltiferys admitted.

"Told you," Iris said, her tone suddenly more cheerful, hopeful. There was no insult or mockery in the statement.

Her mentor gave her a tiny smile. "I fear my personal history with Drake will keep me forever suspicious of him," he said. "It may always be my proclivity to expect the worst from him. Perhaps, in time, I will be proven wrong for it. I once, very briefly, expected nothing but evil from you."

Iris returned the blacksmith's smile. "I remember," she responded, reflecting on her first interaction with him. He had told her outright he would have killed her, but for the intervention of the Hounds. He had recognized her as a demon (and not just as any demon, but as the supreme Devil himself) and had naturally expected her to delight in only wickedness and destruction. Iris certainly had not been a perfect model of goodness since then, having occasionally stumbled into the basest desires of her fallen, demonic nature, but at the very least, she had proven, to both herself and to her mentor, that even an evil spirit might be redirected.

Auraltiferys breathed deeply. "I will say this, Iris," he sighed, leaning his head back and lifting his gaze to the skylights high above. "You are a remarkable example of possibilities that exist beyond the limits of understanding, and if I recognize that, I'm sure Drake has recognized it, too. He may not believe he can follow you, or he may not want to, but you have certainly shown him a path different from the one he has chosen."

Iris likewise directed her eyes to the ceiling, listening to the quiet, graceful voice of the blacksmith. His words comforted her. She had been an example for Loomis, and maybe that was all she had needed to be. As she had already acknowledged, Loomis's damnation or salvation would be a matter for only him and his Creator. She stared through the glass to the sky outside, its dark, silky indigo appearing like a beautiful, blank cosmic canvas, whispering to the imagination of endless promise and potential. She prayed silently for a few minutes in the pleasant stillness, then turned to Auraltiferys.

"What time do you think it is?" she asked him.

"It is nearing dawn," he answered.

Iris closed her eyes and nodded, feeling very much inclined to go to sleep. "Then it's almost time for you to get up, isn't it?" she remarked weakly, relaxing into the column behind her.

He chuckled. "I believe some rest is in order first," he replied. "Work done in exhaustion is rarely worth its cost."

Iris straightened her legs out in front of her and leaned into the blacksmith, resting her head against his muscular arm. She yawned and closed her eyes again, already floating away from consciousness.

"You know," she drawled thoughtfully, "I never imagined I'd be involved in an exorcism."

She felt Auraltiferys nod slowly. "You handled it well," he said, his deep, precise voice creating a relaxing lull. "I worried what effect it might have on you, but in retrospect, I realize that was a foolish concern." He paused and breathed deeply, then added, "Under any other circumstances, I would never have recommended what you did, but...in this particular case, it was quite effective. Perhaps, Iris, with the appropriate training, you could do quite a lot of good out there in the world, considering your...unique understanding of the Devil and his works."

Iris snorted softly. "I'm not a priest," she replied.

The blacksmith shrugged, keeping the motion slight enough so that it didn't disturb Iris's head resting against him. "That wouldn't preclude you from assisting," he retorted. "Of course," he added amiably, "you would have to keep that glove on. That scar would devastate almost any human victim of oppression or possession."

"Mm-hmm," Iris agreed sleepily.

"It's an interesting thought," he added, as if thinking aloud to himself.

"Satan performing exorcisms," Iris clarified. "Interesting thought, indeed. Nice bit of irony."

"I think God appreciates irony from time to time," the blacksmith concluded cheerfully.

Iris opened her eyes and positioned her head more comfortably on his arm. "Were you not afraid?" she asked, seriously. The man seemed completely unperturbed by the event that had just unfolded.

"My only fear," he answered stoically, "was that I might fail to preserve all that God has entrusted to my care."

Amazed yet again by the blacksmith's unceasing loyalty as a servant of God, Iris let the profound wisdom in his words settle into her mind and her heart. A small smile found its way to her lips, though she knew Auraltiferys wouldn't see it. She wondered if he realized just how closely he resembled an angel. Probably he didn't, and even if he did, he'd be too humble to admit it. She closed her eyes again, silently asked God's bountiful favor for the saintly blacksmith-priest, and then let her body relax into sleep.

***

A gentle tapping sound woke Iris from her rest. She opened her eyes to find her face still buried in the blacksmith's sizable bicep, the creases of his sleeve pressing into her cheek as she leaned against him, both of them still sitting on the marble floor of the library's relic room, warmed by the fire he had cast. She sat up as silently and easily as she could, not wanting to awaken Auraltiferys if he was sleeping. He kept a rigorous schedule of work and study and prayer, and Iris had completely disrupted his routine with her latest visit and her unexpected departure for the realm of the damned. He had stayed awake all night for her, enduring her arguments, her death, her damnation, her miraculous resurrection and return from Hell. Even their subsequent battle with the demonic forces attempting to use Loomis's body had, effectively, been her fault. She felt guilty for it all, and she hoped her mentor would get some rest now.

The noise that had woken her was rainfall pattering against the skylights of the grotto. The dawn had broken, turning the sky a clear, dimly luminous gray. It was a relaxing rain shower, beautifully illuminated by the radiance of an only partially hidden sun, peaceful and calming and even healing—nothing like the sudden torrential, gust-laden storms that would arrive behind a wall of dusty, dark brown-gray clouds and spray sharp pellets of dirty water across the poorly draining streets of Iris's hometown. She smiled as she watched the skylights for a moment, thanking God for having willed she should return to see another day, and especially one like this, on this holy mountain. After a moment, she glanced at the blacksmith sitting beside her, surprised to discover he was already awake and enjoying the pleasant rainfall just as she had been.

"Beautiful, isn't it?" he asked quietly.

"It's incredible," she answered. "Did you get any sleep?"

Auraltiferys chuckled. "You worry too much for me," he said jovially. "I have rested enough."

"I feel guilty!" she explained. "I know how disciplined you are with your routine, and I always manage to mess it up for you."

The blacksmith smiled at her, the golden reflections of the fire dancing across his sparkling sapphire eyes. "I am glad to have my routine disrupted," he answered boldly. "It keeps me from becoming complacent. And, frankly, routine gets old after a few hundred years."

Iris grinned and rolled her eyes. Auraltiferys arose nimbly from his seated position and extended his hand to her, prompting her to get up. "I don't know about you," he commented cheerfully, "but I'm famished."

"I could definitely eat," she responded eagerly.

As the blacksmith extinguished the magical flame, Iris turned and stared briefly at Loomis's body, chained to its cold slab. She winced, her facial expression betraying the instant pangs of grief that struck her upon seeing him lying there. *It's not him*, she told herself. *It's just a relic, just a vessel.* She hadn't seen her adoptive parents after they had perished in that awful car wreck, but she remembered spending the last moments of her grandmother's life with her in the hospital, and she vividly recalled having recited the same mantra to herself then—it was only a body, only a vessel; the soul lived on; her grandmother was in God's care. Those beliefs were somewhat comforting when one was reflecting upon the departed members of a human family, but they were no comfort at all to Iris right now as she gazed at the empty vessel of a demon, knowing the once-beautiful spirit that had animated it had been sentenced to perpetual torment and endless, painful separation from its God, all by the spirit's own choosing.

Auraltiferys wrapped a strong arm around her shoulders, giving her a comforting squeeze. "You have done all you can for him," he said, his deep and elegant voice an anodyne to her spirit. "And, should you be called upon again, I know you will yet do more. But that is all in God's hands, and you must trust in Him. Focus now on the living, the ones you might lead away from Hell by your example."

Iris nodded sadly and sighed deeply, then allowed the blacksmith to lead her away, up the steps of the grotto and back into the library. They followed the violet-carpeted path to the library's side entrance, walking in silence. Auraltiferys opened the heavy wooden door and stopped abruptly, his sudden halt immediately impelling Iris to trace his attentive and wary gaze. Stepping beside him and looking out through the delicate rain, she saw what had frozen him in his tracks. An Empyreal Hound, an Alpha, stood regally before them, perhaps thirty yards outside the library door, its huge, brilliantly white lion-wolf form perfectly still. Not even its pristine fur appeared to move under the raindrops. Only in its golden eyes was there any movement, and the movement there was striking. The hypnotic orbs were all but literally on fire, glowing from within with light that burned like a beating heart, their motion, though silent, somehow creating a rhythmic pulse that resounded within the mind.

Iris inhaled sharply, unsure what the strange appearance might mean, and rather unnerved by it. She glanced at Auraltiferys, whose own bright and watchful eyes were fixed so intently upon those of the Hound that Iris imagined all the rest of existence must have eroded from his consciousness for this moment. The blacksmith was as rigid as stone for a few seconds before he blinked and turned to her.

"Go back to the relic room," he ordered, in a tone that, though not unkind, indicated very clearly that no questions should be asked. Iris hesitated only an instant before she turned and ran for the grotto, while Auraltiferys walked purposefully out into the rain to approach the Hound.

In a matter of seconds, Iris had returned to the marble reliquary, her heart racing more from anxiety than from the short sprint. Her mind had been a frenzied jumble of horrendous expectations as she approached. Had a new legion of demons returned for a second attempt at penetrating the mountain's defenses? Had they already broken through? Would she find the chaotic and ghastly aftermath of a silent and evil magical onslaught neither she nor Auraltiferys had foreseen? She stopped in the center of the room and looked all around her. The quiet rush of her breath and the tranquil drumming of rain against the skylights were the only sounds she heard. The grotto was still and cool and peaceful, not even a trace of last night's demonic activity marring its appearance. She waited, alertly, wondering what was about to happen and praying she would be able to help the blacksmith with whatever it was. Seconds turned into minutes, and nothing happened. Auraltiferys had not returned, and Iris considered leaving the grotto to meet him back outside, but his command had been stated with such palpable authority that she in fact feared the consequences of doing anything but what she had been told to do. The authority in that voice, she decided, had been of a divine nature, and so she remained in place, watching and listening and wondering as apprehension stretched a relatively brief time into an uncomfortable length.

Finally, the faintest whisper of a new sound reached her ears, so minute that she wouldn't have been certain she had heard it but for the feeling within her heart. Hardly daring to breathe, she slowly approached the granite slab upon which Loomis's body lay enchained. To a less perceptive eye, the body would have appeared to be dead, unmoving and unresponsive and empty. Iris, however, noted the infinitesimal movement of eyes beneath the closed eyelids and the nearly imperceptible rise and fall of the chest, which caused the heavy links of the magical chains to shift ever so slightly. In contrast to the vulgar, animalistic heavings of the beasts of Hell that had toyed with this relic hours ago, these subtle motions evidenced class and dignity...even grace, perhaps, and Iris had not a single doubt that the body's genteel and inexplicably yet unfortunately demonic creator was returning to it. She stood beside him, a part of her wanting to speed him into his body with magical aid, while the greater part of her was afraid to do so—not because she feared Loomis or his power, but because she feared having to send him back to Hell again. She hoped for him, yes, but she refused to continue being foolish about it. Her obligations were to God and to Auraltiferys and her human family, and she couldn't allow a fervent and blinding hope for the near-impossible to disorient her.

She watched Loomis intently, sensing he was near but struggling to regain the full use of his body. She made no attempt to speak to him, and she pondered what she might do if he asked for her help. Would she trust him? She couldn't trust him completely, but, yes...she knew she would help him if he asked. It might make her the cause of the mountain's destruction, if Loomis was yet bent on evil, but she had too much of an emotional soft spot for him to deny his pleas, and she knew it. Just as Auraltiferys had warned her, she was compromised. Her nervous hypotheticals went untested, however, because no call for help came, and she couldn't decide whether she was relieved or disheartened by the silence.

Time dragged quietly by, and eventually she could no longer see any movement in Loomis's body at all. As complete, inanimate stillness settled again over the stone, Iris felt tears pooling in her eyes. Words could not convey how desperately she wanted Loomis out of Hell, how fervently she believed a trace of God's grace yet abided in him. That he might be trying to reach this body in order to seek a return to goodness and light made her all the more hopeful; that he might fail and then give up completely made her suddenly terrified to let him go. Was it worth the risk, she wondered, to bring Loomis into this body, knowing he might still let his demonic desires choke the angelic spirit she knew still existed within him? She decided it was.

She reached gingerly between two chains and laid her left hand on the expensive fabric sleeve covering Loomis's arm. She began the spell silently within her mind, immediately sensing Loomis's familiar presence at the edge of her awareness. He conveyed no message to her, but she felt him accept her assistance without any resistance. His spirit seemed weakened and apathetic, a stark contrast to the power and strength and purpose that had long differentiated him from the Devil's other subjects and had secured him certain allowances under Satan's rule, and she feared the Devil may have finally broken the seraphic spirit whose journey into Hell had originated from a great love for God and for the human race He had created. If Loomis had rejected an offer of mercy because he believed his return to Heaven to be impossible, it seemed even more likely now he would continue to reject it. Iris felt no hope in him at all; his spirit seemed to have become the hopeless and immaterial essence of Hell itself, and she wondered why he had even sought to reacquire his body, if damnation had finally taken its toll. Demons weren't particularly fond of great effort, and returning from Hell to this relic on the mountain would be a great effort. She had forced the others away; only Loomis had returned to try again, and two possible motives crossed her mind—either the Devil had taken away the luxuries he had once allowed Loomis, and Loomis was now striving a final time to save the one relic that would let him dwell outside of Hell, or...she hardly dared to think it, but perhaps Loomis had changed his mind on acceptance of eternal separation from God. Only the smallest voice in her mind still called out to her to be careful, to question whether Loomis might again be tricking her into aiding a sinister scheme. She felt certain, mostly, that whatever his motivations, Loomis Drake was no longer a threat to her.

Within seconds, Iris had helped Loomis through the invisible folds of the immeasurable distance of existence itself, leading him with magical power to the incredible relic he had designed for himself. His eyes opened, looking exhausted, but still beautiful and brown and alive. They were Loomis's eyes this time, flecked with the same amber hue that not even demonic mutation of spirit had ever completely erased. He blinked several times and then pressed his eyelids tightly together, his face tensing into a grimace as he breathed as deeply as he could beneath the weight of the golden shackles entangling him. Iris stared at him, wanting to free him and comfort him, but still afraid to trust in the hope she had. Who knew how he might yet be fooling her? Even if his spirit had been weakened, who knew how quickly he might regain his demonically oriented ambition and his abundant magical powers? It wouldn't be prudent, she decided, to help him any more than she already had. In fact, she could only hope she hadn't already made a terrible mistake...again.

Raindrops lightly pelted the skylights above, their muted,

staccato taps dampening the weighty silence looming over the relic room as Iris waited, guardedly, for Loomis to speak or move. After a minute, he once again opened his eyes, this time turning to look at her.

"Please," he uttered hoarsely, his voice riddled with pain, "remove these chains, Iris. I can't bear their weight."

Iris angrily forced away the sympathetic, hopeful tears attempting to breach her resolve. "I won't remove them," she replied, in a tone of overcompensating coldness. "Not until I know why you're here, and maybe not even then."

Loomis simply looked at her imploringly, the color and life draining from his face. Iris had never seen him so frail in physical form, and though it worried her, she refused to let human emotion guide her decision-making now. *Better heartless than stupid*, she thought. She allowed a moment to pass in silence, awaiting a verbal response. When none came, she shook her head and said, tightly, "Loomis, if you're here for evil—"

"He isn't," Auraltiferys interrupted, his quiet but sharply precise voice startling her. He had appeared silently and now stood at the foot of the granite slab, drenched from having been in the rain, but as noble and authoritative in appearance as Iris had ever seen him— back straight, shoulders squared, chin lifted, muscular arms crossed rigidly over his chest, silver-blue eyes alert and bright. Iris couldn't read his current expression with any certainty. She knew her own expression was a quizzical one as she looked to her mentor for an explanation, but his gaze was focused on the anthropomorphized demon lying chained in front of him.

"The power from your scar, the residual magic of the archangel's sword, has made that body a purified relic, anathema to demons," Auraltiferys explained. "The impure can hardly stand to touch it, let alone use it for evil."

As the words left the blacksmith's mouth and reached Iris's ears, her heart began pounding so forcefully that it seemed almost to leap into her throat. Sudden hope and nervous excitement raced through her veins, but she remembered she had felt something like that not long ago, when Loomis had come here to the mountain and lied directly to her face, telling her he sought forgiveness when, in truth, he had sought only the great secrets yet hidden on the mountain. She swallowed hard and strove to maintain a calm and neutral demeanor.

Auraltiferys paused for a brief moment, then he breathed deeply, muttered a magical spell, and allowed the unlocked golden chains to fall away from Loomis. Iris watched in disbelief, remembering the blacksmith's own admission about his opinion of the demon he had just freed, and realizing she now seemed like the most unsympathetic being in the room. Loomis took a deep breath and moved to sit up, but his motions were lethargic and pained. Iris reached over and helped him, gently pulling him up by his shoulders and helping him to the edge of the stone so that his legs dangled over the side. He propped his arms at his sides, curling his fingers along the edge of the slab, and hunched over, his chin tucked toward his chest. As Iris released him, she realized her own body was tense with concern, and she questioned why she should have such a reaction. Concern should be unnecessary; if Loomis was here, he wasn't in Hell and suffering, and if the blacksmith was correct about the purified relic...well, then there was certainly cause for great hope.

She remained close beside him, watching his labored breathing with both sadness and expectancy. She didn't want to see him suffer, but she knew it wasn't a physical ailment bothering him; it was a profound spiritual affliction, and she prayed he had come here to find healing for it. After silently asking God to have mercy upon him, if Loomis would accept it, she hesitantly reached over and laid her gloved hand on top of his, her bare fingertips lightly touching his cold skin.

Loomis lifted his chin and looked at her only briefly before dropping his eyes again. "I wouldn't have made it here without your aid," he said quietly, looking down. "Thank you."

Fearing she might cry if she attempted to speak, Iris simply squeezed Loomis's hand as reassuringly as she could, hoping he recognized the unspoken message she wanted to convey. Auraltiferys stepped around the granite slab and stood near her, just in front of Loomis, who tentatively raised his eyes at the blacksmith's approach.

"Auraltiferys," Loomis said stiffly.

"Drake," Auraltiferys replied, in a tone of begrudging neutrality. Iris glanced awkwardly from one to the other. The blacksmith's penetrating gaze was fixed decidedly on Loomis, and she felt uncomfortable on Loomis's behalf. She had been on the receiving end of that stare a few times, and it was never particularly pleasant. Loomis, not surprisingly, maintained eye contact for only an instant before letting his chin fall back toward his chest.

"Thank you for not destroying this body," he said to Auraltiferys, feebly. It was the same tone a servant might use when addressing a generous master.

"Had I followed my own inclinations," Auraltiferys answered firmly, "I would have destroyed it immediately. It is, however, a relic, and it is my solemn obligation to treat it as I treat every relic from Heaven's Forge, with appropriate respect for the great power of God, which was borrowed to create it and still exists within it."

Loomis nodded faintly. "You always do what's right," he replied softly, staring at his own lap. "Had I been half as faithful to my vocation as you have been to yours, I would have saved myself and your human race much suffering."

Auraltiferys's eyes narrowed, and he crossed his arms again as he stared down at Loomis, who refused to raise his eyes. Silence lingered in the air for several seconds. Iris removed her hand from Loomis's and watched as her mentor stood there in somber contemplation.

She sensed he knew something more than she did—possibly something with which he didn't personally agree. He seemed conflicted, as though he had been asked to do something he thought was a bad idea, and, while she wanted to hope the blacksmith's inner turmoil boded well for Loomis, the uncertainty and the waiting and the silence made her decidedly anxious.

"Do you regret all the suffering?" Auraltiferys finally asked Loomis, his voice cutting the air like cold, sharp metal.

Loomis shook his head slowly, almost imperceptibly, then, at length, resolutely lifted his face and met the blacksmith's eyes. "I have deserved all my suffering," he said in a low voice, "and I deserve still more. But…I do regret the suffering I have inflicted on humanity."

Iris inhaled sharply through her nose and pressed her hand over her mouth, in simultaneous disbelief and elation. She tightened her other arm over her abdomen and stood rigidly, trying to stop the trembling in her extremities. Loomis turned to face her, his eyes bright with hope, yet flickering with sorrow and fear. "Is there yet hope for me?" he asked, his voice shaky and barely more than a whisper.

Iris let out a quivering breath, realizing only then that she had been holding it in for too long. She balled her hand into a fist and squeezed one knuckle into her teeth, closing her eyes and quickly praying this wasn't all just some imaginative, torturously vivid dream. Her bite into her own skin assured her it wasn't. She relaxed as best she could, then smiled at Loomis and nodded. "I believe there's hope," she answered quietly. She looked over at her tutor inquisitively.

The blacksmith met her eyes momentarily, then turned back to Loomis. "What is it you hope for?" he asked.

Loomis was quiet for what seemed like a long time. He shifted uneasily on the granite block upon which he was sitting, closing his eyes for seconds at a time and wincing in discomfort. Finally, after a long silence, he looked at Auraltiferys and replied, "I hope for what I don't deserve, and I'm ashamed to hope for it."

"Tell me, demon," Auraltiferys commanded, not angrily or uncaringly, but with cool authority. Iris shot a look at him, upset by the name-calling, but the blacksmith paid her no attention.

Loomis swallowed painfully, looking quite distressed. "I hope..." He faltered, shook his head, then weakly concluded, "I hope Iris has been right about me. I hope for...a chance to leave Hell." He watched the blacksmith's eyes and awaited a response but soon realized there would be none. Auraltiferys's gaze was pressing him for a better answer. After a moment, Loomis took a shuddering breath, closed his eyes, and said, "I hope God will forgive me."

Iris, wide-eyed, looked at her mentor. He nodded at her once, slowly, then addressed Loomis again. "Do you believe God will forgive you?" he asked, his tone gentler now than before, but still heavily serious.

Loomis opened his eyes, which were now bloodshot and watery. "I don't deserve it," he admitted sullenly. "But...I was told I might yet ask for His mercy and be granted it."

"But you refused that opportunity, did you not?" Auraltiferys countered. "Archangels appeared to you and spoke to you, and you opposed God's mercy then. What has changed?"

Loomis glanced briefly at Iris, then returned his gaze to the blacksmith. "I was shown the vanity of every evil thing I had sought," he answered. "I was reminded of the goodness that exists in the human race, and of the goodness that once existed in me. It has taken me far too long to recognize it, and if God should turn me away now, it is only what I deserve, and it is my fault alone. I will accept my eternity in Hell, if that should be my sentence, but...I will yet dare to make this final appeal to His mercy, even in full knowledge that my sins against His creation are indefensible and more numerous than the stars."

Auraltiferys raised an eyebrow, apparently surprised by Loomis's answer. He looked at Iris, who watched him expectantly, then back to Loomis, who looked pale and sickly, but resolute. He sighed, then said harshly, "Personally, Drake, I don't believe you deserve another chance for anything but Hell."

"Auri..." Iris pleaded quietly.

The blacksmith looked at her and sighed again, then cleared his throat and continued, "But my understanding is limited, and I recognize its shortsightedness. God's infinite mercy will always be greater than His creation's finite sins, although for most, the choice for Hell does in fact mean an eternity apart from Him. I suppose you and Iris are different. I credited Iris's humanity for her chance at return, but you..." He paused and shook his head. "I cannot claim to understand why you're being given this opportunity."

"What opportunity?" Iris asked breathlessly.

Auraltiferys looked at her with an intense and serious expression sharpening the already well-chiseled features of his face. He glanced at Loomis, who was shifting laboriously in his body but watching the blacksmith's eyes carefully. "The opportunity for his redemption," he answered Iris solemnly, "if he chooses to pursue it."

Iris turned to Loomis, anxiously awaiting his response. Somewhere within her, there was a confident positivity he would accept the chance this time. Even amid her certainty, though, she felt numbed by disbelief, shocked by the suddenness of it all. *It's not sudden, really*, she reminded herself. *How many thousands of years has he been separated from God?*

"I...want to pursue it," Loomis answered, gritting his teeth. His discomfort seemed to be worsening the longer his demonic spirit remained within the now-purified relic of his body. Iris desperately wanted to soothe his anguish, but she knew there was nothing she could do. Purification was a painful process—she had experienced it acutely on a couple of occasions—but it was necessary. If Loomis could withstand it, the temporary suffering would be worth every ounce of its agony.

Auraltiferys watched silently for a few seconds as Loomis closed his eyes and hunched over even more dramatically, failing to stifle a tortured groan. To Iris's surprise, the blacksmith stepped closer to Loomis and helped him sit upright, bracing one hand against his shoulder and raising his chin with the other, brusquely, but not insensitively.

"This pain you now feel," Auraltiferys asked, "are you willing to abide it until your debts have been repaid?"

Iris's stomach lurched, doubt suddenly flooding her mind and filling her gut with heavy despair. How long would Loomis have to suffer like this to atone for a near-eternity of demonic behavior? What had she expected for him, a ride on the express elevator to Heaven? She understood Purgatory; she understood the need for sinful humans to be made perfect before entering Heaven. Why had she thought Loomis's re-perfection should be any less stringent?

"What are you talking about?" she asked her mentor, unthinkingly. "Why should he have to suffer like this at all? Will God not just forgive him?"

Loomis answered her before the blacksmith could. In a tight voice, he said, "It is right and just that I should suffer, Iris, and…I expected no different." Moving his eyes then to Auraltiferys, he told him, simply, "I'm willing."

The blacksmith searched Loomis's eyes for an instant, then released his shoulder and backed away, muttering some unintelligible, magical words under his breath and making an open-palmed gesture of blessing toward the demon. "God has freed you from death, from the agony of complete separation from Him," he announced. "The relic's purity will no longer cause you such distress."

The visible change in Loomis was instantaneous. He breathed deeply and exhaled slowly, his body suddenly more relaxed and the color already returning to his skin. He looked at Auraltiferys briefly, clearly humbled, then buried his face in his hands. Iris didn't really sense he was crying, but he was certainly overwhelmed by emotion. She wanted to cry on his behalf, out of joy. "This is it, then?" she asked Auraltiferys, full again of exuberant hope. "He's been forgiven?"

"The door has been opened to him," the blacksmith answered reconditely. "The path that leads there, however, is long and difficult."

Iris's forehead creased with worry. Auraltiferys inclined his head slightly to her, his eyes reminding her how impossible it should have been for Loomis to leave Hell at all. She bit her lip and said nothing, understanding the blacksmith must be having as difficult a time with this strange situation as she was, though for different reasons. Iris might prefer for Loomis to be welcomed into Heaven at this very moment; Auraltiferys was having to put aside years of personal odium just to accept that this chance was even being offered to the demon.

"A long and difficult road," Loomis commented in reply to the blacksmith's statement, "is exactly what the archangels had offered me." He was sitting upright now, more composed, looking from Iris to Auraltiferys, his eyes brighter and less bloodshot than before. "Michael told me Heaven had not yet been completely closed to me, but, if I hoped to return, my path would be a difficult one, full of suffering and laced with pitfalls that would lead me directly back to Hell, with no further chance for redemption."

Auraltiferys stared at him. "And you choose now to embark on this path?" he asked, rather coldly. "Though you refused it before?"

"I was not ready for it then," Loomis answered evenly. "I was angry and arrogant and foolish..." He appeared to have more to say, but he let his thought fall silent.

"You should not have assumed the offer still stood," Auraltiferys retorted sharply.

"I assumed nothing," Loomis replied quietly. "I only hoped."

"Auri," Iris implored, "don't be so hard on him. He did use a purified relic to return here, and you understand the pain it brought him—"

"That he is willing to endure pain is hardly an assurance of his goodness," Auraltiferys interjected, his face dark.

Iris didn't try to mask her offense. With a wide-eyed scowl, she reprimanded the blacksmith, asking brazenly, "Is his goodness your judgment to make?" Auraltiferys held her eyes for a moment, then he blinked once, very slowly, and took a deep breath. He knew it was not his place to make such a judgment, and Iris knew he hadn't really intended to pass any judgment. The blacksmith was only human, though, and thus susceptible to words and actions driven by emotion. He was having difficulty remaining impartial.

"I do not deserve to seek your help, Auraltiferys," Loomis stated ruefully, regaining the attention of both Iris and her mentor. "I have given you nothing but reason to hate me, and I will not blame you if you send me away. I came back here not knowing if the offer proposed to me by the archangels would remain. I denied them once, and I didn't expect they would appear to me again. But I hoped a chance might still exist, and I knew, if it did, only you would be able to assist me in accepting it."

Auraltiferys folded his arms again and watched Loomis's eyes as he spoke. After a brief hesitation, he said, "I see not how a human priest should be expected to aid in the salvation of a demon—"

"You aided *me*," Iris interrupted softly. Auraltiferys's eyes darted to her for a moment, and his expression softened.

"I suppose that is true," the blacksmith acknowledged, "although, Iris, you were different." He sighed deeply. "It matters not," he continued. "I may not understand why this has been laid before me, but...I have been called upon to help you, Drake, and I will do as I have been asked."

Loomis gave the blacksmith a small, curt nod, then cleared his throat. "So," he proceeded hesitantly, "you...have been told what I must do?"

Iris looked at him, her mind still struggling to accept this whole scenario as reality. Loomis was here, really here, ready to ask for God's mercy, which God had apparently not completely withdrawn from him, despite the demon's departure from Heaven and subsequent ages-long mire in sin and evil. Part of her was still afraid to believe it was true, not wanting to be made a fool yet again by falling for a ruse, but there was an aura of such sincere humility and uncertainty around Loomis now that she implicitly trusted his motive for being here. This was not the arrogant, self-confident, scheming and manipulating demon who had donned a man's disguise and then spun the intricate webs of deceit and treachery and temptation that had entangled generations of human souls and pulled them away from God; this was a strong and beautiful spirit nearly broken by the weight of guilt upon him, begging for forgiveness from behind as composed a mask as he could wear, knowing he did not deserve any pardon, and reticent to ask for what he did not deserve.

"I have," Auraltiferys answered. He glanced at Iris, whose wide eyes were eagerly awaiting elaboration, then turned back to Loomis. "Saint Michael did not tell you any more than what you have already shared?" he asked. Iris frowned, wondering where this was going and what the blacksmith had been told on divine authority.

"I didn't ask for details," Loomis replied grimly. "I had no intention then of returning."

Auraltiferys ran a hand over the rain-soaked, silver-white hair on his scalp, then rested the hand behind his head and stared out through the skylights above for a moment, the flexed muscles of his arm standing solidly against the damp, dark fabric of his shirt sleeve. He was considering something, but Iris hadn't a clue what it might be. *I'm the one with the demonic power,* she reflected silently, *and yet he reads me so much more clearly than I can read him.* She was glad the Creator had put such trust in him as a servant; neither she nor Loomis would have fared so well without him.

"You may not like the...*penance* that has been set for you," the blacksmith said at length.

Loomis dropped his chin and stared at his hands, interlaced together on his lap. "Whatever it is," he murmured, "it is lighter punishment than I deserve."

"Perhaps," Auraltiferys replied mysteriously.

"What is it?" Iris asked, concerned and feeling very much like a little kid sitting at the grown-ups' table.

The blacksmith shifted on his feet and met her eyes. "Drake's...*purification,* I suppose we shall call it, is not something for which our Church has a prescription," he told her. "Your sins can be absolved through the sacrament of reconciliation, because you are human. He is not."

"So?" Iris retorted anxiously. "He's still being forgiven, right? I mean, God has said he can return to Heaven, right? Just tell him whatever he has to do! You're making me nervous."

"It isn't simple, Iris," Auraltiferys chided gently, "and he may not be as willing as you hope he is, once he hears what will be required of him."

Iris felt her face turn hot, rather embarrassed that she was so much more visibly enthusiastic about Loomis's redemption than he himself was. She pressed her mouth shut and bowed her head, taking a small step away from the blacksmith and from the granite slab where Loomis sat. She primly wrapped one hand around the opposite wrist and let her arms hang in front of her, then she hazarded a glance at Loomis. He looked weary, and maybe even afraid, but he returned her glance with a small, grateful smile.

"Do just tell me, Auraltiferys," he said, in a tone that attempted cheerfulness but was not free from unease. "You are making me nervous as well."

Auraltiferys crossed his arms once more, making his imposing stature all the more intimidating, though not intentionally. "First," he replied, "you are to accept that relic as your true body. It will become your form, and your spirit will be unable to leave it. You will be confined to Earth until either your purification is complete or you choose to return to Hell." Loomis's expression was serious but neutral as he listened. He said nothing, and the blacksmith continued. "You will...feel as humans feel," he explained. "You will be made to know thoughts and emotions as *humans* experience them, and thus you will be made to face the same temptations and challenges that constantly plague the fallen human race. You will not be immune to the works of the Devil or his cohorts."

Iris felt that awful, sinking feeling returning to her gut. This "penance" was sounding...not too enticing, and she understood now why her mentor had cautioned her about being overly optimistic for Loomis's willingness to accept it. Though the cool air of the relic room hadn't changed, she suddenly felt very cold. She folded her arms tightly across her ribs and prayed Loomis would not back out now.

"You are to avoid all sin," Auraltiferys continued authoritatively, "and you are to make what reparations you can for all the destruction you have brought to the human family." He paused and stared penetratingly at Loomis for a moment, then added, "You should be warned, a single grave sin is enough to condemn you for eternity, and the Hell to which you return will be exponentially more agonizing than the Hell you have already known." His voice was heavy and cold, unquestionably sincere. Loomis's eyes gazed far away, at nothing, or at something beyond the visible, as he reflected silently on the blacksmith's words.

"How can that be expected of him?" Iris asked quietly. "To live as a human but avoid all sin? No human can avoid all sin."

"The transgressions of humankind are a debt already paid," Auraltiferys answered. "Drake, however, is not human. You know more is expected of those to whom more is entrusted. You'll do him no favors by seeking allowances for him, Iris."

"I don't seek allowances!" she exclaimed indignantly. "I just know how hard it is to be human and avoid sin! You're telling him he'll have human thought and human emotion thrust upon him, and yet he'll be expected to, what, be perfect anyway? Meet a higher standard than we have to meet? How is that fair?"

"It's only the same standard by which he has measured the human race," Auraltiferys answered icily. Iris recoiled at the blacksmith's bitter response, suddenly afraid Loomis's eventual return to Heaven was, in fact, impossible. She hated to admit it, but her good mentor made a valid point. Loomis had grown to hate the human race because of their quickness to turn away from God and follow worldly desires, because of the ease with which they could be tempted to sin. He had grown to hate their imperfect virtue, and now...well.

"It just seems...so impossible," she returned, deflated.

Auraltiferys recognized her pain instantly; in fact, he had probably known since his meeting with the Empyreal Hound that Iris would feel this way as these events unfolded. He relaxed somewhat and, in a softer voice, replied, "God does not assign impossible tasks."

Loomis roused himself from his contemplation, and his eyes focused on Iris. "It is fair," he said, "and difficult, but not impossible. I will try, Iris, and if I should fail, I will have only the end I deserve."

Iris looked at him sadly, shaking her head. "You don't know what it's like, Loomis," she told him.

"You don't believe I can avoid sin?" Loomis asked.

"Of course you *can*," she answered. "But so could every human being who ever walked the Earth. You know how that has worked out."

"There is still more," Auraltiferys interjected quietly.

"More?" Iris uttered, with extreme exasperation and despair. "What 'more' could there possibly be? Is perfection not enough?"

Auraltiferys looked at her with a somewhat reproachful but kindly and sympathetic sparkle in his eyes. "Purification will make perfection, not the other way around," he said gently. After a pause, he turned back to Loomis. "You are to confess your sins to me, Drake, before you leave here," he told him, closely watching Loomis's eyes. "That is," he continued, "if you are truly repentant. I will not claim to understand why it is required of you. Christ died for the sins of humankind, not for the sins of angels, and my administration of absolution as a human priest is but a shadow of what you need with regard to forgiveness. The sacrament will not wipe away your offenses, but perhaps it is meant to serve you a different purpose. I suppose it is fitting that you be made to humble yourself before a mortal man, the representative of Christ, acknowledging the wrongs you have done against the race for whose salvation He willfully surrendered Himself." The blacksmith nodded slowly, as if agreeing with his own musings, then concluded, "Whatever the reasons, I am to hear your full confession now, and then I am to hear you whenever you might have venial sins to confess. That simple act of penitence, if made with sincerity of spirit, will be enough to preserve you from immediate condemnation back to Hell, although only God knows how He intends to cleanse you of those sins. Any grave sin, though, I remind you, will be the immediate end of this...demonic purification."

Iris watched Loomis for a reaction. He sat very straight at the edge of the granite block and had crossed his arms over his chest as the blacksmith spoke. His expression was hard-set, but not defiant. Perhaps she was seeing only what she wanted to see, but she believed Loomis looked like a soldier preparing for war—fearful of what might lie ahead, yet resolved to fulfill the duty to which he had been called, regardless of the cost.

After a significant pause for contemplation, Loomis met Auraltiferys's gaze and, sincerely, said, "That will be a heavy burden for you to bear, to hear the sins of a demon and have them etched upon your own heart—particularly when you know the confession does not even remove the stains of those sins. You are...willing to do this for me? Even after..." His voice drifted away, leaving nothing but an unfinished question and the hammering of rainfall against glass echoing through the expansive grotto of the library.

"I am," Auraltiferys answered somberly, in a strong voice and without hesitation. "My personal feelings toward you are immaterial. I will do anything God asks of me." Loomis's jaw tensed at the blacksmith's response, and it appeared to Iris as though he were trying to force tears away from his eyes. Although Auraltiferys wore an expression of extreme gravitas, Iris felt a smile cross her own lips as she wondered at her tutor's humility and faithfulness. As much as he hated Loomis, he loved God even more.

"It won't be the first time he's had to hear the sins of a demon," she added softly, graciously.

"That makes it an even heavier burden for him," Loomis answered, a hint of dejection darkening his tone.

"I consider it only my duty now, not a burden," Auraltiferys responded, "and if my service aids in the redemption of another, then it is a glorious blessing to me." Then, turning his silver-blue gaze on Iris, he said, "The duty, however, is not mine alone."

"What do you mean?" she asked.

"It is only a very narrow and difficult path that has been laid out for him," Auraltiferys replied, "and if he tries to walk it alone, he will almost certainly fail."

Loomis took a sudden, sharp breath, causing Iris to turn immediately toward him. His eyes were narrowed and his brow was furrowed. "What are you saying?" he asked the blacksmith, concerned urgency in his tone.

Auraltiferys looked at Loomis for a moment before he answered. "You will need a patron," he finally said. "Someone to guide you rightly, and as Iris is the only other being to have walked a similar path, she is the obvious and appropriate choice."

"I'll do whatever I can," Iris stated emphatically.

"It isn't as simple as doing whatever you can," Auraltiferys rejoined, shaking his head. "This is a serious responsibility, and one you are certainly under no obligation to accept."

Iris frowned at him, her eyebrows squeezed tightly together. "Auri," she said reproachfully, "whatever the responsibility, you know I'll accept it."

"You will be made accountable for him, if you choose this," the blacksmith answered solemnly. "Any sin he commits will be a blemish on your own record, one for which you will have to answer."

Loomis pushed himself off the stone and stood abruptly, eyes flashing. "That's ridiculous," he argued vehemently. "She can't be held responsible for anything I do! That isn't fair to her!"

"Her salvation will not depend on you," Auraltiferys responded calmly. "But she will have to be aware of all you do, and she will have to make it a constant effort to direct you toward the God to whom you seek to return. And you will have to know that every wrongdoing of yours is another cross she has to carry."

"Absolutely not," Loomis stated solidly. "I won't allow this."

"As I said," Auraltiferys replied collectedly, "she's under no obligation to accept the responsibility."

"And, as *I* said," Iris interjected, growing impatient herself, "I'm willing to accept it."

"No, Iris," Loomis said, genuine protectiveness bringing fire to his earthy, amber-flecked eyes. "I won't have you held accountable for my thoughts or actions. You've already—"

"I thought you intended to avoid sin," Iris interrupted him. " 'Difficult, but not impossible,' you said. So what's the problem?" She forced a small, lopsided smile to her lips, though she knew the expression didn't reach her eyes.

"Think about this, before you commit yourself so readily," Auraltiferys warned. "You will be sacrificing any chance at what you might call a normal life."

"That pretty much went out the window when I became Satan," Iris replied, with mild sarcasm.

"Iris," Auraltiferys rebuked her mildly, "this will become a hardship for you, sooner or later." His eyes took on their characteristic, deeply searching gaze as he elaborated, "It isn't just a favor here and there; it may well prove to be a lifetime commitment—one with eternal consequence to you both if ever you should break it. You will have to be available at all times to act as confidant and counselor. You will have to direct your own thoughts and actions constantly toward God, maintaining virtue and holiness. That is no simple task, especially in the society in which you live. And you will become personally culpable for both your own sins and his."

The blacksmith appeared to have more to say, but Iris cut him off. "I've seen what Loomis is capable of being," she asserted, "and I believe he'll surprise you. But I won't hesitate to help him however I can, if he should need my help."

Auraltiferys searched her a moment longer, then sighed and looked toward Loomis, standing an arm's length away from him. "The accountability will not be solely hers," he said sternly, his tone taking on the cold, knife-like edge that left no doubt about his seriousness. "You will have to guide her and others toward virtue, if you wish to atone for your transgressions." Pausing briefly, the blacksmith's expression went dark, and even Iris felt a flutter of intimidation that chilled her. "If ever you should lead her into sin..." He fell silent once more, staring hard at Loomis. For an anxious couple of seconds, Iris thought her mentor might submit to his personal enmity, draw his blade, and bring a final end to the body Loomis had created. The apprehensive instant passed, however, and Auraltiferys concluded his remark. "If ever you should lead her into sin," he repeated stonily, "you will not be forgiven."

Loomis bowed his head. "I have no desire to lead her into sin," he answered. He then turned to Iris, almost shyly. "Neither do I desire for you to pay anything more for my...iniquity," he told her, his baritone voice sounding uncommonly vulnerable. "Had I known my appeal for mercy would only burden you further," he added, "I might have chosen to remain in Hell."

"You are still free to choose it," Auraltiferys declared. The comment was delivered with complete and genuine neutrality; the blacksmith was not suggesting that Loomis *should* choose to remain among the damned. He was merely stating a fact.

"That would pain me far worse than this does," Iris replied.

"Auraltiferys," Loomis said, addressing the blacksmith but still looking at Iris, "I cannot understand why my purification must entangle her like this." His face was neutral, but Iris sensed emotion somewhere behind it. She wasn't certain, however, what the emotion was. Gratitude, maybe? Or perhaps something stronger. He turned to the blacksmith after a moment.

"I don't have an explanation for you," Auraltiferys conceded. "I don't believe your salvation depends any more upon her than hers depends upon you. God judges justly and mercifully, and perfectly. Either of you can choose Heaven or Hell, and the other will yet be free to choose differently." He cleared his throat meaningfully, then added, "But the two of you are...*acquainted* in a very particular and unique way..."

Iris and Loomis both directed their eyes toward the marble floor, knowing precisely to what the blacksmith was referring. Iris imagined, with no shortage of embarrassment, that Loomis must be horrified right now, learning like this that she had confessed it to Auraltiferys.

"Whatever the reasons," Auraltiferys continued, aware his vague reference had been clearly recognized, "I believe God desires you both to join Him in Heaven, and He knows what each of you needs to keep you headed in that direction." After a pause, he commented, in a more benevolent tone, "Perhaps the way will be made easier for you both if you do travel it together." He looked at Iris, and she saw he had relaxed somewhat, as though something had eased his mind. He glanced at Loomis, then returned his gaze to Iris, closed his eyes, and nodded once before reopening them.

Loomis recognized the blacksmith's affirmative gesture. After a deep breath, he addressed Iris, asking quietly, "Will you resent me for this? For asking yet more of you, after all you've done for me?"

Iris felt tears welling up toward her eyes at the simple question. "Of course not," she whispered in shaky reply, trying hard to maintain her composure.

"I've been a terrible enemy to you both..." Loomis reflected feelingly, choking before he could say anything more. Iris wanted to respond, but she knew it would bring tears if she did.

"Though I have seen what evil you are capable of," Auraltiferys announced, recognizing Iris's emotional state, "I yet believe you can return to grace." His tone was cool and precise, but sympathetic. "Iris has been a staunch advocate of your goodness. She has reminded me how little I truly know and understand, and she has shown me God can bestow His mercy as He wills, upon any of His creation—even upon a demon. I admit it will not be easy for me to forgive you, but...I am willing to work on it, though it will be for me a substantial effort. In the meantime, I will help you as I've been told I can, not only because I am compelled as a servant of God, but also because I trust what Iris has recognized in you. She has seen no less of your evil than I have, yet she has found God's grace still within your spirit. What has been revealed to me since your appearance here by way of a purified relic has proven her right." The blacksmith paused and met Iris's eyes for an instant, then concluded, "Even a *chance* at purification is a miracle for you, Drake, and I believe I speak for Iris, too, when I say we are honored to have any part in it." Iris nodded silently at the blacksmith's statement, looking at Loomis with a faint smile.

Loomis folded his arms and lowered his eyes to the floor. "In that case," he said hesitantly, his downward gaze muting his words, "I...would be humbled to have your assistance."

Iris looked up at Auraltiferys with a hopeful, anxious smile and eyes blurred by joyful tears. She instinctively grabbed his nearest arm with both her hands, hugging it close to her. The relic room felt suspended in a dream, and she couldn't believe Loomis was here now and about to accept a call he had been ignoring for far too long. She was overjoyed that the blacksmith had agreed to help him, despite the existing enmity between the two, and her heart was absolutely overflowing with love for her gracious mentor and his unceasing dedication to all that was right and just.

Auraltiferys returned Iris's smile in his modest yet regal way and placed his other hand reassuringly on top of hers as she held his arm. Then, with a meaningful look from his silver-blue eyes, he gently prompted her to release him. Turning back to Loomis, then, he asked, "Knowing the conditions, now, Drake, do you still seek the forgiveness of your sins and the purification of your spirit?"

Loomis looked genuinely afraid, and Iris feared for an instant he might just disappear, not wanting to start down a path he might fail to reach the end of. Instead, however, he closed his eyes tightly and dropped to his knees on the cold marble. Gleaming light from the magical torches of the grotto reflected off the tears that were now flowing down the sculpted cheeks of the body that was about to become for him a permanent and dignified vessel, giving his face a lustrous glow. He nodded vigorously, keeping his head lowered, and answered, "Yes, I do."

The blacksmith looked down at Loomis with compassionate eyes, and though Iris knew it would be a long time before he could personally forgive whatever wrongs Loomis had done to him, she knew Auraltiferys hoped, deep within his own soul, that Loomis would one day regain admittance to Heaven. As he lowered himself to one knee in front of Loomis's humbled and emotion-laden frame, he said quietly, "Please leave us, Iris, and wait at the house for our return. There is much from which he must unburden himself now."

Iris swallowed and lingered for a brief moment, silently uttering a quick prayer of thanksgiving and an appeal for comfort for the fallen angel now seeking his redemption, then she turned and walked away, ascending the stairs of the grotto and proceeding numbly through the library and out into the cool, fresh rain of the mountain's glorious morning.

***

Back at the house, Iris paced aimlessly around the den, her mind bombarded by a churning sea of thoughts and emotions. She was astounded by what had happened, to the point she couldn't even be sure she yet believed it. She was also incredibly and undeniably happy Loomis had braved a return to the mountain—even after being mercilessly beaten by the Devil and his entourage of demons, and through a purified relic, no less—with nothing more than a hope that he might receive, once more, the grace of God. Joy was the prevailing emotion in her heart right now, and that was an uncharacteristic feeling for her...which was probably why the undercurrent of astonishment so swiftly moved to dispel the happiness and replace it with the dark waters of doubt. She questioned whether Loomis would complete his confession to Auraltiferys and accept all the conditions of his journey toward purification. And then, even if he did embark on the journey, would he be able to reach its destination? How would Loomis handle all the thought and emotion of human existence? Iris was barely handling it now...and she was human. And she had agreed to be his patron and his guide, if he chose to pursue Heaven as the chance had been offered him. Some sponsor she would make! Even with the holiest man this side of the pearly gates as her mentor, she had very nearly accepted an eternity of damnation. How could she hope to keep Loomis on the straight and narrow when she herself struggled so ceaselessly with sin?

Perhaps twenty minutes passed before she realized she was trying to wrap finite human understanding around the infinite and omnipotent. She cast a fire into the fireplace, taking the chill off the room, then sat in her usual place on the couch before it, praying silently as she stared into the flames. She reflected on her own journey, on all the strange turns it had taken and on all the painful snares that had caught her along the way, though thankfully for only a short time. She thanked God for it all; she asked that He change her doubts into faith; and she prayed for His divine providence for herself and Loomis and Auraltiferys as they set foot on this new, seemingly impossible journey together. After a while, she felt at ease, and she reclined into the sofa and shut her eyes. The only question remaining in her mind now was how long Loomis's confession might last. She appreciated the significance of what was happening, and she knew she could wait for as long as she had to, but...her body was tired and beyond hungry.

She sat with her eyes closed for a long time, not sleeping, but barely remaining awake. The warmth of the fire relaxed and calmed her, and the easy tapping of the attenuating rain outside made her feel refreshed and hopeful, as though everything would be possible from this time on. She wasn't in the chapel, but she could feel God's presence all around her, and within her. She hoped and prayed all was going well back in the library.

Finally, after what felt like forever, she heard footsteps on the front porch, and she quickly stood and turned to see Auraltiferys opening the door. The rain was just a gentle drizzle now, and behind the blacksmith was a sky of gray, illuminated by afternoon sun that sent a vibrant rainbow arcing over the horizon. He entered the house in silence, his face drawn and his long hair matted by the damp, and he closed the door gently behind him. Upon seeing Iris's expectant and inquisitive eyes, he smiled.

"It has begun," he said with a slight shrug, as though announcing a fact he was sure of but still couldn't believe.

Iris could tell from the brightness in his gaze that he was, though perhaps physically tired and hungry and spiritually wearied, grateful to be a part of the amazing event that had just been set in motion. She smiled broadly and rushed the blacksmith with a tight hug, which he returned with a gentle, paternal squeeze. She had vowed during her solitary contemplation to shed no more tears today, but she felt now it might be difficult to stick to that self-promise.

"Where is he?" she asked as she released Auraltiferys from the embrace.

"He needs some time alone," the blacksmith replied. "Existence is different for him now. He needs an opportunity to process what has changed for him."

Iris tensed her forehead and frowned, wishing she could see Loomis now, but entirely sympathetic to the need for introversion. "Is he okay?" she asked.

"He is far better now than he has been for some time," Auraltiferys answered, guiding Iris alongside him as he stepped toward his chair and then motioned for her to sit on the couch.

"That's not what I mean," Iris responded as she sat. "I know anything is better than Hell, but...how is he doing with, you know, the whole human-feeling thing?"

Auraltiferys slowly shook his head as he leaned into the back of his chair. "I don't know," he admitted. "He has many feelings right now, I'm sure—guilt, remorse, doubt, hope—but I can't say how his perception has been transformed. I imagine it may overwhelm him for a while."

Iris was saddened by the thought, and she stared blankly at the fire in front of her as she imagined the agony of mind and heart Loomis might now be facing alone. It wouldn't be too much different from the spiritual tortures inflicted upon him in Hell, though at least this time there was a distant promise of something truly worthwhile on the other side.

"I hope he can cope with it," she said at length.

"He can," Auraltiferys assured her. "He must. And I do believe he *wants* to. I'm sure, with your help, the emotions will get easier for him to process. It is a good thing you earned that doctorate in psychology, yes?" He grinned.

Iris rolled her eyes and smiled. "Yeah, maybe that will come in handy," she answered, her tone upbeat but skeptical. "But..." She trailed off as her smile faded.

"But, what?" Auraltiferys questioned, staring intently at her. "You fear you might fail to lead him rightly?"

Iris raised her shoulders in a sheepish little shrug. "I'm not like you, Auri," she stated simply.

The blacksmith gripped the armrests of his chair and pulled himself into his typical ramrod posture, his expression announcing he was about to answer Iris's sophomoric comment with some real wisdom. "Of course you're not," he replied, "and thank God for it.

We serve different purposes. One would not use a hammer to fell a tree, nor an axe to fasten a nail. The tools are different, but both are useful. You have done things I could never do; you have taught me things I had yet to learn. And I am fortunate enough to have certain strengths that can supplement your weaknesses. We have both been called upon to help Drake, in our separate and particular manners. My place is and always will be here, and I will aid you both in every way I can, but *you* are what he will need out there in the world, in the midst of trial. You have been appointed to that position for a reason, Iris, and you know God makes no mistakes."

"Yeah, but..." Iris sighed, then caught a look from Auraltiferys that showed her he already knew exactly what she was going to say. She, likewise, knew exactly what the blacksmith's rebuttal would be. So instead of proceeding with her original thought, she said, "It's just a scary responsibility."

"Indeed," Auraltiferys agreed, "but it's one you are prepared for. That won't make it easy, and it doesn't mean you won't make mistakes—"

"But a mistake now could send him right back to Hell!" Iris interjected apprehensively. "That's what scares me most. I don't want to be the reason he fails. If that happens, I will never forgive myself."

"You aren't the judge here, Iris," Auraltiferys answered kindly. "You don't decide his ultimate fate. If you keep your own soul directed toward God, and you rely on Him to guide you, then you will be a sure guide for Drake, in turn. You needn't worry about mistakes—mistakes can be forgiven. What would be unforgivable would be to lead him back into sin, or to leave him without guidance you know he needs. And those would be your transgressions, not his. He knows right and wrong, Iris. He knows virtue and sin. He will make his own choices, aware of the consequences of his actions for both himself and you. Help him to choose rightly; that is all you must do." He relaxed again into his chair and added, thoughtfully,

"It's really nothing you haven't already done. You've just obligated yourself to continue what you've begun."

Iris reflected on the blacksmith's words, nodding slowly and reflectively, greatly comforted by her mentor's unfailing enlightenment. She took a deep, cleansing breath, then settled back into the sofa cushions, a thoughtful, easy smile on her lips.

"Feel better?" Auraltiferys asked, grinning understandingly.

Iris returned the grin. "Of course," she replied.

"Then, if you're ready, go find Drake now," he directed, gracefully rising to his feet. "I'll prepare us a meal, and we will all share it when you return."

Iris's anxiety reappeared suddenly as she stood up, manifesting itself like a cold, sweaty hand clenching her stomach.

"Don't be nervous," Auraltiferys charged her as he left for the kitchen. He had already turned away, yet he still knew exactly what she was feeling. Despite her uneasiness, Iris couldn't help but smile to herself as the blacksmith disappeared through the doorway, and in an instant, she felt calmer. After a quick but fervent prayer, she headed outside.

There was a crispness to the air and a definite chill in the drizzle, but the sunlight was somehow abundant even amid the gray skies, and its radiance gave the mountain a pleasant warmth in spite of the cool rain. The rainbow she had seen briefly a little while ago still shone overhead, and she counted it a wonderful blessing to see such a remarkably beautiful sight. After a momentary pause for appreciation, she closed her eyes and concentrated on Loomis, locating him easily with a simple spell. Continuing in his direction, she soon found him sitting on a rock outcropping near the river's edge, leaning over with his elbows near his knees and his feet resting on a lower surface of the stone.

She approached quietly and seated herself beside him. "Are you okay with some company?" she asked, looking at the clear water of the river and the pine forest beyond the opposite bank. She really had no clue what she was supposed to say.

"Of course," Loomis answered, his attention likewise directed toward the landscape. Iris couldn't understand why she was surprised his voice sounded exactly as it always had. Had she expected some sort of transformation? That was silly; the body was still the same one Loomis had been using for so long.

For a moment, the two sat without speaking, but eventually, Iris broke the silence. "How do you feel?" she asked.

Loomis sighed heavily and hesitated for several seconds before answering. "Different," he replied simply.

"Better or worse?" Iris asked.

Loomis straightened up slowly and answered, "Overall, certainly better."

Iris finally turned and really looked at him. He was, in appearance, still the handsome, undeniably appealing man who, in today's earthly society, was a multibillionaire business entrepreneur and philanthropist. He still had the clear, olive-complected skin; the statuesque features; the thick, dark hair and well-groomed goatee; the expensive, tailored suit. But there certainly was something different about him—something Iris believed only she could really perceive. She felt as though she had just set eyes on him for the first time, like the Loomis Drake she had seen so many times before had been nothing but a counterfeit. He was unequivocally beautiful, though his shirt was still stained with blood and his usually perfectly styled, slicked-back hair was wet and disheveled, and Iris knew without doubt the beauty she saw in him now was no mask, no disguise. It came from a place far more profound than the superficial. She had recognized it in him before, of course, but it was much more apparent to her now, and it was apparent in a new and different way. As she looked at him in this moment, she saw not the glorious seraph of her visions, but a genteel and dignified man whose gloriousness was both limited by and increased in his physical body. For a passing instant, she was nearly overcome by attraction, and she wished Loomis had become truly human. It was only with a strong force of will that she cast the thought away almost as quickly as it had come to her. She loved Loomis; she could admit that without shame, because it was a pure and good emotion. It would be shameful, though, if she were to develop romantic feelings for the fallen angel. She had been tasked with directing him toward God; the last thing either of them needed was for the scandalous whim of her imagination to subvert them.

Blinking away her suddenly starry vision and mentally grounding her thoughts, Iris finally said, rather timidly, "I'm...really glad you're doing this." The statement was true, and heartfelt, but to her own ears, it sounded inappropriately simple for the occasion, like she was standing face to face with Michelangelo or da Vinci and telling him his art was "okay." She hoped Loomis wouldn't find the comment so offensively understated.

He took no offense and instead turned toward her with a subtle smile. "As am I," he replied softly. He looked at her momentarily before his eyes quickly darted away, and he sat in thoughtful reticence for a short time before speaking again, hesitantly. "I..." He fell silent again, faltering with uncharacteristic diffidence. His uncertain stumbling for words made Iris uneasy, and her mind ran amok with indecision as she wondered what she should say or do, if anything at all. She didn't want to appear uncaring, but neither did she want to seem like an overbearing proponent of conversation, especially when the conversation might be a difficult one. She wasn't the type to bare her feelings to others, and she had a sure sense that Loomis, though he was new to the human experience of emotion, would be much like her in that regard. So she decided to remain still and quiet, calming her own running thoughts instead of trying to prompt Loomis for his. He had already accomplished much more challenging feats than speaking honestly; he would continue talking when he was ready.

After a long moment, he gently cleared his throat and said, "I'm afraid, Iris."

It took no more than that unassuming acknowledgment of susceptibility to bring tears to her eyes. She closed them and forced away the visible display of emotion, then asked, "Why?"

He looked at her again, his eyes their usual amber-studded, chocolatey brown, but now full of a depth and inner light that had not been there before. With a sigh, he said, "I don't know that I can handle this."

"If you couldn't," Iris responded, "God wouldn't have handed it to you."

Loomis clenched his jaw and stared out over the river, shaking his head vaguely. "A demon doesn't deserve forgiveness like what has been offered to me," he said tightly. "A demon doesn't deserve a chance to return to Heaven. Do you not think God might set for me an impossible task, only to remind me how weak and undeserving I am?" As he spoke, he was absentmindedly scratching the toe of his pricey Italian oxford across the wet surface of the stone, and a tiny piece of the water-worn rock flaked off. He kicked it idly into the stream as he awaited Iris's reply.

"It isn't impossible," she returned, "and you're not weak. As for undeserving...well, I think that technically applies to all of us." She paused and tucked a group of dampened bangs behind her ear, then added, "I think you know all of this already. You didn't seem to have quite so negative an outlook earlier. What changed?"

Loomis ran his hand through his thick hair, unwittingly leaving it a charmingly tousled mess. After a heavy sigh, he answered. "I've been using this body for a very long time," he explained slowly, "and it has had its...complications. Occasionally, I would realize my spirit was being affected by the perception of the human mind I had contrived. I would, for lack of any better description, feel too human, and I hated it." He went quiet for a moment, inwardly reflecting on his words as Iris watched him sympathetically. "I would leave the body for a short time," he finally continued, "and everything would return to normal for another several decades. But...I can't do that now. I can't run away from feeling human, and that scares me."

"Sometimes humans hate feeling human, too," Iris told him. "At least, I know I do. But it should be some comfort to know you're not alone in that."

Loomis briefly considered her words, his dark, well-manicured eyebrows pressed into a thoughtful look of concentration. "The sensations of weakness and limitation," he said, "I can endure. But...I've spent ages manipulating humankind, preying on their myriad emotions. I've seen how they can react; I've witnessed the terrible things they say and do to one another when they succumb to their passions. What will prevent me from resorting to the same base instincts? You heard what Auraltiferys said—I will not be preserved from the works of the Devil or those who follow him. They will come after me, Iris. They will torment me just as I've tormented the human race, and they won't stop until they've dragged me right back into sin and damnation." He braced his elbows on his thighs and raised his hands toward his face, roughly massaging his temples before resting his head there against his fingertips.

"They can't drag you anywhere," Iris replied confidently. The tension overhanging the beginning of the conversation had broken, and she suddenly felt completely assured in her words. "You're stronger than they are. You always have been. And for a long time, you believed it, too, so don't dismiss yourself now."

"If I had been as strong as you believe," Loomis challenged glumly, "I wouldn't have spent a near-eternity in Hell. I fear you're mistaking my magniloquent arrogance for actual strength."

"Hardly," Iris retorted. "What other demon has done what you've done? I've seen you stand up to Satan; I've seen the insecurity you've caused him. He had you blind, once, but you have your sight back now, and you should recognize you're strong enough to defeat him."

"I do appreciate your confidence in me," Loomis answered quietly, after a long hesitation. "But the truth will always be that he tricked me once and can trick me again. And if I sin because of it, you will pay a price, too." He removed his hands from his face and draped his arms across his lap, leaning on his forearms. "That might be what scares me most of all," he added, not looking at Iris.

Iris was silent for a moment as she reminisced on her relatively short acquaintance with Loomis. He had spent much of it trying to coerce her or tempt her into sin; he had spent some of it trying to shoo her away from Hell, to serve his own purposes. But now, here he was, genuinely afraid of sin and perhaps even more genuinely afraid of the effect his sins would now have on her. She had seen fleeting glimpses of that caring quality in him before, but now it seemed a permanent and unmistakable fixture of his character. She couldn't help but smile at him, despite his current defeatist attitude.

"I've accepted that price," she replied to him gently. "I'm willing to pay it if I have to, so don't worry about that." She repositioned herself on the hard rock, bringing her legs up and crossing them in front of her. "Besides," she continued cheerfully, "not all the tricks and temptations of demons are successful. I should know." Though he wasn't facing her directly, Iris saw a tiny, understanding smirk pass across Loomis's face before guilt quickly replaced the momentarily lightened expression. He stared at the water and said nothing.

"Anyway," she concluded, "my point is, you make all your own choices, and no demon can force you into anything. You know right and wrong; you have wisdom and good judgment and self-control. You've always been strong and focused and driven, and now your goal is a righteous one. All you have to do is focus on your goal—

focus on God, and He will strengthen you all the more. You'll never be left alone to fight Satan or his minions." She sighed and rose to her feet, stretching her back under the cool drizzle and the pleasant, waning sun. "And, for what it's worth," she added, "I'll be here, too, to help you however I can."

Loomis nodded slowly. "I don't wish to be a burden to you," he said, "but...I will be eternally grateful for your help." There was humble sincerity in his tone, and Iris narrowly avoided an outpouring of tears at the comment.

She composed herself in a momentary silence, hoping Loomis understood she would do practically anything for him without considering it a burden at all. *He must know it by now*, she thought to herself. "Come on," she finally said, her tone light and jovial. "Auri's making dinner, and, honestly, I'm starving."

Loomis breathed deeply, then stood and nimbly stepped up to the rock where Iris was already standing. He ran his hands over his hair, slicking it back, adjusted his tie and vest, then looked deprecatingly at the bloodstains remaining on his shirt after his body's victimization by the blacksmith's knife. With a pointed glance at the slashed fabric and dried blood on Iris's shirt, the marks of the same blade, he commented, "We hardly look presentable for dinner."

Iris looked down at her shirt, still torn and crusted in crimson-brown from the fatal stab wound that had sent her to Hell, and sheepishly agreed. "Yeah," she said, drawing the word into a long sigh. "Auri's seen me look worse, I'm pretty sure, but..." Before she finished her sentence, Loomis had cast a spell that instantly repaired the fabric and removed the stains. She looked back up at him, his shirt, too, now as pristine as his exacting fashion dictated, and she smiled.

"Thanks," she said with a tiny snort. "You know, even after all this, magic is not always my first thought when it comes to solving the simplest problems."

Loomis returned the smile, and though she knew he hadn't intended such an effect, Iris went almost weak in the knees from the sheer handsomeness of it. He had smiled at her before—many times, in fact—but he had never looked like this. There had always been a sinister element to it, a subtle, inconspicuous hint that his motives warranted mistrust. Though undeniably attractive, all those smiles had been faked, intended to charm or tempt or otherwise manipulate their recipients. Now, though, the expression was softer—genuine and unforced and *real*—and it brought a captivating glow to his face and a remarkable light to his eyes. Iris couldn't deny it—as alluring as Loomis had been as an evil spirit behind a good-looking mask, he was far more exquisite now. Goodness, and perhaps the experience of human emotion, suited him well.

"I'm gladdened to know I can still use magic," he replied to her, his voice breaking the transitory enchantment that had nearly overcome her. "I had wondered if my powers might be...inhibited."

"Why would they be?" Iris asked brightly as they turned and headed side by side to the house. "You're still you, Loomis. A human body hasn't limited your magic before."

"True," he acknowledged, "but I must admit to feeling a bit...constrained now. It was different before."

"I think I can relate," Iris suggested. "After I returned from my...temporary damnation, I felt insignificant and powerless. But, for me, the feeling lasted only a little while, and truthfully, I wouldn't *want* that unbridled strength I felt in Hell to become my new normal. There's comfort in limitation. It reminds me to rely on God more than I rely on myself." Watching her footsteps as she and Loomis continued along the winding path from the river to the house, she added, "You'll get used to the feeling. And, if it means anything to you, I'll never believe you're anything but powerful."

They walked for several more yards before Loomis replied. "I hope I will not disappoint you," he said quietly.

"I should say the same to you," she answered. "You suffered much to get here, and your purification is only beginning." She sighed, then continued, shyly and hesitantly, "I want nothing more than for you to be welcomed back into Heaven. I hope I can provide the help you need, if you do need help at all."

"Your help is the only reason I stand here now," Loomis asserted, gratitude in his voice. After a pause, he added, "And thank you for the pep talk. I don't intend to make a habit of needing that, but...I do appreciate it."

With a smile, Iris replied lightly, "I'm not usually known for my 'pep,' but, for you, I'll make an effort to dig it out when needed. If it helped, I'm glad." She thought for a moment, then said further, with complete sincerity but also a bit of timidity, "I'm...happy you're willing to speak candidly with me. I know emotions aren't the easiest conversation topic, but...I hope you won't hesitate to talk to me whenever you feel like you need to." She felt Loomis nod almost invisibly beside her.

They continued in silence until they reached the clearing directly in front of the blacksmith's abode. Loomis paused, not far from where his body had met its demise less than a full day before. Iris stopped and held his gaze for a moment, folding her arms. The sun was beginning to set, and the air and drizzle felt much cooler now.

"Hard to believe we were both dead about eighteen hours ago," she mused.

"Indeed," Loomis agreed, his eyes drifting away from Iris's and staring into the distance. "I realize I don't deserve it, but...I am grateful to be alive."

"Me, too," Iris seconded. She waited for a few seconds as Loomis remained lost in contemplation, then asked gingerly, "Did you want to be alone? Do you need more time?"

Loomis roused himself from his thoughts. "No, no," he said. "You're starving, and, admittedly, I'm finding myself rather peckish as well." He grinned slightly, then added thoughtfully, "I suppose I should take better care of this body now that it's...permanent. I used to maintain it more with magic than with actual sustenance."

Iris nodded and smiled. "Well, come on, then," she beckoned. "I get grouchy when I don't eat."

She uncrossed her arms and proceeded across the clearing and up the steps of the porch, with Loomis right behind her. He stepped in front of her as they neared the door so that he could open and hold it for her. She thanked him and entered, the welcoming warmth of the fire in the den quickly chasing away the chill of her rain-soaked hair and clothing. Loomis followed hesitantly and quietly closed the door behind him, a slight air of discomfort falling over him. Iris felt sympathetically awkward, too, as she recalled the bad blood that existed between Loomis and the blacksmith. She felt completely comfortable with her mentor, and she felt mostly comfortable with Loomis now, but she knew neither of them was particularly comfortable with the other. She worried it might be a tense ambience at the dinner table.

Auraltiferys greeted them from the doorway of the kitchen, his cool, steely presence commanding the room but not eclipsing the natural warmth of his gentle and caring heart. A faint smile appeared on his lips as he looked at Iris and then nodded brusquely toward Loomis, and she felt her worries about an uncomfortable dinner largely quelled. He might not believe Loomis deserved a second chance at Heaven, but he wasn't going to argue with it. Even if he didn't like Loomis or couldn't personally forgive him, Auraltiferys was going to be as accepting and helpful as he could be.

"Dinner is ready," he announced, "if you're both ready to eat."

"My stomach is eating itself," Iris joked, though she wondered if it was really all that much of an exaggeration. Auraltiferys rolled his eyes and smirked, waving her and Loomis toward the dining table, where he had already set places for each of them. In the table's center sat a large pot of steaming and wonderfully aromatic stew and a bowl full of crusty, wheat-colored rolls, their tops speckled with a mélange of tiny oats and seeds. Iris headed for her usual chair, eager for the feast to begin.

From behind her, she heard the blacksmith address Loomis, causing her to turn in curiosity. "How are you holding up, Drake?" he asked quietly, his eyes adazzle with their typical impossible keenness. The question wasn't a pretense; he genuinely wanted to know.

Loomis humbly inclined his head, then met the blacksmith's gaze, begrudgingly but dutifully, like a well-mannered child eating his vegetables in submission to a parent's demand. "I'm doing well," he answered tensely. "Apprehensive, perhaps, but...ready for what lies ahead." Iris was surprised by the relative openness of his response, and she was heartened by both Loomis's candor and her mentor's honest concern for him.

With as near an approving look as he could give him, Auraltiferys nodded at Loomis and motioned for him to take a seat at the table. He seated himself to Iris's left, leaving the blacksmith to take his usual chair on her right. Following Auraltiferys's lead, they all bowed their heads as he blessed the food, then Iris waited for a decorous second or two before grabbing the serving ladle from the stew. She respectfully filled her companions' bowls before serving herself, but then she hungrily started in on her meal.

"Thank you for dinner, Auraltiferys," Loomis said, meekly helping himself to one of the rolls. "Thank you both, in fact, for...everything." His voice was taut with formality, but genuine.

"The thanks goes to God," Auraltiferys answered coolly, "but we are both glad to help you as we can."

Iris swallowed a painfully large bite of bread and agreed, adding, "We're both glad you've chosen this." She saw Loomis's eyes dart toward the blacksmith with skepticism in the brief pause that followed her statement, and she felt immediately compelled to address it. "Listen, I know you two have your history," she stated bluntly, "but Auri knows how God loves all His creation, and whenever there is a chance for the lost to find their way home, he wants them to succeed in their return, because of his great love for their Creator." She took a sip from her water glass, catching a rather surprised but concurring glance from her mentor, then she continued, more cheerfully, "Besides, humble service is kind of his job, and I'm pretty sure he enjoys it. I've only followed his lead to get here, and maybe one day, by God's help, I'll be half as charitable and wise as he is. But we're both here for you now, and, personally, I couldn't be happier to be here with the two of you, and I couldn't be happier for the opportunity you've accepted, Loomis."

Loomis stared at her for a moment, appearing both bemused and touched by her words. He finally smiled, seemingly at a loss for any verbal reply. Iris returned the smile and nodded understandingly, and Loomis slowly turned his attention back toward his dinner.

"You may take rather naturally to the spiritual advisor role, Iris," Auraltiferys commented, a small, proud grin on his face as he addressed her.

"She already has," Loomis concurred, taking a delicate bite of stew.

Iris felt her cheeks warm with the sudden attention. "Well, maybe," she faltered. "I'm...just trying to do my best." She suddenly understood how Loomis must feel—she felt almost as undeserving of this current praise as he felt of his opportunity to be purified and return to Heaven. "Actually," she clarified, "that credit is really yours, Auri. I wouldn't make much of an advisor at all if you weren't such an outstanding mentor."

Loomis genteelly dabbed at the corners of his mouth with his napkin, then, to Iris's astonishment, said, "She is probably correct about that, Auraltiferys. I admit, under my demonic motivations, I was most displeased when I confirmed my suspicions that she had been led to you."

Auraltiferys sat as rigidly as stone, but for the glacial stare that seemed to shoot like daggers from his eyes. Loomis sat with equally perfect, unmoving posture, meeting the blacksmith's sharp gaze with a resolved and guileless look of fortitude. Iris blinked her eyes back and forth from one to the other, acutely anxious about whatever strange sizing-up seemed to be going on right in front of her. She believed Loomis had meant the statement as a genuine compliment to the blacksmith—an extending of an olive branch, as it were. But...she wasn't sure if perhaps her mentor had taken it to have some other meaning; he appeared to be searching Loomis most thoroughly for any hint of artifice, and it was uncomfortable to watch. Loomis, however, intrepidly endured the unspoken, internal interrogation without a trace of angst.

Only a few seconds passed, but they felt to Iris like an eon. Finally, Auraltiferys broke the silence. "God has intertwined our paths with very specific purpose, and we have all been blessed by this, even through the pain we've all suffered," he stated objectively. "In retrospect, I see the perfection of His plan. I never dreamed of a scenario such as this, but..." He sighed, gently cleared his throat, then softened and concluded, "Drake, you have not been left alone to complete your journey, and I see you are appropriately grateful for that. I see you recognize the presence of God in Iris and in me, and that gives me great hope for you."

The two nodded once in understanding to each other, then continued eating. Iris, stunned but encouraged by the mysterious armistice that seemed to have just been reached, delightedly tore off another piece of her roll and stuffed it into her mouth. After chasing it with a spoonful of stew, she asked optimistically, "Now that we're all in agreement we're on the same team, we can cut out the stuffy formalities, right? We can all just talk like friends?"

"Formality is sometimes warranted, Iris," Auraltiferys chided.

"I know that," she retorted with good-humored exasperation, "but can't we simply *celebrate* right now? It's dinner, not an inquisition!"

Auraltiferys raised an eyebrow at her, but it wasn't long before a radiant smile lit up his face. Loomis, meanwhile, had watched their brief exchange with real amusement and actually laughed at the end of it. It was a deep and refined, almost musical sound, expressive of authentic mirth—something the demonically inclined Loomis Drake had never exhibited—and hearing it made Iris immeasurably happy.

With the tension between Loomis and Auraltiferys somewhat eased, Iris found their company remarkably pleasant. As dinner went on, the conversation became slightly less formal and somewhat more friendly, though Loomis maintained an evident guardedness for much of it, the charismatic and cocksure demeanor of his former worldly persona notably subdued and far less confident after his humbling experience. Iris remained aware of a certain stiffness in Auraltiferys, too, but he didn't allow it to be too apparent. He was making a supreme effort to let go of the wrongs that had been done to him on the mountain long ago, and, while she understood it would take him a long time to trust Loomis fully, assuming he ever could, it gave her a firm hope that the two of them would get along fine in this arrangement.

After their meal, they moved to the den for tea, where the discussion became a more serious deliberation about what would happen after Iris and Loomis left the mountain and returned to "normal" life. Even that, however, was relatively agreeable. Loomis was nervous about the return, and Iris admitted some anxiety herself, but Auraltiferys was, as always, a calming presence and a wise guide, and his sound and faithful reasoning made the road ahead seem far more navigable than Iris had first imagined. Nothing would be easy, but neither would anything be impossible.

Evening had faded into night, and the trio had convened in the chapel for prayer before bedtime. Iris had nearly cried at the sight of Loomis kneeling before the tabernacle, lowering himself before the presence of Christ, the Word made flesh, the Savior and Redeemer of the race he had so long victimized. Her eyes saw a human man bowed in prayer, but her heart recognized a fallen angel humbly placing himself once more under the divine hand of his Master, asking for mercy and acknowledging the debt he had been asked to repay. Even in his humility, though, he had the bearing of bravery, of loyalty—like a knight scolded for insubordination and now willing to do anything to reinstate his office. She imagined him in seraph form, kneeling, as her obscure, white-light mental rendering of God reached out and conferred on him, again, the honor of service to the one true crown. She hoped, and truly believed, one day the scene would play out in the reality of Heaven.

Now, back at the house, Iris was in the bedroom she always used, perched on the side of the bed and tugging off her boots as she reflected on the first night she had spent here on the mountain and on everything that had transpired since, culminating in the incredible events of the past day's worth of earthly time—events that, she realized, marked only the beginning of a new and important journey. Her first trip to the mountain had set her on a path she had never imagined, one that had seemed impossible and terrifying. She had stumbled along it, and she and others had suffered for it, but God had mercifully transformed every mistake, every sin, every pain into seeds of goodness that would continue to grow under His loving care. And, in His infinite love and forgiveness, He had opened a way by which even a spirit once thought damned could return to Him. As Iris considered the magnificence of it all, she felt her own role in the plan had been only a tiny one. Nothing in her own power could have crafted such an amazing tale, yet here she was, small and insignificant right in the midst of it, serving a purpose she never would have guessed.

She leaned back onto the pillow, lying on top of the bedspread, her mind so engrossed in contemplation of the incomprehensible mastery of the universe's Creator that she hardly recognized what she was doing. Her body was tired, but she didn't really want to sleep, and her mind felt very awake. Her reflections drifted to something Loomis had said earlier in the evening, comparing her to his original human ward. As she, the woman created by God, had been tempted by the Devil and had thus brought sin into the world and upon humanity, Iris, a failed creation of Satan and adopted by God, had remained faithful to righteousness and had thus brought mercy and virtue into Hell—*the Devil's Eve*, Auraltiferys had suggested after listening to Loomis's musings. Iris had been embarrassed by the comparison, because she felt far less important in the grand scheme than such a title would imply she had been. The more she reflected, however, the more she could perhaps see the aptness of the moniker, and she had to admit she felt rather flattered by it, humbling though it was.

A light rap on the doorframe startled her out of her thoughts. By the dim, warm light of the magical bedside lamp, she saw Loomis standing in the open doorway, looking drawn and exhausted and a bit timid, as though he weren't sure he should bother her right now.

"I saw your light was still on," he explained in his quiet, smooth baritone, leaning one shoulder against the doorframe as he folded his arms across his ribs. "I wouldn't disturb you otherwise. I take it you're still awake?"

Iris smiled reflexively at the gentleness in his gaze. She rolled off the bed and met him near the door. "Yes, I'm awake," she answered, realizing she had to stifle a yawn as she spoke. She stood a step away from Loomis and similarly crossed her arms. "What's up?"

He looked pensively at his shoes and then straightened, easing his shoulder off the wood. He breathed deeply, then said, "I know you've asked me to dispense with the formal announcements of gratitude, but there is yet something I would like to say."

"Loomis, you've already thanked me," she replied with a dismissive snicker, "and even that wasn't necessary."

"Not necessary for you, perhaps," he retorted, gently but unwaveringly, "but it feels quite necessary to me."

Iris searched his eyes for an instant, finding bright sincerity and a certain earnestness in them. She gave him a tiny smile and an understanding nod and waited silently for him to continue.

He sighed, then spoke with quiet resolve. "Iris, if not for you," he said, "I would have spent an eternity trying to ruin what God had created, and even success would have brought me nothing but emptiness. I don't know how you recognized anything worthwhile left in me, but I'm fortunate that you did. You saw in me what I could no longer see, or no longer wanted to see, in myself. You appealed to me, and then you led me by your example. Whatever happens after we leave here, you rescued me from Hell, and you have forever changed me."

Iris felt tears preparing to fill her eyes. She sniffled lightly and replied, as breezily as she could, "It was all God's doing, really. I'm only a tool in His hand."

"That is true," Loomis acknowledged, his eyes staring at her with keenness only a few shades less piercing than the blacksmith's, "but God never forced you. It is by your willingness to serve Him that I stand here now, with the hope of complete redemption. And so it is right for me to be grateful to you for all you've done, and to be grateful to God for having worked through you to save me.

You needn't minimize the part you've played in the miracles He has wrought."

Iris sniffled again and then chuckled deprecatingly at her own emotionality as she brushed tears away from her face. "I'm happy to have been a part of this," she answered gratefully, "and I'm happy to still have a part in it." After a final sniffle and a deep breath, she said, more jocularly, "Now, please, Loomis, no more heartrending, formal thank-you's. I swear I've cried more in the months I've known you than I have in the entire decade before, and I don't want to start looking weak."

Loomis studied her gaze for a passing moment, seeming to assure himself that she had understood the depth of his gratitude, then he smiled. "Of course," he replied cordially. "Though I think we both know human emotions are not weakness."

Iris cleared her throat. "Right," she stated in more serious agreement.

After a lengthy pause, Loomis turned halfway as though to leave for his own room, then he hesitated and faced Iris again. "I don't know what awaits us off this mountain," he practically whispered, "but I am glad I won't face it without you."

Iris was overcome by the sentimentality in the simple statement. She expected such occasions of bared feeling would be fewer and farther between once Loomis adjusted to earthly existence with human emotion, and she herself would feel less inclined toward physical manifestations of sentiment. For now, though, she could no longer refrain from an outward display of affection. She stepped over to Loomis and wrapped her arms around his shoulders, squeezing gently as she pressed her cheek against his. He tensed at first, momentarily unsure how to react, but then he relaxed slightly and encircled her delicately with his arms, returning the friendly embrace. After several seconds, Iris eased away, smiled rather wistfully, and bade him a good night. He responded in kind, then departed down the dark hallway to his room.

Iris quietly closed her door and then climbed into bed, drawing the sheets and quilt over her as she extinguished the magical light. Silver starlight trickled through the sheer curtain covering the window above her head, and she smiled to herself in the dimness. She had a feeling Auraltiferys would be in the forge shortly after dawn had broken, working away on some fine relic Loomis might need on the road ahead. Then there would be breakfast, and prayer, and conversation, and eventually she and Loomis would return to the realm of the fallen Earth, where the miracles of God were perhaps more veiled, but no less remarkable. She buried her face into the pillow and closed her eyes, thanking God once more and asking for His unfailing help as she and Loomis would follow Him, together. Though the immediate future was yet unknown, she was uncharacteristically excited for it. Whatever hardship would befall her along the way, whatever tribulations Loomis would have to face as part of his purification, she believed the ultimate ending of their stories would be even more beautiful than this beginning had been, and it filled her heart with peace.

36

The musical tinkling of a little brass bell hanging from the top of the door announced Detective Crane's arrival at the diner as he entered, his eyes scanning the small establishment for his partner as he let the pleasantly warm air and the smell of bacon welcome him out of the cold. This was one of those locally owned, old-fashioned, seat-yourself eateries, with worn red vinyl-clad dining booths and chairs; tables lined with red-and-white-checkered vinyl tablecloths, each one dotted with bright red and yellow ketchup and mustard squirt bottles; and waitstaff who wore white aprons and tiny plastic nametags. Toward the back was a dining counter with red-cushioned metal barstools, beyond which were a series of coffee makers, a soda fountain, and a clear view of the expansive grill where most of the real magic happened. Crane had sat many, many times at that counter, drinking coffee and, unfortunately, adding to his seemingly ever-increasing waistline, and he had often wondered whether he looked like the stereotypical cop-in-a-diner one could find in any number of movies. Frankly, though, he didn't care if he did—this was the only place in town that really nailed the art of breakfast foods, and besides that, they served an apple pie à la mode that could salvage even the worst of days.

He caught sight of Banks sitting in one of the booths lining the walls, grinning and needlessly waving a hand in greeting. Crane had been, guiltily, rather nervous about meeting Banks here today, but seeing his partner with at least a small smile on his face made him feel much, much better about things. After the encounter with Marvin Whitakker in the museum basement had gone south (way, way south), Banks had been put on administrative leave at the behest of the department psychologist, and Banks hadn't even tried to argue it. Only bits and pieces of the actual truth had come out in the final reports—and, somehow, everyone had seemed to accept the "official story" without question—but Banks had awoken in the hospital with a splitting headache and a fragmented and vague but terrifying recollection of what had happened to him, and it was clear he needed some time to cope. There were perhaps a few officers who wondered what could possibly have been so traumatic about a minor run-in with a frumpy academic in a cellar, but, thankfully, almost everyone treated Banks's absence in one of two ways: either with lukewarm, general human concern, or with complete indifference because it wasn't their problem. It was good no one was asking any probing questions.

 Crane plopped heavily into the seat opposite Banks and scooted toward the center of the table. "How you doing?" he asked as he wriggled out of his jacket. His voice sounded gruff to his own ears, though his intent had been to make it sound like this was just another normal day. He hoped Banks wouldn't mistake the slight discomfort in his tone as grumpiness.

 To his great relief, Banks chuckled. "I've been out more than a week, and that's the best greeting you can muster for me?" he joked, prompting a good-natured eye roll from Crane. "For real, though," he continued, more seriously, "I'm doing much better." He nodded, as if to prove the validity of his own statement.

 "That's good," Crane replied, suddenly nervous again. He wasn't sure how much Banks might have remembered by now, or how he must be processing it all. His partner *seemed* normal...but could anyone really be normal after something like...that?

A thin, college-aged waitress with a jet-black pixie cut (streaked in the front with neon pink) and a full sleeve of colorful tattoos approached their table, two empty cups in one hand and a carafe of hot coffee in the other. "Detectives," she addressed them blithely, giving a mock salute after she placed the cups down and filled both. "It's been a while! You want your usuals?" Both detectives gave affirmative responses, and the young woman flashed them both a friendly smile before striding purposefully back into the kitchen.

Crane took a swig of coffee, draining practically half the cup, then looked at Banks uncertainly. "So," he said slowly, hesitancy leaving a question mark hanging at the end of his pathetic attempt at making conversation.

Banks took a less animalistic sip of his coffee and set the cup back down with a small sigh. "I'm still me, Crane," he chided. "I'm still your partner. You don't have to wear the kid gloves, man. Seriously, I'm fine."

"Sorry," Crane grunted, shifting in his seat. "It's just...you know, after what you went through—"

Banks interrupted with a shrug. "It hasn't been all bad," he said solidly.

"Seriously?" Crane asked in surprise, unthinkingly. "Geez, Banks, do you even...I mean, do you remember what happened?"

"Only parts of it," Banks admitted, "but I remember enough. It was terrible, and I can't explain any of it, and I guess I don't really understand most of it, but...I know it was real and not just some weird-ass nightmare. I didn't really believe much in the spiritual stuff before, but I have definitely woken up now, and that's a good thing."

Crane felt his forehead wrinkling as he appraised his partner, but he relaxed slightly as Banks finished his statement. "Yeah," he agreed, "I'm with you on that one. That whole museum case...it...well, I guess it made me think differently about the spiritual stuff, too."

Banks nodded slowly and commiseratively. "Listen," he said in a low voice, after a long hesitation, "I know this will be tough for you, but..." He trailed off and looked out the window to the cold, gray morning sky and the mist-covered parking lot.

"What is it?" Crane asked, figuring he knew exactly what Banks was about to request of him.

Banks met Crane's gaze and then dropped his eyes to the coffee cup he was mindlessly rotating on top of the table. "Can you maybe tell me the truth?" he asked. "I mean, all of it?"

Crane inhaled deeply and slowly blew the air out through parted lips. He had wondered when this inquiry would come, and he wasn't sure Banks could handle the truth. But he thought back to Iris's words to him, to her assertion that he would be an example to Banks with regard to "the spiritual stuff," and he knew he owed his partner the whole truth. Though his brain might be wondering whether Banks was ready for it, something in his gut told him it was time.

"Sure," Crane finally replied, finishing off his coffee as the waitress returned with their food.

"Two scrambled eggs, bacon, and toast for Crane," she announced giddily, setting a large plate of breakfast perfection in front of the senior detective. "And oatmeal and a dry English muffin for Banks," she finished, placing the bowl before Myron. She then removed a coffee pot from her now otherwise empty tray, slipped the tray under her free arm, and proceeded to refill both cups before ordering the detectives to let her know if they needed anything and then returning to the kitchen.

Crane looked judgmentally at Banks's bowl of oatmeal and snickered. "You come back from a near-death experience," he teased, "and you're still eating that damn oatmeal."

Banks smiled and spooned a big scoop of the stuff onto a muffin half before taking a huge bite. With his mouth full, he replied, "So what if I like oatmeal?"

Crane laughed, genuinely laughed, and he instantly felt completely right about telling Banks everything that had happened. This was, after all, his partner and his friend, and he owed the guy the truth when he asked for it. Plus, now that there was food on the table, the conversation would seem far less awkward.

After taking a bite from a bacon strip and washing it down with coffee, Crane was prepared to give Banks the explanation he had requested, but he soon realized he didn't even know where to begin. In fact, as real as he knew it had all been, thinking back on it now, the whole thing seemed like a crazy dream—and a totally unbelievable one, at that.

"Um," Crane mumbled sheepishly, "where should I start?"

Banks ran a hand over the dark, smooth dome of his head and sighed. "Well," he said, "I *think* I remember some inexplicable, paranormal weirdness going down under the museum when we confronted Whitakker about the stolen spearhead. Start there. And don't leave anything out."

"Right," Crane consented hesitantly, wiping his mouth with his napkin as he gathered his thoughts. *Might as well just go for it*, he told himself. "Well, honestly, I don't know *everything*, but..." He stopped and glanced at Banks, whose unamused expression indicated quite clearly that his partner was sick of knowing only part of the story and tired of waiting for answers. Crane sighed and shook his head, mustering his resolve. "Okay," he continued, his voice sturdier. "Whitakker *had* stolen the spearhead, and he had put it in a personal collection he kept in an old, unused part of the museum's basement. That, uh, 'inexplicable weirdness' you saw...that was something like a portal to Hell that he had opened. He was into some, you know, creepy demonic stuff, I guess, and he had some dark powers because of it."

Across the table, Banks was nodding slowly, stirring his oatmeal thoughtlessly as he listened. "I remember we were in trouble," he said quietly. "That girl showed up—the one who had met with you at the station."

"Yeah," Crane confirmed. "Iris Wakefield. She...well, listen, this is where things get even more unbelievable."

"Come on, brother," Banks pleaded, his voice rife with exasperation. "Just spit it out!"

"Fine," Crane begrudgingly acquiesced. "She had told me Whitakker had taken the spearhead and hidden it away below the museum. She warned me to stay away from him and to keep you away from him. She knew he could be dangerous."

"How'd she know that?" Banks interjected. "She some kind of occultist, too?"

Crane massaged his forehead briefly, finished his second cup of coffee, then answered, "Not...exactly. She's...the Devil."

Banks released his spoon, leaving its handle creeping slowly through the viscous oats toward the edge of the bowl, and he straightened up in his seat. He raised one hand toward his jaw and rubbed it thoughtfully. "You're not...I mean, that's...a metaphor or something, right?" he asked.

"I don't think so," Crane replied. "She says she was supposed to be, like, the incarnate Satan, but then God gave her a human soul, and so she's actually human and the Devil at the same time."

Banks stared blankly at Crane, logic and gut-feeling clearly battling for control of his wits. Crane ate a bit of toast before proceeding. "I saw her *melt* a pair of handcuffs, man," he recalled. "And she knew things about me that..." He paused, cleared his throat of its sudden upwelling of emotion, and shook his head. "She knew things about my past that I've never told anyone. Things that happened more than thirty years ago. Things she couldn't possibly know if not for some kind of supernatural power. I know it sounds insane, but...I believe her."

Banks blinked several times, then repositioned himself on his seat and took another bite of his English muffin, seemingly lost in thought as he chewed. After a moment, he roused himself and spoke. "But she *helped* us, didn't she?" he asked. "She was arguing with Whitakker, and trying to get us out of there."

"I'm pretty sure we'd both be dead, or worse, if she hadn't shown up," Crane acknowledged as he piled scrambled eggs on top of his remaining toast.

"If she's, uh, the Devil," Banks argued, "why would she have done that?"

Crane swallowed his food and shrugged. "I don't get it, either, really," he admitted. "She...has Satan's powers, but she's not evil. She's not THE Devil...she's, I don't know...a separate and better version of him. Honestly, she even convinced me to get back to church. And I mean real church, not some twisted, Devil-worshiping cult."

Banks's eyes narrowed, more in thoughtful consideration than in suspicion, though there was a touch of disbelief in his face. "That's...crazy," he said at length.

"Sure is," Crane agreed. "But that's not the craziest thing."

Banks lifted an eyebrow but said nothing. Crane thought his partner was starting to look a bit drained, but there was still an urgent, pleading expression in his eyes that he couldn't simply ignore. All the insanity was taxing, sure, but only the truth would really help Banks recover from what had happened to him.

"The portal in the museum cellar opened again after Iris showed up," Crane explained, getting back to the story. He knew this part would be difficult for him to tell. "I don't know if you remember. Something came out—something from Hell. I...I don't know what it was, but it was definitely evil and definitely *not* human. It...attacked you."

"I don't remember," Banks said quietly, his voice barely more than a whisper.

"Banks," Crane continued slowly, watching for Myron's reaction, "it *killed* you."

"That's...impossible," Banks stated weakly, sounding completely unconvinced of his own words.

"I saw it," Crane argued, shaking his head. "That damned thing passed right through you, and you were *gone*." Focusing on keeping tears from drowning his eyes, he set down his fork and rubbed his eyelids with a heavy hand, not wanting to have this scene replaying in his head. He remembered kneeling by his dead partner and desperately praying for him, and he remembered how sick and scared he had felt the entire time. *It's over*, he reminded himself. *He's alive now; he's okay.*

He looked back at Banks, knowing his own eyes were probably red now. Banks met his gaze and held it for what felt like a long time before finally nodding once, firmly. It was a simple gesture that said, *I believe you.*

"Anyway," Crane sighed, leaning against the cushioned back of the booth, "Iris brought you back. She saved you."

Myron's forehead creased. "Brought me 'back'?" he asked. "Back from where?"

"Back from Hell," Crane replied hoarsely.

A panicked expression crossed Banks's face, and for a moment, Crane feared his partner might have some sort of anxiety attack. Soon, though, Banks's racing thoughts seemed to settle, and he took a deep breath as he massaged the back of his neck. "So...it wasn't a nightmare, then," he said. "I...I was really in Hell."

"You were," Crane confirmed. "That shadow-monster thing stole your soul, and Iris went to Hell to bring it back."

Banks shifted in the booth and had started to say something when a peppy voice from beside their table asked, "More coffee?"

Both detectives were visibly startled, and the waitress giggled as she refilled their cups. "Geez, jumpy much?" she ribbed. "Maybe I should bring the decaf next time!"

Crane managed an embarrassed grin as he thanked the waitress, who smiled and saluted again before trotting off. Banks waited for her to leave, then chuckled. "I guess this stuff *has* rattled us a little, hasn't it?" he asked.

"With good reason!" Crane added defensively. "For you especially! How are you dealing with all this? You didn't even know what had happened to you."

Banks grabbed his fresh coffee and reclined into the booth, thinking. "I didn't know what had *really* happened," he concurred, "but I knew I wasn't crazy, either. I knew I had lost consciousness, and I thought maybe some of the awful things I had seen were just hallucinations or subconscious nightmares or something. I could deal with that. But when I woke up in the hospital...I remembered how I had felt this horrible dread, like complete hopelessness, total darkness...and I just sensed in my gut that there was more to the real story. I guess I understand it now."

"Have you...told anyone?" Crane asked, as gently as he could. "I know you talked to the department psychologist, but...what about Cora?" Crane had given his partner's wife as little detail as he reasonably could, and he had a feeling she had accepted the meager explanation more because she wanted to focus on gratitude for her husband's survival than because she actually believed the story.

Banks shook his head. "Dr. Mays is a decent guy," he said, "and maybe he's a great psychologist, but you know how that goes. He thinks there was an unfortunate row in a dark, moldy basement full of scary-looking museum exhibits, and I got knocked out, and it somehow triggered a series of stress-induced nightmares. I know it's more than that." He paused and sighed, staring into his coffee cup as he swirled it. "Anyway," he continued, "Cora was worried, obviously, but I gave her just the necessary details and convinced her I'd be fine. I asked her to take the girls to her sister's place for a while so I could have some time to myself to process everything." He grinned and added, "They were actually really excited to stay with their cousins for a couple of weeks."

Crane smiled. "I bet," he replied. "But...Myron, are you ever going to tell Cora the truth?"

"The whole truth?" Banks asked. "That I was killed and my soul was trapped in Hell until a human-devil-lady rescued me? No, Crane, I think I'll keep that to myself."

Crane scratched his head. "Probably for the best," he admitted. He opened his mouth to say something more but then thought better of it. As he had explained to Iris, he had never known Banks to be the religious type, and he wasn't sure he was ready to kick off that kind of conversation with his partner just yet. Instead, he concluded by saying, "If there's anything I can do to help—"

"Just pray for me," Banks responded, smirking at the surprised look on Crane's face when he said it. "I know that sounds strange coming from me," he went on, "but...that experience changed me. When I woke up and I knew I was alive, everything felt completely different, like there was hope and happiness in this world that I had never known was there, or at least had never paid attention to. I have a lot to learn, but...now I *know* there are powers way beyond ours, and if there's a Hell, there must be a Heaven, too. I think I'm a pretty good dude, but I've never been the spiritual type. I think it's time I change that. I want to be sure I'm on the right side when my time...my *real* time...comes."

Crane listened, nodding thoughtfully as the initial shock of his partner's sudden interest in religion wore off. "That's a good thing," he answered, doing his best to sound encouraging. Talking about religion and feelings, especially with his partner, was not something he was used to, and, in all honesty, it made him a tad uncomfortable. But he remembered how Iris had spoken to him, and he knew the difference that had made. If he could make that same kind of difference for his friend now, it was worth a little bit of awkwardness. He cleared his throat again and added, "I know Cora's really religious, and the girls are, too. They'll be glad to have you with them at church. And they'll set a great example."

"They've tried before," Banks confessed, staring dejectedly into his coffee mug. "I wish I hadn't wasted so much time ignoring the truth. Honestly, I'm lucky Cora has put up with me for all this time. She's always been a devout Christian, and I know it hurt her that I really wasn't."

"Hey," Crane said, downing the last of his coffee, "religion doesn't make anyone a good person. That comes from you, from your everyday decisions. You're a good man, and Cora loves you. Your girls love you. And whatever hurt they've had, it's because they want the best for you, and if you start on this path now, they won't even remember the pain that came before. This will make you all stronger."

Banks looked at him with raised eyebrows and a small grin, clearly astonished, and only then did Crane realize how easily the words had come out. "Did you become a priest while I was out?" he joked, though there was a clear note of appreciation in his tone.

Crane snorted. "No," he answered, "but maybe I am trying to, you know, get back in with the Man upstairs."

Banks smiled. "Good for you, man," he said. He rested one arm along the top of the banquette and crossed one ankle over the other knee under the table with a contented sigh. "This is nice," he remarked, the twinkle in his eyes telling Crane another joke was on its way. "We should make a habit of discussing spiritual and emotional things like real men," he finished.

"Oh, shut up," Crane answered jocularly, looking down at the table and shaking his head. They both knew there was a seed of sincerity in Banks's statement, but it still relieved them both to be able to varnish things with a touch of comedy.

"Seriously, though," Banks said after a pause. "Thanks for your support."

"You got it," Crane replied. "Anytime."

The waitress popped over to their table and daintily waved the handwritten check. "Whose turn is it?" she asked.

"It's mine," Crane answered, shifting to dig his wallet out of the pocket of his jeans.

"Cool," she replied, dutifully handing the check to him. Crane accepted the piece of paper, and, as was her custom, the waitress pointed two finger-guns at him and said "Have a nice day" before bouncing off with a wink and a smile.

Both detectives chuckled. "You think she'll ever get tired of that traffic cop joke?" Banks asked.

"Not a chance," Crane answered, fishing bills out of his wallet and folding them under the salt shaker before reaching for his jacket.

"Oh, hey," Banks said, donning his coat while he remained seated. "This might sound weird, but...I feel like I should thank Iris. Send her a card or flowers or something. Would that be...appropriate? I mean...you know, I never officially met her, but...she did save my soul, after all..." He trailed off, waiting for Crane's response.

"Um," Crane faltered, unsure how to answer. The thought hadn't occurred to him, really, except that he had found himself on a couple of occasions since the museum hoping he might run into the young woman again, because he, too, felt like he owed her more thanks than she had received.

He was formulating a reply when he saw Banks's eyes move to a figure approaching their table from behind where Crane was sitting. Before he registered what was happening, a familiar voice said, "You don't have to thank me at all, Detective, but, if it would make you feel better, I wouldn't say no to one of those cookie bouquets. I'm not a huge fan of actual floral arrangements."

Crane looked up just in time to see Iris slipping into the booth beside him, looking much like she had the last time he had seen her—intimidating, but with a marked air of innocence. Her auburn hair was piled on her head in a messy knot, her long bangs parted and tucked behind her ears, framing a soft, heart-shaped face bejeweled with two striking green-gold eyes. She wore a partially open, blue button-up shirt over a black tank top and jeans, with knee-high, black lace-up boots and a black leather jacket. A single black leather glove adorned her right hand, a fashion statement Crane didn't remember having seen on her before.

"Iris?" Crane asked in disbelief.

"In the flesh," she replied, turning to smile at him.

"Whoa," Banks said, folding his arms on the table. "Speak of the Devil."

Crane hurriedly corrected him. "Damn, Banks," he exclaimed in a hushed voice, "she's not the Devil!"

Iris laughed. "Well, I see you've finally gotten the whole story, Detective Banks," she said. "I'm glad. But Detective Crane *is* correct, technically. I'm substantially the same, but I'm not the Devil."

Banks drew back in his seat and cleared his throat. "Well," he said slowly, "it's, uh, good to officially meet you, Iris."

"Likewise," she replied. "It seems you're doing quite well."

"Thanks to you," Banks returned with a sigh. "I wouldn't be here if you hadn't done what you did."

With a tiny, affable shrug, Iris answered, "God saved you, Detective; He just used me to do it. I'm happy I was in the right place at the right time."

Banks stared hard at the young woman for a moment, almost as if he were a desert traveler seeing a mirage. Eventually, he nodded and smiled. "I guess He really does work in mysterious ways, like they say," he commented.

"Indeed, He does," she agreed.

"Why are you here?" Crane asked, still stunned by the girl's sudden appearance.

"Are you not happy to see me?" Iris retorted, raising an eyebrow at him.

"No, I am," Crane answered hastily. "I'm just...surprised, that's all."

Iris grinned. "Well, I'm never too far away," she replied mysteriously. "But, to answer your question more specifically, an associate and I are attending to some business matters and just happened to stop by the diner here for some coffee to go."

"No rest for the wicked?" Banks asked, his eyes sparkling with mischief as Crane groaned.

"You'll have to excuse him," Crane interjected, shooting a look at his partner. "See, he died recently, and I'm not sure his brain is back to full function yet."

"Come on, Crane," Banks laughed. "She knows I'm joking."

"How the hell would you know that?" Crane argued. "You've only just met her!"

Banks's confident grin wavered just a little as he looked from Crane to Iris. "You *do* know I'm joking, right?" he asked her, his usual intimidating-authority voice now clouded with insecurity. He barreled full-speed into his next sentence. "I know we just met," he explained, "but...sorry, I shouldn't have said anything like that. It's just...I know this sounds totally freaky, but...I sort of feel like we've been friends for a long time."

Crane looked at the anxious expression on Banks's face as he addressed Iris, and he didn't mean to do anything that might offend his partner, but he couldn't help but laugh. Luckily, he was able to cover his own mouth before any accidental spittle went flying out from beneath his mustache as he guffawed.

"Nice cover, Banks," he japed. "You know, I've tried to warn you about those smart-ass comments before. If I didn't trust her like I do, I'd say you were in some big damn trouble."

Banks had appeared momentarily taken aback by Crane's laughter, but any embarrassment he felt had quickly been replaced by his own hearty chuckle when Iris had joined in the hilarity herself. He realized she was not offended, and the mirth was probably a welcome relief after the self-consciousness he had felt just a few seconds before. It really did feel damn good to laugh.

"Yeah," Banks retorted sarcastically, grinning. "*I'm* the one with the problematic smart mouth."

"You're both wonderfully entertaining," Iris commented with a smile. "I would love to see you both cast in a movie. Anyway, Detective Crane, don't worry about your partner's jokes made at my expense. Yes, he and I have only just officially met in person, but we've encountered each other before, in a very harrowing place. We should all be thankful he has already recovered enough to laugh like this." Turning to Myron, she continued, "And Detective Banks, do know you haven't offended me. I myself have formed some incredibly profound relationships in a very short time, and I'm attributing it to the deeply spiritual aspect of my recent adventures." After a brief pause, she met the eyes of both detectives in turn and added, more somberly, "I must request that you both keep the details about my...nature...to yourselves, but I am glad you've been able to accept the truth so easily. Especially you, Myron. Of course, even a brief time outside this physical realm is enough to change one's view entirely."

"Sure is," Banks agreed.

Iris drummed her fingers across the tabletop and smiled again. "I do feel a certain kinship with you both," she said, "and I hope you'll not become strangers."

"You ever think about joining the department?" Crane asked,

suddenly inspired. "You'd make one hell of a detective." He hadn't intended the word play, but he grinned at it immediately afterward, in spite of himself.

Iris inclined her head thoughtfully, an amused expression on her face. "You're definitely right about that," she returned genially, "but I'm called elsewhere. If you should ever find yourselves truly in need of my assistance, though, I'm just a call or text away."

"Good to know," Crane answered with a nod.

Iris stood from the booth and lingered by the side of the table, placing one bare hand and one gloved hand into the pockets of her jacket. "Well," she announced, "it has been wonderful seeing you both. I'm happy to see you're staying strong, Banks. And, Crane, I'm happy to see you're stronger than ever." Crane didn't even wonder what she meant by that; he knew. And she was right—he did feel stronger now than he had in a long time.

"I should be on my way," she continued, glancing out the front windows of the restaurant to where a tall man in a long, black coat stood waiting for her, presumably with two cups of coffee, though his back was turned. "My associate and I have some important work to do."

Thoughtful furrows lined Banks's brow as he looked at Iris from his seat. "Why do you do it?" he asked. "With what you are, and the power you must have...why are you out here helping people like us? How is it you're good and not evil?"

With an enigmatic smile, Iris answered, "No one can be made a slave to evil but by one's own choice. My life and power come from God, and to Him I will return them."

Crane felt a strange chill in the back of his neck as she spoke, and he wondered if Banks had any similar sort of reaction to her words. It was an eerie chill, but in a good way—like a sudden, profound sensation of self-awareness that prompted him to take stock of his own life and his own decisions and question whether he was on the right path. He knew he was, especially now, and it was an odd but wonderful feeling.

Iris exited the diner amid the gentle, brassy clattering of the bell on the door, and the detectives watched silently through the window as she approached the man in the coat. He handed her a lidded cup of coffee, then opened the passenger door of a gorgeous black Maserati and closed it behind her before returning to the driver's side and entering the vehicle himself.

"She's...definitely something," Banks stated, his eyes fixated on the car.

"Yup," Crane agreed, raking his memory for the identity of the guy in the coat. He looked familiar, but he couldn't place him. Judging by the car alone, though, the man was loaded. He and Iris remained there in the parking lot, conversing about something.

"I recognize that guy," Banks said. "He was a really big deal a few years back, I think. A business tycoon, or something like that. I remember seeing his face on a magazine cover at the grocery store once. Cora made some comment, like, 'A man shouldn't be that good-looking.' " He raised his voice into a feminine timbre as he quoted his wife, and Crane snorted.

"She's not wrong," he replied. "I guess he's Iris's 'associate' now, whatever that means," he added, feeling a little nagging of doubt in his mind. He couldn't help but wonder what a good Christian demon like Iris would be doing with some rich, handsome celebrity, but he didn't want to doubt her intentions.

"You think Iris is really as good as she seems to be?" Banks asked pointedly, as if reading Crane's thoughts. "You don't think she's out there tricking people into evil, do you?"

"I think she's exactly what she claims to be," Crane answered emphatically. As he spoke the words, he felt even more sure of it.

"I think so, too," Banks agreed, watching as the Maserati pulled out of the parking lot. He sniggered quietly, then remarked, "Why are we questioning this, anyway? Conducting business with a rich dude isn't a sin, after all. She's probably convincing him to donate a bunch of money to the homeless and the hungry."

Crane finally put on his jacket and slid stiffly out of the dining booth. "Probably," he agreed. "Or he's just a step away from Hell and she's trying to save him from eternal damnation."

Banks rose from his seat and stretched his back. "Or maybe they're just an item," he suggested.

Crane rolled his eyes with genuine disgust. "I *really* don't think so," he responded, surprised his partner's remark had irritated him as it did. He realized Iris reminded him in some ways of his own adult daughter, and while she was certainly old enough to make her own decisions and more than capable of handling their consequences, the thought of some hunky, well-to-do, magazine-gracing businessman making any sort of romantic move on her had triggered at least a low-level dad-mode alarm inside him.

"Easy, pops," Banks returned cheerfully, spying Crane's authentic irritation. "I didn't *really* get that vibe, and you know I'm good at reading people. It was just a joke."

"Yeah, I know," Crane groaned as they exited the diner. "All the same, though, I'd rather not gossip about it anymore."

"We're not gossiping," Banks said, squinting at the sky as he slid a pair of silver-framed aviators over his eyes. "I trust Iris just like you do. She's a good person, even if she is...complicated. She wouldn't fraternize with bad people. If the rich guy is a friend of hers, he must be all right. Case closed."

Crane grinned and slapped Myron on the back. "Yeah, case closed," he agreed. "Now, go enjoy what's left of your leave, because I expect you back at work soon."

"Sir, yes, sir," Banks replied with a tiny salute. He moved toward his car but then promptly turned back around, shaking his head. "Bring it in, brother," he said, hugging Crane tightly, patting him solidly across the shoulder blades. After releasing him, he backed away and said, "Really, Crane, thanks for everything."

Crane nodded his acknowledgment as Banks opened his car door and waved his goodbye. He waved in response and then walked to his own car. He sat in the driver's seat for a moment, studying the Saint Michael medal clipped on his visor. Feeling uplifted, he checked his watch and then started the engine and left the parking lot. It was his day off, and he had some time before the shopping date he had planned with his wife later—and he knew exactly how he wanted to spend it. There was a church with a nice, quiet chapel not too far from here, and he had lots of people to pray for, and even more thanks to give.

END

About the Author

Lauren is a Lubbock, Texas native and Texas Tech University graduate with a bachelor's degree in economics and a minor in German (don't ask her to speak it, though—she has forgotten most of what she once knew, and she was always better at listening and reading!). She now works as a compliance consultant and occasionally leads group fitness classes at her gym on the weekends. Generally quiet, reserved, and introverted, she listens far more than she speaks, but she will gladly engage in conversation or debate when prompted with an interesting subject. She values and greatly respects integrity and hard work, and she holds herself to the same high standards she demands of others, but she isn't always the rigid and exacting stick-in-the-mud people sometimes perceive her to be. She is wholeheartedly committed to balance and believes one's free time is every bit as valuable as, if not far more valuable than, the time one spends working, and it should therefore be treated with the appropriate appreciation.

In her own free time, Lauren can often be found her stuffing her face while watching television reruns of her favorite shows, though she does like to maintain a disciplined exercise routine to balance that. She enjoys competition in any form, whether in trivia, air hockey, arcade or board games, or arm wrestling (she often loses on that one). Other interests of hers include music (she can play the piano, the violin, and the guitar, though she's admittedly rusty on all of them), online geography quizzes, puzzles of any variety, and drinking all the coffee and hot tea she can hold. She takes no offense when labeled as a homebody or as a creature of habit—food and entertainment are every bit as compelling and often far more enjoyable in the company of one's closest acquaintances, away from crowds, and nothing beats old favorites. If an urge for adventure beckons, it can be satisfied by daydreaming, reading a favorite book, watching a favorite action movie, or replaying a favorite old video game for the fifth or fiftieth time.

Ironically, Lauren always hated English classes in school (she very critically found them subjective and pointless, though she always enjoyed reading and writing and grammar), but she can now count "writing a book" among the highlights of her personal achievements. She can also mark that off her "bucket list," leaving only "appearing on a game show" and "owning a Dyson vacuum" as the remaining items thereon.

CPSIA information can be obtained
at www.ICGtesting.com
Printed in the USA
LVHW021031281022
731799LV00011B/852